VITALERIUM
DESCENT INTO THE VOID

VITALERIUM
DESCENT INTO THE VOID

NICHOLAS KEATING CASBARRO

atmosphere press

© 2024 Nicholas Keating Casbarro

Published by Atmosphere Press

Cover design by Ahmed Geatar

Interior sci-fi graphic by dekiprabowo on vecteezy.com.

No part of this book may be reproduced without permission from the author except in brief quotations and in reviews. This is a work of fiction, and any resemblance to real places, persons, or events is entirely coincidental.

Atmospherepress.com

*Dedicated to my wife, Marisa
& my daughter, Sloane*

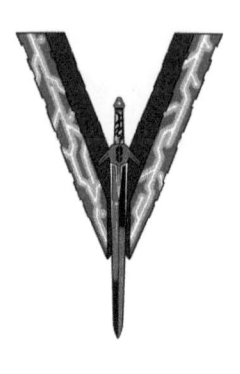

COALITION FOR PROSPERITY (CP)

THE GOLDEN PHOENIX

INTERGALACTIC GOVERNING BUREAU (IGB)

THE SACRED ORDER OF EQUILIBRIUM

WIBETANI MILITIA

TABLE OF CONTENTS

History of the Final, Bloody Frontier 1

Prologue: A Scourge of a Species 9

Chapter 1: Roman Wasn't Built in a Day 12

Chapter 2: The Weight of the World 32

Chapter 3: A New Normal 45

Chapter 4: Home is Where the Heart Bleeds 60

Chapter 5: Fourteen Orbits 75

Chapter 6: Mo-Hawk-Bang-Bang 87

Chapter 7: Courts, Courtiers, and Kings of Kairus 102

Chapter 8: In the Name of Science 119

Chapter 9: The Job 132

Chapter 10: Alchemy… Not Quite 145

Chapter 11: An Unbreakable Bond 161

Chapter 12: Emboldened 177

Chapter 13: Death from Above 193

Chapter 14: Green and Gold 214

Chapter 15: Saving Grace 229

Chapter 16: Quantify, Qualify, Poke & Prod 241

Chapter 17: Reluctant Alliances 263

Chapter 18: A Connection Pure 287

Chapter 19: It's Just Politics 295

Chapter 20: An Obsession Like No Other 313

Chapter 21: The Devil's Dealings 341

Chapter 22: The Hybrid Sensation 356

Chapter 23: Bleed for the Black and Blue 375

Chapter 24: Separate Paths 404

Chapter 25: They Keep to the Tunnels 436

Chapter 26: Glow Worm Hunting 448

Chapter 27: Trifecta 473

Chapter 28: A Heart of Cracked Crystal 502

Chapter 29: Friends in Low Places 522

Chapter 30: Philosophizing and Hard Truths 541

Chapter 31: An Heir of Consequence 561

Epilogue: The Sentinels 572

Leebrus
Dorok
The Apex
Sanctum Tower
Spire
Ytonia
Kairus Prime Inner Sphere
Kairus Prime Outer Sphere
Argos
Luxenia
The Grind
The

History of the Final, Bloody Frontier

In Year 2036: NASA Launched its Collector II space exploration probe to expand our knowledge of that beyond our solar system. This fifty-year-long mission was the most ambitious in years, with goals of surpassing all prior unmanned missions to provide a detailed map of our known universe and discover habitable planets to replace our own. Unsurprising from a species that even considered itself on "borrowed time." Unfortunately, about twenty-four years into its tenure in space, NASA lost communication with the probe. Collector II had all but disappeared, vanishing into the void.

However, in January of the year 2086, the mission thought long lost to celestial collisions saw Collector II's unanticipated return home, despite Earth's failed attempts to reestablish communications. Its preprogrammed course had been fulfilled, although slightly skewed. Its flight ended with a crash landing on Earth's surface in Central Egypt, just west of the Nile River. NASA, excited by their lucky break, immediately dispatched a recovery team to secure their probe. Even more unexpected than its timely return was the presence of a small meteoroid of unknown material and origin found lodged in its hull, imbedded directly in its destroyed communications relay. It presented as a beautiful, blue crystalline substance with a sublime blue glow. The vitreous crystal itself was made opaque by what appeared to be gray smoke continuously permeating throughout its translucent vessel.

It captivated the scientific community worldwide, as well as their governments. A seven-ton boulder of untold possibilities. However, the substance was dangerous and unstable. If investigators even came within a dozen feet of the crystal without proper protection, their skin would quite literally melt off their bodies. Severe burn injuries and casualties were sustained by the entire first-contact team. Their tragic loss of men and women only further piqued the interest of Earth's superpowers. After diligently studying the energy signature at the crash site and correcting their mistakes, NASA and the now-involved United Nations were finally able to secure their precious new space rock. There was no doubt that the power housed within these crystals was immense, and testing began immediately.

A multi-national co-examination of the crystals was authorized by the United Nations, but it proved unlike anything scientists had ever seen before. Just a single ounce of this crystal element had thousands of times the potential energy of a pound of plutonium-239, and harnessing that type of power proved to be extremely difficult. It was a substance not found to be naturally occurring in our solar system, and thus our perspective was limited. After six months of attempting to harness the crystal's ostensibly boundless power, the team had produced no meaningful results, only a litany of opposing theoretical frameworks. As they would come to find out, sometimes, a little bit of rule-breaking is required to make progress in leaps and bounds. Unorthodox situations require unorthodox methods, and it wasn't until the deployment of Dr. Hilkar Mjartansson that we discovered the substance's true potential…

Mjartansson, a bit of a renegade scientist, discovered that

only by "exciting" the crystals on a massive scale could we begin to discover their true power. The energy output of the crystals was massive, he thought. So why wouldn't the need for immense power input be required? Previously, scientists had posited using different light frequencies, vibrational frequencies, radiation, and other methods to arouse the swirling smoke dwelling dormant within these glowing rocks. Dr. Mjartansson would not fall prey to the same suboptimal outcomes. During a not-so-routine round of lead-ion collision testing, he loaded his designated sample of the substance into CERN's Large Hadron Collider and fired; an experiment that was nearly stopped by government officials overseeing the co-examination for fear that this type of drastic collision could cause a catastrophe of unknown proportions. But Dr. Mjartansson triumphed.

It was discovered that upon collision, the crystal substance elicited a unique field around its structure, altering the fabric of local spacetime and rendering the contents of the field "massless." The contents of what later became known as the "V-field" were decoupled from the Higgs field, and gravity itself was observed bending around the crystal. This phenomenon was observed when the hunk of crystal appeared to "teleport" from inside the particle accelerator to the other side of the lab, lodging itself in the concrete subterranean wall. It traveled in the same direction as the accelerated particle that collided with it. The V-field also seemed to produce internal stabilizing properties, preventing the crystal itself from disintegrating due to its inertia, and resultant lack thereof. This marked the first ever recorded instance of exceeding lightspeed travel.

Upon discovery of this species-altering advancement in technology, President Benjamin Robinoc of the United Nations declared these crystals to be "the vital essence by which humanity will colonize space and flourish with prosperity throughout the known universe." The element was dubbed

"Vitalerium" following this speech, much to the dismay of Dr. Hilkar Mjartansson, who had named it "Mjartanssonium." Unfortunately for him, this name didn't have quite the same ring to it, and the layman's name eventually all but replaced it.

After just a few more years of trial and error, refining techniques were developed to expand the generated V-field significantly. Powered by the Mjartansson Higgs Decoupler (or MHD as its mechanism is commonly called), the first light-speed-exceeding spacecrafts had been constructed, tested, and even operated by humans. A single-stage-to-orbit (SSTO) spacefaring vessel the size of a football field could be powered for deep space travel by a vitalerium crystal no larger than your fist. The final frontier was finally traversable, and it would seem, for a short time at least, that our species was saved. Deep space mining operations were not just plausible now—they were frequent and relatively safe. Humanity flourished for generations as President Robinoc had forecasted. Our problems related to the finite resources of our singular planet seemed to be solved, with the exception of vitalerium itself.

As the years went on, humanity realized an opportunity to become the gods they always strived to create. Because of this, research into creating artificial intelligence to mimic or surpass the image of human consciousness all but ceased. With the goal of a "higher" digital life-form rendered obsolete, the focus pivoted to implementing AI applications to merely assist us in our endeavors for interstellar expansion. Of course, at the forefront of human priorities was experimentation to discover other uses for vitalerium. The ability to terraform new planets soon became possible. Entire cities could now be powered by singular hunks of the ultra-rare vitalerium. Then finally, in classic human fashion, research into vitalerium-powered weaponry made its way onto the scene just in case new threats were to ever emerge; or perhaps for the reemergence of more familiar ones...

The Interplanetary Alliance was formed between all

known terraformed planets to achieve the combined goals of the human species throughout space. But access to the final frontier meant virtually endless opportunity. It was a new Wild West, but to an exponentially greater and seemingly unlimited degree. The Intergalactic Governing Bureau (IGB) was established by the Interplanetary Alliance to police the expansion of humanity's boundless ambition. By the year 2350, humans had colonized five new planets in the Milky Way Galaxy. Along with Earth, humans now inhabited Mars, Ventura, Sigmi, Portia Quixote, and Plenathu Viridus. The human race celebrated their success, and the population boomed. But as the new world flourished, the old familiar tensions of generations realizing their anxious complacency began to surface. When the small amount of vitalerium held by the Alliance and the IGB began to deplete, a tipping point was reached. The cycle of empires, it would seem, was ready for its next iteration.

Due to its unique energy signature, methods had been developed to locate more of this vital resource throughout the galaxy. However, humanity's ability to detect and track vitalerium was still limited. Small deposits were discovered and harvested on Saturn's moon, Titan, in the asteroid belt, and on the former planet Pluto. Other locations in neighboring solar systems also provided trace amounts of the precious "blue gold." Although this provided some deterrence to the coming storm, it was not nearly enough to fill the bottomless demands of endless expansionism. As vitalerium stores continued to diminish, humanity searched high and low for a more indefinite option. Desperate times finally led to further examination of the data from the Collector II mission. Using the trajectory of impact from the initial vitalerium meteoroid, scientists and explorers finally made a new discovery: its source.

In the year 2351, the Vitalerium Spatial Fracture was identified. Also known as the "Vital Fracture," this term describes a strange, never-before-witnessed spatial anomaly; a literal fracture in space time, from which clusters of vitalerium meteoroids would intermittently burst into our galaxy. The endless flow of the once-rare element was referred to as the Vital Cascade, originating from an unknown source rumored to be the "center of the universe." For those inclined to folklore, some even believed it to be a place where the gods reside. Though none of the following exploratory missions were successful in traversing through this space-time fracture, the consistency on our side of the anomaly was evident. The Vital Cascade could provide enough raw material to allow for mankind's continued colonization of the universe for millennia.

However, where there is an opportunity for control, there are those looking to take advantage of it. Human ambitions began to collide in the wake of the discovery, and like the Vital Fracture itself, the emergence of secret factions forming in the back rooms of stone buildings began to fracture the once-solid Interplanetary Alliance. Those in power lucky enough to be privy to the information commenced initiatives to position themselves accordingly. The goal: to mine untold wealth in the form of blue gold. Once again, the restless populations were led by the blind ambitions of our elected officials as we approached all-out conflict.

In just two years, the Interplanetary Alliance shattered, splintering into three factions. A one-hundred-year war was waged between the Plenathu Viridus-based IGB, who had designated themselves the bureaucratic overlords of the universe, and the two multi-planetary alliances: The Coalition for Space Freedom (Earth, Mars & Ventura), and the Planetary Vitalerium Alliance (Sigmi & Portia Quixote). Hell-bent on acquiring the sole right to guide progress for the human race, these six planets all vied for planet Deorum.

A planet in the Kalurite 3 system, Deorum was located deep in the Perseus arm of the Milky Way Galaxy's first quadrant. It was just slightly larger than Earth, negating any major gravitational obstacles. Combine that with the presence of water, a similar atmosphere, and a similar orbit around its star Bios, and there stood the perfect Goldilocks planet. Colonizers would not even have to bother with terraforming. Optimally positioned, Deorum was the only habitable planet in the system whose orbit sat directly next to the Vital Fracture, making it the ideal location for the most profitable vitalerium mining operation in the galaxy. Whoever controlled Deorum controlled vitalerium, and could then reallocate power as they saw fit.

Unfortunately for the free world, the IGB had been allowed to become too powerful throughout the prior 250 years. Although valiant efforts were put forth by the planetary alliances, the IGB emerged victorious in the end. The course of fighting had taken its toll, and the blood of over two billion people had been spilled in both space and planetary combat. It is said that the black of space was tinted red for decades following the war. The planets retreated back into their place, although they harbored disdain for the Intergalactic Government's gruesome triumph, and even more resentment for the way they ruled with an iron fist in the post-war era. But to the victor go the spoils, and by the year 2453, the war had ended and Deorum was now the planetary property of the reigning galactic superpower. The colonizing process began, and a government was installed to run the vitalerium trade for the IGB. Over the next 248 Earth-standard years, the constant source of vitalerium from Deorum has poised the IGB to obtain more power than gods, while those who run Deorum's operation experience wealth beyond what one could imagine.

Deorum became home to the megacity of Kairus, a humongous, smoking chrome blemish on the face of the relatively untamed planet and the only portion inhabited by humans. Easily seen from space, Kairus is an almost perfectly circular city. It is comprised of seven city-states, with the largest by far being Kairus Prime and its three spheres: the Outer Sphere, the Inner Sphere, and the Apex and Inner Sanctum. Great steel walls separate the spheres from each other and from the world outside the city. Positioned around Kairus Prime like numerals on a clock lay Argos, Talos, Luxenia, Ytonia, Dorok, and Leebrus, the remaining six city-states. Each has its own great walls that separate it from the undomesticated expanse of the Grind: where the majority of Deorum's inhabitants live between the walls of the city-states and the unforgiving terrain of Deorum's jungles, deserts, and mountains.

Governed by the Coalition for Prosperity (CP), Kairus grew at an exponential rate upward toward the heavens with every ounce of vitalerium they mined. However, not unlike the government that installed them, the government of Deorum is ruthless, corrupt, and harbors ambitions of its own. The people of Deorum live under a constant state of martial law, with only the chosen few free from consequence.

A shift in power to the Aganon family caused massive disparities in wealth as the government consolidated the banking system of the planet. Criminal organizations find themselves emboldened as they capitalize on loansharking and other methods of illegal revenue behind the shield of bribery. The year is 2701, and although humankind has experienced over 240 years of relative peace, the blind ambitions of new players begin to take root, and the old familiar sentiment of unrest begins to bubble to the surface. One man, Zerris Aganon, with his visions of ruling the universe, is the only spark humanity needs to ignite catastrophe. And as spark turns to ember, ember to flame, and flame to inferno, the pendulum swings...

PROLOGUE:

A Scourge of a Species

Humanity... Humanity never changes. A species too young and inexperienced to have earned its place in the universe. How ambitiously they propel themselves into the cosmos. They survive, although barely, fooling themselves into thinking they work toward some ultimate goal of utopia; toiling in the minutia of their short, under-evolved lives with the belief that each step forward will lead to the avoidance of suffering. But for humanity, suffering is unavoidable, merely deferred...

The boredom that eventually accompanies any momentary prosperity only leads them closer to their breaking point; a regression back toward the brink of violence as the pendulum swings. The longer prosperous times last, the more they experience restlessness, indifference, and the deference of individual judgment to the discretion of those in power until it becomes absolute. Weakness... it flourishes in prosperity. Laziness, it spreads like a mind virus. And the politicians, the vultures, and the wolves they foolishly choose to elevate, they capitalize on that weakness.

As if tired from the triumphs of their predecessors, humans lose their affinity for personal responsibility. If simply asked nicely, they willfully give up their rights in the name of safety and well-being for "the masses." It matters not that those responsibilities are shifted to people they've never met, so long as it produces no sweat on their own brow. How easily they throw their freedom to the wind. How unfortunately short-sighted;

well intentions are never well enough for a species so easily corrupted.

While consciousness and inspiration may exist in them, they remain muscles unflexed in the vast majority. Instead, they allow their biological inclinations and reward systems to prevail; mere evolutionary itches in their feeble brains that ultimately fail them. And though it may elicit the drive they require to produce and create—art, science, technological advancements and the like—humanity is still a species that requires purpose through struggle. For without it, their collective consciousness withers and becomes susceptible to the emptiness of the void. However, this universe is not without its obstacles, and colliding ambitions of the powerful eventually evolve into civil unrest; an unfortunately easy sentiment to spread amongst their populations. Unrest leads to turmoil, turmoil to conflict, and finally, when all of their sins align...war.

War is the easy and careless option for the rebirth of a species' purpose. A concept that no individual human seems especially keen on, yet every few generations their restless subconscious somehow allows them to be driven to the brink of abyss. Whether it's culture, religion, money and resources, or a simple idea, it makes no difference. Humanity has always found a way to bait itself into conflict in the name of scratching that primitive itch of psychic disturbance they mistake for progress. An evolutionary flaw driving them forward to some unknown end. Each time promising their collective selves that this time...this time will be different. This time, they will right their wrongs, and never have to resume their seemingly encoded habits of digressing into barbarism against one another. This time, a utopia shall be established.

But what is really gained...? Each time, all they achieve is a departure from one equilibrium to some new "elevated" one. And peace...peace only lasts for as long as their generational attention spans; the curse of a species that dies too young to acquire wisdom on a cosmic scale. Destined to forget the lessons of their ancestors in exchange for progress deemed worthy by those in power, they find themselves once again not as citizens of a civilized world, but as denizens of hell forever searching for heaven... and the cycle repeats.

There is little faith in them or among them, it would seem. The chosen champions of humanity have proven uninspiring. We have received *an aggressively militant stance to our revelations from the would-be champion, the Grand Regent from Plenathu Viridus. And the young proponent from "Deorum," as they've chosen to call it, well...he seems motivated by selfish designs that verge on megalomania. Why we waste our precious little time with them, I do not know. The truth is, they are not ready for the endeavor that lies before them; barely capable of mustering the competency and clarity to ally with themselves, never mind with the cause of all biological life. The human experience remains but a constant, and Humanity...it never changes.*

CHAPTER 1:

Roman Wasn't Built in a Day

The city of Kairus roars day and night. At the rim of the Inner Sphere, giant mega-structures tower over the Guaniton park where children play, emitting a blinding neon glow from their holographic advertisements despite the afternoon light from Bios. The noise of people chatting in the stands and the clamoring of a city still hard at work is accompanied by the sounds of hovercars zipping by just a few dozen feet overhead. Armed Guardsmen of the Coalition for Prosperity patrol the city block wearing their standard, shiny black armor detailed with fluorescent blue lights. The letters "CP" are scrawled across their chests in block font. One hovercar flies in lower as it passes over the field and lands nearby in the stalling section adjacent to the ensuant game. An attractive, long-haired brunette woman in her late thirties steps out of the vehicle and hurries toward the stands where her teenage son plays. Her high heels and business casual attire present an obstacle to quick movement.

"Pass the damn guan!" shouts one of the adolescent boys to another as he runs down the field with his teammates. "ROMAN! Pass it!" he calls out again. One of the teens with brown, collar-length hair furling out of his metallic green

Guaniton helmet races toward the holo-arc at the end of the field. The cries of his teammates fall upon deaf ears, for Roman is focused on imminent victory. Slightly larger than the other boys, and already a surprisingly skillful shooter at the age of thirteen orbits, all Roman has to do is make it to the starboard holo-platform past their first line of defense. If he can just accomplish that, the tie would be broken.

The small crowd of parents in the stands cheers as the Guardians inch closer to their fourth win of the season, this time against the rival Lychrens. Their cheers aren't even enough to penetrate Roman's tunnel vision. He dodges right as a defender hurls a small metal sphere in his direction. A ball-sized charge expands into a multicolored holo-net mid-air. It misses the determined Roman and snags one of its own Lychren players in pursuit of the young athlete, engulfing him and causing him to fall to the ground. Though undoubtedly big for his age, it does not detract from Roman's agility.

While swinging the icosahedron guan in his sling, Roman grabs a bounce charge from his belt and tosses it on the ground in front of him. Upon striking the ground, a similar multicolored panel bursts from the circular charge and illuminates a small square on the field. Roman takes two more steps and hops onto the holo-panel, which launches him into the air toward the floating starboard holo-platform in Lychren territory. He lands on his feet and quickly faces the blue Lychren holo-arc.

The arc-tender stares up at Roman with a look of clear distress. He already knows what fate has in store for him if number thirty-three is allowed to get into position. Roman doesn't hesitate for a second; *as he continues swinging his sling containing the guan above his head, all goes quiet. The familiar icy sensation spreads from his brainstem down his back as his body floods with adrenaline, and time seems to slow. His beating heart syncs with the turning of the world around him. The other players race to his position in a futile attempt to stop him from scoring, but they are too late. Roman targets his opening to the arc, aims, and lets loose the guan...*

All in the crowd are on the edge of their seats as the guan flies through the upper limits of the arc, just missing the arc-tender's defensive net. "ARC!" shouts one of the referees as he makes an arc shape with his arms over his head. The once-blue Lychren holo-arc is now flashing red and yellow, indicating a successful shot. Roman celebrates by throwing his sling-carrying fist into the air and yelling, "YEAH!" The game clock on the floating scoreboard centered above the field counts down "2...1..." followed by a deafeningly loud buzzer. Every member of the crowd adorned in green attire jumps from their seats, clapping and cheering for the Guardians' victory. The members of the crowd dressed in blue attire do not share their enthusiasm, instead participating with indifferent clapping.

The young boy jumps down from the platform as his teammates rush over to celebrate with him. Roman is overwhelmed with hugs and high-fives from his teammates as the field's holographic structures are turned off and begin to blink out of vision.

"Nice shot, Rome!" says one teammate.

"Yea, you smoked that arc-tender!" says another.

Roman smiles from ear to ear, clearly pleased with himself for his third game-winning shot this season. As he thanks his teammates for their praise, his coach approaches the group of elated kids on the field and congratulates them on their big win.

Then, in a serious tone, he comments, "You really need to learn to pass, Rome..." Roman looks at him, slightly puzzled, then back at his teammates, then back at his coach. After a moment of awkward silence, a smirk begins to crack through the stoic expression that bores down on Roman "...but that was one hell of a shot!" the coach yells. The team erupts with cheers as they all celebrate with the coach, some even breaking into goofy victory dances.

Roman's friend Joshua proclaims so the whole team can hear, "Nothing can stop us from getting to the championship this orbit! Not with this guy scoring so much," and pats Roman on the shoulder.

Roman responds loudly for all to hear, "And we'll win when we get there!"

Coach Alan interjects with a humbling announcement. "Alright, alright, we are only four games into this season, let's not get too excited. Only the fool celebrates before the buzzer. We're still a long way away from the playoffs, and even further out from the championship game. That is the *true* final buzzer. But we've got great momentum! So, let's keep that momentum moving into next week's game. I want you all to remember this feeling...what it feels like to win. Chase that feeling! I'll see you all at practice tomorrow."

The teammates exchange a few more remarks, and a few more celebratory high-fives before clearing the field to meet their parents. The coach stops Roman as he is about to leave the field. "You know..." he says, "you really do need to learn to pass more. You're a great shooter, but you can't just carry the team on your back all the time. When we start playing tougher teams like the Comets or Desert Lightning, you are going to have to make use of your allies on the field..."

Roman nods in agreement, then looks at the ground before responding, "Yea...but I saw an opening, Coach Alan. I had to take it."

"Well, what if that net charge had hit you like the defender intended it to?" retorts Coach Alan.

"But it didn't! I dodged..." Roman is cut off before he can continue.

"It's not always gonna work out that way, bud. Sometimes you need to utilize your other teammates to move the guan forward."

Roman knows he is right, though he has never been fond of letting the guan out of his control. If he had his way, he would have the guan every second of the game. But there is no sense in arguing with his coach at this point. "Ok, I guess..." replies a skeptical Roman.

Coach Alan sighs, then, looking up, notices Roman's mother approaching them from the stands. Though she arrived late, she had made it just in time to see the winning goal. She starts to walk onto the field but then stops to allow the conversation to continue uninterrupted. Coach Alan finishes with, "Hey, rest up tonight. Because we're doing transfer drills the entire practice tomorrow. You're a great shooter, let's start working on some other areas of gameplay."

Roman smiles meekly, then nods and concedes, "Yes, Coach," before turning toward his mom to leave.

Clearly proud of her son's great showing in the game, she greets him with a big hug; one that lasts a little too long for his liking. "Come on, Mom... Everyone is still here. They're looking!"

Roman's mother Alora puts her hands on his shoulders and says sarcastically, "Would you rather a crotchety old mother who doesn't love her son?"

Roman responds immaturely, "No...we're just in public; my friends will make fun of me."

Alora raises one eyebrow and smiles as she shakes her head at her embarrassed teenager. "Let the prying eyes of the field do as they will. They don't concern you in the slightest. There's nothing wrong with giving your mother a hug. Now get in the hovercar, my not-so-little champion."

Before moving, Roman looks around and asks, "Wait, where's Dad?"

Alora glances down and sighs. "Unfortunately still at the store. He's engulfed in some project for one of his high-priority clients...had to work late tonight. But I know he wishes he could have been here. He always loves to see you play. Now please, let's get a move on. I actually need to stop by the shop before we head home tonight." Roman nods, picks up his gear bag, and walks with his mother.

The two make their way over to the plain black vehicle with deep red accents parked next to the field. The hull shines as the light from setting Bios reflects off it. As they approach, the side hatch hisses as the hydraulics release, allowing the door to open toward the sky. It is not a luxurious vehicle by any means, but is always cleanly kept and well taken care of. They enter the vehicle, each sitting in one of the four seats that face each other. As they sit down, Alora says out loud, "Take us to the Outer Sphere, Crystal's Edge downtown."

When she finishes, the vehicle hatch immediately begins to close as an attractive virtual voice emits from the speakers. "Welcome back, Mrs. Matthews. Your estimated time of arrival is eighteen minutes and thirty-nine seconds from now." Alora seems to ignore the response as she turns her attention back toward Roman. The hovercar lifts off and swiftly joins the traffic above the field, heading toward their destination.

Roman looks, smiling out the window as they fly, scanning the buildings of Kairus and the glow of their many advertisements. A beautiful, scantily clad woman dances on the side of the Amorton building, advertising the club on the upper levels. Spinning cologne bottles from Sigmi Scents shine like diamonds as they spin in front of a blue neon backdrop, while another hologram depicts a scene from an AI Helper commercial promoting their personal home assistant robots. Roman has always loved the city. To him, it is a glorious playground of endless opportunity. And flying above it is one of his favorite parts of the day. Like most kids his age, he couldn't wait to have a hovercraft of his own. It meant freedom in his mind. He looks up through the transparent roof of the hovercar at the thousands of holograms that illuminate the dimming sky. *One day, maybe I'll even be lucky enough to fly manually,* he thinks.

"I think I'd like to be a pilot... Like on a real starship," he says into the window that his forehead is pressed tightly against.

Alora responds somewhat disapprovingly, "You either need to be in the Guardsmen or part of the transport union for that. A boy with your capabilities should shoot higher..." But her words barely penetrate his skull as he sits lost in thought. Roman simply stares out the window, continuing to smile as if he didn't hear her. A few moments pass in silence as the hovercar sails toward the Outer Sphere.

His mother breaks the silence with, "So... I saw your winning arc! Sounds like you had quite the game today. Coach Alan and the team seemed very happy with you...and what better day to have such a good performance..." Alora opens a compartment next to her seat and pulls out a small black box with a white bow on it. This he takes notice of, and Alora smiles as she hands it across the cabin to her excited son. "Happy birthday, Rome," she says sweetly. Roman smiles as he takes the box and starts untying the bow concealing its contents. His mother looks just as excited for him to open it as he does. After discarding the bow on the seat, Roman opens the lid to reveal a beautiful silver chain, from which hangs a small, silver pendant in the shape of a shield. Small markings adorn the shield, but Roman is too excited to read what they say. He immediately removes it from the box and puts it around his neck. Many of the kids at school wore chains like this, and his mom had obviously paid attention to his incessant requests for one.

"I love it," Roman says, smiling from ear to ear.

"Are you sure? I can return it if it isn't the one you want..."

Alora is cut off by Roman's immediate response. "No, really. It's great, Mom, thank you," he says shyly. He was almost always shy when receiving gifts. Roman reaches across the cabin and gives his mother a hug and a kiss on the cheek. Alora smiles contently as the car flies through the Outer Sphere checkpoint and makes its way toward the family's shop.

The flight seems to pass in the blink of an eye while Roman catches up with his mother, talking about school, friends, and

Guaniton. The vehicle slows into its descent, landing next to a shop with a small hologram sign reading: "The Crystal's Edge Emporium" with smaller letters spelling "Luxury Décor, Fine Jewelry & Custom Artisanal Pieces." Roman's father's store. Despite its location in a decent part of Kairus's Outer Sphere, small bits of trash litter the street. The sidewalks are grimy, except for the small strip of walkway in front of the Emporium. As a whole, Kairus is dirty and rough around the edges. But Roman never minded that; he even liked it. It is home to him and provides a sort of edgy charm. Only the city's center is notably clean. The Inner Sanctum, where the great Sanctum Tower rises higher than the eye can see. Though he's never seen it with his own eyes, he always hoped that, one day, he might get a chance.

The hatch hisses open and Roman and Alora exit the vehicle and walk through the glass doors. The ring of a bell fills the room. As the sound clears, a wavecast emitter in the back of the shop transmits Cyrus Bolan, a wavecast host speaking in satirical and critical tones about current political events. Despite the low volume, his stentorian voice travels across the room unfettered.

"...I mean, it hasn't even been a month since the sudden death of Baxter and Roland Gamera, CEO and CFO respectively of Kairus Spheres Bank. And we're just supposed to believe that they died of natural causes two days apart from each other? At the ripe old age of fifty-six and sixty-two orbits? Don't pay attention to constant attempts to absorb them by our lovely CP Bank. Or the fact that their deaths caused a spiral of doubt that saw the bank's stock droop like a lancor's cock! Don't pay attention to the CP Bank who picked up their assets for pennies on the dollar shortly after. No, it's all just a solemn coincidence, I believe. *I BELIEVE! BELIEEEVE*, PEOPLE! I mean, this is crazy news, but the state-run media hasn't covered that. NO, they'd rather talk about Overseer Gannon's newly imported pet cordfish collection. Ha! Separate note, he does kind of seem like a cordfish guy, doesn't he? Just cold and unfeeling..." Roman had become used to hearing this familiar voice after hours. He smiles and shakes his head, aloof to the political ramblings and eventual commentary that would inevitably follow from his father. It provides him with a sort of free entertainment: his father turning a talk show into an unrequited two-way conversation.

The mumbles of Frank Matthews can be heard across the room: "No one with half a brain would believe that garbage..." right on cue.

The shop is filled with interesting oddities for sale from all over the galaxy: hunks of rare gemstones from Ventura polished into decorative tchotchkes, an ancient mammoth tusk from Earth adorned in scrimshaw, the skeleton of a small Reebish posed in an aggressive stance with metal posts, decorative centerpieces, and hologram projectors. Glass cases line the room, filled with everything from ancient ceremonial knives to beautiful artisanal jewelry. As a young child, Roman fondly remembers walking the length of the store in awe at the treasures his father was able to curate; each piece with its own story. He would become attached to many of the pieces and remembers crying when some of his favorites were ultimately sold to patrons with enough coin to afford one of Frank Matthews's decorative focal points.

Behind the counter at the far side of the room, Roman's father works on an ornate diamond necklace with precision tools. The burly man sits quietly at his work bench, aware of his guests but locked in on his task. He wears jewelers' loupes so he can see clearly as he makes fine adjustments to the beautiful piece. He has a thick coif of short brown hair, and a graying brown beard that juts out from his chin a few inches. The muscles in his forearm dance beneath a thick layer of dark hair as his fingers work meticulously. He dons casual clothes, which are more worn than usual. Roman can already tell he has had a long day.

Alora asks him, "Frank, what are you wearing? That's hardly client-facing attire..."

Frank doesn't skip a beat and responds slyly with a smile, "The customers may not like it, but you're the only one I need to impress." He leans back in his chair, tilting his head back as Alora walks behind him and kisses him quickly on the lips.

Roman rolls his eyes, saying, "Get a room..."

Frank ignores this classic teenage response. He turns to Roman with a stern look and bellows out a trivia question. "In the Hundred Years War, who was it that guided the fleet to victory over the Planetary Vitalerium Alliance in the Battle of Mendora?"

Roman huffs and puffs as if he just walked off the Guaniton field after practice. "Captain Marcus Singer," he utters, feigning boredom.

"Hm...not bad. But perhaps too easy. Let's try a different subject. What do you do if you come face to face with a bevy of cave plods?"

Another sigh from the tired Roman is followed by a response that has seemingly been rehearsed and reiterated numerous times. "Cave plods are a small but aggressive species that rove in groups called bevies. Due to a lack of eyes, they can't see, so they go by their sense of hearing and tactile sensation. The best thing to do is quietly find a place out of their path and remain as still as possible until the bevy passes."

"And what if you can't stand still? What if they become alert to your presence?"

Roman recounts in a snarky, undulating tone commonly used by teenagers, "Cave plods are sensitive to drastic changes in temperature, so the best deterrent to use would be fire. The heat will cause the bevy to disperse, providing you with a window for escape."

Frank looks up at Alora, and a smirk replaces his usual stoic expression as he is overcome with paternal pride. Looking back at Roman, the same smirk morphs into a wide grin as he chuckles to himself. "Can you believe this kid? Like he's reciting it from the godsdamned manual. Well done. How'd the game go, champ!?" His voice is deep and far-reaching.

"I scored two goals and we won," replies Roman, seemingly tired of talking about it after the flight.

Frank feigns an unimpressed look and replies, "Scored two goals and you won, huh...and that's your level of excitement?"

Roman fakes a smile and shrugs his shoulders. A feeling of exhaustion is beginning to set in, unsurprisingly. He had been on the field for almost the entire game.

As Alora walks into the back room labeled "Employees and Those with a Death Wish," his father leans in and says, "Well that's just unacceptable." He pauses, looks around, and follows up with, "Maybe this will cheer you up a little..." He reaches under the desk he's working at and produces a thin, rectangular box about six inches long. Scribbled on the box in red ink are the words "To my son, Roman." He wheels over in his rolling chair to the jewelry counter and pushes it across the glass surface to Roman.

Roman pauses, trying to imagine what might be inside. He looks up at his father, who raises one eyebrow and says, "Well?" and then nods toward the mystery box on the counter, motioning for his son to open it. Roman reaches out and picks up the box, which is heavy for its size. He shakes it, but nothing seems to rattle inside, and his curiosity only grows. Roman opens the lid to reveal a sleek, shiny silver handle. Inlaid on its chrome frame are ornate black metal accents that create an hourglass shape of sorts. At the top end of the handle is a red crystal cut down to the shape of planet Deorum, with the Sanctum Tower extending visibly into the sky. Someone had gone through painstaking efforts to capture such detail on a stone this small.

"Whoa! A knife!" Roman exclaims.

Frank nervously shushes him and whispers, "Hey now, don't let your mother hear!" Roman can barely hold in his excitement but manages to calm down and nods to acknowledge his father. "Took a long time for me to get those accents right... I had one of my own when I was your age. Wasn't as nice as yours by any means, but it's a good tool to have."

Roman is unable to take his eyes off the beautiful work of art. "You made this? This is so awesome!" he says quietly, trying to contain his enthusiasm.

"Here, let me show you how to use it," says Frank as he beckons for the blade. Roman hands over the box and watches with unwavering focus. Even his post-game exhaustion cannot stifle this second wind. His father removes the handle from its foam inlay, holds it firmly, and presses down on the red crystal. The second he pushes it, a silver blade protrudes from the handle as fast as lightning. "You wanna be *really* careful with this, because it's very sharp. Never put your hand in front of the opening. It's perfectly balanced..." Frank places the end of the handle with the red crystal button on the edge of his finger. It teeters back and forth at first, then eventually stills, remaining completely level while the blade is open. "And when you're done..." Frank pushes the red crystal button again. Just as fast as the blade appeared, it retracts back into its handle.

"This is SO COOL!" exclaims Roman, absolutely beaming.

"Settle down, you little homunculus. Now, don't go flashing that around with your friends. And you can NOT take it to school. Not unless you want the both of us to end up in a CP jail cell. Remember, this is a tool, not a weapon; unless the situation is ABSOLUTELY dire," says Frank sternly. "Dire means to protect yourself, or to protect your loved ones from an imminent threat to life. And that doesn't mean just any acquaintance either—I don't want you running around playing hero. That'll get you nowhere..." he looks around as if what he tells Roman is confidential information, then locks eyes with his son to finish his thought, "...to protect yourself, or your family. Do you understand?" Frank gives Roman a serious look as he hands the closed blade back to him.

Roman swallows the saliva in his mouth, then responds equally seriously, "Yes, I understand."

Frank smiles, crosses his arms, and scratches his bearded chin, saying, "Good." Looking down toward his feet, he pauses and thinks for a moment. After a few seconds' pause, he says, "I'm going hunting again next month with an old friend... Lancites, maybe a trophy Vitornial Ankonyl if we come across a pack. We'll be going just beyond the outer ring toward the Vitornial Mountains. Maybe it's time you finally joined me. You can take it with you then, and I'll really teach you how to use it."

This is new. Roman stands flabbergasted by the suggestion. He had never been invited on one of his father's hunting trips. "Whoa, really!?" asks Roman, hardly able to believe what he's just heard.

"Yea, why not? You should know how to handle yourself in the open planet, it'll do you some good. Put all those survival guides and Deorum fauna books to good use." The confirmation of his suggestion prompts Roman to walk briskly around the counter and embrace his father. Frank returns the hug and gives him two pats on the back. "Happy birthday, kiddo. Now go do your homework in the back. I've got some more work to do before we head home."

As they let go, Alora emerges from the back room and notices the silver handle in Roman's hand. "And just what is that, Frank?" she asks disapprovingly. Roman looks up at his father, who is at a surprising loss for words. "Eh... I uh..." He searches for an explanation, but Alora's face is telling. The secret is out. He knows the woman he married all too well and is immediately forthcoming. "I mean, I had one at his age. He's a responsible kid. He can handle it, can't you, son?"

Roman nods like a bobblehead, reaffirming, "Yes. Yes, I can." Both father and son gaze at Alora's unchanging, disconcerting expression. She looks at Roman, who ineffectively hides his elation. He is clearly pleased with his father's gift.

After a moment her expression lightens. She lets out a deep sigh and extends her hand, saying, "Let me see the knife." With some hesitation, Roman hands her the blade's handle. Alora takes the knife and inspects it. Roman's shoulders bow, sure that his gift is as good as gone. Alora presses the red Deorum-shaped button and ejects the blade; from the sound alone, one could tell it was masterfully crafted. To Roman's surprise, she twirls the blade downward and grasps it with the blade facing the floor, then twirls it back upward and retracts the blade.

"Whoa!" gasps Roman, surprised by his mother's display of dexterity. He looks back at his father, who only smirks.

His smirk turns to a toothy grin as his eyes meet Alora's. He proudly extolls, "That's my lady."

His mother taps the closed blade on her free palm, all the while shooting Frank a cross look. Frank only smiles back. She then places the handle back in its case and hands it to Roman, stating, "This is NOT a toy." Roman nods gratefully. Alora follows up with, "And it is to stay at *home*."

Roman lets out a victorious "Yes!" as he runs past her to the back office and closes the door.

Alora walks up to Frank and puts her arms around his shoulders, retaining concerned eye contact with her husband. Still unsure about the situation, she says, "A knife, Frank? He's thirteen orbits."

"Fourteen orbits today," he corrects her, smiling. She does not seem settled by his answer. "I had one when I was his age," he repeats reassuringly. "He may be a boy today, but he's becoming a man. He needs to be prepared for what's out there. This city...this planet...it can be a dangerous place. We can't shield him from that forever. I don't want him to have to learn the hard way."

Alora sighs once more, then says, "Just...take care of him, Frank. I'm going to go shut off the hologram," and walks toward the entrance of the shop. Frank sits down in his chair and continues his work. As he starts to make more adjustments to the necklace, he hears the ding of the shop doorbell, signaling someone has entered, followed by Alora speaking in a nervous tone, "Oh, uh...hello. Um...please come in..."

When Frank looks up, a pit forms in his stomach as he watches three armored CP Guardsmen walk through the front door. Two of the Guardsmen are wearing the standard jet-black metal armor with blue trim. Blue lights gleam from the face masks on their plated helmets. However, the third man wears black armor with green trim; a lieutenant. Just by the presence of a lieutenant, Frank deduces that this is no ordinary check-in.

The lieutenant in green approaches the counter slowly, scanning merchandise in the room as he walks. He reaches up and presses the right side of his helmet, causing the face mask to retract and reveal his face. He is shorter than the other two Guardsmen, with a bulbous nose and thinning hair. Despite his appearance, there is a cocky sort of air about him. Calmly, he places both hands on the counter and, in an insincere tone, proclaims, "Good evening, sir. My name is Lieutenant Forgs. Please forgive the intrusion, but I'm sure you're aware of the new directive that was passed this week, C-301A?" Frank stares back blankly, shrugging his shoulders. Forgs continues, "The expansion of the blue zones from the Inner Sphere to include the Outer Sphere of Kairus?"

Frank's expression changes. "No, I was not aware."

The stout man in front of him goes on, "Well, you see...it takes effect today. We are here to collect any firearms present on the premises. It shows here..." the lieutenant places a large holoscreen on the counter "...that there is one registered firearm to this location under the name...Frank Matthews?"

Frank is clearly disturbed by the hassling presence of the Guardsmen, and even more perturbed by the inquiry. He stands up, collects himself, and replies, "Yes, I'm Frank Matthews."

"Oh good," retorts Lieutenant Forgs. "It also says here..." pointing to his holoscreen again, "that this firearm is a PX80 pistol."

Frank begrudgingly replies, "That's right."

Forgs continues, "Then if you'll just hand over your formerly legal firearm, we'll be on our way." The cocky tone of his request does not sit well with Roman's father, whose blood begins to boil. The CP has made it hard enough to run a business with their policy changes this orbit, and now he can add confiscation of property to the long list of intrusive laws and regulations.

"Do I get any sort of compensation for this property that you are taking from me? This wasn't a cheap purchase, as I'm sure you're aware," Frank asks in an irritated tone. "There have been two attempted burglaries this orbit alone. How am I supposed to protect my business?" Alora glares at Frank from behind the visitors, silently signaling for him to stop. The CP Guardsmen grip their rifles and take half a step toward the counter.

Forgs lifts his hand lazily with an index finger extended, signaling for the two Guardsmen to remain calm, then states in a casual tone, "Unfortunately you will be granted no such luxury. Laws are laws, and you will hand over your firearm immediately."

Frank recognizes this situation is not one he will win. He nods and slowly reaches under the counter, producing a sleek black pistol and accompanying magazine. He carefully places the weaponry on the jewelry case in front of him. The PX80 is top of the line for civilian-authorized gauss-powered weaponry.

The tension in the room is palpable. Frank then steps back from the counter with his arms crossed and grunts, "There it is."

One of the Guardsmen remarks to the other just loud enough for Frank to hear, "That'll look good in my collection." Frank says nothing. He only looks down in disgrace.

The holoscreen behind the desk is still on, emitting a low-volume rant from Cyrus Bolan. It is the only sound for a few moments as the lieutenant assesses the forfeiture, checking the firearm's serial number and inspecting its action.

Forgs hands it to one of his men and motions for him to pack up the firearm. The Guardsman places it in a large plastic bag and seals it shut. With that, they begin to make their way to the door with Forgs in the lead. Before exiting, Forgs turns and utters, "Oh, and turn off that Cyrus Bolan nonsense. It's sure to lower your IQ. That man is no patriot..." then turns and begins to leave.

Frank, overcome with disdain and having reached his tipping point, utters under his breath, "Neither are you."

Forgs stops with one foot out the door, and slowly turns back around. Frank had not meant for him to hear this, but Forgs, with his face mask still retracted, was just able to pick up on the dissent. "What was that, Matthews?" he shouts back into the shop. Frank stands silently behind the counter, still looking at the ground. Alora is as still as a statue. Her heart races. Forgs marches back into the boutique, scowling with his eyes ablaze. Frank and Alora do not move a muscle, but Frank remains outwardly calm. He refrains from redirecting his gaze toward Forgs, which infuriates the lieutenant.

"You know...you look familiar..." The man looks Frank up and down. He ponders for a moment, then says, "You wouldn't happen to be the Frank Matthews, formerly of the CP Guard, would you?" Frank finally raises his eyes to meet Forgs. The lieutenant does not even wait for his response. Frank's worried stare had already betrayed him. "Hehe, you are, aren't you? Oh, I've heard about you," remarks Forgs smugly. "You were that commander who was discharged for insubordination. You're practically a traitor."

Frank hesitates to respond. He flashes back to his days in the CP Guard, which at one point he was proud to be a part of. Unfortunately, evolving leadership had pushed the Guard in a new, lurid direction. The martial law implemented at the onset of Deorum's colonization was never abolished as promised; only expanded. The covenant of a society unfettered from the pressures of an omnipresent authority remained the stuff of dreams; consistently deferred until the next "milestone of accomplishment," then deferred yet again.

As the party took a more bureaucratic approach from governing to ruling, deception and subterfuge became the norm, and authority became the only currency that carried weight. Jaded by their practices, a feeling of misanthropy replaced Frank's sentiments of loyalty to the party, and the truth of the matter became clear: he was part of the problem.

At the final juncture of his service, he was asked to make a "problem" disappear for the Coalition. Although Frank had seen plenty of action in his time, he was no murderer. It was not a problem he intended to solve, and so he turned in his resignation on the spot. However, rather than accept his peaceful departure from service, he was dishonorably discharged, reprimanded, and charged by the government. Through the help of a high-powered connection, he was able to escape banishment from Kairus, though he was blackballed from every major employer within the city walls. Opening the shop was his only option. Despite having acted in accordance with his values, it brings him shame recounting this part of his past.

Frank knows the kind of man standing before him; he is not uncommon. Venomous, vindictive, and power-hungry; lacking in any sort of human empathy. Cowardly by themselves, but resplendently aggressive when the odds are stacked in their favor. This was the type of person that the CP had continuously recruited and elevated in the Guard over the orbits. This is what Frank's former organization has deteriorated into. There is no point in arguing or explaining at this point. Frank's response is short and succinct. "Forgs, you and I are cut from a different cloth."

Forgs snickers at his comment, then his face returns to a

scowl. "I'm sure a man of your 'former' stature has many connections in this city...perhaps even some clandestine ones." He had emphasized the word 'former' as an insult to Frank. Without breaking eye contact with Matthews, Forgs calmly says to the Guardsmen, "Search the place."

One of the Guardsmen orders Frank and Alora into the small space in the back of the shop near Frank's desk. He stands guard with his rifle raised, pointing ominously at the couple as Forgs and the second officer begin to tear the place apart. Alora looks apprehensively at Frank, who shares her sentiment but does not express it. The two wait anxiously at gunpoint while their store is turned upside down.

In the back office, Roman is doing anything but his homework. He drops his gear bag near one of the desks in the back, then flings his backpack beside it. The glint of the office light reflecting off his birthday present encompasses his entire attention. He ejects the knife from its handle and then retracts it. Ejects it again, turns it in the light, and then retracts it. As he sits back in one of the office chairs, he feels the light thud of his new necklace hitting his chest under his padded Guaniton jersey. In all the excitement surrounding the dagger, he had almost forgotten about his mother's present.

He pulls the pendant out from under his shirt and takes a closer look. The kite-shield-shaped pendant is slightly larger than a coin, but clearly carved in its metal are four squares, each containing an etching. In the top left square is the letter "R" in a fancy font that Roman has never seen before. The top right square contains an etching of a gem. The two squares below contain two crossed swords on the left and the letter "M" in similar font on the right. He loves the initials but would have to ask his mother what the other symbols stood for. He turns the shield over to reveal a fierce-looking creature with wings. *An eagle?* he ponders. He had learned about these in school during the semester his science class covered Earth biology, but he had never seen one like this. Eagles are not indigenous to Deorum.

An inscription has been engraved below the eagle. The font is extremely small, and he must squint to read it. The inscription reads: "On life's road exist challenges plenty. Hold your head high, for the path will become clear. Walk tall, so none find reason to look down. Speak truth, for truth's voice is bold. Brave the storm, for the brave will reach shore. Believe you're bound for greatness, and the universe will listen. Love, Mom." He reads the inscription over and over as he rotates the blade handle in his palm with his thumb and index fingers. There's a warmth to the words etched in the pendant's cold silver.

A chime from his backpack prompts him to rummage through its pockets for his commscreen; the messages had been building up since before the game. He turns on the screen to find a notification for seven new text messages and two new school assignments, but he is too fatigued to check them; he can always answer tomorrow. A few voices can be heard from the shop floor, but they are too muffled to break his preoccupation.

Slipping the commscreen back into his pocket, he continues to admire his gifts. Suddenly, a loud crashing sound of impact and broken glass erupts from the shop-room. It startles Roman, causing him to eject the knife. The blade slices his right index finger, and the knife drops to the floor. Roman grunts, clutching his hand as a drop of blood flows down his finger to his palm. The cut is not deep, but he could not let his parents see this, especially his mom. Roman collects the knife, then wipes his blood off the blade and retracts it, returning it safely to his pocket. Putting pressure on the wound with his thumb, he shoves his hands in his pockets to avoid detection. *I wonder what is going on out there*, he thinks to himself.

CHAPTER 2:

The Weight of the World

Outside the door to the back office, a CP gauntlet presses Frank's head into the glass jewelry case, which cracks beneath the pressure and begins to cut into the skin of his cheek. The Guardsman holds him there, with his rifle now pressed firmly into the back of Frank's neck. Alora screams as the scene unfolds before her eyes. A trickle of blood leaks from Frank's left cheek into the newly formed crevices in the glass. It would seem Forgs and the other Guardsmen have found something.

"You STUPID motherfucker, Matthews! We've got you now!" taunts Forgs. He cackles to himself as he struts over to Frank, pointing back to the second Guardsman, who is holding a vitalerium rifle and a vitalerium canister in his hands. The rifle is the same standard-issue firearm that the CP Guardsmen carry. "You know damned well vitalerium weaponry is illegal for civilian scum like yourself. You lost those privileges when you were kicked out of the SERVICE." As he finishes his sentence, he slams his fist down on Frank's head, causing the glass beneath his face to shatter. His face is cut gruesomely by the glass, and he slinks to the floor beside the case. He has no time to react before the first officer delivers another blow to his opposite cheek. Alora begins sobbing uncontrollably and slinks to the floor where she stands.

"Not to mention..." continues Forgs, "...harboring pure, unrefined vitalerium!?" he says, referring to the cold metal cylinder with reinforced transparent sidings, revealing a glowing blue crystal with gray smoke raging within it. "That's two cardinal felonies I've got you on. And you can't call on your buddies in Argos to bail you out this time," he says as he kicks Frank in the back, causing him to recoil in pain. Alora continues bawling loudly in the corner, which diverts the attention of Forgs, who is mad with power.

"And you, bitch! YOU are complicit in this too!" he says as he starts toward her, pointing aggressively at Frank's wife. Both Guardsmen make the mistake of momentarily turning their attention toward the sobbing woman in the corner and away from Frank. Frank takes advantage of this lapse in judgment. The mention of his wife causes his adrenaline to instantly surge. He jumps to his feet, hooks the leg of the Guardsman next to him, and tosses him over the broken glass showcase. The man flips over the display and lands heavily on his head. Before the second Guardsman can react, Frank has already closed the distance, grabbed Forgs by the shoulder, spun him around, and delivered a punch directly to Forgs's bulbous nose.

"ARGH!" squeals Forgs as he falls to the floor with blood gushing from his face; his nose is clearly broken, with its bridge angled to one side. In the commotion, the second Guardsman turns to Frank and begins to raise his rifle at him, but Frank is one step ahead. He grabs the rifle, blocking it from rising to the Guardsman's shoulder, and throws an elbow to the officer's neck, the only part of him not fully protected by armor. It sends him off balance, allowing enough time for Frank to disarm the man, who he then flips over his hip to the floor. Frank was well trained by the CP and is still effective even today. During his time in the service, he was known as one of the most capable in combat. However, even the best combatant cannot win if overwhelmed, and his rebellion is quelled as the second Guardsman strikes him in the back of the head with the butt of his gun. Frank falls to the floor on top of the legs of the first fallen officer.

A few feet away, Forgs covers his nose and winces in pain. He looks at his bloody hands and cries out, "You son of a bitch, Matthews! You broke my fucking nose!" His voice is muffled and nasally from the injury sustained. Frank begins to crawl, groaning from his own pain. The two Guardsmen work together to restrain him. The first officer holds him while the second removes a thin black strip from his belt and slaps it on Frank's back. A bright orange light bursts from the strip, engulfing Frank's arms in a gleaming orange net as the holo-restraint binds him. They pick him up by his arms and drop him to his knees at the feet of the now-standing Lieutenant Forgs, who wipes the blood off his face with paper invoices from the nearby countertop. Even badly beaten and cuffed, Frank is hard to restrain. The Guardsmen must each press down on his shoulders to keep him still.

"Now you've gone and done it, Matthews..." Forgs says in his muffled voice. "Now you're dead." He pulls his pistol out from its holster and aims it point-blank at Frank's bloody forehead.

Amidst the chaos ensuing in the shop-room, Roman opens the door of the back office. Upon catching a glimpse of the scene that unfolds before him, he immediately pulls the door back toward its frame, leaving a crack just wide enough for him to peer through. Roman remains as quiet as a mouse. The shock of confusion and fear glues him to the edge of the doorframe. He hasn't the slightest clue as to why it is happening, but knows that it's always bad news if the CP is involved. His father had taught him that much. Due to the tension of the situation, no one outside seems to have noticed his presence, though that brings him no relief. Roman peers into the ransacked shop-room in horror. His hands begin to quiver as he looks upon his father's merchandise tossed about the room carelessly. The broken wares, the shattered glass...he has no idea how it got to this point, but the bloodied man holding a gun to his father's head shakes him to his core.

"NOO!" screams Alora as she runs toward Forgs, attempting to save her husband. She grabs the lieutenant's head and digs her nails deep into the cornea of his left eye. Again, Forgs screeches in pain, then pushes Alora off him and strikes her in the face with his pistol. She falls onto the desk behind her and curls in pain. Once again, adrenaline kicks in and Frank makes a valiant attempt to get back to his feet, but the Guardsmen's hold is too strong.

Forgs, despite only having one eye open, notices how his actions have affected Frank. His painful grimace soon turns to a devilish grin. "It seems our plans have changed. You're dead, but not before you watch," he says in a sinister tone. He steps over to the desk and strikes Alora again in the face.

"DON'T, FORGS, IT'S ME YOU WANT," bellows Frank. It takes the full strength of both Guardsmen to restrain him now. Alora lays there on the desk in agony.

Forgs retorts, "You two obviously need to be punished..." as he strikes her again with the back of his hand.

"DON'T YOU FUCKING DO IT FORGS YOU PIECE OF SH—" Another blow from the first man silences him, and blood begins to pour from his mouth. Alora scrambles across the top of the desk, trying to escape, but Forgs pulls her back by her pants. The mad lieutenant winds up again to put a cease to the woman's struggling, but as he does, Alora's hand finds Frank's welding tool. Her thumb presses the red button on its handle, sparking it to life. Forgs's backhand is batted away as she swings the metal torch to meet his assault. She quickly pushes herself up toward the slimy beast, grabs him by his armored collar, and presses the white-hot flame into his cheek.

"YOW!" wails Forgs as he steps back in agony, smoke rising from the charred ring on his face.

From the back office, Roman gawks as his mother fights back against the slovenly monster. He is terror-stricken;

unable to move, let alone look away. Control of his bodily functions evaporates, and his knees begin to shake as he urinates through his uniform pants. It forms a small puddle at the base of the door. As he continues to watch, a rage boils within him that he is unable to act upon. He clutches the handle of his blade in his hand, but it too shakes uncontrollably. His mind races. Every fiber of his being, down to his very soul, yearns to rush out into the shop and kill these men...to attempt something, anything at all to save her. But he remains frozen: a deer in the headlights.

Forgs recovers and plants his titanium greave into Alora's stomach, sending her careening into the side of the desk. The moment of rebellion, although short, lasts an eternity in Frank Matthews's eyes. Alora is unable to lift herself from the floor after having the wind knocked out of her. Her eyes meet Frank's, both filled with tears. She reaches out to him with her left hand and attempts to call to him. But before she can, a gunshot rings out as a vitalerium charge takes the back half of Alora's head off. She falls limp to the floor as the embers continue to burn her face to ash. Forgs stands above her body, panting with his vitalerium pistol extended. A thin plume of smoke rises from its glowing blue barrel. With an evil smirk and one eye still scratched closed, he mutters, "Good riddance, bitch."

A look of utter disbelief washes over Frank's face. For a moment, he is unable to process the gravity of the terror that has unfolded before his eyes. His devastation is immeasurable, but not yet realized. "Alora?" he whispers. His head begins to shake as his sorrow gradually turns to pure, unbridled rage. He grinds his teeth despite them being broken and chipped. His gaze focuses on the human waste that stands before him. His knuckles turn white, and the veins bulge from his forehead as he lets out a primal roar so loud that it startles everyone in the room, including the Guardsmen restraining him.

"AAAHHRRRRRRRRRRRRRR!!!!" His battle cry lasts at

least ten seconds long. And when it is done, he bellows out again, "AAAAHHRRRRR!!" as he forces himself up. The men are barely able to hold him, but once again force him to his knees.

The lieutenant struts over to the broken man on the floor before him and raises his pistol. Frank stares daggers into the eyes of the devil himself. He knows death is imminent, but he is without fear. His final words, like bullets from his bleeding mouth: "Your judgment lays just around the corner, you fat little swine." Frank spits a glob of blood and saliva directly onto Forgs's forehead. "Now send me to my wife like a good little soldier."

Forgs responds disdainfully, "That's enough out of you..." and fires his pistol once more into Frank's face. The blue flash of the vitalerium charge eviscerates Frank's head, spraying blood and ash across both of the Guardsmen's shiny black armor.

The sight of his parents' violent deaths is too much for Roman, who experiences a near out-of-body experience that causes his legs to give out beneath him. He falls backward with his face frozen in contorted horror. The sound of his body crashing to the floor is just loud enough to be heard in the shop. Immediately alert to the presence of another possible threat, the Guardsmen release Frank's shoulders. Roman watches as his father's body falls to the floor, the image forever seared into his mind. Life as he once knew it is over, and his face turns white as a ghost. But there is no time to process the events, for now, he has another problem. As he focuses his gaze upward through the sliver of the cracked office door, three armored CP Guardsmen now stare back.

"Go investigate that!" barks Forgs. The Guardsmen quickly retrieve their weapons and start toward the office. Roman has no time to grieve his loved ones. His only option is to run.

His legs feel like lead, but he is able to scramble to his feet. He rushes through the office to the exit at the rear. As he reaches it, the office door flies open, and the Guardsmen spot him. He turns and his gaze is met with the fluorescent blue lights beaming from their helmets; their armor as black as the night. Roman throws open the door and bolts onto the metal platform outside. He races down the stairs to the alley below street level. The Guardsmen begin to chase him, but the man in front slips in the puddle of urine collected at the foot of the door. The second officer trips over his fallen comrade clumsily.

"What is it!?" calls out Forgs nervously.

One of the Guardsmen shouts back, "It's a kid! He just ran out back!"

"Well, go get him! We can't have witnesses," barks their superior. Forgs runs for the front door, calling out, "I'm going to head him off at the street level!" Both parties pursue Roman with the intent to silence with deadly force.

The Guardsmen's timely spill has given Roman the head start he needs. Tunnel vision and adrenaline have taken over. He sprints down the narrow alleyway for his life, hurdling over trash heaps littering the path. A group of young vagrants, clearly enjoying a substance of choice and oblivious to their surroundings, prove to be no obstacle as Roman runs straight through them, knocking one man over.

"Hey man!" he calls out, confused as he lifts his head from the ground, but Roman does not stop. He keeps running with life-or-death urgency and turns the corner, disappearing behind the off-white cinderblocks of another building. The Guardsmen, who follow closely behind, also come across the group of vagrants who now block the way in an attempt to discern the situation. The man who was knocked over yells at the Guardsmen, "Hey man! What the hell is going on?"

The officers have no time for this. "Out of the way!" one Guardsman shouts, but the vagrant puts his hands up in front of them and persists, "Nah, nah, man, I was just assaulted! I got rights! Some kid just ran right through me..." He goes on and on, blocking the route to their target. The Guardsmen look at each other, then raise their rifles.

As Roman turns another corner, he hears the grim, familiar sounds of vitalerium rifle fire; multiple shots. It only fuels his survival instinct, and he continues sprinting down the alley, turning another corner. The system of alleyways is complex and confusing. *I might have a chance to hide and lose them back here*, he thinks. He would just have to find a good place and then wait it out before he exits to the street.

He turns a corner once more and comes across an elderly homeless woman sitting against the dirty foundation of the back of a warehouse. She's covered herself in a tattered blanket, and her odor is pungent. She stares at Roman with a surprised look on her face, which is weathered from age and a rough life on the streets of Kairus Prime. It's not every day she sees a panicked teenager in a Guaniton uniform racing through the back alleys.

"The HELL are you rustlin' on about? You in some kind o' trouble, kid?" she asks in a raspy voice, just as weathered as her features. Roman nearly runs by her, but stops when he notices the large waste container she is propped up against. He tries to speak, but his sprinting catches up with him and he vomits at his feet. The old woman does not look fazed at all by this.

Roman pants and tries to explain, "Please! They..." He's not even sure how to describe what happened. He racks his brain for the words through labored breath. Panting heavily and wiping the spit from his mouth, he finally gets out, "... they killed my parents." Once again, the old woman seems unmoved. She looks to the garbage container to her left, then looks back at Roman and quickly tilts her head to the side, motioning for Roman to get in. Unable to think, Roman simply complies. He quickly climbs into the garbage bin. It is not very full, but the stench is foul. It makes him gag loudly.

From outside the container, he hears the old woman speak, "I can't help you if you don't shut up." Roman chokes back his gag reflex, pulls some of the trash over him to hide, and lays as still as possible. The sound of heavy footsteps approaching his location is now audible. They get louder and louder until they are just outside the bin. The thuds of their boots against the pavement slow as they begin to approach the old woman.

The CP officers address her aggressively, "Vagrant! A boy just ran through here. Tell us where he is. Which way did he go?"

First, feigning disappointment, she complains, "Oh, that little TWERP—he vomited in my alley! Got some right on my shoe, he did. Oh..." She notices the first Guardsman eyeing the dumpster and decides to switch gears to regain his attention. "CP, huh? You know, when I was a young little lady, I used to date a boy in the Guardsmen..." She flaps the blanket covering her in a flirty manner and purses her lips. "I just loved that black and blue armor...quite the lover he was! What are your names, officers?" The men look at each other, likely exchanging expressions of disgust beneath their black headgear. It's just enough to distract them.

"JUST TELL US WHERE HE WENT," the second Guardsman shouts as he leans in aggressively with his rifle gripped tightly.

Instantly, she reverts back to disappointed support. "That way!" she shouts. "He went down that way and took the third left turn. Go give him what he deserves, the little twerp! Oh, and come back and see me when you do..." she finishes with a smile and a wink.

To Roman's surprise, the woman's ruse works. He hears the footsteps of the CP Guardsmen running away from his dumpster hideout, becoming less and less audible until he hears nothing. Suddenly, there is a jarring knock on the side of the dumpster, followed by her raspy voice.

"Come on out, kid, they're gone," she calls. Roman is hesitant to reveal himself. *What if she is actually giving me up? What if the guards are still right outside!?* He can barely control his racing mind. "You'd already be missing a chunk o' ya' chest if they knew you were in there. Now get out here," she replies as if to read his mind. Roman cracks the lid covering the trash and peeks out. She wasn't lying; the Guardsmen were gone. He proceeds to climb out of the dumpster and falls to the concrete ground on his back. It nearly knocks the wind out of him, but he sits up, facing the old woman. Roman has no idea how to thank her for her kindness.

"Can you believe those klangs fell for that? Got rocks for brains, I tell ya. No need to thank me, though I could'a won an award with that acting..." she says nonchalantly as she lights a cigarette. Roman just stares at her, speechless and grateful. She takes a drag from her cigarette, inhales deeply, and then speaks as smoke pours out of her nose and mouth, "I sent 'em on a wild goose chase. That third turn is a winding maze. I live here and I even get lost back there sometimes...when I'm drunk at least."

Roman still says nothing. He just sits there, a lost soul unsure of what to do next. Strategies on how to hide from the law are not something he has any experience in. Luckily, she decides for him. "Well? What the hell are you waiting for? You said they killed your parents? Don't wait for those tin cans to run back here, GO!" she barks bluntly. She points to the first right-hand turn and says, "Take that right. There's a ladder to street level." As his wits return and the memory of his situation resurfaces, Roman gets up with a nervous urgency and begins to run in the recommended direction. As he runs, he hears her raspy voice call out once more, "And lose that uniform! You stick out like a Lancor's cock!" He turns back, nods approvingly at her, and then disappears down the alleyway; yet another lucky break.

After running a few hundred meters, Roman reaches the ladder the old woman had spoken of. *Without her, I would be dead...*he thinks to himself...*like my parents. And I didn't even thank her.* But there is no time for regret, and no time for mourning; only focus. He glances up at the street light that peeks over the top of the ledge. The ladder before him is tall. There is at least forty feet between him and street level. The ladder ends about seven feet above the alley floor. As Roman jumps up and grabs the cold steel of the ladder's first rung, flashes of the grim scene at the shop plague his mind. *No, not now. Survive now, mourn later...*he thinks, repeating a lesson learned from his father, fighting his own mind. He pulls himself up to the second rung, then the third. He can now hear the familiar sounds of the city street; the chatter of pedestrians, the hum of hovercars. Roman climbs a few more rungs and then looks down. It is a long way down, and the thought of falling only adds to his anxiety. He quickly looks back at the metal ladder, not daring to look down again. A few more seconds of climbing and he hangs just a few rungs from the ledge. But when Roman looks up, what he sees frightens him more than any fall.

That slimy grin. The gnarled, swollen bloody nose. His charred cheek, scratched eyelid, and bloodshot cornea; it is the face of Lieutenant Forgs that stares back at him. He crouches to the ground above Roman and reaches down to pluck the boy up by his jersey. His fat hand grasps Roman's collar and begins to lift him upward, but Roman fights back. He has no choice now; it's fight or flight, and flight is not an option, considering the height he hangs from. Roman tries to push his hand away but is unsuccessful. His grip is too strong.

"Come here, you little shit!" shouts Forgs. "Mommy and Daddy want to see you!" His face is grotesque, and he spits as he talks from the pressure of his gut against the ground. Roman bites his hand and Forgs lets out a groan of pain as his grip jostles free from the jersey. Roman loses his grip on the ladder, but as he is about to plunge downward, he grasps the only thing he can get ahold of: the sleeve of Forgs's armor.

The weight of the boy pulls Forgs closer to the edge. His chest is now hanging off the ledge, stopped only by the metal railing of the ladder above. A worried look comes over his face. "Let go of me, you little shit!" he yells down at the boy, but Roman is in no position to obey his order. He dangles from freefall, swaying back and forth on the arm of the devil that destroyed his life. Letting go would mean, at the very least, broken legs, and if the fall didn't kill him, Forgs certainly would.

"That's it! I'm done playing around with you," yells Forgs as he reaches for the pistol in his holster. "I'm gonna kill you like I killed your bitch mother and traitor father!" But when he attempts to pull the gun out of its holster, it catches against the junction of the ladder's railing. The pistol is stuck, and so is Forgs. As he visibly struggles to dislodge his firearm, Roman sees his opening. The words of Roman's father flash through his mind. *"Remember, this is a tool, not a weapon, unless the situation is ABSOLUTELY dire."* Roman, forced into a state of pure focus, uses Forgs's arm to swing back to the rungs of the ladder and grabs one with his left hand. He quickly moves up one rung, pushing Forgs's hand out of his face as he closes in. Roman reaches into his pocket and grabs the knife, then, with one quick motion, swings the handle into Forgs's neck and ejects the blade.

Forgs's eyes bulge out of his head. For a moment, Roman is unsure if his attack has even worked until the lieutenant spews blood from his mouth onto Roman's face. Roman pulls the blade from his neck and blood shoots out in spurts like a cannon. He had stabbed the lieutenant through his carotid artery and down through his throat. Forgs wheezes and coughs, spitting up more blood. Roman had never hurt anyone before. Never in his life had he thought he would be in a position to kill someone. But after seeing what this monster had done to his family, he cannot deny that seeing Forgs in this state gives him a rush. So, he stabs Forgs in the neck again. A similar response as Forgs wheezes in pain, his life force pouring out of him onto Roman's head. Another stab. Then another. And another. Now faster. Every jab adds a spark to the fire inside Roman that eventually erupts into a primal scream, like that of his father. He loses count of how many holes he has put into the neck of the man above him. Roman stabs and stabs at Forgs's face and neck until his head is nearly severed. The blood pours out of him like a faucet, staining Roman's entire green uniform crimson red. He continues until his arm aches to the point he can no longer lift it to puncture the man again.

When he finally stops, the man's head dangles by a fleshy thread from his body. Roman does not make any attempt to move. His physical and mental exhaustion have hit a breaking point. So, he just grips the ladder motionless as blood continues to drip down on him from above; his baptism of violence. He can't go home. He can't go back to school. He can never play Guaniton again. He couldn't possibly trust any of his friends to keep this secret. He will never see his parents again. Just as all these thoughts begin to barrage his brain, the skies open, and it starts to rain. Cold, alone, and on the run, Roman only knows one thing for sure, and only because he had been told so. He has to lose this uniform.

CHAPTER 3:

A New Normal

As the light of Bios creeps over the horizon of Deorum, the familiar sounds of people chatting, the humming of hovercars, and the clang of metal on metal begin to erupt with the bustle of daily life. Roman sits awake on his makeshift bed fashioned from flattened cardboard boxes. His dingy, long-neglected surroundings create a stench even worse than his own in the abandoned warehouse. From the second story, he stares out the broken glass of a window that once sheltered its workers from the elements. His gaze follows the citizens; citizens of a city he once loved. They simply go about their day, completely unaware of the events that occurred just days before; unfazed. Life seems to have moved on around him.

Roman's eyes burn from exhaustion. If there were any moisture in them at all, he surely would cry. He rubs them vigorously to no effect. Sleep is not an option, for when he dozes off, the nightmares return. Roman is miles away from anything familiar, without a shred of hope or dignity. However, some force...something undefinable within him persists that he must keep going. And so Roman packs up the few supplies he has gathered on the dirty streets of Kairus and plans his next steps.

It had been five long days since that dreadful night. Roman learned quickly how unforgiving the streets of Kairus could be to an unkempt boy with no money, no support system, and no shelter. His parents' home was not an option. He had returned there shortly after the incident to find the street below his building already littered with CP hovertanks, their flashing blue lights engulfing his street with an ominous glow. His only bathing had been that of the rain five days earlier, conveniently washing most of the lieutenant's blood from his person. He had dug through countless trash bins in countless alleyways to find food scraps and the tattered clothes he now dons. But the waste of others was not enough to keep him going forever. He could not buy food, or anything for that matter, without universal credits. Stealing had crossed his mind, but within the limits of the city, surveillance is omnipresent. And in his mind, the CP Guardsmen were around every corner, just waiting for him to turn up...to slip up.

Roman walks down the rusted metal steps of his latest domicile and sneaks under the broken board that blocks what used to be a front door; a lucky find even in this part of the Outer Sphere. He emerges to a street much dirtier than the streets near his father's shop. This street has its own stench; that of rotting waste, rust, and smog. He hops over a pile of empty energy drink cans and alcoholic beverage containers in the street, accidentally crunching one underfoot as he lands. He can barely see the sidewalk through the garbage. He looks up to see a square, illuminated hologram emitting an orange glow at the next corner. The sign reads "Kairus South Gate 2.1 Miles," with an arrow pointing to the right at the next street. He thinks to himself, *If I can just get outside the city, I might be safe.* So when he approaches the corner below the orange sign, he turns right and follows the path, weaving between the disheveled denizens of Kairus's slums toward the Grind.

A CP hovertank zips by overhead with its blue lights flashing, likely heading toward some call for backup. Roman nervously hides his face from the sky above him, looking down into the torn pocket of his tan, stained jacket. His heart beats out of his chest, and his pace quickens as he shirks the thought of what might happen if he's discovered. The streets are swarming with unfamiliar faces, and any one of them might be the one that recognizes him.

As he passes the open door to a convenience store, something catches his eye. A holoscreen blares behind the counter with no one paying attention to it except for Roman. On it, a news story flashes before him as a beautiful, blonde female anchor reads the latest in local news from her teleprompter.

"Still no leads on a burglary gone wrong in Sector 472 of the Outer Sphere that left two dead in their family-owned and operated jewelry store. A tragic story, merely reaffirming the need for new initiative C-301A, to further control the spread of firearm-related violence in the Spheres…" she declares for the world to hear. She continues on, providing more details about the situation, but the words fall on deaf ears within the store. A sinking feeling hits Roman's gut as two familiar faces appear on screen. The first, an attractive woman with long, dark hair and piercing blue eyes. The second, a man with a graying beard; Roman's parents.

"A burglary?" Roman mutters under his breath in confusion. He focuses closer on the lies pouring out of the screen. His hands begin to shake as his anxiety builds into rage. The political rants from his father's programs begin to show merit as he watches the deception play out before his eyes. The spinning of the state's execution of his parents into an act of random violence forces his hands to clench into fists.

"And still no sign of the couple's son, one Roman Matthews…" she continues. Roman's heart skips a beat as his school picture illuminates the screen for all to see. A woman glances up at the screen as she checks out at the counter of the convenience store. Roman freezes as she finishes and turns toward him to walk out, looking him directly in the eyes as she does. Roman feels as frozen as he felt in the back office of his father's shop five nights ago. But to his surprise, the woman exits the store and walks right past him without so much as a second look.

She didn't recognize me, thinks Roman to himself. Perplexed by what just occurred, he turns toward the glass siding of the shop he stands beside and realizes that *he* barely recognizes himself. Five days of dust and grime cover his face, and his thick, furling hair now presents as matted and greasy. Tattered, dirty rags cover him that barely pass for clothes. His current state is a vast departure from the clean-cut boy displayed on the screen. However, the disparity in appearance is not enough to comfort him. The paranoid feelings of impending capture or, worse, the thoughts of what might follow prevail. Without further hesitation, Roman expeditiously makes his way toward his destination with his head down.

After walking another few blocks, the city limits come into view. A tall, hulking metal wall appears in the distance over the nearby buildings. Its charcoal-gray-colored panels loom over him, dwarfing everything around it. He stops and stares at the final milestone between him and freedom, contemplating what life outside of Kairus would have in store for him. He knew little about the expansive sector people called "the Grind," and the little he did know was only schoolhouse rumors and media ramblings. A place where criminals ran free and even the CP was afraid to go. Frightening as it sounded, the lack of military law enforcement was enough for Roman to believe the Grind could offer him sanctuary from those who hunted him.

He starts forward again, but as he takes a step, the crackle of broken glass under his feet stops him dead in his tracks. As he looks down at the jagged glass reflecting below him, Roman is enveloped by an uneasy feeling. First as a drop, then as a flowing river, blood begins to fill the spaces between each fragment. Within just a few seconds, the river flows over and becomes a lake beneath him. Startled by the sight of these crimson-stained shards, Roman's face turns as white as a ghost. He jumps back as fear grips him with the tightness of a vise. The bloody pulp of his father's face and the lifeless, blank expression of his mother splayed out on the office desk fill his thoughts. Roman screams and falls backward into a pile of trash, covering his eyes from the horrible visions. Feelings of fear and guilt pierce his brain like pins and needles. "Why didn't I help them!? WHY COULDN'T I HELP!?" he cries.

"Hey! Hey kid!" shouts a feminine voice from Roman's right. Roman looks to the source of the sound and sees a portly middle-aged woman in high heels scurrying toward him. With his mouth still agape and a look of defeat in his eyes, he thinks to himself: *This is it. She has recognized me and will surely turn me in. The CP will kill me, without a doubt. Oh no... Will they torture me too!?* Roman is only able to conjure the worst.

The woman's curly red hair swings as she approaches and kneels beside him. The buttons of her shirt scream with stress as she leans forward and grabs Roman by the shoulders. "What happened? Are you hurt?" she questions him. Her concerned tone surprises Roman, who glances back at the glass shards, expecting to see the pool of blood, but there is nothing; just a scattering of glass pieces that once formed a bottle.

Roman's mind churns with questions he has no answers to. *Where did the blood go? Did I imagine it? Am I going insane!?*

The woman breaks his train of thought by asking him, "Honey, where are your parents?" There is a sincerity to her line of questioning that somehow breaks down the walls of Roman's paranoia.

"I... They're..." He struggles to search for a response that will not give away his secret. He is too scared to think. At least ten seconds pass as his eyes rapidly dart from side to side, switching back and forth between comprehending his visions of blood and violence and how to answer the stranger beside him. Finally, he is able to blurt out, "I don't have any." He anxiously awaits her response. *Will my answer be good enough?* thinks

Roman. He studies her expression, hoping his answer will satisfy her curiosity and cause her to leave.

"Oh no, you poor thing!" the woman exclaims as she pulls him in for a hug with crushing force. Roman lets out a low sigh of relief but stays on alert in case things turn. Before he can say another word, the woman says, "I know a place for boys like you. Don't you worry your little self! You come right along with me, and I'll take you somewhere safe." Roman is slow to trust, but quickly realizes he has few options to choose from. Making a run for it could get him out of this situation, but it would also draw more attention to him; and for reasons he cannot grasp in the moment, his instincts guide him toward her.

The woman is adamant with her suggestions. "Come on now, get up! When's the last time you ate? Good Prime of Balance, you look famished!" She pulls Roman to his feet with surprising strength. "Oh..." she says as her face scrunches in repulsion, "...been a while since you had yourself a shower, hasn't it? Oh, you poor thing!" The woman talks incessantly. Her mouth moves as fast as a CP hoverbike. Roman barely has time to get a word in.

"Wait, I don't know if I should..." Roman starts to retort, looking over her shoulder at the great wall standing just within reach. But he is interrupted by her high-pitched voice once again.

"Oh, hush now. A good shower, a nice hot meal, a roof over your head! You'll be feeling good as new. And definitely that shower part..." At the mention of food, Roman feels his stomach growl with pain. All he has eaten in the past five days is an old apple and a candy bar he had found. *Maybe I could at least eat something before continuing on,* thinks Roman to himself.

She leads Roman by the arm around the corner, never once ceasing to talk. As they turn, a small green hovercar comes into view. Rust eats away at the paneling toward the bottom of the vehicle, leaving holes and gaps in its metal. Splotches of silver shine through the puke-green paint job in several places. The paint has been chipped off from the dings of a lifetime of street parking. The hydraulic door rises as she approaches, and she beckons him inside. Roman takes one last look at the wall, then reluctantly climbs into the car. The unnamed stranger squeezes in after him, plopping herself down in the seat next to his as she commands her vehicle, "Ion Street and the corner of Drucon, pronto!"

An upbeat computer-generated voice echoes through the cabin, "Sure thing, Sh-sh-sh-Shelby! Arriving in five minutes and fifty-one se-e-econds." The speakers crack loudly at the end of the announcement. She had clearly chosen the "cheery" setting for her car's AI. Roman inspects the interior of the hovercar. The mud-brown material lining the cabin is worn, and in some places even torn. Dirt and crumbs cover the floor where his feet rest, and crumpled candy wrappers are tossed haphazardly throughout. Roman looks at the woman, apparently named Shelby, who had so quickly convinced him to join her. She smiles back at him, then rambles on. Roman is still not sure why he decided to go with her. Maybe it was the promise of food in his stomach, which was starting to slowly eat itself. Maybe it was the way she smiled at him despite his stench, or perhaps it was the fact that she didn't stop talking for one second, giving him no time to think it through. The car makes a loud CLUNK sound, shaking the two in their seats, and lifts off. Whatever his reason for following her, he was now stuck with his decision.

Five minutes and fifty-one seconds of a Shelby-monologue later, and the car sets down in front of an old building just two blocks from the Kairus wall; very clearly a rough part of town. Shelby had talked nonstop the entire ride, and Roman had drifted in and out. All he can say for sure is that she is obviously overtly religious. And though Roman had been to mass a few times throughout his childhood and had nothing against religion, he cannot match her enthusiasm for it. She spent most of the time talking about three of the four Primes: Balance, Confidence, and Interconnectivity. Though she continues to ramble whether he listens or not, Roman finds himself wondering how it is she's yet to mention the Prime of Consciousness.

The door to the hovercar hisses and starts to open, then catches about three-quarters of the way ajar. "Oh, Consciousness, this always happens!" she exclaims as she reaches up and forcefully pushes the door fully open.

"Well, never mind then…" Roman mutters under his breath as he follows her out of the car. The building before him stands five stories tall, made of old-style red brick like many of the other structures around it. Four cracked concrete steps lead up to a dented metal door with no window. There are only four windows in the entire edifice that he can see; one on each floor directly in line with the door. The property itself looks to be in total disrepair, also similar to the other buildings on Ion Street. Cracks snake through what is showing of its foundation, and the entire area around the building seems to have collected a film of light-red brick dust. Four dead bushes greet Roman and his stout new friend as they walk up the steps. The sign on the door reads in small letters, "Ion Street Home for Boys."

Roman glances over at Shelby with wide eyes and a look of betrayal. She just smiles and nods to him reassuringly, then knocks three times loudly. There is no response for a few seconds. She knocks again five times, even louder, and chuckles to Roman nervously; still, no response. She frowns, then rails her fist against the door continuously as hard as she can until finally, around the tenth knock, the door swings open furiously. A man in a disheveled brown suit answers the door and begins to scream, "WHAT DO YOU WAN… Oh, Shelby…" He turns to Roman, sizing him up through frameless corrective lenses. They connect to crescent-shaped metal implants at the corner of his eyes. "Found another stray, have we?" he asks sarcastically.

"Don't call them that! He's a poor lost boy who needs our help, and he hasn't got any parents!" she yells back. Based on the rapport these two clearly have, this is not her first time delivering lost children to the orphanage.

"Well, obviously he's got no parents! Otherwise, why would you bring him here? And don't you mean he needs MY help?" says the man, his second remark just as biting as his first. Shelby does not seem to find this amusing.

"You would have an empty orphanage and no funding if it weren't for the poor souls I bring here! It is by the will of the Primes that I do their work to heal the lands and bring about blessed Equilibrium! You know I break my back..." she begins to go on a tirade.

"Yeah, yeah. You'll get the usual two hundred UCs. Just... just come in already, kid," says the man impatiently, clearly done with Shelby's rambling as he turns his attention to Roman.

Once again, Roman reluctantly steps inside, although this time he is sure it is to escape the talking. As Shelby waves goodbye to him from the front steps, she calls out to him, "Let the Prime of Confidence be with you and hold yourself high! OH! And let the Prime of Interconnectivity bring you many new friends!" Roman looks back and waves awkwardly as the heavy metal door is shut in her face.

The man quickly brushes past Roman and walks five paces ahead of him. Without stopping or turning around, he calls back commandingly, "Follow." Roman, unsure of what he's gotten himself into, hurries after him, trailing just behind up a metal set of stairs. They creak just like the steps in the abandoned building he slept in the previous night. The slender man leads Roman into an office on the second floor where two large men in wrinkled blue polyester uniforms sit in folding chairs. The room is tight and equipped with multiple holoscreens displaying views of the interior and exterior of the building. Utility belts with keycards and handcuffs adorn their blue jumpsuits. They look up with an expression of disinterest as the slender man and Roman enter the room.

"We need this one processed and shown to a bed," the man in the suit says sternly, before turning to face Roman. The two men nod and slowly stand up behind him. As he stares down through the strangely shaped corrective implants, he furrows his brow and says, "My name is Bodan. I make the rules here, and you follow them. You don't want to follow my rules, you can try your luck back out there. Do you understand?"

Roman nervously scans the man who stands before him in the dusty tan suit, then the two large men scowling just over his shoulder. Their overbearing presence is frightening, but he does his best to think his way through the situation. His plans to get past the security checkpoints to the Grind were flawed to begin with. He wasn't sure how he would be able to leave the city without being scanned. Finding himself influenced by the three men towering over him, he thinks, *Maybe my best option is to try my luck here...* As the anxiety builds, he finally looks up at Bodan and nods in response.

"Good. This is Rhodes and Melling; they'll be getting you acquainted with our facilities," says Bodan as he walks out of the room, leaving Roman with the two large individuals.

Melling walks over to Roman and begins to pat him down, but stops and takes a step back, remarking, "Kid you smell like a turd took a shit." Rhodes chortles behind him. When Roman has no response, he simply shakes his head and continues the pat down. He stops at Roman's right back pocket. "What's this now?" He pulls out Roman's blade, marveling at how it glistens in his hand. He presses the red crystal sphere at the end and jumps as the blade ejects out the end.

"Whoa!" exclaims Rhodes, who has already sat back down in his chair behind Melling, clearly impressed with the equipment smuggled in by Roman. "How'd a street rat like you get a fine piece like that?" asks Rhodes. Roman has no time to respond before Melling accosts him.

"First rule, no weapons in Ion Street Home!" barks Melling

before continuing to admire the blade he has confiscated from Roman.

"My father gave me that! It was a gift. It's mine!" Roman cries out in protest. He seethes at the sight of Melling toying around with the last material possession from his father.

This time, Rhodes chimes in. "Either you follow the rules, or you try your luck out there. You deaf or somethin'?" He leans forward in his chair, glares at Roman, and says, "The streets are rough. People die out there all the time. And look at ya...you wouldn't last more than a few days out there. Now, unless you want to be out on the streets with the rest of the animals, pipe down."

"You can always have it back when you leave," remarks Melling insincerely.

Roman's stomach growls intensely as he discerns his next move. *Is this really my best option? I have no idea what I'm getting into,* he thinks. He knows what lies outside; he's lived through it with uncertainty for the past five days. The idea of one of his last prized possessions being in the dirty hands of Rhodes and Melling repulses him, but another painful twist of his stomach leads Roman to decide that it's a battle he can fight another day. "Fine," replies Roman, defeated.

The two men continue to process Roman, which includes documentation and photographs, a rundown of the house rules, and the issuing of a yellow uniform. Now the decontamination phase begins. Melling had not noticed the silver chain dangling from Roman's neck beneath the filthy rags he wears. When it comes time to disrobe in the shower room connected to the office under Melling's supervision, he does so slowly and carefully. He discreetly removes the shiny metal as he removes his shirt and cups it delicately in his palm to avoid detection. Melling unravels a hose and begins the unsavory decontamination process.

A blast of frigid water erupts from the hose and sprays down Roman, which immediately causes the hairs on his skin to stand up. He lathers himself with the gritty soap from the dispenser on the wall, angling himself carefully so the guard does not catch a glimpse of his final possession. When he notices Melling isn't looking, he moves his hand behind his backside and tucks the chain between his clenched buttocks. Just a few moments later, the water shuts off and a towel and a jumpsuit are thrown at Roman's shivering body. He dries off and dresses quickly, then walks awkwardly back into the office. He takes short steps, being extra careful not to drop the jewelry as he moves. As unenjoyable as the experience was, Roman cannot deny the comfort that comes with being showered and in clean clothes.

The two security guards lead Roman up the narrow set of metal stairs to the fourth floor, passing a small, engraved sign that reads: "Living Quarters." As he reaches the final step, Melling opens the only door available and Roman is faced with four rows of bunk beds that stretch back to the edge of the far wall. The building, he realizes, is a lot longer than he had initially estimated. Dozens of boys inhabit the room, some older than him and some younger. They huddle in packs around the bunks, talking loudly, trading things, and playing card games. Most of them stop what they are doing to gawk at Roman as he enters the room, and a hush falls over the quarters.

Roman feels queasy as he browses the faces staring back at him. The expressions are not welcoming ones. He can tell right away that they are measuring him, searching for signs of weakness. Despite his uneasiness, he straightens his posture and holds his head high, maintaining a stern expression. He knows that he must show confidence. His mother always taught him that first impressions are everything, and here, they matter most, it would seem. Rhodes and Melling walk him past rows and rows of blank stares to his bunk. Roman does not make eye contact with anyone, his eyes focused directly ahead, locked in a staring contest with the far wall. About six bunks before the end of the room, Rhodes and Melling stop, pointing to a top bunk on his left.

"This one's yers," says Melling as he throws a blanket and a thin pillow onto the mattress. "Breakfast is at O-eight hundred. Don't be late or you won't get any." The two men turn to leave and start back the way they came. The Living Quarters door slams shut behind them, and once out of sight, the chatter erupts again.

Roman reaches into the pants of his yellow jumpsuit and removes the silver chain from between his legs. He stares at it for a moment, fighting back flashes of his mother's untimely demise. Thankful that he was able to smuggle it in, he lays it to rest around his neck and tucks it under his shirt, then climbs up to his bunk and spreads out. The springs of the old mattress groan as they press sharply into his back. The electronic clock on the wall reads "7:58 AM" in red numbers, only two minutes to breakfast. His stomach churns, and he fantasizes about eggs and game sausage like his father used to cook in the morning. He would miss his father's cooking...but before his thoughts can go any further, a hand grabs the collar of his uniform and yanks him from his top bunk, sending him crashing to the floor onto his side. Pain shoots through his left shoulder blade as it hits cold, hard concrete.

"Ain't no rest for the weary, newbie!" shouts a large, muscular boy who cackles with a group of others who form a circle around Roman. The boy, if you can call him that, is at least six feet tall with a shaved head. He cracks a maniacal grin, baring a set of yellow, crooked teeth, some of which are missing. "What? You think you'd just walk in here and not expect a welcome party?" he asks rhetorically as he grabs Roman by his collar again and lifts him off the ground. "Well, what do you think? Should we show him a warm welcome?" he asks his crew.

His cronies cheer the boy on with "YEA!" and "SHOW HIM!" Roman has no time to react before the fist of his assailant lands square in his left eye, sending him back to the ground in agonizing fashion. The group of boys around him laugh hysterically. Roman braces himself on the floor but does not attempt to get up yet. The boy approaches him again. Jeers from the bunks behind him echo throughout the room. "Show him, Jace!" Roman prepares for his moment. His father had shown him how to box in their apartment, but he had never been in a real fistfight before. He would have to time it perfectly.

The boy approaches him again and squats down next to him, saying cockily, "If you ain't heard yet, the name's Jace. And when those two fat bozos aren't in here, I'M in charge. And if you're thinkin' 'bout snitchin', don't. Unless you want to wake up with an eye gouged out. And just so you remember that them's the fuckin' rules..." Jace goes to lift Roman up again, but before he does, he notices a glint of silver peeking out of Roman's uniform collar. "Wait, what's that around your neck?" He reaches out to move Roman's collar to see more clearly, and that's when Roman sees his moment.

Roman grabs Jace by the wrist and pulls him forward onto his knees. Jumping to his feet, Roman cocks his fist back and lets loose a punch that lands square in Jace's nose. The blow sends him stumbling backward. Roman, thinking he landed the perfect knockout punch, smiles as he waits for his foe to drop. However, to his dismay, Jace regains his balance. The tall juvenile wipes the small bit of blood from his nose. Like every other boy in the room, Jace is wide-eyed at first, but after recovering, he eventually howls with laughter. The boys standing around him join in the laughing as well. The smirk slowly evaporates from Roman's face.

Jace's cocky tone calls out to his friends, "Man, get this stupid bitch. Teach him how things go 'round here." The circle of boys around Roman begins to close in on him. Overpowering him, they take him to the floor and unleash a barrage of kicks and punches that set his nervous system on fire. Just as the last kicks are being thrown, a bell rings, followed by a voice over the PA system.

"O-eight hundred, breakfast. Everyone, report to the third floor." A clicking sound ends the announcement, and everyone filters out of the room as if nothing happened, including the boys who had just given Roman the beating of his life. As Jace walks by, he lifts the silver chain from around Roman's neck and fits it around his own. "Thanks for the glitz, newbie," he says as he delivers one final kick to Roman's stomach, then uses his rib cage as a stepstool and exits with the others.

It is hard for Roman to tell how long he stays there on the floor. It feels like a lifetime passes as he labors with each breath. Breakfast is no longer an option. In this condition, Roman will be lucky just to make it back to his bunk a few feet away. But deep down he knows he cannot lie on the floor forever, and that same unidentified force inside him presses him forward.

Roman spits blood onto the concrete. Every inch of him throbs. He is barely able to pull himself to his knees as pain radiates through his bruised limbs. He grips the metal post of the bunk next to him and cries out in pain as he uses the siding to stand. Slowly, step by agonizing step, he makes his way back to his bunk. Using the ladder this time, he lifts himself to his top bunk. Though he has been physically beaten to a pulp, somehow the pain of guilt is what hurts the most. Guilt that he did not win the fight. Guilt that he had let his mother's gift be stolen. Guilt that he had trusted the woman who brought him here. Guilt that he did not try to save his parents; the crux from which this series of dominoes began its fall. As he weeps into his pillow, he makes a deep, powerful promise to himself.

Never again. Never again will I trust. Never again will I back down. Never again will I lose...

CHAPTER 4:

Home is Where the Heart Bleeds

Nightfall. The room is pitch-black save for the sliver of starlight that peeks through the single window across the Living Quarters and the crimson red glow from the numbers of the electronic clock on the wall. Roman lays awake in his top bunk with his eyes glued to the gleaming numbers: "11:59 PM." They burn like embers in the darkness. Waiting patiently for the number to change, Roman focuses on his breathing. Although energy flows through him like a roaring rapid, he is calm on the exterior. The room is silent except for a low snoring just a few bunks down, and the creak of a bed as one of his roommates shifts in their sleep. He has been ready for this moment for weeks, but is too focused to let his excitement rile him.

Tonight is special, for one minute from now will mark his anniversary with Ion Street Home for Boys. A full orbit here has broken him more times than he can count. However, he has healed stronger at the fractures to become a more hardened version of himself. The beatings sustained have become but a daily tedium, their pain numbed by the sheer force of prevalence. After all the months that have passed, Roman now sees Ion Street for what it truly is to him: an unintentional training ground for the unforgiving world in which he resides.

One that he soon plans to reenter...

The clock turns and beams a brilliant "12:00 AM" into the room. Without wasting a second, Roman quietly reaches down to the bunk below him and taps his bunkmate on the shoulder. A head pokes out from below, his eyes meet Roman's, and he nods. Carefully, the two get out of bed, followed by three others from bunks nearby. The crew of five, led by Roman, make their way down their respective aisles, moving almost in synchrony toward the front of the Living Quarters. Each member had slept with their socks on, which softens their footsteps as they creep. They halt beside a bunk about twenty feet from the door where a large, muscular boy with a shaven head snores. Roman looks down at him, scowling in disgust at the face of Jace. Drool leaks from his cavity-ridden mouth, staining his pillow. It is finally time.

Without breaking his gaze on the slumbering behemoth in front of him, Roman signals toward the boy standing to his right. The boy removes the socks from his feet, rolls them together, and places the ball in Roman's palm. On the other side of the bunk, one of the two boys removes the thin drawstring from his orphanage uniform and works with the other to slip it around Jace's ankles. A knot is formed and tightened, binding Jace's ankles together. Upon tightening the knot, Jace jostles awake and, with tired eyes, looks down at the rope constricting his movement. Roman acts quickly.

He shoves the ball of socks into Jace's gaping mouth hole, stifling the call for help that Jace attempts to let out. Roman leans into the bottom bunk and kneels on his left shoulder, immobilizing it. The other boys each grab one of his limbs and lock him in place as Roman delivers blow after blow to Jace's skull. Jace moans painfully, his voice muffled by sweaty cotton. One final elbow connecting directly to the jaw knocks Jace out cold, and his eyes roll into the back of his head. The five collect on Roman's side of the bunk and roll Jace onto the floor in unison. After using another drawstring to tie his hands together, they drag him through the door of the bunk hall. One of the boys closes it gingerly behind them, then takes the stolen key card from his pocket and locks it from the outside. No reinforcements would be coming for Jace tonight.

They drag Jace's limp body down the stairs to the second floor and prop him up against the wall. From his pocket, Roman pulls out a second key card, liberated from the security staff earlier that day. He quickly moves down the hall to the supply closet. Swiping the key card on the flat black surface above the handle, he unlocks the door, revealing cleaning supplies. He grabs the rolling mop bucket, the bottle of bleach on the middle rack, and the bottle of ammonia on the top rack.

Roman and his bunkmate bring the supplies over to the cracked office door where Rhodes and Melling are enjoying their nightly dose of smut on their set of small holoscreens, radiating light through the space in the doorframe. With rehearsed stealth, Roman's bunkmate slowly pours the bleach into the mop bucket. He looks Roman in the eye to confirm his job has been completed. Roman nods back as both boys proceed to tie their undershirts across their faces, covering their noses and mouths. Without further hesitation, Roman dumps the ammonia into the bucket, which begins to emit a noxious gray smoke. He then kicks open the door to the small office, rolls in the bucket of smoking liquid, and closes it, locking the door from the outside with his key card. Both boys grab the handle of the door and hold it shut with all of their strength.

Sounds of confusion and panic echo from Rhodes and Melling inside the office as the security guards begin coughing from the smoke. Attempts to get out of the office prove futile, and as they scramble to open the door, banging and fumbling for their key cards, they eventually succumb, and the noise stops. The boys hear them both collapse with a THUNK to the floor on the other side. Roman unlocks it and opens the door, releasing a thick plume of smoke. He then quickly moves in, leaving the other boy behind.

Holding his breath in a race against time, Roman runs to the still-smoking bucket and rolls it to the shower, where his "decontamination" had occurred just over an orbit ago. He dumps the contents down the massive drain in the floor, then closes the glass door to the shower room, confining the smoke within it. Next, he must clear the room. He runs to the window and opens it hastily, gasping for a few deep breaths of fresh air, then runs back and opens the door to the smoky office. Two of Roman's bunkmates appear, donning their undershirt face masks, and help Roman drag out the unconscious Rhodes and Melling. They strain under the weight of the two large men, but together the three of them are able to move the security guards one at a time. Roman takes the zip ties from Rhodes' belt and cuffs both men to the hand railing across from their office. One of the boys closes the office door, and the group returns to their captive, Jace.

Roman, however, does not follow. He firmly motions to them across the hallway to continue the plan. Roman's bottom bunkmate, second in command, leads the others as they drag Jace down to the first floor. Roman takes a few more deep breaths, repositions the undershirt over his airways, and reenters the office, this time searching for something.

The smoke in the room is mostly cleared now, having flowed out the solitary open window. Roman holds his breath anyway. He throws open the drawers to Melling's desk and rummages through the junk inside. Nothing. He exits the office, takes a few deep breaths, then reenters. Roman moves over to Rhodes's desk and does the same, but what he is looking for does not turn up. Rage begins to replace the levelheaded demeanor that he has maintained throughout his mission as Roman turns the office upside down, searching high and low for the object of desire. Then, it hits him.

Rhodes... Rhodes had made a remark about his blade when he was first processed. Roman abandons the office and runs to the security guards, who wheeze in their slumber. He targets Rhodes and begins patting down the unconscious orderly who remains zip-tied to the hand railing. Roman shoves his hands into the large man's front pockets but feels nothing but polyester and a crumpled-up receipt; no luck. Roman wheezes as he tries to flip the large man over. Again, he searches through the contents of his pockets, turning up a wallet. Roman removes the universal credit chip from it and returns the wallet. UCs are useful, but still not what he needs. As he attempts to flip him back over, he notices the outline of a long, thin object in the side pocket of his blue cargo pants. *Bingo*, he thinks.

Roman un-does the Velcro and reaches in. He is filled with delight when his fingers grasp the cold, familiar steel of his blade handle. He removes it and admires the shining silver and black work of art. An entire orbit has passed since he last saw his knife. To his surprise, Rhodes seems to have kept it in good shape. He ejects and retracts the blade to test its durability. Its mechanism is still as smooth as ever. *Good man, Rhodes*, thinks Roman as he gives the unconscious orderly two playful taps on the cheek. Now that his first prized possession has been rightfully recovered, he walks down the stairs to meet his team and reclaim the second.

The boys wait for him at the bottom of the stairs. Roman descends the last few steps and speaks his first words of the night to his bunkmate. "Go fill a cup with water and meet us out back," Roman says decisively. The bunkmate runs to the restroom to fulfill his wishes. "Let's go," says Roman to the other boys as he helps them pull Jace's body down the first-floor hall and out the back door.

The courtyard behind the orphanage is not big, but its walls are tall, and they shroud the deeds to be committed within their confines from the prying eyes of the world around. The boys drop Jace to his knees just as he is starting to come to. His head rolls from side to side, and his eyes blink repeatedly, trying to capture familiar surroundings. Mumbling unintelligibly, Jace's eyes focus on the silhouette of a tall boy standing in front of him. The spotlight above the back door shines on Roman's back, making it hard for Jace to discern his identity. All he can see is a blurry, dark figure. All he can feel is the throbbing of his head and jaw, and the wet dirt soaking through his uniform to his knees.

Roman's bunkmate returns with the water he had requested. Roman tosses the liquid into Jace's face, startling him fully awake. "Who…whoa what? What is this? YOU! YOU FUCKIN' STUP—" A kick to his solar plexus stops any sort of rebuttal from Jace, whose eyes bulge as he gasps for air. The boys holding him to his knees do not laugh, but instead tell him to pay attention. Roman speaks with the calmness of someone who has exorcised fear from his emotional spectrum.

"For one orbit… One full orbit, you have tortured me in this place. Four hundred and one days…you created a brand-new hell for me in this building." Roman's eyes are filled with disgust as he glares at the massive boy, who offers no response. "But it wasn't just me who you bullied and beat. Everyone has suffered under you." He points to one of his bunkmates, who lifts his shirt to reveal a bruise spanning the length of his entire midriff. The blue and purple skin is covered in scabs from an obviously recent beating. Another boy lifts his shirt to reveal a multitude of scars across his midsection, including one scar in the shape of a crudely cut smiley face on his chest. A rusty piece of an old bedframe had been Jace's paintbrush. "Take a good look at your work."

"Aw BOO HOO!" jeers Jace mordantly. "Did you boys get some booboos? Man up…"

"You locked Ryan in a closet for almost three whole days," Roman says, pointing to another boy who restrains Jace.

"Now you're crying about a time-out? Ha-ha! You better let me go…the longer you hold me here, the worse it's gonna be when I get loose and even the odds on you little bitches."

"He had to be hospitalized! By the time those idiots Rhodes

and Melling finally got to him, he almost died of dehydration. You're bigger than everyone else, older than everyone else, so no one ever challenged you. Not even your cronies who follow you out of fear because it's a safe bet. You claim to be the 'boss' when the adults aren't around, but what do you do with that power? What do you provide that makes you worthy of that self-given title? Bloody noses? Broken teeth!? WHAT KIND OF PERSON DOES THAT!?" exclaims Roman, pointing to a third boy holding Jace's left shoulder, who smiles with three teeth missing.

Jace cackles and retorts back to his captor, "Hehe...hey, he looks kinda' pretty, just like me," as he smiles big for everyone to see, displaying multiple gaps in his own jagged smile. He wears them proudly. Again, he chuckles in cocky mockery of his captors. However, Roman is unmoved by his mocking. He simply looks down and continues.

"People like you don't deserve the life you've been given, even if it's a shitty one," Roman says as he reveals the silver and black handle and presses down on the red crystal. Its razor-sharp blade ejects with lightning speed and Jace's face drops. His cockiness is immediately blunted, and a look of worry washes over his face when he sees the glint of the blade in Roman's hand moving toward him. "You know, you took something from me once," continues Roman as he slowly inches closer to the thug.

Jace struggles to get up, but the force of four boys is too much even for him to overcome. Jace writhes under their control, but with his hands and feet tied, he cannot stop what is coming. With each slow step from Roman, the blade gets closer and closer. The knot in his stomach twists tighter as all hope evaporates. No more jokes escape his lips. The only option now is to bargain, and he nervously blurts out, "Fine! You... you want your chain back!? Just take it! TAKE IT! HERE!" He leans his head forward and jostles his neck, revealing the silver chain tucked under his collar. "Just take it, man! You win!

You got your chain back. Ju... Just let me go, alright? Let me go, I won't cause no trouble no more, bruh." Roman lifts the chain from his neck with the point of his blade, nicking the back of his head as he does, which causes Jace to shudder and scream "AH!" more so in fear than in true pain. A slim trickle of blood inches down his neck.

Roman grasps the pendant on the end of the long silver necklace, pulling it from the edge of his knife. He reads it to himself first. The words on its back side bring him a comfort he hasn't felt in a long time. Though it had been a full orbit since he last held it in his hands, he hadn't forgotten a single word. He reads aloud for the group to hear, "On life's road exist challenges plenty. Hold your head high, for the path will become clear. Walk tall, so none find reason to look down. Speak truth, for truth's voice is bold. Brave the storm, for the brave will reach shore. Believe you're bound for greatness, and the universe will listen. Love, Mom." Jace looks up at the man who controls his fate, and his face contorts into a confused, perturbed kind of expression. "That's what the inscription says. Did you ever read it?" asks Roman sincerely as he turns and paces away from his nemesis.

"What? No, man! What the fuck are you even talking about!?" cries Jace, confused and scared. His head is spinning, but despite his condition he is still able to contemplate the imminent danger he is in.

"This pendant...is the last thing my mother gave me... right before CP Guardsmen blew the back of her head off as I was forced to watch," proclaims Roman. Jace's eyes shoot wide open. The boys holding him down even look a bit surprised by the revelation despite their vague prompting beforehand. "Then they killed my father...blew his head off with a vitalerium pistol. And this..." he flips the knife in the air with his left hand and catches it with his right, "...is the last thing that *he* gave me before they turned his face into ash."

Jace, a boy that everyone thought was made of steel, begins

to cry before Roman as he once again inches closer, one step at a time. "Please, please don't kill me, please! Please... Please... Don't fuckin' kill me, man. I... I'll be better! I won't bother you guys a bit! You-you won't even know I'm here! Come on man, please! I'll do anything!" sobs a broken Jace.

Roman now stands just a few inches before his bully. He kneels until their eyes are level. Having adjusted to the light, Jace's teary eyes finally lock with his captor, and what he sees terrifies him. He looks into the eyes of Roman and sees darkness only comparable to the void of space itself. It sends a chill down his spine.

Roman holds up the chain next to Jace's face and says, "You turn eighteen orbits in a few months, don't you?" Jace nods quickly in response, too afraid to speak. Roman calmly says, "Almost made it out of here." Jace's face turns white, but to his surprise, Roman opens the clasp on the chain gifted by his mother and puts it back around Jace's neck. As it dangles in front of him, the pendant jingles from Jace's rapid breathing. Roman is so close that Jace can smell his breath.

"What...what are you doing? Come on man, please just let me go!" begs Jace.

Roman's responses remain muted and calm. "Don't worry, Jace, I'm not going to kill you," he whispers.

Jace's shoulders relax. "You're not? Oh, thank you, thank you man..." He exhales in relief.

"But we're far from done," replies Roman as he continues to twirl the blade between his fingers. He cups Jace's cheek and squeezes it. "Now, hold still. I need a good view..."

"Wait...why? What do you mean..." Jace moues in confusion, trailing off as the shivers of uncertainty return.

"Because if I want to leave you with a reminder of this lesson, I need a good view of my inspiration," replies Roman casually. And before Jace can even ask what that means, Roman's left hand extends with lightning speed and grasps Jace's chin, forcing his head backward and locking it in place.

With Roman now standing over him again, horror consumes Jace as he glimpses Roman's blade-wielding hand move above his eyeline, then...

Screaming. Pain. Continuous, searing, soul-deadening pain courses through Jace's nervous system as Roman carves into his shaved head with the pointed tip of the knife. Roman holds back nothing, and strains as he presses into Jace's forehead, incising down to bone. Jace's screams are almost melodic to Roman as he watches the bully's eyes dart back and forth, his reaction equally based in both pain and fear. His pitch rises and falls as Roman's blade changes directions, tracing the shape of the pendant that gyrates from the end of the chain on Jace's neck. Blood gushes from his open wounds and pours down his face. Despite the viscous fluid that flows into them, his eyes remain wide open. His agonizing howls persist, but so does Roman's knife. As he traces up into the top of his head, the outline of the shield is completed. Unfortunately for Jace, the design on Roman's pendant is quite intricate, and so will be his masterpiece, which requires a unique inscription of its own. Blood continues to gush from Roman's head-skin-canvas, but the cutting is far from done.

Minutes pass, and the slicing continues. The boys restraining Jace notice that he no longer fights back with the same intensity. His screams deaden as his blood-soaked eyes roll back into his head. As Roman puts the finishing touches on his gruesome, artistic life lesson, Jace passes out from pain and falls limp. Roman's crew release their captive, who collapses to his side as if the bones have vanished from his body. The blood is already beginning to congeal in some of Roman's first cuts on Jace's forehead, which now displays a spitting image of the pendant with the word "ASSHOLE" scrawled through it. Roman bends down and removes the chain from the once-powerful Jace and returns it to its rightful place around his neck. He had forgotten what the weight of the chain felt like. It taps lightly against his chest as he maneuvers, providing a subtle delight to its owner. Its once-perfect silver sheen is now discolored and tarnished from lack of care. A splattering of dried blood turns the pendant a slight brown hue, but it's nothing a little rinse can't fix.

Roman lets out a long sigh of relief. His mission had been successful. He turns back to his partners in crime and attempts to smile, but it almost pains him to do so. He takes a moment to internalize what just happened, and what it means for him...or at least what it means for the person he's become. He finds himself torn by his own actions. He cannot deny there is a certain feeling of accomplishment that permeates after delivering retribution to Jace, a boy who had beaten and degraded him and his friends day in and day out for an entire orbit. However, another feeling lingers as well; one that scolds him for the fact that he found pleasure in causing harm to another. The combination of warring thoughts depresses him, and no real joy comes from the climax of his months of planning. Too many emotions swirl around his head for him to achieve any sort of closure.

The only things that uplift him slightly are the reclamation of his property, and the presence of his friends, who had meticulously planned the events with him. Without them, he would not be standing here, finally holding the last mementoes of his parents. For the first time in a long time, he actually feels thankful for something. "I, uh... I couldn't have done this without you, so..." Roman stumbles over his words as he tries to thank his compatriots sternly, but one of the boys finishes for him.

"We never *would have* done this without you, Roman," says David with a tone of deep gratitude. Roman looks at the ground in response to the words of praise. He cannot handle adding another emotion to the litany he already feels. He reins himself in and deflects with humor.

"Yeah... Well, David, we had to do it. Roland can't afford to lose any more teeth." Despite the joke being mediocre at best, the boys all howl with laughter. They revel in their victory as the feeling of accomplishment courses through their veins. Adrenaline is a funny thing like that.

"At least I don't have to worry about getting locked in the commissary cabinets like Ryan's scrawny ass!" retorts Roland. They rear their heads back in laughter once more.

"Shit, after Jace wakes up and looks in the mirror, I think my days in the cabinets are over!" Ryan chimes in. The only one who does not say anything is Jerrick, Roman's bunkmate; the only one who had shown any concern after the massive beating he incurred on his first day at the orphanage. He just smiles wide and laughs with the rest. As the boys begin to settle down, there is an awkward silence as they think of what to say next. The silence pierces Roman's ears like nails on a chalkboard. He breaks through the awkwardness by posing a question to the group.

"So...what will we do with our newfound freedom?" he asks. The boys look back, perplexed, as if they had not even considered it. Jerrick, Roland, David, and Ryan all look at each other, hesitating to respond.

Finally, Roland speaks up. "I mean, I always figured we would just go back and blame this whole thing on you," he says, chuckling. The laughter is short this time.

David and Ryan respond simultaneously with, "Yeah..."

Roland follows his prior quip with a more serious response when he sees Roman's defeated look. "Man... Jace will be outta here in a couple months. And his crew? They ain't worth shit without him. Especially after they hear about what we did!" His excitement does not transfer to Roman.

Roman looks down, unable to understand their position. "Don't you want to join me? We'll go out to the Grind and start something of our own...like we talked about..." His suggestion is met with four heads looking toward the ground. Roman begins to realize that maybe they just don't have the will to escape the orphanage. They had been there long before Roman ever arrived, and perhaps the cage had already taken form in their minds. His heart sinks to his stomach, knowing they would not be convinced. In a last-ditch effort, he looks to his bunkmate, his best friend Jerrick Sparx, and asks, "What about you?"

Jerrick, who also looks at the ground, hesitates to respond, kicking the dirt patch at his feet. Then, after a long pause, he looks up and says, "I mean...come on. Getting past the city walls and the CP Guard? Trying to make it out there with nothing?" Roman nods solemnly and stares at the ground in utter defeat. But Jerrick smirks and finishes with, "...can't let you take all the glory by yourself! Count me in!"

Roman's head shoots up with excitement. He reaches out and grabs Jerrick's already extended hand, pulling him in for a one-armed hug. He slaps Jerrick twice on the back as he releases, then finishes their handshake with slaps, fist bumps, and other strange hand maneuvers. Looking back to the others, Roman can see on their faces that they have not changed their minds. And so, they embrace each other, one by one, for the last time. As Roman and Jerrick make their way to the back door of the Ion Street Home for Boys, something catches all of their attention and makes them pause.

They glance up at the fourth-floor window, now illuminated from the inside. Dozens of eyes gaze out the window from the Living Quarters where the other teenagers now gather. It's hard to tell how much they have seen, but they gaze upon the group that brought down Jace in awe. Roman turns back to the three boys still standing in the middle of the courtyard near Jace, who has begun mumbling unintelligibly again.

"What will you do about Rhodes and Melling when they wake up? You sure you're going to be ok here?" Roman calls back to them. David looks over at Jace, who is beginning to awaken, then back toward Roman.

"I think we'll be just fine here." He smiles. "And don't worry about those two. There're almost no cameras in this shithole, and the two oafs never saw us. We'll break a window or two. Make it look like a sloppy break-in. I bet we'll have the other kids' support when they find out Jace got a taste of justice."

Roman smiles for a moment, then looks down as the thought occurs to him: *I may never see them again...* There are so many memories he would like to rehash with them. They were his first friends since his parents' tragedy. However, the thought of Rhodes and Melling waking soon fills him with the burning urgency to make haste. After a brief pause, he finally responds, "I'll never forget you guys..." He feels awkward saying it, but when he looks up, the sentiments he receives from David, Roland, and Ryan are warm. It allows him to feel like he can finally exhale. His smile returns, and he makes one more request of the group before he leaves.

"Just do me one favor..." The three wait patiently for his response, listening intently. "Now that you're in charge, take good care of them." He points up to the illuminated fourth-floor window, the bottom of which is filled with the heads of the other orphans. They peer out the window over one another, attempting to get a view of the ruckus outside.

David replies, "Like they're my brothers," as he gives a single nod back to Roman and Jerrick. Ryan and Roland nod in agreement.

Roman then follows Jerrick through the door, down the first-floor hallway, and out the heavy, dented metal door to freedom. They descend the four cracked steps that lead to the street, but Roman stops at the last step, realizing in an instant that a full orbit has passed since he has even left the premises of Ion Street. He pauses to think for a moment.

Jerrick, who has already made his way to the sidewalk, turns back and calls out to Roman, "Hey man, what's the deal?"

Roman looks up at Jerrick, then looks up at the sky, which is brightly illuminated by Deorum's three full moons: Cindis, Beryllia, and Dontra. He responds softly, "It was my birthday a few days ago..."

Jerrick grins even bigger than before. He holds both of his arms out to his side with his palms up and sashays a slow, one-hundred-and-eighty-degree turn, gazing cheerfully upon the rest of Ion Street despite all its disrepair. Without lowering his arms, and never losing his grin, Jerrick yells, "WELL MERRY FUCKIN' BIRTHDAY BROTHA!"

Roman smiles back bigger than ever. He straightens his posture and dusts off his jumpsuit as the sole of his shoe crushes the dirt below the last step.

CHAPTER 5:

Fourteen Orbits

Deorum, though sharing many similarities with Earth, embodies many differences as well. For instance, it takes 401 standard Earth days for Deorum to complete one orbit around Bios, the Kalurite 3 system's equivalent of Earth's sun. Although this seems close enough to operate on the Earth-standard system of timekeeping (like five of the other six colonized planets), the Plenathu Viridus-based IGB would have nothing of the sort. After winning sole ownership of planet Deorum and its vitalerium trade, the IGB took every step possible to ensure complete separation, both literal and symbolic, of its prized Deorum from the jealous reaches of the planets. Even the concept of the word "year" had to be altered, and thus the standard unit of measurement became the orbit; roughly 1.1 standard Earth years. Fourteen orbits have passed since Roman's audacious departure from Ion Street; fourteen orbits filled with the hard lessons of a life detached from the safety and security of the Spheres. The Grind is unforgiving for all, but for those who are smart enough to survive it, one can expect they will emerge changed; cultivated in the experience of ruthless hardship... Evolved, in a sense. And though time has left its scars, his tissue regenerates tougher, and his shell harder.

As the black of a starless sky is pierced by the orange hues of Bios peeking over a nearby hill, Roman's eyes snap open, only to shudder closed again from the blinding light. The warmth of the soft ground beneath his back seems to get hotter by the second, and his tongue brushes like sandpaper against his cracked lips. A deep throbbing in his brain antagonizes him as he lifts his head from where it rests, releasing a dusting of sand to the ground as his matted hair sways. *Where did this sand come from?* he thinks to himself. After wiping the crust of a night's debauchery from his eyes, his vision adjusts, and his breath leaves him as his surroundings come into focus. His gaze darts from side to side, attempting to find some familiar landmark or point of reference in the vicinity. He finds none. The slow, rhythmic pain continues to pulse in his brain, only intensifying as his heart rate increases.

He now knows why sand is in his hair. Sand is all around him; the *only* thing around him as far as the eye can see. He shakes his head and vigorously massages his eyes with his knuckles in pure disbelief at his position. When he opens them again, the same desert stands before him. He slaps himself in the face, still unsatisfied with the answer that the universe has provided him. *How did I get here? Where even is here?* are the only thoughts his aching mind can muster. Besides the steady thumping of his headache, the whoosh of wind-blown sand is the only sound that fills the air, an unnerving omen.

His confusion is interrupted by the slight motion of small, tan digits entering the bottom of his view. Roman lowers his gaze to reveal bare feet, then further to reveal bare legs. He's not wearing any pants…any clothes at all, for that matter. Roman's hands sift frantically through the sand around him for his missing garments. When he lifts his hands from the ground, nothing but desert grains filter between his fingers… unsuccessful. Roman pauses, glancing around once more at the shockingly barren terrain with seemingly no end. A pit forms in his stomach, and his mouth is as dry as the sand beneath his hands and knees. Finally, reality sets in and his logic returns: *I don't know how my drunk ass got outside the city, but I have to figure out where I am to find my way back to the Grind.*

Roman pushes himself to his feet and stands as tall as he can, looking for some semblance of footprints or tracks that could lead him home. Unfortunately, the wind pummeling the dunes around him had made fast work of any traces that once were. *Maybe higher ground is the solution.* The sun beats down on him with unrelenting force, a reminder that time is of the essence. After looking around for the best vantage point, he makes his way to the tallest dune as if drawn to it. His legs feel like lead when he walks, as if he wades through deep water with ankle weights. Despite his curiously heavy limbs, he continues on, driving his feet into the hot sand with each laborious step. As he approaches the peak, the horizon comes into view. However, what he sees provides no respite from his situation, only despair.

More desert, in all directions; almost unnaturally so. No matter where he looks, there is never-ending sun-scorched land. He paces in a small circle, attempting to find a landmark, something...*anything* that could lead him from certain doom. His anxiety builds as he walks in circles, gaping at the surrounding landscape. He tries to talk but finds his tongue to be as heavy as his legs. Finally, a raspy voice escapes his lips: "No... No... NO..." He circles faster and faster until dizziness sets in.

Suddenly, his right foot catches in the sand and begins to sink, causing him to stumble, but he is able to pull it out before falling. Upon planting his left foot atop the sand dune, it too begins sinking deeper, this time up to his ankle. With a concerted effort he is able to free it, only to have the ground beneath his feet open up to engulf both feet like quicksand. Anxiety becomes fear as he helplessly sinks into the depths of the dune, the terrain swallowing him like a ravenous beast. Roman struggles but is rendered immobile as the sand begins to reach his knees, his thighs, and then his waist. "WHAT IS THIS!?" he cries out as he looks down in despair. As the sand reaches his navel, he finally stops sinking; completely immobilized. He digs through the sand with his hands to free himself, but with every handful of sand he moves, another falls into its place. Just before his panic hits a breaking point, the sudden appearance of a shadow breaks his preoccupation as it eclipses his view.

An ethereal silhouette descends from the sky as if originating from Bios itself, moving toward him with an unnatural, unsettling grace. It is encompassed by the aura of Bios's light as it hovers in the sky before him. Roman freezes, although this time from curiosity, attempting to discern the shape of the object that approaches him. Tendrils of black matter extend from its center, waving like currents and playing games with the light as it bends between them. It descends quickly, blocking more daylight with each second that passes until the shape of the object comes into view. *A person? It can't be... Those proportions...* Roman tilts his head to the side in confusion as the being approaches from the sky. The visage enthralls him, and his focus on the strange silhouette is unwavering. Mesmerized, his feelings of panic and fear regarding his surroundings seem to melt away, immediately replaced by an unexplainable warmth.

"You think everything happens for a reason?" speaks a calm, familiar voice beside him. Roman turns to his left to see his best friend Jerrick standing just an arm's length away, gazing up toward the same vision in the sky. His pristine, black Klipper jacket ripples in the wind; its white and red Wibetani Militia patch in the shape of an ornate helmet and crossed daggers boldly displayed on the left breast padding. He continues speaking in his familiar, confident voice. "Part of me thinks that's garbage talk...but then again, the way things play out sometimes, really makes you think...you know what I mean?" Jerrick redirects his eyes to meet Roman's.

Roman retorts, "Are you gonna go into one of your delusional fate rants again? You're crazy, Klip. Fate is just a calming distraction for the simple-minded. Something to take their minds off the chaos that's..."

"Everything?" Jerrick finishes his sentence, smirking as he chuckles to himself.

"Yea, exactly," Roman responds agreeably as he returns a smirk. But his calm feeling is short-lived, as Jerrick's face drops and he speaks to Roman, looking through his brows.

"Looks like you're just as predictable as me. Except it's *not* everything." His tone becomes serious. Roman furrows his brow but cannot seem to come up with a response. He just stares at his friend, whose eyes burn holes through Roman's. "She comes bearing gifts," Jerrick says, tilting his head back toward the sky.

Roman turns back on his cue and is startled to see the humanoid silhouette is right on top of him, hovering just above the ground his feet are buried beneath. He shields his eyes as blinding light emits from around the being as if it produces its own. The aura burns Roman's eyes. He squints at the searing visage, but despite its proximity to him, it is just as hazy as when it was miles away. All he can see is a towering feminine silhouette encompassing his field of vision, her limbs like tree branches, long and spindly—inhuman in proportion. "Who... What are you?" Roman calls out to the figure.

"It's going to hurt," yells Jerrick over him. Just then, as if it hangs on his words, the hot wind that whips sand against the dune ceases to blow in an instant. The air is hauntingly still, and all becomes silent. Roman looks back to his friend, but it is not the same Jerrick that stood before him just moments ago.

His black Klipper jacket is now torn and tattered, revealing patches of mauled flesh, sinew, and bone of his torso. Blood trickles down his clothing in thick streams of deep red, collecting in a puddle beneath him. No shoes cover his gaunt, bony feet, and his black skin is now pale and lifeless. A chunk of his neck is missing, with the area around it charred to ash and scab. Two eyes stare back at Roman, but they are not the eyes of his friend. Bright glowing orbs of pure hellish red now pierce straight through him, sending an icy chill down his spine. The feeling of crippling fear returns as Roman's psyche descends into a downward spiral. Though he is submerged in sand, he can feel his legs trembling at the incorporeal vision of Jerrick.

"You...you shouldn't be here!" stutters Roman frightfully as he stares at the face of death in its ghoulish form, which glares back at him menacingly. The decrepit limb of his friend lurches forth with unnatural speed, cracking into position to point at Roman. The tip of Jerrick's index finger hangs by a thread of flesh.

Jerrick speaks, but the sound of multiple voices echoes out of his ghastly mouth. "The old way carves the path, the primordial home instills strength, and the guide shall return to judge the tribulation of champions." When he finishes, the haunting silence prevails. Roman is frozen still. He racks his brain for meaning but is unable to make sense of Jerrick's cryptic message. He repeats the words over and over in his head to no end. All he can do is stare back into the bloodred glow of Jerrick's eyes. Before he can make a remark, Jerrick's jaw shoots open and the voices of many resound a terrifying cry. "The astral tides will conform to the might of a soul reborn from the ashes of sorrow. AND THAT SOUL'S SPARK WILL UNLEASH UPON CREATION AN INFERNO WITH THE DEVASTATING GRACE OF UNNATURAL DISASTER!!" screams Jerrick's standing corpse.

Overcome with fear, Roman once again frantically attempts to free himself from his desert shackles. But before he can, the hand of the mysterious astral silhouette reaches out and, with one long, slender finger, touches Roman's forehead, and all goes black.

Searing pain courses through his brain as horrid images strike through his mind with unfathomable speed. The city of Kairus flashes before his eyes as a dilapidated hellscape; its once tall, magnificent skyscrapers appearing before him as burning scaffolds. The sky, now crimson red, rains ash onto his war-torn home. The screaming of men, women, and children, the echoing of vitalerium rifle shots, and the scraping of metal on metal flood his ears at an unbearable decibel. Explosions shake the earth with the magnitude of earthquakes as megastructures collapse to the ground. Flashes of blood and gore rape Roman's mind. Piles of skulls and mutilated armored bodies fill the city, and rivers of blood replace the familiar concrete of the streets. Visions of space littered with the fractured scrap metal of destroyed warships floating next to severed body parts and corpses, which spin freely in zero gravity. A blue vitalerium crystal floating in the backdrop of the abyss begins pulsing faster and faster until it vibrates, its carapace overflowing with gray smoke. Voices begin to whisper in his ears, speaking in undiscernible tongues. As the blue shard edges closer, the voices get louder…and louder…until the crystal cracks. The voices multiply and fill his eardrums until the vitalerium crystal splinters and finally bursts with a mighty force, sending shards of vitalerium in all directions. Roman lets out a scream of agonizing fear. "AAAARRGGGHHH!!!"

Roman shoots up like a rocket, silver pendant swinging from his neck, still screaming from images no mortal mind was built to endure. His bloodcurdling screams are met with the light from Bios gleaming through the small glass window above him. His body drips with sweat, soaking the sleeping bag he sits in. He pants heavily as he copes with his surroundings, different from just moments before. The familiar sheen of curved steel walls creates a small domed space around him, meeting at a transparent peak. Roman clutches his silver shield pendant, takes a deep breath, and sighs. "Just a dream… just a fucked-up dream," he mutters to himself, rubbing the large raised scar on his right shoulder.

Swinging his legs out of the sleeping bag, he scratches at the large gash on his right calf; a new one from his latest adventure coming to a close. It will add nicely to his collection of souvenirs from past bounties. He had been too exhausted the prior night to take care of it. The cut burns as his fingernails scratch the surrounding skin; this is a good one. He reaches into the gear bag beside him and retrieves a small silver vial containing a green fluid. The red block letters scrawled across the container read "MEDISEAL." It sloshes as he brings it to his lap. After prepping the disperser, he aims its nozzle at his leg and sprays the viridian film over the open wound.

"ARGH," Roman groans. It feels as if someone brands him with a hot iron. He stares at his leg as the skin begins to bubble and release pungent steam. Though painful, the edges of the wound quickly meet at its center. A small scab flakes off onto the floor as the wound is healed in a matter of seconds. He breathes heavily, partly from the pain of the Mediseal serum and partly because he is still reeling from his unusually vivid nightmare. Reaching into the back pocket of his pants, he produces a small flask from which he takes a long swig. His eyes wince as he swallows the warm swill. *What shitty whiskey*, he thinks to himself, placing the container back in his pants. His body aches, and he rubs his eyes as he lifts himself from the ground. Every movement is lackluster and labored, but Roman has a job to complete. So, he slugs back some water from his canteen, dresses himself, and slings his gear bag over his shoulder before exiting the makeshift domicile.

At the push of a button, the metal walls retract into themselves around Roman, each panel fitting snugly into the next one until finally collapsing into a small, two-by-two metal plate at his feet. Bios light shines through the trees caressing Roman's face, blurring his already tired vision. He picks up the heavy metal slab from the ground and dusts the dirt from it. He stands in a clearing surrounded by a forest of foliage. The sounds of creatures small and large filling the atmosphere does not faze him in the slightest; this terrain is practically his second home. Roman walks the retracted metallic hovel over to a small, open-topped hoverbike parked against a nearby tree and loads it into a side compartment. The brown of dirt and the green of crushed warm-weather foliage cake the bike's black and purple tarnished paint. What was once colored chrome had become red with rust throughout the orbits on his vintage vehicle. With a gloved hand he wipes away some of the grime on its profile, revealing silver lettering spelling "OMARA" and, beneath it, "LANCER," the make and model. Roman smiles at the vehicle he kneels next to, which has gotten him out of many a predicament in the past.

"Let's fire you up, Rooster. And don't give me any shit today; we've got an appointment." The nickname had been bestowed upon its purchase, named after some feathered Earth animal that Roman had never heard of. He thought it had a nice ring to it, and according to the salesman he bought it from, it was a fierce Earth beast. There was no AI in a bike of this model; no guiding voice, which brought about a kind of affection for his silent partner in crime.

A bike like Rooster requires skill to ride, and Roman is certainly adept. He slaps the left shoulder panel on his terrain armor, out of which springs a black metal strip from the thick armored collar. It curves around his head and then expands into a helmet encasing his face.

"Give me some music to work with. Play Infiniti Inferno." Roman's voice echoes into his helmet. His ears are instantly flooded with a blaring heavy metal rift that spikes his adrenaline. He smirks as he's filled with a newfound energy; reinvigorated by the sounds of his favorite band. In cadence with the melody, he hops into the seat of the bike and presses the ignition. The bike roars to life, launching sparks and smoke onto the dirt behind him. A neon purple glow flickers through the engine as Roman is lifted about a foot off the ground. With the dirt kicking up around him, he jams the throttle back and takes off through the forest...back toward the Grind.

Small branches and leaves whip against the bike as Roman

races home for the handoff. He skillfully navigates the vehicle between the hoop trees and forest thickets at high speed. He does not have to check the time; he is already over a day late for the drop. *After what I just went through for this thing, they'll get it when they get it,* he thinks to himself. Despite the treacherous terrain, he races through the forest at a shocking speed; not because he is late, but because he loves the thrill. His adrenaline gets the best of him and he twists the accelerator as he zigzags around each barrier. Throttling under an arc-shaped rock formation, the speedometer projects the numbers "113" onto the HUD in his helmet and continues counting up.

Though the heavy metal blaring through Roman's helmet makes his heart race, conversely, it calms his mind. The music eventually turns to white noise in his head, and the stress of life and all its responsibilities dissipate into the ether. Time itself seems to slow around him, and tunnel vision takes over as he weaves left and right. He does not focus on the obstacles in his way; they mean nothing to him. He only focuses on the path through them.

Finally, as the tree line breaks and the foliage begins to thin, the skyline of Kairus peeks into view. It produces a distinct gradient as the buildings grow taller toward the center of Kairus's Inner Sphere, a city so massive, they say it can be seen clearly from orbit. Its gargantuan structures seem to brush the very atmosphere of the planet. Even though the city is in view, it will be at least another two to three hours of travel before he reaches the Grind. It is but a great, smoking mole marring the surface of the green planet, surrounded by barren, cracked terrain, his regrettable home. The smile leaves Roman's face as he looks upon the monstrosity in the distance, but his pace does not slow. He travels on, hurtling through the arid plains between him and his destination: the southeastern block of the Grind, between city-states Argos and Luxenia.

The flat terrain provides no obstacles other than an occasional boulder or stone pillar. With nothing to keep him busy, the memory of his nightmare begins to creep back into his idle mind. Roman is used to nightmares, but even the horrid dreams of his parents' deaths do not compare to this night terror... nothing had ever felt this real before. It plagues his mind the entire ride home, like a seed planted deep in his subconscious.

After hours of travel, Roman finally reaches the city limits. The makeshift panels haphazardly welded together to form walls surrounding the Grind look like a joke compared to the massive walls surrounding the city-states. Two CP Guardsmen approach Roman on his bike as it slows to a stop at the gate. Their rifles hang at their side, and the boredom that accompanies their station is apparent as they begin to question Roman.

"ID," says one Guardsman in a low, jaded tone. His partner stands beside him with his arms folded. Roman slaps the left shoulder of his armor, retracting his helmet to reveal his face. His long hair falls out past his collar. He steadies his head as the second Guardsman extends an arm, holding a small scanning device. It beeps as it registers Roman's eyes, prompting the Guardsman to check the device's screen. "Darryl... Frost?" asks the Guardsman. Roman nods yes. His face is expressionless, but his eyes harbor a secret hatred for the CP armor worn by the two men. The first Guardsman continues to grill Roman. "Any contraband or artifacts in your rig, or on your person?" Roman slowly shakes his head in response. "Then what's your business beyond the walls?" retorts the officer.

Roman says nothing in response, simply reaches down to one of the large compartments on the side of his bike. The Guardsmen take notice of this and bring their weapons up at the ready, worried that he might produce a weapon. Roman looks back as he hears the clink of guns lifted against their armor. His expression does not change; he simply raises both hands halfway. Then, more slowly this time, he reaches for the release latch on his bike compartment. The compartment hisses, then extends laterally, revealing three frozen Lancite heads with their long teeth bared, caked in blood—some of it Roman's, most of it theirs. Steam rises from their yellow-brown skin as the Bios heat beats on them. Even while frozen, the aroma is practically corrosive.

"Ugh..." One of the guards flaps a hand in disgust at the beast's carcass.

"Hunting," replies Roman sharply. "Meat's in another compartment. Wanna gawk at that too?"

Roman's heart races as the Guardsmen look at each other, deciding whether to search further. Then, to his relief, one of the men blocks his nose and mouth with the crux of his elbow and delivers a muffled reply. "Definitely not. PRIMES, lock up that disgusting Grind cuisine already!"

Roman slams the latch with his fist, and the steaming rack of Lancite heads retracts back into his vehicle. While one keeps a watchful eye on Roman, the other Guardsman with a seemingly sensitive nose walks to the entrance and scans his own retina on the green pad beside it. It chimes to confirm his credentials, and he steps back as the hydraulic systems engage to lift the large hangar door outward. The dusty streets of the Grind come into view with its dilapidated buildings and crowded, trash-covered streets. Roman shifts back into drive and zips in past the CP officers, leaving a trail of dust in his path. *Fuckin' Klang's,* Roman thinks to himself, chuckling. He passes them and hovers down the tan street toward his drop. Home at last...though a home provides little respite for those who live in the Grind.

CHAPTER 6:

Mo-Hawk-Bang-Bang

The Grind as a whole is colored a rust brown. It reeks of a combination of combustion, sewage, and street food. No skyscrapers grace the clouds above like in Kairus Prime. Most buildings here are crafted from the salvaged remains of destroyed starships that were in abundance after the Hundred Years War—with the majority not built from choice parts, either. The high-tech, clean surroundings present in the city-states seem to have eluded the residents of these parts. Roman has seen just about every section of the Grind, and not a single inch of it is pretty. Not quite a city-state of its own, the Grind has always been more of a "no-man's-land" that encircles the entirety of Kairus Prime and its city-states, housing about half of the planet's population outside of the protective walls of the Spheres.

It first began as a place for those banished from the great walls of Kairus Prime. For individuals seeking to escape the hand of the government, it also served as a respite; a sanctuary of freedom for those who simply wanted to live in peace apart from the CP. However, the small settlement expanded over the years following a surge in planetary migration in the early days of Deorum's booming economy. The Grind was suddenly filled with a massive influx of residents who required low-rent living to get their new lives started. And as the city-states became more expensive, more and more people began to move outside the protective walls of Kairus Prime: low-level mechanics, street merchants, blue-collar workers, petty criminals, hybrid humans and all the like. The Grind became a home for those looking to get by, those looking to come up, and those simply denying their inevitable decline into cogs of the great Kairus machine. It has no representation in the court of Kairus, and only loose connections to the city-states.

As decades passed, the community grew more rapidly, and a bustling economy of its own began to form. Despite its less-than-opulent conditions, the Grind began to thrive in its own way, with freedom as its mark. But the court of Kairus, greedy as ever, wanted their piece of the little success that the Grind had produced—despite giving nothing in return. Slowly but surely, the long arm of the CP began to reach its way into the Grind; first with walls surrounding the boundaries of the enormous circular expanse, then with the Guardsmen, and finally with taxes.

Despite their best efforts, the presence of the CP Guardsmen, although ever-increasing, has never been enough to provide the same magnitude of pressure that the city-states experience. This lack of oversight made the Grind a breeding ground for gangs to proliferate and build their own books of business, a response to the unwelcome intrusion of the CP. However, due to the vastness of the Grind and its circular shape bordering the walls of Kairus and its city-states, no real leadership ever emerged within these gang factions. With too much ground to cover and not enough brains to go around, they remained simple satellite operations, forever expanding and contracting as they war with each other and the CP.

Gulcher is the name ascribed to small-time Grind outlaws who squabble with each other over territory and resources.

Essentially anarchists, they exercise influence in their respective territories, dealing primarily in extortion, theft, drug trafficking, and black-market trade. Though Roman has little respect for the Gulchers, he finds them useful for freelance work when he needs a payday. So, with his credit account low and a Gulcher gang's package in his possession, Roman makes his way to the hand-off for his payday.

The street hums with the chatter of street merchants bartering with residents. Roman navigates slowly through the crowded dirt road on his Lancer. The denizens make little effort to move out of his way, and do so at their own pace. Small tents and makeshift huts line the street filled with all sorts of goods and wares, trinkets, scrap metal, food, and animals. It is hard for Roman to see past the herds of people conducting business in the street, but he is able to identify a low arch-shaped entrance adorned in red neon lighting. A small hologram of a beer bottle spins in front of the entrance, reading "The Tontine."

Roman glides to a halt in front of the building and sets his Lancer down. Rooster lets out one final huff of air as Roman powers the hoverbike down, expelling a cloud of dust around him. Hopping off the bike, he circles around the back and kneels by the rear exhaust. Carefully reaching beneath the chassis so as to not touch Rooster's hot mechanisms, Roman flips a hidden switch. Mechanics whir as the seat of his bike lifts upward, revealing a small satchel in the hidden compartment. He grabs the bag and makes his way to the Tontine's entrance. As he approaches the archway, a large man sitting in a plastic lawn chair takes notice and removes his oversized black headphones. He sets down his bottle of Sham, a grotesque liquor the color of nuclear waste. The opaque green fluid sloshes about the bottle as it hits the dirt. It stinks of engine grease, which to some may be considered more appetizing than the drink itself.

The man stands to meet Roman as he nears. Even Roman,

who stands at six-foot-one, is dwarfed by the figure before him. The man's head is shaved, which brings attention to his oddly shaped skull. Scars cover the brute's cheeks, and muscles like boulders bulge from beneath his dirty, brown t-shirt. A block of gray metal emitting a small red light covers his orbit and merges with his skin, which curls over the metal edges crudely: a bionic ocular implant. It scans Roman up and down. Definitely an archaic model, it sticks out on his face like a sore thumb. Unlike other planets, cybernetics were outlawed on Deorum unless medically necessary, and even then, the state-of-the-art technology was reserved only for the political class and the most elite of soldiers. Judging by the character this device is implanted in, *medically necessary* was likely the case. The bouncer looks as if he has never seen a fight he didn't love...or participate in.

    Roman gazes up into the man's cyborg eye and calmly says, "G'mornin', gorgeous." The man does not seem to find humor in the remark and balls his fists as he stares daggers into Roman. The veins in the bouncer's arms thicken as his muscles tense. Roman looks past him at the bottle of Sham propped up against the mud-brown lawn chair, then back at the thug, asserting, "Getting an early start this morning, I see. Don't listen to the naysayers—toxic sludge *is* the breakfast of champions..." The man's nostrils flare and his lips curl into a snarl. He steps forward aggressively and starts to lift his hand to strike Roman for his moderate insolence. Before his hand is fully raised, Roman calmly states, "Tarley needs a trinket," which stops the modded thug in his tracks. Roman dangles the satchel from his outstretched arm, allowing it to sway back and forth in front of the bouncer.

    The man glares at the satchel, annoyed by the fact that Roman has a reason to be there. It eliminates any hopes of delivering an AM beating. He looks anxiously up and down the street, scanning for CP Guardsmen. "Why the fuck didn't you start with dat!?" the man bellows. "Put dat away and get inside. You're late. Tarley *hates* lateness. And you're late..." he repeats himself. Intellect is clearly not one of his strengths. Roman swings the bag over his shoulder and struts through the archway, which houses a dark stairwell leading down to a dank basement barroom.

As he descends, the sound of heavy electronic music being played through crackling speakers becomes audible. Upon reaching the bottom, a dimly lit room opens to reveal a grimy, poorly attended venue. No bartender stands behind the bar. Only a handful of people occupy the space: five men packed around a single table in the back of the room. Three men stand watching as two others sit playing holo-games on the bar table. Two small, illuminated figurines stand on the holo-board, exchanging blows controlled by the two men as they mash the buttons of their controllers. All of them wear dirty, disheveled clothes like the bouncer, except for one. One of the sitting men dons a distinct, bright orange mohawk and a bandolier with no shirt. Baggy black cargo pants with orange pockets meet his spotless black army boots at the ankle, and he looks as if he is running out of flesh to tattoo.

As Roman strolls past the bar, he notices that all the men carry weapons, and at least four have guns; one of which is a staggeringly large revolver that rests on the table by Tarley's ink-stained arm. The man sitting across from him displays a long bowie knife sheathed on his belt. Another man standing behind him holds a long rifle, and the two men beside him carry pistols holstered at their hips. Infatuated with the ensuant game, the men do not notice Roman enter. They're too busy yelling obscenities at the challenger and cheering on their boss. But their game is interrupted as Roman drops the satchel onto the holo-board in front of them, which lands with a heavy thud and blocks their view of the miniature characters in combat. All shift their attention to Roman, whose arm is still extended above the holo-board.

Tarley restrains his anger behind a grimace. Not used to

being disrespected in his circle of thugs, he speaks to Roman through his teeth. "I was winning…"

Roman smiles without showing his teeth, then walks to a nearby table and drags a chair over to the group. Its metal legs scrape against the floor like nails on a chalkboard. He spins it around and sits down, resting his crossed arms on the backrest. "I'm sure you were. But I don't have all day, so if you'll simply pay me, I'll be on my way," replies Roman.

All the men remain silent. Tarley stares at Roman, maintaining his grimace, then snickers as he looks around at his goons, who follow him in laughter. Tarley shrugs his shoulders, then retorts, "Well! Let's see what you've brought us then," as he un-does the leather straps of the satchel. From inside, he pulls out a small, stone-carved statuette and rests it on the table before him. The figurine is chiseled in the shape of a humanoid warrior with wings and a metal mask. Tarnished metallic accents are inlaid throughout the statue to form its armor, and the eyes of the figure are crafted from yellow gems. They reflect the light of the holo-board it stands on.

Tarley extends his hands toward the statue as if to present it and exclaims to the group, "Now isn't that a beauty! That'll fetch a nice price from my buyer." He glances back at Roman, who looks to be growing more impatient. Tarley asks, "Where'd you find it?"

"Where you said it would be," replies Roman bluntly.

"Well *obviously*. My intel is always premo. That's why I'm sitting where I am." Tarley shoots a cocky look toward the others, who nod like drones. "I mean, where was it exactly? What else was there? What was it in?"

Roman grunts loudly. "In a cavern. Lodged in the wall at the end of a tunnel. Looked like some kind of shrine… Hey, can I get those UCs now?" Roman can feel his temper rising, but Tarley is too enthusiastic about his artifact to notice.

"You know, some of these artifacts are tens of thousands of orbits old…and do you know why Gleph artifacts are illegal for citizens to possess, Roman?" When Roman provides only a blank, uninterested stare in response, Tarley continues, "Not a fan of history, I see... They're illegal to possess because the CP, with all their insecure power-mongering, seeks to control us by limiting our access to the history of our planet. They want the secrets locked within these artifacts all to themselves. It's *aaall* about who's swinging around the biggest dick." Roman still looks unimpressed and now slumps in his chair. Tarley continues, "The Gleph were here millennia before us. Imagine a civilization lucky enough to be birthed on a planet with near-infinite access to vitalerium right from the get-go. One so advanced and so refined in their utilization of vitalerium, they say, that they gained access to the multiverse and disappeared to an entirely new reality."

"Great story. Can I go now?" Roman finally answers sarcastically.

"I bet those politicians up in their ivory towers in the Inner Sphere look for these to study so they can gain access to the same knowledge that..." Tarley is cut off by Roman, whose agitation has reached its limit.

"From a dinky stone statue? A hunk of planet rock bedazzled and carved in a fancy shape?"

"This is an artifact!" shouts Tarley, who is now the one losing his restraint.

"Yea, one that I spent four days in the fucking forest retrieving for your sorry ass because you couldn't do it yourself. Some rich fuck probably just wants it so he can show off at his next debutant ball."

"Watch it, *freelancer*! I'm the one who hires *you* for jobs and gives the orders. THAT'S why I don't go running around in the forest like you..." Roman rolls his eyes as Tarley holds the artifact up to the light and turns it, eyeing the gems and accents as if mesmerized by its form. "They say that the Gleph are still out there somewhere. They left this planet in search of brighter horizons than these. Just imagine what they must have found... I bet one day they'll come back to collect their history, only to find us squatting on their planet; their former home. Rumor has it, some of them are ten feet tall..."

Fed up with the thug, Roman lays into him. "Ugh... Rumor has it they're probably dead! They're probably extinct from bombing themselves to shit with their own vitalerium weaponry. You ever thought of that? We've colonized seven planets and never seen the Gleph. You think they wouldn't have noticed us by now? Besides, I didn't come here to listen to your lancor-shit conspiracy theories. Pay me now, *please*."

"YOU THINK THIS STUFF IS A JOKE!? YOU THINK I'M JUST PLAYIN' AROUND!?" Tarley shouts at Roman, whose disinterest he cannot seem to grasp.

"No, Tarley..." Roman adds politely before letting out his real sentiments, "...I think you're psychotic... And I think you dress like a gay porn star at a BDSM convention for middle-aged punk-rockers. And I *also* think your little *crew* who waits to laugh at all your little *jokes* has given you a big head to house plenty of these garbage ideas you concoct. But most importantly, Tarley, I think that I want to get my money and get the fuck out of here so I can drink the rest of my SHIT whiskey and get some actual sleep on a bed that isn't a FOREST-FUCKING BUSH. NOW PAY ME, TARLEY!"

Tarley seethes with anger, insecure that Roman insults him in front of his crew members. Every muscle in his body tenses to the point that he looks as if he'll pop. His face begins to turn red as blood is forced to his head, returning a look so angry he almost looks sick. Finally, he mumbles angrily to the man behind him, "Pay the stupid mongrel." The rifle-toting man reaches into a bag hanging from the back of Tarley's chair, pulls out a credit chip, and walks it over to Roman. Roman grabs the blue-tinted transparent plastic from him aggressively, then scans it on the TAB monitor wrapped around his left forearm. The TAB chimes as the universal credits are registered, and a holographic image is projected just inches from his wrist. An orange-red number spins above the device, reading, "+Ж10,000." Roman's face twists as his demeanor swaps from relieved to infuriated in an instant.

"What the fuck, Tarley. THIS IS LESS THAN HALF!" he yells at his small, ginger-haired employer, who remains seated. Tarley almost looks proud of himself as he smirks back at Roman.

"You're over a day late on delivery… And thus, I've deducted what I feel appropriate for the wasting of my time. My buyer was expecting this *yesterday*. So, what you get…" retorts a snide Tarley as he extends a middle finger toward Roman, "…is what you get! Hahaha!" His maniacal smile exposes his two chrome-colored canine teeth, each with a small red LED light gleaming at its center. His minions laugh along with him as he flaunts his position over Roman.

Roman's jaw clenches as he glares back, but the voice that responds to the insult is a calm baritone. "Either you produce another credit chip from that grab bag of yours and hand it over, or I'm going to make you *eat* your middle finger for wasting *my* time." The room goes silent. They pause their laughter for a moment as they exchange looks, unsure of the seriousness of Roman's threat. The moment passes, and the room erupts in laughter again, only louder this time. Roman's expression does not change.

Tarley, after having a good howl, finally says, "You can fuck right off, *Klip*." Roman's former title, a term used within the Wibetani Militia; the straw that breaks the camel's back.

Roman inhales as if he prepares to hold his breath underwater, but lets out a long sigh as his gaze falls to the ground. His teeth grind, and the gall of Tarley screwing him out of his payday causes his heart to beat out of his chest in anticipation of what comes next. When he finally looks back up, Roman's expression is haunting. His eyes look as if they have grown three sizes beneath his furrowed brow. The crew looks upon him, puzzled by his persistence. A silence falls over the room, and the men begin to slowly move their hands closer to their firearms. A pin drop can be heard as they await Roman's response, which is succinct. "Let's hope you don't choke..."

Gunfire fills the room as two flashes erupt almost simultaneously from the end of Roman's pistol, which he unholsters with incredible speed. The next sound they hear is the thud of bodies collapsing limp to the floor. The two pistol-toting thugs that once stood beside Tarley fall dead, one with a bullet to the center of his chest and the other with hot lead through his forehead. Before their corpses even start to bleed, Roman grabs the rifle from the man to his left, preventing the barrel from rising. He then plants his right hand firmly on the ground next to him and wraps his lower limbs around the aggressor's legs, performing a scissor sweep that folds the man to the floor.

Unable to aim in time, the goon's head slams off the linoleum, causing him to involuntarily discharge a spray of bullets into the ceiling. The sound is deafening as it echoes off the subterranean walls of the small bar. Dust and ceiling debris hit the ground just as Tarley falls from his seat, covering his ears and scrambling to safety. The other seated man unsheathes his bowie knife and races to put a stop to Roman, who has already kicked the rifle from the downed man's hand and wrapped himself around his extended arm. With a sharp thrust, the thug's elbow snaps between Roman's knees, exposing bright white bone and crimson red flesh. A guttural, agonizing cry bursts from somewhere deep in the gangster's gut but is silenced instantly by Roman, who fires his pistol point-blank through his right temple. Blood and brain matter splatter across the already grotesque floor of the tavern.

Out of the corner of his eye, Roman sees the sheen of a serrated blade screaming toward his midsection as the seated man finally reacts to the chaos and bloodshed terrorizing their base of operations. His face is gnarled in aggression, and his greasy hair thrashes side to side as he hurls his weight at the freelancer who murdered his cohorts. The blade sinks deep into torso flesh, making a horrid squelching sound. However, the flesh he stabs is not that of Roman, who was able to roll the corpse he lays next to into the path of the man's knife.

In the commotion, Roman's pistol slides under a barstool out of reach. With his arms now burdened by the weight of the body that shields him, Roman delivers a swift kick to the last thug's knee, which buckles from the blow. Roman has just enough time to push the corpse off him before his last foe recovers. He rolls to the left, narrowly dodging the second blade attack. The blood-drenched bowie knife instead becomes lodged in the linoleum flooring next to its intended target.

Frustrated by his failed attempts, the thug presses forward toward a now-standing Roman. However, he pauses his advance when Roman produces something else from his hip. The shine of silver and black steel reflects the dim, multicolored light of neon signs and small holograms illuminating the bar. And as Roman's black-gloved thumb presses down on the round red crystal toward the edge of the handle, a long blade ejects. The thug, attempting to hide his fear, shouts out, "COME ON!" as he swings his blade around him furiously. The Gulcher exhibits his dexterity with the knife as he steps back and circles Roman, who stands firm and calm, following the movements with only his eyes. Tarley remains pressed against the back wall of the room, awaiting the outcome of the standoff. Finally realizing that Roman is not going to make the first move, the gangster pumps himself up, produces a final war cry, and begins to charge his freelancer opponent. Then...

THWACK! The man does not even take a full step before Roman hurls his balanced blade through the air, which pierces the Gulcher's throat and lodges deep in the crevice of his Adam's apple. The thug's serrated blade bounces off the linoleum flooring as he wheezes and falls like a brick to his flank. He squirms involuntarily as he chokes on his own fluids. With his hands grasping his throat, he tries to cover the wound but cannot stop the flow of blood, which pours down his windpipe. The blood that escapes forms a puddle on the ground beside him.

Tarley stares in horror as the last of his crew perishes before his eyes. The shady runt of a gang boss lets out a short, high-pitched whimper as his gut sinks to the floor. He chokes on air like his underling chokes on bodily fluids. As Tarley frantically plans his next move, Roman reaches down to pick up his pistol from under the bar and returns it to his holster. He then walks swiftly across to the man who quivers as he gags on Roman's blade. The gurgling of blood in his airway is the only sound in the bar other than the low, steady beat of electronic music. Roman dislodges his blade from the man's throat, removing it slowly and releasing a river of blood and saliva. Roman wipes off the blade on his pants, then retracts it and tucks the handle back in his belt.

Turning his attention back to the coward Tarley, Roman shouts, "What did I tell you, Tarley!?" He breathes heavily, exasperated from the calamity that leaves four dead. He marches quickly toward the convulsing orange mohawk at the rear of the bar. Tarley's heart and mind race as he searches for an escape. His eyes fall to the large revolver resting on the holo-board where he sat. In a last-ditch effort to evade the wrath of the freelancer, he dashes for the gun. Reaching the table before Roman does, Tarley grabs the weapon, but his nerves cause him to fumble with it between his sweaty palms. By the time he is finally able to get a grip on it, he raises the gun and aims it at Roman, a futile attempt at self-preservation.

Before Tarley can pull the trigger of his oversized hand cannon, the toe of Roman's boot collides with the butt of the gun, sending it soaring straight up in the air. Petrified, Tarley's eyes can only follow the careening steel as Roman's arm extends to catch it. Tarley winces and leans back, lifting his hands to block his face from Roman's aim and pleading,

"NO, PLEASE DON'T!" With his eyes forced shut, he does not realize that Roman is not aiming at his face.

The ear-shattering crack of the revolver echoes through the room as bright orange fire expels from the gun barrel. A large-caliber bullet collides with Tarley's left hand, severing his middle finger and practically splitting his palm in half. Tarley collapses to the bar floor in a fetal position, bawling as he grasps his hand, which now spurts like a red fountain. Tears stream down his face, following his frown lines into his mouth, and his detached digit rests just a few feet from his head. Roman stares down at Tarley with his lips pursed. He almost feels pity for the Gulcher, who continues to writhe and cry on the floor. However, he cannot allow himself to be taken advantage of. In these parts, reputation is the only thing keeping a steady flow of work coming in; especially in Roman's profession. Weakness is not well rewarded in the Grind, where word is bond. And so, intent on fulfilling his promise, Roman picks up the detached middle finger, then kneels beside Tarley's head. He grabs the leather strap of his bandolier and shakes him to regain his attention.

"Do you know why the last three amateurs you sent on this little artifact witch-hunt failed? The fucking thing was in a Rachidna nest. RACHIDNAS, TARLEY! You know damn well that lancor-shit timeline wasn't set in stone when we negotiated—I made that crystal clear! I NEARLY DIED GETTING THIS THING FOR YOU!" shouts Roman.

"I'm sorry... I'm sorry... I'm sorry..." Tarley whimpers repeatedly.

Roman sighs deeply as he looks upon the sorry state of the man at his feet. "So am I, Tarley...but a deal's a deal. And I *always* hold true to my word," he replies before shoving his hand into Tarley's mouth and forcing open his bottom jaw. Tarley attempts to scream in rebuttal but is unable to form words. His eyes widen, and his legs flail as Roman forces his once-attached middle finger down his gaping throat hole.

Roman then covers his mouth with his gloved hand, pinches his nose, and holds his jaw shut. Tarley tries to breathe, but the force-fed digit curls down his esophagus, blocking his airway. After a few seconds of fighting and moaning through closed lips, he is forced to swallow. He closes his eyes and sobs.

Roman pats the weeping man on his shoulder. He retrieves a green vial of Mediseal serum, opens the applicator, and places it on the floor by the broken Tarley. "Better apply that ASAP before you lose more blood. You'll be fine; you've got nine of them left to jerk off with." Roman lifts himself up and walks toward the Gulcher's bag still hanging from the back of his barstool. He rips it open and rifles through it, retrieving two more credit chips, which he scans on his TAB. A hologram display projects upward, and the spinning numbers read "+Ж30,000." Roman smiles and says, "I'm taking thirty thousand UCs on top of the ten you gave me before, uh...you know..." Roman makes a gesture, pointing around the room full of bodies, "...yea. Anyway, that's ten thousand more credits than we agreed upon at the beginning. That's for the move you tried to pull, and I think that's more than fair considering the rules of engagement. But don't worry, I'm not leaving you empty-handed. You can keep your toy soldier, which I'm sure your buyer will still happily take off your hands for a sizable margin." He then grabs his empty satchel and makes his way toward the exit. As he walks up the stairs, he hears Tarley yelp once more as the hiss of Mediseal serum misting from its canister reaches his wounds.

Upon reaching street level, Roman notices to his left that the giant bouncer still sits in his lawn chair, blissfully unaware of the situation that unfolded below. His head bobs up and down, and his hand taps rhythmically to the music blaring through his oversized headphones. Roman shakes his head, then walks by, giving him an ironic salute, to which the bald-headed man scowls in return. The satchel is returned to its compartment before Roman fires up Rooster. A cloud of dust wafts from its undercarriage, then disperses as Roman makes his way down the dirt road toward his home. Another job completed. Another check cashed. Just another day in the Grind.

CHAPTER 7:

Courts, Courtiers, and Kings of Kairus

Situated 221 stories above Sanctum Core sits the grounds of the Apex, a platform that few buildings' peaks surpass. Unhindered by the blockade of the city's countless structures, the Apex's magnificent view of Kairus Prime stretches for thousands of miles, and is a treasure to behold; enjoyed by few. The majority of Kairus residents live lifetimes without ever getting a glimpse of the artfully manicured grounds, or the breathtaking sight; a testament to humanity's power to beautifully create. At this altitude the air is thin, but the Apex compensates with atmosphere-modulating beams. These tall, thin structures are dispersed across the grounds, creating the perfect environment for those residing within it. The foliage of ornate trees from different planetary origins are carefully shaped. Artistically sculpted bushes decorate the paths of passersby, each positioned perfectly to accent the next. Grand statues of stone and metal reach toward the heavens, serving to celebrate the heroes and heroines of Deoran past. Luxury hovercars and spacefaring vessels pass by quietly above, interspersed with CP craft patrolling to maintain the safety of residents.

An attractive, impeccably manicured middle-aged couple

wearing ornate white tunics traverse a spotless concrete sidewalk lined with luscious blue grass. Another couple passes by them in their carriage. The vehicle, like a halved silver sphere providing just enough room for two seats, hovers along the walkway with a delicate hum. Its occupants also wear tunic-style garments, almost indistinguishable from the first couple, aside from the color. Fine silk and satin adorn others on the street in differing fashions as they stroll leisurely through the Apex of Sanctum Core. The Apex's hyper-wealthy citizens gather in the sprawling park to socialize and gossip as their day begins.

The chatter varies little. Most talk about their positive sentiments for the CP, and excitement regarding recent initiatives that contributed to universal credits in their bank accounts. Others brush shoulders with representative members of the court, lobbying for changes in their favor and paying homage to their policymakers. Some even boast about their part in the passing of recent initiatives. The Apex, in general, is the mecca of ever-evolving political discourse. Upon passing by, the middle-aged couple overhears a man conversing with another. "I told Representative Case, my pockets are zipped shut. We've been contributors for years, but I need to see some progress on these permits moving forward if you want to see another UC!"

The couple looks at each other and smirks. The man chuckles softly as he looks away and mutters, "Heh. Good luck dealing with that snake, Case," under his breath. As they continue walking, a glossy white sphere hovers toward them. It approaches with the quiet hum of automated grace and stops beside them. At the sight of the hovering orb, the two turn toward it and stand still. They are immediately encompassed by a wave of green light emitting from a pinprick hole in the side of its hull. It shines brightly and quickly across their faces.

An automated female voice emanates from the small floating vessel with a friendly tone. "Good morning, Matrinas family! My records show that all criteria are in order. Can

I offer you anything today?" A black crevice forms in the sphere's hull, splitting it in two. The hull doors slide open to its flanks, revealing a plethora of gourmet hors d'oeuvres and beverages, hot towels and amenities, intoxicating agents and medicines. The couple reviews the day's many options, then they reach inside the cabinet display. Each grabs a small pink square topped with tiny, pearlescent yellow spheres and prepares to ingest them.

"You've chosen Imptia fish pate garnished with Frezan roe, a delicacy imported from Portia Quixote; well known for their oceanic cuisine. Exquisite taste!" the feminine AI commends their choice. The couple savors their snack, then they reach back into the orb's cabinet and remove two small patches. Each removes the backing and places a patch on their wrist. Within seconds of applying the patches, their pupils dilate, and the world around them brightens. Their smiles widen. "Two doses of Ephena Lotus. Feeling is freedom with Ephena! Your account will be invoiced. Enjoy your day, Matrinas family!" With that, the compartment closes, and the sphere floats away to continue its journey of service.

The utmost upper echelon of society resides in the Apex, where politeness precedes, leisure prevails, beauty radiates, and safety is paramount. If Sanctum Core is the gem of Kairus Prime, then the Apex gleams like an opus diamond fitted delicately at its center. Populated by royalty and politicians, corporate barons, oligarchs, and business moguls, only the worthy may call this place home. And all have one thing in common: ties to the CP. Life is joyous, orderly, and automated. The high-class revel in their perfect society that treats them to lavish convenience; and pay for it, they do.

A great fountain gives forth intermittent bursts of water in visually pleasing patterns. Holograms dance just above it, depicting a beautiful contemporary ballet that passersby may enjoy, or perhaps take for granted as they view the world through their augmented realities. The beautiful architecture of the few evenly spaced towers that do surpass the Apex platform only add to the pristine aesthetic experience. Blue accents across each edifice showcase support of the CP, and the most expensive of designer brands proudly display their wares in evenly spaced boutiques, all adhering to the aesthetic of the grounds, of course.

At the very center of the Apex stands Sanctum Tower, which dwarfs all surrounding structures. It houses not only the vitalerium providing power to Kairus and its city-states, but the court that presides all-powerfully over Deorum. Despite the pearlescent white theme that permeates the Apex, Sanctum Tower is a pitch-black obelisk of governance. At its pinnacle floats a massive icosahedron comet of vitalerium, spinning freely in its transparent casing and casting a blue glow in all directions. It is the single largest hunk of vitalerium ever recovered from the Vital Fracture, and the lifeblood of the civilization.

Sanctum Tower stands over 350 stories tall, and the black monstrosity of opulence and order is broken only by a single, glowing blue stripe cascading down its exterior from the pinnacle, which casts its shadow on all. Six transit tubes connect to its edifice from different directions at the three hundredth floor, allowing for safe travel of courtesans from their respective city-states surrounding Kairus Prime: Argos, Talos, Dorok, Luxenia, Leebrus, and Ytonia; each an oasis of opulence in its own right.

At floor three hundred and thirty-three, just a few dozen stories below the rotating vitalerium beacon atop the tower, the Court of Kairus meets. Today, they discuss the newest initiative proposed by the CP's Overseer. The amphitheater is filled to the brim with representatives, including the six chief representatives who act as governors of their respective city-states. The room is silent as a tall man with dark, feathered haired stands from his seat, which hovers effortlessly at the center of the room. His steps echo off the marble walls as he approaches the metallic podium. Placing his hands on the gold-laden surface before him, he browses the hundreds of faces that stare back at him. An aura of confidence exudes from his presence as he addresses the court.

"The last governor to speak on the item at hand, Initiative 919, will be the Chief Representative of Argos, Arpen Delgato. Chief Representative Delgato, you have the floor..." says the man with a hint of disdain on his tongue before returning to his garish, floating throne.

Arpen Delgato, a man of short stature, approaches a second podium at the base of the stage. With a loud thud, he drops a holoscreen onto its surface. "Thank you, honorable Overseer Aganon. I have no doubt that most of you in this courtroom see yourselves as the voice of all citizens residing in your respective city-states. Or at least it is my hope that this is how you view yourselves, because nothing could be closer to the truth. I, myself, hold a certain level of pride and respect for the weight of the responsibility that comes with holding an esteemed position in this court. Although a certain amount of responsibility should always fall upon the individual to maintain or advance their position in life, we hold in our hands the ability to significantly improve the lives of all Deorans, both within the walls of our cities and beyond the barriers that divide us. However, we must always remember that this responsibility—this duty to govern—is a double-edged sword. For we also bear the ability to cause great detriment to the society that was built before our time, and to those who call this planet their home. Which is why I'm sure you all can understand on some level, or perhaps even mirror my sentiments when I say that this series of laws..." he pokes aggressively at the holoscreen before him, "...is utter nonsense. A joke in poor taste at its best, and a scam of the highest order at its worst."

The crowd erupts with chatter over Arpen's remarks. The Overseer presses a button on his chair, triggering a loud tone that chimes throughout the room. Slowly but surely, the chatter dissipates.

"Ahem... Would you care to clarify, Arpen?" asks Overseer Zerris Aganon, who masks his anger in placidity.

"Overseer Aganon, with all due respect, it was your team that wrote this initiative. No matter how carefully worded and positively spun this initiative may be, what we are voting on is a staged annexation of all residential property for the state outside of Sanctum Core and relevant central metropolis zones! And you've even included the Grind in the plan's progression? As if we didn't have enough trouble keeping the citizens of the Grind in check as it is? Not to mention, one would think that with goals this ambitious, this *drastic*, an appropriate transition period would be allotted for its execution. Yet, it is clearly stated in this bill that 919 will be made effective today, and achieve full transition a mere three months from now! What exactly is your goal here, to encourage a rebellion?"

Overseer Aganon sighs. He has come to expect this sort of opposition from Delgato. He squints his eyes at the politician, responding as if annoyed by the opinion voiced. "Chief Representative Delgato, I doubt that anyone in this room lacks respect for the magnitude of the responsibility placed on their position. The way I see it, this initiative places an even greater responsibility on our shoulders. Following the banking consolidation, the CP Bank took over the vast majority of loans that exist. Additionally, given the events over a decade ago with both Deorum National Bank and Kairus Spheres Bank failing, we find ourselves in a unique position; one where we have the opportunity to give the majority of our citizens a break. And assuming you've scoured through this initiative cover to cover like I've come to anticipate with you, you'll see by our census calculations the vast majority of Deorans living inside the walls are bound by lease. The state-appointed, and state-subsidized rates that would replace them would not only account for a reduction in monthly costs for our renting citizens, but it would also account for installments that are significantly below the national average for mortgage payments for owners. This would allow for..."

"By forcing our citizens into indefinite debt to the state? And don't get me started on the circumstances around bank failings in recent years past... The drop in Deorum National Bank's stock after certain connected investors publicly announced their pulling of funds was convenient at best. And the untimely deaths of Kairus Sphere's executives set off a similar chain of events," retorts Delgato.

The Overseer stiffens as he leans forward in his chair. A somewhat scathing tone coats his words. "I don't know what you're insinuating, Arpen, but business is business, and we narrowly avoided financial recession through our efforts to stabilize the situation. But if you want to spin it that way, everyone is already indefinitely in debt to the state through taxation. That has never changed, nor will it. A government is not operated on buttons and strings. It is run on currency, and this initiative will create a new revenue stream for the state; one to improve the lives of the very people you stand here defending today. You are not alone in your quest for benevolence, Arpen."

"I would certainly like to think so, Overseer Aganon. But I'm not so sure. Because the bill you're proposing seems to me like one big power grab for the CP, and namely for Overseer's chair." Another low chatter breaks out in the courtroom. "*For instance*, one hefty allocation, eleven trillion universal credits no less, of this new income stream feeds directly into the newly created 'Board of Residence and Livelihood' which, and I quote, 'the Overseer, and the Overseer alone is charged with appointing members'? I don't know about the rest of you, but this doesn't seem very democratic to me. Another large chunk goes toward bolstered defenses against the pirating of unrefined vitalerium from the Vital Cascade. That part is somewhat understandable given our recent troubles. Although, in my opinion, you attach to it an unreasonably inflated price tag... But by far the largest allocation of funds is to 'Expanded Vitalerium Research,' which remains entirely undefined, by the way. It's not that I am opposed to the idea of expanding insights into, undoubtedly, our most important resource. However, the repetitive string of vague *ifs* and *maybes* listed here only dance around any specifics of what this *research* actually entails! And I, for one, am no writer of blank checks." Arpen is successful in flustering Zerris. The Overseer's right hand, which bears a large, raised scar across its dorsum, clenches into a fist until his knuckles turn a bright white. He shields it from the view of the court between his leg and his chair's large armrest.

Despite this, Arpen continues his inquiry. "Do you care to elaborate on this open-ended vitalerium research that we are signing onto?" Arpen then turns and addresses the entire court in disappointment. "Did anyone else even read this two-thousand-page monstrosity? Am I the only one overcome with a disconcerted curiosity here?" Arpen's eyes scan the now-silent court in search of support. He finds that support in Nataliya Yoon, Governor and Chief Representative of Luxenia, who stands from her seat across the room.

"I don't agree with Arpen on many things, but even I concede that the language in this Initiative is entirely too vague to put into action. It's simply not ready." Nataliya's input stirs the crowd again, and within seconds the chattering elevates to shouting amongst the hundreds of courtesans. Another blast of the tone echoes through the room as Zerris mashes the button on the right arm of his chair. The crowd is tougher to quiet this time. Zerris looks for his allies in the crowd and motions subtly toward Tye Brenzen, the young, portly Governor of Ytonia, who stands to voice his rehearsed take.

"I know this is a big change, everyone, but as we begin to put more money toward infrastructure, our power requirements are going to increase significantly, which will require us to find new ways to utilize vitalerium. Think of the Grind, for instance. To be able to bring them into the fold will require significant resources. But imagine the quality-of-life improvement for residents of the Grind once we do! It will have countless benefits, but it will require contribution and sacrifice from every citizen. That's a fact that I'm sure both Chief Rep Delgato and Chief Rep Yoon can agree with. That is why I would like to gently remind the esteemed court that progress is not free, nor is it cheap! It is my opinion that Initiative 919 serves to achieve this goal sufficiently, and I would once again like to voice my avid support of its passing, along with all of the representatives of Ytonia!" His seemingly rehearsed presentation is followed by hearty applause from the Ytonia representatives and select others in the court. Arpen, being a cunning and experienced politician, can smell exactly what Zerris is up to with his "yes man" from Ytonia.

"Oooh! Thank you, prince of Ytonia. I'm glad we can all be happy with a solution that is simply *sufficient*. If you'd not spoken, we wouldn't have had the slightest idea how much good we are doing with this legislature. Boy, does it feel good to be good!" Arpen chimes in sarcastically as he rolls his eyes. Brenzen takes his seat, blushing with embarrassment. Arpen's interrogation proceeds. "And just how do you plan to sell this idea to the citizens of this planet? That the homes they've made are now the property of the state? Homes that they own and have already paid off?"

This time, the Governor of Dorok chimes in. An intimidating house of a man, he is named after the city-state itself. Zerris has no ally greater than Governor Dorok Ferrous Benson XIII, who also holds the title of acting General of the CP Guardsmen. Dorok does not even stand as he smugly adds to the conversation.

"Probably the same way we've always done, old man. In the name of supporting your neighbor, the preservation of the Party, and for the good of Deorum. If you had read the damn thing, you should already have concluded that!" he shouts fervently.

"Old man...heh. Chief Representative Dorok, I think every person in this room would be surprised to discover that you could read at all," replies Arpen. A low chuckle emanates from the rest of the court. Benson's grip tightens on the arm of his chair as the muscles bulge from his neck.

Arpen glances around the room, doing some quick mental math as the representatives continue to argue. He already knows that Nataliya Yoon from Luxenia is on his side. He can count on her votes. Tomlin Cornathus of Talos, stubborn as a mule, sits silently grimacing amongst his representatives as words are exchanged around him. The most senior member of the court, his political leanings have always been more old-school, more preservationist than his own. He would never vote in favor of passing laws this extreme. Together with his votes from Argos, they might stand a fighting chance.

However, Zerris has Ytonia's votes in his pocket thanks to his puppet, Tye Brenzen. Dorok's votes in favor of the initiative are as sure a thing as his low IQ, and the representatives of Kairus Prime would always go in the way of the Overseer's chair. With this in mind, he estimates 110 votes for passing vs his 115 votes to strike. It would seem that the fate of this legislation hung in the hands of the final city-state, Leebrus. The thirty representatives of Leebrus, headed by Triconius "Trike" Gunderson, could either make or break this case. Arpen, a cunning politician, placates his fellow governor.

"Chief Representative Gunderson, we have not heard from you yet on this initiative, but you are an outspoken champion of your people in the cultured city-state of Leebrus. What you have done for the Hybrid community of this planet alone has been nothing short of saintly. I implore you to consider your citizens, and the harm this initiative would cause them. Perhaps not in the short term, no. The average citizen has not the time to read through thousands of pages of dry legal documents. Given the options without fully understanding the concepts, many would happily save a credit where they can, and I acknowledge that. But I ask of you, do not simply consider your citizens. Consider the children of your citizens and their future children who will never know the meaning of true ownership or experience the responsibility and growth that it brings. Would you trade their long-term potential by putting a cap on their future? I humbly ask you to be honest with yourself. As an owner of multiple homes, Chief Representative, what do you believe they would say if they knew what we know?"

Trike Gunderson stands and responds, "Thank you for the kind words, Arpen. I have always had great respect and admiration for your service, and I do not doubt your wisdom, nor do I doubt that there are shortcomings to this type of approach. However, I also believe that any approach will have its flaws. With the number of citizens renting versus owning in Leebrus, which far exceeds any other sector, I feel that this initiative would not necessarily put a cap on my people. With the amount of money that will be put back into the pockets of every citizen, we have an opportunity to raise the standard of living on a massive scale and provide a much-needed stimulus to commerce. And while I appreciate your kind words, and your impassioned views, I can't stomach the idea of facing my citizens with the knowledge that I turned down an opportunity to put universal credits back in their pockets. I'd be a hypocrite to consider myself a champion of my people if I do not serve their needs here and now."

Arpen sees his resistance to the bill's passing begin to fall apart at the seams, and chatter once again erupts in the court. This time, the Overseer does nothing to interrupt it. Arpen makes a last-ditch effort to sway the minds of his fellow representatives. "Please, Chief Representatives, I don't think you understand the potential repercussions of actions this drastic..." But as Arpen begins to elaborate, he is interrupted by Zerris.

"Chief Representative Delgato, I'm sorry but your time has concluded. Thank you for voicing your opinions; I'm sure we will all take them into careful consideration."

"Zerris, please... What about those who have made real estate their business? We've yet to even tread those waters. *This*...is bald-faced stealing. I..." Arpen trails off as he searches for some way to relate to the young ruler. "I knew your father well when he was alive. And I don't have to tell you that we rarely agreed on anything. You grew up around the court, so you know all too well. You've probably even been privy to many of our heated arguments. But even *he* understood that people by nature are resistant to change, and that *gradual* progress was not just politically sound, but *absolutely necessary*. And if he were here today, I know in my heart of hearts that we would both agree on that. These radical changes you're proposing...they could undo us all. If this is truly the direction that you plan to take the planet, then let us take the time to get this right."

"First, *Arpen*, I believe you find yourself becoming too familiar. You will recognize me as Overseer Aganon while we are in the court, and outside of the court, for that matter. Second, my father is no longer with us, and thus the opinions of a dead man carry no weight in this courtroom. You speak as if he lived in the same world as we do now, and I assure you, that is not the case. Perhaps you, yourself, are stuck in the past. What I *can* tell you is that no one knew the man more than I. So, why don't you save your pontifications on his potential leanings for sessions of reminiscing your glory days over after-hours cocktails? The fact of the matter is we have an opportunity today to make a lasting impact on our planet as a whole. One that could catapult us into a new age of prosperity. So, I implore *you*, sir, to reconsider your stance on the initiative at hand."

Zerris, though usually more reserved and tactful with his responses, refrains from holding back today. Each domino has been neatly arranged prior to this congress of the Kairus Court. He knows he already has the votes he needs and intends to squash any voice that aims to shift those votes. The stakes of his plan are simply too high.

"But why now? You say these things as if we don't already have enough prosperity on our hands...as if we are a nation in decline rather than in growth! We are a planetary nation made rich by the vitalerium trade. We act as a separate and *independent* arm of the IGB. Deorum is granted all of the benefits of a free nation while experiencing remarkably less strife than other planets in relation to the intergalactic hierarchy! We have but only the Grand Regent to answer to! Why implement such a radical reorganization now? I need everyone to understand that drastic changes like these..." Arpen tries to continue, but the crescendo of his speech is interrupted by the amplified voice of the Overseer.

"What I need *you* to understand is that you have taken enough of the court's time already. Your allotted time has been far surpassed, and you may take your seat, Governor!"

With that, Arpen sighs and looks down at his feet, muttering under his breath, "...usually come with a civil war attached..." then grabs his holoscreen and returns reluctantly to his seat.

Zerris smirks with relief as Arpen finally finishes. He announces to the court, "If everyone is done airing their grievances, let the voting commence." The room is silent except for the tapping of holoscreens in each representative's seat. All representatives simultaneously cast their votes, which tally in large holographic numbers displayed above the podium before Zerris. After a few seconds go by, the totals are tallied and a bell chimes: 124 votes against, and 131 votes for. Arpen lowers his head once more, filled with disappointment.

"It is settled then! Initiative 919 shall go into effect immediately. Let this Coalition for Prosperity Party Court Session adjourn," announces Zerris as he rises and walks through a door behind the Overseer's chair. He is followed by three armed Guardsmen wearing white armor with royal blue trim. The RoGuard, short for Royal Guard, is the most elite of the CP Guardsmen. Their reinforced, mechanized armor—or mech armor, as it is commonly called—is significantly more robust than the standard Guardsmen armor. His chief administrator, Mingen Arellot, approaches the podium as Zerris departs. He angles the microphone downward to meet his face, and, in a shrill voice calls out to those in the court, "May we serve the Party for Deorum's Prosperity!"

In unison, the room responds with, "And may the party prevail!" The representatives all rise and move toward the exits closest to them, chatting with their peers as they walk. Arpen does not move from his seat; he simply observes as others around him stroll carelessly by, patting themselves on the back for another perceived job well done. Out of the corner of his eye, he sees Nataliya Yoon staring in his direction. She delivers a solemn glance as she shakes her head in disappointment, then departs with the others. Arpen knows in that moment that she still shares his concerns. Tomlin Cornathus says nothing. The seemingly permanent scowl is still etched on his face as he storms through the crowd, practically knocking over anyone unlucky enough to be standing in his path. For a man of his age, he is surprisingly spry.

A young man holding an oversized holoscreen and brimming with nervous energy approaches from the aisle and takes the seat beside Delgato. Ram Sandiam, chief administrator to Arpen Delgato, knows all too well the look that has washed over his superior's face. It was no longer one of disappointment, but one of contemplation. "Governor, I'm sorry to see the outcome of the vote. I know how strongly you felt about this initiative. What would you like me to do, sir?"

Arpen does not speak immediately. He looks off into the distance as he scratches his trimmed gray beard. After a moment passes, he places his hand on the shoulder of his colleague and friend, replying, "It's alright, Ram. There are always other options on the table, even when the situation seems hopeless. Remember that. Let's set up a meeting with Yoon and Cornathus. Make it a *private* one. Sooner rather than later, if you would."

Ram nods, taps at his holoscreen a few times, and replies, "Right away, sir."

Outside the Court of Kairus and many floors below, the TABs and commscreens of the Apex's residents buzz with notifications. A unique tone plays on all devices, signifying a government update. Every resident simultaneously ceases their activities, all lifting their screens to their faces to listen intently as Overseer Aganon makes his royal address. He exudes confidence as he speaks regarding the outcome of the vote and the benefits it will provide to all Deoran citizens. Every citizen in the Apex is silent as their faces illuminate with the glow of their devices.

One man lets his arm go limp, allowing his commscreen to swing by his side. Leaning over to the man next to him, he unloads his dissatisfaction. "Can you believe this cocky Overseer we've got? I mean what is he, thirty-five orbits? The unbridled idiocy of this 'new way forward' marks the end of an era, I'm telling you! Don't you think?"

"I think you should continue watching the royal address, you know it's mandatory..." warns his friend.

"I can't listen to him anymore. He makes my blood boil with his foolishness!" continues the man. "I mean, does he have any idea how this is going to affect investment potential? Is he that far removed from real life? He must have his head up in outer space! Floating around in the Vital Cascade..."

The white floating orb glides gracefully over to the two men and stops before them, facing the outspoken man. Its gentle female voice offers a suggestion. "Citizen, please produce your transmission device to view the Overseer's important message."

"I've seen enough. I've got the general gist of it," replies the man, clearly miffed by the intrusion.

"Citizen, please produce your transmission device immediately to view the Overseer's important message. This is your second warning," says the orb. The man's friend begins to slowly edge away from the malcontent.

"Look, I'll watch it later. I've got plenty to do today, including preparing for the implementation of this *glooorious* new set of laws. If I need some foie gras, I'll let you know."

The man begins to walk in the opposite direction but stops when the white orb emits a cascade of green light, which scans the disagreeable man. He squints and looks away from the blinding illumination. Behind the HUD of the floating orb, its systems process the facial structure of the individual to produce his identity. *Citizen: Goran Kyvach, Age: 58 orbits, Profession: Software Entrepreneur, Compliance Score: 358*, a precariously low score, indicating this individual is known to exhibit displays of malbehavior. With a score that low, even the slightest misstep might cause it to cross the threshold into Non-Compliant Status... The AI voice responds more loudly this time. "Citizen Goran Kyvach, scans indicate that you have not taken your prescribed Ephena Lotus in some time. Please administer your dose." A compartment containing the small, white patch extends toward Goran.

"I don't need medicine to feel better! Just let me tend to my business. I've work to do!" he shouts.

A new, ominous sound bellows from the floating orb that shocks Goran. Two nearby CP Guardsmen take notice and begin to approach from across the street. The orb continues, "Citizen Goran Kyvach, a careful review has produced discrepancies related to your business' 2698 taxation records that require further investigation. Please await the arrival of CP Arbitration to settle this issue."

"What!? That's ridiculous. My taxes are always in order! I have entire teams that look into these things!" he says nervously as the two CP officers march closer.

"Citizen Goran Kyvach, you are displaying exacerbated behavioral responses. Please remain calm," replies the device as a plume of white mist expels from the orb and envelops Goran's face. Immediately, he becomes weak in the knees and begins to stagger where he stands. Before he can fall, the Guardsmen, clad in black armor with blue trim, each grab one of Goran's arms and carry him back to their hovertank. His feet drag along the street as they move.

Goran's body is limp, and his lips go numb. Barely audible to those around him, Goran slurs his words as he pleads, "Pleash...not da Cuubve!" But the Guardsmen do not respond. They load him into the back of their armored vehicle and then take off into the sky. Except for one or two people, no one around the incident even notices. They watch on their devices intently, oblivious to their surroundings, as Overseer Aganon perseverates on the benevolence of the party, and wondrous future with the enactment of Initiative 919.

The Apex of Sanctum Core, where politeness precedes, leisure prevails, beauty radiates, and safety is paramount. Life here is joyous, orderly, and automated. Excess is encouraged, if not insisted upon. The unspoken tenets of the aristocracy value chemical ecstasy over enlightenment, for to live in convenient bliss is better than to worry about the intricacies of how their society runs. Besides, an enlightened aristocracy has proven to be a dangerous mindset, and a utopia with omnipresent danger is but a lie, is it not? Danger is the antithesis to safety, and so these dangerous thoughts are shunned. The high-class revel in their perfect society that treats them to lavish convenience that only high kings could command; and pay for it, they do.

CHAPTER 8:

In the Name of Science

Zerris and his RoGuards enter an elevator behind the court, accessible only by the Overseer and his personal security. As the doors close behind them, a blank blue screen with no markings appears next to the door, floating freely just inches from the glass elevator wall. Without any prompting, one of the RoGuards traces an hourglass pattern across the hologram, which turns green as he finishes. The elevator promptly begins to descend, increasing in speed as the floors pass. Rapidly approaching ground level, the elevator does not slow. The view of the city through the glass disappears behind cold, black steel as the elevator descends below ground level. The small screen above the door flashes numbers as they enter the subterranean levels: "S10... S15... S20..." Finally, the elevator begins to slow, and the screen stops at the number S73; seventy-three stories below the surface of Deorum.

The doors slide open to reveal a gigantic oval-shaped room lined floor to ceiling with chrome machinery. Dials and meters attach to long tubes that cool the supercomputers housed against the far walls. Two women wearing lab coats and goggles walk with urgency to complete their next task. Dozens of others in white coats are scattered around the space, all working on various projects. At the center of the space, a large chunk of vitalerium hovers in its containment capsule, permeating its light blue glow over every surface.

Zerris exits the glass vessel and makes a beeline toward the center of the room with his guards following closely behind. As he passes, every person in his vicinity immediately stops what they are doing and faces him. They place their right fists over their hearts and their left fists over their navels: the CP salute. The scientists only relax and return to work once the Overseer and his RoGuards have passed. Zerris approaches a young, thin-framed man in a gray lab coat at the center of the room. His curly, dirty-blond hair is uncombed and sticks out in multiple places. With a mechanical glove, the man manipulates the robotic arm inside a room behind a transparent, vitalerium-proof barrier. With each movement he performs, his female colleague reviews the charted data from his experiment on their dock's holographic display, both so focused on their trial results that they do not notice Zerris and his muscle standing behind him.

"Norvel Mathis..." says Zerris in a low voice with patronizing cadence. Norvel immediately recognizes the voice behind him. He slams a button on the dock to pause the experiment, quickly removes the mechanical glove, and swivels around with haste.

"Oh, uh... Overseer Aganon. I heard you would be checking in on us today, I just didn't realize it would be so early." Norvel's tone is shaky, and pressured.

"Well, when my lead scientist expresses problems with my highest-priority project, I make it my priority to find out exactly what is stalling said progress. Especially when the issues reportedly expressed are those of morality," Zerris replies coldly.

Norvel looks away anxiously, then attempts to redirect the conversation. "Well...uh...you will be happy to find that Project Sky-light is complete and fully functional. We-we've already set up a site test for you to trial the weapon yourself!"

"Wonderful news. I look forward to seeing what you and your team have crafted for me. Although, you know that is not the reason for my visit... What of Project Touch of Ra?" asks Zerris.

"Ye-yes... Touch of Ra... That project, um..." Norvel hesitates and looks to the scientist he was previously working with. She only stares back like a deer in headlights. He kindly motions for her to leave, and she promptly gathers her things and walks across the room. Norvel continues, "It's moving along..." He points awkwardly to the room behind him. "Working on it right now, actually... I'd really like to talk with you about what you're asking us to accomplish with this endeavor..."

"Are you having problems getting the item in question to work? Because I would be disappointed to learn that you are incapable of completing your task, especially given the magnitude of investment I've put into this venture and the amount of resources I've laid at your disposal."

"It's not that. I mean there have definitely been some challenges in completing the project given its...ambitious nature. We're still perfecting it...the trouble is finding a way to transfer that much raw power without destroying everything in its path from user to target. We've dampened the transference of energy, but it is not perfect. We are also trying to find a way to improve its homing capacity at long range, which is proving to be a challenge..."

"Well, lucky for you, I've secured significant funding for whatever it is you need to accomplish your goal."

"It's not that... I have a potential solution that we will be trialing soon. It's just..." Norvel anxiously pushes his unkempt hair out of his face as he works up the courage to speak his mind.

"Just what?" probes Zerris.

"It's just that, what you're asking me to build...could have severe consequences. There has never been anything like this before. And the range you're asking for?" Norvel's concerned tone is met by Zerris's blank stare. "It would essentially allow you to selectively target anyone within a planetary radius... the implications of something like that could be, well..."

Zerris furrows his brow in frustration but maintains his composure. "Could be what, Norvel?"

Norvel sighs, then responds, "It just lends itself to the possibility of massive abuse. I mean...what do you plan to use this for? And how will the next Overseer choose to use it? Or could you imagine if it got into the wrong hands? And Primes forbid if the public ever found out about it..." Norvel tries his best to relay his point without becoming emotional, but his sentiments begin to bleed through his words.

"It sounds an awful lot like you are questioning my intent, Norvel." Zerris grits his teeth and tilts his head toward Norvel. The large vein in the Overseer's forehead begins to bulge as his blood pressure rises. "Which is interesting, because one would think that a young man in your position would be grateful for the opportunity they've been given. Especially considering where I pulled you from..."

"Grateful? I fully understand the opportunity I've been given, and yes, I'll be forever thankful for you getting me out of...my situation. B-but gratitude has nothing to do with it! I've completed every task you've given me for the past two orbits to the tee without a complaint. And we've made some incredibly powerful tools to add to the CP arsenal...but this!? What are we trying to prove!?" As the words leave his mouth, he immediately regrets them. A pit forms in Norvel's stomach in response to the sinister expression that washes over Zerris's face. The RoGuards take a menacing step closer to Zerris, ready for action should the order be given. The room becomes eerily quiet as every scientist and technician looks on in suspense.

Zerris takes a deep breath and calms himself. He now displays a light smile, and breaks the silence by saying, "Such is empathy... I understand your concerns, Norvel. And I will take them into consideration. But right now... I need you to focus on the task at hand. How complete would you say the project is, Norvel?"

Norvel, who had been expecting a much more aggressive response, shoots a puzzled glance at his second-in-command, Mirene, who stands just twenty feet away. Her worried expression provides him no comfort. The tension in the room is felt by all, especially Norvel, whose heart is still beating out of his chest. Turning back toward Zerris, he replies, "We've hit about eighty percent of our milestones, so..."

"And can I trust that your team is still fully capable of fulfilling the task at hand?" questions Zerris, calm as ever.

Still unsure of his aim, Norvel responds, "Of course, Overseer. I trust my team; I hand-picked them myself."

"That's good to hear, Norvel," responds Zerris.

A feeling of relief rushes over the nervous scientist, who exhales and then coughs into his hand. But the feeling is short-lived, for Zerris's next comment is, "Because it has become clear to me that I can no longer trust you or your loyalty to my cause, your team can finish your masterpiece without you." Each word from Zerris's mouth feels like a dagger piercing Norvel's chest as the fear builds inside of him. "And given your access to privileged information and top-secret project knowledge, I'm afraid that you are now no longer allowed to leave." Turning to his guards, Zerris barks, "Show our friend to one of the max security cubes until I can figure out what to do with him."

Norvel shudders as the RoGuards march toward him in uniform motion. Mirene yells out in concern from across the room, "NOO!!" as she runs over to Norvel and embraces him. Trembling from the idea of an unpromised tomorrow, he returns her embrace and holds onto her for dear life. As he holds his loved one, he feels a hand reach into his lab coat pocket, followed by the tug of its fabric. Something heavy has just been dropped inside. Noticing this, he pulls back slightly and gazes into Mirene's eyes, unsure of the gift she has bestowed. Mirene's expression, now a silent, stoic one, relays a wordless message.

Norvel, with his mouth still agape with fear, turns to the approaching RoGuard. His voice cracks as he says, "It's fine, Mirene... I'll go willingly."

The RoGuards stop just a foot from Norvel and look back to Zerris for approval. With a bored sigh, Zerris nods his head, prompting the guards to give him space to walk on his own. Norvel solemnly walks toward the elevator with white and blue armor following closely at his side. Every eye in the room is on Norvel Mathis as he is escorted to his prison cell. The only sound is the beeping of machines and the footsteps of the incarceration procession. Norvel does not lift his gaze from the floor as he walks. He cannot bear to take in the concerned stares of his peers.

Zerris now addresses the room. "As you can see, we do not tolerate dissent in this organization! There is no room for it in our pursuit of acme. I assume everyone here understands this, and understands the consequences?" He looks around the room to a host of fearful, blank stares. No one speaks. "Good," responds Zerris with a fake smile. He then turns to Mirene and changes gears, asking, "I also assume that you are familiar with my project and know what must be done to complete it?"

Mirene holds back her emotion as she lets out a meek, "Yes, my Overseer." She wipes a tear from her eye as she looks down, fearing for the safety of Norvel.

"Get it done. I expect bi-weekly updates. Should you complete your task as delegated to you, you might just get your Norvel back in one piece," he responds coldly; a bald-faced lie, but a motivating one. His blue mantle flutters through the air as he turns to leave.

Across the room, Norvel steps to the back of the elevator and inserts his hands into the pockets of his gray lab coat. His right hand grasps a small, cold sphere in his jacket where he had felt the tug earlier. A chill runs down his spine when he discerns the object rolling between his fingers, and adrenaline courses through his body as the realization hits him: he only has a few seconds to act. The guards stand in a row before him, and Zerris approaches rapidly from the lab's interior. Norvel, unable to catch his breath, closes his eyes. He knows that a trip to the Cube is as good as a death sentence. Incarceration by the RoGuard meant one of two things: either he dies in his cube or is executed for treason. His breath quickens further as he feels an asthmatic episode coming on. There is no more time for hesitation.

As quickly as he can, he presses the small button on the metallic ball in his pocket and tosses it against the wall of the elevator with all his might. The ball bounces an inch off the glass frame, then hovers in the air, vibrating intensely. The blue light of its button blinks with increasing speed as it beeps ominously. Norvel retreats to the corner of the elevator and crouches, hiding his face in the crevasse and covering his head. One final angry beep is emitted from the orb before it unleashes ripples of orange energy, arcing like lightning bolts into the armor of the RoGuard. A blinding light bursts from the elevator doors, causing every onlooker in the laboratory atrium to shield their eyes. The beams of energy course through their armor, seeming to target it specifically. The men lock up as they experience jolts of agonizing pain but are unable to make a sound. The three RoGuards begin to levitate from where they stand, and their armor steams as the electronic systems housed within them fry to a crisp. Within moments, the orb bursts, and the bright orange light that filled the space dissipates, letting the Guardsmen fall to the floor incapacitated.

Zerris uncovers his eyes and looks upon his fallen RoGuard, their white armor now scorched a grayish black. His rage boils over as he sees Norvel's unscathed face pop out from the corner, and he begins to sprint down the long hallway toward his prisoner. Despite the Overseer's formal court attire, he moves with impressive speed.

Norvel races to the elevator console, fumbling with controls as he rushes to input the code to close its doors. After entering the code, the illuminated blue screen of the holopad flashes red as a large "X" appears. Denied. He enters it again with haste, but again the floating screen flashes red as the elevator is filled with the noise of a loud buzzer. Norvel looks down and realizes one Guardman's arm is blocking the elevator door, setting off its sensors. Zerris is just moments away from the elevator door, running at full speed to prevent the scientist's escape. Norvel reaches down and quickly pulls the RoGuard's limp, armor-clad limb into the elevator, then scrambles to reenter the code a final time. As Zerris reaches the only elevator in or out, he slams into the elevator doors, which close just in time. Norvel catches a glimpse of Zerris's sneering face through the crack of the doors just before it disappears behind the sliding metal barrier, and the elevator shoots upward.

"FUUUCK!" screams Zerris with unbridled rage.

Meanwhile, inside the rapidly ascending elevator, Norvel is still attempting to catch his breath. He can hardly believe his own actions. His adrenaline registers at an all-time high, and he tries desperately to wrangle his thoughts. "Holy shit, holy shit, holy shit..." he repeats to himself. The elevator floors whiz by on the screen above the door, and he realizes once again that his time is in short supply. His eyes fall to the bodies lying motionless on the floor in the center of the elevator. He slaps himself in the face in an attempt to snap himself back into action, and then pulls an inhaler from his pocket and breathes the medicine in deeply.

"Ok...ok..." he says anxiously as he begins to drag the passed-out Guardsmen to the front corners of the elevator, stuffing them as tightly as possible in the space to avoid detection once the doors open. He labors as he pulls them, gasping for air as he strains. Once all three of them are moved, he stands nervously before the door. "Come on, get it together, Norvel! You have to look calm... Like nothing is wrong," he says to himself. He closes his eyes, waiting for the chime from the elevator as his heart beats against his chest wall. He still cannot catch his breath, and so he holds it instead.

The elevator slows to a stop, and the screen above reads "S4" as the metal doors open before Norvel. He cautiously steps out toward a group of Guardsmen standing a few feet from the shaft with their backs to him. Their attention is focused on one Guardsman's small holoscreen as they watch a video, laughing and neglecting their duties. Norvel, still holding his breath, walks by and flashes his ID card to one of the officers with an awkward nod. The man barely glances at it before replying, "Yea, go ahead," and returning to the video. Norvel picks up the pace as he passes them, heading straight for the back wall housing two circular openings connected to long tunnels: ports for escape vessels. Designed to allow for safe departure from Sanctum Tower should the Overseer's life ever be in danger, they are now Norvel's best and only chance of escape. He would have to disengage the nav system to avoid being tracked, but if all goes smoothly, it just might work.

The gigantic room is filled with dozens of mechanics in dirty, oil-stained clothing; all tending to hover tanks, mechanized war machines, and spacefaring vessels housed on S4. Attempting to remain unnoticed, he walks briskly across the room with his head down. Upon reaching the first black escape vessel, he lifts open the compartment below its open hatch. Grabbing a screwdriver from the tool bench next to him, he rummages through the exposed wiring until he sees a small metal square bolted to the back of the compartment. Sweat begins to bead down his forehead as he unbolts the device.

The guards by the entrance just a hundred meters from Norvel continue to laugh at the video that distracts them; that is until the sound of an armored hand striking the concrete floor by the elevator startles the group. They turn around and are shocked to see one of their comrades, with his white armor stained black with ash, crawling from the elevator. The man points across the room to Norvel, who is climbing into the open hatch of the escape vessel. The three men race across the room with their rifles drawn, shouting for Norvel to halt.

Shots ring out from their vitalerium weaponry and spray across the back wall as Norvel closes the hatch and engages the system. As the vessel comes to life and the thrusters roar outside, a voice alerts Norvel in the cabin: "Warning: P-nav systems offline." Norvel's hands scramble across the holographic console as the Guardsmen continue to close the gap. Again, the vessel's computer relays the message, "Warning: P-nav systems offline."

"I KNOW THAT!" shouts Norvel as he slams the throttle forward. As the vessel's thrusters roar, blue fire bursts from the back, scorching the blast plate behind it. The small black vehicle begins to rocket down the tunnel. The officers in pursuit continue to shoot at the vessel as they approach the circular port. A few well-aimed vitalerium charges connect with the rear thrusters as Norvel speeds down the tunnel, causing him to shake violently in its cabin. Red lights flash and alarms blare inside the vessel as the tunnel angles upward. Norvel ascends into darkness until a motorized door opens, revealing a light at the end of the tunnel.

Daylight illuminates the black vehicle as it explodes out of the ground and into the air, soaring upward above the tall buildings of Kairus at alarming speed. Norvel is sucked back into his seat as if pulled by an invisible hand. The G-force is strong, forcing his right cheek into the headrest. From his position, he catches a glimpse of the city as he soars over it. First the inner walls come into view, then the outer walls. He struggles to turn his head forward-facing. But when he does, his stomach drops as a transparent blue hue comes into view. First, only small spots are visible in the distance, but suddenly the film covers the entirety of the sky visible through the small canopy. *Oh no! I forgot about the Skyshield!* Norvel panics internally. His stolen vessel is seconds away from broaching the Vitalerium Skyshield, an energy matrix that covers Kairus Prime and its city-states. Powered by the great spinning vitalerium icosahedron, it provides a protective barrier from attack, as well as a border creating a private airspace of sorts for Kairus. Nothing can penetrate it while it is active, which means crashing into it would mean oblivion.

"Shit! SHIT! SHIT!" he screams into the echoing chamber of death he finds himself trapped in. His reactions are anything but voluntary. His ship has almost reached the barrier and Norvel remains stuck to his seat, helpless to avoid the outcome. All he can do at this point is wince his eyes shut and pray. Closer...and closer...imminent... But for a split second, a section of the blue transparent barrier blinks and disappears, allowing his escape pod to pass through, then reappears behind him.

Norvel struggles to look back, overcome with confusion as to why he is not feeling his skull smash into a thousand pieces. When he finally realizes what happened... "WOOHOOOHOOO!! YES! HAHA!" he cries out in pure joy. *The vessel launch must have set off a timed deactivation for its trajectory!* he thinks to himself. The expanse of the grind passes almost in an instant, and as the small ship passes the city limits and reaches peak altitude, a sense of calm suddenly washes over Norvel. He had escaped the impossible, and as he glances out of the canopy, for a split second he marvels at the beautiful view before him. Bios gleams over the distant mountain peaks, casting light and life onto everything in sight.

WHOOP WHOOP sounds another alarm as the vessel's cabin shakes again with a vengeance. The starboard thrusters give out, sending the small ship into a spiral. "WARNING: CRITICAL THRUSTER FAILURE, STARBOARD. CRITICAL THRUSTER FAILURE, STARBOARD." Norvel's state of serenity is short-lived as he descends into panic all over again. The ship veers off course, and Norvel loses all control of his trajectory. He fumbles with the controls, fighting against the G-force that pummels his body from the ship's velocity. All attempts to regain control fail as he is thrashed about the cabin. As the nose of the ship turns toward the ground, he knows that no timed deactivation will prevent this collision. Nothing will save him. So, he shuts his eyes, braces himself in his seat, and accepts his fate.

CRASH!! The vessel hits the ground at an angle with immense force, tearing through dirt and foliage. The metal undercarriage shears against the ground with an ear-shattering screech, unearthing rocks and spraying sparks into the forest greenery. After skidding the length of a Guaniton field, the escape pod is finally stopped by a large tree trunk, which crumples the black metal on collision.

As the seconds pass, the smoke rising from the front of the pod turns to flame. Norvel snaps to life, hacking from the smoke that begins to fill the cabin. His disoriented state is only outshined by his survival instinct as he searches frantically for the hatch release. The smoke stings his eyes and burns his lungs, but his hands finally find the lever on the console above him. His eyes water as he pulls downward on the steel handle with all his might.

The hatch flies off the top of the vessel, and a battered and bruised Norvel claws his way out of the cockpit. He lands on the ground with a painful thud. Blood drips from his nose onto his coat, staining it red. He looks around, confused by the fact that his life remains intact. But as the fire in the vehicle behind him begins to roar louder, reality sets in and he runs for cover behind one of the nearby trees. Pain shoots through his left knee as he runs, but it does not slow him. Just moments after ducking behind the nearest large tree, the vessel explodes into a ball of fire, knocking Norvel to his hands and knees as the concussive force hits him with a wall of hot air. A plume of black smoke rises from the wreckage, and fragments of flaming metal and debris cover the ground around him. As the dust settles, Norvel rolls to his back and begins to sob from the combination of stress and exhaustion.

What bothers him most is not the stress from his multiple near-death experiences, or the fact that he is now a fugitive of a vindictive state led by an aspiring autocrat. It is not his cuts and bruises that bring him the most pain. It is the shining locks of strawberry-blonde hair juxtaposed with her white lab coat. It is her emerald-green eyes that reflect the blue flashing lights of the lab equipment surrounding her. Her bright red lipstick, which never seemed to be applied perfectly to the shape of her lips, as if put on in a hurry. The way she held him before he was apprehended. Mirene. And now that he has somehow escaped, her life is surely in danger. The tears stream down his face as the forest burns around him. They will likely infer that she must have had something to do with his escape, and Zerris is not a forgiving man. Norvel wallows in the thoughts of Mirene's imminent fate.

Then, as he lay there in the dirt, a realization hits him with the force of a hammer, and his crying instantly ceases. She is the only other person who knows how to finish Zerris's project. He needs her, so he can't get rid of her; he cannot kill her...yet. Norvel shoots up from where he lies, ignoring the pain in his leg. *I have to get her out before she can finish the Touch of Ra...* It is the one saving grace he and Mirene have in their favor; Norvel's sole bit of integral leverage.

With a new wind at his back and a daunting clock ticking in his mind, Norvel Mathis hobbles back toward the skyline of Kairus. All fear replaced with focus; all doubt traded for intent; all hope not lost.

CHAPTER 9:

The Job

Roman gasps as he quickly sits up in bed, knocking his guest's arm off his chest. A cold sweat covers him from head to toe... another nightmare. This time, more in line with his normal night terrors, he relived the night of his fourteenth orbit. He wipes whiskey-scented droplets from his forehead, then looks at the clock displayed on the wall of his domicile. The time reads "15:24." He had slept into the latter part of the day; not all bad considering the debauchery that ensued the night prior. Roman slinks off the bed and kicks the empty bottle of whiskey off his pants where they lay on the floor. As he pulls them on and begins to buckle his belt, he hears a soft moan coming from his bed.

As he turns back to take stock of the night's conquests, he sees a head of long blonde hair poking out of the bedsheets to his right. Her beautiful features are smooshed into his pillow as she starts to wake. He looks down at her feet that poke out from the sheets on his bed. He counts one, two...wait...three feet. *Fuck, am I still drunk?* he thinks to himself. Based on the empty bottles and cups scattered around his mess of an apartment, probably yes. Looking back, the lump of sheets next to his blonde guest begins to shift and moan as well. With his head tilted in curiosity, Roman carefully reaches down and pulls the sheets away, revealing a woman with long green hair, her face covered in freckles that emit a bioluminescent blue glow; a hybrid woman.

"Ah... Almost forgot about you, our late addition to the party," mumbles Roman as the woman comes to, stretching and yawning in his bed. Roman pulls the sheets down further to reveal her large breasts, smirking as they poke into view from beneath the covers.

"Mm... Hey! Are you creeping on me, Roman?" she says playfully as she pulls the covers back up to her chin. "I was warm under there..." Her voice is raspy and tired, worn out from the long night.

"Only fair after what you did to me last night," replies Roman, rubbing one of his bloodshot eyes. He stumbles to his left as he reaches for his boot on the floor; definitely still drunk.

"You should be *thanking* me for what I did to you last night, mister," retorts the green-haired woman as she sits up in bed, letting the sheets drop to her waist. The blonde woman next to her now begins to stir from the noise of the conversation.

"You kick me square in the spheres and I should be thankful?" he says, half laughing as he stumbles to a sitting position on the foot of the bed and begins to strap on his boot. The green-haired woman crawls to the edge of the bed behind him and presses her chest against his back. Wrapping her arms around him, she rests her chin on his scarred right shoulder with a giggling smile.

"I told you, that was an accident!" she says insincerely as she laughs. He can feel her warmth against him as she shifts and wraps her legs around him.

A voice comes from behind them as the blonde woman wakes from her slumber and embraces Roman around his opposite shoulder, saying, "Besides, didn't we kiss them better afterward?" She follows her remark by kissing Roman on the corner of his mouth.

Roman secures the final strap on one of his boots, then looks to his left at the blonde woman; then to the right at the hybrid woman. "Oh, you mean that. That is true, I guess..." He trails off. After a brief pause, he booms loudly, "I guess I can forgive you!" as he turns and tackles the two women playfully back into bed. They erupt in laughter as he rolls over them, tickling and wrestling. But he stops suddenly, and kneels up in the bed, feigning sadness in his tone. "But...unfortunately, Club Roman is now closed." Roman points to the steel door at the front of the apartment.

"What!?" shouts one girl. "You're making us leave!?" cries the other.

Roman rolls over his shoulder across the bed, flipping to his feet and grabbing a shirt that was tossed haphazardly over his lamp the night before. As he puts it on, he replies, "Not that it hasn't been fun, I just..." His response is interrupted by the ringing of his commscreen somewhere in the room. He looks around for it, knocking trash off of surfaces and kicking around the clothing that litters the floor. He lifts up a bra from the ground and finds it vibrating and chiming underneath. The name on its orange screen reads "MM."

Roman swipes his hand over the screen to accept the comm, saying, "If you're calling to tell me you're sorry, I just want you to know that I accept." He releases the device, and it begins to hover, following his face as he moves.

"SORRY!? The only one who should be saying they're sorry is you, motherfucker! Do you know who I just got a comm from?" replies the voice over the commscreen.

Roman turns toward the two women who sit gorgeously dumbfounded on his bed. Whispering at a decibel just loud enough to be picked up by his device, Roman says, "Sorry, the devil is calling," and motions for them to go.

"What the fuck, Roman!" yells the blonde woman. "What

about lunch like you promised!?"

"YEA! This happened last time, you asshole! What the fuck!?" the hybrid woman shouts.

"WHAT THE ACTUAL FUCK ROMAN! YOU SHOT OFF TARLEY'S FINGER!?" screams the voice on the commscreen.

"TOO MANY PEOPLE YELLING!" shouts Roman, whose head begins to spin as his hangover kicks in. "Ok, first off, this is work. Please leave, and I'll make it up to you and buy you both some street-meat another time. Second, you don't have the whole story, Modus..." The disgruntled women begin to gather their things and head toward the door. Roman's good-bye-waves are met with considerably more vulgar gestures; clearly not the first time the women had been let down by him. They slam the door behind them, and the voice on the commscreen continues to berate Roman.

"You fuck with another one of my job prospects and I will shoot all your fingers off!" shouts Modus over the commscreen speakers.

"Hey now, would you speak to one of your sons like that?" replies Roman sarcastically.

"If you were one of my sons, I'd have drowned your disrespectful ass a long time ago!" Modus shouts.

Roman snickers at his response. He has known Modus since his early days as a teenager in the Grind. He can feel the familiar tension building through his commscreen, and knows that he has reached the limit of Modus's patience. Running his fingers through his matted hair, he sighs and says, "Look, you *know* Tarley, he's your contact. So, I'm sure you're familiar with his business tactics..."

"I don't want to hear about business tactics, Roman!" replies Modus.

"He tried to short me more than half of our agreed-upon rate! That comes out of *your* cut too! You know how word spreads in this town," Roman complains.

"Not an excuse! I have my own reputation to uphold here.

What am I supposed to do? How am I supposed to keep getting info on jobs when everyone's got it in their head that it'll literally cost them an arm or a leg!?" Roman rolls his eyes, knowing what is coming next. "When you run into a problem with a contact, you come to me, and I take care of issues on the back end. That's how this works!"

"Yea, yea...got it. Run to daddy when there's a problem..." concedes Roman reluctantly. "Forgive me if I'm a little hazy on the rules. It's not like we talk every day."

Modus's voice changes from angry to disappointed. "You've developed a real attitude problem. To be frank, you're lucky your success rate is 100%; otherwise you'd have been out of work long ago. No doubt you've got talent, but talent without discipline is—"

Roman interjects, "A death sentence on this planet? Yeah... you've mentioned that." He paces the room with a staggered gait, looking for his other boot.

"You never used to be like this before. Before Jerrick...well, when Jerrick was still around..." Modus stumbles over his words, trying to bring up the topic without setting Roman off. "You two...you were special. My rising Wibetani Militia stars...and when you left afterward...brings me shame to think about it."

Roman stops his search for his boot and slumps down on the edge of the bed. His hair falls over his face as he leans forward toward the phone; his silver chain and shield pendant dangle before him, jingling quietly. He looks up at the wall across from him where another lone silver necklace hangs, displaying a small dagger pendant and a red feather. He can only stare at the totem to his fallen friend for a moment before he must look away. A few more seconds pass in silence as Roman shirks off the urge to remember his best friend and partner in crime from Ion Street.

"Rome, you there?" asks the voice over the commscreen.

As if all the energy had been sucked out of him in an instant, Roman says solemnly into the phone, "That all you commed for, then?"

"Actually, no...believe it or not, despite your recent indiscretions, I've got another job for you."

"I don't get a word from you for almost ten orbits, and you find two jobs in the same week for me? I've told you before, Modus, I'm not coming back to the Wibetani."

"Psh...like we'd even have you! You've burned that bridge," returns Modus's snarky tone. "Anyway, it just came in this morning, 'bout the same time as the comm from that mohawked fuck, Tarley. At first, I was inclined to hand it off to someone who's less of a loose cannon, but no one has your rate of success... Only reason I still keep ya' contact in my comm. Apparently, it's...sensitive in nature. Some top-level CP defector hiding out in the South Grind trying to find a courier for some pretty heavy cargo. Been turned down by half the Gulcher gangs in the west quadrant. Even Golden Phoenix turned it down, so I'm told. Surprising, considering he wants to pay in raw-V. And according to this contact, he used to work for the *almighty* Zerris Aganon."

At the sound of the name, Roman's ears perk up. His teeth grind involuntarily, and his knuckles turn white as he grips the sheets of his bed tighter. "Don't you say that fucking name to me," growls Roman.

"Hey, easy! Relax. I thought given the circumstance..." But Modus is unable to finish his thought.

"What would you want with a job that the Goldens turned down? And raw-V? A CP *defector*!? That's sketchy, even for you, Modus..."

"The GPs thought he was puttin' them on, as did I in the beginning. But I looked into it. Got some intel that others aren't privy to...confirmed it legit."

"And where did this magical intel come from?" asks Roman, unconvinced by his ex-boss's confidence.

"My sources are of no concern to you. If you had the contacts I had, you'd be the one doling out the jobs now, yea?" retorts Modus.

Once again, Roman rolls his eyes as he collapses backward onto his bed. "Forgive me, o connected one. How lucky I am to be in the good graces of the great Modus Magni."

"Enough with your smart ass. Now, the raw-V is extremely important to…other aspects of the Wibetani's growing business, so I'll be paying you myself on this one. That means there'll be no need for you to dismember any more of my clients. You copy that, Roman?"

"Copy that," replies Roman, as if his old habits as a member of the militia resurface.

"Alright. Consider that my *final* warning on the matter. So? You in or what?"

"What're you payin'?" asks Roman.

"Your cut? Heh…how's two million in UCs sound?" replies Modus smugly over the commscreen speakers.

Roman promptly sits up in his bed. His hair follows behind him wildly, covering his furrowed brow. "I'm sorry, you're gonna have to repeat that," responds Roman, convinced that his ears are playing tricks on him.

"Haha, I figured that'd perk you up," laughs Modus, but his jocular tone is short-lived. "But this ain't no average haul, Rome. This is gonna require some serious equipment, and absolute discretion. That means no scar stories for the women at the local drinking hole. I assume that wasn't a Lancite screeching on the other end when you answered?"

"Hey! You're…not wrong in that assumption," replies Roman, half smirking, still bewildered by the offer.

"I'm serious as the void here. You speak a word of this to the wrong person, and you'll have a CP gun barrel stuffed into that smart-ass mouth of yours. Life-or-death silence, promise me."

Roman thinks for a moment as Modus repeats himself, looking for an answer. But something does not sit right with him in his gut. He thinks to himself, *I've never been paid this* much for a job...that kind of money could last me two orbits, maybe longer. Game-changing payday... Roman is enticed by the deal; however, he cannot shake the uneasy feeling that envelops him as he contemplates the gravity of the gig. Raw vitalerium is the most regulated element in the galaxy by the CP and the IGB. *How does this client have access to it without their knowledge?*

After thinking about it, he sighs and responds, "Think I'm gonna pass on this one, Modus. Sounds like way too much heat."

"What!? Roman, this is the gig of a lifetime! This could change your life if you don't piss it away on booze and women like you usually do. Plus, I don't trust anyone else to get this done but you. I need you on this, Rome." Modus's dumbfounded voice echoes out of Roman's commscreen.

"I'm sorry, but something feels off about this whole thing. Not to mention, you know what happened the last time I tried to get into the raw-V game. You *know*..." Roman looks down again, trying with all his might to fight off the memories of his friend.

"Yea... I do. I know. But your little tandem side project with Jerrick was entirely unsanctioned by the Wibetani Militia, namely ME. You know damn well your eyes got too big for your stomach. We only put trust within our ranks. How many times did I tell you two? But no, you let your ambitions get the best of you and tried to come up on your own. You lost your fellow Klip, and Jerrick...Jerrick just lost."

"Then I'm sure you can see why I'm wiping my hands clean of this. Appreciate the offer," replies Roman unapologetically.

"But just think, doing this job would be like giving the middle finger directly to Zerris himself. Stealing vitalerium right from under his nose? It's the ultimate payback for what him and them goons did to your friend all those orbits ago."

"That would barely be a start. That monster deserves to have his fucking head cut off. Actually, he deserves worse."

"But like you said, it's a start...a big ol' 'fuck-you' to the man who sanctioned the death of your Klip," replies Modus, sensing that he is breaking down barriers. In all the orbits he had spent giving Roman orders, Modus had figured out exactly how to motivate him. "I've always said you have massive potential. Here's your opportunity to really make something of it. You want revenge? It has to start somewhere."

Modus has clearly hit a nerve with Roman. Remembering his past requires unpacking a pain too great to endure. The swirling brown liquor at the bottom of opaque glass bottles provides a temporary blissful ignorance that keeps his mind's eye forward facing. But, as strong as the urge is to crack another bottle, he has never seen a payday this large. The desire for riches wars with his gut over the decision. Roman now stands and paces back and forth across his small Grind apartment. "I don't know about this..." he finally says.

"Look, I'll bump it up to two-point-one mil. I told you I need *you* on this, no one else. Without you, this doesn't happen. And besides, you owe me after the whole Tarley-finger debacle."

Now Modus really had Roman's ear. He had never heard Modus beg before. Somewhere deep down, he feels a switch flip as he contemplates the amount of money he would make from this gig. For once, he is the one with leverage. Not needing to force his way through a situation is a new concept for him, but he can certainly see himself getting used to it. After another moment, Roman replies, "I'll do it for two-point-five."

"Two-point-two, and now I'm just being generous," counters Modus.

Enticed by even the slightest budging, Roman eagerly replies, "Fine. Consider it done."

"My best freelancer, comin' through for the big one! You'll be receiving coordinates soon for a rendezvous location. Payment will be transferred upon confirmation of job completion by the client. And remember; discretion, Roman."

The light on Roman's commscreen goes dark as Modus ends the transmission.

As he looks across the room, Roman spies his second boot hanging from the shelving unit toward the ceiling of his domicile. Scratching his head, he mutters, "Four Primes, what the fuck happened last night?" before retrieving it. He then suits up and sits down by his dock. With the swipe of his arm, he clears the top, knocking the collection of empty bottles, cans, and other garbage to the floor. The motion engages the dock, which projects an orange screen just above its surface. Roman taps the holographic display with his fingers to open his encrypted messaging system. Like clockwork, the details are already in his inbox. Modus Magni is always punctual, if anything.

The message only includes coordinates, the phrase "Out of the frying pan and into the flames," and a code name: "The Alchemist." Roman transfers the data to his TAB, then pulls a small case from the shelf next to him. He opens it to reveal contact lenses lined with faint electronic wiring: his profile veils. "Time to work, Darryl Frost," says Roman to himself as he places them in his eyes. Then, with a wave of his arm, he disengages his dock and gets up to grab his cloak.

The number "Ж2,200,000" encompasses Roman's entire focus, adding an energy to his step as he walks. He imagines celebratory drinks flowing, VIP service at any high-end club he wishes, and how the crowd will cheer his name when he buys a round for everyone in the room. *I've always wanted to do that... And the women that will come? Oh, how much fun I'll have...just as soon as this job is done. I could live like a king for months, get out of this crappy apartment, maybe even move back beyond the walls...would have to change my name, though...*

Despite his high-flying daydreams, he cannot seem to shake the sense of dread ever-present in the background; it permeates his subconscious. Modus is one of the few people in the universe that Roman trusts. Even still, he is overcome with a bad feeling about his opportunity. As these thoughts flood Roman's overstimulated brain, he grabs his cloak from where it rests, covering the upper half of his full-length mirror. The thick material slides off the glass, revealing his reflection in the mirror... But what he sees is not himself. Pallid, decayed skin fills the mirror between its black metal frames. The familiar tattered Klipper jacket...that charred, black neck wound...those blazing red eyes.

"WHAT THE SHIT!!" he exclaims as he falls backward onto the floor, white as a ghost. He scrambles to eject his blade as his eyes dart frantically around the room, looking for an intruder, but none appear. Unsure of what he saw, he looks back to the mirror, but the image that had flashed before him was gone as quickly as it appeared. He only sees the frightened expression of his own face, gasping for air as sweat trickles down the back of his neck. Roman wipes the sweat from his neck, nervously talking to his reflection. "Get your shit together, Rome. Get it together..." The glint of silver catches his eye, reflecting the small amount of light that breaches the apartment's metal shutters. Jerrick's necklace hangs on the wall behind him, swaying ominously from the shock of Roman's fall. It raises the hair on his arms and sends a chill streaking down his spine. He feels a presence that he cannot explain and cannot see. All he can think is that he must get out of his apartment immediately.

Kicking open the door, he quickly descends the two flights of makeshift metal stairs to street level, trying all the time to shake the image of his dead friend from his thoughts. It was just like his dream the other night... *Am I losing my mind?* He tries to think about the money instead; the good times that lie ahead of him. The metal creaks and groans under his weight, and as he reaches the alleyway next to his apartment, he is able to regain his senses. Parked just a few feet from the stairway sits his hoverbike.

As he walks toward it, an old voice calls out, "Hey! Roman!

Que paso mi amigo?" Roman turns to see the landlord stuffing the alleyway dumpster with large garbage bags. They seem far too heavy for the old man's frail, small frame to be moving. His shoulders bow forward, and only a few white hairs still remain on his balding head. He wears pressed black slacks that drag on the ground behind his heels, and a short-sleeved button-down shirt curves around his protruding gut. The man dresses as if he actively fights the times he lives in.

"Hey, Big Juan. What's up? Let me help with that before your spine shatters, you old geez." Roman welcomes the distraction from his landlord, if he can even call him that. Roman is the only tenant in the building that lives there rent-free.

"*Gracias*, Roman. You can move these bags but don't get cocky. I could still wipe the floor with you," remarks Juan as he steps back from the pile of rubbish. Juan, though far from big, enjoys the nickname Roman ascribes to him, as well as the banter. He also enjoys the protection that Roman provides by simply living in his building. In the past he has been easy prey for Gulchers, but those problems evaporated shortly after Roman moved in.

Roman makes quick work of the trash bags and then faces Big Juan and retorts, "Yea, yea...maybe in your prime. When was that anyway, 2500?"

"Laugh it up. I'll make you start paying for rent again..." chuckles Juan.

Roman has a good laugh at this remark. "Grendon's crew giving you any shit lately?" asks Roman sincerely.

"Hah! Not since you blackened his eyes for him. That coward won't even show his face on this street anymore. I don't foresee any more problems from him. At least not while I've got my good luck charm in-house." He gives Roman a playful slap on the arm.

"Good to hear. I gotta run. I've got a job. Better get back inside before the wind blows you away," replies Roman as he walks away.

Juan swats his hands in Roman's direction, mumbling, "Ah, pft...go on, get out of here."

Roman hops on his Omara Lancer and links his TAB to his helmet. The GPS coordinates from Modus begin to load, and the system pinpoints a building about forty miles southeast of his location. "Lower-lock?" he says out loud. "What kind of CP scientist hides out in a shithole like Lower-lock... This should be interesting... Play me some tunes." Roman's ears are instantly filled with the heavy sounds of his favorite band. He fires up Rooster, pulls out into the street, narrowly missing pedestrians, and makes his way southeast to meet up with this so-called "Alchemist."

CHAPTER 10:

Alchemy... Not Quite

Lower-lock. It truly doesn't get much lower than this. Likely one of the oldest parts of the Grind; the complete dereliction of maintenance makes it stick out even in the scrapyard that is the Grind. A vagrant haven, and home to some of the lowest-tier Gulcher gangs on the planet. Anyone who made their start here, even at the incipience of the Grind, would have moved out long ago—if they had any sense, at least. Gigantic gaping holes litter the hulls of the shipwreck buildings, and there are hardly any intact windows in sight. The entire section of Lower-lock is practically falling apart.

The grains of sand pelt against the visor of Roman's black helmet as he flies down the streets toward his destination, uninhibited by the lack of pedestrian traffic. Unlike his home near Market Circle, which spans the entire length of the Grind, the inhabitants here keep to the shadows of their makeshift tents, which line the street like an impenetrable wall. Roman can barely make out their dazed stares as he speeds by. Handfuls of disheveled denizens shuffle around the gloomy alleyways like zombies, completely unaware of their surroundings as if in another world. *Probably off their ass on Lotus-fly*, thinks Roman to himself. Lotus-fly, the drug of choice for those who've lost all hope; concocted from fermented Ephena Lotus and cut with everything under Bios. Roman presses down on the accelerator. It is best to traverse these parts as quickly as possible to avoid trouble.

Suddenly, Roman's visor flashes brightly and chimes over the hum of Rooster's engine, signaling that Roman is approaching his destination. He pulls to the side of the road in front of a small shop. It is surprisingly intact for its location, nevertheless an eyesore if it were anywhere else. Powering down his bike, he notices a hodgepodge group of letters in various fonts lining the metal doorframe, obviously from various sources. They spell "SaM's ElecTroniCs." He starts toward the shop entrance but stops, feeling the gaze of many burning a hole in the back of his jacket. He turns back to see at least a dozen faces shaded from daylight by the tents, makeshift hovels, and burned-out buildings that line the street, all of them focused on Roman. Each stare relaying the same silent message: you shouldn't be here.

Roman taps his left shoulder to retract his helmet and calmly walks back to his bike. From one of its compartments, he removes a small metal cube. Placing it on the seat of the bike, he taps the flat black circle on its surface twice. In an instant, the sides of the cube expand and open outward. A buzz of mechanical motions erupts from the device, which forms a small double-barrel turret that rotates on its base toward Roman, and then shines a small green light from its apex. The light scans Roman, followed by a loud electronic voice that addresses its owner: "DIRECTIVE."

"Deter intruders. Radius two meters," responds Roman. The device whirs and clicks a few times after he speaks.

"AFFIRMATIVE," responds the small swiveling gun as it turns toward the street. The green light turns red and begins sweeping the small perimeter at regular intervals.

Roman glances up at those who stare back at him and addresses the entire street with a loud, stern warning: "Don't even try it..." At this, most eyes turn away, now voluntarily ignoring the newcomer. A few still stare on in anger, but it does not faze Roman. Content with the safety of his property, he turns back toward the store and makes his way through the open doorframe.

The inside of the shop is covered floor to ceiling in dust, though its contents seem fairly organized. The merchandise displayed could hardly be categorized as "electronics." Exhaust pipes, small combustion motors, wires, and random paraphernalia line the shelves of the wall. Everything in the shop is practically an antique, and in rough shape to boot. *Clearly a front*, Roman thinks to himself. He glances over at a dark-skinned man who stands behind a cashier's counter cleaning a TAB device at least forty orbits old, seemingly oblivious to Roman's existence.

Roman blinks his right eye twice and instantly his vision turns to gray scale, allowing him to see a silhouette of the shopkeeper's legs behind the counter. The only color in Roman's view rests on the shopkeeper's hip; a bright red light forming the shape of a vitalerium pistol tucked into his waistband. "Whoa..." mutters Roman under his breath, knowing how rare it is to find vitalerium weaponry in the Grind, especially in a place like this.

Most of the common civilian weaponry operates on gauss platforms, where magnetic fields are utilized to propel projectiles at incredible speeds. The template is vastly inferior to vitalerium tech in accuracy, recoil, and power. Additionally, vitalerium weaponry requires no reloading until its power core is completely drained, providing the wielder up to three hundred rounds per light-weight core. The gauss platform is an old technology, but it tends to get the job done. Wasting no more time, Roman approaches the counter.

Without looking up from cleaning his junk, the man says, "You know how to make an entrance." His words carry a callous, biting sarcasm.

Roman replies sarcastically, "Yea, I'm a real people person. Out of the frying pan and into the flames." He stands idly at the counter for a response but receives nothing in return. Perplexed, Roman leans in and repeats the line more clearly, "Out of the frying pan and into the flames..."

"That supposed to mean something to me?" asks the man, entirely disinterested and still refusing to look up from his task.

Roman's face twists in confusion as he lifts his wrist to check his TAB for the phrase again. He confirms it, then reads it directly from the encrypted message, this time practically yelling. "OUT OF THE FRYING PAN...AND INTO THE FLAMES," Roman shouts in an almost robotic cadence.

"Sure, say it again, dummy. That'll make something new happen," the man retorts, emotionless.

"Alright, look guy, this is the phrase I got. Are you the Alchemist or not?" Roman's short fuse is burning fast, and he feels that his patience will run dry very soon.

The man finally turns to face Roman. Placing his hands lazily on the counter to support his weight and resting his gut on its surface, he stares Roman directly in the eye. A dirty baseball cap covers his graying black hair, and his face is as weathered as the rest of the shop. A name tag on his worn, dusty button-down reads "SAM KERRIGAN." His response is short. "Nope."

"Well then, where is he!?" shouts Roman. It is like speaking with a brick wall. The man's demeanor does not budge. He simply gawks back at Roman as if bored. Living in Lower-lock and dealing with the locals has obviously left Sam more than just a little jaded. This character was not easily rattled.

"Sorry. What I meant to say is... I don't know what the fuck you're talkin' about, kid."

"Look, if I were CP wouldn't I have CP armor? Wouldn't I be with backup? Or ransacking this place with little regard for scrutiny? WOULDN'T THEY JUST SEND A DRONE OUT TO

THIS SHITHOLE TO—" again, Roman's complaining is cut off.

"Fire," says Sam, deadpan as ever.

Dumbfounded, Roman pauses before asking, "What??"

"Fire. The saying is, 'Out of the frying pan, and into the fire.' That what you meant to say, dummy?" Sam does not seem intimidated by Roman in the slightest as he leans forward onto the counter.

Roman gives up, raising his arms sharply and letting them go limp to slap his sides in defeat. "Yea, sure. That's what I meant. Out of the frying pan, and into the fire."

Suddenly, a new voice echoes over an intercom in the shop. "Alright, Sam, cut him some slack. He's clear."

Sam sighs and walks to the wall behind him, stopping at a floating shelf at shoulder height. First, he grabs a remote from the shelf and, pointing it toward the front entrance, presses one of its buttons. Immediately, sets of metal shutters slam to the floor with a BANG, blocking all windows and doors. Roman staggers back a step, startled by the sound. He grows increasingly uncomfortable with the situation at hand, and with the realization that all exits are now blocked, he reaches to his hip for his pistol. The gun gets only halfway out of its black, carbon fiber holster before Sam addresses this coldly.

"Calm down, stupid. You don't need that thing in here. Besides, mine'll blow the tits off your little pebble sling of a gun. And you *won't* beat my draw," Sam says in a more serious tone. Roman hesitates for a moment as he contemplates his predicament. Realizing no imminent danger, he slides the gun back into its holster. He keeps his hand perched firmly on the weapon's grip, still reluctant to trust this Sam character. Better safe than sorry in situations like these.

Sam returns the remote to its original resting place as he mutters some indistinguishable insult under his breath. His oil-stained fingers move to an old radio on the same shelf and grasp the rusted tuning dial. He cranks it back and forth to the left and right multiple times in a sort of rhythm. It produces a somewhat satisfying clicking as it turns. After a few turns of the knob, an audible CLANK bellows from behind the wall as if gears shift on the other side. It is followed by a barrage of metal on metal, each sound louder than the last. Sam steps back calmly with his hands clasped behind him, and Roman stares in awe as the entire wall disappears into the ground, revealing a large, circular metal door. It is reminiscent of an old bank vault and in pristine condition. Its chrome doors reflect the fake yellow glow from the shop's cheap lighting.

Roman's jaw drops at the sight of the monstrous vault covered in pistons and gears. He watches as Sam scans both of his retinas and then both of his hands on the light of the green console at the door's center. Upon completion, the console chimes daintily and a symphony of whirring and clicking ensues as the gears spin on the face of the door. Four gigantic latches retract backward and release the door from its frame. It cracks open toward Sam, who grasps the edge and labors considerably to pry it open the rest of the way. The hatch, crafted from pure steel, must be at least four feet thick. Behind it lies a small, descending stairway illuminated by a weak, white light.

Roman, still astounded by the crafty safehouse stashed in the broken-down shop, walks behind the counter to the precipice of the stairwell. He gazes down the poorly lit corridor, unsure of what this descent has in store for him.

"This door closes behind you. On you go," says Sam, impatient with Roman just standing around. Roman says nothing back, knowing that any response will be met with yet another snarky remark. So, he walks through the precipice and descends the dirty concrete stairs. A thin strip of lighting along the ceiling guides his path. About halfway down, a loud thud followed by a gust of air reaches Roman as Sam seals the gigantic door. He pauses to shake his head, pondering once again why he accepted this job, then continues his descent to the sound of whirring gears.

At least forty steps later, Roman finally reaches the bottom, finding himself in a much larger, much cleaner room. Wires cover the majority of the floor space, making it complicated to navigate. They converge at four large electronic towers, two on either side of the room. Pipes snake around the room and connect to machines with indiscernible functions. High-tech docks and cheap tables displaying strange devices with flashing lights cover what little floor space is left open. In the far-right corner of the room lays an unmade bed. To the far left, a small door remains slightly ajar. Yellow light peeks out from the crack, and the sound of running water can be heard faintly over the ambient sounds of the computers and devices.

The door swings open, and a man with unkempt, dirty-blond hair emerges from the small room. He wears brown cargo pants and a matching tactical cargo top, a strange juxtaposition to his surroundings. His clothes look like they haven't been changed in some time. The mysterious character wipes his hands with a small towel and then hangs it over the door before walking briskly toward Roman, who places his hand on the hilt of his gun once again.

Noticing Roman's uneasiness, the man says, "Uh...hi... you must be Roman. I understand your hesitation...especially given the small amount of information you were provided with for this mission. I can only imagine what you must be thinking of all this."

Roman says nothing in response; he gives the man a once-over, then calmly paces around the room, investigating every inch. His eyes scour the specs of the impressive outfit of floor-to-ceiling supercomputers. Clearly uncomfortable with the silence, the man nervously blurts out again, "Oh, uh... I see you're eyeing my Titans. Th-there's enough processing power in these four builds to break into the IGB Currency Reserves, hehe...or hide indefinitely. I call them the Four Horsemen." Roman does not make eye contact. He simply continues to pace the room, scanning his surroundings. The man's pressured speech once again breaks the silence: "Like, of the apocalypse? Kind of a dated reference. And not that I want to bring about the apocalypse! It just seemed fitting considering there are four of them..." His eyes follow Roman's hand on the grip of his gun.

"Uh...look, I'm sure you're well trained and all, but...you're safe here. I don't intend to cause you any harm. No need to, uh..." He points at Roman's hip.

"If I'd felt at all threatened, you'd be lying in a pool of blood by now," replies Roman bluntly.

The man recoils slightly, instantly reminded that he is dealing with a mercenary. "Um...ok then. Well, in any sense, I am the Alchemist."

"Yea, that's a cute nickname and all..." retorts Roman, who locks eyes with the man and steps decisively toward him, "...but who am I really dealing with?"

More of a sharp recoil this time as Roman stands just inches from the Alchemist. He looks up at Roman, who towers over him, and says meekly, "I would...rather not say, given my hiding and all? That part I'm pretty sure I already mentioned. Probably better you don't know."

"Hm..." grunts Roman, looking up and to the right as if contemplating. "Well, that's not gonna work for me." Then, without another word, Roman walks toward the exit.

"Hey, wait!" shouts the Alchemist. "What, you're just quitting? Can you...even do that? You already agreed to the job! This is a matter of life and death! It involves EVERYONE!"

Roman stops, then turns back and marches toward the Alchemist, feigning intensity to get what he wants. "I don't care who it involves; I don't work for shadows! I like to know who my clients are, in name *and* in character. And right now? I don't see either of those in you. This job already has a bad vibe, and I won't be getting myself killed for some pencil-pushing computer nerd with a shitty code name. Last time

I checked, not many in my line of work were exactly *jumping* at this opportunity. So, be my guest! Feel free to try and get someone else to do your dirty work." With that, Roman once again heads swiftly toward the exit. Just as he reaches the first step, like clockwork, the man's voice calls back in concerned fashion.

"Wait," calls out the Alchemist, followed by a heavy sigh. Roman, with his back turned to the man, smirks as he realizes his leverage has worked.

With much reluctance, the man states, "My name...is Norvel. Dr. Norvel Mathis... I was the former Physics Director and Principal Investigator for XSEC. I escaped from Sanctum Tower about two months ago." Upon finishing, he sits down in defeat in his computer chair. "And you're right, I am out of options."

"That's better...but I thought you worked for the CP," replies Roman.

"No...well, I mean, yes. Sort of. The CP includes all the governors and representatives. I worked directly for Overseer Zerris Aganon. XSEC is...a little more discreet than the CP. It's not exactly an organization they advertise the existence of. Officially, it doesn't even really exist. Only a select few trusted members of the government know about it, and XSEC answers *only* to Zerris."

"And you left because...?" asks Roman.

"Short answer? I guess fear for my life...and guilt," replies the doctor.

"And the long one?"

Another heavy sigh leaves Norvel before he explains. "Look, Zerris is a madman; a tyrant. You have no idea what that psycho is planning. The things I had to do for him in XSEC...the experiments, I..." Norvel looks down and pauses, the weight of his past clearly hanging heavily on his shoulders. "I built something for him that I never should have. I left before it could be finished, but Mirene, my Senior Research

Coordinator...she could finish it if given enough time. I have to get her out..."

"Ah, so there's a girl involved too. Great..." responds Roman.

"What does it matter to you!?" responds Norvel with an unexpected ferocity that almost impresses Roman.

"Easy there, big man. Just thinking to myself that this is *definitely* not what I thought I signed up for," replies Roman. "So, what, you want to commit suicide by breaking into CP headquarters?"

"Wouldn't you do the same for your loved ones? I mean, isn't there anyone you would set the world on fire for to save?"

Roman looks away, uncomfortable with the images of those who come to mind when he ponders the question. He deflects, "So you're some kind of...super-genius, then? You build physics shit for Zerris?"

"XSEC stands for Explicit Scientific and Explorative Contingencies. We work on the cutting edge of science you never knew existed; weapons being the main focus since Zerris took the throne. *Extremely* top secret. So yea, I *build physics shit for Zerris.*" Norvel pauses for a moment before continuing, trying to find his words. "I started building Zerris a very particular weapon...one that could literally strike fear into the hearts of *any* of the powers that be—even the IGB itself, if they were to find out about it."

"What kind of weapon?" Roman asks as he pulls up another rolling chair and sits across the table from the physicist, his interest now piqued.

"One with dire consequences, I'm ashamed to say. Imagine if you could identify an individual...any individual, enemy leaders, political rivals... Hell! Anyone who even shows the slightest hint of discontent toward the government...and kill them with the proverbial press of a button?"

"Yea, it's called a gun. Here's an example," interrupts Roman as he unholsters his gun and points it lazily at Norvel, mouthing fake shooting sounds: "Pew! Pew!"

"NO! Ugh...and can you put that away, please!?" says Norvel nervously. Roman purses his lips in disapproval but obliges him. "What I am talking about is a weapon where you don't have to be standing in front of your enemy to kill him. You wouldn't even have to be on the same side of the *planet* as the target you're trying to eliminate. And it doesn't involve lasers, missiles, or projectiles of any sort. It's pure energy transference."

Roman raises a brow, perplexed by the concept. "Alright, go on."

"It's called the Touch of Ra," says Norvel as he grabs a screwdriver and a wrench from the neighboring desk. He places the screwdriver on one end of the desk in front of Roman and continues, "Let's say this is Zerris Aganon, and he has the Touch of Ra, which is more of a room and a console than a gun." He then takes the wrench and places it on the other side of the desk. "And let's say this is you and me in this very basement. The Touch of Ra essentially compacts vitalerium energy and transfers it anywhere within a planetary radius and causes it to appear in a confined, predetermined spot." Roman nods, following along with him. "Do you know what happens when humans without the proper gear come into contact with vitalerium energy?" asks Norvel.

"Cell death from rapid protein coagulation or something," responds Roman, recalling his schooling from orbits past without missing a beat.

"That...whoa, yea that's...surprisingly accurate..." Mathis sits back in his chair, impressed. "Anyway, once charged, the device can harness and transfer the energy from an extremely small source of vitalerium and transfer it to an exact coordinate, and I'm talking down to the *inch* of where you want it to go. It doesn't pass through anything on its way, causes no destruction as it travels, and it doesn't leave a mark externally. The target just DIES. INSTANTLY. An autopsy would only show cardiac and surrounding tissue death, but there would literally be no ties to the CP. No evidence. Just dead adversaries...or citizens." Norvel looks back at Roman's concerned expression and finishes by pointing to the screwdriver, stating, "So Zerris locates us, presses a button here, and we..." he knocks the wrench off of the table, "...cease to be."

Roman's brow furrows as he contemplates the potential for such a weapon. The CP had already taken so much from him. The thought of countless others succumbing to the same fate as his parents is too much to bear. He knows more than most about the treachery the CP is capable of, and his fists involuntarily ball in anger. "And you built this fuckin' thing for him? For that MONSTER!?"

"Hey, come on, man, take it easy. I didn't have a choice! You don't just say no to Zerris, not when you're in XSEC. That's how you disappear for good. Why do you think I ran!? Plus, I already told you the weapon isn't complete yet. They're still in the prototype phase. The signature identifier works, but it isn't infallible. It becomes less accurate as the target gets really far away. And the vitalerium transfer module? It's still...wonky. As it stands, he can locate and identify a target down to the centimeter by their unique heart signature. Anyone plugged into the mainstream Fabric in the last few orbits would have their heart signature recorded in the CP's database through their devices: their TAB or commscreen, whatever they have. Which, granted, is nearly a hundred percent of people within the walls of the seven city-states. But if you're operating your comms equipment dark? If you've been off the main Fabric and running on the Fray? It's different. The console can see the location of your heart signature, but IDing you is nearly impossible if you're not out in the open."

"Then how come Zerris can't simply find you now? I can't imagine he'd have someone potentially as dangerous as you go unregistered in this heart database thing," asks Roman.

Norvel pulls the collar of his shirt down, revealing a small black circle stuck to his chest. It is partially implanted, and its black metal shines in the dull light of the room. "This is an SA Node Detection Shield. It blocks the CP from using the weapon to locate me. Not fun to self-implant, by the way..." He picks at the edge where his skin meets the device. "A month later and it still itches... Anyway, that's not the only problem with the Touch of Ra. The transfer of vitalerium energy is still not completely clean. As it stood when I left, when the energy transfers to its target, it still causes collateral damage to organic life in its path. It's less harmful than direct exposure, but it leaves a trail. He has half a weapon, which does him no good. And the reason it's STILL nonfunctional is because I escaped!"

"Yea, you never mentioned *how* you escaped exactly," replies Roman with an air of suspicion.

"Mirene helped me... It's a long story. I'll tell you sometime," he says, attempting to act cool at first. "Pretty badass actually, if I do say so myself..." Norvel tries to play it down humbly but is now visibly bursting at the seams with excitement. "Ah, what the hell! So, I'm there in the sublevels of Sanctum Tower, and these three RoGuards have me! And they're taking me to the Cube—that's this secret prison they have in the Tower, it's where they 'disappear' people to—and then... oh wait, well the *reason* I was being arrested in the *first* place was—"

Roman has heard about enough. "Good Primes, stop! Forget I asked...can we get to the part where I do the thing then get paid in money and leave?" says Roman, rolling his eyes.

Norvel frowns and leans back in his seat, swiveling away from Roman and looking as if the wind has just been stolen from his sails. "Fine...maybe for another time then," he scoffs. He waves his dock to life and taps the projected screen a few times. Spinning the view toward Roman, he says, "Here...is where a rogue vitalerium meteor struck the surface of Deorum just five nights ago. I need raw vitalerium to get Mirene out of

Sanctum Tower and crush any hopes of that weapon coming online. My escape only stalled progress on the Touch of Ra. Mirene is incredibly bright...so I have no doubt she will figure out how to perfect Zerris's weapon without me. In due time she will be forced to complete what I started there."

The illuminated screen shows a 3D map of the planet with blinking red rings emanating around coordinates a good distance from Kairus. Studying the map, Roman calculates the rough distance in his head based on the terrain. "That has to be two thousand miles from the city limits, at least!"

"Let's see...yes, one thousand nine hundred and fifty-six miles. Pretty close, heh. But that's nothing for a freelancer like you, right?" asks Norvel, trying to distract from the long trip Roman has ahead of him.

Roman closes his eyes and sighs in annoyance. Then he says, "Hold on. The CP tracks these impacts. They literally have teams armed to the teeth specifically designated to salvage these raw vitalerium meteors. How do I know I'm not gonna run into one of these death squads while I'm out there? How do you even know this meteor is still there!?"

"Well, thanks to these babies..." Norvel turns and points to the four computer towers, two on either side of the room, "...they never even knew it existed. With the Four Horsemen, I was able to access their tracking systems and simply erase this landing from their database. Then the more complex part was creating an emission sequence in their vitalerium signature scans. I actually had to ghost malware into the system through one of their satellite nodes..." As Norvel talks enthusiastically about his methods, he looks over and notices Roman's eyes beginning to glaze over. He switches gears: "Right... essentially, I created a hole around the meteor and its trajectory where their systems didn't scan for vitalerium. It will be essentially invisible to them for at least another two or three days."

"Thank you, *Hilkar Mjartansson*. Except that still leaves one problem. How am I supposed to deliver this hunk of raw-V? How am I even supposed to get near it?"

"Oh geez, didn't think of that. Guess we should just cancel the whole mission," replies Norvel sarcastically. "Oh wait, I'm a genius, not some armchair influencer! Look behind you," he says, pointing to a corner of the room where a large locker stands.

Roman purses his lips. "You better check that attitude. No one likes a smart ass," says Roman as he gets up to investigate. He opens the rusted metal door of the mustard-yellow locker. Tucked inside is a clear plastic suit with metal rings incorporated throughout, and a bubble-shaped helmet with a transparent blue hue. At the center of the suit's thorax is a fist-sized metal transponder with a blue button at its center; an anti-V suit. "How the hell did you get this?" asks Roman.

"Through painstaking effort…and the expenditure of a lot of UCs," replies the scientist as he gets up from his seat. "After entering the atmosphere, the meteor itself should only be about the size of your head. Oh, and to house it, you'll need this…" He walks over to another table and retrieves a large metal cube with two transparent sides; a vitalerium canister larger than Roman had ever seen before. Norvel struggles with the weight of the container as he delivers the cube to Roman. Placing it on the floor by Roman with a thud, he exclaims, "There ya go! Modified it to scramble vital-energy scans so it should pass through the border stations just fine."

With nothing left to say, Roman collects the gear and makes his way to the exit. Before he leaves, Norvel calls out to him: "Hey, so…as you can imagine, this is incredibly time-sensitive. Every minute that goes by is another minute Zerris gets closer to completing this weapon."

"Yea, I got it. Retrieve quickly so you can save the day."

"Ok! So… I'll just send the encrypted coordinates to your TAB? And I'll check in periodically throughout the mission in case you need anything?"

Roman turns back toward Norvel at the base of the stairwell. "I've already got the coordinates. I took a picture," he says, tapping his orbit, referring to the lenses. "And as far as 'checking in,' please don't."

"O-ok then! Wait, when will you be back then?" asks Norvel.

"When I'm back," replies Roman as he disappears up the stairs. "Tell smiley upstairs to open the hatch...and tell him I'll need some gear."

CHAPTER 11:

An Unbreakable Bond

Due to dangerous working conditions associated with infrastructure maintenance in the city of Kairus, radiation burns are an affliction commonly seen in Deorum's hospitals. When human tissue encounters high levels of radiation, the generation of hydroxyl free radicals in oxygenated water occurs. The higher the water and oxygen content in the tissue exposed, the greater the injury to the cells. Being that human bodies can average between 45-75% of their weight in H2O content, high levels of radiation exposure can cause massive bodily harm and detrimental side effects for the individual. Even at low doses of exposure, protein and DNA cross-links can begin to form that destroy the body's rapidly dividing cell lines, leading to bleeding and neutropenia secondary to thrombocytopenia. This is usually seen over the course of a few weeks. More drastic doses of radiation will lead to cell membrane damage and, ultimately, death within as little as six hours. Most often affecting the skin and mucous membranes, patients will often experience hair loss, erythema, severe inflammation, large skin lesions, and ultimately necrosis of the affected tissue. If rad exposure is intense enough, as with acute high-energy penetrating radiation cases, the necrosis can begin to spread beyond superficial layers to muscle, bone, and even organ tissue.

This type of injury can be extremely painful and must be treated immediately. Despite advances in medical science, the cellular damage caused by this type of injury can be irreversible if treatment is not sought in time, requiring affected tissue to be removed through surgical excision. Often accompanied by acute radiation syndrome, otherwise known as "radiation poisoning," systemic symptoms that accompany radiation injuries include nausea and vomiting, diarrhea, fever, headache, dizziness, disorientation, bloody vomit and stools, internal bleeding, infections, and low blood pressure. Patients who experience severe acute radiation burns from high-energy exposure require a significant amount of medical care to live through the ordeal.

However, as morbid as this type of injury can present, it cannot hold a candle to injuries sustained from direct vitalerium ore exposure...

The day after his meeting with Norvel, Roman's eyes open early. No alarm wakes him, and no light from Bios shines through the metal slats shielding his apartment windows. Anticipation provided him little sleep that night. The dull pain in his right shoulder, which grows worse with every minute he lays on it, finally annoys him into rising. He massages the scar on his right shoulder as he sits up in his bed. Walking sluggishly to the window and peering outside, he gazes upon dark storm clouds covering the already dim sky. His stomach aches from hunger. He removes the flask from his back pocket and takes a swig. It burns as it reaches his gut but removes his urge to eat. Roman never eats before a job.

"Lovely..." he mutters to himself, irritated by the less-than-ideal weather conditions. There was once a time when, despite the condition he woke up in, Roman would start his day with a workout. Nothing serious; some push-ups, sit-ups, lunges, and pull-ups would do the trick. Perhaps he would run a combat simulation on his dock, which would render a faceless holographic opponent he could spar with in several choice martial disciplines. But somewhere along the way, pessimism and waning discipline had caused training to become less frequent. Luckily (or unluckily, depending on how one frames it), the life of a freelancer is often fraught with "forced" bouts of intense physical activity. So, despite not having a formal workout in about a month, Roman remains well conditioned.

His gear for the job is splayed out neatly on his dock's gray surface. Necessary survival gear for the voyage accompanies an array of weaponry, including a long-range gauss rifle equipped with an electronic scope, a pistol next to its holster and belt, Roman's knife, and two E27 fragmentation grenades. The anti-V suit rests neatly folded inside his open gear bag with the vitalerium canister. "Good a time as ever," he says in a gravelly, tired voice as he suits up. He latches his black terrain armor in place, straps his TAB to his wrist, and finishes by throwing his black hooded cloak over his shoulders.

As he opens the heavy metal door to his apartment, he hears a jingle to his left and looks over to see his friend's red-feathered dagger pendant swaying and softly tapping the metal wall. The familiar, ominous feeling once again encircles him, filling the gaps of his tiny apartment from wall to wall. Roman fights off the chill that starts in his neck and travels downward. His eyes shift anxiously to the floor, intentionally ignoring the mirror to his right. He forces the bad feeling down, and exits, repeating to himself, "Two-point-two million...two-point-two million credits..."

Roman travels quickly through his section of Market Circle. The people who usually fill the streets are nowhere to be found in this early hour. Rain begins to pelt the streets of the Grind. As the shops and alleys fly by, Roman runs through possible scenarios of CP encounters. Vitalerium Salvage Teams are relentless and ruthless, acting with full impunity should they encounter anyone within an impact zone. He will need to conduct significant reconnaissance of the terrain from afar before approaching the meteor. It is always prudent to assess possible hiding places, cover, and...

His thoughts are interrupted by a soft blue glow in his peripheral vision. As he passes by an alleyway, Roman slows his hoverbike after noticing a young girl crouched alone beneath a makeshift rain cover fashioned from scrap. No older than twelve orbits, her bioluminescent freckles gleam through the soot on her face. Her arms are extended toward the mud at her feet, where a few dirty marbles levitate and swirl before her with the motion of her hands: a telek. On Deorum, a small percentage of hybrid-born humans possess weak to moderate telekinetic abilities. Although the term "abilities" may be an overstatement, with the majority of teleks only able to express this trait to the magnitude of moving a few sand pebbles. Once a source of hybrid segregation at the onset of Deorum's early colonization, it has become a generally accepted phenomenon, and teleks no longer find themselves shunned from society as they once were.

However, it is not the girl's telekinetic abilities that cause him to slow his speed. Nor is it her poor state of affairs that causes him to bring his hoverbike to a stop and reverse back to the mouth of the alley. It is who lingers in the shadows a short distance behind her that compels him to quickly dismount his hoverbike and trudge through the mud to stand beside her. The sudden approach startles the girl, and her marbles immediately fall into the mud. She doesn't move a muscle as she stares up at his hulking, armored frame.

The two rain-drenched, disheveled men, who stand just fifteen feet behind the child, immediately stop in their tracks; their careful approach halted by the sudden arrival of Roman's intimidating silhouette. His presence is a stark warning to deter any cruel intentions harbored by the sketchy pair. Judging by their jittery movements and tics, Roman discerns they're at least four or five days since their last Lotus-fly fix. *Desperation phase. Fucking junkies,* he thinks. Their darting eyes size up the figure before them, calculating their next move. Roman decides to make the choice for them.

He unholsters his pistol and fires it twice in the air, which instantly causes one of the men to sprint in the opposite direction. The crack of the discharge startles the second man so severely that he locks up and falls into a deep puddle. He scrambles to get away, but his erratic movements turn the muddy ground beneath him into a waterslide. Roman easily catches up with him at a brisk walking pace, grabs the man by his grubby collar and presses his back into the sludge with a knee to his chest.

"I'll be coming back this way *very* soon. And if I don't find *that* girl sitting in that *same* spot as contently as she was just a minute ago, I will find you *and* your friend, and I will rip out your tongues through your assholes! Nod if you understand," growls Roman. His stare burns like a fire through the man's fearful eyes for a long moment. When he finally obliges with a jittery head nod, Roman releases his tattered garments. The tweaker lets out a high-pitched squeak before clawing himself upright and scurrying away.

Roman watches the man disappear into the darkness as quickly as his feet will carry him. When he is sure they are gone for good, he shifts his attention back to the little girl. Only a sliver of her face is visible as she hides behind the scrap metal of her hovel. Upon noticing her, the rest of her face quickly disappears behind the rusted panel as well.

Roman sighs, then slowly kneels beside her, doing his best not to frighten her further. "Are you ok?" he asks, softening his gravelly voice. The girl's freckles illuminate the corner where scrap metal meets the building's edifice in the alley. Though she refuses to look up from where she cowers, she responds with a quick nod. "What are you doing out here? Don't you have anywhere to go? Anyone to stay with?"

This time, she turns to him solemnly. Roman recognizes the look in her eye. He had once known that same hopelessness many orbits ago. Up close, thin, malnourished limbs can be seen peeking out of her ragged clothing. As her gaze falls to the ground, Roman grunts to a stand before trudging back to his hoverbike. She watches as he rifles through one of its compartments until his hands find what they are searching for. Moments later, he returns with a small pouch of jerky, and another item concealed in his left hand. "You hungry?" he asks, extending the shiny package to her.

Without hesitating, the girl grabs the snack and retreats into her corner, where she rips open the package and sinks her teeth into the preserved meat. Roman can't help but chuckle at the speed with which she finishes his food, but his expression turns serious again when he extends his left hand and opens his palm to reveal a small, folding karambit. At the sight of the knife, the girl drops the empty pouch and curls up in fear again, but Roman puts a stop to her reaction.

"No! None of that," he says to her sternly. "There's no room for fear in the Grind. Now take it." Though he pushes the knife closer, she does not budge. It takes him a moment to remember how slow he was to trust when he was first cast into the streets; how scared and alone he felt in the beginning. Roman lets out an exasperated grunt as he lightly slaps the karambit against his palm repeatedly. He stares into the darkness of the alley as he ponders how to reframe his offering.

"You know, uh…when I was just a little older than you, I lost my parents…both of 'em… Wasn't long after that I was out here alone, just like you. My father, before he died…he gave me this knife." He moves his jacket to reveal the silver and black handle on his hip. Though the girl watches with a skeptical eye, she follows his words closely. "He taught me never to use it unless I had to protect myself. And then he died protecting me…" Roman trails off, wincing as he pushes shop-room flashbacks out of his mind. He barely notices the girl's posture begin to change as she is calmed by his sincerity.

"Point is, I learned early on that this place…it'll swallow you up if you don't learn to protect yourself. There's no place for the weak in this world." Once again, he slowly extends the knife in his open palm. "Choose to be strong."

Cautiously, the girl takes the defensive knife and begins

inspecting it. After fiddling with its mechanism for a moment, she is able to unfold the blade from its handle. For the first time since he showed up, she almost finds the courage to speak to the mysterious man who protected her. But when she looks up, all she sees is the blur of his hoverbike speeding off into the rain.

As Roman returns to the mission at hand, the little girl's image conjures memories of his departure from the Outer Sphere. The orphanage. His friends... Daydreams fill the space in his mind, turning the minutes into seconds. He only snaps back to reality upon realizing he's reached the Grind's city limits. Roman shakes the memories from his head to refocus.

He signals to the CP attendant, who does not even ID him before opening the large gate outward and retreating to the cover of the guard shack. *Maybe this weather is a good thing*, he thinks to himself. *Smuggling raw-V back into the city might prove easier if the klangs provide less resistance.* Droplets of rain pelt against the visor of his black helmet as he cranks on Rooster's accelerator and races into the open terrain.

"Just two thousand miles to go..."

As dusk approaches and the last light of day peeks over the horizon, Roman's bike halts at the edge of a cliff. The rain had stopped hours back when he passed the storm clouds, but the black volcanic rock of the ridge he stands on is still wet. He approaches the edge and lies prone. The ground drops downward drastically at his position, but the rocky terrain below transitions gradually to a valley thick with foliage. Directly across the valley stands a mountain, its sharp, rocky angles juxtaposed with lush greenery. A magnificent waterfall cascades down to a small river that runs through. This is the Bando Basin. His father used to dream of taking a hunting trip here one day, but never got the chance. Roman pauses for a moment to take in the natural phenomenon, gazing upon the surreal-looking patch of green land surrounded by black, barren terrain. "Well, I made it here, at least..." Roman mutters as if speaking to his father. Glancing down at his TAB's nav system, he confirms he is a mere four miles from the anticipated impact site. He looks back to the mountain and thinks this has to be it.

He speaks a directive into his helmet: "Zoom." The visor magnifies his view of the mountain, and he scours the surface for signs of impact. Starting from the top, he scans the mountain itself, but sees nothing but green-covered boulders. As he meticulously works his way down, he notices a U-shaped gap in the top of the tree line just before the base of the waterfall. "Zoom," he says again with anticipation as he focuses closer on the treetops. As his view magnifies again, he can make out broken branches in a relatively even trajectory. Again, Roman calls out: "Zoom." Upon closer examination, it looks as if the edges of the broken tree branches are black, as if burnt. "Found you," says Roman smugly as he tags the area on his visor. "Now...how do I get to you?"

He scans the perimeter for a way down to the basin. After a few moments, he locates a break in the ledge about a quarter mile away with a much more manageable grade to the valley below. Getting down will be no trouble, but he will have to traverse the thick foliage by foot...quickly. Daylight is in short supply. He tags this as his starting point and then waits as the visor calculates a general path to his first tag through the woods. Roman scans the area once more looking for hostile forces, but finds no sign of them. Luckily, the area looks untouched by CP forces.

"Looks like you were right after all, mister 'Alchemist,'" says Roman sarcastically as he mounts his hoverbike toward the charted path.

Upon reaching the basin, Roman parks Rooster between two large bushes. He glances back at the sky and determines that tonight he will have to camp. Traveling through an environment like this one in darkness is extremely dangerous, not to mention he's grown tired from a long day's travel. He packs all the provisions needed into his gear bag for a night under the stars, then collects fallen branches and leaves to cover his vehicle from sight. As the little light remaining continues to fade, Roman swings his gear onto his back, clutches his gauss rifle firmly in his hands, and makes his way into the forest.

He hikes quickly and quietly. This basin is a breeding ground for many of the planet's dangerous beasts; best to try and avoid any contact if possible. After about thirty minutes of stepping through thickets and climbing over obstacles, Roman checks his progress. His visor reveals that he still has about two miles left to the burnt trees at the base of the mountain. He sighs and adjusts the weight of the heavy pack on his shoulders, then continues.

A few minutes later, Roman comes upon a small clearing that encircles a large rock formation. Its shape is strange and foreign. Stone tendrils arc upward as if reaching for Bios like a flower. *This is no natural structure; it's a ruin.* Overgrown from millennia of neglect and likely Gleph in origin. The ornate carvings on its surface are now worn to indiscernible scratches by the sands of time. A small cavern is visible at its base, and just above, one can make out the shape of a face in its stone. Despite the weathered nature of its ancient masonry, the strange proportions are a clear departure from the human form. Fascinated, Roman takes another step closer as he scans the structure, then freezes.

A black sludge covers the ground before the small cavern entrance, and at its sight, Roman immediately darts behind a nearby tree. Creatures often use the empty ruins of the Gleph for shelter, and black sludge means that this particular ruin is a Vorkrill nest. Roman takes a deep breath, then peers out from behind the tree. He cannot see into the dark cavern, but when he slows his breathing, he can hear the hum of the creature's wing mane rubbing against itself. The hum is slow, rhythmic, low; it is sleeping. Relieved, he carefully begins to walk around, hugging the tree line that surrounds the clearing. If he wakes the Vorkrill, he will surely have a fight on his hands. Vorkrills are incredibly territorial and will tenaciously protect their nests with their razor-sharp, spear-like appendages. Only the boldest of poachers look to hunt them. The meat of a Vorkrill is poisonous, rendered inedible by the toxic black ooze that it secretes. However, the black ooze itself is used in multiple medicines, and its organs are considered a delicacy to some. Thankfully, Roman had brought food with him. Better to save his ammunition for a fight he can't avoid...

As he creeps by, he peers into the dark opening, looking for a glimpse of the slumbering creature. A few steps further and he is just able to make out the top of the Vorkrill's emerald-green husk, covered in clumps of dried black sludge and patches of moss. Its wing mane is collapsed and protrudes vertically from its back like an antenna. It vibrates intermittently with a low hum, revealing the multicolored wing blades behind its chitinous shell every few seconds. Vorkrills cannot fly but will reveal their wing mane as a warning before attacking. With careful treading, Roman reaches the end of the clearing and disappears safely into the forest. The Vorkrill's hum slowly but surely disappears from earshot.

Another stint of uninterrupted hiking brings Roman to the far edge of the basin. The sound of running water gets louder and louder until he steps beyond the forest limits, revealing the mountain's great waterfall. Its runoff careens downward and crashes into a river that divides the base of the mountain from the wall of trees standing before it; a marvelous scene to behold. Roman wades through the shallow water of the river and trudges up the other side. The burnt, broken trees tower above his head, only visible by the light of Deorum's moons Cyndis, Beryllia, and Dontra and the twinkling of distant stars. But as he steps out of the water, dripping wet up to his waist, he notices another faint glow emanating from over the nearby hill. It casts a dull blue hue on the side of the mountain. Roman attempts to smile, but his feelings of accomplishment are immediately dampened by memories of his last raw-V encounter.

Atop the hill, the blue crystal meteor comes into view, lodged firmly in the ground at the mountain's base. Gray smoke courses throughout the crystal shell, producing mesmerizing patterns. It is a small meteor, not much larger than Roman's helmet, but a chunk of vitalerium that size is worth untold credits on the black market. The soil around the meteor is black with ash, and any foliage nearby had either died on impact or withered to dust from vitalerium exposure shortly after. A near perfect circle of scorched black terrain surrounds the crater, after which the overgrown grass is permitted to grow. It provides a perfect indicator of exposure limits; not to be crossed without the appropriate protection. Roman finds a space about twenty feet from the cusp of the dead grass and sets up camp. He pulls his anti-V suit over his clothes and presses the button on its chest, which causes the rings in the suit to begin glowing a deep blue. After erecting his metal hovel, Roman sets up his small portable range and pulls a bottle of whiskey from his provision bag. He could collect the ore in the morning.

The darkness of night unfurls upon the basin as the hours pass, and with little to do but rest, the whiskey drains until the last of the alcohol sloshes around the bottom of the bottle. Roman tosses the cap into the black of the vitalerium exposure zone. Within seconds the few drops of condensation harbored within it begin to steam. Roman takes a swig directly from the bottle where he sits next to the edge of the blackened earth, mesmerized by the blue aura of the meteor. He spits the liquid from his mouth into the dead land and watches as it immediately evaporates with a loud sizzle and a plume of steam. He laughs out loud at the reaction, head swaying side to side as if his neck were rubber. He talks aloud as if to converse with the forest: "Fuggin' Alshemist things vitaderium will...save his lady... Heh!" He hiccups, then pauses as the dazed smile is wiped from his face. "Shit doesn' do anyfin' but kill..." He attempts to focus his eyes back on the single hunk of glowing crystal, but two of them are visible through his eyes. "Onkay... Time fer bed," he says to no one, sounding as if his tongue is swollen. He tosses the bottle and what little contents are left onto the black ground. It shatters and sizzles on contact.

Roman struggles to rise, but eventually comes to a stand. He takes three slanted steps toward his hovel but stops when a rustling sound comes from his left. He stumbles into a defensive stance, gaining back a sliver of sobriety as his adrenaline kicks in. Searching up and down, he sees nothing but nature. He looks to his right, but no opponent makes its presence known. Only the sound of a light breeze blowing through the clearing and the ambient sound of the forest fill the space he defends. He softens his stance, hiccups, and giggles to himself.

"Never knew you to be wasteful when it came to the brown liquid..." says a voice as clear as day from behind Roman.

A chill runs down Roman's spine as he spins sharply around to see a dark figure standing directly in the middle of the exposure zone. The shadow of the mountain just blocks his identity from the glow of moonlight. Only a set of red eyes glow through the darkness. As the figure steps into the moonlight, the black skin of his face comes into view.

"No... NO! I'm not fuggin' CRAZAY!" Roman cries out as his mutilated best friend Jerrick stands before him. "YOU CAN'T BE HERE!!"

"And yet here I stand, unlucky enough to see what your grown-ass has become," replies Jerrick coldly. His voice, multiplied and distorted, echoes through Roman's head.

Roman paces back and forth, rubbing his eyes and slapping himself in the face as he reassures himself, "I'm just drunk... I'm JUST DRUNK. HOW? TELL ME HOW!?" cries Roman.

"Only you can answer that question for yourself, Klip," replies Jerrick.

Stumbling closer to the black circle, Roman has no answers. He searches what is left of his functioning consciousness to explain what he is seeing but just finds himself more lost. His head pounds as his frustration builds. "AARGH!" he screams at the ground.

"We were supposed to take over Kairus, become kings together...but I see no king. I see a drunk errand boy doing others' dirty work."

Roman's pacing stops. He turns and steps toward the exposure zone, antagonized by Jerrick's critical rant. "FUCK YOU!"

"All sense of the bigger picture lost down the bottom of a bottle. Letting your talents wither in a shallow existence of a life. You gave up, Rome. Just another drone."

"SHUT UP! SHUT! UP!" he screams back at the judgment of his friend. "You don' even have a life! YOU LEFT ME HERE!"

Jerrick's bloodied face curls in disappointment. "Always feeling sorry for yourself. Drowning your sorrows in whiskey and women. You think I did this to you? YOU DID THIS TO YOU!" Jerrick's voice travels with such force that it physically knocks Roman to the ground and echoes throughout the basin.

Shaking his head, Jerrick continues, "You used to unite those around you, used to be a leader. That's the Roman I used to know. Don't you remember Ion Street?"

Roman crawls to his knees. Drunk and exhausted, he gives in to the impossible presence of the man before him. "The... boys' home. I rememer..."

"That Roman was destined for greatness. He knew the value of the people around him, had the capacity for friendship and camaraderie. He was a leader! You...are weak, alone; depressed. A pitiful, perverted shell of the person you once were. You disgust me."

Tears begin to stream down Roman's cheeks as the emotion elicited by his memories becomes too much to bear. He struggles to fight back against what he knows deep down. "No...'at's not true!"

His words have no effect. Jerrick continues to dig into Roman. "Thank the Primes your parents weren't around to see what you've turned into. Imagine what your mother would think; what your father would think. The honorable Frank Matthews... Shit, he'd disown your sorry ass."

Roman can no longer withstand the punishment as his sorrow turns to anger at the mention of his parents. He jumps to his feet, wriggles his pistol loose from its holster, and screams, "I SAID SHUT DE FUCK UP!" as he points the barrel at Jerrick. It trembles in his hand.

"What shame it would bring them, to know that their deaths were in vain at the expense of a sorry sack of..."

BANG, BANG, BANG! Three gunshots erupt from the barrel of Roman's pistol in Jerrick's direction. But with each shot, Jerrick's figure shifts position with unfathomable speed, disappearing and reappearing from the path of Roman's projectiles. Roman drops the gun in disbelief.

Jerrick stands before Roman unharmed, laughing in his face to add insult to injury. "Such a glaring display of your lack of self-control. You haven't learned a thing...you can't handle what's comin', Klip."

"YOU WANNA SEE SELF-CONTROL!?" cries Roman as he removes one of the grenades from the gear bag at his feet. He rips the pin off the handheld explosive, cuing a small, orange light to flash a countdown. In his drunken rage, he throws the grenade at Jerrick's morbid image. But before it leaves his hand, he loses his balance, slipping over the bag at his feet and releasing it high. Roman falls to his back but quickly recovers. However, when he looks back, no more insults are hurled his way. No voice disparages him; only the trees and the ambient noise of the forest surround him. Jerrick is gone. Roman's head swivels around in confusion, trying to find who (or what) he has been talking to, but he is alone. Before he has a chance to think any further, his attention is grabbed by the quickening flashes of orange light in his periphery. He struggles to focus through the blur of orange and blue in the distance. His eyes bulge with horror when he discerns where his grenade has landed. The orange light flashes directly on top of the vitalerium meteor lodged in the base of the mountain.

"Oh fu—" Roman starts to blurt out...

Blinding light sears his retinas as an explosion erupts from the impact site. Roman attempts to jump for cover but there exists none nearby. The orange flames turn to blue as the grenade fragments the vitalerium crystal beneath it, sending razor-sharp shards of vitalerium shrapnel in all directions. The shockwave from the blast lifts Roman off the ground and sends him flying backward. Searing pain shoots through his arms, legs, and torso as the deadly crystal shards penetrate his skin and lodge themselves inside him. Another shockwave of pain as Roman's body slams off the metal of his hovel and falls to the ground on his side.

Intense heat courses through his body. Burning; such incredible burning pain radiates through his limbs and torso as the vitalerium begins to react with his living tissue. He writhes in pain, tearing off his useless anti-V suit as steam and smoke begin to pour from his wounds. The unbearable stench of burnt flesh fills his nostrils. He tries to scream, but when he opens his mouth, smoke pours from it. He is barely able to bring himself to a crawl as his body begins to break down from exposure. His nerves scream messages of pure agony to his brain as if every inch of him is engulfed by an inextinguishable conflagration. He crawls with urgency to the river behind his camp. He looks down at his hand as it hits the ground and sees the blue glow of a vitalerium shard sticking through his palm. The skin of his hand looks as if it becomes looser by the second. With each labored crawl forward, lesions begin to open on his arms as his skin peels back, melting from his bones. A few more steps and his clothes have completely burned off, and a trail of his flesh and blood line his beaten path. Overcome with the unfathomable level of pain, he falls to the ground and rolls to his back. A steaming creature of liquified flesh and muscle, Roman takes one final look up at the heavens. He can feel the sinew on his face burning through as he musters one last primal scream of agony... "AAAARRRGGHHH!!"

The pain begins to subside as the fire in Roman's veins is replaced by a cold sensation. His view of Deorum's three moons flutters in and out. A face appears above his, looking down sternly; his bloody brow furrowed, his dark skin aged, beaten and singed; his infernal red eyes as bright as the moons in the sky. The last words Roman hears are the words of his best friend, Jerrick.

"I told you it would be painful, but don't worry, Klip. Pain is only temporary. Transcendence, on the other hand...hmph. Now that's a different story..." Jerrick smirks and then disappears from Roman's view in the blink of an eye.

Then...all goes black.

CHAPTER 12:

Emboldened

Which organ is the largest in the human body? If you guessed the brain, you would be incorrect. Perhaps the intestines? A valiant attempt but another wrong answer. The largest organ in the human body, believe it or not, is the skin. The average human has about eighteen to twenty thousand square centimeters of dermis and epidermis covering their bodies. Along with adipose tissue, blood vessels, nerves, hair follicles, and sweat glands, the amalgamation of structures comprises the integumentary system. Integral to maintaining body temperature, protecting and maintaining water content, and acting as a physical barrier to infection and trauma, the skin serves to protect in many ways. It is also largely a sensory organ, housing millions of nerve endings that allow individuals to feel sensations and experience a spectrum of temperatures. This is also why injuries sustained to the skin can be extremely painful.

Another interesting facet of the integumentary system is its ability to repair itself through something called the healing cascade. For instance, a laceration sustained to the skin would first, after eliciting obvious pain, bring about something called the hemostatic phase of healing. Platelets in the blood create a clot to stop the bleeding. Eventually this clot will form a scab to create a sort of protective cover over the site of injury. Next comes the inflammatory phase, in which blood flow increases to the site of injury. With it, the blood brings macrophages and other healing cells that *remove pathogens, damaged cells, and bacteria. The blood also provides nutrients and growth factors to aid in the healing process. The proliferative phase follows, where the wound is rebuilt from collagen and extracellular matrix. Cells called myofibroblasts, also known as anchor cells, begin to contract on either side of the wound, pulling the edges of intact skin toward each other to close the laceration. Finally, over the course of months and years, the remodeling phase serves to realign and reorganize the collagen of the scar tissue, providing strength.*

The ability to heal, recover, and ultimately grow from injuries sustained is truly a marvel of earth-derived evolution...

"PSST...yo, Rome!" whispers Jerrick loudly. "Hey... Rome, get up, Klip! We have to go now before Runner Yarrow gets here. If he sees us leaving, the hand-off is screwed, and this deal is as good as done!" Despite his attempts, Roman does not budge. He simply lays in his cot facing the wall with the sheets pulled up to his forehead. Only a low snore vibrates from Roman's sinuses underneath. Jerrick pokes him roughly in the back with the butt of his rifle to rouse the sleeping teenager. Still nothing. Jerrick sighs, lowering his weapon and hanging his arms limp by his sides.

Without warning, the covers fly off of Roman and into the air, revealing that he is already dressed in his Wibetani Klipper jacket and uniform. He points two shiny pistols at Jerrick with a huge grin. "Pew! Pew!" says Roman, louder than he should. "Never let your guard down, Klipper!"

Jerrick jumps back, startled. "Shit, man! SHHH! Quiet down. You're gonna get us pinched!" Looking around the room, Jerrick sees a few low-level recruits rustle in their beds. One of them looks toward them with tired eyes, then nestles back into his pillow.

"What are the recruits gonna do anyway? They take their orders from us now," replies Roman, pointing proudly to the patch on his Klipper jacket.

Laughing quietly and shaking his head, Jerrick responds, "Phew... You scared the shit out of me, man! That's gonna merit some payback for sure. Now, you ready to stop fucking around and make some real-time UCs, brotha!?"

"I'm just getting it outta my system before the meet. We gotta button this shit up when we get in front of this guy. He's, like, royalty or something...seriously connected. Either way, his pockets run *real* deep. You and I will be able to start our own militia if we play this right." Roman gets serious as he holsters his pistols and grabs his rifle and gear bag from under the bed.

Jerrick rubs his hands together and smiles. "Fifteen million creds, man... We'll live like kings! Get ourselves a compound, a couple of Banari hovercrafts, have all the women we want...like boss man Modus."

"Even *better* than Modus. Which is why he can't know. You and I? We're gonna use that money to build something. I'm talking run-this-city one day type of deal. Now...shall we?" replies Roman as he produces a rope and tilts his head toward the window across the room. Jerrick grins, then grabs Roman's forearm to lift him up.

After descending from the third floor of the barracks to the alleyway, the boys ride their Lancers outside the main gate of the Grind and throttle across the sun-scorched sands toward their big meeting. Both boys are brimming with adrenaline and excitement, and both think the exact same thought: *This might really be it...our big break.* Their shot in the dark at elevating in a harsh world. Young and filled with ambition, in their own minds the city of Kairus was just a gold mine waiting to be prospected. All they had to do was provide a CP Salvage Team with the location of a raw-V cache they had happened upon by accident and become rich overnight. As Bios begins to rise over the horizon, a few figures begin to take shape in the distance.

"You see that? They're already at the spot!" Jerrick says

into his helmet's microphone.

"I see them! Just let me do the talking," shouts Roman in response. "We don't trust these CP klangs as far as we can throw 'em 'til they show us some collateral. Only reason we're going to them is they have the creds to pay us."

"Copy that, Klip," replies Jerrick.

The two pull up to a tan hovertank surrounded by half a dozen heavily armed men. None move as the bikes approach, except one man. He wears a black and blue officer's uniform, much fancier than the clothing worn by the rest of the mercenary types that accompany him. He is a tall man, not much older than Roman and Jerrick, with thick, feathered brown hair. As the boys pull up and power down their bikes, he speaks confidently and directly with them.

"Welcome and good morning, gentlemen. I assume that you two will be leading us to this, as you quoted, 'fuck-ton' of raw vitalerium ore? Who am I dealing with here, exactly?"

Jerrick lets his excitement get the best of him. "Yea, it's gotta be at least..." but is interrupted before he can overplay their cards.

"Half now, half when we show you the location. We won't say another word unless we get some assurance," interjects Roman.

The tall man chuckles at his forward response. He glances around at his salvage detail, who follow him in laughter. "Wow, well aren't you quite the negotiator? Unfortunately, that was not our deal. You show us the location and provide proof of this vein, and only then do we pay you what was promised."

"All due respect, Commander Zerris, we don't know you all that well. The raw-V is out there, and you'll never find it unless we show you where it is," retorts Roman.

Zerris Aganon thinks for a moment and then asks, "And why won't I be able to pick up this supposed vitalerium mine with our V-sense satellites?"

"Because the V's too deep, and the entrance ain't close to

the source. You need to know *exactly* where to look. And right now, seems like we are the only ones who know that."

Zerris takes a moment to think, then says, "Hm...no deal. Let's pack it up," and begins to get back into the tank. The mercs begin gathering their things to leave as well. Roman's stomach sinks. Had he just tanked their chances of making this deal happen?

"Wait!" shouts Jerrick, nervous at the idea of their lucrative future slipping through their fingers. The men all stop and stare at the teenager. Zerris stops just before taking his last step into the tank and stares at the boys, awaiting a change of heart. "Just give us something. Some kind of collateral. I know that wasn't part of the deal, but we need a show of good faith...that you klangs won't screw us."

Zerris pauses for a minute, then calls out to the largest man in his group, "Lieutenant Benson! Would you give these boys a show of good faith?"

The hulking, bald-headed mercenary approaches them with a scowl. Roman and Jerrick both take a step back as he closes in, unsure of what is about to unfold. To their surprise, he raises his TAB, taps a few times, and then swipes the screen toward Jerrick. Jerrick's TAB device chimes and displays the numbers "+Ж50,000," which hover in red above its screen. It is already more money than the boys have ever possessed. Jerrick shoots Roman a smile, but Roman is unconvinced.

"That is as good as the collateral gets until I see something glowing blue. Now, if you'll stop wasting our time...?"

Roman is overcome with a bad feeling from their interaction with Zerris, but the mannerisms of royalty always seem to rub him the wrong way. He usually knows when to trust his instincts, but this time is different. The stakes are higher than usual, and he can feel the promise of fortune discombobulating his senses. Unfortunately, without a buyer, his information is useless. He and Jerrick have no knowledge of how to harvest the material themselves, never mind the money needed to buy the equipment to do so. Without much of a choice left, he simply nods in agreement.

"Good. Let's get a move on, shall we?" And with that, Zerris hops into the cabin of the Desert Hovertank. Jerrick and Roman hop on their hoverbikes and lead the salvage crew to their secret cache of blue gold.

After hours of travel through the desert, two mountains emerge in the distance. The boys lead Zerris and his crew to the base of the mountains and then down a winding path between the two. At the sign of their landmark, a grouping of rocks they had stacked on top of each other, the boys pull over and power down their Lancers. Once the CP Salvage Team catches up, Roman and Jerrick lead the men through a crevasse in the stone to a narrow path. The path goes on for at least a mile, with the stone walls that guide their path rising higher and higher until they become the ridges of the mountain itself. After a long trek, the path finally ends at a small atrium. At the far side of the space, the mouth of a tunnel opens into the mountain cavern.

"This is it," states Roman. "It goes down about another mile or so, at least. Your V-scans probably wouldn't have picked it up through the mountain with all the rock in between."

"Is it one path, or are we dealin' with a fuckin' maze here, kid?" asks Lieutenant Dorok Ferrous Benson aggressively.

"One path. Almost looks like it was carved by someone... who knows when," replies Jerrick.

Zerris motions to three of his men to search the tunnels. The men open a case containing a number of anti-V suits and pull them on over their clothing before departing down the tunnel. "You two will stay here with the rest of us while they confirm the validity of the vitalerium cache. Settle in, boys," barks Zerris.

Two hours pass, and as the group of mercenaries sits around, Roman and Jerrick wait with bated breath for their dream to come to fruition. Lieutenant Benson paces back and forth with his rifle in hand, having become seemingly angry with boredom.

"This better not be some trap, or you two are in for a world of pain!" he shouts at them.

"Calm down, Dorok," Zerris says calmly, looking Roman and Jerrick up and down with disdain. "I'm sure these two... upstanding gentlemen know better than to lie to us." Just as he finishes, the three men emerge from the mouth of the tunnel, all of them smiling ear to ear. Upon seeing their expressions, Zerris stands up with excitement, actually displaying emotion for the first time during the exchange.

"Report?" he asks them.

The first man to exit laughs and then replies, "You're not gonna believe this. It's all there! It's bigger than you can imagine, at least forty- or fifty-ton's worth visible, and who knows how deep the vein runs."

Jerrick and Roman embrace each other and begin to celebrate. The thoughts of rich living and bright futures fill them in a way they've never felt before. It's finally time to get what they deserve.

"Well, you boys certainly do have something to celebrate, don't you?" asks Zerris coyly. "Unfortunately, given the size of this mine and the nature of its contents, I can't risk the possibility of its location being known outside of the CP. We can't have the likes of you Wibetani scum double-dipping on a supply of state-owned resources now, can we?"

A shift from pure joy to absolute fear causes Roman to feel sick to his stomach; the bad feeling he initially had proven right. They should never have trusted the CP. Looking over at Jerrick, the same expression of fear and panic is painted on his face.

Zerris looks over at Dorok and gives him the order, "Dorok, would you mind taking care of this problem of mine?" An evil grin replaces Dorok's scowl, as if he has been waiting for this the whole time. He raises his rifle and aims directly at the two boys. Vastly outnumbered and outgunned, Roman and Jerrick do not stand a chance in a fight against these mercenaries. In that moment, they read each other's minds. They have to get out, and fast.

Both take to sprinting down the narrow path from which they came. The wind rushes past Roman's ears as he tries to escape certain death. He looks back, and his spine turns to ice as he sees Dorok's rifle pointed at Jerrick. Slowly but surely, Dorok's finger squeezes the trigger. The ear-shattering screech of a vitalerium rifle charge pierces the air of the canyon and echoes off the surrounding stone.

"LOOK OUT!" shouts Roman as he shoves Jerrick out of the way. Searing pain envelops his entire right side as Roman falls to the ground, limp. His right shoulder smokes from sustaining the charge intended for his friend. The pain runs so deep that his vision blurs, and his sense of hearing dulls to a low ring. Roman tries to scream, but his voice vanishes from his throat. It feels as if the blood has left his entire body, and for the first time since the back room of his father's shop, his body trembles as he begins to urinate in his trousers. Jerrick continues to run but does not get far. Another high-pitched screech from a vitalerium rifle fills the canyon, followed by a cry of pain and a thud. Roman looks ahead to see Jerrick lying on the ground. A massive hole in the side of his neck and shoulder; dead.

Looking back, Roman stares down the barrel of Dorok Ferrous Benson XIII's vitalerium rifle. Another shot rings out, and as if in slow motion, the blinding flash encompasses his entire field of vision. As the light gets brighter, a familiar black silhouette flashes before him like a short-circuiting hologram, its black tendrils delicately caressing the light. Voices begin to fill his eardrums again, speaking in indistinguishable tongues. The humanoid silhouette reaches forth to touch him. Her long digit extending closer to his face. The voices become louder and louder, until...

"HHUUUUUAAHHH." A great gasp erupts from Roman's

lungs as he regains consciousness. Laying on his back in a field of green, his eyes burn as he stares directly into the blinding light of Bios. He attempts to lift his head but is restricted by immense pain; every movement another dagger piercing what little is left of his flesh. Roman's eyes scour his surroundings, wincing through the agony to take stock of the damage. His anti-V suit rests in the dirt a few feet away, torn to shreds by the vitalerium discharge. Only a few scraps of his clothing remain intact, which barely cover the sinew and muscle now exposed to the world. Steam rises from his body, climbing toward the heavens before dissipating into the woodland air. With great struggle, he reorients himself to his current situation: badly burned in the Bando Basin. *How? How am I still alive!?* His mind races.

A wave of panic washes over Roman as he tries to conjure an answer to why the sweet embrace of death has not yet arrived to deliver him from pain. As he struggles to move, he painstakingly lifts his arm into view. The vitalerium shard that once protruded like a spike from his palm is now flat and flush with the contours of his body, looking as if it has melted into him. He stares in awe as the gray smoke housed within the crystal sparks to life and morphs into a swirling neon green color. The crystal itself follows, now emitting an unnatural green glow. His eyes widen as he watches the transformation in color, which moves from the center of the stone to its edges. The burning heat he feels begins to cool as the bloody sinew surrounding the crystal masses begins to change... First to yellow, then to pink, and then finally to flesh; permeating outward from the smooth vitalerium that tiles his skin. Threads of hair slowly emerge as the follicles push through his epidermis. Looking down at his abdomen, he notices the same phenomenon occurring around the large shard lodged in his chest...and the smaller pieces embedded in his stomach.

As the pain subsides and his ability to ambulate returns, Roman scrambles backward until he is stopped by the metal shell of his hovel. He stares in fear and confusion at his skin rapidly regenerating—healing before his eyes around the flattened shards of vitalerium until finally, the edges meet. His hands slap to his head, expecting to feel bone, but instead are met with the healthy flesh of a human face. He palpates his cheeks in disbelief as his fingers stop at a small, flat sliver protruding from below his left eye: another piece of vitalerium that has become flush with his new skin. No steam and smoke rise from him anymore. The searing pain that once plagued him begins to dwindle to a feverish body ache.

"What the...?" he blurts out, only to be surprised at the sound of his own voice as a small, final plume of smoke crosses his lips and disperses before him. Holding his hands in front of his face and scouring his body for answers, he watches as the raging green smoke within the vitalerium shards settles; first retreating to the center of each new crystal "implant," then disappearing entirely. Finally, the green glow emitted by the crystals dissipates to nothing before his eyes, leaving nothing but a shiny blue surface...and leaving Roman speechless.

Roman glances back toward the impact site to find little trace left of the once-present meteor. He investigates the area around him, marveling at the destruction his stupidity had caused the night prior. Finally coming to terms with the notion that he is, in fact, alive, he cautiously lifts himself to his feet. The second he stands, he is hit with a dizzy spell so strong that he falls backward in the exact same spot with a nasty THUD. An immediate feeling of exhaustion sets in, and he does not make another attempt to rise for some time. While he recovers and waits for the vertigo to pass, he gives his body another once-over.

Though his tissue has mostly regenerated, he has not completely healed. A few larger scrapes, bloody gashes, and bruises still remain on his aching body. Though his heart still beats, he feels as if he's been hit by a speeding hovercar, and a febrile chill stings his bones like a winter frost. Whatever happened to him seemed to have reached its limitations, leaving him feeling completely drained. Finally, he fights through the exhaustion and attempts to stand again.

Small patches of black surround him where other shards of the meteor had landed. Although his wits return to him now that the pain has subsided, his head fills with questions he hasn't the answers to. *How am I alive? How did I heal? What was that green smoke inside the crystals? Why the hell have I been seeing Jerrick!?* The barrage of mysteries leaves him with an unsettling feeling that reaches deep into his stomach...too deep. Grabbing his knees and leaning forward, he retches and vomits on the ground before him.

"Ugh...why...?" he says, feeling insult added to severe injury. But as he looks away from the puddle of brownish puke, Roman's eyes rest upon the vitalerium cube sitting by his range that lies tipped over on the grass. Force of habit leads him to revert back to things he can wrap his head around. "Shit...need to see if there's any meteor left for the alchemy wizard." Looking down again at his compromised anti-V suit, he realizes that collecting it may not be possible. If the distraction of his newly implanted crystal accessories and their consequences were not enough to deter him from completing his mission, the idea of experiencing a similar ordeal of pain certainly was. "Fuck this. I'm out of here."

Roman hastily collapses his unused metal camper and packs up his things. He reaches into his gear bag and pulls out a change of clothes to replace the ones turned to tattered ash on his person. Kneeling beside his belongings, he starts to pack up his range with nervous energy, fearing what the crystals might mean for his lifespan. He may have healed... somehow, but he now walks with pure vitalerium in his system. *That can't be good,* he thinks to himself. *Will I even be able to be near people again? Or will they simply melt if I get too close?* None of the hypotheticals present themselves positively in Roman's mind.

A sudden rustling sound from behind Roman gives him a startle, causing him to tightly grip his metal range and fall forward from where he kneels. His balance is still off, and his nerves have put his stomach in knots. But Roman does not turn around, simply pulls himself back to the balls of his feet and calls out, "You back to deliver another cryptic tongue-lashing, or can we just skip to the part where you tell me what is going on?" Another rustle and hum from behind him finally elicits a reaction from Roman, who turns around and yells, "JUST TELL ME WHAT I...oh..."

This time, Jerrick is nowhere in sight. Instead, the sheen of emerald-green, mossy chitin and the hum of a wing mane prove to be much more frightening. Just fifty feet from Roman's position, a gigantic beast stands twelve feet tall. Its shimmering exterior strikes fear into Roman's heart. It is the Vorkrill he happened upon during his trek through the woods, and this time, it is very much awake and aware of his presence. The wing mane on its back is no longer collapsed. It instead fans out to rapidly hum a dire tune. The glossy wings display a blur of yellow, red, and orange above its bumpy, moss-covered exoskeleton. Black sludge drips from its mandibles and splatters onto its sharp, spear-like appendages as they extend further from its body. The beast inches closer. Its four black eyes fixate on Roman as its six legs creep forward with a predator's grace, delivering a bone-chilling warning as its insect-like wings beat faster and faster.

Roman does not move a muscle. Without shifting his head, he looks down at his rifle on the ground next to his bag. He will have to dive for it if the Vorkrill decides to attack. "Please don't screech, please don't screech," whispers Roman to himself, remaining as still as a statue. "Just move on...nothing to see here," he whispers again. This interaction could go one of two ways for Roman. Either the Vorkrill will attack and tear Roman to shreds, or he will have to be very, very lucky...

The Vorkrill stops in its tracks just twenty feet from

Roman, its eyes never leaving his figure. It begins to swiftly strafe around him, sizing him up from a different angle with each sidestep. The chitin of its legs makes a hollow sound with each step, and the decibel of its angry hum grows louder. Its long, armored neck swivels precariously as it studies the potential threat. It stops one last time to Roman's left, and then crouches...

"Oh fuck..." mutters Roman. Just as it leaves his lips, the wing mane's hum heightens to a blaring screech, and the Vorkrill launches itself to his position. Its leap is impressive, and it covers ground incredibly fast. Roman is just able to dive out of the way in time, falling to the ground and rolling to a standing position with rifle in hand. The crack of the rifle echoes off the mountainside as he fires one shot from the hip, striking one of the Vorkrill's legs and piercing its armored shell. The Vorkrill screams like a banshee but barely recoils as blood and toxic sludge spray into the air. It leaves a small hole from which the green and black fluid leaks out, but it is not nearly enough. The Vorkrill swings one of its sharp appendages at Roman, who just barely dodges it. But the Vorkrill moves quickly, and as it closes in for its next attack, Roman is unable to respond in time. A second swing of its spear claw knocks the gun from Roman's grip, leaving him defenseless. The beast then uses its momentum as a weapon and charges him. The side of its dense husk collides with his chest.

Roman soars back at least ten feet before colliding with the ground. "AARGH!" he cries out in pain as the wind is knocked out of him. "That all you got..." wheezes Roman as he claws himself to a crouch. The Vorkrill circles around, changing directions to face Roman once more. Vorkrills are incredibly fast when moving forward, but they cannot turn quickly. Their crab-like leg fixtures don't allow for it. Roman only has one chance to get this right. He must dive for his gun again and deliver an accurate shot to one of its weak points to save his own life. As the Vorkrill faces him and lets out another high-decibel screech, Roman sprints for his weapon while still wheezing for air.

As he covers the ground, the Vorkrill rushes him with lightning speed, intent on sinking its razor-sharp talons into his flesh. Roman dives to the ground, landing on his right flank with a heavy THUD and a grunt of pain. He grasps the butt of the rifle and pulls it in close, then rolls to his back to aim at his aggressor. But he is too late—before he can raise the rifle to fire, the Vorkrill is already on top of him. He looks up to see both spear claws descending toward his head. Instinct kicks in, and all Roman can do is throw his hands up in defense, squeeze his eyes shut, and scream as horrid death approaches yet again.

Adrenaline surges through his body, and he feels the ice course down his spine and radiate outward to his limbs. A cold energy surges through every muscle in his body. The only sound he hears is the beating of his own heart, and time itself seems to slow.

"AAAAAHH!" he cries out as the sound of the Vorkrill's spears strike solid matter. But no pain follows...

When a bloody mauling does not ensue, Roman's eyes squint open one by one to a bluish glow. What he sees first is the shard of vitalerium lodged in the dorsum of his hand, within which gray, vaporous smoke rages. The shard now gleams a radiant blue within the confines of his skin, but it is not the true source of the light that seemingly casts a blue hue over his entire body. He opens his eyes further to see the Vorkrill's talons hovering just above his forearms, trembling as they press into...something. A blue aura permeates beneath their toxin-stained tips, enshrouding Roman in what looks like a transparent blue eggshell. "What the hell!?" His words slip between clenched teeth. His eyes fall back upon the gray smoke swirling inside each vitalerium shard lodged in his hand, forearms, and torso as they emit a familiar glow. It is similar to the swirling and glowing they emitted when his skin had miraculously regenerated earlier, only this time, blue in color.

Frustrated, the Vorkrill raises its spear-like appendages back into the air, and the blue light disappears. This time, the Vorkrill winds up to ensure it kills its victim and stabs even harder at Roman. Another surge of adrenaline shoots chills down Roman's spine as he tenses and squints, watching the spear claws descend toward him with frightful speed. But once again, they are stopped just inches from Roman's extended arms, blocked by the strange blue aura that forms between him and certain death. Black sludge leaks from the Vorkrill's mouth onto Roman as it attempts to push its sharp appendages through the aura, but even the slime is stopped by the blue energy flowing around him. The sludge rolls around the barrier and pools beside Roman's flanks. The creature, now enraged by its inability to annihilate its target, rears back on its four hind legs and extends its appendages to the sky one last time. This time, Roman does not hesitate.

Pulling the gauss rifle to his shoulder, he uses the extra milliseconds he's been granted to aim the barrel straight at the Vorkrill's head, and pull the trigger…

A light blue flash bursts from the end of the gauss rifle as its projectile passes right through the creature's mandibles and out the back of its chitinous skull. It lets out a painful shriek before falling backward and crashing to the forest floor. As it hits the ground, its legs curl and twitch with involuntary contraction. After a few seconds of writhing, one last huff of air passes through its mangled mandibles, and the Vorkrill expires.

Roman sits up, astonished not by the fact that he survived, but by *how* he survived. The strange blue aura, whatever it was, had protected him from the strength of a fully grown Vorkrill. His muscles relax as the adrenaline slowly flushes from his bloodstream. Looking down at his hands, he notices that once again the gray smoke slowly begins to disappear, and the glow of the vitalerium dims to nothing. Roman shifts to get up, but a sharp prodding in his buttock prompts him to investigate the area in which he sits. The grass is blackened and dead beneath him... *Oh no*, he thinks. Too exhausted to react quickly, he reaches behind him and lifts a small shard of vitalerium to eye level. With fascination, Roman rolls the bright crystal between his fingers. However, this time the blue glow induces no pain. His skin does not melt, and his body does not smoke. Instead, he watches the gray smoke dance just inches from his nose while he remains seemingly immune to its exposure. "What the fuck happened to you last night, Roman...?" he asks himself out loud.

The ever-growing mountain of unanswered questions creates a burning urgency within the young freelancer. Without any need for an anti-V suit, Roman collects a handful of vitalerium shards scattered about the campsite and dumps them into the heavy containment cube. He collects his gear and practically sprints the distance back to his bike. He is powered by a second wind from his all-consuming need to consult someone for answers. That someone, an XSEC scientist slumming it in Lower-lock, is not only the person who brought about this curse; he is possibly the only one who can remedy it. Finally reaching Rooster, Roman clears off the branches and rubble that hide it and speeds back toward Kairus with feverish intent. If anyone can figure out this unnatural marvel...this strange evolution...it is Norvel Mathis.

CHAPTER 13:

Death from Above

Sweat, rhythm, bass. The boom of impossibly loud resonance pairs with screaming melodic decibels to pummel the crowd as they jump, wind, and gyrate. Each shockwave from the subwoofers is enough to lift the glistening perspiration from the young ravers' faces at the stage front. Hundreds. Thousands. Tens of thousands. It is impossible to say just how many dance in the chaos of the concert. Every last one of them moving in time with the sounds of an electronically crafted symphony; their hearts beating in sync with the downbeat. Anticipation builds as the song's drop approaches. Laser lights cut through the manufactured fog like hot knives through butter, bursting from the fantastic display. Spotlights shine so bright they even rival the light of Bios, which bends around the bowl of the arena. Stories above the crowd, holograms of dancing women arc overhead in sweeping technological fashion. A steep release of dopamine begins to grip the fans as they await what's coming. They can hardly wait as the music climbs and climbs, yearning for the rush of their melodic heroin.

The music builds and builds, faster and faster as the people scream for what they want. The DJ lifts his masked head from his decks to gaze upon the crowd, displaying his gem-covered visor. It sparkles in the glow of the dancing lights. He lifts his hand into the air as the rhythm reaches its climax, then...

Suddenly, the music cuts. The system goes silent as it is replaced by the sound of thousands of moving feet and confused chatter. At first, they all look to each other in the crowd, as if to see if everyone else is experiencing the same phenomenon. As the seconds pass and no music returns, the fans begin to turn their confusion toward the stage.

"WHAT HAPPENED TO THE BEATS!?" yells one concert-goer toward the DJ.

"WHERE IS THE MUSIC!?" yells another young raver covered head to toe in glowing attire.

The DJ does not falter. He does not even move from his position. He simply stands with his index finger pointed to the sky before thousands of people who grow more confused and disappointed by the second. After a few more seconds his arm drops, and his finger points to his left. As he does, a polished chromite boot steps into view from backstage, and a second character joins the performer on stage. He is followed by two armor-clad men donning white and royal blue. As the spotlight hits him, the DJ mashes the play button.

Music explodes from the speaker as flames erupt from pyrotechnic cannons on either side of the stage. The young crowd celebrates with a new wind of excitement as they are graced by the presence of the Royal Overseer himself, the honorable Zerris Aganon. He smiles and waves to his crowd as he approaches the stage. Today, he wears a slightly different royal garb in keeping with the setting. A glowing mantle hangs from his shoulders and flows through the air as he walks. A hologram surrounds him, emitted from small lenses in his collar, that dances to the beat, creating an almost mystical aura. As he walks, he takes a few steps to the beat and mimes a simple dance move in coy fashion. The minor gesture is a success as measured by the woos and cheers from the audience. The DJ gives a shallow bow as he hands his Overseer a tiny device and lowers the volume of the music. Zerris raises the mic device to his cheek, and releases it as it attaches to his face. The crowd goes silent, and the Overseer addresses his subjects.

"I don't know about all of you..." he says, once again building the anticipation of the crowd. They wait with bated breath for his next words. He points back at the DJ as he finishes, "...but I love me some Holofiend!" The crowd screams in approval as they jump up and down. The DJ responds with more shallow bows to both the audience and to Zerris.

"And I want you to know that in my earlier orbits before my days in the court, I would have been right out there on the dance floor with all of you!" More screams of approval erupt from the crowd in response to his relatable statements. His beaming smile provides a feeling of hope and comfort to all. "But I'm not here today just to enjoy the music, although I most certainly am enjoying it. I'm here today to tell you all that I am continuing the fight, day in and day out, for your futures! I want each and every one of my supporters to know that I deeply appreciate your warm welcome. The love you show does not go unnoticed, and I can honestly say that the love is a mutual one. As Overseer, it is my job to care for all Deorans! And while I can't give each of you a hug...that would take all day, wouldn't it?" he says, looking back at his RoGuard escorts. The sound of thousands of forced laughs from the crowd fills the stadium. "With Initiative 919 passed, I will be able to show each and every one of you my love... Love that you will feel in your wallets and your bank accounts!!"

The arena is overwhelmed with screams that gradually evolve into a chant: "ZE-RRIS! ZE-RRIS! ZE-RRIS!" they cry.

"Thank you for allowing me the time to stop in today, and again, thank you all for your undying support. I thank you sincerely, from the bottom of my heart, for the opportunity to fight for you. Holofiend, take it away! May we support the party, and may the party prevail! And to everyone in the arena..." He waits for the DJ's cue. Just before the music starts up again, Zerris finishes, yelling into the mic: "Rave on!" The crowd, acting as if they all simultaneously lose their minds, frantically cheer and dance as waves of electronic music fill the air once more. With that, Zerris returns the mic, walks off stage, and is escorted by an armed guard out of sight. The party continues.

Upon leaving the stage, Zerris's beaming smile is immediately replaced with a scowl and a sigh. Escorted by a half-dozen RoGuard, he enters his heavily armored hovercar parked in the security tunnel leading toward the arena's exterior. He seats himself in the opulent, blue interior of the vehicle and begins ripping the glowing attire from his person. He tosses the mantle to the floor, then looks up at the seat facing his. Mingen, his chief administrator, sits across from him with his holoscreen in hand.

"How are you feeling, my Overseer?" Mingen asks enthusiastically.

"Relieved. I feel relieved to finally be out of this clown suit," responds Zerris sharply. Then, with a hint of sarcasm, he comments, "I should have you tarred and feathered for putting me through this, Mingen."

"I understand your frustrations, Overseer. However, their response was overwhelmingly positive! I monitored the entire speech from my holoscreen. Your delivery was impeccable! Perfectly short and sweet to adapt for those enjoying substances, mentioned the benefits of the new initiative, and positioned yourself as a man of the people. And most importantly, you used "love" four times. That always seems to poll well with this particular demographic. Aside from your clear... opposition to this leg of the tour, I think this was an absolute success!"

"Successful or not, it would behoove you to have these burned," says Zerris, pointing to the rave-themed clothing on the floor. He sits back in his chair, pontificating. "We don't even require their votes to rule and yet, still, we must perform this charade... Still, I must dance for them."

"It's a small price to pay for a consistently docile populace, my Overseer," his chief advisor replies.

Zerris bites the inside of his cheek as he looks out the window. He knows that despite his disdain for these types of duties, Mingen is right. Still, it irks him that there are dozens of other tasks more important to his goals that remain undone. "That concept is not lost on me, Mingen. Understanding doesn't require my enjoyment. Just get me far away from this place... What's next on the docket?" he asks as he begins to change into his usual black and blue mantle. The hovercar lifts up and floats down the tunnel to the city, followed by six CP hovertanks.

"Well..." responds Mingen apprehensively.

"Well, what? Spit it out, Mingen, my time is valuable."

"... Well, we were supposed to head directly to the quarries for XSEC's testing of your new satellite-based ion cannon..."

"Oh, good. I might actually enjoy something you put on my schedule for once," replies Zerris, who is only half paying attention as he fumbles with his shirt cuffs.

"But..." continues Mingen.

Zerris begins to grow aggravated with Mingen's indirectness. "But *what*, Mingen?"

"Grand Regent Wyngor has requested—er...demanded an emergency meeting in the Fabric. So, I've redirected us back to your office so you can take it comfortably. I've already postponed the XSEC testing two hours to accommodate."

"What!? WHY!?" yells Zerris.

"I'm sorry, Overseer! He refused to say. I didn't have a choice in the matter..." Mingen becomes nervous as he senses the Overseer's stress level skyrocket.

Zerris rises from his seat slowly, deliberately to match the cadence of the questions that follow. "Tell me, Mingen. Why is it you think it prudent to schedule a meeting with my only...

my *sole* superior...one whom we are actively trying to undermine...without clearing it with me first?"

"I'm sorry, my Overseer! He requested the meeting directly! I have no authority to deny the Grand Regent his wishes, er... no one does!" replies Mingen apologetically.

"That menacing bastard...it's eight weeks before his shipment is due. And he wants to meet in the Fabric? He couldn't simply comm!? What in the hell could he possibly...ugh. Never mind that. Call XSEC and reroute us back to the quarries. I'll take the meeting from here. I will not have that *Plenathuen* brute ruin my day."

"Right away, Overseer Aganon." Mingen begins to hastily tap his holoscreen to alter the schedule. Zerris, still fitting a cufflink into the sleeve of his shirt, walks across the spacious hovercraft to a full-length mirror on the wall. He inspects himself from head to toe for any imperfections, repositions a hair, and flattens out a wrinkle in his pants. Then, he moves toward the center of the hovercraft and steps onto a small, circular platform. Its steel-mesh pattern glows upon receiving his weight, and a wave of his hand causes a set of holographic controls to display in the air surrounding him.

"While I'm in there, I want you to jack into the feed and record everything," orders Zerris as he taps floating buttons to select his settings.

"As you wish, Overseer," replies Mingen. Immediately jumping to action, he uses the controls on his seat to float forward toward the platform where Zerris stands. He reaches down toward Zerris's feet and opens the maintenance compartment, removing a long, thick wire. Mingen then removes the black glove from his right hand, exposing a small electronic square implanted in his wrist. Upon pressing on the square, it pops up to reveal an input socket and an output wire. He connects the wire from the platform to his wrist, then reels the other wire outward from his forearm and connects it to his holoscreen. After a few taps on his device, he nods to

Zerris that he is ready. Mingen sits back in his chair, adjusts his glasses, and closes his eyes. Zerris hits one last button, then stands still as a large, black metal tube descends from the ceiling above him, enclosing him inside a shell of darkness.

The whirring noise of increasing gear RPMs steadily rises within the equipment that encases him until, suddenly, a great flash of light bursts from the inner walls of the Fabric shell. Zerris opens his eyes to find himself in a giant room. The floors, ceilings, and walls are all colored the same bright white. No furniture decorates the space. No windows or art adorn the walls. It takes a moment for his eyes to adjust to the light. Once they do, he looks around the space for his superior, but all that can be seen is a sea of white as pure as creation itself. He clenches his fist, stretching the scar on his right hand in frustration at the impromptu meeting. Minutes go by without a sound as Zerris waits with his hands clasped behind his back. As his patience begins to wear thin, he begins pacing back and forth.

Suddenly, "I always know when to start my meetings with you..." barks a loud voice from behind Zerris, startling him, "...because as your distress builds, you begin to pace." Zerris turns to see a gigantic man sitting behind a tall pulpit, his image vastly enlarged and extorted to nearly three times the size of Zerris by the Fabric. The voice belongs to a large bald man with an oddly shaped cranium. Tubes protrude from his armor and insert into the pale flesh of his neck. Like most from planet Plenathu Viridus, the planet's atmosphere affects his pale skin with a slight green tinge. His bionic eyes glow a nuclear-waste green, and external processing chips protrude from his temples. His unfeeling stare pierces through Zerris as he speaks, and his ornate green and black armor is so clean it practically sparkles. "Back and forth, back and forth...tell me. Is there something distressing you, Zerris?" the Grand Regent Wyngor continues. His probing questions come with an accusatory tone attached.

Zerris regains his composure in the presence of his only superior, and assumes a power stance with his hands behind his back. He speaks as calmly as possible, choosing his words extremely carefully. "Your Eminence, Grand Regent Wyngor. Thankfully, you may worry not. And while I doubt anyone in the verse retains the capacity to interpret the human psyche like you, I can assure you that no distress plagues me."

"Then are you asserting that your Grand Regent...IS LYING!?" he shouts as he leans forward aggressively over Zerris. He has never been the charming type, but today the Grand Regent seems more vitriolic than usual.

Zerris blinks at his rise in tone but remains composed as he responds, "Of course not, your Eminence. I humbly ask your forgiveness for the unintentional slight. I meant nothing by it. I was simply wondering what type of emergency would precipitate such an early meeting this quarter."

Wyngor leans back in his chair, never breaking eye contact with his subordinate. His rage calms and his face relaxes to its usual scowl. "You can coat your responses with fancy wording all you like, but it wouldn't be the first time I caught your planet hiding something from me. I needn't remind you of your father's unauthorized and secretive construction of a sentient Artificial General Intelligence, or the consequences that followed... You would do well to remember who put your family in power. I can revoke that gift as quickly as it was given. So, I hope, for your sake, that you are not hiding anything from me, Zerris."

Zerris bites his top lip to prevent it from quivering in anger. His blood boils as he lets the Regent's words marinate for a moment. His father, Gannon, had made a discrete attempt at constructing AGI sentience on Deorum, but was discovered acquiring the obscure materials to complete it. The only true AGI in existence in the galaxy was under the control of the IGB. Zerris, though fuming on the inside, pushes the images of his father's corpse hanging limply off the edge of his bed from his mind, and retains his poker face. Though a relatively young politician, he is exceptionally adept at masking his emotions, as well as his intentions. Rather than react from a powerless position, he swallows his pride, believing with ferocious certainty that one day, he will be the one sitting in Wyngor's seat. He swiftly attempts to redirect. "The Aganon bloodline is forever in your debt, and I am happy to serve, your Eminence. Should there be anything I can provide…"

"Enough of the chatter. I have no time for it," interrupts the Grand Regent as he shifts in his seat and looks into the distance. "We will need our usual shipment doubled this quarter…"

The immense request baffles Zerris to the point of stuttering. "Doub-doubled? Your Eminence, I-I…"

"Yes, Zerris. I'll repeat so you can keep up. I need my raw elemental provisions doubled. And before you ask, your weapons shipment…will need to be postponed."

Zerris is bewildered by the statement. "Your Eminence, please understand that I mean no disrespect when I say this is an immense request. It will require substantial resources and manpower to fulfill so close to the carrier arrival."

"Of that, I have no doubt. I trust you will have your hands full. If I were you, I would get to work," responds the Regent coldly.

"And the weapons…? Your Eminence, we are already understocked…"

"As I mentioned, *delayed*," responds Wyngor as if annoyed by the question.

Zerris, due to the Vitalerium Accords that placed the CP in charge of the raw vitalerium trade, is forced to rely on the IGB to refine the vitalerium that Deorum mines. From there, it can be utilized for a multitude of different exports; one of which is the vitalerium weaponry that every CP Guardsman carries. Although this is inconvenient, it is not Zerris's main concern. For a few orbits now, his own small vitalerium refinement plant operated under the radar in the subterranean levels of Sanctum Tower, hidden from the prying eyes of the paranoid Grand Regent. What bothers him is the why... *Why is the Grand Regent in need of such a large quantity of raw element so urgently? For what purposes? And if he has the raw vitalerium at his disposal, why delay the weapons shipment? What is he preparing for?*

Zerris attempts to dig deeper. A move like this is likely preceding something much bigger. "But Grand Regent, what could possibly require such a drastic alteration in plans? Perhaps turmoil in the other planets? Perhaps if I had more time—" Zerris's ask for a grace period is immediately interrupted.

"Your Grand Regent has made his demand of you. I don't care how you do it. I don't care if you must force half of Deorum into *indentured servitude* to get it done! Either make it so, OR I WILL FIND SOMEONE ELSE THAT WILL COMPLY!"

Zerris remains confounded by the interaction. The Vital Cascade mining operation is ripe with vitalerium this quarter, but for a drop-shipment of this magnitude, it would require Zerris to delve into his own off-the-books vitalerium allocations. *Does he know? He couldn't possibly know...he would have to have a spy in my top ranks. There are few who even know the broad strokes of our goals, and even Dorok himself remains ignorant to the full extent of our efforts and the benefactors involved*, thinks Zerris to himself. He tries to think of a way to requisition more time, but his mind is pulled in too many directions, and he draws a blank; a rare occurrence. It doesn't help that his internal fire is fueled by every word from the Grand Regent's spewing mouth. What irks him most is his inability to respond due to position. Not a soul in the known universe could rebut the commands of the Grand Regent of the IGB, Kodo Wyngor.

"Consider it done, Grand Regent Wyngor," he finally concedes. As he finishes, the faint noise of short-circuiting electronics emanates from a distance. Zerris looks behind him to investigate the origin of the sound but sees nothing but the distant white walls of the Fabric.

"Good," replies Wyngor. His icy expression curls into a nefarious smile as he asks, "Oh, and Zerris?"

"Yes, Grand Regent?"

"If you ever try to record me again, I will have you emulsified in a vat of acid on a live emergency-broadcast feed to all IGB planets," he says with a disturbing hint of joy as he jabs the controls on his pulpit, abruptly ending the Fabric connection.

All goes black, and Zerris once again finds himself inside the dark tube of his Fabric shell. After a few moments, a hydraulic hiss gives way to the light of the room as the tube retracts back into the hovercraft's ceiling. Again, Zerris's eyes struggle to adjust to the light. This time, however, an unbearable burning stench fills his nostrils. The tube finally passes his line of sight to the room, but plumes of black smoke block his view. Zerris coughs and frantically waves away the noxious fumes to reveal a horrid scene.

Mingen, chief administrator to Zerris, sits slumped in his seat connected to the Fabric platform in a pool of congealed blood. His skin is charred beyond recognition, his jaw angled into an unnatural position. His left eye rests on his cheek below its socket, and the smell of burnt flesh permeates the vehicle cabin. Zerris coughs as he tries to process his surroundings. The leads from the platform are burnt black as they enter the contorted wrist of his former subordinate... The Grand Regent's associates had penetrated the system's firewall and somehow short-circuited his video feed, causing Mingen to receive a fatal electrical current. The only word Zerris can muster is a gravelly "Wyngor..."

Zerris looks at his former administrator discerningly, then glances up at the smoke collecting on the ceiling of his hovercraft. His jaw clenches, and he balls his right fist, stretching the scar on its dorsum. He walks briskly to the navigation dock and hits "VENT." The smoke is swiftly pulled from the cabin through metal grates on either side of the ceiling. Before settling, Zerris approaches Mingen's carcass. Moving his charred arm from the directional controls with a disgusted look, he turns the chair to face away from his own, then returns to his chair and sits upright.

Zerris massages the scar on his hand while he stares at the back of Mingen Arellot's chair. *Poor Mingen, he will be hard to replace,* he thinks to himself before directing his energy toward the more pressing issue in his mind: *What is Kodo Wyngor up to?* As Zerris contemplates his predicament, the hovercraft continues its trajectory toward the quarries, speeding by the outer walls of Kairus with his RoGuard escort in tow.

Minutes later, the convoy of royal ships lands by a small testing facility on a rocky ridge. The raised facility sits at the very edge of a cliff overlooking an enormous abandoned quarry. Zerris exits his ship after the hatch opens and steps out to a small group of RoGuard and two men wearing lab coats who await him. Zerris barks at the first guard he sees, "Take care of my problem in the cabin," then follows the scientists up the stairs into the small building.

The heavy metal door swings open to a single room outfitted as a makeshift lab with a viewing atrium. Floor-to-ceiling windows cover three of the four walls, presenting a magnificent view of the quarry below, where a large herd of Lancors graze on bales of foliage and hay placed intentionally to distract them. Men and women donning XSEC security badges all turn to greet him with their right fists over their hearts, and their left fists over their navels as he enters. Only one man does not give the salute: Dorok Ferrous Benson XIII. He busies himself with his commscreen while he sits facing the quarry in his general's armor. He only budges when Zerris steps to his side to enjoy the view.

"Overseer! Good to see you, brother!" shouts Dorok as he gives Zerris a quick salute, then a hard pat on the back.

"Likewise, Dorok," replies Zerris unenthusiastically.

"Looks like these science drones finally finished a new toy for us!" replies Dorok with the excitement of a child. He looks around the room as if searching for someone, then asks, "Hey, where's Mingen? I owe that little wimp a good dead-arm."

"Unfortunately, indisposed," says Zerris without looking away from the windows.

"Huh… I didn't take Four Eyes for a big drinker…"

Annoyed, Zerris sighs and responds, "Indisposed as in dead, Dorok."

"Whoa… HA! The little twerp finally pushed you to your limits, huh? What'd he do to get you so murderously pissed off?"

"Unfortunately, it was not of my own volition this time. Can we proceed with the testing, then?" Zerris is clearly done discussing the topic.

"Hey, you're the boss…" replies Dorok before turning to the diligently working scientists and yelling, "HEY! BRING YOUR OVERSEER THE CONTROL PANEL, STAT!"

A young woman approaches Zerris with haste and presents a metallic chrome piece of hardware with a brilliant blue screen. He takes it and inspects, admiring the beautiful sheen and contours of the device as the scientist looks on with anxious excitement.

"Alright then? How about an explanation there, Brina!?" barks Dorok at the nervous woman.

She visibly jumps at his remarks before quickly segueing into a description of the weapon. "So sorry, General Dorok! Uh… Ok! So, we call the system the Vitalerium Orbital Ion Cannon, or the VOIC for short," she says, pronouncing the acronym like the word "voice" with excitement. "The device you hold contains a perfect topographical map of planet Deorum. With this you can select any location on the planet, and one of our uh…hehe, I mean *your* Ion Cannon-mounted satellites will fire a continuous beam of vitalerium energy at your target's location," she says as she focuses the blue screen near their location. "It can also target objects in proximity to Deorum space."

"...and?" replies Zerris, seemingly unimpressed.

"...and eliminate them, my Overseer," the woman responds.

"*And*... What if my target is right in front of me?" Zerris probes, still unmoved by her presentation. Dorok stares at the scientist as if she were a T-bone steak.

"GREAT question! So, it does have the ability to strike locations relatively close to your own. And there's a built-in safety measure that ensures you can't target anything within one hundred meters from where this device is, i.e., where you are! Would hate to have you caught up in the crossfire! To use this feature, you access the menu here and press this..." she says as she taps the screen in his hands. The screen now depicts the view from its camera, which displays Zerris's feet below him. "Then, you point it up at your target..." she lifts Zerris's arms up to face the quarry and taps the screen on the Lancors. A red triangle appears over one of the large animals toward the center of the group. "The camera triangulates the position of the target based on your position and where the satellite is. Then, when you're ready, you just flip the safety switch and hit this button here! Now, just let me clear the field and we can..."

"Interesting. Well, let's see what your efforts have achieved..." says Zerris as he flips the switch and presses the red button labeled "Engage" on the screen.

"WAIT ZERRI...uh, OVERSEER! THERE ARE STILL TWO MEN OUT THERE WITH THE HERD!" she screams in fear. But her warning comes too late. Red lights flash throughout the facility in a circular pattern, and a siren blares a final warning to anyone in the path of the orbital cannon. Zerris and Dorok look around in confusion.

"Well then cease it!" responds Zerris bluntly.

"We can't!" yells another scientist scrambling in front of a control panel.

The siren's cry echoes throughout the quarry, prompting

two men to emerge from a pillbox at the center of the Lancor herd and begin rushing toward the facility. Moving as fast as they can, they barrel through the herd at their own peril.

Brina presses her hands and face against the glass as she watches in horror. "OH, PRIMES! THEY'RE NOT GOING TO MAKE IT!"

Most of the beasts do not notice as the two men run unprotected through the herd. The gall of such a move is almost too much for the hulking four-legged animals to process. However, one large Lancor closer to the middle of the pack does take notice. It lets out a bellowing groan before charging the men head-on. Its yellow-brown, sinewy flesh ripples with musculature as it picks up speed. The first man rolls to his left, just barely dodging its advance. However, the second man is unable to redirect his momentum. His eyes bulge as the Lancor gores him through the stomach with one of its massive horns and flings him into the air like a rag doll. His legs shatter like glass upon impact with the ground. Immediately the aggravated Lancor begins to pummel him into the dirt under the weight of his massive feet. Others begin to join in. The second man continues to sprint like the wind, knowing there is nothing he can do to save his colleague. He has merely a few more rows of Lancor to run through before he makes it to safety...

A continuous, iridescent blue beam of pure vitalerium energy bolts out of the sky quicker than the eye can follow with the circumference of a large hovercraft. It lands just feet away from the man with unrivaled force, instantly incinerating him and continuing on as it disintegrates the herd of Lancor, which groan in fear as they try to escape. But they don't stand a chance. Hundreds of animals are turned to dust as the beam makes its way through them.

"NOOO!" screams Brina as she collapses into a ball on the floor. The rest of the scientists look on in horror at the blackened floor of the quarry. Small fires break out on whatever material is left to burn, and thick, dark smoke rises from the path of the laser. Only twenty seconds later, its circumference begins to thin until it slowly dissipates.

"Whoa-HO! Holy shit, did you see that, Zerris? This thing is a fucking GAME CHANGER! I can't wait to have this active in our arsenal." Dorok practically jumps up and down as he watches the carnage. He glances over at the whimpering Brina on the floor and reels himself in. "Oh...sorry about your, uh... friends."

Zerris motions for the RoGuard to remove her from the room. She does not move from her spot on the floor as they approach. She simply stares out the window at the destruction with her mouth agape. They lift her gently and walk her to the back room. Zerris turns to the rest of the scientists, who stare at him in disbelief. "I suggest you follow them... now," he says coldly. The scientists scurry to the back room with their colleague and shut the door behind them.

Only Zerris and Dorok remain in the viewing atrium. Zerris stares blankly out the window before him. He remains completely silent. Dorok decides to break the silence after a few seconds.

"Hey... You ok? Overseer?"

"I'm fine, Dorok," says Zerris without breaking his gaze on the quarry and seemingly aloof to the situation.

"Yea, I mean...it's not like you meant to kill them, so don't stress yourself. Honestly, it's kind of their fault. They should have cleared the testing site before handing you the damn controller. All the book smarts in the world and no damn sense..."

Zerris thinks for a moment, then looks over to Dorok and asks, "Have I ever told you how I received this scar?" Zerris lifts his right hand, showing Dorok the large, raised scar on its backside.

"Actually no. I've always wondered, but you never brought it up," responds Dorok.

He pauses before responding to his general, "Hm, the wind and the leaves..." Zerris mutters as he looks off into the distance, then begins pacing the room.

"Wind and...? I don't understand... There's no way some leaves did that to you?" replies Dorok.

"No, Dorok." Zerris's expression remains stern as he explains. "When I was a child of only eleven orbits, my father started taking me into the city with him on his Initiative Campaigns. I was fascinated with the position of Overseer even at a young age, and loved to listen to the way he framed his speeches. He had a way with words, my father..." He stops his pacing and looks down at the floor, massaging the scar on his hand. Dorok says nothing, only listens.

"On one particular tour, we were visiting the edge of the Outer Sphere. At the time there were some relatively serious anti-CP sentiments brewing in the eastern region. My father was intent on realigning them with the cause of the party non-violently... He wanted to make them understand the goals he had for Deorum, and the greater good that could be achieved with unwavering support of his initiatives. Really, the goal was to prevent any further descent into dissidence. He always had an affinity for *diplomacy first*. But, during this speech, there was an attempt made on his life. A man stepped through the crowd and fired a vitalerium pistol at the podium. Thankfully, one of the Guardsmen in the crowd grabbed his arm as he went to fire, and his shot missed my father. Instead, the charge was redirected toward me and grazed my hand as I ducked for cover. I still remember, even to this day, the feeling of gut-wrenching pain...and my inability to react to it. I simply stared at the exposed bones of my hand as the RoGuard charged the man and subdued him."

"Whoa, I remember hearing about this, but I never knew you got hit in the exchange," comments Dorok, surprised.

"It was never reported. I was brought back to the Sanctum Tower infirmary immediately, and the man was arrested. I spent all day in that ward, silent. The pain of my injury and even the subsequent treatment was not enough to get a peep out of me. The physicians said I was in shock. I had never experienced fear like that before." Zerris goes quiet for a moment as he recaps the memory.

"We ought to get you a Blue Drop for that one!" Dorok chimes in, referring to the badge awarded to CP Guardsmen for injuries sustained in combat. Zerris simply shrugs off the comment.

"After being informed of my state, my father visited me later that night in the infirmary. He checked me out of my room, still bandaged, and took me to the sublayers of Sanctum Tower. We stepped out of the elevator on level S100...the Cube. He walked me to a holding room where five RoGuards watched over my assailant, who was restrained to a chair. He was badly beaten...weak, yet the sheer force of his disdain for the party prevailed...yelling obscenities towards the Guardsmen and my father. That is until he saw me. Then he went quiet."

Zerris sits down and finally looks Dorok in the eye. "Do you know what my father said to me that night?" he asks rhetorically. Dorok simply shrugs his shoulders.

"He said: 'Zerris, I want you to know that despite what happens here tonight, I am not angry with this man. Nor should you be angry. He is simply doing what is in his nature. In this world there are different types of people. Most of them, this man included, are like the leaves on the tree. As in life, there are many trees, each with hundreds if not thousands of leaves. Thus, people like him, whether guilty or innocent, productive or not, are plentiful. The next type are individuals who are like the great trunks of the tree. The strength of their roots and their far-reaching branches hold the leaves together; organized and content. These types are fewer in number and are extremely useful, but not uncommon. Finally, there are the few; those who strive to accomplish more for this world, and push the boundaries of what is possible for humanity. They are like the wind, which blows the trees with their leaves in the direction that it wills. All leaves are destined to eventually wither and die with the seasons. Yet, some cling to the tree for dear life; fighting the wind and yearning for the time they were once vibrant. Try as they may, and valiant as their attempts may be, they always succumb to the forces of nature. Remember this: the wind cares not for the leaf that it blows into the stream, or for the brush fire its gusts feed, turning the tree to ember and ash. Its destination...its purpose is of greater importance to the world than the debris caught in its current. The wind must blow without fear so it may alter the course of life...' I remember every word as if it happened yesterday."

"So...? What happened then?" Dorok pries.

"After that, he walked me over to the restrained man and handed me a dagger. My father, Gannon, instructed that I must erase my fear and regain the strength of my wind..." Zerris pauses for a moment to reminisce as Dorok waits with bated breath for the story's conclusion. "With his guiding hand, I drove that blade through the man's chest and watched him choke until his last breath... My hands trembled with terror at first, but eventually the quivering stopped. Once he expired, I turned to my father and spoke for the first time since the incident."

Even the battle-hardened General Benson looks impressed. "Whoa. That's young for your first confirmed kill. What did you say to him?"

"My response was simple. I looked my father in the eye and said: 'I understand now.' The fear I felt seemed to evaporate, and I left that room changed. My point is, Dorok, our benefactors have charged us with something far more important than the mere protection of individual people. With my plan in place and with my newest project almost complete, we will be the winds that guide not just our planet but the entire human race into a new era... One where loyalty will be the most sacred of virtues."

Dorok stands up straight with his feet together, facing Zerris, and slams his chest and his navel with a quick, devoted salute. "I'm proud to be part of the movement with you, Overseer Aganon. Should anything or anyone try to block you, you can count on my wind to be the one that knocks them off a fuckin' cliff!"

With a smile of satisfaction, Zerris approaches General Benson and lays his hands on Dorok's shoulders. "Your loyalty will pay dividends in our new world, Dorok. And it shall not be forgotten," he says encouragingly. Dorok gives a stern nod in response.

"By the way, how are we coming along with vitalerium allocation for this quarter's shipment?"

"We should be right on target by the time the fleet shows up. Why?"

"I just spent some lovely bonding time with our Grand Regent in the Fabric before arriving here today. He has informed me that he is expecting his drop shipment to be...doubled."

"DOUBLED!? Do you think he is on to you?" asks Dorok, concerned.

"I can't be certain. It does fall strangely in line with the passing of Initiative 919...either that or the brute is planning something substantial in the near future. Perhaps both... Whatever the case, I want us to be prepared."

Dorok thinks for a moment, then responds, "I don't know if we can double his batch without digging into the stockpiles... I can put some pressure on the Vital Fracture Mining teams to increase output, maybe push for the VRTs to pick up the slack on any planetary findings. But the VFM can only fill so much of that void. I still think we're going to have to supplement with our own."

"Just ramp up your efforts and I'll tend to how we ultimately divvy up our supply. Get it done, and hopefully by the fleet's arrival, I'll have another card in the deck." Zerris begins walking toward the door as he finishes. "We may have to get the ball rolling earlier than expected..."

"Understood, Overseer."

The doors open to the testing facility and Zerris descends the ramp toward his hovercraft. A few of the RoGuards carry the rigid body of Mingen away from the vehicle as he steps on board. The hatch closes, and the royal hovercraft lifts off and angles toward Kairus. As it elevates, Zerris looks out the window as the RoGuard drop Mingen's corpse off the cliff into the quarry.

"Another leaf blown from the tree..." mutters Zerris to himself. "Worry not, Mingen, your death will not be in vain. Soon, I'll answer to no one."

CHAPTER 14:

Green and Gold

The silence of the early morning is cut like a knife by the delicate chimes of an alarm clock resonating throughout a large room. A small hologram of a beautiful tree with falling leaves shines brightly above the alarm, illuminating the dark room with vibrant color. Its electronic tune bounces off the white and gray marble of the walls and floors, brought finally to an end by a hand that reaches out from beneath the covers of the bed at the room's center. A middle-aged woman emerges slowly from beneath the sheets and reties her silk nightgown at the waist. Wiping the sleep away from her eyes, she looks across the room at a man who sits at an elegant dock by a large, floor-to-ceiling window. He works diligently, squinting through his glasses to try and decipher the screen on its lowest brightness. His appearance is disheveled and tired. He scratches his trimmed gray beard while switching between reading and typing.

The woman approaches him slowly with her arms folded. "Up before your alarm again?" she asks before yawning.

Without taking his eyes from his work, the man replies, "Yes dear...for quite some time now..." His distracted state is immediately clear.

"Arpen, you need sleep. You're not a young man anymore, your heart is going to explode in your chest. Widowhood doesn't suit me," she responds. Her tone is concerned, though she coats it with sarcasm. She sits at the edge of Arpen Delgato's dock and stares at him patiently with arms folded.

"No rest for the weary, my dear...and times like these require those with influence..." he pauses to squint again at the screen, "...to be vigilant."

The woman unfolds her arms and reaches across his workspace, turning up the brightness on his dock. The holographic screen before him blazes with electric light, causing them both to squint. The woman then declares, "Home, illuminate!" into the open room. The room steadily glows to life, revealing an elegant room decorated with marvelous attention to detail. Hints of gold and black accent the mostly white décor. An array of items is displayed in corners and sporadic places around the room. An old, engraved violin from Earth, a crystal sculpture from Portia Quixote in the shape of one of their many oceanic creatures, a cyriax crystal partially encased in rock from Sigmi's moon, and many other treasures; totems to their galactic adventures and well-traveled past.

"Times like these require a man with a beating heart. You need to take care of yourself."

Arpen breaks from work and swivels his chair toward his wife. "Well, I would. But honestly, I think you're better at it." He smirks as they make eye contact.

"Truer words have never been spoken, husband. Except, I have my own agenda to worry about. I address the town hall this afternoon regarding the changes our *lovely* Overseer has forced through, which should prove to be a less than enjoyable experience, and I must greet delegate Charsi on his arrival from Ventura before that. So, if you don't mind, I'll be passing those self-care duties on to you today." She stands up from the dock, steps toward Arpen, and rests her hand lovingly on his shoulder.

"Wow, leaving me home alone. That's a bold move. Maybe I'll have ice cream for breakfast when the boss is gone," replies Delgato with a wide grin.

She removes her hand from his shoulder and lands a playful slap on his chest. She leans down toward Arpen so her face is merely inches away from his. "That's inadvisable, Governor," she says, before giving him a peck on the cheek. As she walks toward her wardrobe, she calls back to Arpen, whose attention has returned to the holographic windows above his dock. "Do you have your meeting with Yoon and Tomlin today?"

"Hm... I do, in fact. Any words of wisdom for me, Leyona?"

"Knowing your propensity for gabbing, I'd say listen first and then speak. Reel them in with the highlights, and then hear them out before elaborating. Let them guide you to what they need to hear."

"Good advice, my wife. I knew I chose well," he replies, referring to her.

Leyona Delgato smiles, then returns with, "Yes, yes, you're a lucky man. Oh...and Arpen?"

"Hmph?" he grunts in response.

"Turn your alarm off if you're not going to use it, please? Mine wasn't set to go off for another fifteen minutes." Silence follows from the governor. She calls out again, "Arpen?"

"Hm? Oh...yes. Apologies, dear," he says, clearly distracted yet again.

Leyona sighs and shakes her head, knowing it would more than likely happen again. As she turns to enter her wardrobe, an ethereal-sounding doorbell interrupts her task. She pivots, walks to the door of their room, and unlocks it using the control panel at its side. The frosted glass double doors slide open, revealing their visitor, Ram Sandiam. He is well dressed and, per usual, holds his oversized holoscreen in hand.

"Good morning, Mrs. Delgato. Do you always look so lovely this early?" Ram says with a smile.

"A bit early for flattery, Ram, but thank you. Has that

charming girl made an honest man of you yet?"

Ram blushes. "From the moment I met her, Your Grace. Although, we are yet to be wed. I assure you that you will be the first to hear about it, and you both will be the guests of honor at our wedding. On a more work-related note, is this a good time?" he asks politely.

"Of course, Ram, come in, dear. And what a surprise, he's already knee-deep in it at his dock..."

Ram acknowledges with a nod and enters. Not being one to waste time, he walks quickly across the room to Arpen and sits in a second chair near the dock. "Good morning, Governor Delgato. Did you sleep well?"

"Not at all, Ram, and for the last time, we're not in court. Call me Arpen. It's too early for titles and lancor-shit. We've known each other too long."

"Apologies, old habits die hard, sir," replies Ram. "I have the images you requested from our satellites, and the data associated..." he says before placing his holoscreen on the dock beside Arpen. The governor takes them and inspects the images provided, swiping through the dated photographs.

"Hm... What am I looking at exactly? Is it as we expected?" Delgato asks.

"Actually, it's more. Significantly more. I've documented the number of vitalerium mining convoys entering Sanctum Tower for the past few weeks, compared it with prior quarters, and cross-referenced that with the reported numbers from both the IGB's dropship demands and Kairus's reported utilization. The discrepancies are...glaring, to say the least."

"So, he is stockpiling vitalerium! I knew our *benevolent* Overseer was up to something... How glaring are we talking?" Arpen is clearly exhausted. His skin shines in the overhead lights, coated in oil from working through the early morning. His white hair protrudes in all directions, styled by his pillow. The bags under his eyes are heavier than usual.

Noticing this, Ram tries to be as direct as possible. "About triple the expected haul."

"Wow, wow, wow... Now that's quite a bit of blue rock, Ram. Although I have heard rumblings that the IGB is demanding significantly more raw element this quarter..."

Ram taps his holoscreen to bring up another chart. "That's not all, sir. When I was comparing historically, I noticed something else. These anomalies date back much further than the passing of Initiative 919. It was easy to spot the recent ones because I could simply count the convoys from our satellite imagery and compare. But after digging into the convoy traffic from the past orbit, I unearthed similar discrepancies. There are instances of 'double-weigh-ins' that were initially deleted from the weigh station records, but the deleted weights don't match. I have a feeling these weren't duplicates at all, but extra barges in the convoy that were erased from the record. These discrepancies aren't as drastic as recent ones, but they go back much farther."

Arpen is intrigued. The new information pumps life into the old man. "So, you're saying...?"

"I'm saying that there are two sets of books that don't match. Kairus Prime has been stockpiling its own off-the-books vitalerium for more than a full orbit...at least. And that's only as far as I've investigated."

"Great work, Ram. I think it's about time we brought some of our skeptical friends into the fold, don't you? Let's get the Fabric up and running!"

"Uh, sir, it's nearly an hour early for your meeting with Yoon and Cornathus," responds Ram.

"Oh..." says Arpen, looking down at his TAB, then into the mirror on his left. "Well, probably for the best. I look like hell. Let me sort this and we'll continue... Oh, and Ram?"

"Sir?"

"Better run our meeting on the Fray. We ought to keep this one off the books. Ping the others and tell them the same," replies the ever-wary Arpen.

"As you wish, Gov...er...Arpen."

With that, a tired Arpen stumbles from his dock and disappears into the bathroom to prepare for his meeting. Ram busies himself by setting up the Fray for Arpen's meeting, transferring the images and figures on Zerris's activity to Arpen's dock.

The Fabric is the quantum communication network that ultimately replaced the internet and cellular frequencies after the onset of space exploration. It utilizes quantum entanglement of photons to allow for instant communication across vast distances, including communication between planets. Particles accessed by these devices are forced into a state of quantum entanglement, which makes them act dependently of one another no matter the distance between them. For instance, let us say that a mother on Sigmi wishes to speak with her daughter on Mars. When the particles within her Fabric device are shifted on Sigmi, their quantum-entangled sister particles also shift on Mars in her daughter's device, resulting in familiar images and sounds.

Though the Fabric connects the galaxy virtually, the Fray is the underlying mass of dark sub-connections that operate off the map of the majority of Fabric interactions: a way to escape the prying eyes of those watching. Once the connection is secured, Ram messages the chief correspondents of the other governors about the change of plan.

Next, he lays out a few choice outfits for the governor and waits patiently for Arpen. A mere twenty minutes later, a door opens at the opposite end of the room. Steam pours from the threshold as Arpen emerges draped in a white bathrobe and looking like a new man.

"Now, isn't that better...oh. What do you have for me here?" he asks Ram as he gazes upon three outfits splayed out on the bed: a gray tunic, a red and black set of robes, and a green and gold outfit.

Ram explains his rationale behind the outfits. "Just a few

options for your meeting attire depending upon what sentiment you'd like to relay. The gray is unassuming and elegant, yet simple. The red and black is a bit more of an aggressive statement to the business at hand. Might be useful if you're looking to take a strong stance. And the green and gold tunic for the colors of Argos."

"Hm..." Arpen thinks for a moment, then replies, "Let's go with gray—I like unassuming. I feel like making a bold statement before I have all the answers would prove unwise." As he goes to grab the gray tunic, Leyona emerges from the far side of the room, dressed and ready for her day. Noticing the two deciding on outfits, she offers her perspective.

"You're going with the gray, I see...understated," she intervenes with a delicate hint of judgment.

"I suppose you have your own opinions on the matter?" Arpen listens with his arms folded.

Leyona's response is matter-of-fact. "The gray is boring, and black and red is certainly out...you're not giving a war address. I would choose the green and gold."

"Hmph. And your reasoning?" asks Arpen.

"Besides the fact that the other choices are in poor taste, green and gold are your colors, dear. You wear them well." With that, she gives him another kiss on the cheek before gathering her things.

Arpen looks back at the wardrobe choices on his bed and, with a smile, says, "You always do know how to sway me."

"That's why I won you," she responds with a sly grin.

"Hehe...oh, by the way, we were right about Zerris and the convoys," says Arpen, changing the subject as time grows scarce.

"That's unsurprising..." responds Leyona warily. "The you-being-right-part, that is. I am a bit surprised that our young Overseer has the guts to pull a move like that. Perhaps he truly is his father's son..."

"I fear he's worse than that, Leyona. You've not seen him

in some time. The young are always more drastic, less tactful... more rushed with their ambitions."

"Agreed...but for now I must go. We can discuss more later." As she turns to exit, she gives a wave to Ram and her husband without looking back. The frosted glass doors of their quarters slide open automatically as she approaches them. "Good luck with the city-states, boys..."

"Same to you. And tell delegate Charsi he still owes me a thousand universal credits from last month's Guaniton bet," shouts Arpen across the room.

Leyona's words just slip through the crack of the doors as they close behind her. "I'll do no such thing, Arpen!"

Delgato dresses himself in the green and gold tunics quickly, then exits his quarters. Descending the spiral staircase to the first floor of his home, he enters his office, where Ram sits at a second dock, unlocking the Fabric chamber housed within the room. A giant sphere of white and gray metal panels, the chamber hums and hisses as it boots up. Ram enters a command into Arpen's dock, causing it to roar to life.

Its spherical edifice rotates quickly, revealing an arched doorway. A brilliant white light fills the office from the chamber's opening, overpowering even the light from Bios that begins to peek over the horizon and fill the office through its large windows. As Arpen approaches, Ram gives him the signal that everything is set up for their meeting. The governor enters the rig and stands on the meshed platform at its center. Upon receiving his weight, the platform begins to glow, and the edifice spins in the opposite direction to seal him inside.

The blinding white light that beckoned Arpen inside goes black in an instant. The machine's humming grows steadily as the machine renders his meeting with the governors. He closes his eyes as the noise grows louder. A thin, blue light fans past his eyelids slowly at first, then increases in speed until the blue practically stains the backs of his retinas. Then, suddenly, a burst of white light erupts before him.

Arpen opens his eyes to a beautiful setting of lush greenery in a forest clearing. A rendering of Bios's light peeks through the tree cover, illuminating the meeting space. A large round table sits at the center of the clearing with three chairs. Their pure white metal creates an interesting juxtaposition to his surroundings. Avian creatures chirp lightly in the background. The sound of a light breeze through the forest leaves provides a calming ambiance. Dirt, leaves, and twigs crunch under Arpen's feet as he walks toward the center of the clearing. Only one sits at the table, Tomlin Cornathus, early as usual. His military-like promptness has been practically engrained in the fiber of his very being.

"Good morning, Tomlin. Enjoying the sights?"

"I find the forest soothing. It's much more pleasing than the moon setting you chose last time. Brings back too many memories of conflict from my time in the Guard..." Cornathus's response is monotone, emotionless.

"I'm glad it's to your liking. Thank you for joining me." Arpen takes his seat at the second white chair. "When are we expecting Nataliya? Did she reach out—"

Arpen's sentence is cut off when the image of Nataliya Yoon bursts into view, already walking toward the table before her digital rendering has finished. An electric aura surrounds her even as she sits down with the two men. "Good morning, gents. Forgive me if I seem rushed, but I have a full day, so let's make this brief. Although, I have to say I am very interested to see what you've uncovered, Arpen."

Even Tomlin cracks a smirk, responding, "Yoon hasn't had a free day since she was birthed."

"A pleasure as always, Cornathus," responds Nataliya with a feigned smile. "What do you have for us, Arpen?"

"Unfortunate news, I'm afraid; news of actions by our Overseer that could potentially put our planet at odds with the IGB. I don't need to tell you how precarious of a situation that places us in as top-ranking CP officials, or what it could mean for the stability of Kairus. Given the severity of the potential sanctions, I believe it merits our utmost attention and concern."

Tomlin Cornathus leans back in his seat and purses his lips. "Out with it, Arpen. I may not be as busy as Yoon pretends to be, but that doesn't mean I want to hear you postulate all morning." Nataliya rolls her eyes in response to Tomlin's brash remarks.

"It would seem that I was correct in my assumption regarding uncharacteristic VFM convoy activity. As you can see here..." Arpen looks behind him and raises a hand to display multiple satellite images, charts, and graphs. Their holograms float gently in the forest air. "...the discrepancies are significant. For more than a full orbit now, the number of convoys severely outnumbers the amount needed to fulfill our trade with the IGB. Recently, the discrepancy rate has nearly tripled since the passing of Initiative 919. Zerris is and has been stockpiling vitalerium for some time, that we know for sure. For what reason...well, that will require more significant digging."

"How do we know they aren't just half-full shipments?" responds Cornathus.

"Thank you, Tomlin, something I was definitely skeptical of initially. However, that would go directly against the data we have pulled from the weigh stations in line with shipment timing. All convoys were either at capacity, or over capacity. In this case, the devil is in the details: specifically, the deletion of 'duplicate' weigh-ins. However, the duplicate weights don't match the barges they were supposedly copies of, and the time stamps of deleted duplicates don't match either. This only confirms the merit of our findings. The fact is: Zerris has been misreporting to the IGB. It also means there is likely someone at the weigh station who is involved in his plot. Discovering who will be the next step in our investigation. All of this leads me to believe that Zerris is planning something big."

Tomlin furrows his brow and grunts. He crosses his arms as he contemplates the information before him. "How do we know it's Zerris and not just some bad actors? It wouldn't be the first time someone was caught skimming off the top of the VFM convoys…"

"Another possibility I considered, until I calculated the amount of missing vitalerium. The sheer quantity of vitalerium that would account for these discrepancies would require an unprecedented level of logistics. We're talking warehouses for storage, barges and spacefaring vessels for transport, industrial-level jamming of state V-sense signal tracking, and black-market buyers on a planetary scale. This is no small skimming operation, Tomlin. Let us not forget, raw vitalerium is the most regulated element in the known universe, and an operation this large would not go unnoticed."

Arpen can see the gears begin to turn in Tomlin's head. "But someone with direct oversight of the VFM *could* make it go unnoticed if they needed to…"

"Based on your findings, Arpen, exactly how much raw element are you suggesting is unaccounted for?"

Arpen takes a deep breath and responds, "Over the past orbit, somewhere in the neighborhood of three thousand five hundred tons."

The meeting space becomes silent in response to Arpen's revelation. Only the chirps of rendered birds and the light whoosh of a manufactured breeze can be heard in the background. Nataliya Yoon, Governor of Luxenia, sits in awe with her jaw dropped. Even the stone-faced Governor of Talos, Tomlin Cornathus, leans forward in his seat. The veins in his temples visibly bulge from his skull.

After giving them time to absorb the startling information, Arpen Delgato breaks the silence. "I know this is a lot to take in, but this is the reason I asked that we meet in the Fray. This is a deadly serious issue."

"Wait, wait... What about the possibility of the IGB requisitioning a higher quarterly order? I've heard from multiple contacts in Kairus Prime that an elevated quota has been placed on the CP. The IGB can and will do as they please. How do we know this isn't just evidence of the Grand Regent's increased demand? I don't think any of us need proof of Wyngor's insatiable power-lust...or his violent proclivities."

"I had thought of that also, Nataliya. I, too, have heard rumblings of a higher requisition order this fiscal quarter. But as you alluded to, the lips of Kairus representatives are not sealed all too tightly, and this quarter is the first I'm hearing of a higher requisition order. The occurrence of such discrepancies goes back much further. It doesn't give us answers to the history of these coincidences..."

"I'll give you that, but what if your focus is wrong? What if it's the IGB that is planning something big, and Zerris is just their instrument?" Yoon interrogates.

"I'll admit the potential is there, and we should all keep our ear to the ground for anything in line with that narrative. But let us not forget that Zerris, although limited by even his position, is no fool. And after his display at the court ruling, I believe we can all agree he is an authority with an authority problem..." Arpen waves away the images above him and looks down at the ground as he ponders. "I called this meeting in response to Initiative 919 being rushed into effect; an initiative all of us were opposed to. After reviewing these findings from my surveillance, I'm more convinced than ever that we need to be ahead of the curve. Something doesn't add up, I don't think that can be discounted anymore. There is something larger at play. I just don't have a full view of the chess board yet..."

"I agree, Arpen, but correlation is not causation. The accuracy of our moves is determined by the information we get. And if that information is not precise, we put ourselves in danger. I need more if I am to act on what we discuss," retorts Nataliya.

"Speaking of 919, I can't tell you how many constituents are up my ASS about what is to come with these ridiculous transition timelines. How the hell are we supposed to convince people that this is in their best interest? I certainly don't believe it myself. Why should they?" interrupts Tomlin. Nataliya's sigh follows as evidence of similar pushback from her city-state.

Delgato takes a deep breath, then adds, "I agree, Governor. We are having our own issues with that in Argos, and I'm sure the situation is no different in Luxenia. But we need to focus on getting in front of this right now. If we can get a vote of non-confidence in Overseer Aganon, we can wipe this thing out before it starts..."

"A vote of non-confidence!? That would require an overwhelming majority in the court! We would need a majority from both Leebrus and Ytonia to be able to push that through! It's never even happened before in Deorum history!" Nataliya practically shouts at the suggestion.

With reservation, Arpen responds, "You are correct, it would be a historical level of cooperation. However, we cannot forget that our planet is a young one, Nataliya. And there is a first time for everything. That is why we need more solid, incriminating evidence before we bring them into the loop. I assure you both, I am working on it."

"Now this is starting to get interesting..." responds Cornathus with a chuckle as he sits back in his chair.

Nataliya leans forward onto the table, taking a more aggressive stance as she retorts, "You better have *rock-solid* evidence before we go that route. I am not staking my career and potentially my LIFE on a hunch, Arpen."

"Nor would I expect you to, my dear. But I will need your connections to Trike Gunderson, and Tye Brenzen when that time does come. And Tomlin, I'll need something different from you..."

"Speak it," Cornathus says bluntly.

"I assume a man with your background in special forces has informants in Sanctum Tower?"

"Interesting assumption..." Tomlin Cornathus leans forward, placing his elbows on the table. He folds his right fist into his left palm and smiles. "Let's suppose that, hypothetically, that was the case. What would you want with that?"

"I need more than a bird's-eye view into Sanctum Tower to find out what's really going on there." Arpen turns back to Nataliya Yoon, who sits stoically in her seat. "Our fellow governor says she needs some hard evidence. Let's get her some."

The machinery of the Fabric whirs as the lights go dark in front of Arpen's eyes. The arched doorway of the machine appears once more as the spherical chamber rotates. Arpen blinks a few times before stepping back into the reality of his office. The beautiful scene of Bios rising illuminates the room.

"How did it go, Arpen?" asks Ram Sandiam, who greets Arpen with bated breath.

"Oh, good. You remembered," responds Delgato.

"Remembered what, sir?"

"To call me Arpen," replies Delgato with a smirk. "And as far as the meeting, it was certainly a start. But we have much work to do, Ram. I have a list of items I'd like for you to get started on. But before you do, go on and review the Fabric meeting. See what little bits of wisdom you can pull from the interactions. It will be good for your development."

Excited by the opportunity, Ram gleefully answers, "Of course, sir! Happy for any chance to gain new knowledge and insight!"

Arpen interrupts his glee. "No, Ram, I said wisdom. Knowledge is to know that a tomato is a fruit. Wisdom is knowing not to put it in a fruit salad." Ram raises an eyebrow, chuckles at

Arpen's response, then listens as he continues. "It is knowledge practically applied. That is how you make something of yourself in the world of politics, my friend."

Ram nods before responding, "Thank you, Arpen."

"Don't thank me yet. After you're done in there, you're not going to be happy with the size of this to-do list..."

CHAPTER 15:

Saving Grace

Roman's heart races like a sprinter as he splashes water on his face. He knows his task, but how he will accomplish it, he hasn't a clue. His reflection in the pond stares back at him dauntingly as he begins pacing the water bank. The smooth vitalerium shard in his cheek beneath his left eye gives off an undeniable sheen. The blue splatter in his reflection mocks him in the rippling water. Roman hastily looks for a solution at the edge of the forest line. Barely visible through the trees, the city of Kairus takes shape on the horizon, filling his chest with anxious energy.

His tired brain jumbles his thoughts, and hopelessness radiates through him like a fever. After a few moments of frantic pacing, his eyes fall back on the front of Rooster with its rusted Lancer emblem. Like a ton of bricks, the eureka moment hits him, and Roman rushes to remove a panel from the side of its hull. After fumbling through the wiring inside to reach the mechanics, he scoops some of the black lubricating grease from its internal workings and smears it over his face. The smell is putrid, and it certainly does not provide perfect coverage, but it does make the deformity less obvious. *It will have to do.* He slaps the left shoulder of his armor to engage his helmet and mounts his hoverbike, preparing to ride back into the lion's den. The compartment inside his bike would hide the raw vitalerium signature. But the shards of element lodged in his body are a different story; one Roman does not know the ending to.

A few short hours later, Rooster's purple gleam approaches the hydraulic door to the Grind. A number of rough-and-tumble individuals returning from their own adventures sit on their vehicles waiting to be scanned. The cracked concrete landing glows multiple shades of blue, green, and red from their respective rides. Roman keeps his distance from the person next in line for fear that the vitalerium in his body might harm them. Sweat begins to drip down Roman's forehead behind his visor, prompting him to tilt his head to his right to avoid moisture making the grease run.

The line shortens as two men in a dual-passenger hovering buggy are allowed to enter. Its delicately balanced frame hovers gracefully along the road up ahead. Another man in a small, orb-like vehicle is let inside and disappears into the streets of the Grind. Only one woman remains in front of Roman now. The rhythmic pounding of his heart becomes more erratic as he edges closer, eyeing the large Concussion Turrets pointed in his general direction. If caught, he knows that the cost of raw vitalerium smuggling could be his life; and a trial would be unlikely.

"Remove your helmet, citizen!" barks the first Guardsman to the woman perched tensely on her hoverbike. She wears a skin-tight riding suit made from Lancor leather in lieu of armor. Roman watches carefully, evaluating their level of scrutiny. In doing so, he notices that the woman's hoverbike is much newer than his own and fiercely modified. Illuminated wires, tubes, and valves all protrude from its rear-situated gravity resonator, and red and white stripes streak across the sides of its jet-black hull; the colors of the Wibetani Militia.

"Oh, yea...of course, officers," she replies flirtatiously. The woman is slow to react but complies with the officer's request, removing her red and black helmet. Dyed crimson red, her short hair unfurls from beneath its covering, resting at her jawline to one side; the other side shaved to her temple. The Guardsman steps closer and lifts his handheld scanner to her face. A wave of green light flashes across her face followed by an off-tone chime. The Guardsman checks the device, puzzled by its response.

"What's wrong?" calls a second Guardsman as he slumps lazily out the threshold of his guard post's open window.

"It didn't fully register," returns the Guardsman who stands beside her. Turning back to her, he orders, "Stop blinking your right eye. Both eyes must be scanned for a positive ID."

"Sorry, got a little sand in my eye. Or maybe I just wanted to wink at you..." she responds coyly again. Her flirting is forced; pressured. Roman's ears perk up. *Is she using profile veils?* he thinks to himself. He watches intently, sliding his right hand discreetly to his belt line near his gun, just in case. The Guardsman once more lifts the scanner to her face and activates the device.

An intermittent alarm sounds from the scanner. The officer reads the screen and shouts frantically to the other, "WE GOT A DOUBLE ID HERE!" Red lights flicker to life in the turrets above the gate as they target the unidentifiable rider. The CP Guardsman reaches for her arm in an attempt to apprehend her, but before he can get a solid grip she throttles through the open gate with impressive speed. The turrets immediately rotate to track her, each firing in her direction. The ground shakes from their concussive forces, which emit non-lethal energy waves that ripple through the air at the woman. She maneuvers in a zigzag pattern, dodging the first projectile. Dust and concrete soar into the air as the wave connects with the pavement. She maneuvers sharply again to dodge the second blast, but despite her impressive handling, the second round connects with the back of her large hoverbike. The impact sends the woman and her hoverbike careening into the barrier just past the gates, causing the hull of her bike to scrape violently against the divider.

Miraculously, the woman regains control of the bike after the collision and maintains her forward trajectory. Arching, blue electrical currents strike the ground around her gravity resonator, which now releases thick black smoke from the turret's precise strike. Sparks shower the street from loose parts that drag behind her. She punches the accelerator but is unable to increase velocity. Her hoverbike barely makes it around the nearest corner before the turrets are able to finish her off. They hurl waves of energy into the edifice of the nearest building, splintering shards of glass and debris into the street.

"DRONES! DRONES!" the Guardsman shouts to his counterpart, who immediately straightens up behind his post and fervently pushes buttons on his console. Two small doors embedded in the cracked concrete landing retract, launching two small white orbs into the air. They levitate for a split second, then race past the wall in pursuit of the mysterious fugitive. While calling for backup, her would-be apprehender races toward his own CP hoverbike to join in the pursuit. He too speeds past the gate after the woman. The man in the guard station frantically tries to raise alarms, rushing from one side of the station to the other. However, overcome with nervous energy, he trips over his own feet and falls to the ground inside. His armor clatters against the metal floor of the station. In all the commotion, the gate is left open.

Roman's grip tightens on Rooster's handles. The excitement of the situation causes every muscle fiber to activate. *She's not going to make it. Not on that hoverbike anyway,* he thinks. The turrets perched above his head begin to reset, turning back to the untamed environment beyond the walls. The door remains wide open, almost welcoming him in, and the urge to aid begins to flood his brain as if injected with a needle. *Don't do it, Roman, she dug her own grave...* he thinks, fighting against his own instincts. But the realization hits him that his own entry is not guaranteed. When the men return to their station, would he be next? Would their sensors pick up the vitalerium in his body? Was the grease even still covering the visible piece in his face?

His window of opportunity is quickly closing. So, as the remaining Guardsman begins to lift himself from the ground, Roman mutters, "Fuck it," and twists the throttle. He flies through the threshold of the gate and down the streets of the Grind. The Guardsman yells after him, but as the distance grows his words are drowned out by the sounds of the city. From behind him, an earth-crushing BOOM emits from the cannons as they fire in unison. Roman hits the brakes as hard as he can and ducks, allowing the concussive waves to pass overhead and strike the ground before him. His ears ring as the air flutters around him from remnant energy. Punching the throttle once more, the structures begin to blur in his peripheral vision as he accelerates. Tunnel vision takes over, and time seems to slow. He takes the first turn, following the same path as the two before him, driving as fast as Rooster will carry him to close the gap.

Farther ahead, the woman struggles to maneuver her damaged hoverbike. She glances back to see blue lights blazing from the CP vehicle, which gains on her with every second that passes. She knows that if she maintains this course, she will surely be caught. With few options open to her, she takes a dangerously sharp turn down the nearest alley to try and lose him, then again down another alley. But the Guardsman maneuvers with equal skill and remains on her tail. A buzz above her head prompts her to look up from the path ahead. Directly above her, she can see the two white drones following her movements over the buildings she navigates between.

"CP! PULL OVER OR I'LL SHOOT!" the Guardsman yells through his PA system.

She makes another narrow turn, trying desperately to find

a way to escape her fate of incarceration. The woman weaves around the obstacles in the back alleys, dodging trash shoots and heaps of garbage. Suddenly, a vitalerium pistol shrieks and a charge flies just over her head. Startled, she glances back at the Guardsman, who now fires in her direction as he closes in. She unholsters a pistol from the side of her bike and fires two shots back. The gunfire echoes throughout the narrow passage, and its projectiles ricochet off the black and blue hull of the craft and into the surrounding buildings.

Swiveling her head back to the path ahead, a pit forms deep in her gut when she sees a heap of metal scrap just a few feet before her. She squeezes her brakes as hard as she can, but it is too late. Her hoverbike collides with a terrible **CRASH**, bringing it to a screeching halt and sending her soaring over the handlebars. Her heart all but stops as her limbs flail helplessly through the air. Before she can comprehend her situation, she careens into another trash heap ahead; a lucky break. Just a few feet shorter, and she likely would have been dead.

The CP hoverbike slows to a stop nearby and the Guardsman dismounts, chuckling through his helmet. He does not run but rather meanders slowly toward her with his gun focused on his mark. The crimson-haired woman struggles to escape as she practically swims through trash. She feverishly pushes bags and old rubbish out of her path until she is able to crawl to the pavement. Clearly in pain from being catapulted from her vehicle, she strains with each movement. After finally standing, she starts to run in the opposite direction. But again, she is stopped dead in her tracks. The two drones that had followed her quickly descend from the sky to street level and block her path. With an ominous humming they float in place, as if daring her to pass. She attempts to run by them, but one of the drones discharges an orange holo-net, which engulfs her, rendering the woman immobile. She falls to the ground with a painful thud.

The Guardsman approaches with an arrogance in his

cadence. Kneeling just a few feet beside her head, he retracts his visor just to laugh in her face. "Hehe! I'm not going to lie; I didn't even know they made Wibetani scum this attractive. What's your haul, smuggler?"

The woman groans in pain as the orange holo-net constricts her body progressively tighter, but she says nothing. She tries to hide her emotion, but her eyes betray her; a mix of fear and hate is written in her gaze.

"Did you really think you could escape? Just storm through the front gate and get away?" he pries again. Tears now stream from her eyes, yet she retains her silence.

"Hm...doesn't matter, I guess. You fired back at a CP Guardsman. That's attempted murder of a CP official. You're not just going in; you're going to the cube." The man stands, re-engages his visor, and states, "By authority of the CP, you are under arrest—"

Three blaring gunshots interrupt his apprehension as he watches the drones hit the ground like scrap metal. Loose electronics rattle inside them as they roll around the pavement, sparking from the new holes in their exterior. The holo-net immediately disengages, releasing the woman, who sprawls out on the ground and gasps. The officer raises his gun and turns to address the new threat, but before he can react, a large blur of black and purple collides with him at high speed. Roman's Lancer sends him flying like a rag doll into the concrete of a nearby building. Rubble and debris crumble from its edifice as the Guardsman's armor impacts the siding, then falls to the ground. No movement follows. He lays there motionless on his stomach with his leg twisted to the side.

After circling back around, Roman parks Rooster a good distance from the woman in the riding suit. He is still unsure whether he is a danger to other humans. He keeps his helmet on as he dismounts. She now stands in disbelief at her own luck. Despite her pain, she even cracks a smile as she begins walking toward him.

"WHAT THE FUCK ARE YOU STILL DOING HERE? GET

OUT OF HERE BEFORE MORE COME!" shouts Roman, brimming with adrenaline.

The woman stops dead in her tracks. She is clearly taken aback by his demeanor, expecting a different interaction from the person who just saved her from the Cube. "Whoa, that's some hello... I was only going to say thank you for..."

"Save your thanks, change out of that ridiculous riding outfit, and blend into the crowd back on the main streets. Use the abandoned buildings to travel until you hit the fourth row."

"Hey!" she yells in return. Ignoring his advice, she continues walking toward him. "No, seriously, thank you. I owe you one. More than one, actually... If you ever need anything from the Wibetani..."

Roman takes a step back and interjects, "Seriously lady, what don't you understand about *get the fuck out of here!?*"

His words do nothing to change her course. With her curiosity piqued, she looks him up and down as she takes another few steps forward and asks, "Who are you?"

Roman slaps the left shoulder of his armor and retracts his helmet. "I said don't come any closer! I'm warning you!" he shouts. He moves backward again but bumps into his hoverbike. Before he can move away, she is already within arm's reach.

She starts to respond but stops when her eyes fall upon his cheek, where the grease has begun to run down the side of his face. It exposes the smooth blue sheen of the crystal's surface. "Whoa...what is that, some kind of bio-implant?" she asks, reaching out to touch the strange material on his face. She practically has him cornered at this point. Roman pulls back as her skin nears his, but she persists. Her fingers gently brush the surface of the crystal. "I've never seen implants like this before!"

Roman grabs her hand and removes it from his face, but realizes that she is already in his personal space. *It doesn't seem to be hurting her,* he thinks. Roman looks up from the ground and begins to soften his grip on her hand. For the first time his eyes connect with hers.

Her ice-blue irises practically sparkle. They pierce through his and immediately command his attention, as if subtly whispering to remain calm through her grace. Her crimson hair shimmers in what little light sneaks its way into the dark alley. Despite only just returning from outside the city walls, her tan skin is radiant. Two delicate lines are tattooed below her left eye, and a dainty golden ring pierces her septum. A strange, unfamiliar feeling of helplessness seems to gently embrace Roman as she gazes back. It is as if she can see how the gears churn inside of him.

"Argh!" The Guardsman groans painfully back to life, breaking the trance of the two. They watch as he attempts to move, but instead recoils in pain.

Refocusing their gazes on each other, Roman again insists, "Yea...we really do need to go." He releases his grip on her hand and hops back on his Lancer. It hums to life with a purple glow that illuminates the dark alley.

"Wait! Um... I'm Monique." Her response is sweet and unrushed.

Every cell in his body itches to tell her his name, but the words of his mentor, Modus, flash through his mind. No one could know anything about this mission, or it could mean being hunted by the CP. Whether the cube or execution, none of the potential outcomes were preferable. He would be especially vulnerable if this woman were to end up in CP custody on her escape journey. He looks down in disappointment. *Godsdamnit, you old goon, Modus...* he thinks to himself before finally responding, "I'm sorry, Monique. But you never saw me." Roman's response is even surprising to him, given the circumstances. He re-engages his helmet, lifts off, and speeds down the alley in the opposite direction.

Monique watches until he disappears down an adjacent

alley. Once reality sets in, she walks over to the officer who struggles to activate his TAB device from the injuries he has sustained. His hand quivers with pain, trying to tap the device on his wrist to call for backup. Monique kneels beside his head in the same manner that he had done with her just prior. Gently, she slides the device off his arm before he can alert his fellow Guardsmen. She looks at him as he cringes back in pain.

"Hm... Looks like you'll live. I'm sure a CP klang like yourself is well covered...probably throw you in one of their expensive recon chambers and heal you right up." She smirks with her tongue pressed into her cheek. Saliva involuntarily drools from the Guardsman's grimacing mouth. "Doesn't matter, I guess...because you got outsmarted by a Wibetani woman. And now *all* your little klang buddies are gonna know about it once they eventually find you. Good luck with that shitstorm, champ! That is some strong armor, though...definitely need to get me some of that."

"BITCH!" the Guardsman strains through clenched teeth. But she is already gone.

After adding insult to injury, Monique runs back to her smoking wreck of a hoverbike. Covering her nose and mouth from the noxious smog, she pries open the bike's side compartment and retrieves a small package. Once acquired, she runs to the nearest building and hunches over to cough, clearing her aching lungs from the assailing smoke. Once recovered, she breaks the window and disappears inside.

After two hours of riding, Roman's Lancer floats to a stop beside the "SaM's ElecTroniCs" sign and drops to the ground with a loud CLUNK. He quickly retrieves the vitalerium containment cube from Rooster and runs inside, neglecting to set up any protection from the onlookers in Lower-lock. He bursts through the entrance and looks over to Sam Kerrigan, who sits behind the counter in his usual spot, endlessly cleaning some antique contraption of little value. Immediately, Sam drops the device on the counter and, in one fell swoop, hits the remote to shutter the metal doors of the shop closed and draws his vitalerium pistol. He remains seated with his gun pointed in Roman's direction and waits silently.

With a stern look, Roman says, "Out of the frying pan, and into the fire. Let's do without the small talk. Just open the vault and don't give me any shit about semantics and secret phrases."

Sam stares in his direction with the same unfazed expression from their last exchange. But this time, as if understanding the situation through Roman's pressured tone and unbreaking eye contact, he simply sighs and places the pistol back in its holster. He stands with significant effort and cranks the dials on the old radio to reveal the vault door, muttering, "Only 'cause you said it right this time…" The secret wall disappears into the floor once again, allowing Sam to scan himself. The giant door swings open, revealing the dimly lit safehouse stairwell. Roman purses his lips as he walks behind the counter and through the threshold.

"Nice face, dumbass," mutters Sam as he notices the blue sheen of the vitalerium in Roman's left cheek.

"Always a pleasure, you old lancor-shit heap," responds Roman in a similarly unenthusiastic fashion as he descends the steps to Norvel's hideout. Sam closes the door, shaking his head, and gets about as close to a smile as he is physically able to achieve.

As Roman rounds the corner of the stairwell, Norvel comes into view. Waiting at the bottom of the stairs in anticipation of Roman's arrival, his hair protrudes in every direction, and his brown tactical clothes look as unwashed as ever. The scientist brims with excitement to see the vitalerium meteor Roman has procured for him. He beams through his glasses as his eyes train on the cube-shaped canister the freelancer totes. But instead of a full meteor, he sees only a few shards of raw vitalerium floating around the container. Immediately, his face drops.

"Aw man, that can't be the whole meteor! Roman, what hap—" his voice ceases to work as the light from the room illuminates Roman's face, and a familiar blue sheen comes into view. Norvel's jaw drops like an anchor.

"Forget whatever you were doing..." responds Roman to the flabbergasted scientist. "I need you to tell me what the fuck is going on with me," he says, pointing to the vitalerium lodged in his cheek. For a moment, Norvel does not speak, only gapes at Roman.

Attempting to ease the tension of the situation, Roman declares, "Don't worry, it's safe. I've already tested it at the guard station when I entered the Grind. You won't burn up. Not like I did, at least..." Norvel's eyes are as large as bowling balls behind his glasses. "Did you hear me? I need your help here, Mister Alchemy. I have no idea..."

Norvel cuts him off by rushing toward Roman with his arms outstretched. He presses and probes the tissue on Roman's face, hesitantly broaching the borders of the glossy crystal in his cheek. He cranks Roman's head backward, bringing the vitalerium into the light. His hesitance evaporates, and his fingers prod the shard with intent. It blends seamlessly with Roman's skin as if it is smooth sea glass. "Remarkable!" shouts Norvel. "I... I-I I've never seen anything like it!" But his excitement is interrupted. He takes a step back, and a puzzled look washes over his face as he does some mental math. Pointing at Roman's cheek, Norvel asks, "Wait, that was a sizeable meteor. Is this...the only one?"

With a sigh, Roman drops the vitalerium canister to the ground, then removes his armor, which falls to the concrete floor with a loud CLUNK. Looking down, he removes his shirt, revealing the numerous vitalerium shards scattered throughout his body. They spot his flesh like a cheetah's coat. Norvel is beside himself with excitement.

It takes Norvel's brain a few moments to process what he sees. Finally, he is able to muster up a response. "Well, that's new..."

CHAPTER 16:

Quantify, Qualify, Poke and Prod

Norvel Mathis paces the small room, sporadically tripping over wiring as he walks. His missteps do nothing to slow the gears from turning in his head. As he tries to process what he's just been told, he scratches the patchy five o'clock shadow that has grown on his chin. Across from him, Roman sits in one of the rolling chairs, bouncing his leg anxiously. He runs on the fumes of nervous energy as he watches Norvel mull around the epic adventure retold.

"Tell me something, Norvel! It's been almost thirty minutes!" says Roman, growing impatient with the lack of answers provided.

"Don't rush me!" retorts Norvel, turning toward Roman with surprising zeal. "Respect the process…" He continues pacing a few minutes longer before finally organizing his thoughts. "First off, very impressive that you killed a Vorkrill up close and personal. Most hunters won't get within a Guaniton field's range of one of those."

"Yea, thanks. I'm really basking in the glory of my hunting prowess after *almost dying*! Twice, by the way!" Roman replies sarcastically.

"But that's the thing. You described some kind of…blue

forcefield that prevented its attacks. Tell me everything about that situation. What did you feel when it happened? What were the circumstances? What was around you?"

Roman tries to recap the events in his mind but keeps getting stuck on the memory of searing pain from the vitalerium explosion. His thoughts are scattered, and painful to relive as he tries to recollect the mission. He deflects by saying, "I felt like I was about to die by impaling in the forest. What the hell else do you want me to tell you, Norvel?"

"I know that, but I'm trying to discern what brought about the phenomenon. So, I'll say it again—BE SPECIFIC!" Norvel shouts back.

"I don't know! It all happened so fast... I couldn't lift my rifle fast enough, and I only had a split second to react. I saw it rear up with its talons, so I raised my hands." He scratches his head, struggling to recall more details. "I felt...cold...but full of energy? It was weird... I've been through a lot of tough scraps in my life, but this time, I really thought I was gonna die."

"Cold! AHA! See, this is good!"

"Yeah, this whole situation is just perfect..." replies Roman.

"I mean it's good to have all the details so we can evaluate your situation, you ass... A near-death experience is sure to be an insanely stressful ordeal. Maybe there's something to that. Some kind of...process, or reaction. One that activates the vitalerium your body miraculously accepted."

"*Accepted*!? I FUCKING MELTED, NORVEL! I SHOULD BE DEAD!" yells Roman at the prying scientist as he stands with his fists balled by his sides.

"Alright, alright! Calm down. I'm trying to help but I need you to be open with me while we think this through." With his hands above his head in a non-threatening pose, Norvel tries to calm the agitated freelancer back to a steady state. Roman rubs his face with his fidgety hands and pushes the hair away from his brow.

"Just sit down and we can talk this through. What else can

you tell me about the interaction? What happened after you shot it?" questions Norvel once again.

Roman falls back into the chair. His elbows rest on his knees as he hunches over. "I killed the thing, it fell, and I sat up..." As he explains, he begins to recall the aftermath, and then it hits him, "I was sitting on a shard of raw-V."

"Wait what? Did it hurt you?" asks Norvel.

"I mean, it was uncomfortable. Thing was poking me right in the ass cheek..."

"What I mean is, did it harm you like it did before? Were there any of the same symptoms as with your first exposure?" Norvel questions fervently.

"No. That's when I realized I could touch it. All the shards in the container were picked up by hand."

"Holy shit. That is incredible! Ok. Wait...just wait here!" shouts Norvel as he begins scouring the room for something.

"What are you looking for?"

"One second!" responds Norvel as he continues his hunt through the clutter. The clunking of machines moving and metal tools falling to the floor fill the safehouse. Finally, "AH! Got it," comes Norvel's voice from the far side of the room as he emerges with a red-tinted plastic case. A large white cross is etched on its front.

"Don't you think it's a little late for first aid?" says Roman sarcastically.

"Hehe, very funny, but no...well, yes, it is too late. But I want to run some tests. There must be something different about your makeup that allows you to bond with an element that literally kills anything organic it comes in contact with. I'm going to sequence your DNA and look for any unique traits." Norvel opens the case on the desk next to Roman and removes a long syringe. It's archaic-looking, not one you would likely find in any CP hospital. The needle alone is at least five inches long. "Sorry, this is the smallest one in the kit," Norvel apologizes before sterilizing the tip.

Roman's eyes grow to the size of Deorum's moons. "What kind of fucking first aid kit is that? Are you taking out my spleen?" asks Roman, shocked by the gruesome-looking device.

"We're in a hole in the ground. This is all I have! Now, take off your jacket so I can get to a vein. I need a blood sample to analyze," responds Norvel. Roman sighs, then reluctantly stands and removes his long black jacket. He rolls up the sleeve of his shirt as he sits back down, nodding to affirm he is ready. Norvel approaches and kneels beside him, saying, "Ok. Just look away. It will only take a second."

Once finished, Norvel removes the needle and places a small piece of gauze over the pinprick. He takes the syringe over to a machine near the center of the room and injects it into a rubber port in the side of the device. As he presses the plunger down, Norvel begins chatting again.

"Genomics is a fascinating science. For instance, most people think that Hybrid people are the way they are because of their proximity to vitalerium. But that's not the case! It actually has to do with the body's interaction with the native species of this planet in-utero. Humans developed on Earth consuming plants and animals that developed alongside them. And although the vast majority can process the sources of macronutrients here normally, a small minority of us have interesting interactions with the nutrition provided by our mothers during pregnancy!"

As the plunger reaches the end of the syringe and ejects the last of Roman's blood into the device, Norvel connects the sequencer to the base of his dock via a long cord. "I have to say, I'm feeling lucky I was talked into getting this DNA sequencer, and now I have a reason to use it. The Gulchers I bought the equipment off basically forced me to buy this and a few other devices, along with the computational towers and dock I asked for. 'A full stock purchase or no purchase,' they said. Ha! Actually, came in quite handy. Idiots had no idea how expensive these devices really are..."

Rather than tell Norvel to shut up like he usually would, Roman lets the scientist ramble. His mind is elsewhere. Flashes of his last forty-eight hours distract him from his surroundings. The vitalerium meteor, his visions of Jerrick, the Vorkrill, the fugitive woman on the hoverbike...processing it all is too taxing to be completely present.

Norvel types commands into his dock with lightning speed. The holographic screens switch back and forth in front of him faster than most people could follow. After another few moments, he smiles, smashes the "enter" button, and leans back in his computer chair. "Done!" he proclaims with a tone of pride in his voice.

"Did you find out what's wrong with me?" asks Roman, stirred out of his haze.

"Oh! No. But the DNA sequence *is* underway. You might want to rest for a bit, this is going to take a little while. From what you've described, it sounds like you could probably use some sleep..."

The suggestion prompts Roman to take inventory of how he feels: completely exhausted. His joints ache from the stress he has placed on his body, and a headache begins to set in from lack of sleep. For the past two days he has essentially done three things: drink heavily, fight for his life, and frantically search for a solution to his newly implanted problem. Too tired to make a snarky remark, Roman simply responds, "Yea...maybe you're right," before walking to Norvel's mattress in the corner of the safehouse and collapsing on top of it.

Roman's head throbs as he lays his head on the pillow. The dirty concrete wall of the safehouse stares back at him in Norvel's bed, but all he sees are visions of the dark events of days past. They play like reruns through his mind's eye; unshakable regrets of his own making. Strong as they are, his need for sleep prevails. The cacophony of electric white noise that surrounds him dulls to silence, and the gray of the concrete wall slowly but surely fades to black as he drifts off. As sleep begins to take hold, Roman briefly feels a singular moment of peace, and then...

"Roman, wake up!" shouts Norvel with the excitement of a child. He grips Roman's shoulder and shakes him aggressively to wake.

A weak, gravelly voice returns from Roman as he comes to. "Come on, I was just falling asleep. You said it would take a while for your genetic sequins or whatever..."

"You've been out for nine hours! And its genetic *sequence*; we're not making dresses down here," chortles Norvel.

"Nine hours..." confusion washes over Roman's face as he squints up at Norvel's disheveled head through the room's yellow lighting, "...felt like nine seconds." As his vision adjusts, the room and its hazy contents finally begin to take shape. Norvel stands over him wearing an intact anti-V suit.

"Yes, nine hours. You haven't budged an inch all day, I almost thought you were dead for a minute. And it's a good thing you got some rest too, because what I've found...well let's just say we've got some serious testing to do!" His ear-to-ear grin does not transmit enthusiasm, as evidenced by Roman's blank stare. "Er...just come see for yourself!" he finishes, before rushing back to his dock to display the results.

Roman, still aching from his adventures, rolls painfully off the mattress and lifts himself to his feet. Although he experienced dreamless sleep, his clothes are soaked with sweat as if he had just awakened from a night terror. He stumbles over the wiring that lines the floor as he makes his way to the dock where Norvel stands. The scientist frantically types on its metal surface to prepare his presentation. Roman sits on one of the adjacent work benches, and scratches at the large scar on his right shoulder. "Alright, Norvel, master of alchemy... what did you find?"

In his elation, Norvel ignores the snub. He brings up a rendered image of two strands of DNA intertwined with each other, then uses his fingers to enlarge the floating holographic image. "Look at *this*!" he exclaims, staring eagerly at Roman, who seems nonplussed by the graphic.

The multicolored DNA strands spin freely above the dock, with scrolls of information streaming by continuously at either side. Numbers, letters, symbols, and equations, all undiscernible to Roman's untrained eye. Shaking his head, he asks, "What am I looking at here?"

"Ok! I had some time after the DNA was sequenced. So, I started doing a deep dive into the data. This is your genome... or to be more accurate, *these* are your genomes."

"And?" replies Roman ignorantly.

"*And*, you're only supposed to have ONE! Genome is not supposed to be plural for a singular person, Roman! But look at this, right here!" He taps the dock to make the image stationary, then points toward the bottom of the first strand, where one of the strands breaks off slightly and hooks outward from the rest of the chromosomes. "This hook right here on your eighteenth chromosome...it's not uncommon, but not exactly common. It's one of the genomic deformities that hasn't been associated with any specific genetic trait. Most geneticists will refer to these as 'family heirlooms' because they're often passed down through your bloodline. But no one really knows what they do, because they aren't necessarily outwardly expressed, so to speak. But look at what is connected to it..." He points to the second, shorter strand of DNA that winds beside it, connecting to the hook on the first.

"What is that?" asks Roman, beginning to shake the sleep off and listen.

"Human DNA is formed of four bases: adenine, guanine, cytosine, and thymine. They're the building blocks of you, me, and everyone else. But this strand here...is a mixture of human DNA, yours obviously, but with an additional fifth base. You want to take a wild guess at what that is?"

"Vitalerium?" asks Roman attentively, folding his arms across his chest.

"Yes! There are traceable levels of vitalerium that are somehow bound between your base pairs! And the weird part is, over the few hours that I've been evaluating your blood, you've actually gained another base pair on the second strand..."

Roman unfolds his arms and points to the hologram, asking, "So what does all of this mean?"

"Small picture, it means your DNA is still rapidly changing. Big picture, I have no idea! I've never seen anything like it!" replies Norvel, practically bursting with excitement as he removes his glasses and runs a hand through his wild hair. "Not that I'm an expert in genomics...it's more of a hobby, I guess."

"So, what you're telling me is you've been working on this for nine hours, and all you can tell me is that I'm changing, and you've got no idea how or what's going on?" asks Roman, agitated by hitting yet another perceived dead end.

"What did you expect? That I would have all the answers about a, before now, unseen natural phenomenon? Science doesn't work like that, Roman. This isn't a comic book! Do you have any idea how groundbreaking this is? No one has ever done this before. It's rapidly changing your DNA...no, I take that back. It is literally *rewriting* your DNA this very moment, as we speak! And no, I cannot fully explain it. Not yet, at least..."

"So how the hell do we stop it!?" cries Roman.

Norvel stops what he is doing as if affronted by the question. It is as if someone just hit *control+alt+delete* on his brain. Perplexed by Roman's response, Norvel sits down in his computer chair and fits his glasses back on the bridge of his nose. After regrouping, he asks Roman, "Stop it? Why would you want me to stop it? Even if I knew how, we could literally be looking at the next stage of human evolution here! And you want me to just simply stop it?"

"Yes, I want you to stop it. I want you to take these blue crystals out of me and stop it. I want to collect my two-point-two million UCs, and I want to continue living my life. Couldn't this stuff be killing me?"

Norvel leans over and taps on his dock, which brings up a second hologram with an electrocardiogram reading and other vital signs. "Well based on your vital signs, you're the perfect image of health. I put a set of monitor pads on you while you were out," he says, pointing to Roman's forearm.

Roman looks down at his forearm, and for the first time, notices four small foam circles placed in a square formation on his wrist. They connect to a small black chip at the center by four metal wires. Roman rips them off his skin and tosses the crumpled ball of wires and sensors to a corner of the room; his childish protest at being tested on while asleep.

"Look, Roman. I don't know what exactly is transpiring yet, and it's going to take a lot longer than an afternoon to figure it out. So, you're going to have to be patient and work *with* me, not against me. I mean you literally described creating a forcefield around yourself! You have two distinct sets of DNA that are rewriting themselves! Usually when people have extra chromosomes, they are...well, let's just say they're *special*."

Norvel's pep talk succeeds in bringing Roman back to baseline. Despite that, he sinks into the work bench he's perched on, feeling his hopes evaporate. His lack of options leaves him feeling undeniably defeated. After all, it's not like he can waltz into a state hospital with an illegal element lodged in his skin and expect the staff to treat the situation lightly...or treat him at all given his record. Although part of him clings to the idea that his condition can be cured, he starts to settle into the fact that this might be his fate. "So, you're saying I'm retarded now?" he finally responds with a forced smirk.

Norvel sighs, exasperated by Roman's childish response, but smiles back, saying, "You know, sometimes I wonder, Roman. I really do."

For the first time in a while, Roman lets out a half-hearted chuckle. He can't even remember the last time he had laughed. It feels good, a slight abatement of the daunting situation at hand. It is not a feeling he is used to, which brings about an almost anxious reaction. To detract from this, he quickly picks the conversation back up with Norvel. "So...what's next then?"

"Well, considering you experienced some pretty remarkable 'side effects' in the field, I'd say it's about time we do some more practical experimentation; see if it's reproducible. I've got to see this forcefield for myself."

"Alright..." responds Roman apprehensively. "What does that entail, exactly?"

Norvel beams in response before reaching over to his dock and pressing a square labeled "Intercom." After a loud beeping sound fills the room, Norvel speaks into the console. "Hey Sam, do you have an energy-field sensor or something comparable stashed away in your private collection?" He waits patiently for a response.

A few moments later, Sam's voice responds on the intercom, "Yep."

"Yes! Alright, can we borrow that please?" Norvel returns.

After a long pause, Sam's jaded voice fills the small concrete room. "Not fer free you can't."

Norvel sighs, then asks, "Ok then... How much to rent it for a few hours?"

Another long pause persists before Sam responds bluntly, "Ten thousand."

"TEN THOU...uh... Sam, I already paid you a fortune to use this space. And credits aren't exactly easy to come by down here in this hole."

"Yea, well, hidin' from the government ain't cheap. And amenities ain't free. This ain't a hotel."

"Uh...shit," mumbles Norvel off air. He hesitates, then presses the intercom button again and responds, "Fine...just add it to my tab, I guess."

"Send the dummy up to get it," retorts Sam, in classic

Kerrigan fashion, to which Roman rolls his eyes.

"Sorry, do you mind?" asks Norvel, nodding toward the stairwell. "I'll set up the room while you grab it from our *gracious* host."

"Fine," says Roman before trudging back up the stairs to retrieve the device. Upon reaching the top of the dimly lit stairwell, Roman knocks on the gargantuan door between him and the shop-room. The sound of desks dragging and tools banging echoes up the stairwell from the safehouse as Norvel rearranges the furniture. After a few moments of silence, he raps on the metal door again.

"HOLD YER FUCKIN' HORSES!" echoes Sam's voice through the crack as his hand sneaks through the opening with a small device shaped like a radar gun. Roman grabs it and descends the stairs without wasting another word. Sam's voice calls back once more, shouting, "A THANK YOU WOULD BE NICE," before the vault seals shut with a clunk and a hiss. Roman can't help but chuckle to himself.

By the time he returns, the entire room has been reorganized. The tables, benches, and machines have all been pushed against the walls, and the room is essentially cleared, barring the dock, which is fixed to the ground. Even the mattress had been forced to fit into the small bathroom. It sticks out past the threshold slightly with the door left ajar. The room looks twice as big with the new space provided for Norvel's "experiments."

Norvel stands in the center of the room panting and sweating through his shirt, visible beneath his anti-V suit. However, the look of excitement is still plastered on his face. He tosses a distinct, apple-sized icosahedron in the air repetitively, catching it with both hands as it descends. It had been a long time since Roman had seen a guan outside of a professionally broadcast game. As he approaches the room's center, Norvel fumbles with the rubber ball, which drops to the ground and hits a bundle of wires. A chase ensues as it bounces erratically about the room like an untrained puppy. The pursuit ends as he awkwardly corners the guan against a wall, knocking several tools off one of the work benches as he finally traps it.

Norvel Mathis chuckles nervously. "I, uh...was never much of an athlete, as you probably could have guessed. Whoever stayed here last, or I guess *hid* here last must have left it behind..." says Norvel, looking down at the guan in embarrassment.

Roman walks toward him and silently and takes the ball from his hand, studying it as he's overcome with nostalgia. As he rolls the guan around his palm, he recalls the energy of the crowd while on the field, the thrill of dodging charges and scoring against his rivals. He remembers his teammates, his family, his childhood, an uncomplicated and blissful era in his own story. Fighting off a smile, he tosses the guan back to Norvel, who catches it against the anti-V suit covering his chest.

"So, are we having a catch or what?" Roman asks, gently handing him the device lent by Sam.

"Well, as you can probably guess, I want to see if we can reproduce this 'forcefield' you described so I can measure it. Hopefully, I'll be able to qualify exactly what kind of energy you're giving off, and how much. And this..." he lifts the guan in his hand to eye level, "...is the projectile I want you to stop."

"Easy enough, except I have no idea how I did it to begin with," replies Roman.

"Well, that's all part of the experiment! We have a lot to unpack. Also, I'm going to need you to put this back on." Norvel hands him the set of wired foam pads that were previously discarded from Roman's wrist. "This will allow me to measure your vitals, electrical signatures, hormones, basically anything that shifts from baseline when you successfully conjure up this thing."

While Norvel sets up the detection device on his dock, Roman reattaches the pads to his wrist, walks to the center of the room, and stands idly. His arms hang lazily at his sides, preparing to play the role of guinea pig while watching Norvel toggle the sensor and pair it with his dock.

Once Norvel finishes, he practically jumps over to the base of the stairwell and says "Ok! Svetlana, record experiment A, test subject Roman, first iteration, test number one."

"Recording, experiment A, test subject Roman, iteration number one, test number one," radiates a sultry electronic voice from the polished metal dock.

Noticing Roman's judgment toward his AI's seductive persona, Norvel quickly pivots to directives. "OK! Roman, I am now going to launch this guan projectile at your person, and I want you to block it without using any part of your physical body. Are you ready?" asks Norvel as he fits the helmet portion of his suit over his head.

"Yup..." responds Roman unenthusiastically.

"Here it comes!" yells Norvel as he winds up overdramatically, cocks the guan back behind his head, and launches it at Roman with all his might. The guan wizzes above Roman's head, completely missing him to the left. It connects with the ceiling, ricocheting multiple times off walls and tables before rolling toward Roman's feet at the center of the room.

Roman grabs the guan at his feet and tosses it back to the uncoordinated scientist. "Why don't you slow it down a bit. Try and keep this one under control, huh?"

"Hehe...yea," comes another nervous chuckle from Norvel. "Test one result, inconsequential. Reason, assessor human-error."

"Recorded," responds his dock.

"Ok, a little slower this time. Test number two..." replies Norvel. Noticing Roman's lackadaisical posture, he adds, "...and take this seriously! You look like you're waiting in a long line for a holiday sale or something. Let's see what you've got!" He winds up to throw again, although less dramatically this time.

Roman sighs, then shakes out his shoulders, and takes a

more aggressive posture facing Norvel. Attempting to recreate the blue aura that he experienced during the Vorkrill attack, Roman tenses every muscle in his body. His jaw clenches, and the blood forces to his head, turning his face bright red. The guan releases from Norvel's hand and flies directly at him. Roman's eyes follow the ball as it careens through the air, then...

THWACK! The guan strikes him directly in the chest then falls to his feet. Roman coughs a few times from impact, then picks up the ball and tosses it back to Norvel. "This is going great..." he mumbles.

"Test two, failed attempt. Reason, subject unsuccessful at producing energy field," calls Norvel to his electronic assistant, to which it promptly acknowledges. The inquisitive scientist asks Roman, "What happened that time? What did you feel?"

"What happened is you hit me in the chest with the guan. And what I felt...was the guan hitting me in the fucking chest." Roman's frustration becomes apparent.

"Oh, come on! You knew it wasn't going to happen on the first one. Try and do exactly what you did when you were in the basin. Even the little things. Let's try again," says Norvel as he winds up for another round.

Another unsuccessful attempt hits Roman in his torso. Then again in his thigh. Test five also ends unsuccessfully. Then test ten. Test twenty-three fails in similar fashion, and test thirty-one ends with the guan slamming off Roman's forehead and ricocheting into one of Norvel's supercomputer towers. "COME ON! SUMMON THAT VITALERIUM ENERGY! FEEL IT, ROMAN!" cries Mathis as he winds up for yet another throw. Growing disappointed with the lack of results, and even more bruised than when he first arrived, Roman grabs the guan out of the air during test thirty-two and slings it back at Norvel, hitting him directly in the solar plexus and knocking the wind out of him. Norvel's knees hit the floor, and his arms clutch his stomach as he gasps for air. Unable to restrain himself, a low chuckle escapes Roman.

When he finally rises from the ground, Norvel wheezes, "Ok...you're probably owed that one."

"I owe you about twenty. Why don't you throw it back to me?" returns Roman, who is now the one grinning from ear to ear.

Norvel responds with a sarcastic fake laugh. "Yea, *ha-ha*, Roman, but we still haven't gotten anywhere. What are we missing?" responds Norvel as he paces the length of the room, going back and forth between crossing his arms and rubbing his chin in confusion. "Are you sure what you described is really what happened out there?"

"Yes, I'm sure! You think I avoided getting shish kebabbed with the power of my imagination!?" shouts Roman in return.

"Well then, why are we having so much trouble repeating it?"

"I don't know...maybe it was a fluke? Maybe it was a one-time thing, you know? Like there's nothing left in the tank. Maybe I can only do it with Vorkrills? Who fucking knows, man!"

Norvel stops in his tracks and drops the guan, which bounces toward Roman. He pauses for a second, then crosses his arms. "Wait what was that last thing you said?"

"That you're not a Vorkrill? I was being sarcastic, Norvel. Now who's the ass..."

"No, not that! It's not the Vorkrill itself, but the situation the Vorkrill put you in!" he shouts as he runs over to his dock. "Svetlana, summarize the difference between subject's vital responses during tests and between tests."

"Heart rate: 2.1% average increase during trials. Blood pressure: 2.3% average increase during trials. Temperature: no statistical change. Cortisol levels: no statistical change..."

"That's enough, Svetlana. Do you see? It's essentially the same! You mentioned when you first got here that you felt a kind of 'chill' when it kicked in, didn't you?"

"Yea, so?"

"Were you afraid for your life?" Norvel follows up.

"Yes, obviously, Norvel..."

"Did it feel like your nervous system was suddenly coming to life?" Norvel questions again.

"Yes, Norvel, YES! What the hell are you getting at!?"

"What I'm saying is maybe it's some kind of chemical interaction! A response to stimuli of some sorts. Maybe high levels of adrenaline or cortisol? Maybe to reproduce what happened out there, you require a similarly stressful situation; like one you would experience if your life was in danger from a deadly creature." Norvel's arms are now outstretched toward Roman, as if presenting him with a gift.

"How are we gonna do that? Go find another Vorkrill to scare the shit out of me?"

"Well obviously not! All we need to do is try to induce a state of stress in you!"

Roman throws his arms up and lets them fall limp to his waist. "Fine...what do you suggest?" asks Roman, sincerely this time.

Norvel restarts his usual thinking-while-pacing ritual. After a moment he provides Roman direction. "I want you to think of a very stressful or exciting event in your life, something that brings up heavy emotions. Focus on that thought. I want you to really *live* through that moment with conviction."

"Alright I'll try..."

Norvel, growing tired of Roman's transient attitude, storms toward Roman, removing the helmet from his anti-V suit with haste. He stops abruptly, leaving only a few inches between them. Looking up, he leans in close enough that Roman can smell his breath and yells, "Try? We've been working on this for hours now. Don't just try, DO IT! SHOW ME! CAN YOU DO WHAT YOU SAID YOU CAN DO, OR ARE YOU FULL OF SHIT, ROME!? COME ON!" Norvel takes both hands and slaps Roman's bulky shoulders with all his might, and although it doesn't make him budge, it is certainly enough to demand his full attention. Roman's eyes snap wide open. "I SAID LET'S SEE IT! WHAT KIND OF FREELANCER ARE YOU!?" screams Norvel once more, followed by another hard slap delivered to Roman's shoulders. It leaves an uncomfortable stinging sensation.

Roman's nostrils begin to flare as his face contorts into a scowl. He delivers a cold warning to Norvel. "You better slow your roll, science boy. Or else..." But this only seems to embolden the aggravated scientist, who continues to berate him.

"OR ELSE WHAT!? YOU'LL MAKE ANOTHER SNARKY COMMENT?" yells Norvel, landing another slap on Roman's frame, causing his fists to ball up by his sides.

"COME ON! ARE YOU WEAK OR ARE YOU STRONG? WHERE'S YOUR PASSION?" yells Norvel as he moves in again.

Something clicks in Roman's mind. Norvel's last words send him back to Guaniton practice with his father, which makes him think of his parents...his mother, that fateful night in their Outer Sphere shop. It touches a nerve, setting off a cascade of anger that courses through him like electricity.

An involuntary influx of intensity rages through his blood like a tsunami washing over him. With fire in his eyes, his blood pressure soars as he feels the familiar icy sensation conducting through his spine. Starting first in his neck, it travels down his back and then outward to his limbs until he can feel his fingertips tingle. As the ice spreads, it's as though time slows around him, but in reality, it is his mind that moves faster...

Roman has had enough, and as Norvel lifts his hands for yet another slap, this time Roman is first to respond. His arms extend like pistons to deliver a powerful shove to Norvel's midsection, but his hands never connect with the scientist.

Norvel's strike lands, but not on Roman's person. He

stands before the freelancer with a look of bewilderment as his hands connect with something solid, and rest in midair at the level of Roman's clenched jaw. An intense blue light now fills the dimly lit room as a thin, glowing veil instantly separates them, halting both their advances. Roman stands with his arms bent at a ninety-degree angle encased behind the transparent wall that arcs around him. Its egg-like shape extends just above his head and ends at the concrete floor. The vitalerium shard in his cheek glows bright blue, and a swirling gray smoke rages within its confines. Beneath his ragged clothes, a similar blue glow penetrates the fabric and shines through brilliantly. Shades of azure energy radiate outward from the edges of Norvel's hands where they touch with the semi-transparent barrier.

It takes Roman a moment, but as he stands engulfed in blue light, his expression softens as he's overcome with awe. Dropping his hands to his sides, the blue veil disappears, and the glow of his vitalerium shards dissipates. He looks down at his hands, rubbing the smooth crystal surface that protrudes from his palm. Despite this being the second display of the sort, he cannot fight the feeling of disbelief as he tries to comprehend what has happened.

"It worked..." Norvel says, practically whispering.

Roman nods in response. Overcome with a feeling of accomplishment, he repeats back slightly louder, "It worked..."

Norvel throws his hands in the air in celebration, screaming with infectious excitement, "IT WORKS!" while dancing around the room as if he holds a winning lottery ticket.

"IT FUCKING WORKS!" laughs Roman as he celebrates with him.

"I... I can't believe it. THIS IS INSANE!" says Norvel, placing his hands on his head in exasperation. But as he does, he realizes that his gloved hands touch his own hair. He pats around his head a few times in confusion, then looks over at the floor where his anti-V helmet lies. "Wait, I wasn't wearing my helmet..."

Concerned, Roman asks, "Are you hurt?"

Patting his face and then allowing his hands to rest on his chest, Norvel responds, "...I don't think so." A sigh of relief follows. Norvel's gaze finds the detection device sitting on his dock, and he immediately runs to the console and begins scrolling through the findings. After skimming the data, Norvel says, "This is so strange—the readings are off the charts, but it's like your body has rendered the energy inert. As if it's processing the energy...refining it?"

"What does it all mean?" asks Roman, now standing over Norvel's shoulder.

"I don't know yet...but for now we can at least confirm that this energy you're conjuring isn't causing any immediate harm to those around you."

"That's good, right?"

Norvel spins around to face Roman, replying, "Of course it's good! You're safe to..." But he stops mid-sentence as his eyes fall upon the cube resting on a desk against the wall. Only a few measly shards of vitalerium inhabit the transparent cannister. "Oh shit...what are we going to do about the vitalerium? Modus is going to be expecting his portion of the take soon, which is half the meteor. And that is..." he looks up at Roman with his mouth awkwardly agape, "...less than promised."

"Yea, Modus isn't big on delivering anything less than what was agreed upon."

"Shit, shit, shit...uh...what are we going to do?" asks Norvel frantically.

"Look, don't you worry about him. Lucky for you, Modus and I have history. What I need you to worry about is how you're gonna get us into the Outer Sphere."

"The Out-OUTER SPHERE? If you haven't noticed, I'm in hiding, Rome. If I so much as set foot inside the walls, I'm a target! If I even get scanned once there will be a swarm of Guardsmen, then it's straight to the Cube for me. I-I can't!" Norvel immediately begins fidgeting with his hands and darting aimlessly from side to side.

"First off, settle the fuck down. I'm asking you to come with me to the Outer Sphere, not deliver a package to Zerris himself. There are ways to get inside. Second, weren't you talking about rescuing your lady friend from the *Inner* Sphere last time I was here? Because that's going to be way, WAY harder. And third, I'm going to have a hard enough time getting Modus to accept that we're short. I need you there to help me explain why the majority of his take is lodged in my chest. You understand this stuff better than anyone, right?

"Yes, but I... I can't. I just can't yet. I'm not prepared to go back into the city. It's too big a risk." Norvel sits down in his computer chair and folds his arms. Staring at the wall, he continuously shakes his head from side to side, as if to drive the point home.

Roman walks over to him and calmly lays a hand on his shoulder. "Norvel, I appreciate what you've done for me. I do. But perhaps I wasn't clear enough." He begins to increase the pressure of his grip on muscles connecting with Norvel's neck. Norvel squirms as Roman's hand acts like a vise grip on his pressure point. "If you don't come, it's going to bring up a lot of questions as to why. Now, if I don't have you there to help me answer those questions, Modus will begin to fill in the gaps himself, which we do not want. It makes you and I both look bad. And I promise you, one thing you *do not* want is the Wibetani Militia thinking that you screwed them. Especially since they know exactly where to find you."

"ARGH-OW, ROMAN!" squeals Norvel as Roman's grip continues to tighten.

"The way I see it, you don't have a choice here. So, what do you say we get you some natural light for a change?" finishes Roman as he finally releases his death grip on Norvel.

"Shit man! Fine! Fine... I'll go." Norvel shakes out his arm, trying to reduce the pain. "But you better protect me."

"You just figure out how you're gonna keep a low profile. I'm..." Roman's head spins as a dizzy spell hits him like a club. The room turns like a top in his eyes, and his balance starts to fail him as he sways back and forth where he stands. He tries desperately to grab for something to stabilize himself, but all the furniture has been pushed away from the center of the room.

Norvel notices this and stands just in time to provide support before Roman comes crashing to the floor. "Whoa are you ok?"

With Norvel's help, Roman lowers himself into one of the chairs off to the side of the room. "Ugh... Yea. Just need a second. Got a little lightheaded there. I'm just...tired. Gonna head home and get some rest."

"I mean...yeah. You literally just produced a forcefield! There's no telling what kind of energy expenditure that took! Are you sure you're ok to leave? I really should monitor you for longer. This is all uncharted territory..."

Roman takes a few deep breaths, and after a few seconds, the vertigo finally passes. "I'll be fine. Just figure out how to hide in plain sight," Roman responds sternly. After a few more deep breaths, Roman finds his center and recovers. He stands slowly, grabs his jacket off the floor, and heads for the stairwell. Before climbing the dark path out, he shouts back to Norvel. "Tomorrow, we reenter society."

"Roman, wait..." calls Norvel.

Roman sighs. Without facing the scientist, he calls back, "What is it, Norvel...?"

"If we're going to figure this out... If I'm going to help you with your...condition, I need you to make me a promise."

Roman sighs. "And what promise might that be?"

"I need you to promise that you will help me get Mirene out of Sanctum Tower."

"Uh... HELL no. You can count me out."

"Roman, come on! Look at the bigger picture! With your help I can save Mirene *and* we can stop that psychopath Zerris together! Look at me... I don't stand a chance alone. But with you? With what you can do now? Maybe we have a shot... Besides, I thought you hated Zerris. Don't you want to snatch the rug out from under him?"

Roman's eyes droop with exhaustion. He turns back to Norvel and says, "It's not that simple..."

"Roman, you're special. You're the only human who has ever been able to harness the power of vitalerium biologically. And we don't even know to what extent yet! For all we know, you might...shoot laser beams out of your eyes! This could be just the tip of the iceberg! I want to help you navigate this. But I need your help in return. Please...help me."

Roman pauses. He imagines the face of Zerris and his blood boils. Many a night, oftentimes at the bottom of a bottle, he had imagined in brutal detail what he would do to that face if ever given the opportunity. Now, faced with the opportunity and risk, he finds himself unsure. But why? *Isn't this what you always wanted?* he thinks to himself. A battle rages within him between two voices that argue back and forth; one for vengeance and appeasement, and one for safety and longevity. He shakes them out of his head, too exhausted to reach a conclusion. He has no energy left to combat Norvel's pleas. He tries to think of an excuse to reject the scientist's argument but is unable to conjure one.

Finally, he replies, "I'll see what I can do."

CHAPTER 17:

Reluctant Alliances

As Bios sets on the Deorum horizon, the glow of Cindis, Beryllia, and Dontra begins to power the night sky. The evening hum of the Outer Sphere livens as citizens filter into the streets. Not far from the great wall separating the Outer and Inner Spheres, a heightened level of excitement fills the air of District 111: The Club District. The workweek comes to a screeching halt and the masses race back to their vices, fulfilling their deep-seated urges to escape daily life.

Holographic advertisements dance on the sides of structures extending upward from street level and into the sky like flares. Lines form outside of clubs comprised of young men and women who wait patiently for their turn to enjoy the night, basking both in anticipation and the multicolored glow of curated influence. Some talk amongst themselves, though most stare at their devices or immerse themselves in augmented realities through AR contact lenses.

Street-level patrols keep the peace to a beat, consisting of small groups of Guardsmen and their G-BOKs. Short for "ground-based order keepers," these bipedal mechanical AIs often accompany their human counterparts as support. Their gait is robotically intermittent, and though standing only about four feet tall, the shiny dual cannons mounted on either side of their rounded hulls make them fatally effective. Their jet-black armor reflects the surrounding holograms like a mirror.

Among the dazzling lights and attractive depictions, a starship-sized holoscreen spanning half the length of District Center Tower stands out brighter and louder than all. It projects the evening news, made visible to all passersby within a five-block radius where the streets conjoin.

Jennifer Baine, the elegant and beautiful CP media anchor, graces the screen as she brings the nightly news segment to a close, saying, "Criminal factions are still causing trouble for the Vital Cascade Mining routes. Believed to be a sect of rogue 'space pirates,' and yes, I said it, *space pirates*; these well-organized, well-equipped terrorists are finding new and creative ways to pilfer the state's vitalerium harvests and disrupt deep-space mining projects. An unsettling scenario to further complicate these uncertain times. Tune in later tonight for more on that story." The camera shifts, showing Jennifer sitting before her "special guest of the week" for a one-on-one interview. Her perfectly fitted white and blue dress leaves little room for the imagination, and her voice transmits to the masses with soothing cadence.

"Joining us tonight, we have someone who truly needs no introduction. He is a fan favorite in the court of Kairus, and someone who is no stranger to the limelight. A man well respected amongst his peers and beloved by his people in the city-state of Leebrus, please welcome avid supporter of newly passed Initiative 919, Governor and Chief Representative Triconius Gunderson!"

The camera cuts to the governor, who lounges in his chair casually. "Thank you, and please, Jennifer. My friends call me Trike. This is hardly our first interview, no need for the formalities at this point," replies Gunderson coyly with a brilliant smile. He is dressed in high fashion casual attire as if to relay that despite his station, he is also current, and in tune with his audience. Shiny material and juxtaposed patterns clad his person from head to toe, accompanied by tasteful touches of jewelry on his wrist and around his neck. The classically handsome man, despite approaching his late fortieth orbit, has kept himself in remarkable shape. It only adds to his charisma, which flows from him like the tide and is enough to fluster even the veteran anchor, Jennifer Baine.

She projects a phony laugh before continuing. "So, tell us, *Trike*, if you insist... Why do you support Initiative 919? Why is it good for our people and what can we expect from these changes?"

"Jen, this new initiative graciously proposed by our Overseer puts money directly back into the pockets of our beloved citizens. By taking on the burden of property management, the CP takes the headaches away from the individual and delivers the savings directly to the average consumer by operating the housing market at scale. You see, Jen...the average citizen has enough on their plate to worry about. Work, family, trials and tribulations, putting food on the table...and paying exorbitant prices to have a roof over their head shouldn't be one of them. There are a lot of people who struggle even in this modern day. And if we can reduce that struggle even the slightest bit, well...that's an initiative that I can get behind."

"Wow, now that is admirable!" proclaims Jennifer Baine, tossing her hair back gingerly with her left hand. "And as I understand it, this greatly affects the minority races on this planet as well—for instance, the hybrid population?"

"Oh absolutely. The hybrid population on this planet has suffered greatly for generations. Deorum is where we saw the first hybrids in the galaxy birthed after humans colonized, so this is their home just as much as it is any of ours. And anything I can do to aid that community; I certainly make my personal obligation. I'd be wary as a citizen of any who aren't in support of helping those who need a hand up, hybrid or not. As a matter of fact, I'd venture to say that anyone who does not support Initiative 919 likely doesn't care about those who it helps the most."

Jennifer tilts her head in admiration and smiles wide, baring her pearlescent white teeth. "And as I understand it, you have quite a vested interest, so to speak, in the well-being of the hybrid community?"

"Well, of course. The hybrid community is not an insignificant portion of the population in my city-state of Leebrus. Although only eight percent of the population on Deorum may be Hybrid, thirty-one percent of the residents of Leebrus happen to be Hybrid-born. They deserve to live happy lives of prosperity and fulfillment."

"I doubt any of us would disagree with that statement, Trike. But I was referring to your more *personal* interest in the hybrid community?" she replies with a devilish smirk.

Trike smiles as his gaze falls to his chest, as if suddenly shy. "Ah, you refer of course to my wife, the beautiful Zalina Gunderson. She is most certainly my Bios and moons, my world." As he talks, a photo of Zalina appears above his head to the right side of the holoscreen. It depicts a beautiful woman noticeably younger than Trike. Her platinum blonde hair cascades down to her waist, and unmistakable blue freckles glow with bioluminescence on her cheeks and forehead. "Sure, being that my partner is a hybrid woman, I would fairly say I have more of a front-row view of the struggles that the hybrid community has dealt with and continues to deal with even today. It's an issue that is very near and dear to my heart, just like my wife herself."

"I'm sure it breaks a whole lot of single hearts out there to learn that you are a happily married man!" jests Jennifer, who tosses her hair again. "And just where is the magnificent first lady of Leebrus tonight? We thought she might be joining us here at CPN with you?"

"Unfortunately, she is an entrepreneurial social butterfly, that one. She's currently doing a meet and greet with a number of the galaxy's celebrity musicians as they gear up for Beat Galacticus, the biggest music and entertainment festival in the galaxy..." Gunderson becomes animated with excitement as he discusses the event, "...which we are lucky enough to be hosting on Deorum this year in my home city-state of Leebrus!"

"Wow! That's one event I know our whole planet can get excited about! And what exactly can we expect from a Leebrus-based Beat Galacticus?"

Trike responds definitively and confidently, "Expect the performative experience of a lifetime. All the biggest musical artists in existence today will be in attendance, including a once-in-a-lifetime headlining performance by intergalactic superstar and Leebrus native, Valeriya!"

"That is so exciting! For those of you out there watching, this is not an event to be missed! So, tell us, what role will you be playing in this mega festival?"

The interview continues, but even the noise from the gargantuan holoscreen begins to drown in the growing clamor of weekend debauchery. Hovercars fill the airspace, delivering partygoers to their destinations, and the streets begin to fill with more and more intoxicated individuals. Surveillance cameras stationed on every corner record their antics, unbeknownst to them.

One such camera picks up two odd-looking individuals walking side by side, weaving between pedestrians as they approach Earth Mode, one of the large popular clubs in District 111. The first is a short, portly man dressed in clubbing attire. His shiny red jacket fits tightly to his frame, and a netted shirt covers his midsection. The other man is older and slender. His clothing glows neon yellow, pink, and blue from the hat on his head to his chrome-plated sneakers. Through the camera's lens, they look somewhat nervous. They speak out of the sides of their mouths to each other, but the ambient noise shrouds their conversation completely.

"So, you're telling me we're basically invisible to surveillance cameras? Just from these dinky little bracelets?" says one to the other, raising his wrist to reveal a metallic steel bangle laden with dozens of chips embedded in its surface. Its design is rough, as if haphazardly thrown together.

The slender man swats his hand down frantically. "NO! And put that away! It's not exactly legal tech, you moron," he whisper-yells at the portly man. "What I'm saying is it gives us a different form through the surveillance system. In layman's terms, the cameras pick up a sort of electromagnetic aura that the bracelet surrounds us with rather than *us* ourselves."

"How *layman* of you. What about the Guardsmen? What if they spot you? You are highly wanted...they probably have your cute little headshot posted up in their lockers."

"Their helmets operate on cameras too. The visors in the Guardsmen's helmets will pick up the exact same image as the surveillance cameras."

"What if they aren't wearing their helmets?"

"When have you ever seen an on-duty Guardsman without his helmet on?" whispers Norvel sharply.

"Good point... So, what do I look like?" asks Roman inquisitively, yet again playing with his bracelet against Norvel's suggestion.

"Why does it matter, Roman?"

"Just curious... All these people can see me though, right?"

Norvel, visibly sweating, replies, "Yes, Roman. Yes. Everyone else here sees us as we are. Those watching through city surveillance, however...those that could use AI to run our faces through their database and ID us? They see two of your average, middle-aged club rats. It's a recreation of a little invention I built back in XSEC that never saw the light of day...for obvious reasons."

"And you just made these in your basement!?"

"Yes. I had to take apart half the machines I had there just to gather the right parts. Then I *still* had to ask Sam for more components. If by some miracle I ever rescue Mirene from Sanctum Tower, we'll both be in crippling debt to Kerrigan..."

"You forgot the part where we have to live through this Wibetani ordeal first. Don't expect a welcome party from Modus. As a matter of fact, expect the opposite of a welcome party."

"A...farewell party?" replies Norvel.

"More like a firing squad. Just keep your smart mouth shut and let me do the talking," snaps Roman. "Oh, and when I do ask you to talk, don't go too in-depth about my new blue accessories. Keep it vague." Despite his sharp retort, he seems careless and calm. His placid state confuses Norvel, who audibly gulps as he follows the freelancer to the entrance of Earth Mode.

The club's entrance is dazzling, attracting partiers to the venue like mosquitos to a bug zapper. A triangular neon arch extends upward to the fifth story of the building, emitting a stimulating neon glow. Its color changes steadily to the beat of the music radiating from inside. With each thump of the bass, a holographic pyramid travels outward from the glowing triangular entrance and shrinks until it disappears to nothing in the middle of the street. A long line extends down the sidewalk from the frosted glass doors that periodically sink below ground level to allow patrons inside. Three large men barely past their teenage orbits stand guard and tend to the line in shiny black suits. The upscale attire peeks out from beneath red and black body armor that covers their midsections.

Norvel watches in awe as Roman skips the line and walks directly up to the bouncers, who stir defensively upon noticing him. They block his path to the entrance in unison, each presenting the same dissatisfied scowl. Norvel is so close to Roman that he practically hugs his back. Roman says nothing, merely stands before them, emotionless. He waits for them to speak first.

"You got a problem with the line? Cuz you obviously have a problem with the dress code," says the bouncer standing in the middle. The other two chuckle in response.

The remark causes Roman to look down casually and take a self-inventory. He wears his usual long black coat, which is dusty from his last adventure. His dirty white shirt with holes in it certainly doesn't meet the dress code, nor do his dirt-stained gray cargo pants and his worn leather combat boots. Roman glances at the people who wait in line, all of whom are dressed stylishly and impeccably. *This is a nicer spot than I expected. The Wibetani's moving up,* he thinks to himself, raising an eyebrow as he admires what Modus has built for himself. He decides to ignore the question and get to business.

"Which one of you here is Klipper?" he asks.

The three men glance at each other, surprised, then the man in the middle replies, "That's me." He signals to the other bouncers to get back to handling those in line. "Whatchu need with a Klip, huh? What business you got?"

"Shit, you're already a Klip? How old are your recruits now…eleven?" responds Roman. Norvel shrinks behind him as if to attempt a disappearing act.

The man's jaw drops, and he takes an aggressive step toward Roman. "Man, fuck off with that! You got business or what!?" he says angrily as his young ego surfaces.

"I got a meeting upstairs. Top-top biz for M. Tell him R is here," responds Roman frankly.

The young bouncer's eyes open wide, and his demeanor changes instantly from defensive to professionally polite. "Oh, ok. Just give me a second," he says before turning around and speaking into his TAB device. After a moment, he turns around and ushers Roman and Norvel into the club. The two enter, receiving glares from the rest of the smartly dressed people who wait patiently behind holographic barriers.

The two enter a hallway shaped like a tube decorated to imitate hyperspace. Before continuing onward, the Klipper gives them directions. "Walk in and go to the bar on the right. Ask for Runner Idrys, he'll handle you from there."

"Did you say Idrys?" yells Roman over the loud music that echoes down the hallway. "Idrys is a runner now!?"

"He's Runner Left Hand now," replies the Klipper before waving him onward and disappearing behind the frosted glass doors again.

I guess a lot can happen in ten orbits, thinks Roman as he walks Norvel down the hallway to the club. Idrys had been one of Roman's recruits back when he was a Klipper with the Wibetani. Not only has Idrys surpassed him in the years since Roman's departure, but he now holds one of the most powerful positions in the militia. The only higher-ranking member than him would be the Runner Right Hand, whoever that is now, and the General himself, Modus Magni.

The hallway opens into a grand, long club room. The hall's perimeter is lined with balconies on each of the club's five stories. Each tier has its own party raging. Roman and Norvel are immediately bathed in laser lights and holograms that spin around the room. Sporadically placed throughout the club are metallic statues of earth creatures, along with other pervasive and gaudy "Earth"-themed décor. Several platforms spaced evenly on the dance floor extend above the crowd, serving to elevate a scantily clad dancer on each. A silver-painted woman dances on a set of mechanical chrome calves. The people around her cheer as she removes her top and taunts the crowd with her garment. Further ahead, a man bounces up and down on his hands, performing acrobatic dance moves as he tends to his own patrons in nothing but a thong. At the end of the great dance floor, an elevated chrome bubble partially encases the DJ, who hypes up the crowd as he switches between songs. The wall behind him, a giant holoscreen, displays mind-bending images that dance along to the music. At the center of the great hall hangs an enormous globe in the likeness of planet Earth. It spins delicately as beautiful holograms encircle it, bringing the planet to life. Roman stands wide-eyed as he takes in his surroundings. He has never been in a club this nice. It is miles beyond the humble beginnings of the Wibetani he remembers.

Norvel nudges him out of his trance, shouting, "Hey! Your face...it's showing." He points to Roman's cheek, where the flesh-colored plate Norvel had fashioned him is beginning to slide off, revealing a sliver of blue crystal that gleams in the ambient club lighting. Roman readjusts the covering, then grabs Norvel by the shoulder and leads him to the bar. He pushes people in shiny coats and LED clothing out of the way with no regard for their groans. Resting his hands firmly on its back edge, he leans forward and beckons the bartender.

"Someone's in a rush," she says to Roman through the green-glowing face shield that covers her head and ends at the bridge of her nose. "What can I get you?"

"You can get me a double whisky, and Runner Idrys," replies Roman, whose head is on a swivel. The bartender nods and then signals to two militia men in red, black, and white clothes. Their recruit jackets display distinct bulges at the hip, a dead giveaway. They barely even try to hide their weaponry. Nodding in return, they disappear into the crowd.

Moments later a tall man emerges and walks toward the bar. He wears the same colors as the recruits, but his clothing speaks to someone with status. His brown hair is buzzed short, and the left side of his head has three distinct lines shaved into it. His dark eyes light up when he sees Roman, and upon reaching him, he forgoes the formalities and greets him with a big hug.

"ROMAN! It's been too long, my exiled brother!" he shouts over the electronic melodies.

Roman returns the gesture and embraces his old friend. Idrys had been his favorite and most promising recruit at the time. "Ten orbits is far too long. And by the way, people who leave by choice aren't usually referred to as exiles."

"And it ain't often that the Wibetani let people leave by choice alive. Shit, to be honest, I ain't sure what to call you!" replies Idrys with a smirk.

Roman smirks back with pride in his former brother-in-arms. "I just heard what they call you now...and I see you've got the haircut to prove it," he says, pointing to the three lines on the left side of his head.

"Yea well, a lot has changed since you left us. I got bumped up last orbit. You surprised?"

The bartender slides a large glass of brown liquor across the bar to Roman. After grabbing the glass and taking a quick swig, he retorts, "Of course not... I'm a great teacher." He downs the rest of the whiskey, exhales loudly, and finishes with a wink.

The smile slowly disappears from Idrys's face. "You *were* a great teacher until you bailed on us. A lot of us weren't too happy with you for that. Now I knew you better than that, so I never held a grudge. Some others, though, they wanted you dead for leaving. They don't like it when others are treated differently...like they're above the rules."

Roman presses his tongue against the inside of his cheek, biting down as if to literally hold his tongue. He slides his glass back across the bar and squares up with Idrys again. "Yea, well, I guess it's a good thing they weren't calling the shots then." The friendly interaction begins to tighten, and an air of tension fills the gap in conversation.

"Hey, like I said, I don't hold a grudge. I knew how close you and Jerrick were. But I'm doing you the courtesy of being honest. Not everyone's gonna be happy to see you up there."

"Heh, if you only knew the half of it..." replies Roman as he ponders how he is going to address the delivery issue with Modus.

"Well, let's not keep the top waiting." Idrys leads Roman

and Norvel along the perimeter of the dance floor. About halfway across the club, they approach a small platform lined with red lights and guarded by four more gun-toting recruits. Roman and Norvel follow the Wibetani officer onto the platform.

Idrys waves his hand to bring up a set of holographic controls, which prompts railings to rise around them from its base. After a few quick hand motions, the platform lifts off the ground and begins to hover up above the dance floor. It soon becomes clear that the giant spinning globe is its destination. As they ascend, Idrys whispers to Roman, "You brought the contact with you? I thought he was in serious hiding. Isn't he ex-CP?"

"You'll see soon enough..." sighs Roman.

The platform docks on the edge of the massive glowing sphere, and a door becomes visible behind the delicately spinning holograms of the faux planet's oceans and land masses. A code entered by Idrys causes a hatch to slide open on its surface, allowing the three men to enter a tiny foyer inside the globe. They step inside and the door behind them promptly closes.

While they wait for the second door to open, Roman stares at the screens that display views from cameras around the club. One of the screens displays the room they stand in, and for the first time, he gets a look at the portly image Norvel crafted for his virtual surveillance avatar. Glancing up at the short, pudgy man wearing clothes far too small for his frame, and the tall, lanky raver that stands in Norvel's place, he squints as if his eyes deceive him and grunts, "You've got to be kidding me..." Norvel smiles innocently and shrugs but is unable to respond before the second hatch opens.

The three men enter a much larger room that spans the circumference of the globe. The entire club, everything underneath and around the sphere, is completely visible, as if there are no walls or floors. Every step looks as if they are walking on thin air; able to see everything that goes on in the club, though no one can see inside. Four couches sit cozily at its center around a low table with at least six Wibetani troops of different ranks standing nearby. Only two occupants sit.

One man leans forward with his elbows resting on his knees. A sleeveless leather jacket the color of red wine exposes the black, tattooed flesh of his arms and chest, and fatigue-style cargo pants meet his worn combat boots. Dark sunglasses cover his eyes, just visible around the dreadlocks that hang from his head. He clutches a cigar between the index and middle fingers of his black metal hand. Both arms below the elbow are bionic replacements, and not the legal kind. Modus Magni, General Premier of the Wibetani Militia, is an unmistakable figure. He argues with someone sitting across from him who is blocked from Roman's view.

Modus yells across the table with tenacity, "When are you going to listen? When you pull a move like this, you put yourself in danger, and our business with it. You were not sanctioned to run that job. You could have been killed! Or worse, captured, tortured, THEN KILLED! WHAT THE HELL WERE YOU THINKING!?"

"I was thinking that when you promoted me to Runner, I would have some godsdamned fucking autonomy!" shouts a female voice in return.

"Hehehe...autonomy. You speak of autonomy like you act in a manner that is deserving of autonomy. You'll get the freedom to run your own segment when you prove to me that you make smart decisions!"

"The haul from that job alone was a higher yield than half the jobs your little pet brings in through his contacts!" the woman retorts, pointing behind Modus.

The man who stands directly behind Modus perks up, and his eyes widen in response. He lets out a cocky chuckle, as if unfazed by the woman's insinuations. Four lines are carved into the right side of his buzzed haircut, and a familiar, smarmy grin is etched across his face. Roman recognizes him instantly. *Drezz? Drezz is Modus's Runner Right Hand!? What is the old man thinking putting someone like him at his side?* thinks Roman as he continues to ponder who this woman is and how she is getting away with speaking to the General in this manner.

"Yea, you right. It was a good haul. Impressive even. Until you consider the cost of your lost hoverbike! AND the favors that I had to call in to clean up the absolute fucking MESS that you left behind at the West Gate! Do you know how much it costs to pay off a CP lieutenant? Don't worry, I'll fill you in... ENOUGH TO BLOW YOUR FUCKING HAUL!"

Wait a minute... thinks Roman, as the female voice rebuts the verbal assault, sounding more familiar with each word.

"BECAUSE YOU DIDN'T PROVIDE ME THE GEAR I ASKED FOR!"

"THAT'S ENOUGH OUT OF YOU!" Modus grips his cigar so tightly that it splits in half and flakes to the ground at his feet. He looks down and exhales with despair, then retrieves another cigar from the front pocket of his jacket, and lights it with the thumb of his bionic hand. "All Klippers get the fuck out of my sight..." says Modus calmly before taking a few puffs of the fresh cigar. Almost all the men in the room exit past Roman and Norvel, leaving only four Wibetani in the room with them: Modus, Drezz, Idrys, and a young woman with short, crimson hair who sits on the edge of the couch.

Modus collects himself, then continues. "I'm so tired of your constant disobedience. I thought putting you in a leadership position would evoke some leadership behavior from you. But your work is sloppy! And you have no regard for any hierarchy or protocol! I mean shit, you left a trail of breadcrumbs behind you like Hansel and fuckin' Gretel. How the hell did you even manage to escape?"

"Like I told you, I got lucky this time. I..." She turns to the entrance, and her heart skips a beat at the sight of Roman. Her jaw drops, and for a moment she is left speechless. But her look of surprise morphs into a smirk as she remarks, "I had help from an unexpected friend."

Modus's attention shifts as he notices the arrival of his guests. "Ah, Roman, welcome. Monique, meet Roman Matthews. Once a member of the Wibetani Militia with unlimited potential, now my top freelancer. And although he chose to stay slummin' it in the Grind where the Wibetani found their humble beginnings, at least he knows how to run a solo job... Roman, meet my hardheaded daughter Monique."

Monique rises to greet him and extends her hand. She smiles the same way she did after Roman came to her aid in the Grind. "Nice to see you again, unexpected friend."

Roman takes her hand and smiles, forgetting to shake it as her palm rests in his. "You too..." His eyes lock with Monique's, mesmerized not only by her but by the circumstances that bring them together. Somehow, by some stroke of cosmic luck, they cross paths again.

Modus's face curls in confusion. "You two know each other?"

Without breaking eye contact with Roman, she replies, "Roman, huh? So that's your name..." She beams back, equally surprised and elated by the second-chance meeting.

"Does someone want to fill me in here!?" shouts Modus.

"Uh..." Roman starts but is interrupted by Monique.

"Roman here is the reason I'm standing here in a sphere and not in a cube... He's the one who helped me escape," responds Monique, finally releasing Roman's hand and turning to face her father.

Modus leans back in his seat. "So, *you're* the one who pulled her out of the shit?" he asks in utter disbelief.

Roman simply shrugs. "Right time, right place is all." As the interaction unfolds, Drezz adopts an expression of jealous discontent.

"If that's truly the case, then I owe you one. You can put that feather in your cap," he replies bluntly. "I'm glad you were there. BUT..." he shifts his focus back to Monique, "...you may not be so lucky next time. So, until you can learn how to delegate and use your team rather than running around like a one-woman army, you're on base duty."

"WHAT!?" shrieks Monique.

"You heard me. You should thank the Primes that's all I'm doing, because any other Runner that acted as reckless as you would get a group beat-down...or worse. So, you can show the new recruits the ropes with the Klippers for a while until I feel like you have a better understanding of the organization." Monique's jaw drops. Drezz, who is now perched behind Modus on the couch's backrest, stifles a laugh.

Monique fumes and retorts, "OH, GET FUCKED, DREZZ!"

"Let me know if you need any help with the recruits, Klip... I mean Runner." Drezz winks at her following his snarky remark.

Monique moves forward aggressively but stops as she feels a light touch on her arm. She looks back to see Roman's hand gently pressed against her bicep. It is not force that stops her, but the message he relays silently as their eyes meet. The gesture is like a lithium pill, and her rage subsides slightly; just not enough to stifle her rebuttal. "You can't teach me anything that the average street whore couldn't teach. If I need any tips about fondling my superior's balls, I'll ping you." With that, she storms out of the room, followed closely by Idrys.

Now it is Roman who fights back laughter as Drezz seethes. Even Modus looks down to hide his subtle expression of amusement. Drezz's face turns red as his jaw clenches like a vise. "What are you laughing at, you exile piece of shit?" he snaps at Roman.

"Drezz. I see you got a new haircut. It's too bad your barber-bot couldn't do anything about your short fuse or that hatchet face of yours," replies Roman, straight-faced. Drezz shoots up from his seat with his hand on his hip.

"Alright, that's enough!" Modus interjects. "Drezz, calm the fuck down. Roman, shut your smart mouth. Now, please sit...and I'm guessing you're the XSEC runaway? Surprised to see you out in the open, but I'm glad you made it here. Come, join me." He gestures toward the couch across from him. Roman and Norvel take their seats.

Modus leans forward with excitement. The smoke of his cigar fills the air around him as he exhales, then smiles widely. "I apologize for my daughter's outburst; you weren't meant to see that. She's fierce and capable, but a touch insubordinate... a work in progress."

"Honestly, I didn't even know you had a daughter. She, uh...looks nothing like you," replies Roman.

"*Adoptive* daughter... From Reeva, my first, may the Primes rest her soul. And I didn't tell you scoundrels everything. My personal life was on a need-to-know basis. Besides, she was just a kid when you were in the ranks."

Roman smiles, responding, "Yea, well, I was just a kid when I was in the ranks too."

"Good point... There was a time when I didn't mix business and family, but that was a luxury. When her mother, Reeva, died...hm..." he pauses as if the thought of his late partner actually brings him physical pain, "...someone had to be there for her. So, the Wibetani became her family." Modus takes an introspective pause, then snaps back into business mode. "So! I believe you have something for me?" he says, now beaming through his dark shades.

Roman nudges Norvel, signaling nonverbally to produce the vitalerium. Norvel, who is sweating through his shirt from nerves, removes his heavy backpack and drops it onto the table like an anchor. Norvel's hands shake as he unzips the bag and removes the cubic vitalerium canister. Its bright blue glow illuminates the table and everything around it. Modus leans in further for a closer look and removes his sunglasses. As his eyes adjust to the container's contents, his smile slowly turns into a snarl.

"What the hell is this? Where's the rest?" he asks, perturbed.

"We have it with us, but you're not gonna like it..." replies Roman succinctly.

"What's not to like about the most sought-after element in the galaxy? I put over two million creds to my name with the understanding that you would live up to yours. Now, stop fuckin' around! Where's the raw-V?" Modus's patience begins to wear thin.

Roman sighs and removes the flesh-colored plate from his face and rests it on the table next to the vitalerium canister. Modus's face twists in confusion as he tries to comprehend what he sees. The smooth blue chunk of vitalerium shines in the light of the spherical room. Modus mutters, "What in the names of the four Primes is that..."

"HA! Holy shit! And you wanna talk about *my* face..." remarks Drezz.

In this moment, Roman decides to bend the truth. "There was an incident with the meteor. It turned out to be a bit more volatile than expected..." He lifts his shirt to reveal the numerous blue crystal shards embedded in his torso.

Modus now leans over the table to gape at the crystals in Roman's body. "How is this possible?"

"You wanna explain, Norvel?" asks Roman rhetorically.

"OH, um...well, it would seem that Roman has some sort of genetic anomaly that allowed his body to accept the vitalerium...which is remarkable for sure, but what is really remarkable is what he's able to do with the vitalerium post-integration!" Roman kicks Norvel under the table, urging him to change the talk track, but he's too late.

"What is he talking about? I saw that move, Roman. What are you hiding from me!?" pries Modus.

Too nervous to lie, Norvel blurts out, "Well, we don't have all the answers yet, but... Roman seems to be able to express the energy from the vitalerium. When we tested it in the safe house, he was able to create a kind of protective energy barrier around him. This allowed him to stop projectiles that we simulated in the lab. He successfully used it in the field to stop a Vorkrill attack!" Norvel is filled with shame as he looks to Roman, who covers his face with his hand in disappointment.

"A Vorkrill huh? Now that is some serious power..." Modus paces the room as he stares down at the two men sitting on the couch. "I want to see this so-called *energy barrier*."

"I'm not a circus act," replies Roman bluntly.

"And I'm not a chump! I'm a businessman. You're sitting there with *my* haul lodged in your fucking dome, and you want to try to dictate terms to me? What's to stop me from cutting that fuckin' crystal out of your face right now!?" he says, producing a large knife from its hilt. At the sound of his raised voice, a few recruits enter the room from another door, each with a rifle in hand.

Roman grits his teeth, but Norvel interjects for him. "He's still learning to control it! I-it's a very novel situation we have here, and it's something we are working on studying as we speak. But we did find out that it seems to react to a heightened state of stress!"

Roman purses his lips in annoyance. "What happened to letting me do the talking?" he asks Norvel.

"You better do more than talk. Because neither of you are leaving until I get a demonstration." Modus sits back down in his seat and puffs on his cigar. Swirling smoke pours from his lips as he puts his sunglasses back on and finishes, "Now show me."

Norvel searches the backpack on the counter until he produces the guan that Roman has become all too familiar with. "Great, this again..." he says, as he takes his position at the edge of the sphere. Modus and his group of thugs watch intently as they prepare.

"Ok, Roman! Focus like we practiced," he says nervously.

Roman pumps himself up by slapping himself in the face. He then closes his eyes and lets his mind journey to the past. He thinks back to the day in the desert with Jerrick, the shady dealings with the CP, and his friend's ultimate death. The memories elicit anger as he imagines the faces of those who have wronged him. Soon, the icy sensation travels down his spine as adrenaline surges through him. After a moment, he opens his eyes and gives Norvel a stern nod. Norvel cocks back and throws the guan. It hurtles through the air at Roman, then...

Roman lifts his hand and the blue aura explodes outward from him, casting light in all directions. The guan ricochets off of the energy surrounding him and bounces around the room. The recruits all cover their eyes, and Drezz practically falls off the back of the couch in horror. Modus's mouth hangs open like he just saw a ghost. Norvel picks up the guan as it rolls back, and beams at the Wibetani General. Even Roman smiles a bit after producing the aura on his first try. No one in the room speaks as they try to decipher what just unraveled before their eyes.

After a few moments, Norvel breaks the silence once again. "See!? This is a magnificent scientific breakthrough!"

"I'll be damned..." mutters Modus in disbelief.

Drezz quickly wipes the expression of bewilderment off his face and scoffs with exasperated jealousy. Roman and Drezz have their own history within the organization and have never seen eye to eye. Looking around the room, he takes stock of the others' expressions: all of them enamored by the "exile" and his talents. "Yea so you can block a guan. Not like that will hurt you..." Roman ignores him, and none of the other Wibetani pay his comment any mind.

"How'd you fuckin' do that!?" asks one recruit excitedly.

"Yo, your face is glowing!" shouts another.

This infuriates Drezz, who decides to test Roman's abilities himself. Removing the knife from his hilt, he calls out to everyone, "So what!? He stopped a toy! Let's see him stop something dangerous this time..." and then hurls the blade at Roman.

Roman's eyes shoot open in horror as the blade tumbles through the air at him in slow motion. The familiar ice shoots down his spine yet again, and his hand instinctively rises to cover his face. The same blue barrier appears with a vengeance. As the blue energy forms around him, it strikes the ground with such force that it shakes the room slightly. The knife connects with the barrier, and ricochets back from whence it came with more force than it had arrived. It lodges in the couch directly next to Modus, who sits frozen in horror, a remarkably close call. Modus says nothing, only stares at the handle protruding from the cushion.

Overcome with embarrassment, Drezz struggles to find words. "Boss, I... I didn't..."

"Leave us. Now." Modus's response is as sharp as the blade in the couch leather. "You've got work to do. And you can start with acquiring us a new couch...off *your* credit ledger."

Speechless, Drezz looks down and shuffles shamefully out of the room. The others watch as he exits.

"What an ass..." speaks Norvel out of turn.

"If I were you, I would keep your mouth shut. That *ass* you speak of has earned more UCs for this organization than half the militia in the club tonight combined! You question him, you question me. Norvel, is it? Are you questioning me, Norvel?"

"No! No, no of course not," Norvel babbles.

"Good. You're in no position to be making remarks. Neither of you are! As a matter of fact, you both have a serious short to answer for! Amazing as this power...is, or whatever you want to call it, it doesn't make up for the lack of raw-V sitting in front of me. So, tell me how you're going to fix this, and why I shouldn't make you two disappear."

This time, Roman steps in more tactfully. He walks back to the couch and sits down across from Modus. He looks his former boss in the eye and speaks concisely, and without fear. "We are without a doubt short. That's obvious, and we have no excuse for it. And there's nothing we can do to make more of it appear on this table." Roman taps his knuckles lightly on the transparent surface of the low table where the vitalerium canister rests. "That's the unfortunate part. But what we can offer you is something more valuable." With that, Roman removes the steel bracelet from his wrist and tosses it to Modus, who snatches it from the air and inspects it.

"That little trinket is how we made it into the Outer Sphere right under the noses of the Guardsmen without a trace. Every CP klang in the city is out looking for this guy, yet we waltzed into your club at street level like it was nothing. It makes us appear as different people through any surveillance network. And he built that in the dirty basement of some Lower-lock shithole in a day."

Norvel smiles meekly as he lifts his arm to reveal his own steel bracelet. Modus sits back in his seat and crosses his arms. His biceps bulge as he grits his teeth, and awaits Roman's offer. For a middle-aged man, he is surprisingly fit. "Hm... I'm listening..." he grunts.

"Well, the top XSEC scientist on the planet is sitting in your club...someone who can turn a pile of lancor-shit to a space-worthy vessel if given the right resources. If my memory serves me well, you're a man with an imagination, and plenty of resources...so he works for you until his debts are paid."

Norvel's jaw drops. "Uh, whoa... Roman? Can we talk about this...?"

Modus takes a long puff from his cigar and blows the smoke around him. With a discerning grunt, he thinks about the proposal. "Hm...and what of your portion of the debt?"

"I've always known you to be a man of your word. You said you owed me one for saving your daughter... I think I'd like to call in that favor now."

Modus twitches slightly. "Damnit, Monique..." he mutters. His jaw clenches as he looks away from the two, regretting his words at the beginning of their meeting. After a moment, he looks back and says begrudgingly, "Fine. If you're willing to consider this job pro-bono...then we'll call it even."

At the mention of this, Roman begins to lose his calm, collected self. "What? Come on! It's not like you didn't get anything out of it! That vitalerium is still worth a ton of UCs! And if I know you, you probably have more than one iron in the fire to source raw-V for whatever it is you're scheming at!"

Modus smirks, then laughs at Roman's comment. "You're right, I never put all my eggs in one basket. Maybe you did learn a thing or two back in the day... Still, that means nothing for your situation. Because if you had remembered all the lessons I taught your ass, you'd have remembered the one about leverage. I've made my offer."

"Fuck..." mutters Roman as he processes his position. His fists ball with anger and the blood vessels in his neck become more defined. "FUCK!" he screams as he comes to the solemn conclusion: he has no leverage. He stands in a room outmanned, outgunned, and with all of his leverage sitting on the table or lodged in his abdomen. He seethes at the prospect of defeat but knows well enough to realize when he's arrived at it. "FINE! Take your winnings. Good luck finding me next time you need a freelancer."

"Um... What is going on right now?" comes Norvel's shaky voice from behind Roman.

"What happened is you've got a new job, and I'm out of a small fortune!" yells Roman sourly in defeat.

"Don't worry, Roman, you'll get your *big score* yet," Modus chuckles as he tosses the steel microchipped bracelet back at Roman. He motions to the recruits, who begin to approach the freelancer. "And don't go far... You're not off the hook yet. I might still need you and your blue magic yet. I want you right where I can see you. Why don't you enjoy a night in the club. On the house! Primes know you earned it!" He continues laughing, this time joined by the recruits.

Roman storms through a room that echoes with amusement at his expense, followed closely by a trio of Wibetani recruits. As he passes the threshold of the door he entered through, Norvel runs to him and stops the door from closing. In a frenzy, he squeaks, "Roman! What am I supposed to do? I just work for this guy now!?"

"Yea, I told you I needed you to come. Would you rather be working for the Wibetani, or dead in Sam's shithole beyond the wall?"

"But Roman, what about the plan? The weapon!? I need to get Mirene out of that tower!"

"Well, then you better make Modus happy. Go build him some fun toys and you'll be out of here in no time," responds Roman coldly.

"But Roman..."

"But nothing! You made a deal with the Wibetani, and you didn't deliver. Own up to your debts! As far as plans go, I've had a hard week, which means I have some serious drinking to catch up on. I've got a mind to wake up in a bed I don't recognize. So, until the weekend's up, don't bother me. I'll ping you on encrypted comms then..."

"Mr. Scientist! Come, let's talk business... I think you'll find I'm a reasonable man," calls Modus. Norvel watches Roman wave sarcastically at him as the door closes abruptly between them. With no options left, Norvel obliges the General, and sinks into the couch's red leather to discuss his fate.

CHAPTER 18:

A Connection Pure

The platform hovers down to the dance floor, carrying a fuming Roman and his escort team. Below him, the club patrons dance uninhibitedly to the electronic airwaves that echo through the hall. As the platform approaches its destination, Roman spies a familiar face. Her red hair refracts the laser lights like a mirror, and her golden septum ring gleams in the darkness. Their eyes meet as the platform locks back into place, and the railing retracts into its base. Monique's hypnotic smile somehow permeates through Roman's hardened exterior effortlessly, loosening his white-knuckled fists by his sides. He walks down the steps toward her as if involuntarily drawn to the woman. As he approaches, her hand extends one of the two small glasses she holds.

"I heard you're a brown liquor guy," she shouts over the noise of the club.

Roman inspects the gift offered briefly, then takes the drink. "Who told you that?"

Monique nods toward the bar. "Just a friend of mine." She waves at the blonde woman with the bright green face visor behind the bar, who waves back with a smile. Monique takes stock of Roman's defeated look, then suggests, "C'mon, drink up, freelancer. Looks like you could use it."

"You would need a drink too if you just lost out on two-point-two million creds…" replies Roman, looking deep into the shiny brown fluid that sloshes around in his shot glass.

"Fucking Primes! Holy shit, two-point-two mil? That's the great Modus Magni for you… A shrewd *businessman*," she says sarcastically with a devilish smirk. Her eyes lock with his, piercing through him with mystifying fascination.

Roman stares back until his face can no longer hold the stoic expression. He cracks a smile and chuckles with her. He notices her glass is filled with Sham, which glows lime-green in the same lasers that dance on her hair. "What about you?" he says, pointing at her drink. "You trying to shave some years off your sentence?"

"Maybe I just don't like to waste any time," replies Monique, as she clinks her glass against his and downs the green liquid, barely wincing as it drains. Impressed, Roman follows suit, taking his shot. She smiles and shouts, "Come on, freelancer, we'll drink to our sorrows." Without warning, she grabs Roman's hand and leads him through the crowd.

Their feet traverse the sticky floor in tandem as they weave through the dancing mob. The seemingly oblivious clubbers collide with their surroundings as they dance without a care in the world. They bounce off Roman's sturdy frame like ping-pong balls. Monique finally stops at a door near the back of the club. The letters "VIP" made of glowing, opaque glass decorate the ingress. Two men in black suits stand on either side of the door like stone statues, but upon seeing Monique, they assume a friendly posture. After exchanging hugs and cheek kisses, the door slides open.

The lounge section is much quieter than the main room, and the booth they occupy is far more posh than those on the club level. A half-empty bottle of green fluid sloshes as it's passed between Monique and Roman, who drink straight from the bottle with little regard for decorum. Although they no longer need to yell over the loud music, they find reason to in each other's company.

"Wait, wait, WAIT! So, YOU... YOU'RE the Klip that Modus...I mean my dad... HA! No sense in hiding that anymore... But seriously, you're the one he's always going on about? The Klipper who left the Wibetani!?" shouts Monique as she hands the bottle of Sham over to Roman.

Roman takes a swig of jet fuel and winces before responding, "Guilty!" and raising his hand like a fool. He laughs at his own stupidity before rolling backward, deeper into the cushions of the couch.

"No FUCKING way!" she laughs back. It takes them both a minute to compose themselves before continuing. Monique reaches for one of the hoses that droops down from the ceiling and inhales deeply from its tip. She expels a thick plume of sweet-smelling smoke, talking through it as she does. With each word, smoke pours from her nose and mouth. "You know he talks about you all the time, right?"

"What? No, I don't believe that for a second..." replies Roman.

"No, I'm serious. I mean, he doesn't mention you by name... but he does talk about you. You're the only person who was ever allowed to leave like that. I think he misses you."

"Not a fuckin' chance. Modus only has one emotion..." Roman reaches over the table and grabs a pair of cheap LED sunglasses that are strewn about the lounge. He puts them on in an exaggerated fashion, then jostles his hair so it falls over the edges of the frames. Finally, he grabs the hose from Monique and, holding it like a cigar, says, "Let's talk business!" imitating Modus's voice.

Monique doubles over laughing. But when she finally stops, she insists, "No, but seriously, I think he does. You like... set the standard for the Klipper role the way he talks. Plus, he gets kind of sad when he talks about it."

"Come on..." replies Roman, still in disbelief. He hands the bottle back to Monique, who takes yet another gulp of the green fluid.

"Yup." She nods confidently. "He even gets that undeniable Magni sad face, like..." Monique removes the glasses from Roman's face, and places them on her own. She contorts her face, attempting to recreate Modus's "sad face," but fails miserably, eliciting a deep belly laugh from Roman that infects her as well. The two roll into one another, practically tying themselves up in elation as they lay on the L-shaped couch. Their server walks by to check on them but notices the state they're in and promptly leaves.

"That was an absolutely *awful* impression. Probably because you look nothing like your old man. And I'm just gonna say it...thank the Primes you don't! Seriously, how could Modus Magni be a father to someone as beautiful as you? I would have imagined his daughter more...ogrish."

"Well thank you kindly, freelancer. And that's because I'm his adopted daughter, you goon. I look like my mother." Monique affects an exaggerated model pose on the couch. "A very high-class and alluring lady. Never knew my real father, though. Modus, despite his obvious flaws, has always been that for me."

"Ah, that explains it," replies Roman, who inhales deeply from the hose and creates his own smoke cloud. He lays back on the couch next to Monique, completely relaxed. "The grit of a Wibetani and the...non-Modus part, ha-ha..." The Sham is really starting to flow through his veins now.

Monique laughs hysterically despite the lack of effort in Roman's humor, then decides to change the subject. "So...why did you leave then?" asks Monique curiously.

Roman's smile slowly starts to fade as he thinks back to his final days in the Wibetani. He hadn't spoken of them in many orbits; a sore subject, and one he does not tend to enjoy revisiting. But something about Monique makes him feel uninhibited; an open book. And like an open book, the words just seem to pour out of him. "My best friend was killed. And it was my fault, I was the one who got him into the situation. He was a Klip like me, but I... I knew him before we even got wrapped up in the militia. We got in over our heads because I thought we were unstoppable...invincible. I thought we found our ticket to the next level...but all he found was death. And all I got was a vitalerium charge to the shoulder, a scar that gets stiff, and a nightmare I can't shake. Actually, the nightmare part might be getting even worse..."

"Wow, that is...dark." Monique's concerned voice slurs from the liquor.

"Yup...anyway, when I finally healed up enough to confront Modus about it, he didn't take it well. He beat my ass good...like REAL good. I fell back in line...eventually got back into the good graces of Modus. Even ended up getting nominated for Runner. But after Jerrick died, life in the Wibetani never felt the same."

"So you just left?" she pries.

"Before I became a Runner, Modus and I had some...differences in opinion in regards to growing the business. On the day of my Runner initiation, we got in a huge fight. And... I don't know what came over me, but I actually struck him."

"Wait. You punched my dad? Modus Magni, leader of the Wibetani Militia. You punched him?"

"Actually, I kicked him. Right to the jaw." Roman makes a clicking sound with his tongue as he taps his chin with his knuckles.

"I am literally beside myself right now..." exclaims Monique with her jaw hanging open. "Color me impressed, freelancer!" she says as she takes another swig from the bottle of Sham and then passes it to Roman.

"Yea well he wasn't. I'd never seen anything like the look he gave me. It was..." Roman struggles to find the words through the Sham that cartwheels through his synapses, "...disgust. Like the sight of me caused him pain. I ran out of there and never looked back. He never sent anyone after me, I...figured he must have pitied me." Roman pushes himself up to a seated position and stares off the balcony of their booth.

Monique, whose head now rests on Roman's lap, reaches up and gently touches his chin; tracing his jawline with her long nails, running her fingertips over the scars that speckle him. "You're a beautiful, tortured soul," she says sweetly.

Roman looks down at her with a fake smile. Her face is a beautiful distraction from his recent failure, and the disturbing dive into his past. The warmth of her hand on his face soothes him, and his fake smile slowly turns legitimate. For just a moment as he stares into her ice-blue eyes, he forgets.

Monique breaks the silence by sitting up and saying, "Sorry to bring down the vibe like that. But..." she takes a swig from the bottle and slams it back down on the table, "...I think I know how to repair the damage."

"Oh yea? What's the solution, repairman?" asks Roman sarcastically.

Monique leans in with a devilish grin until she's only an inch from Roman's face. Just above a whisper, she says, "You wanna go somewhere *really* fun?"

A series of doorways, a meshed mural of street holograms, and a blur of unidentifiable faces pass by them, and suddenly thirty minutes disappear. Roman and Monique find themselves at street level walking arm-in-arm toward another large building, its edifice constructed of jet-black glass with opulent golden accents. A hologram extends twenty stories high, hugging the contours of the building, depicting the gold silhouette of a woman performing a sultry dance. The word "Xanadu" is etched in gold above its entrance.

The two laugh at a joke that Roman cannot even remember the punchline of as the Sham continues to loosen their grip on reality. Monique leads them to the doorman, skipping the line entirely. Once again, Roman feels the eyes of those waiting in the long line burning holes into his coat.

While Monique releases Roman's arm to whisper something into the ear of the doorman, Roman takes this time to address the onlookers.

"Could any of you fine gennelmen help me? I've been kidnapped by dis horrible girl and she's threatening me with the time o' my life. I think her intentions...are NOT honorable, hehe." His stoned laugh and slurred speech are a dead giveaway to his condition. A few patrons at the front giggle. Most do not. Monique runs back and grabs Roman with an excited grin. "Come on!" she yells as she leads him through the tall doors.

The music is loud, even in the empty atrium. As they walk down the corridor to the club, Monique pulls Roman into the wall against her, and a jolt of dopamine floods his brain as she kisses him passionately. Her lips are supple, and the warmth of her tongue massaging his excites him back to life. In their shared state of inebriation, he feels as if he flows with her, and takes control by pressing her hands against the concrete. She bites his lip hard, providing an exciting little jolt of pain, and then releases, staring through him with her penetrating gaze. Freeing a hand from Roman's grasp, she searches for something in her pocket. Monique places a blue triangle into her mouth and swallows. With a devilish smirk, she gives Roman his orders.

"Open up," she says, tempting him with her fingers. He chuckles, then obliges her, opening his mouth and sticking out his tongue. She places another blue triangle on its tip, and he gulps it down.

"And... What did I just take?" Roman asks curiously.

Monique never loses her devilish grin as she replies, "Does it matter? You took a chance with me, you're already screwed," and winks.

Hallways turn to dance floors and darkness turns to bliss as their faces are covered with the blue and gold flashes of fluorescent ecstasy. A gigantic mass of people dances around them, circulating like the currents of an ocean. Seconds turn to hours, and suddenly, Roman finds himself jumping...moving...dancing under a monstrous Tesla coil perched at the center of the club. Its tendrils of electricity arc over the sea of people in mind-bending patterns as holograms give life to the very air they breathe.

Roman and Monique, both drenched in sweat, flow simultaneously to the magnificent melody of an electronic symphony. As his heart rate rises, his smile only widens as they move in sync with one another. Roman's gaze moves across her gyrating body, and he's almost certain that he witnesses Monique's aura as clear as day, and as natural as Bios's light. It expands and contracts outward from her center of gravity, which grinds steadily against his. Her light glows with incandescent beauty and grace, growing by the second and changing in hue with each thump of the bass. His eyes lock with hers, and hers lock with his, each knowing with certainty they can read the thoughts and yearnings in each other's mind; a connection pure. The surroundings become ambient noise and suddenly, it is only them. Their hands navigate each other's bodies with ravenous intent. Monique's skin glistens brilliantly beneath her black and red Wibetani clothing as if producing her own luminescence, and the arcs from the Tesla coil bend and break at her will.

As radiance expands, hours shrink to seconds. Time elapses at the rate of pure chaos. Thresholds are crossed, and blank faces pass in a blur; the fatal flow of memories unremembered. Pain, excitement, then elation. Darkness. Warmth. Skin to skin, and then finally, black.

CHAPTER 19:

It's Just Politics

Four consecutive horns sound a familiar jingle from one of the many brightly lit screens in Leebrus, distinctly marking the start of the morning news. "You're watching CPN Daily News, and I'm your host, Jennifer Baine." The news anchor smiles and gives a slight head nod as she finishes enunciating her name, then returns to her rigid posture. "Today's top story: the IGB and their increasing demands. Everyone knows of the Intergalactic Governing Bureau. It's a household on every colonized planet in the Galactic Alliance. They give shape to the untenable universe we reside in by governing through strength, wisdom, and the might of the IGB fleet. In short, they bring order to the untamable chaos that is space. But what is it that they ask of us, the planets, in return?

"Many of the colonized planets provide support in the form of tariffs to the IGB, while other planets provide support through ongoing trade relations with the Bureau when the benefits of economic growth through resource exchange outweigh the value of the currency itself. Sound familiar? That's our own planet, Deorum, which partakes in trade relations with the IGB. It's no secret that our relationship with the Bureau is heavily focused on the trade of our most precious resource, the elusive and powerful vitalerium crystal. For generations, the IGB and the CP have enjoyed prosperous trade relations, and both parties have benefited massively from the partnership. But a trade relationship is just that, a relationship. What happens when one party begins to ask too much of the other, or begins to renege on their allotted responsibilities in that relationship?"

Jennifer Baine flips her luscious red hair and faces another camera before continuing. "For the past five orbits, the IGB has consistently and exponentially increased their vitalerium demands of the CP, putting stress on both our leaders and our infrastructure. Just this quarter alone, the IGB requested a one hundred and fifty percent increase in output from the Vitalerium Mining Operation run out of Doral Space Station. Not a bad thing, right? If I go to a coffee shop and ask for double my usual coffee, I just pay double the price and everyone wins, right? Unfortunately, that is not the case here. Sources report that the IGB will be paying nothing for this inflated shipment. You heard right, absolutely nothing. And it's not like we can simply deny them—they're the IGB! In the coffee shop there is justice. Apparently, we are no longer worthy of the same justice in our dealings with the IGB. So why the sudden changes in demand? Why the delay in payment? Are they simply going to pay us back next time? It would be understandable if the IGB simply needed time to pay off a shipment that large, but that brings up the question: why can't they pay? Has the IGB hit hard times? Tough questions asked of a tough situation. More on this after these messages. As always, thanks for watching. I'm Jennifer Baine."

Even from space, Leebrus appears a slight green hue. The vast majority of structures in this city-state house lush greenery in their edifices. Trees and bushes trimmed to perfection spill out beyond the sharp borders of concrete, metal, and glass, a beautiful juxtaposition of man-made marvel and natural spectacle. But upon zooming in, one would see this northwestern-most ellipse of Deoran civilization glimmers an amalgamation of every color palette imaginable. Asymmetrical architectural works of pure artistic inspiration spiral upward toward the sky, painted like canvases by the most creative among artists. They twist and curve around each other as if to dance. Leebrus: the arts and fashion capital of Kairus. Where everyone goes to make a statement, and the louder the better.

Some make their statement with experimental fashion; adorning themselves in bright colors, eye-catching patterns, and risqué cuts of material as they utilize the autonomous streets as their own personal catwalks. Others find an outlet in flaunting luxury hovercars, which line the streets and skies like bright pieces of candy. If performance is your medium, the streets and squares are filled with Deorans displaying their magnificent talents. The songs of vocalists mesh with the preaching of soapbox-saints as actors portray characters, and acrobats put on high-flying shows. Artists and musicians alike peddle their works on the street, creating a sort of melodic cacophony that fills the sweet-smelling air. Entrepreneurs from Sigmi, models from Ventura, Hybrids from Deorum, movie stars from Earth, influencers from Mars, politicians from Portia Quixote... People from all planets, economic levels, and walks of life gather to bask in artisan bliss. For those who harbor wealth with intent to display, there's no better place than the Design District of Leebrus. Conversely, for those who have but a fraction of a credit to their name and dreams of stardom and fortune, Leebrus is their destination. It oozes with promises of potential; their hopeful ticket to the top.

An enormous, mirrored structure shaped like a wind-warped dome sits at its eastern flank. The building is not particularly tall in comparison to the megastructures surrounding it, but it covers an enormous plot of land, wider than anything else in the city-state. The deep waterways that carve through the grounds around it reflect a bluish light that arcs up the mirrored outer walls, making it gleam like a giant blue gem. Caerulleum Showcase is where every performer hopes to one day entertain the masses of fans that flock to Leebrus to be dazzled. On this day, the grounds bustle with activity as workers prepare the venue for the galaxy's ultimate entertainment festival: the much-anticipated Beat Galacticus.

However, the convention center is not the only place filled with action and excitement. Just opposite this blue behemoth stands the Leebrus Government Spire, a great conical building ending in a sharp, narrow point over one hundred stories in height. At its base, thousands of citizens gather behind hologram barriers guarded by at least a hundred well-armed CP Guardsmen. The sentiment expressed by the crowd is one of aggravation. Tension fills the air as the citizens press themselves against the holographic barriers that block them from the front doors of the spire. They yell chants in unison as they wave handmade signs and stand under holographically projected banners that guide the crowd in disdainful slogans.

"Nine-one-nine takes yours and mine! Poor until the end of time! Nine-one-nine takes yours and mine! Poor until the end of time!" they shout at the CP Guardsmen, who grip their rifles tighter with each second that passes.

"Don't fall for their charity! Nine-nineteen, theft by the CP! Don't fall for their charity! Nine-nineteen, theft by the CP!" others chant at citizens who slink by on the automotive sidewalks that carry them to their destinations. Most citizens pay them no mind, either buried in their devices or wrapped up in conversation. Those who do notice do nothing. Their faces relay a sort of apathetic pity before looking down or away from the spectacle.

At the spire's pinnacle, Triconius Gunderson stares down at the crowd through the translucent glass edifice of his office. The group of protestors seem only a speck from where he stands, but it does not settle him. He scratches his wrist with his nails compulsively and begins pacing around his office, flapping the outer layer of his stylish outfit repeatedly in an attempt to quell his sweating. It does little to help.

Trike's office makes up the entire one hundred and twentieth floor, a beautiful circular space bright with natural light thanks to the floor-to-ceiling windows that surround the entire room. Everything is colored white, beige, and gold from the office furniture to the elevator platform. At the room's center, Trike's chief advisor and his publicist sit on swanky minimalist couches that hover in place. The young colleagues argue back and forth, trying to loop the jittery governor into their conversations.

"I think we should double down on the hybrid-hate tagline. If people want to oppose the new initiative, not only are they unpatriotic, but they are clearly bigoted people," says the publicist as she crosses her legs and leans back in her seat. "It certainly resonates with our base. The Jennifer Baine interview was received well according to the polls, Governor Gunderson."

His chief advisor chimes in, "That rhetoric by itself isn't enough! It's not his base we should be worried about. His base isn't down there protesting right now! We have to put out a spin that's a bit more even-keeled to resonate with the middle, and maybe even some of the unhappy few. Maybe some numbers showing savings over time? Or an example of what that money could be turned into if invested? Most people are still on the fence regarding Initiative 919. We need to bring them over to our side before some angry mob brings them to theirs! Come on, back me up, Trike! Trike?"

The governor says nothing at first, only continues pacing. The inside of his bottom lip is raw from hours of continued biting. After a few moments, he responds without looking in their direction. "No, no, I like it... We double down!" he says, moving his hands in small, jerky motions in front of him that match his spoken cadence. "If they want to be on the opposite side of this issue, we need to let everyone know that they are on the wrong side of history! And we need the citizens of Leebrus to know what these kinds of people are really like... Radicals! Yea, yea, no... I-I like it. Good job, Sayla." He shakes his finger in the air close to his chin, and nods rhythmically at his own remarks.

Sayla smiles in appreciation, then looks back across the couch. She shoots her colleague a smug grin, and mimes an explosion by making a fist then splaying her fingers out and wiggling them in the air. "Hear that, Rod? He likes it. Looks like we go with my plan for the address."

Rod grits his teeth in jealousy. "At least I have original ideas, *Mz. Predictable*. You've been preaching the same exact thing since the passing of this initiative."

"Yea, because it's working! Why are we trying to fix what isn't broken? You're just mad because the plan didn't have your stamp of approval on it," responds Sayla with venom in her voice.

Rod stands up and points toward the window with renewed energy for a fight. "You call *that* working!? We have protestors! We haven't had a protest *against* Leebrus's governing body in thirty orbits! And that's *aaall* following your recommendations. YOURS! Sorry if I'm trying to adapt here."

As the two bicker back and forth, Trike's anxiety reaches a peak threshold, and he shrieks, "STOP IT!" so loud that his voice cracks. "That's enough out of both of you. I'm going to start losing my hair if I have to keep listening to this." He turns toward the window and reaches into the pocket of his jacket, removing two red and black capsules. Being careful not to reveal himself, he covertly pops them into his mouth and dry swallows them.

The two cease their quarreling and sit back in their seats. A few seconds pass in relative silence except for the sounds of nervous fidgets coming from the room's occupants. As they sit in silence, a tone echoes through the room, signaling the arrival of someone via the elevator. Next to the couches where

Trike's senior team members sit, a cylindrical platform rises from the white marble floors as the elevator reaches the penthouse office. The frosted glass doors open, revealing a man in a royal blue mantle accompanied by two RoGuards. Their white armor matches well with the surrounding aesthetic as it gleams in the natural light of the office. Sayla and Rod immediately stand and give the CP salute as Zerris Aganon strolls in with his personal security. Trike follows shortly after.

"Overseer Aganon! Go-good to see you sir, er—my honor. I mean your honor! Uh..." Rod fumbles with his words as he attempts to address the most powerful man on Deorum.

Sayla rolls her eyes at his failed greeting. She then smiles wide and squints her eyes practically shut before chiming in, "Ugh, so sorry about him, Overseer Aganon! He gets excited. It is just an absolute pleasure to see you in person, your honor! How was your trip over? Uh, easy flight?" She takes a meek, respectful step forward and breaks her salute to extend her hand to shake Zerris's.

As Zerris walks by, he stops beside Sayla and glances down at her hand. He does not look her in the eye, or even face her; rather, he simply raises an eyebrow as he stares at her quivering palm. Without acknowledging the gesture further, he speaks to Trike directly. "Are you going to, or do I have to?"

Trike nods, breaks his salute, and commands the two, "Sayla, Rod? Out. NOW, thank you."

The two look at each other nervously, then quickly gather their things from the coffee table and disappear behind the doors of the frosted glass elevator, which sinks back into the floor of the office.

"Interesting people you choose to run your operation," remarks Zerris sarcastically.

"Yea, they are a quirky duo, those two. I find the competition they have amongst themselves produces good concepts occasionally," replies Gunderson as he sits down behind his large white desk.

"I'm sorry, I said interesting, but what I meant was annoying..." Zerris pauses to notice the sweat stains under Trike's arms and around the collar of his shirt. His face has a moist sheen to it, and his head nods endlessly. Trike hides his hands from view, but based on his movements, they were almost certainly writhing beneath his desk. Zerris squints, then sits down across from Trike with his legs crossed casually. "Having a rough week, are we? Am I sensing trouble in the Trike Spike?" he says, referencing Trike's self-given nickname for the Leebrus Government Spire.

Trike laughs nervously, then lets out a long sigh. "It's been a bit more stressful than usual, what with the music festival coming up and with the first wave of property annexations; not to mention these protests starting... But we are managing, yea. Yea. I've got my best people on it. We'll come out of this one on top like always!" Another forced chuckle follows.

Zerris fake-laughs along with him, then responds, "I meant with your drug problem. You don't hide it well."

Fear washes over Trike's face as he gulps audibly. He looks down shamefully, then attempts to rebut the accusation. "Dru-drug problem? I don't..."

"Spare me! You dare lie to your Overseer? Any street walker would be able to spot the signs on you!"

"It-it-it's not a problem... I've got it under control. It's just a social thing, a lot of the musical talents like to partake when they're planet-side and...well, I mean I am their host! So... It's just we haven't had a protest in some time, and we are trying to deal with it without making a scene or sparking violence... and then it turns out a few of our performers dropped out of the festival with just a week to go, and you...you know and those two...my team? Those two advisors of mine, they can really stress me out with the bickering sometimes..." His ramblings get more fragmented and less coherent the more he continues.

Zerris, who grows tired of the incessant chatter, calmly interrupts his blathering. "So, use."

Trike falls silent and gapes at him with wide-eyed confusion, his face now ghost-white. His response is like a skipping record. "Um... I don't... I'm sorry, what? I—"

Zerris interrupts again, his voice no louder than a whisper. "Go ahead and use. You're obviously stressed, and I'm sure you keep a stash somewhere in your office." When no response follows from the stunned governor, Zerris pushes again. "It's no secret to anyone here in this room, so why don't you just go ahead and plug up. Hell, I'll even join you with a bit of my own substance of choice..." he says as he walks over to the office wet bar, pours himself a glass of clear liquor, and takes a sip. "After all, the weekend is upon us, my old friend and cohort."

"I... I can't do..." Inside he is dying to use. The familiar itching has taken over with a vengeance, and he finds himself unable to hide his look of shame. But still he persists, trying to fight the urge. *Is this a test? It has to be a test...* His thoughts run wild as he tries to decipher Zerris's angle.

The fake smile disappears from Zerris's face and is replaced by a grimace. His voice starts in a growl and ends with a roar. "I said, get out your stash, plug up your arm with that poison, and relax. Because if you aren't stressed already, you will be after you hear what my demands are of you!"

Trike's eyes bug out of his head, and he cowers back into the cushion of his office chair. "You don't mean...you need more?" he asks in a weak voice. "No...no, I-I can't, Zerris. This can't go on..." He begins frantically searching through the storage under his dock.

"You can and you will. I need you to speak to your contact. I need fifty more."

"Oh Primes, *fifty*!?" replies Trike, who now rifles through drawers and tosses items to the floor until he comes across a small, thin tube with metal sidings. An opaque, black liquid sloshes around inside the safeguarded syringe.

"Yes, fifty. The last batch has expired, and we need another so we can continue to conduct our research."

Trike rolls up his right sleeve, orients the tube, then jabs the syringe into his wrist and presses the button on its side. The liquid disappears from the syringe as it empties into Trike's bloodstream, turning the veins in the governor's forearm momentarily black as it spreads up his extremity, and then throughout his body. Trike breathes heavily for a moment, then gives one long exhale, releasing a small cloud of black smoke that quickly spreads and dissipates. His anguish is replaced with a smile of pure relief. He sits back in his chair and looks up at the ceiling as Zerris walks behind his dock, peering down at street level.

"Fifty...is going to be tough. That's a lot of people to go missing at once..." Trike now talks more slowly, more controlled; the smile remains plastered on his face despite the gravity of the conversation. "...works better if it's piecemeal. Probably have to do it a few at a time."

"Unfortunately, that is not an option. I need all fifty at once, and I need them before the start of the festival."

"Psh! Yea right, ha-ha. Impossible...probably..." replies Trike through his drug-induced grin, apparently not grasping the nature of the demand.

"Oh Trike... If I know you, you will get it done," Zerris says patronizingly, pointing at the politician, who sits slumped in his chair, completely limp. "You're a smart man! Maybe you can come up with some kind of small-scale catastrophe to explain their disappearance. Just an unfortunate accident. We all must make sacrifices from time to time. And please, understand. This is *not* a request," the Overseer replies. However, Trike merely laughs through his grinning mug.

Changing strategies, Zerris walks over to Trike's dock, and enlarges a hologram displayed on part of the projected screen: a beautiful woman wearing a jet-black dress. She has platinum blonde hair that is almost heavenly, and bioluminescent freckles. "A stunning partner, your Zalina. Does she still not know about your little habit? Or how about our little business arrangement, is she privy to that?"

Trike struggles with his haywire emotions through the manufactured joy brought on by the Lotus-fly flowing through his system. He winces painfully while laughing involuntarily. All the while, still smiling wide. "No... She knows what I tell her. She's...too busy to notice...too happy to. I love her too much to burden her..."

"And what you mean is you couldn't face her with that information. I have to say, I was surprised when an old man like you landed a young beauty like her. Amazing are the youthful...so unassuming, optimistic, naïve. Often easily taken by the limelight provided by a popular figure...willfully ignoring the red flags. It's almost as if they actively try to avoid seeing the darkness of the world that surrounds them." Zerris taps his wrist TAB a few times, then swipes the screen toward Trike's dock, causing a video to pop up. "Shall we watch?" asks Zerris politely as he starts the video.

Holographic horror plays out before the stoned politician as he watches dark, yet identifiable footage of himself fornicating with two young women, both with brunette hair. Clearly high in the video, his naked frame thrusts wildly on camera as he tells the two girls what to do: an absolutely embarrassing spectacle. As he watches his own slimy acts reenacted, the expression in his eyes alternates on a dime back and forth between pure joy and shame as a single tear runs down his cheek. The smile, however, never leaves his face. He lets out an involuntary half-laugh, half-cry and slaps his thigh with a limp hand as he looks away from the screen.

Zerris leans down so his face is level with Gunderson's. "Why, you're a mess, old friend! Shame what these drugs can force us to do at times..." Grabbing Trike's face, he repositions it back toward the screen, forcing the governor to watch as the video plays out. "What do you think Zalina would think of your indiscretions? Or of your junky habits? Or how about the fact that you willingly kidnap people like her and send them off to be used as guinea pigs?"

Trike's face contorts in pain and his teeth grind. His limp body writhes in his chair as he whines back, "You...you told me you were healing them! So many health problems...the hybrids... I wanted to help..."

"Hmph...yes, perhaps at first. Be that as it may, you've known the truth for some time now. I'm sure Zalina will have a hard time believing your line of reasoning; that you were too stupid to realize what was really occurring." Zerris leans in closer and whispers into Trike's ear, "I own you, Gunderson. If I say I want your votes for an initiative, you get me your votes. If I say I want *a thousand* hybrids for testing, you will oblige me. If tell you to cut your cock off and present it to me on a silver platter like a New Orbit's Day present, then you better sharpen your FUCKING BLADE!" Zerris stands up straight and wipes his spittle from the side of Trike's face. Returning to his calm state, he says, "Now...you will reconnect with that Golden Phoenix creep, and you will get me my test subjects."

Trike nods as he smiles like a circus clown, tears streaming down his face. Even the Lotus-fly cannot keep his fear and shame locked away during this ordeal. He reaches for his dock and retrieves his Electrovapor, which he begins smoking from compulsively, filling the vicinity with thick blue smoke. Nothing takes away the pain of his predicament, and the same thought runs through his mind on a loop: *I'm trapped. A pawn...a slave...*

"Oh, and as far as your protesters are concerned, I believe I can help with that. We're having a bit of a similar situation in the Outer Sphere as well. Just leave it to me, old friend. Though it is true I expect much of my loyal team, I do not lack in generosity..." As Zerris finishes, his TAB begins to chime. "Ah, there's our solution now," he remarks lightly. Zerris taps the device, which projects a visual of Dorok in front of him.

"Overseer Aganon!" shouts Dorok enthusiastically.

"General Dorok Ferrous Benson. I'm glad you holo'd, you're just in time. How is the protest situation faring in the Outer Sphere?" asks Zerris directly.

Dorok responds indirectly, his cadence different from that of his usual. "Funny you mention it. My men just picked up on an interesting group of pro-initiative enthusiasts who have planned a celebration march in the vicinity. If my intel is correct, they are poised to march right past the protest in District 341."

"Well, I imagine that situation might get tense..." replies Zerris in similar cadence. "Do we have any Guardsmen nearby to keep the peace should things get out of hand?"

"Fifty strong, and ten G-BOKs, your honor. I'm forecasting a...short day."

"Fantastic news. On a similar note, I have another request of your special teams. We're having a similar protest...*situation* here in Leebrus. It's causing our friend Trike here a great deal of stress..."

"Hm... I see. Please give the governor my regards. Leebrus is a different beast, too many do-gooders and self-involvers," replies Dorok. He thinks for a moment, grunting as his gears turn. After a moment, he replies in the same discretionary tone, "You know, Overseer, it's cold out today. And wouldn't you know it? I think a few of my men forgot their coats. Overseer, what are your thoughts on these men having *no-coats*?"

"I think they should be fine without their coats," remarks Zerris with a smile.

"I'll tell the *no-coats* you said so," replies the General.

"Will that be all, General Benson?" Zerris asks the floating image of Dorok.

"Unfortunately, no, my Overseer. I have some unfortunate news to report..."

"Report it then, Dorok. My time is precious."

"I was called out to the Bando Basin by one of our Vitalerium

Meteor Reconnaissance teams for some 'uncharacteristic' anomalies with a retrieval mission. I'm here now and have just confirmed them for myself."

"What are you doing wasting time with a VMR team? I need you focusing on the mining operation. And what anomalies?"

"Well, Overseer, it appears that someone else has cleaned up the remains of a pretty sizeable hunk of raw element...happened before the VMR got here. And whoever they are, they did a pretty shitty job of retrieval. I thought they were amateurs...at least at first, but..."

"But what?"

"Well, half the land around the base of the mountain is dead, and I mean way outside of the impact zone. It's almost as if they tried to blow it up or something...that's the amateur part. But I had XSEC do a deep dive into Vital Signature Logs from our satellites and...something didn't add up."

"General Dorok, speak frankly, please. I've already told you my time is short," responds Zerris.

"Someone hacked our system is what I'm saying. The thing appears on our scanners above orbit, then as soon as it breaks atmosphere, it disappears. According to XSEC monitoring, they tracked the original trajectory of the meteor and discovered that someone was actively blocking the signature at its impact site for multiple days before lifting the code. But by the time that happened, the signature wasn't there anymore. Which means someone had already come here and snatched it."

Zerris clenches his right fist until his knuckles turn white, stretching the scar on the back of his hand until it hurts. Although Zerris's technological background is limited, he knows just how complex it would be for someone to hack into their XSEC orbital monitoring systems. A knot in his stomach that he hasn't thought about in a while begins to rise once again. He knows exactly who has the capability of accomplishing such a complicated task, and the motive to do so.

Zerris cuts the holo short. "That will be all, General Benson. Thank you for the update. I want a report on the Vital Cascade forecasts by tomorrow."

"Understood, my Overseer," replies Dorok before his image disappears.

Although calm on the outside, Zerris fumes on the inside. It takes everything in him not to remove the glass-blown sculpture from the nearby coffee table and smash it against the wall. *Norvel, you sneaky little cunt, I see you've been busying yourself. Enjoy it while it lasts...* thinks Zerris. Before leaving, he turns to Trike to solidify his orders. "Well, old friend, the no-coats will help solve your protest problem. Give it a few hours, no need to thank me. It should free up some bandwidth so you can focus on the other issue..." He pauses to ensure that Trike can sense the urgency in his voice. "Fifty. You have five days. Are you going to remember this little interaction, or will I be required to send you a reminder?" asks Zerris ominously.

Trike, beginning to even out after the initial rush of Lotusfly, wipes the sweat from his forehead and looks up from his lap for the first time in minutes. In a somber tone, he reluctantly replies, "Fifty..." He then leans back in his chair and stares off into the distance with the mental presence of a zombie. Without saying goodbye, Zerris and his Guardsmen call the elevator and depart.

As the lunch hour passes, the protests continue with renewed strength outside of Leebrus Government Spire. The crowd has grown, and although still relatively small in comparison to the size of the courtyard, it begins to attract more attention. Three more unassuming men filter into the crowd. Two of them wear black hats, and the third wears a hood. They join in the chants that echo off the walls of the metal spire. The men wearing black hats move to opposite sides of the crowd's edge, and discreetly plant devices near the holographic barriers when no one is watching. When activated, the small devices begin emitting subsonic frequencies at irregular intervals. The binaural beats permeate the unwitting ears of the protestors, and the crowd begins to gain steam with each repetition that they complete.

"Nine-one-nine takes yours and mine! Poor until the end of time! Nine-one-nine takes yours and mine! Poor until the end of time!" and "Don't fall for their charity! Nine-nineteen, theft by the CP! Don't fall for their charity! Nine-nineteen, theft by the CP!" they yell.

The new members in the crowd turn to the other protestors and begin to raise the intensity. "Come on everyone! Louder so Trike Gunderson himself can hear us!" shouts one.

"They stole from us!" shouts another. "Let's show them we really mean business, people!"

A few impassioned speeches and thirty minutes later, the crowd has begun shaking the holographic barriers that separate them from the Guardsmen who now grow anxious, feeling more threatened with each minute that passes. One of the CP Guardsmen calls for backup as he notices the crowd growing bolder. Fifteen minutes later, three CP hovercraft arrive and land behind the barriers. Their hatches hiss open, dispatching BARI Drones: Bipedal Autonomous Riot Intelligence, equipped with anti-riot measures. Their black and blue metallic hulls shimmer in the afternoon daylight as they walk in perfect unison toward the growing threat. They take their position in front of the CP Guardsmen and deploy their holoshields. Shock batons buzz with blue arcs of electricity in their cold, steel hands. Their processors evaluate the situation and report back to the Guardsmen who gear up for a fight.

The man in the hood now stands on the barrier and faces the protest, shouting, "ARE WE GONNA LET THEM STEAL FROM US? THE GOOD ONES? THE HARD WORKERS? THE ONES WHO EARN FOR THEM? SO THEY CAN LIVE IN THEIR SILVER SPIRES?" The mob yells back in agreement as the thermometer on the protest reaches a boiling point. "I SAY WE SHOW THEM EXACTLY WHAT HAPPENS WHEN YOU STEAL FROM US!" screams the man.

The CP Guardsmen and the BARI drones stand in formation, dozens of them at the ready with their holoshields deployed and their weapons drawn, ready for whatever trouble may come their way.

One of the men wearing a black hat removes a small bottle from the lining of his jacket and begins to light the rag that plugs up its opening. Once lit, he lobs it over the barrier at the Guardsmen. As the Molotov crashes into one of the multicolored holoshields, one BARI's black armor is engulfed in flames. As this takes place, another man in a similar hat pulls a small baton from his own black jacket and pushes through the barrier with a war cry. A sea of protestors follows him, spilling into the concrete courtyard of the spire with the fire of insurrection burning in their eyes; escalation intentionally interpolated.

An electronic voice blares over megaphone upon their approach. **"YOU ARE ENTERING A RESTRICTED ZONE. PLEASE TURN BACK,"** orders the lead BARI drone as his shock baton connects with the head of a protestor. His body falls limp to the ground immediately. The hordes of protesters descend upon the CP forces, colliding with their holoshields; many receive similar beatings or are shocked into submission. Tear gas grenades fly through the air, producing noxious fumes that disperse portions of the crowd. More protesters fall as blue arcs of pain connect with their bodies. Screams erupt from the courtyard as the CP forces begin to push the crowd back. Shots ring out, and one man falls dead. The onslaught of the angry mob is quelled in mere minutes, transforming it into a fearful, retreating mass of men and women. Ten minutes pass, and the Guardsmen begin to arrest all those who still remain as Medivacs load up the injured. Before the hour is up, the only remnants of the day's events are the holographic barriers that have been put back in place, and the dissipating clouds of smoke that climb up from the empty courtyard. The Leebrus protest annoyance: resolved.

Hours later, in the Leebrus metropolitan area, people go about their lives blissfully unaware of the recent events. A large commscreen emits programming in the center of a shopping mall for passersby. Four distinct horns play a familiar jingle.

"You're watching CPN Nightly News, and I'm your host Jennifer Baine. Tonight's top story: Tempers flare as protests turn violent outside Leebrus Government Spire. Below the city-state's capital building, a small group of anti-patriots who gathered to protest the passing of Initiative 919 displayed their shocking lack of empathy for those that the initiative helps. The enraged insurgent group bit off more than they could chew as they faced off with CP Guardsmen, who stood boldly by to protect our benevolent government officials, and, by proxy, our liberties. According to the lieutenant on-site, it would appear empathy was not the only thing they lacked, for they also showed a glaring dearth of preparation and organization, attacking CP officials with rocks, batons, and rudimentary homemade firebombs. But not to worry, folks. Our brave CP Guardsmen prevailed once again. Our protectors were able to deter the senseless violence and made quick work of the would-be revolt, returning the beautiful city of Leebrus to a state of peace. Let's go to our field reporter, Nathan, who is currently outside the Leebrus Government Spire for more. Nathan, back to you."

CHAPTER 20:

An Obsession Like No Other

Roman's eyes flutter open in Monique's bedroom. His eyelids track like sandpaper over his cornea, breaking through the crust that lines his tear ducts. His shoulder aches as it usually does, but he is too tired to even bother adjusting his position. The apartment is still dark, and Roman's eyes land on a blurry figure across the room, only visible from the waist down. The person stares out the window, shrouded by the soft orange glow from the street outside. Roman's head pounds, undoubtedly from the liquor. After much laboring, and with his head still buried in his pillow, he finally speaks.

"Monique..." he calls. His voice is weak and muffled. It barely projects past the pillow his face is plastered to. *Last night must have been really rough,* he thinks. When Monique does not respond, he tries again. "Monique..." he calls out, barely louder than before. Every syllable is elongated with exhaustion, and his throat stings from sleeping with his mouth open.

Finally, Monique turns around and takes a step toward him. He can barely make out her clothing through his blurry vision, which slowly improves as he blinks. As she approaches, her figure becomes clearer. Her pants are baggy, and she wears rugged terrain boots...his own?

"Hehe... Why are you wearing my clothes?" he asks in his same muffled voice. He tries to move but finds it extremely hard. His fingers twitch first, then a slight movement from his wrist, but no further. Monique now stands beside the bed, looking down on him, but all Roman can see are her knees. "Come back to bed..." Roman whispers, finally clearing the last of the sleep from his eyes.

The final request prompts the baggy pants to kneel beside him, which sends a chill down his spine and forces Roman's eyes wide open.

"That's a tempting offer. Looks pretty comfy from where I'm standing," responds the figure in a bellowing voice, clearly not Monique's. Two blazing red eyes meet with Roman's, their glow projecting from the lifeless tissue enveloping Jerrick's skull. "At least you've been living the high life...and with the former boss's daughter no less? Got to admit... I'm kind of impressed."

"You!" Roman forces out, but his voice is still labored as ever. He tries to jump out of bed, but his limbs are like lead. No matter how hard he fights, he remains frozen. Only his eyes move freely.

"Someone's been shirking their duties. Chasing the party and running around with women while the plan unfolds without you."

Roman's mouth fights to speak, but even his jaw feels like cement. He is barely able to muster the question: "Who are you!?"

"Man, you're like a broken record, you know that? Same shitty, stubborn greeting every time..." responds Jerrick through his teeth. "You know who I am already. But I'm trying to talk to you about the plan, and you keep asking all the wrong questions."

"What plan?" asks Roman.

Jerrick nods toward the far corner of the room and says, "Her plan..."

Roman, still unable to move, follows Jerrick's cue with his eyes. What he sees sends another jolt of terror down his spine. Fear grips him like a vise, and he feels his skin tighten as every hair on his body stands on end. Out of the corner of his eye, he is able to make out a shadow. As he attempts to focus on his peripheral vision, the shadow morphs into a black silhouette floating at the room's edge. Its proportions disturbing... inhuman. As if shocked by an electrical current, the visage strikes pure terror into Roman. He sweats profusely beneath the sheets of the bed where he lies imprisoned in his own body, his heart beating out of his chest. Black tendrils extend from its figure and caress the boundaries of the room, though whether they are appendages or waves of pure dark energy, he is unable to distinguish. As the form undulates by the wall just out of direct eye contact, Roman fights to regain control of his limbs...control of anything.

"Who is she?" Roman moans.

"She is the one who decides," responds Jerrick bluntly.

"Decides what?" asks Roman.

"Who survives to fight," replies Jerrick.

Both the bluntness of his response and the cryptic nature of his answers give Roman another wave of goosebumps. He cannot take his eyes off the black silhouette that suspends itself in midair across the room from him. Defense against the unexplainable sensation that envelops him proves futile.

"Stop trying to stave it off, you'll only succumb to it. Accept it and you will succeed!" shouts Jerrick just inches away from Roman's face.

Roman begins to recognize a different side of Jerrick's tone as commands are shouted in his face. *Is he helping me?* thinks Roman. Rather than continue to attempt escape, he gives into his circumstances and searches frantically for the right questions despite his heightened sense of fear.

"Survive what?" he finally asks.

Jerrick takes his time answering. He looks to the nightmarish presence as if it holds the answers. His crimson eyes return to Roman. The exposed bit of muscle in his jaw clenches as he responds bluntly, "The ultimate trial."

"What ultimate trial?" asks Roman, still frozen in bed.

"In time, you will come to know. For now, you need to focus on the task at hand. Or else this will become your fate, and the fate of everyone..." Jerrick shifts to the side and points, revealing the window behind him and the source of the orange glow. Roman's eyes are filled with the flickering light of a fire that engulfs entire sectors of the Outer Sphere. The conflagration extends as far as his watering eyes can see. As he falls into a trance by the sight, his ears begin to define the ambient noise that sneaks past the walls of the apartment. The dull hum of voices speaking in an unrecognizable language grows in his ears until they begin to ring. It is hard to tell, but they seem to be emanating from the shadow being.

Beads of cold sweat stream down Roman's forehead, stinging his eyes. The insanity that unfolds before him becomes too much to bear, and he now fights with every ounce of his willpower to move. His muscles tense but fail to budge more than an inch or two. The veins in his neck bulge as if he's being choked. Slowly, his face lifts from the pillow. He spits as he forces the words from his locked jaw.

"WHY...ME!?"

Jerrick chuckles, then nods his head approvingly. "That's it. Now you're asking the right questions, Klip."

"WHAT DO...I DO, JERRICK!?" he shouts over the voices that fill his ears.

Jerrick nods as if to approve of Roman's effort. Rising to his feet, he takes a step closer to Roman, blocking the orange light from view and casting a dark shadow over him. The light shudders from the room, replaced by a ghastly darkness; only two gleaming red eyes shine through. He extends his hand toward Roman's face. "Get off your ass and follow the path, Klip." The words roll off Jerrick's tongue with almost no emotion. As he finishes, the sound of voices speaking in foreign, almost alien tongues rises to an intolerable decibel; one yelling over the other as if shouted directly into his ears. The dusty, dead tissue of Jerrick's hand covers Roman's eyes...all goes black, and...

The crystal shards in his skin ignite. A blue aura explodes outward from Roman's body as he sits up in bed, launching the covers across the room. The sweat-soaked comforter lands on the floor with a wet SLAP, and the aura dissipates. Roman sits naked on the silky black sheets of Monique's bed, panting as he recovers from the shockingly vivid dream. Yet another in the three-day streak of night terrors. The afternoon sun shines through the glass edifice of Monique's apartment, illuminating the room and caressing Roman's skin. The smell of fresh coffee fills the air, providing a placid, welcoming atmosphere to quell his heavily beating heart. Across the small, yet organized space, Monique stands in her underwear and a long t-shirt with two black mugs. She stares at the wet sheets on the floor next to her in the kitchen, then glances back at Roman with a look of concern.

"Another nightmare?" she asks.

A heavy sigh follows from Roman, who is still processing his surroundings. "Yea...this one was...more intense. Felt like sleep paralysis."

"I heard you talking. You mentioned a Jerrick? Something about a plan?"

"Yea...the old friend of mine who died... It's a long story. I'll fill you in sometime." Roman shakes his head as if to try and jostle the image of Jerrick from his mind. It only exacerbates his headache.

With a sympathetic frown, Monique replies, "I was going to wake you up...but you sort of did that yourself..."

Roman only grunts in response, rubbing his eyes with his fists and wiping the sweat off himself. Monique gazes upon him inquisitively, prompting Roman to ask, "Well, out with it then; what do you want to know?"

"How does it feel? Does it hurt? You know, when you...go all blue mode?" she asks sincerely.

Roman thinks for a moment, trying to figure out how to put into words that which is still so foreign to him. He finally responds, "No. I mean, not really...it stings a little bit at first, like I can feel the crystals in my skin. It's kind of invigorating actually...at least at first. But doing it a lot becomes tiring...it takes a lot out of me. Does that make any sense?"

"I guess...yea." Monique nods, trying to empathize with him. She uses a coffee mug to point at the bedspread on the floor. "You know one of these days you're gonna launch me across the room. Might have to start making you sleep on the couch..." Her voice is sweet and playful. The sunlight dances on her features as she brings Roman a liquid dose of caffeine. Despite her lack of clothing, every detail of her appearance is perfectly in place. She has clearly been up for a while.

Just the sight of Monique is enough to bring Roman's blood pressure down. He quickly falls into the playful vibe that she has spun. In a gravelly, tired voice, Roman responds, "We could try, but I doubt that would last very long. You're insatiable." He leans back on his hands and smirks.

Monique hands him one of the mugs and crawls into bed, straddling Roman with a devilish smile. As Roman takes a careful sip of his deliciously bitter black water, Monique rebuts with a devilish smile, "Maybe someone should do a better job at satiating..."

Roman nearly spits out the hot liquid. "Liar!" he says, grinning and squinting in disbelief. "You wouldn't look this well-rested if I wasn't doing my part," he jokes.

Monique chuckles and smiles sweetly. Her eyes gaze into his as she leans in, whispering, "Don't get cocky now..." before she teasingly bites Roman's bottom lip. She slides over to his side and rests her head on his shoulder as she sips from her own cup.

Monique's fingers caress Roman's skin until she reaches

his right shoulder. She pokes and prods the large raised scar that covers his shoulder blade and curls around his deltoid. "This must have been one hell of a scratch. How'd you get this scar?"

"Same day Jerrick died...got shot with a CP vitalerium rifle, just like he did. Only he wasn't so lucky... The charge only grazed me, but it still tore through my armor and nearly killed me. Then they left me for dead out in the Korr Desert." Roman sighs as the memory returns, but the anger that usually festers inside him from reliving the traumatic event seems calmed by Monique's touch.

"Holy shit... How did you survive?" she asks, concerned.

"Stroke of luck. I was found by a Seer of the Sacred Order. Crazy old man took me back to his church and performed surgery on me. Saved my life."

"Uh, wait...how? What was a Seer doing in the Korr Desert, of all places? And surgery? By a Seer!?" she asks in disbelief. To her credit, the scenario described seems a highly unlikely one, if not impossible.

"Hehe, yea... Emannuel isn't your average, run-of-the-mill holy man. Crazy bastard was out in the desert doing some kind of holy pilgrimage for 'clarity,' as he described it... Anyway, the CP torched my hoverbike before they left. Must have put out a hell of a smoke trail after the grav-resonator blew, because it got his attention as he was passing. When he came to investigate that, I wasn't too far away from the wreck. Or so I've been told..."

"But...surgery?" she exclaims.

"Guess he was a surgeon before he became a Seer. Never really asked him. He always seemed reluctant to talk about his past. But he kept a bunch of tools in his church from his doctor days. Took care of me 'til I was on my feet again."

Monique kisses the thick, raised scar on his shoulder. "Well, I'm glad he found you. I'd like to meet the man who saved my *lover* from death's grasp," she says with dramatic inflection as she brings her lips to Roman's cheek.

"Trust me, you wouldn't. I'm grateful to the man and everything, but save yourself the hassle..." Roman's commscreen chimes on the coffee table across the room, but he ignores it as he casually imbibes the much-needed caffeine. Each sip reinvigorates him slightly. His tired eyes scan Monique up and down. Her short red hair cascades down his shoulder, and her soft, tan skin presses against his despite his unbathed condition. Her presence provides a warmth not simply from her physical body. Roman's eyes close as the weight of the world seems to lift itself from his shoulders. He would stay here for an eternity if he could. And with the way things have been going, he just might. However, another chime from his commscreen echoes through the high-rise apartment and brings the moment to a stark end.

"Aren't you going to get that?" asks Monique.

"Not until I piece together whatever happened last night." Roman slides backward to lean against the cold metal headboard, and Monique shifts backward along with him. Neither of them can get enough of each other's touch. Massaging his temples to ease the headache, Roman tries to recollect the events of the previous night. "Could use a little input if you've got it..." he says to Monique.

"We hit Bastion and Xanadu again last night, but that was after stopping by Portal. Maybe start there, Mr. Show-off?"

"Portal...that's right," responds Roman with a tilted head. "Hey, what do you mean show-off?"

Raising an eyebrow, she replies, "C'mon. Are you serious?"

Roman takes another sip of his coffee as he dives into the fragments he is able to salvage from the night. All he can remember is...

...

......

Roman tilts his head backward as he throws back a shot of green Sham.

"Rome, I want you to meet two friends of mine, Lonny and Tram," replies Monique as she approaches him at the blue-lit, circular bar of Portal.

"What's up, cowboy?" Lonny greets him with a jocular grin and a head-nod. She is a small girl with jet-black hair in a high ponytail hairstyle. She wears an outfit that resembles suspenders and covers just about as much of her as suspenders alone would.

Tram introduces himself next. He wears sunglasses inside, and his reflective gold sport coat is an interesting juxtaposition to his baggy pants and high-end sneakers. A Wibetani patch is etched into his shirt. "Sup, freelancer." They each extend a fist to Roman.

"Hey," replies Roman, who finds little else to say. He awkwardly fist-bumps the two newcomers, then asks, "So...how do you two know Monique?"

Tram is the first to jump in. "Ah, man! Long time we been knowin' Monique now. Probably since..."

...

......

"A REEBISH!? So the fuck what!?" yells Roman, sloshing his beer about as he stands by a blue-lit bar. With an arm around Monique, he yells back at another large individual. Although he wears the clothes of a roughneck, he's too clean-cut to be the real thing. His boots are too shiny to have ever seen the world past the walls, and his eyes say the rest: A blade that's been over-sharpened and underused. "You wanna compare scar stories, and you follow up my story with a measly Reebish? A Reebish can't hold a candle to a Vorkrill. Might as well be a fucking Dagling you're bragging about killing."

The man snarls and retorts, "Yea, yea, we heard about your trophy Vorkrill already. It's not a competition, we were just sharing stories. Besides, it was a PACK of Reebish. Not just one."

"No, you're right. It ISN'T a competition, because one

Vorkrill could easily take on your pack of Reebish, then the next pack of Reebish it comes across, and still have time to devour you and a Korr Ankonyl without breaking a sweat!" yells Roman, half jesting, half flexing. With a chuckle, Monique rolls her eyes while Lonny and Tram attempt to hide their laughter at the stranger's expense.

The man becomes aggravated by the response. "OH, LIKE A VORKRILL COULD TAKE ON A KORR ANKONYL! Do you know how many pounds of pressure a Korr Ankonyl's jaw can create? He'd bite right through the chitin armor and tear a hole in him. Plus, they are highly intelligent! It would have set a trap for the Vorkrill!"

"Says the armchair survivalist! I bet you've never even..."

...

......

"Deflected a knife? With a barrier? What the hell is this guy even talking about?" laughs a thuggish club-goer covered in garish jewelry and tattoos. He shouts over the music from his VIP couch by the dance floor. A close group of his friends laugh along as they're bathed in the glow of holograms that dance above the crowd. Only a table filled with liquor and a short holographic barrier stands between him and Roman's group, which has seemingly grown larger since he last checked.

"Yea, that's right, he did," Monique jumps in, playing along.

"You heard me *Hiccup*...right. I'll tell you what..." Roman pulls out his silver blade and tosses the closed knife onto the lap of the VIP. "I'll do it again too. You a betting man?"

The man picks up the knife and inspects it. The blade ejects while in his hand, and the speed with which it reveals itself actually startles him.

"Here's the bet: If I can do it again, you have to let us drink off your table."

The thug smirks, then shouts over the music, "Hey everyone!"

...

......

"DO IT AGAIN! DO IT AGAIN! DO IT AGAIN!" shouts an enormous crowd around the VIP table, stoked on by Lonny and Tram. Even the VIP, who lost his bet and now watches as Roman drinks directly from his bottle of vodka, joins in the chant.

Monique nudges Roman, shouting, "Come on, freelancer! You gonna give the people what they want and keep this party going? Or are you going to let everyone down?" Her lips curl into a smirk as she finishes her sentence.

Roman stops drinking and smiles as he passes the bottle back to the jewelry-clad man. "How could I disappoint my people?" he says before standing up on the couch and closing his eyes with intense focus. Although a hush falls over the crowd, heavy music still blares in the club. After a few seconds, a flash of blue light covers the crowd as Roman manifests the vitalerium barrier around him. The crowd cheers in response as the blue light blinks until it goes away.

"Alright, I'm done! I don't have any left in me!" he shouts, crossing his arms to show that he's about finished with his party trick for the night. The crowd's cheers eventually transition to normal chatter as everyone jumps to the beat of the song again.

...

......

"Hey! Hey... I just wanna say I...ugh...thank you for... letting me stay with you. It's been a while since I've lived anywhere what wasn't a rusted-out dump," he says, pulling Monique in close for a kiss.

"Hehe, I think someone's a little drunk!" whispers Monique into Roman's ear. Though she makes fun, she sways from intoxication herself. The thud of bass echoes down the hallway they stand in; their faces illuminated in ambient multicolored light.

"Now let's go back in there and dance, my Grind-goon!"

"No, no, wait!" he says with a laugh, grabbing her by the waist and pulling her back toward him. His tone changes this time, as if to say this is serious. "You...uh... It's just... I haven't felt this good in a long time. Maybe ever actually." Roman's face swells with warmth as he tries to talk through the booze. "I think I..." Roman starts.

Monique places a finger to his lips and leans in close. Her lips brush against his cheek as her sweet voice caresses his ear. "Shhhh. I know where you're going, and it's too soon." She pulls back and her eyes meet his. Like mirrors, they reflect the incandescent light beaming from the club. "But... I'm happy too." Her smile is like heroin to Roman. She feigns a stern look, and shouts like a drill sergeant, "Now get back on the dance floor, Klipper! That's an order!"

Roman does not move from his spot, perched against the wall of the tunnel. "I'm not a Klipper anymore. You can't tell me what to do." His cocky tone prompts Monique to approach again.

"Then I'll just have to convince you," says Monique, pressing against him and beginning to undo Roman's belt.

"Whoa... Uh...here?" says Roman nervously.

"Good a place as any..." replies Monique as she continues to undo his pants. Then in one fell swoop, she removes the belt from its loops and drops Roman's pants to his ankles, exposing his underwear. She then jumps backward with his belt and laughs. Roman stands there like a fool with his pants around his ankles as two women walk by giggling. Roman gives them a goofy wave, as if unfazed.

"Oh, so this was your plan all along?" he says to Monique, as he wobbles slightly from the liquor.

She laughs hysterically as she taunts Roman with his own belt, which dangles out in front of her. "Yup. I've been playing you since the very beginning."

"Well *Hiccup* I'm sorry to inform you, but your plan

has backfired. FOR THIS IS MY MOST POWERFUL FORM!" he shouts, extending his arms forward and affecting a sort of Frankenstein walk toward Monique. She lets out a shriek of joyous laughter as Roman chases her ineffectively back toward the dance floor with his pants down.

"NOW I'VE GOT..."

...

......

"WOOOT!" shouts the crowd as Roman stands on the DJ table, slugging liquor straight from the bottle. The DJ swats at Roman's feet, and tugs at his pants, but nothing gets his attention. He can see a few large men pushing through the crowd, but he can't tell what they...

...

......

Roman punches a person whose face he cannot make out. People surround him. He cannot tell who it is, or why he assails him, but...

...

......

"What're you mad about, even!?" Roman shouts in slurred words after Monique as he stumbles after her on street level.

"Don't even try!" she says, pushing through the crowd. Her speech is just as slurred as Roman's.

"C'mon! I just meant..."

...

......

"I love you..." she says as she tears off her top, then jumps up and wraps her legs around Roman. The force of her pounce causes *them to stumble backward into the nightstand and send the decorative crystal statue crashing to the floor. Then...*

...

......

Roman snaps back to reality and leans to his left, looking over Monique's head to view her side of the bed. Pieces of the crystal statue still lay broken next to her nightstand against the wall. He leans back against the headboard and smiles. "Hmph..." he grunts. "Oh, I remember now. I remember that you said you love me," he says with a goofy face.

Monique's head snaps up with surprise, and she blushes. "Did not!" she retorts, unable to cover her embarrassment well.

"Oh yes you did. And you meant it too!" he says as he playfully wrestles her to the other side of the bed. "Admit it!" he shouts, tickling Monique into submission.

"NEVER!" she shouts as she fights back. She is surprisingly strong for her size, but Roman eventually gains the upper hand and she succumbs to laughter. Another continuous chime from Roman's commscreen interrupts them and brings their play to a screeching halt.

"Answer him please? He's your friend, isn't he?" Monique pleads with Roman.

Roman releases his hold on her and pushes himself from the comfort of Monique's bed. He drags himself across the room to find his device. "He's not my friend, he's work. And he should be helping me figure out this blue crystal scenario, except he's busy helping your father." He picks up the device which reads "Unknown" across its screen. "Ugh..."

"Hm...helping you. Sounds like a friend to me. Also, you didn't seem to be crying about your health while you were showing off your crystally talents for everyone last night..."

"Yea...probably should hold off on that for a while now that you mention it." Roman taps on the screen, then releases the device, which hovers in the air, following him around as he collects his clothes. The image of Norvel's face fills the screen.

"Roman? Is that you? WHERE THE HELL HAVE YOU BEEN!? You said you would get in touch with me after the weekend. It's been almost a whole week! What the hell, man!"

"Hey now relax, it's too early to be yelling like that..." Roman replies.

"It's three in the afternoon, Roman!"

"Shit, is it?" he says, looking back at Monique. She simply rolls her eyes in response, then hops off the bed and walks into the next room. "Oh..." replies Roman, slightly embarrassed. "Well, you've got me now. What's up, Norvel?"

"What's up is you basically handed me off as slave labor to Modus without any sort of help negotiating a 'start-stop' date, and then you disappear off the face of the planet for a week! What is wrong with you!?"

"Alright, alright, godsdamnit, man. I'm sorry, alright? Cut me some slack. I've had some pretty life-changing shit occur in the last week or so. I'm...working through it," Roman says.

"Yea? Tell me, how's that going? Getting plenty of deep philosophical revelations from all those liters of Sham!? ARE YOU FUCKING KIDDING ME!? PRACTICALLY EVERYONE IN KAIRUS KNOWS YOU'VE BEEN ON A BENDER THROUGH THE ENTIRE CLUB DISTRICT!" Norvel's frustration reaches a fever pitch, and his voice cracks as he paces in front of a dock at an undisclosed location.

"Um..." just then a fragment of his memory returns to him, and Roman remembers being tackled off the stage by a bouncer wearing a black and gold suit, "...it's certainly taken me to some dark places, I'll grant you that... Wait, did you say *everyone* knows?"

"I... Ugh... Forget it, Roman. Just forget it. The point is, I need your help now! Modus has been asking me to craft some really strange things for him. Please, just get me out of this sorry excuse for a Wibetani lab. I can't be in the Spheres for much longer. It's a dangerous place for me...and for you too in case you've forgotten!"

"Alright, alright. Just, let me clear my head and I'll think of something," Roman finally concedes as he zips up his pants and begins the hunt for his other boot, which eludes him once again.

"And after this shit you put me through, you are DEFINITELY helping me get Mirene out of Sanctum Tower..." As Norvel speaks, Roman's commscreen begins chiming again as another comm comes through, this time from "MM."

"Eh, hold on there, buddy. I've got another comm. We'll talk about this later..." replies Roman as he hangs up on Norvel mid-sentence and answers Modus, opting to keep the video off this time.

"Modus, how can I help you?" Roman says in a strangely positive tone that even he regrets immediately.

"Hiding for any particular reason?" comes Modus's suspicious voice through the device. "Afraid to show your face? Or perhaps just your surroundings?"

"Nope, just..." Roman pauses as Monique walks around the corner, shirtless this time, "...just juggling a few things right now, trying my best to multitask. Uh... What is it you need?"

"Lose that buddy-buddy tone when you're talking to me. I need you to get down to the Earth Mode. I've got a *high-priority* job for you. I imagine romping around in the Outer Sphere must be getting expensive for a Grind-pup like yourself. Especially considering you don't have a home inside the walls. Those *hotels* must be getting...*expensive*."

Although looping in Roman on yet another high-priority job is suspicious, especially given the result of his recent gig, he realizes that he's stuck like a mouse in a trap. He has no choice but to accept the offer. He has no other friends in the Outer Sphere, and he knows that Modus has eyes everywhere. *I just hope he hasn't figured out the full story, yet,* he thinks. "You know, the timing couldn't be better... I actually could use a payday."

"Good. I'll expect you here within the hour."

"Ok. I'm on my way," replies Roman, reaching up to try and end the comm. But before he can, Modus's voice continues.

"Oh, and Monique, baby?" calls Modus in a fatherly tone. Roman's stomach sinks as he realizes the secret is out. It sinks even further again when Monique responds.

"Yea, Dad?"

"Why don't you come with Roman? I want you involved on this HP. It's about time you get some schooling on how an appropriate job is run. Make me proud and you'll get your Runner privileges back."

"Affirmative. I'll be there," she says before turning around and disappearing into her wardrobe. Roman's face reads a look of worried confusion.

"See you soon, *Rome...*" is the last thing he hears before the comm abruptly ends.

Roman grabs the device out of the air and tosses it behind his head onto the bed. He grunts, then looks to his right to see Monique is already suited up in black and red leather. The Wibetani helmet-and-daggers signet is stitched skillfully on the back. "Are you trying to get your father to have me killed?" Roman says, shooting her a disappointed look.

"He was bound to find out at some point. By the sound of it, he's already known for a few days and had some time to cool off. He's the leader of the Wibetani. Did you think information about his daughter wouldn't get back to him?"

Roman only grunts in response, placing his hands on his hips and looking out the window disapprovingly.

Monique reassures him. "He'll be fine, and you'll be fine. He likes you, remember? At least somewhere deep down in that black heart of his. It's weird that you worry so much about what he thinks. You certainly don't do that with anyone else."

Roman faces Monique again and sighs. "Fine. You're right,

I'll be good. We'll see about him, though. You're not the only one who knows how he can be."

She picks up his missing boot from behind the couch and tosses it to him, followed by his jacket. "C'mon. Let's go get my privileges back."

The two descend to the ground level of Monique's building. The elevator doors open to reveal a lobby filled with vagrants. Some seeking shelter, some simply mumbling to themselves. They have to step over people just to get to the front door. Though Monique's apartment is not in a rough part of town, this type of scene is commonplace for any building like hers in the Outer Sphere. Only in the Inner Sphere would you find respite from sights such as these.

Rooster is parked out front near a number of other hoverbikes. A glossy sheet hangs from the windshield, attached by two magnetic binders: a parking ticket. He produces his blade and removes a small panel from the first magnetic binder, then begins cutting through its inner workings. Roman makes quick work of the annoyance. Prying the magnets from the windshield, he tosses the device and its attached ticket it into the nearby gutter. Roman's stomach growls, which halts him from mounting the bike with Monique. *If I don't eat something, my stomach is going to eat itself.* Scanning his surroundings, he spies a food stand across the street with a hologram that reads "BAO!" *Perfect,* he thinks to himself.

"I'm gonna grab a meat bun. You want one?" he says.

"Sure. Just not the Dagling ones. The critter meat never sits well with me at that spot."

Roman walks across the street and waits as a stout man in an oversized business suit orders five bao buns from the electronic vendor, then waddles away with his bounty. Roman, after ordering a few for Monique and himself, swipes the screen of his TAB device toward the ledger to pay.

"Two hundred universal credits, accepted. Thank you! Have a BAO-tiful day!" responds the automated vendor.

After the transaction, the statement that appears over his TAB displays a shockingly low balance. With all the stress he feels about his upcoming interaction with Modus, he pushes the thought of his waning funds to the back of his mind and takes his bao buns.

Before getting to the sidewalk, a blur of blue and white in his periphery causes him to abruptly stop. His path is cut off by a group of Seers from the Church of the Sacred Order of Equilibrium. Roman actually has to step back to avoid being struck by the first man in the procession. They walk with their shaved heads facing down, closely huddled together. Two by two they trudge in their pearly white robes with fluorescent blue lines woven throughout, looking almost like the etchings on a microchip. On each set of robes, the blue lines conjoin on the four-pointed pendulum sigil displayed prominently on their chests. Each pendulum is fitted with a bright blue, diamond-shaped crystal at its center.

Roman does not apologize for almost bumping into them, and they refrain from acknowledging him, or anyone else on the street for that matter. He simply watches as they pass, slightly perturbed by the solemn vibration that seems to follow them. The hunger pains in his stomach disappear as his attention is redirected. The crowd ahead parts to allow the monk-like servants of the Order to pass. Roman looks to the right and watches them as they walk down the street. Readjusting the flesh-colored faceplate that hides the vitalerium in his skin from the world, he starts back toward Monique. With his eyes still focused on the robes to his right, he only takes one step before bumping directly into someone on his left and dropping the bao buns to the ground.

"Oh, come on! Watch—" He stops midsentence as he comes face to face with two more men in white and blue robes. A tall young man with a shaved head guides another, much older cleric of the church. The old man's eyes are clouded with opaque gray cataracts, making his irises barely visible. The tall man shoots Roman a dirty look, but before he can deliver his scathing comments, the old man hushes him. His face, wrinkled with age, holds the weight of constant pain. Nevertheless, in a hoarse voice that expels more air than sound, he speaks calmly to his counterpart.

"Be at ease with the tangible environment, brother. Every interaction in the universe occurs in perfect harmony with itself. It only requires that we contemplate our reflection in it all." He pats the arm of the cleric who guides him delicately. But when he turns his unseeing gaze toward Roman, his expression changes dramatically. The wrinkles of time that laden his face relax as if his pain seems to suddenly alleviate itself. His voice shakes with excitement as he proclaims, "Now this, a rare gift. Bestowed by itself unto itself." A small chuckle from the old man is followed by a rattling cough. The stark change in demeanor takes Roman by surprise and puts a knot in his stomach. Despite the awkward feeling filling the space between them, Roman finds he cannot seem to escape the situation.

"Like the swing of the great pendulum that has reached its apex, the universe ultimately delivers itself from chaos. And we, the consciousness of carbon and universal experience, are part of the plan. Equilibrium incarnate shall apply the force that initiates the pendulum's reciprocal motion." The old man extends a feeble hand up toward Roman's face. Like some sort of mystical force, the intense resolve in the cleric's beliefs seems to cement Roman to the cracked sidewalk where he stands. The Seer's eerily joyous smile causes Roman to enter a state of unnatural focus as a tingle travels the length of his spinal cord.

As the shaking hand of the elder inches closer to Roman's face, he whispers, "The point at which all forces converge... The crux of the swinging pendulum." As he finishes, the cracked, callused tips of his fingers brush against Roman's faceplate.

The contact is just enough to snap Roman out of his trance,

and he pulls his head back. His face contorts into a mash of emotions. Between the creepy smile still plastered on the old man's face and the ominous nature of his strange message, he cannot get out of the situation fast enough. Shoving his empty hands into the pockets of his black coat, he steps over his breakfast, which lies strewn about the street, and power walks toward Monique.

She sits on the back of Rooster and checks the messages on her TAB, blissfully unaware of the interaction that has just occurred behind her. When she notices Roman arrive and abruptly mount the bike without any food, she asks, "No bao?"

Without stopping, he quickly replies, "They only had Dagling left," as he fires up the gravity resonator on his bike, which emits its usual purple glow. Monique has to tightly grasp his jacket to avoid falling as Roman takes off in a hurry.

After a few short minutes, the two arrive at Earth Mode. This time, Roman takes his bike down the narrow alley to the right and rounds the corner to access the rear entrance. He parks his vehicle next to a number of other bikes, all clad in Wibetani sigils and colors. A few recruits sit on the staircase by the door, smoking Electrovapors and laughing. Drezz stands before them, telling a story, but stops when he sees the two arrive. With a disgruntled look, he turns to deliver a less than polite Wibetani greeting.

"Well, well! Look at the two lovebirds here. Looks like daddy's girl is back to work. Must have been good behavior." He snickers after mocking them, though this time the others refrain from joining in. They watch the exchange unfold carefully.

Monique approaches and says, "Mhm, that's right, Drezz. And with a high-priority job no less."

Drezz's look of confusion says it all: he was not looped in. "An HP? Fuck off. I didn't hear anything about an HP gig."

"Maybe he thought you were busy...or didn't feel you were up to it," replies Roman nonchalantly, knowing full well what the reaction would be. He smirks at the seated recruits as he and Monique scale the steps to enter the club. Drezz fumes, and as the heavy door opens, he runs up the steps and enters with them.

"What's the matter, Drezzy? Feeling left out?" asks Monique, who shoots a coy look at Roman.

Huffing and puffing, Drezz replies, "I just...as Runner Right Hand, I should be looped in on all jobs, especially HPs. I'll join you. I have to give boss-man some news anyway."

The club is empty this time of day, and the only people inhabiting the space are preparing for the night to come. Some of them recruits, some of them just club employees. The three board the floating platform and ride it up to Modus's office: the giant spinning globe suspended above the club. The doors hiss open and Roman, Monique, and Drezz enter. They find Modus and Idrys sitting across from each other. Modus discusses something serious with him but breaks to welcome the others.

"We'll finish this later, Idrys," he says before turning to the door. "Ah, Monique and Roman. I'll be honest, you got here faster than I anticipated. And... Drezz. What can I do for you, Right Hand?"

Drezz steps in front of the others and places his hands on his hips as he states, "Uh... Yea. I heard there was a high-priority job. Just wanted to..." he pauses when he sees the blank stare on Modus's face, noticeable even behind his dark sunglasses, "...just wanted to get briefed. See if I could offer any help in strategizing. Maybe even join if it's—"

"No," replies Modus bluntly. "I need you on something else. You'll be briefed after the fact with Idrys." His words are followed by a cold silence that makes Drezz squirm where he stands. When he does not follow Idrys out the door, Modus ends with, "That'll be all, Drezz."

After an awkward moment of silence, Drezz reluctantly replies, "Alright then...affirmative," and promptly exits, meeting Idrys on the platform outside. A drop of water would have sizzled to steam if it were to land on Drezz's skin. Monique hides her feelings of joy behind a façade of seriousness.

"That man could give a headache a headache..." mutters Modus under his breath as he leans back on his couch. He looks tense today, as if exasperated, which is uncharacteristic of the man. "Come in and sit. I've got a unique one for you this time, and it involves an old friend of yours, Monique. Which is why I need you both, at least for the first part."

"I'm just glad you came to your senses about—" Monique is cut off before she can finish her sentence.

"Before your confidence spills over into cockiness, know that you're not out of the woods yet. I'm still disappointed about the previous mishap, and you've yet to prove yourself. So just sit there and listen."

Monique crosses her arms and sits in silent, reluctant obedience. Roman merely leans back in his seat, trying his best to stay out of the family quarrel.

Modus stands and begins pacing as he collects himself. "Right. I need you both to keep this one quiet. I'm working some things out internally... Don't want jealousy to start interfering with the results of my teams, especially regarding the magnitude of the assignment. So, not a word from either of you. Do you understand?" asks Modus with concern. After exchanging glances, both Roman and Monique nod in acceptance of Modus's terms.

"Good. Now this job is a little different than the run-of-the-mill cash grab. We've got a chance to do some good here for someone close to the Wibetani. Monique, I'm sure you remember your old friend Asa-Valeriya... She'll be back in town for this music extravaganza thing taking place in Leebrus. Apparently, she's co-headliner this year."

A new side of Monique reveals itself as she becomes visibly excited to the point of letting out a short high-pitched scream, which she immediately reins in and apologizes for. Roman raises an eyebrow, surprised by the note that escapes her vocal cords.

Modus flashes a stoic look at the pair to reaffirm the seriousness of the meeting, then continues. "Valeriya filled me in on some very troubling details over holo. She tells me that a number of hybrid people have gone missing lately in Leebrus. According to her, this phenomenon has gone under-reported, and under-investigated by the CP. Now usually I take what your childhood friend has to say with a grain of salt, given her anarchist streak. But apparently her cousin, another hybrid girl and a Leebrus native, is among the missing. She has requested our help in finding her. Here are two tickets to the show." He tosses two clear cards on the table. Upon inspection, holographic words spin inside them, reading, "Beat Galacticus," and the letters "VIP" spin in gold underneath. "These were delivered here this morning by two of her couriers, along with partial payment. You'll be expected to meet with her backstage tonight after her performance." Modus then takes two fingers and swipes them across his TAB toward Roman.

Roman's wrist chimes, and the holographic numbers "+Ж100,000" spin in red above his own TAB. "Hm... Not bad," grunts Roman.

"That's just a taste for the consultation. Should you find her cousin, she'll pay her second installment, and you'll get your full cut: another nine hundred K UCs. More than that, we get to help one of our own without involving the Coalition."

Another big payday; not quite the Ж2.2 million he was expecting from the last mission gone wrong, but enough to grab his interest. Roman's ledger is certainly in need of a credit infusion. This time, however, he does not let the number get to his head. A lot can go wrong during these missions. He had not collected a single credit from his last so-called "big break" mission, and his energy is better utilized to maintain his focus. He simply sits back and listens to the details.

Monique is so excited that her feet tap. She tries to maintain her serious attitude, but her smile betrays her, peeking through at the corners of her lips. Roman asks her in disbelief,

"You know Valeriya? Like *the* Valeriya? Intergalactic popstar Valeriya?"

"We were friends when we were little. Then her singing took off and she started touring off-planet. Fucking Primes! It's been so long—I'm so EXCITED!" Her eyes gleam as she talks about it.

"Alright then. This should be interesting…" replies Roman.

"Didn't think you'd be one for keeping tabs on pop culture, Roman," says Modus plainly.

"I don't live in a cave. I mean it's not like I'm buying merch and waving signs, but I still hear things," replies Roman.

"Then hear this. The shit that Mz. Valeriya filled me in on? Her suspicions? I did some digging of my own before accepting her proposition. She's right, there's a lot of hybrids missing out there in Leebrus. Based on my own intel and the details provided by little miss pop star, I have reason to believe this thing runs deep. I've got my own thoughts as to who's involved, but do your own investigating. I don't wanna bias your search. But, whoever it is, they have an immense amount of resources. So, you two better tread real fuckin' light. It also means I only want you there for negotiation and strategy, Monique."

"WHAT? What is the point of involving me if I won't have any part in the retrieval?"

Slamming a fist on his desk, Modus yells, "Because I said so! Godsdamnit you are just like your mother!" This time Modus is the one who has to rein himself in. He pauses for a moment, softens his tone, and says, "Are you still oblivious to the reasons why I run things the way I do? It's so we act as a unit! When you learn to stop questioning my authority and start taking orders like your position requires, my faith will be reinstated. Now pipe down or I'll pull your involvement entirely and you can stay at Klipper rank!"

Monique, who now stands at her father's level, starts to speak but catches herself. She itches to say something smart but realizes nothing she says will provide the outcome she wants. And so, reluctantly, she sits back in her seat. "Yes, General Magni," she finally says.

Modus, who was ready to receive more lip service, actually has to recollect himself at the sight of his adopted daughter acting with respect toward him. "Uh... You'll report to me after you've met Valeriya and have had time to strategize. I'll approve and we'll provide support as necessary. Make sure you make it to the showcase before midnight. I want you two to be early and have your shit together. No mistakes."

"Understood," replies Monique in a sort of depressed, robotic tone.

"Dismissed," says Modus as he swivels away from them in his suspended chair.

"Oh, and one more thing. Valeriya is a control freak. I guess fame will do that to a person...but she's got the credits, so do what you can to keep her happy. Make her *feel* like she's running the show, just don't be stupid on her account."

Roman and Monique get up to leave while Modus stares blankly in the opposite direction. He gazes down at the club through the transparent globe siding. "Roman, hang back," he calls out.

Roman turns around, letting the door close between him and Monique. He takes a few steps closer to the desk, expecting Modus to speak, but the room remains silent. Modus simply watches as the workers prepare the club below him. After a few moments pass, and the anticipation builds, Roman finally gives in and blurts out, "You know we, uh...Monique and I...we didn't, or at least I didn't expect to..."

Modus interjects, "The first person to speak in an exchange like this is usually the more desperate person. Just a tip for ya'...something I've picked up along the way." He swivels around in his chair to face Roman. "So, what is it that you want? You don't strike me as the old-school *permission-asking* type. But then again neither was I... Maybe that's why I always liked you, Roman."

"I just don't want any trouble," replies Roman.

"I didn't ask you what you *don't* want. I asked you what you want. And I imagine the answer to that question is: you want to keep seeing Monique," stresses the General from behind his desk. For the first time since they arrived, Modus removes his sunglasses and sets them down. His elbows rest firmly on his desk's surface with his fingers interlocked.

Roman looks Modus dead in the eye and responds, "Yes."

Modus snickers, then shakes his head. "Back on Earth, more orbits back than I care to admit, I lost my parents young, same as you did. Except my home wasn't quite as warm as yours may have been. It hardened me, life alone at that age. Made me effective, but it also made me cold. Drove me to join the military, same as it drove me to get kicked out of it. When I started the Wibetani I had no one. And the Wibetani was nothing more than an aimless Gulcher gang. Wasn't 'til I met Monique's mother that I gained the perspective I needed to grow...the clarity I needed to hone my values and define what the Wibetani stands for aside from simple cash flow and a lawless life. A good woman will do that to you... Suddenly the goal wasn't just creds. It wasn't just thrills from breaking the laws of the system. It's about true independence and separation from an ever-encroaching state that doesn't give a fuck about us. It's about creating an organization that looks out for its own no matter what. One that its members can own a piece of and find purpose in. But when Reeva died..." Modus gets lost in thought as he pontificates. Roman does not interrupt; rather, he allows time for Modus to find the words that he searches for.

Rather than pick up where he left off, Modus suddenly hardens his expression and starts down a different path. "No one's allowed to leave the Wibetani; not before you, and not since you. The only reason you're still alive is by my good graces, and because at one point I looked at you like a son." He swivels his chair away from Roman again before continuing. "But if you hurt my actual daughter, Roman, you make an enemy of the Wibetani. Do you get me?"

Roman answers simply, "I won't."

"Good. Now go find that glow worm and make me proud," Modus finishes.

Roman steps out the back door of the club to find Monique already sitting on Rooster. The sight of her breaks the bout of introspection that Modus had initiated, and his mood elevates in an instant. The other recruits have gone back to work and no longer loiter around their vehicles. Monique slides forward provocatively on the seat of Roman's hoverbike and lifts up the tickets, saying, "Hey there, boy, you're pretty cute. You ever been to a VIP show?" She then splits the cards so he can see both of them with their holographic letters spinning.

"Not this side of the walls," replies Roman. A smile spreads across his face, and the two laugh before taking off for Leebrus. Their problems evaporate with the gusts of the wind that whip at their free faces as Roman speeds away on Rooster. A care in the world was not to be had as she grips his cloak, and he twists the throttle.

CHAPTER 21:

The Devil's Dealings

Miles away in Leebrus, Trike Gunderson orders his staffers around in the offices of the Caerulleum Showcase. Everyone works frantically to prepare for the start of the music festival as the lines outside grow longer and longer. Some employees tap on their screens, while others communicate orders via comms to staff elsewhere. At least twenty people fill the noisy space as Trike coordinates the group.

"It's too late for that! Just see if you can get one of the local groups to fill in for them. Tell them it's their chance of a lifetime to hit the stage or something..." he shouts across the room at Rod.

"Working on it!" Rod shouts back.

Trike's attention is grabbed by a blinking light on his dock. *A call to Fabric...who could that be?* he thinks to himself. He walks over and taps the surface of the dock to see who could possibly be bothering him now. The screen displays an encrypted request. The requestor is simply listed "G," with no further information provided. The sight of the letter alone burns a sense of dire urgency into his actions. The governor immediately addresses the rest of his staff. "Alright! Listen, everyone, we need to head down there now! First acts start in two hours. I want this to go smoothly, so heads on a swivel everyone! Don't let me down, and good luck out there!"

Everyone stands, and the group begins to quickly file out of the room. Once the final staffer exits, Trike quickly grabs his things and rushes out of the building through another exit. He races across the street to the Leebrus Government Spire, beginning to break a sweat as he finally reaches the elevator to his office. He bends over and places his hands on his knees in an attempt to catch his breath and collect himself. By the time the frosted elevator doors open, he has perspired through his clothes.

He sits at his dock by the windows overlooking the city. A few taps on its controls powers up the large, circular machine to his left. The small, metal pieces that complete the sphere begin to shift and rotate, opening a doorway to its center. He takes a puff of his Electrovapor and exhales a cloud of blue smoke as he prepares to enter the Fabric. His hand trembles as he places the device back on his desk. Before building the courage to begin the meeting, he looks down and mutters to himself, "Come on, Trike. Get it together! He'll have good news. He has to have good news... FUCK." Not wanting to keep the mysterious "G" waiting, he grinds his teeth and enters the sphere, waiting for the darkness to engulf him as the sphere spins closed.

A blinding flash of light prompts Trike to cover his eyes. It takes a few moments for them to adjust to the environment he finds himself in. The wind blows discarded trash by his feet across the cracked concrete street of an old world. He discerns that he's definitely outside. Compacting dumpsters line the edifice of the buildings on either side of the narrow street. *Must be some sort of alley?* The road behind him leads to a dead end, blocked by a tall chain-link fence. The one before him leads to another street. He is definitely somewhere in the city, but the strange, deafening silence of the environment makes for an all too uncomfortable scenario. It looks like Kairus if all signs of humanity had vanished. It sends a shiver down Trike's back. Looking up, he is put further on edge to find himself standing under a harrowing red sky.

Up ahead of him, someone walks into view and starts down the alley toward him. His silky black suit is pristinely pressed with shiny gold accents. Golden bracelets adorn his wrists and jingle against his bionic golden hands. He holds his arms out to the side as he walks. A golden chain hangs from his neck over his black dress shirt. From the necklace hangs a large pendant in the shape of a flaming bird with a skeletal face. The man is well aged, and though he walks slowly, it is not due to feebleness. His speed is intentional, symbolic. He takes his time, for he knows the man he meets with shall wait patiently. The man's eyes glow an unnatural yellow in their metal sockets, and the skin of his face is marred with numerous illegal implants and a long, wispy beard. The wind whips at his long, black and gray hair and sends it cascading to his right.

Finally, he stops ten feet from Trike and stands completely still. His arms remain extended laterally with his golden palms facing the sky like hell's polished savior. A wide grin curls from ear to ear as he greets his guest.

"Welcome, my always prompt business partner, Triconius Gunderson. Thank you for joining me at my polite behest. I find myself humbled by your presence." The man articulates as if histrionics were his first language.

Trike gulps at the sound of the man's voice. Though seasoned, and rich, it carries with it a certain insincerity; one not intended to be hidden. Rather, it is a fakeness meant to openly mock. "Good to see you too, Riku," lies Gunderson, who is physically sickened by the sight of the gangster. "Couldn't you have picked a better environment to meet in? I feel like I'm in a bad movie..."

"Ah, but is it not a fitting scene for the clandestine business at hand? A dark environment to match the dark deeds asked of me by you, a *government official*," asks Riku Yamasaka, whose bionic eyes pierce like laser beams through Trike's.

Trike ignores the sarcasm, and frantically asks, "So were you able to acquire them, er...the full package?"

"Has my business partner begun to doubt the efficacy of his hired outfit? Do you doubt the consistency that has been shown by the Golden Phoenix thus far?" Riku steps closer and lets his hands drop to his sides. "Or is it me, personally, that you doubt? Tell me, Triconius. Do you doubt me?"

A bead of sweat rolls down Gunderson's forehead, which only causes the gangster to smile again. "Let's not pretend that we're happy-go-lucky business partners, Yamasaka. You provide a service that I pay for. And I pay well, so I expect results," he says unconvincingly.

"Oh, do not misread my line of questioning, good governor. I certainly have no problems with our current arrangement, for you do pay well for my services. And fear not, for I plan to deliver just as I have historically throughout our... relationship," responds Riku in a patronizing tone.

Trike wipes the sweat off his forehead. "Oh, thank the Primes. Ok, good. Now I can finally focus on this music festival. You really worry me when you..."

"When I what?" asks Riku poignantly. "When I kidnap fifty hybrid citizens from different parts of the city and transport them through the city of Dorok for secretive government testing?"

Triconius is visibly shocked by the bluntness of the leader of the Golden Phoenix. The tactic actually renders Trike speechless. "I, uh...um...what are you...?"

"I find that my feelings are hurt when you fail to acknowledge me as your business partner given how much I could hurt you with the information I am privy to. You see, people expect these sorts of actions from a person like me. I act in the nature of my being, perfectly content with the consequences of my actions, and the actions of my organization. People fear me, because they know me." Riku takes another few slow steps toward Trike. "You, on the other hand...you act in complete opposition of your nature. A bacterium choosing to live in the shade of hypocrisy rather than expose yourself to the light of Bios, afraid to test your own immunity."

Trike takes a few steps back as Riku continues to advance. An unsettling feeling fills him as the gangster approaches, knotting his stomach like an old yarn.

"You see, I've developed a sort of immunity to that same starlight." Riku now stands inches from the governor, who continues to retreat. He grabs the governor's shoulder with his cold, cybernetic hand and pulls him in closely. With his other hand, he grabs Trike's chin and physically positions it to face the sky. "Because of my reputation, people expect me to act terribly and thus the terrible nature of my actions falls on a populace that grows numb to them. Because they expect *just* that of me. But you...you present yourself as a saint though you involve yourself in the acts of a sinner. Such a precarious position you have agreed to place yourself in." Riku cranks on Trike's jaw, forcing him to face the gangster. "How...unfortunate," he says, before shoving the government representative to the trash-covered ground.

"AH! Please...what do you want—more credits? I'll pay you more. It's fine... Just stop, I..."

"Money is the LEAST of my worries!" yells Riku as he strikes Trike in the cheek open-handed. Trike spits out blood and begins to crawl toward the chain-link fence behind him. "Imbecile! You see, I have outgrown my quest for UCs. I find myself more than comfortable in the reapings of my businesses... I feel that, unfortunately, I have also outgrown you, my dearest Triconius. I see so clearly now that you gather these subjects for your Overseer, and the Overseer will have his fifty test subjects... Worry not, should keep you comfortable for a while. But in my old age, I've grown quite tired of dealing with middlemen. I now seek...the source; a referral of sorts," Riku finishes as he follows Trike, who crawls down the alley toward its dead end.

"No! Stop!" cries Triconius, who crawls his way over to the chain-link fence and uses it to bring himself to his feet. A painfully tight grip on his shoulder swings him around and presses him against the fence, preventing his escape.

"You see, Triconius, I wish to be introduced to your superior. As the political landscape changes, the top-tier members of each organization should, well...match up. And being that I am the leader of the Golden Phoenix, I should be doing business with the *leader* of the CP. Especially given their new and interesting approach to ruling. I feel that Zerris and I may find much in common... Don't you agree, Triconius?"

Trike, who fights to pry Riku's bionic grip from his shoulder, shows a moment of strength in his whimpering. Through tears, he actually laughs at the request. "ARGH...hehe. HA! Zerris would never do business with you! He gains strength from his distance from scum like you. You're stuck with me!"

"Ah! But that's where you're wrong! For unlike you, these yellow eyes of mine pick up on opportunity in all its forms. And their sight spans beyond your puny city-state." After finishing his sentence, he points to the wall of the building beside them with his free hand. A video plays against the side of the building as if a projector is shining on it. It depicts a club filled with people surrounding one man, who suddenly surrounds himself with a godly blue aura.

"What is that!?" begs Trike desperately as the pressure of Riku's grip begins to crush his collarbone.

"Oh, governor... The correct question is *who*, not what. That, my old and dear friend, is my collateral. Did you think I don't know why your leader experiments with Hybrid people!? He seeks the answers to the mysteries of the universe. He seeks what all with power seek...to become gods." Riku Yamasaka tightens his grip yet again, which causes the governor to squeal with agonizing pain. "Zerris will want to know more about this man, and I am the only one who knows how to find him. Get me a meeting with Zerris. And speak highly of me. If you don't, I'll find a way to get this message to him without you. It's only an educated guess, but I imagine you wouldn't want your paranoid ruler thinking you were hiding information from him...would you?"

Riku begins to loosen his robotic grip on Trike's shoulder, providing relief with each pound of pressure released. With two cold, metal fingers, Riku gently repositions the governor's view by turning his chin back toward him. "Would you, Triconius?" asks Riku in feigned empathy.

"Mmm...no!" squeaks Trike. The grip immediately releases on his shoulder following his response, and Triconius Gunderson falls to his knees and moans in agony.

"Phe-nom-en-al!" says Riku. Every emotion that he displays is manufactured. "I will expect that you connect us within the next forty-eight hours. As always, my old friend, a true pleasure to conduct business with a gentleman such as you. I look forward to our communication. And as always, may you have good fortune in your endeavors." With that, Riku begins walking slowly down the alley away from Trike. As he walks, the environment begins to repackage, and the images of his surroundings begin to pixelate and fold in on themselves, quickly dissipating to nothing. Within a few seconds, the entire landscape is blank white, then immediately all fades to black.

Triconius falls out of the opening to the Fabric chamber and hits the ground with a thud. Though the pain immediately subsides upon leaving the chamber, he still clutches his shoulder from the violent interaction with the head of the Golden Phoenix. As he brings himself to his feet and dusts himself off, the elevator at the center of the office opens and a beautiful woman with platinum blonde hair exits. Her arms are looped through dozens of gift bags, and an elegant silver sequin dress fits tightly to her thin frame. A distinct blue glow emanates from her cheeks.

Trike immediately turns to greet the woman. "Zalina!?" he gasps.

"Baby!" she yells as she drops the gift bags to the couch and runs to him. She embraces him warmly. "The first lineup of musicians are already warming up in the green room across the street! What are you still doing here?"

Triconius laughs nervously in response, following with, "I uh... I just needed to tend to some court business before I headed over. Is everything panning out alright? How are our performers? Are these the gift bags for the afterparty?"

"YES!" she shouts with unbridled excitement. "Only about half of them, though. My girls should be bringing the rest up shortly and...oh! There they are. HEY GIRLS!" she shouts as the elevator opens and another four beautiful women exit with arms filled with gift bags. "This is going to be the best Beat Galacticus EVER! The whole galaxy is going to be raving about how amazing the show was this year. And that means Deorum, and more importantly, *Leebrus*, is going to be in the galactic spotlight for the next few orbits! Zerris ought to give you a promotion after this!" she says playfully with a flip of the wrist while she runs to greet her friends. Although her statement is playful, Trike knows her intent is literal.

"Yea... I don't think that's how it really works, sweety. Unfortunately..." replies Trike, with a hint of shame in his voice.

"Oh, come on! If he hasn't realized what an asset you are to this planet, then what kind of Overseer do we really have. Right, girls?" Zalina asks, addressing her youthful friends.

The group of women, each more scantily clad than the next in their music festival attire, respond in unison, "RIGHT!"

Zalina skips back to her husband with a naïve grin and a soul full of party energy. "See? You're the envy of all of Deorum." Placing her arms around Trike, she spins around with him joyfully. "And I'm lucky enough to call you mine..."

she says with a coy smirk before planting a loving kiss on his lips.

Trike feels as small as a jungle Dagling in her arms. Her tantalizing perfume fills his nostrils, providing a momentary respite from the nightmare at hand. He closes his eyes and loses himself in her warm embrace. But when he opens them, he faces the windows behind his dock and sees Bios setting on the horizon, which turns the sky a harrowing red color. Reality returns, along with its harsh problems, and as Trike hugs Zalina closer...a tear streams down his face.

Two city-states from Leebrus, the men and women of Argos gather in the Grand Galleria of Government Center for their state forum. The marble floors and stone walls echo with voices of dissatisfaction, which grow louder and more irate with each passing minute. They shout their grievances at the stage, where Governor Arpen Delgato stands stoically behind his podium. He absorbs their outraged objections with composure and understanding, for he too opposed the same initiative that brings them here tonight.

"And what are we supposed to do in the meantime while we wait for the Court of Kairus to fix this mess!? It's not like they're even offering us market value for our equity in these units! How are we supposed to make a living when the CP thinks they can steal from us!?"

"As I have mentioned before, this outcome was not my intention. Your reasoning is sound, and I am in full agreement. However, now is not the time to lose our heads. My team and I are constructing a plan in collaboration with select other city-states that..." His response is cut off by the rise in volume of the crowds shouting. He shoots a glance to his wife, who stands to his right, then to Ram Sandiam on his left. Their expressions relay concern, for never in their lifetimes have the people of Argos been so up in arms. Glancing back to his people, Arpen only sighs. *How can I even blame them? It's too soon for this conversation,* he thinks as he looks upon the thousands of angry faces that gather.

Realizing that he has reached a stalemate with the constituents of Argos, he gives his parting words. "For now, there is much work to be done. Please exit peacefully and know that I am fighting this tooth and nail until we can resolve this diplomatically. I will not leave the people of Argos in the dust of what's to come. Thank you all."

With that, Arpen, Leyona, and chief administrator Ram quickly exit the stage and walk back into the offices of Argos's government center. As they walk, Arpen hangs his head in silent contemplation. Only the sound of their footsteps fills the space between them as they twist and turn through the halls to the governor's office. Though Arpen can feel his wife's stare burning a hole through his back, she does not speak until they are behind closed doors.

"Why did you leave them like that? Do you want them to riot their way out of the government center!?"

In the space that follows, a holoscreen projects the CP news just low enough to still be heard. Exasperated, Arpen plops into the chair behind his dock and speaks sincerely to his wife. "Because, Leyona, I sympathize with their aggravation. The people need a chance to get this off their chest before any cooperative progress can be made. They need to blow off steam before they will listen."

Leyona shakes her head, maintaining sharp eye contact. "No, I don't accept that. You have always been a man capable of swaying the sentiments of the people. Where was the inspirational speech? Where's that silver tongue of yours? How do those people know they can trust you to bring their concerns into an actionable plan?"

When Arpen only looks down, Leyona tosses her hands into the air and storms out of the room past Ram, whose mouth remains sealed shut. When the door slams behind her and the two are left alone, Ram slinks over to the seat across from Arpen's desk.

"You know she is right...there is more I could have done. Perhaps, in my old age, I am losing my touch..." The faintest of smirks crosses his face as he looks across the desk at his loyal administrator.

"I don't believe that for a second, Governor Delgato," Ram responds, his lighthearted expression meant to hide the anxiety the forum bestowed on him.

"Arpen is fine, Ram. There are no cameras in here," he says as he stands and begins to pace the room. He practically treads a divot in his office floor before speaking again. "To craft an effective plan, we must first understand the reasoning behind the initiative itself. Though it may seem a foolish one, Zerris is no fool. He must have reason to have implemented a seemingly nonsensical initiative so quickly..."

The two men ruminate on the subject for nearly an hour, every so often exchanging ideas. However, none of the possibilities seem to bear any fruit of reasonable motivation. When Arpen finally sits down in his seat again, he reclines in his chair and stares at the ceiling. Scratching his white beard, he suggests, "We may have to sleep on this. Why don't we shift our focus to something else? Were you able to get a copy of the Overseer's official schedule history like I asked?"

"I did, in fact, sir...Arpen. And unfortunately, there were no meetings with any planetary governments that might suggest he is trying to offload the extra vitalerium stockpile. Actually, there has been very little off-planet travel or communication at all..."

"Damnit..." responds Arpen as he spins around in his chair. "We have to be missing something. Something important..."

Another fifteen minutes pass in silence. As Arpen continues to spin in his chair, Ram begins listening to Jennifer Baine's monologue on the CP State News network. She drones on about a story regarding the IGB's mishandling of a diplomatic dealing with insurgents off-planet. "Let's hope the IGB doesn't find out about Zerris's stockpile...they may just label us terrorists when they visit," mutters Ram as he turns his attention back to the litany of messages on his holoscreen.

"IGB...visit..." mutters Arpen in response. His brow furrows as Ram's words begin to swirl around his head. "IGB...visit," he mutters again, louder this time. The words bounce around his thoughts of deciphering Zerris's motives until they become stuck in the whirring gears of his brain. Suddenly, Arpen's eyes shoot open as a shocking sense of clarity travels from his cortex to his cerebellum, stimulating his body into movement. He stands from his seat and proclaims, "Ram! You're a genius!"

"I uh... I am, sir?" His baffled response only seems to invigorate Arpen, who rushes around the desk and pulls the young administrator from his seat.

"The two are related, don't you see!?" He shakes Ram and hugs him, then recoils for a moment and continues conservatively. "Although I don't believe we should be celebrating if I am right..."

"Arpen, I'm sorry, but I don't understand."

"The IGB are visiting relatively soon. Yes...and how often have you seen the IGB on the news lately?"

"Quite often—" Ram starts to say, but he is cut off by his boss.

"Quite often indeed, Ram! And in quite a capricious manner, I might add. Tell me, what is the light they have been portrayed in? Would you say the general sentiments have been particularly scathing lately? Perhaps even to a surprising magnitude given the way they typically deal with planetary dissent?" His line of questioning is not one in search of answers. Rather, it is to have Ram produce the answers for himself.

Ram thinks for a moment, and then nods as he begins to track Arpen's logic. The CP News Network, essentially the only primary news network on the planet, *has* provided an excessive amount of coverage on IGB dealings in the recent past. "Ok, but how does it connect to 919? Or the stockpile?"

"Ram, let's run a hypothetical scenario. When a government wants to start a war, what do they need?"

"Er... Resources, a strong army, uh...the technology to compete with their intended opponent?"

Arpen shakes his head. "Hm... Ram, I thought better of you. You're only two for four, my friend. Allow me to fill in the gaps. A government needs a strong army no doubt. Although the CP is no sheep in the military world, facing off against the IGB in open warfare would be suicide. The government would need resources, and when discussing our own situation, we have an off-the-books vitalerium cache to fill that gap." Ram nods as he follows along. "A government also needs the support of its people. A disillusioned, indignant populace is likely to provide trouble at home. It needs the people united under a common goal to prevent being destroyed from within. The machine has to keep running. And finally, Ram, a government needs funding to pay for its conquests."

Arpen's words settle on Ram, and the picture takes form in his head all at once. He places his holoscreen on the desk and sits down as he tries to contemplate the gravity of what Arpen is suggesting. "Are you saying...that Zerris is pumping out propaganda to unify Kairus into conflict with the IGB? And that the vitalerium stocks are in preparation for war?" Ram crosses his arms in disbelief as he thinks it through, but there are still unanswered questions in his head. "Then what about the funding? I checked myself. Our communication with other governments has been minimal, reclusive, even! And taking on the property debts of the planet may provide a steady revenue stream, but it actually puts the CP in debt!"

Arpen smirks. "Tell me, in that royal schedule you retrieved, are there any meetings with the universal or global banks from other planets?"

Now along for the ride, Ram scours the meeting lists on his holoscreen as Arpen watches his fingers scroll. He stands by Ram with anticipation, thinking, *If I am right about this, we are all in a great deal of trouble...*

"Oh..." replies Ram. Arpen awaits his response with bated breath. "All of them... He's met with all of them...multiple times just over an orbit ago. They visited *here* on Deorum, that's why I must have missed it!"

Arpen smirks before asking, "And when did you trace the discrepancies in vitalerium reporting back to?" While Ram reviews his notes, Arpen grabs his cloak and packs his belongings into a large case in preparation to leave. Upon closing the case, it illuminates a bright gold color and begins to hover, following Arpen's every step.

"Just over one orbit ago," responds Ram woefully.

Arpen leans in and asks, "Did you also know...that the property value of Deorum is estimated at a value of ninety-two quintillion universal credits?"

Ram reacts as if struck by lightning. "He's leveraging the planet to pay for his war!?"

"It would seem we've been put up as collateral, my old friend," replies Arpen succinctly.

"But that still doesn't account for the army! I mean... Without the help from other planets, Zerris would have to quadruple the CP Guardsmen to stand a chance! Even with funding, resources, and support! There would have to be..." Ram stops talking because the answer becomes imminently clear. He comes to the realization that the number of people who would be out of work in the wake of Initiative 919 plays perfectly into the plan. If Zerris isn't worried about so many people being jobless, it is likely because he already has another job in mind for them. "...a mass conscription. A draft!?" shouts Ram.

Arpen pushes through the door of his office and storms down the hall with his trusted administrator following close behind. "Set up a meeting with Yoon and Cornathus ASAP. If they say they're busy, tell them I said to hell with their schedules! And Ram..." Arpen suddenly stops in his tracks and turns to young Ram Sandiam with a fiery glow in his eye, "...prepare for war, my boy."

CHAPTER 22:

The Hybrid Sensation

Roman and Monique take their time, indulging in the benefits of their VIP passes as they navigate through the maze that is the interior of Caerulleum Showcase. They drink, dance, and lose themselves in each other's company as the music of bands and electronic artists carries on the air. Twelve separate stages showcase the performances of an eclectic collection of artists under a single roof. The domed canopy itself is an absolute visual masterpiece. The image of a star craft traveling at lightspeed through the universe paints itself across the entire ceiling as it passes planets and galactic anomalies present only in the furthest reaches of space. It tells the visual tale of bravery, adventure, and beauty narrated by the melody of talents that take to the stage; the perfect ambient backdrop for Beat Galacticus. Behind holographic barriers, artists and celebrities rub elbows with people of great influence amongst the millions of fans who have come to experience momentary bliss in their favorite songs played live.

Monique's TAB device chimes, emitting an orange holographic timer that shakes and buzzes above her wrist. "Shit! We have to head to the main stage!" she shouts to Roman, who grinds against her.

"What time is it... We still have half an hour!" he shouts over the deafening music.

"It's going to take us ten minutes just to walk there!" she shouts, tugging on his black jacket.

"I kind of like this stage. What's the rush? Who's even playing over there?"

"Um, let me see..." she says as she scrolls through the event schedule on her TAB. "Infinity Inferno? I don't know them, but I don't want to miss any of Valeriya's set..."

"WHAT!? I didn't know they were playing here!" cries Roman with excitement. His elated response surprises Monique.

"Yea, they're playing right before Asa!" she says with a cupped hand to Roman's ear.

Roman promptly switches gears. "You're right. Let's go right now!" he says as he grabs Monique by the hand and practically tugs her out of the crowd. She follows him to the main stage, tickled by his giddiness. They walk at a brisk pace, and within a few short minutes they arrive at a wall of people that separates them from the main stage.

"This crowd is crazy! Let's go to the VIP section!" yells Monique over the heavy metal rifts that energize the rowdy fans.

"Not for these guys! You have to be in the crowd. It's half the experience! I've never seen them live before, but I've heard their show is insane!" Roman shouts back with a smile before pushing his way to the front. Although the crowd is densely packed, it provides little obstacle to a determined Roman. After shoving their way to a decent space, Monique finds enjoyment in the expression that lights up his face.

Fire explodes from pyrotechnic machinery; not holographic fire, but real fire. The flames bend and twist into shapes that dance above the band and shower the crowd with blazing heat. First, the fire forms a perfect circle, like a great red portal to hell. After a few moments, the flames bend and twist into an infinity symbol with a fiery spear through its center; a burning effigy of the Earth-based band's sigil. A heavy guitar rift riles the crowd, which dances aggressively around Monique and Roman. They push and shove each other with no regard for the assault they receive in return from others. Roman wraps his arms around Monique's shoulders and pulls her close to his chest, protecting her from the chaos.

The lead singer projects his deep, gravelly voice into the microphone protruding from his cheek with such force that he hunches over, as if using gravity to expel his lyrics with greater intensity.

<u>Lead Singer:</u> *"When the embers of bravery burn out in our hearts,*

Then the poison that they feed becomes preferable 'cause"

<u>Band:</u> *"A weak mind is predictable!"*

<u>Lead Singer:</u> *"We take the weight on our back, division crafted by the souls that have turned black"*

<u>Band:</u> *"As the void!"*

<u>Lead Singer:</u> *"Ambitions driven by fear,*

Their cancer bleeds through and spreads to everything held dear!

Measure your faith or you'll be traded like gold,

And feel the darkness of the void with the death of your soul!"

<u>All:</u> *"Fuck them who lie!*

Fuck them who take!

Fuck them who tell!"

<u>Lead Singer:</u> *"'Cause when the sword swings back it wields the fire of your manufactured hell!"*

Monique's eyes widen as she takes in the lyrics. "Uh... These guys are a little intense. I'm surprised they are allowed to perform on Deorum with lyrics like this! Isn't this a state-sponsored event?" yells Monique at Roman.

"Yea, but look at this crowd! Guess credits speak louder

than lyrics. What do you think!?" asks Roman, grinning wide, awaiting her validation like a sprightly young puppy.

"Not bad, not really my style... I like that it makes you excited though," Monique says with a wink. She turns around to face Roman and presses against him, pushing his long, dark hair out of his face and tucking it behind his ear with her fingers.

Another explosion of fire coincides with a guitar solo as the crowd's intensity increases. Roman becomes infected by the energy and begins to jump with the others in the pit. Another song goes by, and even Monique begins to join in. When the band finally finishes their set, the crowd cheers for minutes. The lead singer thanks the fans, and the band exits stage left. Monique and Roman make their way to the VIP section in preparation for the headlining act.

They are led to a small metal square surrounded by a railing that houses their fully stocked VIP booth. Once the gate closes, the platform begins to rise, gliding smoothly up the wall it connects to and stoping far above stage level with other VIP platforms. From the elevated position, they enjoy an exceptional view of the main stage. Almost every person in Caerulleum Showcase now stands in wait for the final act to start.

Shortly after they settle in, the lights are cut, and the entire showcase goes black. Even the images on the great ceiling showcase fade out momentarily. Another few moments of relative darkness begin to spark whispers amongst the enormous crowd. However, the whispers evaporate as a single white-hot spotlight pierces through the darkness. It shines down on a stage that has changed drastically since the last act. A woman crouches on the ground, covering her face from the light. Aside from the long, braided ponytail protruding from the back of her head, she has no other hair. A number of small stones cut into runic shapes surround her on stage, making her look like the human sacrifice in a pagan ritual. An ethereal melody fills the air, and she lifts her shaved head toward the beam of light that shines down from above. Even through the bright light, her blue freckles glow brilliantly for all to see.

Monique screams at the sight of her friend, and the crowd begins cheering as Valeriya's face comes into view. The spotlight fades to a shade of deep purple, masking her bioluminescence and softening her sharply defined facial features. Her fingers, with their long, spindly nails, play in the purple light as if she's seeing color for the first time. Her exaggerated movements create a display of dramatic curiosity.

Her mouth opens, and a heavenly voice serenades the room, not with words, but with resounding, angelic notes. After a few melodic measures, wings resembling a dragonfly's extend from beneath the white garb on her back. The light that engulfs her turns a deep red shade. Her bioluminescent freckles come back into view, then begin to glow brighter and brighter. As she continues to sing, her feet suddenly lift off the floor and she begins to levitate above the stage. One by one, the stones around her levitate as well, as if her voice tantalizes them into spontaneous motion. Ten stones now spin around her, moving with the vibrations of the song as she floats nearly ten feet from the floor of the stage.

"Whoa, is that real? I didn't know Valeriya was a telek," exclaims Roman, referencing the term used for hybrids who display moderate levels of telekinesis. "I've seen a few hybrids move sand or lift small objects, but I've never seen anyone that strong before!"

"Yea it's a huge part of her live act! When we were young, she had to keep it a secret. By that point, they weren't rounding up hybrids anymore, but it still wasn't safe to practice openly, especially with how gifted she was. Then she became famous and moved off planet. Now I feel like she makes a point of showing it off." Monique begins waving her arms with the music as she cheers on the performance.

As she sings, Valeriya scans the VIP tables until her eyes

rest on Monique, who waves frantically at the edge of their platform next to Roman. She lifts a hand to them and gestures subtly, as if to acknowledge their presence without breaking from her act.

"We love you, Asa!" screams Monique over the noise of the concert. Two hours breeze by as Roman and Monique enjoy the rest of the enthralling show from their balcony. When the encore finishes, Asa-Valeriya bows gratefully to her fans. But when she gazes back at Monique and Roman, the smile disappears from her face and is replaced by a solemn stare. She turns and walks backstage with a gait so smooth it almost seems she glides. Monique nudges Roman that it's time to follow Asa backstage, then calls their platform back to ground level. After showing their VIP passes to the bouncers, Roman and Monique are led backstage. They stop outside a greenroom labeled "Headlining Act: Valeriya / Infiniti Inferno," and the bouncer opens the door to announce them.

"Valeriya! Your guests are here for you," he proclaims confidently, then makes space for them to be seen through the doorway.

The room is dim, lit mostly by neon lights. It is a large space, equipped with everything an artist could possibly need: a full bar, couches and tables, screens, and even a bed. An eclectic mix of performers and their entourages celebrate a successful night of performances with toasts and an array of substances. Against the back wall of the room, Asa-Valeriya kisses the lead singer of Infinity Inferno on the cheek as they prepare to leave, then returns to sulking in her love seat. She leans to one side and throws her legs over the opposite armrest, matting down the fake green fur that covers the chair. As the band walks toward the door, Roman cannot help but address them. Not only was he able to see them play live, but he also now stands face to face with the members of his favorite heavy metal band.

"That was one hell of a show!" he says, trying his best to

dampen his excitement while he fist-bumps each of the band members as they pass. Each of them responds with a grateful nod as they exit the room.

Upon reaching Roman, the lead singer, dressed in all black, ignores Roman's extended fist. He simply replies unenthusiastically, "Thanks mate," with a stern look. He stops to give Monique and Roman a once-over, taking in the details of their attire, which, clearly, is designed for utility rather than fashion. "Hmph..." he grunts. He then turns back to Valeriya and asks, "So these are the ones, eh Asa?"

Asa-Valeriya's smooth, high-pitched voice responds, "That's right, Winston. They're here to help me solve my family matter. Supporters to the cause."

The lead singer grunts again in response, then turns back to Roman. His serious expression does not change, but his tone does. "Any friend of Asa's is a friend of mine." Rather than fist-bump Roman, he reaches out and grasps his forearm, a militia handshake. Repeating the same gesture to Monique, he addresses them with concern in his voice, "You take good care of her; both of you. And make whoever did this pay. Windi was a friend to us all..."

"*Is* a friend to us all," Asa corrects him, staring daggers in her friend's direction and revealing just how fragile the situation has left her.

"Right...of course," he replies apologetically. "I'll see you at the afterparty, Asa." Turning his attention back to Roman, he finishes, "And you? It's always good to meet supporters of the cause. Others who remain unblinded. Godspeed." The lead singer briskly exits to meet his band members who wait for him outside.

"Supporters to the cause?" asks Roman, slightly confused.

Valeriya sighs. "Part of the underground. They fancy themselves freedom fighters of sorts, as if the concept still even exists in the universe... It's easier to have them believe you're on their team than to explain the nuances of being blissfully neutral..." While Roman takes in Valeriya's comments, Monique rushes across the room to her childhood friend.

"You were so great out there! I've missed you so much!" shouts Monique, bearhugging the pop star.

Valeriya's freckles reflect off Monique's cheek as she tightly embraces her back. She responds solemnly, "I missed you too, moon bug. Forgive me if I'm not in a celebratory mood. As I'm sure you're aware by now, my little cousin, Windi..." Tears stream from both her eyes and sparkle as they roll down her cheeks, momentarily breaking the musician's aloof façade.

With sympathy in her voice, Monique responds, "My father told me... I'm so sorry..."

Valeriya wipes her eyes, desperately trying to shelve her emotions for when she can express them in private. She quickly collects herself. "Thank you, Monique... And you must be Roman," calls Valeriya across the room.

"Yea that's me," replies Roman, who, having to stave off the excitement of meeting his favorite band, tries to match her somber tone.

"It's nice to meet you, Roman. Please, sit with me. I'll tell you everything I know," she says sweetly. The two women sit, Valeriya in her fuzzy love seat, Monique in another chair next to her. "I have to thank you both for agreeing to help me with this sensitive issue. Obviously, I can't trust the Leebrus Guardsmen with something like this. They could care less about a missing Hybrid girl. And given their abysmal response to the number of Hybrid disappearances this orbit alone, I expect minimal action. For all we know, they're involved."

Roman walks to meet them, resting his hands on the back of a chair that faces the musician. He has too much energy to sit, and he knows himself too well. He thinks better on his feet, where he has room to pace while the gears turn. "Alright. Let's hear it."

A voice deep as a bass drum barks an order at Roman as he

stands there. "Valeriya asked you to sit. So why don't you do yourself a favor and sit your ass down?"

Behind Asa-Valeriya stands a hulking human, possibly one of the largest Roman has ever seen. He steps into the light, revealing implants not commonly seen on Deorum. His bald head shines in the neon glare, and a neatly groomed goatee represents the only visible hair on him save for his eyebrows. He wears a white cut-off sweatshirt, from which extend gold metallic pistons with mechanocontractible musculature. Emerging from his rolled-up sweatpants, his shins display the same golden framework that taper into mechanical feet. All limbs are fully bionic and high-tech too; the new models. These are miles ahead of the "medically necessary" types of implants available for civilians on Deorum. He takes two loud steps closer to Valeriya, which echo through the room as his prosthetic feet connect with the grated metal floor.

"Sorry Roman, this is my longtime friend and personal bodyguard, Aramis Goldeys. He gets protective of me at times and can *forget his manners*," she says as she shoots a disappointed look into the side of the man's head. "So, let's agree not to fight those who've agreed to help us? Settle down, Aramis. For me, please."

"Just making sure the newcomer shows you the respect you deserve. And you can call me Strider like everyone else. Only Asa calls me by my government name."

Roman does not falter; rather, he saunters around the chair and plops down in his seat as he's told. He ignores Valeriya's apology, and with a smirk on his face replies to Strider, "So, is your dick metal too? Or did you just stop at the beach muscles?"

Recognizing his attempt to stir the pot, Strider's booming voice returns, "Nope. That appendage already packs enough power." Upon finishing his sentence, he leans against the wall behind Valeriya and crosses his arms with a grunt and grimace.

Roman chuckles in response. He points at Strider and says

to Valeriya, "He's fun. I like him."

"I'm told by Modus that you're very effective, and I'm sure that means you're very tough. But please, don't antagonize my team, Roman. Time is of the essence. The more of it we waste here, the more unlikely it is we..." Valeriya trails off. She does not want to finish her sentence, nor does she have to. The message is relayed.

Roman straightens up in response. He looks down as if to apologize without using words. Switching gears into work mode, he asks, "When was the last time you saw or spoke with your cousin?"

The noise of others in the room becomes too much for Valeriya, who proclaims loudly for all to hear, "Everyone, please give us a few moments alone." She lifts her hand toward the door and holds it outstretched. The door swings open by itself, and more than a dozen artists and members of Valeriya's entourage cease their partying, and leave.

Roman scans the space to find only six remain in Valeriya's green room. Roman, Monique, and Valeriya sit around a small holo-board with its display turned off. Strider, the pop star's cyborg muscle, still hovers closely over her shoulder. To Roman's right, two other men remain by the bar. The first, a more eccentric-looking individual, stands behind the bar pouring liquor directly into his mouth from a bottle he holds a foot above his head. He then gargles the fluid before swallowing. A sleek electric guitar is slung around his back, and his clothes are baggy and tattered. Chains dangle from his Lancor leather jacket and flamboyant orange parachute pants. His hair is cut into five parallel mohawks that travel from the back of his neck to his hairline. Each lane of hair is dyed a different color and protrudes a good six inches from his head.

The second man sits on a barstool watching with a smirk as the other guzzles vodka. He is plainly dressed, almost surprisingly so given the setting and company. Everything about him seems average, from his stature to his short, cleanly cut brown hair. The only thing that stands out is his unnaturally placid state, and a circular black implant under his occipital bone behind his skull. *A chemical modulator?* Roman thinks to himself. When the man turns to face the others, it becomes evident that he has an alarming amount of cybernetic hardware in his head and face. Black cognitive enhancement chips line his forehead from one temple to the other. Reflex boosters protrude from above his ears next to Fabric access ports and quantum decryption relays. Silver and black metallic implants line his face, creating his features, alluding to more cybernetic enhancements beneath his skin that Roman cannot even identify. They travel around his jawline, and down his neck below the collar of his button-down shirt. His eyes are neon blue, encapsulated by an unnatural glossy sheen; clearly implants as well. He lifts a martini glass to his lips, exposing a number of implants in his wrist commonly used for interfacing with docks and other technology. *Whoa...that has to be at least a few billion UCs worth of tech*, thinks Roman.

"We gettin' down to it then, yeh!?" shouts the colorful man in an obnoxiously nasally voice and an accent that Roman cannot quite place. He slams the vodka bottle on the counter and walks over to the group.

Valeriya wipes another tear from her eye and introduces the first man. "Roman, Monique, this is Nails, one of my most trusted confidants and tour mates. He's been with me since the beginning, and he's loyal to a fault. Don't worry, you'll get used to his energy level."

The very paranoid, clearly drunk Nails crouches between Roman and Monique's chairs. Putting a hand on the back of each seat, his eyes practically bulge out of his head as he questions them. "You two CP? Couple of no-coats, are ya!?" he shrieks.

"No," says Monique, leaning away from him in discomfort.

"How 'bout you, cunt!? You a no-coat lackey? IGB? SECRET SERVICE!?"

Roman raises an eyebrow, which surprisingly seems to be enough of a response for the inebriated punk. He chuckles and slaps Roman on his shoulder. "AY! All goodies then, the lot of us!" Nails exclaims. He sits on Monique's armrest and pulls a large knife from his waistband, causing Monique to shrink uncomfortably in her seat.

Roman's instincts prompt him to immediately stand when he sees the knife. However, the belligerent musician lets out a deranged cackle and playfully lifts his hands to either side of his face. "Ay, ay! Easy mate! It ain't for stabbin'!" He reaches into his front jacket pocket and pulls out a small bag of orange powder, then sprinkles a small pile onto the knife's flat surface. "Just a bit o' the Kraken!" he shouts with excitement before snorting the small mound of powder off his weapon. Roman rolls his eyes and removes his hand from his own knife.

Noticing her guests' expressions, Valeriya continues to introduce her cohort out of perceived necessity. "Nails was an orphan back on Earth. He grew up on the streets of Sydney, Australia, after he was essentially discarded by the foster system. A lot of families couldn't handle his...rambunctious nature. Found his home in one of the mole societies that live underground. He may not be as domesticated as some, but I trust him. To top that, he's one of the most skilled guitarists and meglaphronon players in the galaxy, a true savant."

The fidgety musician pours another small pile of orange powder onto his blade as if completely unaware of the ongoing conversation about him. He brings the blade closer to Monique to offer her some of his mysterious "Kraken." When she declines the offer by turning her head in disgust, he simply shrugs and makes the orange dust disappear up his nose. Roman shakes his head.

"My other colleague sitting by the bar is Dieter Wuntz. He's been lying low with us for quite some time now."

"Yes, just about one standard year now," replies the man in a strange monotone voice.

"Dieter is..." She pauses as her eyes connect with the neon blue irises of the heavily modded man. Her glance is one that implies a question: *Is it alright for me to tell them?*

"It's fine, Asa. You can tell them. I've already done my own research and background checks. I feel I can trust them."

"When? You just learned we exist five seconds ago..." asks Roman, perturbed by the tone and level of confidence in Dieter's statement.

"Just now. I may access the Fabric as I please," replies Dieter bluntly. His monotone, nonchalant responses are unnaturally consistent, likely relevant to the plethora of implants actively assisting his cognition.

Asa-Valeriya continues, "Dieter is one of the most wanted men you will never hear about. He's a biohacker, and as you can see, outfitted with more illegal tech than an IGB evidence room. Our bureaucratic overlords have been hunting him for many orbits, but he's a Blackhat ghost. No one can hide their signature quite like he can. He found respite with us, and in turn, he helps us obtain certain things." Roman notices a very slight change in her tone, like the presence of admiration.

Roman looks the man up and down, somewhat uncomfortable by his presence. "What sorts of things?" asks Roman warily.

"Information, mostly," replies Dieter, who takes another dainty sip from his martini glass.

"Which is the only reason we have any idea about Windi's whereabouts," finishes Valeriya. She reaches out and taps on the small, conical table. The touch causes its surface to illuminate, then project a picture of Windi just above it. She is young, no older than twenty orbits with strawberry-blonde hair, and the anticipated blue freckles of a hybrid. There is a sort of naivety behind the eyes that exudes from the young girl's smiling picture.

Roman starts his probing. "Tell us about your cousin, Asa."

"My closest family member... That sweet girl means the

world to me. She attends Leebrus University to study bioengineering and agriculture. Windi always had a good head on her shoulders…"

"When is the last time you heard from her?" asks Roman.

"A week ago. I holo'd her to tell her I'd be headlining the festival, and that I would have VIP tickets for her…the same ones I gave to you. But during the journey here she went completely dark."

"And how did she seem when you spoke with her last?"

"She seemed fine…happy even. That's why it was so strange when she went MIA. She always keeps in touch with me, *always*. Especially whenever I'm making a trip back home. If she doesn't holo or comm, she's messaging constantly."

"Where does she live? I'm assuming you checked her residence…" Roman probes.

"Here in Leebrus. I sent people to check on her as soon as I arrived planet-side, but she wasn't there. Her apartment looked untouched, almost staged. Her holoscreen, her TAB, and all of her possessions were still there. But no Windi…" The fear of her hopeless situation begins to emerge again, and she sobs for a moment into her hands. The tears stream down her tattooed fingers. Roman feels his own discomfort creeping up on him, and he looks away. He never knows what to do at the sight of women crying. His reaction stems from a combination of his action-oriented personality, and a lack of example in his own life. Although he wishes to help, he knows not how.

"What about friends? Does she have any close friends that might know something?" asks Monique.

"Her two closest friends haven't seen her for days. I wouldn't have called you otherwise," responds Valeriya.

Roman sits back in his chair and scratches the scruff on his chin. It had been a while since he shaved, but the self-stimulation helps him organize his thoughts. "Was there anyone new in her life? Was she seeing anyone?"

"I don't know… Maybe? She's a vibrant young girl. She's

always out and about with new people. Although..." Valeriya trails off as if deep in thought.

"Go on," replies Monique. She places a comforting hand on her friend's shoulder. "Any information will be helpful to us."

"She briefly mentioned someone who was helping her and her friends get into clubs a while back, um..." Asa struggles to recall the name that eludes her. After a moment, she exclaims, "Reggie!"

"Maybe there's something there. Where can we find this Reggie?"

"I don't know for sure..." she responds, deflated.

Roman starts to become frustrated with the lack of information. Valeriya is not giving him much to work with, and they will be nowhere without a starting point. "So, what leads do you have? What makes you think you know where she is?"

"We don't know exactly where she is. She doesn't have any implants we can track, and all her devices were left in her apartment. The messages were wiped, but Dieter was able to decrypt data from her devices related to her most visited recent locations."

Dieter steps into the conversation and lifts a hand toward the table between them. The dock's image changes from Windi's picture to a map of Leebrus. A number of blinking red dots litter the image. They disappear one by one until only three remain. His monotone voice fills the silence. "I was able to identify a few locations that seem to fall outside the norm of her usual activity. Based on the data I reviewed, these three locations stick out based on the number of visits and the landmarks associated. The first dot is a residential highrise, the second is associated with a club..."

Monique chimes in, "I know that club. That's Pyramid. It's a Golden Phoenix front." She shoots Roman a look, relaying concern with her eyes.

"That is correct, Monique. This is the location of Pyramid.

Interesting that you mention a connection to the Golden Phoenix. Please allow me to research something quickly." Dieter places an index finger to his right temple and closes his eyes momentarily. When they open, the map suddenly disappears and is replaced by a mugshot. The individual depicted has neatly buzzed brown hair that meets a sharply defined jawline. Both his nose and eyebrows are laden with multiple piercings. His face is a canvas of small tattoos, the most notable of which is a tattoo of a flaming bird that curls around his right orbit. The man frowns in the picture as if he harbors severe disdain for the photographer. Beneath the image reads: "Reginald Karnock / 27 orbits / 5'8" / Brown Hair / Brown Eyes / Known Affiliations: Golden Phoenix / Arrest Record: Solicitation, Possession, possession with intent to distribute, Assault / Charges: N/A."

Roman leans in closer to the floating hologram of Reginald. The curve of his cheekbones, his nose, the way his forehead sinks inward at the temples...it all seems vaguely familiar. Roman is overcome with a strange, unshakable feeling that somehow, he knows this man. He stares at his picture, trying to discern how, but despite his efforts he cannot seem to place the face. *How would I know some GP midlevel? Maybe in passing from my Wibetani days? No, can't be...* thinks Roman as he scours his memories for answers, but one never arrives.

"Weird..." mutters Roman, after reading through the biography displayed before him.

"Why do you say that?" asks Valeriya, impulsively on the edge of her seat.

"CP don't usually let people off without charges after they've been arrested. I think we'll have to pay our friend Reginald here a visit," says Roman.

Dieter is quick to respond. "His last known address coincides with the third marked location. I'll forward the GPS coordinates to your TAB." When the buttoned-up man turns his gaze to Roman's wrist, his TAB chimes, confirming the coordinates have been received.

"Uh...thanks," replies Roman uncomfortably before turning his attention back to Valeriya. "This should at least give us something to work off. Monique and I will follow up on this lead and report any information we find. How long will you be planet-side?"

"I'll be here as long as it takes. I'm not going anywhere until my Windi is safe. You can find me in the Gaia Hotel. I'm staying in the penthouse."

Roman and Monique both stand and prepare to leave. Monique embraces her friend once more, then wipes a tear from her face before confirming sincerely, "We'll find her, Asa." A faint smile appears as a glimmer of hope is restored to her fragile psyche. She nods affirmingly and watches them leave.

Both Dieter and Strider give a wordless nod as Roman and Monique depart. Nails, ever the gracious host, stands and pulls his orange pants up to his navel, shouting, "Have fun kids! Don't crack any skulls without me, yea?" His head tilts back as he speaks, revealing his orange-coated nostrils.

As they walk through the grand foyer of Caerulleum Showcase, Roman picks up on Monique's mood: solemn and silent. He hesitates before asking the question on his mind. "Do you think she's still alive?" His voice is calm and low as if to soften the inquiry.

She crosses her arms and digs her nails into the skin above her elbows. She wants so badly to say yes, but the potential reality of the situation hovers in the fore of her mind. "I don't know," she responds.

"I mean, what would an innocent, university type like her want with some GP scumbag?" asks Roman, genuinely curious.

"I have no idea, Roman, but we need to be careful. We don't even know for sure if this Reggie is our guy. Even if he is, he's GP; that means he's protected. He won't give up that information willingly, and he probably won't be rolling alone."

"Just leave the interrogating to me." He checks the coordinates on his TAB and begins preparing himself mentally for the upcoming challenge. A cordial encounter with a GP mid-level would be an unlikely event, but the strange feeling of déjà vu returns as he stares at the face of Reginald Karnock on his TAB. *Why...why does he look so familiar?*

"What's wrong? You look kind of distracted..." asks Monique, immediately picking up on Roman's shift in attitude.

"It's nothing... Let's just get you home," replies Roman as he strides toward his hoverbike.

Monique steps in front of Roman, cutting off his path. She stands facing him with burning intensity. "I'm coming with you," she says firmly, with the type of fierceness usually shown to her father, not to Roman.

Roman starts to respond, but his voice never leaves his throat. He can see by the furrowed lines in her brow and the depth of her stare how emotionally involved she is in this mission. *Emotional involvement makes for missteps,* he thinks. But for some strange reason, he cannot deny her. Feeling as though he has no choice in the matter, Roman sighs and concedes. "Alright..." His acceptance of her terms prompts her to peck him lovingly on the lips.

As they navigate through the late-night traffic brimming with concert-goers looking to keep the party alive, Roman and Monique make their way toward the coordinates on his Lancer. As they slowly make their way, Roman holos Modus to give him a mission update.

Upon answering, Modus's face displays on the inside of Roman's terrain helmet, taking up the top right corner of his peripheral view. "What's the word? You come up with any leads?" asks Modus, sitting behind his desk in the globe. The club rages in view behind him, deafened by the transparent inner walls of his office.

"You were right to be wary about this one. GPs likely involved. I'm making my way over to a lead we uncovered from Valeriya and her...*team*. I'll send an update after I exhaust this lead."

"Who's the target?" asks Modus.

"Some GP midlevel, Reggie Karnock. Lives a few miles south of Pyramid Club. Seems to be pretty good at getting tacked by klangs then getting off unscathed."

"Hm... I'll ask around about him. What's Monique's status?" Modus asks poignantly. "I don't want her waiving the Wibetani flag around Golden Phoenix territory if you're expecting trouble."

Roman feels Monique's grip tightening around his waist. He knows he will live to regret it if Modus finds out, but he finds himself hopelessly beholden to the arms embracing him. "Sent her back toward the Outer Sphere." A bald-faced lie. For reasons he would rather not explore, it bothers him that he withholds the truth from Modus.

"Good. Keep yourself in one piece out there."

"Acknowledged," responds Roman, finding a break in the traffic and speeding off with Monique on Rooster. Their precarious meeting with Reginald Karnock awaits.

CHAPTER 23:

Bleed for the Black and Blue

A thundering noise shakes the hull of a CP spacefaring vessel as it makes its way through Deorum's atmosphere. As the color of the sky steadily deepens from blue to black, the violent noise is replaced by a calm, eerie silence. General Dorok Ferrous Benson's military transport creeps through the vast emptiness of space toward Doral Space Station for a routine inspection. On this day, the trip will be a relatively short one. The current position of Deorum in its orbit around Bios places the planet closer to the deep-space vitalerium mining operation.

"How long 'til we reach the docking bay?" barks Dorok at the ship's pilot. His loud voice pierces the silence so sharply that the armored man noticeably jumps in his seat.

"Affirmative, General! Arrival in t-minus four hours," responds the pilot, harnessing every ounce of focus he can to appease his bombastic superior and maintain composure.

"Good. And land gently this time. Knock me off balance with your shoddy landing skills again, and your next station in the CP will be a bombing range!" Just as Dorok settles into his seat positioned at the back of the cabin and elevated above the rest of the crew, a chime from his TAB device grabs his attention. Looking down at his wrist, its glowing screen alerts him that an important comm is queued. Overseer Aganon requests his immediate presence. He rises from his seat and moves to exit the command deck with urgency. "Lieutenant! Take over while I handle something." The man nods and begins to address the crew as Dorok disappears behind the automatic hatch.

Once inside his quarters, Dorok taps his device and transmits the queued comm directly to his eye lenses. Zerris appears as if sitting directly in front of him. He is dressed in his typical royal blue mantle, which flows down the edge of his chair and gently brushes the metal of his greaves. He grits his teeth as he flexes the scar on his right hand repeatedly, a tic brought about by stress.

"Overseer, you'll be happy to hear I'm en route to Doral Station to get an update on our vitalerium quotas. I have already delivered orders to Project Black Flag. Everything should go in accordance with the...anticipated plan. They will reach the target just prior to our arrival."

"Good to hear. This will be a test run of the new technology installed in their vessels. Make certain to communicate that we want *minimal* collateral damage. Our move on the IGB is just around the corner, and that means our private vitalerium stockpile needs bolstering. But this plan doesn't work if the repairs cost more than their haul is worth." Zerris stares off into the distance as if deep in thought.

Dorok stands proudly, filled with joy to bring good news to his superior. "Understood, Overseer. Are we making good progress with our other initiatives as well?"

Zerris ignores the inquiry and begins his own line of questioning by first asserting, "What is your title, Dorok?"

At first, the general is confused by the question. "Uh...my title is General of the CP Guardsmen... Governor and chief representative of—"

"So, your title is not Overseer, correct?" asks Zerris bluntly.

"Er...no, I..." Dorok's words begin to jumble as they escape his gullet, flustered by the unexpected line of questioning.

"Allow me to make this clear, General Dorok. I ask the questions, you answer them. Do you understand?" Zerris's holographic image finally looks up from the floor and makes eye contact with the General; his face is a plastered visage of exhausted stoicism.

Dorok's cheeks turn beet-red with embarrassment, a feeling he despises. It triggers an anger response that, due to his station, he must suppress. The feedback loop only makes him angrier, and his knuckles turn white as his hands ball into brick-sized fists. "Understood, my Overseer," he responds, seething inside.

"Good," Zerris responds. He crosses his legs and shifts in the chair he's perched in, then immediately changes the subject. "There's another item I need you to work on as well. I need a story. Our attempts to shift opinion seem to be falling short. We need someone internal to take a hit...someone with rank. I want to relay to the people how serious the situation is with our so-called *handlers* in the IGB. The people need an example to make the situation real for them...a defector, perhaps. Do you follow?"

Dorok gazes out the small viewing window of his quarters and thinks for a moment. As he contemplates options for the request at hand, he begins to release his fists from their white-knuckled death-grip at his side. After a moment, he smirks and returns his gaze to Zerris. "Actually, I think we might be able to kill two birds with one stone on Doral Station. I have someone in mind. Someone hig-ranking..." he responds, tickled by his own cleverness.

"Good. I expect a report in-person upon your return. I know I can always count on you for sensitive issues such as these. Get it done," responds Zerris.

The arrogance... Dorok stands emotionally torn. He despises being talked down to and knows the value of his own talents.

Though he is semi-aware of the mind games Zerris plays, he cannot deny the recognition of his efforts. It is a constant battle raging inside the renowned general. Finally, through tightly clenched teeth, Dorok responds, "Thank you, Overseer. Your directive is understood." Then, without a goodbye, the transmission is terminated by Zerris.

A few astronomical units away, the terminals of Doral Station become ripe with activity in preparation for a turnover in shift. In Terminal Twelve, the many doors of the crew's sleeping quarters slide open simultaneously as uniformed men and women spill into the hallways and jog to their stations. One door, however, remains closed. It is the door to a private dormitory, a luxury typically reserved only for officers of the CP's Interstellar Operations. Within the privacy of the room, and just loud enough for its occupant to hear, the distinct voice of Deorum's most notorious wavecast host permeates the space with his usual satirical tone.

"Hello lady boys and gentlebots, welcome to the Cyrus Bolan show. It's a foggy, shitty sort of day here on Deorum, or wherever it is that I'm transmitting from because I'm in fucking hiding! And I find that it sets the perfect tone for the special segment we have for you today on PIRATES! That's right, the pirates of the vitalerium mining operation that is so near and dear to the hearts of the CP. Now, this is a topic that is also near and dear to my heart, considering my own pirate status. That is because, as of two orbits ago, I was designated as a wavecast PIRATE by the Coalition for Prosperity. In the eyes of our gracious autocrats, I TOO am a pirate. Which is why I now transmit from beautiful none of your fuckin' business! So, as you could imagine, I feel like these fine people are my *brothers* in some way. BROTHERS IN AAARMS! I'm joking, obviously. Anyone who knows me, and they are few, would know that I am about as effective with a weapon as I am with a woman!"

Cyrus's voice intensifies, affecting a more serious note as he begins his tirade on the circumstances surrounding vitalerium piracy; a topic that has become a commonly covered mainstay in state-sanctioned news. "Back to my point... As everyone knows, the main source of income for our planetary government overlords is, in fact, the interstellar mining operation surrounding the Vital Cascade: the source of the vibrant blue crystal, vitalerium, that we harvest so we may sell it to the IGB. We exchange it with them for money and the vitalerium weaponry they ultimately convert it into after it's refined. Literally the most important resource for humanity AND the most heavily regulated element in the known universe.

"So, my first question is a rhetorical one: why wouldn't there be pirates? An obvious question at first, until you understand how hard it would be for pirates to do anything with the vitalerium once they have it in their possession. The last three thefts of vitalerium from these pirates amounted to a whopping forty-two tons. But who are they selling raw vitalerium to? The IGB would sooner blow up a planet than allow for that amount of vitalerium to be sold on the black market. Especially one of its planets that it views through a paternalistic set of demon eyes, the light of which burns with the fires of HELL ITSELF.

"I mean look, a generation ago, Ventura was practically invaded by those greenish IGB goons when their government attempted to purchase twenty tons of unrefined crystal from an undisclosed buyer. Plus, with the distinct and easily traceable signature of vitalerium, it would be nearly *impossible* for these pirates to pass that amount through IGB space without being detected, detained, and probably liquified. Or drawn and quartered. I don't know, pick your torture...maybe they're forced to watch videos of the Grand Regent shining his armor with the tears of children until they die of dehydration. Either way, it certainly raises some other questions, the most important of which is this: 'Who do they work for, and how are they able to accomplish this?'

"Well, ladies and gentle man-beasts, I have a theory. I said I HAVE A THEORYYYY! And it comes down to this, a simple, delectably human concept: follow the money." Cyrus begins to sing into the microphone in his best sarcastic karaoke melody: "FOLLOW THE MONEYYY! FOLLOOOOW THE MONEYYYYY! That's right! Funny enough, written into the blatant government theft that is the new CP Initiative 919 is a huge new reallocation of universal credits for vitalerium research. HMM...now isn't that interesting? The beautiful Jennifer Baine, who is without a doubt a soulless cyborg witch...and I'm talking *one hundred* percent a cyborg, people. That ice-cold shell of a woman's got a full-on robot brain.

"ANYWAY! She's been the keynote speaker on a number of anti-IGB narratives over the past few orbits on the state news network, which have very recently returned with a vengeance. So around the same time that we spend fifty trillion UCs on undefined vitalerium research, we also have the state media stoking anti-IGB fires. I'm talking thirteen separate stories in the past two weeks alone! Coincidence? I DON'T THINK SO! Not that I'm a fan of *those* guys...they're complete monsters! Intergalactic Governing Bureau? More like Insane Green... Bitch-ass-motherfuckers!" Cyrus's wavecast technician can be heard laughing in the background at his ridiculous improvisation. "Shut up, Pulthis, you're fuckin' up my groove here. Hehe...

"Point is, I believe we could be looking at an inside job here, folks. Not that I'm sure or anything, but my guess is that these pirates are nothing more than a false flag operation so Zerris can stockpile vitalerium for an eventual conflict with the IGB. I mean, it wouldn't be the first time Deorum tried to make a power play against the IGB. Look at what happened to our last Overseer, Gannon Aganon! He tries to build a sentient Artificial General Intelligence controlled solely by the CP, and then wakes up with a hole in his chest the size of the pirates' last vitalerium haul. AND FOR WHAT!? Trying to fashion himself a girlfriend that can actually carry a conversation!? All joking aside, that's what you get for crossing the IGB, folks. All I'm saying is that in the next few orbits, I'm expecting *big things* to go down. BIG THINGS. I'm talking invasion! I'm talking war! I'm talking dog collars on your children so they can track whether or not they're VITALERIUM PIRATES! I'm talking literal ball gags in the mouths of the dimwitted aristocracy to prevent their lips from flapping! Not that they need them—they're already pumped full of enough drugs to prevent any sort of enlightenment or intellectual development beyond the type that's beneficial for the economy to keep flowing... Ugh..."

Cyrus takes a dramatic pause before switching topics.

"Well, what are you gonna do... We wish them well, folks. That's what we do here, *we wish them well*! Good luck with your dystopian endeavors, whoever..." The monologue emitting from the wavecast, receiver fades out.

"Hehe, Bolan, you damned psycho. You haven't changed a bit since primary school..." says a man affectionately as he lays with the device resting on his chest. "How can they ban you with content that entertaining?" The question bounces off the walls of the Commander's quarters, meant for no one's ears but his own. He glances around the room, taking a moment for pause, then mutters, "Let's just hope you're way off on that theory, old friend." He pushes the wavecast receiver into a small safe in a compartment under his bed, then lowers the panel to conceal it. The man hops out of the small bed carved into the gray metal wall of the Commander's quarters with renewed energy from a restful night of sleep. Promptly dropping to his haunches, two sets of fifty make for one hundred push-ups, and a set of one hundred sit-ups completes his morning ritual. He lifts himself from the floor, alternating between flexing his impressive physique and stretching to reduce the burning sensation in his muscles.

"Bes, open the blast shields," he calls out to the empty, metal-clad ten-by-ten room.

"Opening blast shields, babe," returns a voice with a unique Earth accent. He had chosen the "Old American-south" accent option because he found it amusing, and for reasons he could not define, comforting; same as the name and affectionate tone he had given the basic AI that governed his room. As soon as the computerized voice finishes responding, the far wall behind his dock begins to segment into small triangles, which first delineate and then fold in on themselves until nothing is left but hex-glass between him and the vastness of space. He has a beautiful view from his quarters. Stars twinkle in the distance, and a sliver of Deorum sits in view through the bottom corner of his hexagonal viewing window. Though beautiful, they are not the focal point. Another spatial anomaly commands the viewer's full attention.

A gigantic sliver, shaped like a preternatural crack in space-time itself, sits in center-view. Its edges shimmer with golden light, but its contents, the space within the narrow slit, seems somehow even darker than the actual space around it: the Vital Fracture. Representing the mouth of the Vital Cascade, it is the point from which all vitalerium originates in the form of meteors that burst from the space crevasse like coins from a winning slot machine. The anomaly, although aesthetically analogous to a black hole in all but shape, certainly does not behave like one.

The Commander, a handsome man just shy of six feet tall, walks past his wall of accolades and awards from a lifetime of dutiful service to the bathroom for a morning shower. A wall-length screen displays images of him with his team on a loop next to his trophy wall. Some pictures are professional, with the team standing together in their uniforms. Others, not so much. Next to it, a wilted house plant sits on a floating shelf, its leaves tan from dehydration, its soil as coarse as gravel. For a dry climate succulent such as this to die, one would almost have to be actively trying to kill it.

Lukewarm water cascades downward from multiple showerheads. It rinses through his dark brown hair and neatly trimmed beard to a drain that actively sucks down the runoff for filtration and repurposing. Accommodations like these were reserved only for officers. The rest of the crew had to use communal showers. It takes him no longer than four minutes to complete his bathing routine before he is toweling off and standing before his wardrobe.

Four identical outfits and two empty hangers dangle from the rack before him. He grabs one of the black nylon outfits with golden accents. After slipping into the uniform, he zips the outfit up to his chest, just next to the blue CP sigil and name embroidered on the breast. The blue writing reads "Cmdr. Braxton Hughes, CP-IO," with the "IO" standing for "Interstellar Operations."

The main deck of Doral Space Station bustles as shifts end, and the next crew is briefed before taking over. Handover is always somewhat entertaining to watch, as exhausted crew members sleepily update their fresh replacements, who are often grumpy at the starts of their shifts. Chrome control panels and pearly white machinery gleam, whirring away before the glorious spectacle of the void visible through the station's main viewing window. The space before them extends ostensibly forever; out past the stars that sparkle in the background. However, no one seems to notice the beauty as they go about their work. Prevalence surely does breed indifference, and everyone has a job to do.

"COMMANDER ON DECK!" shouts Sergeant Litt, who snaps a crisp CP salute at Braxton. The other crewmates immediately stand erect and salute in unison.

Braxton wastes no time, returning their razor-sharp salutes with a much more casual walking salute as he approaches the

Commander's dock at the center of the room. He addresses his crew in the familiar, the way one would to their family. The crew is and always has been that to him. "Who's taking over now, Gama Squad? Who the hell let you lot out of the brig?" he jests.

The sergeant lightheartedly returns, "Hehe, that'd be Micah, Sir. She said as long as we behave, we can go outside and play."

A slender woman with her hair tied neatly in a bun walks toward the main door at a brisk pace. "Someone's got to be work-mom for you grunts. Besides, I just pulled a double and it's my turn to hit the sack. You boys have fun," she says to Litt. Before exiting, Lieutenant Micah turns toward Braxton. "Commander," she acknowledges. Her eyes sparkle when they connect with his. The Commander nods in response then continues hitting buttons on his dock, unaware that she has not left yet. She stands there silently for a moment as Braxton sets up his workstation.

"Permission to speak freely, sir?" she asks, waiting patiently.

"Granted. Shoot, Lieutenant," he replies without looking up.

Her smile disappears, and she says bluntly, "*Water* your *plant*." The tone of this command is half playful, half threatening.

Braxton looks up from his dock and smiles, then with a nod replies, "If that'll be all, Mom..." gesturing her toward the door. Once the door closes behind her, he looks down at his dock and mutters so no one can hear him, "Shit..." having yet again forgotten to take care of the plant gifted to him.

Turning his attention back to Gamma Squadron, who now mans the station, he shouts, "Alright everyone, listen up! Got an announcement before we get into it. I just received notice that our delivery of rations is running late. On top of that, due to resources being stretched thin, we will no longer have access to soda and a number of other food items in the commissary...they're tightening the belt on us, folks."

A collective groan of disapproval fills the room as the news hits Gamma Squadron. There are few pleasures to be enjoyed while on tour at the base, so even the small ones become important to the crew in maintaining their sanity.

"Aw, what the hell? First I can't own my house with this new 919 nonsense, and now I can't even enjoy a soda!?" shouts one of the men.

"919 doesn't affect you if you were already homeless to begin with, Jarvis," replies Braxton. The comment elicits a half-hearted laugh from the team, though it is quickly followed by a somber silence. Braxton understands how hard it is to maintain morale even without worsening regulations and miserly approach to their benefits. "Ugh... Look, I'm no fan of the situation either. If you ask me, it ain't right. None of it. I'm no high-powered representative from the court, but I will be fighting to get these items back on the menu for all of you. For the time being, we've got a job to do. And I, for one, am damned good at my job. What about you, Gamma Squadron?"

A resounding, "Sir, yes Sir!" follows from his loyal crew.

"That's what I like to hear. Now, Team, Sitrep? Let's hear it! We're expecting a visit from General Benson at eleven hundred hours, and I want good news to deliver. We've been waiting on this vital expulsion for nearly forty-eight hours. Where's my raw-V?"

A step below the captain's dock, a uniformed man sorts through a steady flow of data and figures hovering before him. He answers immediately, "Vital fibrillations are reading steady at thirty-second intervals now, with minimal fluctuation. Have been for the last forty-two minutes. We're due for a gravitational retraction any minute now."

"Alright, let's catch some big blue fish. I'm looking to hit full haul today. How about you, grunts?" asks Braxton.

"Sir, yes Sir!" yells Gamma Squadron dutifully in unison.

"That's what I like to hear! Bring up comms with docking bay. They better be on their game today!" Braxton bellows.

"Connecting now, Sir," replies another member of Gamma Squad. A moment later, a pilot's face appears on the viewing window. His black flight armor gleams in the light of the docking bay, somewhat sleeker than a normal Guardsman's armor. Tucked under his arm is a helmet with the letters "CP-IO" stamped in fluorescent blue. Behind him, members of the flight crew dash back and forth in the background as they prepare their ships for departure. The vessels they prepare are Brillus Carriers, essentially transport ships equipped with large, bulky hulls meant for stowing large quantities of harvested minerals. The ships are certainly not designed for battle, but due to recent events, they have been outfitted with cannons bolted haphazardly to their exteriors. This pilot sports a head of short brown hair gelled neatly into place. His voice is peppered with a sort of endearing cockiness commonly seen among the pilot ranks.

"Commander," the pilot says coolly over the frequency. "Reporting sir!"

"At ease, Captain Rillos. Not that you weren't already taking it easy... How's the weather out there, Lex?"

"Well, it's cold, empty...pretty dark. Normal void conditions. I mean it's space so...you know. How you doing, Ol' Smoke Drive?" The pilot winks at the screen as he finishes his sarcastic weather report. "Ol' Smoke Drive" had been the Commander's nickname when he was still piloting vessels, on account of his multiple times landing ships just moments before his grav-drive quite literally exploded.

Commander Braxton Hughes and Captain Lexoran Rillos had once been classmates in the CP-IO academy. Both were exceptional pilots; however, Braxton was always seeking more. He chose a different path, and steadily climbed the ladder in the CP-IO until he reached the rank of Commander. He had achieved everything he wanted; or at least what he thought he wanted. Positions of leadership within the CP are not always as they seem from the outside. Over the years, they remained the closest of friends; more than a few close brushes with death together will do that.

Because of this history, Flight Captain Lex gets away with a lot. Not to say that Braxton doesn't maintain an unorthodox relationship with his crew, especially when compared with other more draconian CP outfits. However, Lex is often allowed to step much further over that line than others. In other companies, this might create jealousy among the ranks, but the two seem to navigate these waters effortlessly. The real fact of the matter is: the pair are just too likeable for anyone to stay mad at. Living on the Vital Cascade Mining Operation is a tough life. For most, their banter brings about a sort of free entertainment for the crew who devote themselves to living in the dead of space.

One of the crew hands Braxton an angular white mug filled to the brim with black coffee. He takes it graciously, then slowly sips the near-boiling black liquid. Having finally begun satisfying his caffeine requirements, the Commander grunts before starting his sentence. "Sounds delightful. I'm well... Wish I could be out there with the fleet. I miss it some days..." He masks the hint of regret in his voice with theatrical exhaustion, then pivots to the task at hand. "By the way, you will address me as Commander while we're working. Now, how about a serious status report, Captain Ass-clown?"

"Just making sure you're awake, Commander," he says, grinning. "We're twelve Brillus Carriers strong and three X48s ready for liftoff on your mark, Sir."

"I want fifteen Carriers and two extra X48s guarding the formation," replies the Commander, who wishes to leave no room for error. They will need as much firepower as they can possibly muster...just in case. "Wake people up if you have to; we need a big day today. I want a fifteen-point global formation, all possible directions covered. I don't want a single dust speck of vitalerium passing our nets. We should be experiencing the retraction any minute now, and the expulsion won't be long after that, so get out there ASAP. We've got the General visiting today, no mistakes."

"You got it, Commander!" replies Lexoran before signing off. As the video feed disappears, the viewing window returns to the usual view of space.

"Lucky bastard..." mutters Braxton, remembering his days in the cockpit. He had spent countless orbits flying an array of different ships; R350s, X47s and X48s, even the Tritan L-5. *Oh, the Tritan L-5, what an absolute mechanical and technological marvel.* He lets his mind slip into sweet memories of adrenaline-pumping flights for a moment as he sinks into his command chair. The rush is what he misses most. He remembers feeling the adrenaline filling his blood, shooting fire up his neck and ice water down his veins, muscles tensing to counter the g-force during a take-off... The excitement of a hunt that ends in success... The freedom... He gives himself five seconds with the memory before snapping himself back to reality. Wiping the coffee from his top lip, Braxton returns to his duties.

"Talk to me, team. What are we seeing out there on the scopes?"

A crewmate uses his station to sweep for signs of other ships on his screen but finds nothing. "No sign of any foreign ships, sir."

"I want your eyes glued to that screen. You alert me the second you get even a whiff of pirates. I want updates every five minutes, then every minute following expulsion."

"Copy, Sir!" the crew replies.

"Commander Hughes, Captain Rillos has departed and is en route!"

Braxton nods silently. *Good hunting, old friend.*

Thirty minutes pass by painfully uneventfully. The heavy anticipation makes the passage of time feel longer for those on duty in the command deck. The crew sit in their seats, fading quickly as they monitor changes in the Vital Fracture. Unfortunately, there are no changes to be observed. Commander

Braxton Hughes sits slumped in his chair with pursed lips, staring into space. The white coffee mug dangles from his index and middle fingers, emptied of its contents. He counts the stars to pass the time, ignoring the uncomfortable silence that permeates the command deck.

Braxton exhales loudly. "Sitrep?" he asks, his voice flat with boredom.

"Still holding steady at thirty-second fibrillation intervals."

"Scopes?" Braxton asks again in monotone.

"We're clear for at least twenty astronomical units," returns a voice from Gamma Squad.

Braxton stares at the time on his TAB, which reads "08:14." He swivels in his chair, grunting as he does so. "Ugh...what does a guy need to do to get some action around here?"

Just as he starts to reposition in his chair, a voice bellows out from the deck, "SIR! We've got a twenty-four-second fibrillation!"

Braxton's blood pressure surges, and he jumps to his feet. "It's about damn time! Get Captain Rillos on the common freq, now!" The room comes to life at the sound of his voice. Everyone at their stations moves on double-time. Captain Rillos appears in the cockpit of his X48 combat vessel. "HUNTER-01, we just hit twenty-four-second intervals. Keep your nugget on a swivel. It's coming..." says Braxton, referring to Captain Rillos by his call sign.

Captain Rillos's voice echoes through the speakers of the command deck. "Funny, that's what Sergeant Litt's mom said last night."

All of Gamma Squad enjoys a hardy laugh. Even Sergeant Litt chuckles, "Yea, yea...hope you don't crash your ship out there, Lex!" Then, under his breath he mutters, "Cheeky bastard..."

"Sergeant Litt knows I'm just kidding. Everyone knows his sister is the real prize anyway," retorts the pilot.

"Eleven-second interval!" shouts the tracker from Gamma Squad.

Braxton starts to grin with excitement but forces it back to redirect his energy toward focusing the team. "Save the jokes for after the collection! This is going to be a big one—the intervals are dropping fast! Keep your eyes peeled for bogies. You should be seeing the expulsion any second now."

Lex nods silently, his clear visor snapping opaque for combat as he signs off. He could have done that after, but he did always have a flair for dramatization.

His image fades to show the carriers repositioning around, above, and below the massive spatial anomaly. Its shimmering gold outline now seems to pulsate like a slow, beating heart. The deep black of its center begins to turn a deep shade of purple, which then transitions to a deep blue. Then, light blue. Soon, the light from the center of the Vital Fracture becomes so intense that it floods the entire command deck with an extra-galactic brilliance. It flickers as the pulsation quickens and the golden edges draw inward.

"Two-second intervals!"

"Holy shit, this might be a record, Commander!" shouts Sergeant Litt as he runs to man his station.

Every eye in the station is on the gigantic blue and gold crack in space-time. The pulsation of the fracture's edges becomes more pronounced, until the anomaly seems to ripple erratically in the dead of space. Suddenly, the opening of the Vital Fracture collapses in on itself until it's reduced to a small blue orb floating in space. Braxton waits with bated breath for what's to come next.

A flash of light erupts from the Vital Fracture as it returns to its normal shape with unfathomable speed. The brilliance forces the entire CP deck squad to cover their eyes despite the polarized shield of the viewing window. When the light finally dulls, Braxton looks back to the window to see the glow of dozens of vitalerium meteorites of varying sizes cascading outward in all directions from the Vital Fracture; after-images from the flash still obscuring his vision. All members of Gamma Squad momentarily pause to take in the beauty of the scene before them. They marvel through the viewing wall at the blue glow of space-derived energy that peppers the space before them.

"Get me a count on that expulsion!" shouts Braxton.

"I'm reading seventy-two crystalline meteors, with thirty-seven in the focus range! Fourteen in small scale, seventeen medium scale, and six *huge* ones, Commander!"

"Get on tagging all those meteors so we can relay tracking to the pilots ASAP! We haven't had a release like this in almost an orbit!" The energy in the room is electric, and adrenaline levels run high as the room rallies around the Commander's directions. Braxton presses a button on his command dock to switch back to the pilots' feed.

Captain Lexoran Rillos's voice comes through the comms, cool as ever. "Commander, looks like an Orbit's Day Celebration out here with all this blue." He speaks in the same tone he might use when ordering coffee.

"HUNTER-01, we've got a total count of seventy-two rocks out there with thirty-seven high priorities, relaying tracking now. Focus your efforts on the big boys before you begin collecting the marginal-scale meteors."

"Yeah…" says Lex with a smirk, "I've done this a *few* times before, boss-man." He taps a few keys on his multi-function display to forward the data to his formation, calls on the formation frequency, "HUNTER Flight, punch it!" then firewalls his throttle before disappearing from the viewing window.

Everyone on the command deck watches as the fifteen carriers scramble like flies. They dart from their original positions to track the numerous glowing rocks hurtling through space in all directions from the Vital Fracture. Gamma Squadron provides the field technical support as the carriers each lock onto individual vitalerium meteors, and race to come within tractor range. The five X48s follow behind, each guarding zones of three Brillus Carriers per fighter. The pilots inside diligently scan their surroundings for anything out of the ordinary.

As the first carrier comes within suitable range of its target, the pilot releases the inventory hatch and activates their ship's tractor beam. A stark white arc of electrical magnetism bursts from the interior of the hatch and connects with the vitalerium meteor. The meteor immediately begins to lose speed, then comes to a complete halt before moving in the opposite direction of its trajectory. It then follows the path of the tractor beam toward the ship's compartment, where it is captured and stored safely inside. Another Brillus Carrier in the second group makes contact with its target and tractors in a second meteor from space. Then a third. Each ship redirects toward another meteor once it acquires its target vitalerium crystal.

"Talk to me, HUNTER-01!" says Commander Hughes over comms.

"Seven down, thirty more to go before we scavenge the marginal-range objects."

"Good! This is a sprint, keep up the pace. I want a running count every sixty seconds until we clear the field. Let me know if you spot *anything* out of the ordinary."

"Wilco. Make that ten—my squad is on a roll."

Braxton can no longer hold back his grin. The expulsion in progress is without a doubt the biggest in recent memory. This would surely put them back on track for the quarter, which tickles his affinity for perfectionism. *General Dorok better give me a damn promotion for this,* he thinks to himself. For a fleeting second, the weight of the expectations set on his station are lifted from his shoulders, and for the first time in a long time, he almost feels like celebrating.

However, a blaring alarm and flashing red lights interrupt his feelings of bliss, immediately putting everyone on high alert. "Scopes, what's the alert for?" asks Commander Hughes, but before the navigator can respond, the answer to his question appears through the viewing window. Four small points in the space above the Vital Fracture suddenly begin rippling with color. At first the waves are subtle and intermittent, but within a fraction of a second they increase in frequency until space itself seems to boil. Suddenly, a barrage of bright green plasma charges descends on numerous carriers with frightening velocity. Two of the carriers are immediately caught in the firestorm, and as plasma connects with their hulls, they explode into massive conflagrations of green, blue, and purple. The light reflects off the faces of Gamma Squad as they twist in horror.

The rippling space reaches a tipping point as four ships burst into existence from the empty void of space. Immediately, tractor beams begin to arc from the newly arrived enemy ships and connect with nearby vitalerium meteors, pulling the loot into their own compartments. The vessels are long and dagger-shaped. Wide storage compartments with forward-reaching, angular wings taper into narrow cockpits at their bows. Another four long, vertical wings protrude from the rear of the vessels and extend forward past the cockpits, ending in sharp points; two dorsal, two ventral. Embedded in each of the six wings are massive, military-grade vitalerium cannons. The black and white paint strewn sloppily across the hulls of the invading ships is immediately recognizable.

Braxton's stomach drops as his worst fears suddenly come to fruition. But the cortisol that stings his brainstem forces him into quick action. "We've got pirates incoming! Initiate Protocol Black, now!" he barks, prompting the members of Gamma Squadron to snap out of their trance and react. The Commander slams his fist onto the comms button and relays the dire message to the ships: "HUNTER-01, we've got four bandits with cloaking tech incoming from Vital Fracture North! All ships engage with deadly force!"

"I see 'em," Lex responds, "HUNTER flight, defending."

"HUNTER flight, PRESS," says Braxton.

"HUNTER, engaging," Lex replies, remaining even-keeled despite the chaos.

HUNTER flight surges forward in pursuit of the vessels that threaten their crew and haul. Within seconds, the beautiful scene that was the Vital Fracture expulsion erupts into a firestorm of red, green, blue, and orange. The space around the crevasse ignites with the ballistic discharge of almost two dozen ships. The CP-IO X48s follow closely on the tails of the agile pirate vessels, which zigzag across the expulsion field, grabbing every vitalerium meteor they can while they work to evade aerial assault. As another two chunks of glowing blue space mass disappear inside the hulls of the pirate ships, Braxton begins to sweat.

The command deck falls into a sort of organized chaos. A Gamma Squad member calls out from behind her console, "Commander, should I engage stationary cannons to target intruders?!" Her voice cracks from the stress of the situation.

"No!" orders Braxton the exact moment she finishes her sentence. "Do not engage weapon systems. Our ships are too close. That would have been an option if we had seen them coming... Scopes! Did we pick up on anything prior to their arrival?"

"No sir! They just appeared out of thin air!" shouts the man, scrambling through his data and tapping his holoscreen.

"We're in space, Watson! There is no air! And what the hell kind of stealth tech avoids detection without making so much as a blip on our sensors?"

Meanwhile, outside the station, a maelstrom of fire ensues. While in hot pursuit, two bright blue blasts from Lex's cannons splash across the black metal hull of one of the pirate ships. It engulfs the cockpit, turning the high-tech piece of machinery into a fireball of dismantled panels and components. Lex narrowly misses the debris as he flies through the fiery wreckage, already tracking his next target. "Splash one bandit, three to go..." Lex growls over the common freq.

Braxton wants to respond, but the sight of black and white ships engulfing another four meteors from space as they outmaneuver his forces prevents his mouth from functioning.

Another chill runs down his spine as he sees a pirate vessel adeptly maneuver behind one of the X48s in his fleet. The CP-IO ship's attempts to escape are futile, and it eventually succumbs to the green firepower of the pirate vessel, then explodes. A few seconds later, another carrier suffers the same fate. The Commander's mouth dries, and his throat clamps shut as the three remaining pirate ships then instantly disappear into the rippling nothingness of space.

"HUNTER-01, Sitrep!" he calls into his console as he stares out the viewing window. Blackened pieces of ships' metal and carrier fragments litter his view of the Vital Fracture. A few ships can still be seen chasing down the last vitalerium meteorites while the intact carriers with full inventories race back toward Doral Station. The captain does not respond.

"HUNTER-01, REPORT!" he shouts again as he begins to dread his captain's fate. Only garbled static returns, leaving the Commander with a pit in his stomach as if a knife had just pierced his gut. The lack of response from Captain Rillos invokes the ominous silence of a graveyard amongst Gamma Squadron. Braxton wipes the sweat from his brow, then interlocks his fingers behind his head. He takes long, deep breaths, trying desperately to calm his pounding heart.

Suddenly, the intercom static breaks and a voice emerges. "SCHCH... How... read."

The Commander races back to his dock and speaks to the incoming voice. "Commander here, HUNTER-01, is that you?"

"HUNTER-01, got you five-by-five. Pursuit led me to the dead zone around the far side of the fracture, over."

"Is your ship compromised?" asks Braxton.

"Negative sir. We lost contact with the three remaining bandits, but I saw them escape. I don't know about you, but I've never seen cloaking tech act like that before...you want us to RTB?"

"Affirm RTB. We'll debrief when you're back onboard. I need a status update on the retrieval crew!"

"It's not good... They got the jump on us, Commander. They made off with at least a third of the expulsion. Worse than that, we lost carriers two, six, and eleven, and they got... Polandus, Sir..." The captain pauses for a moment, adrenaline ebbing enough for his brain to process the events. The loss of the pilots, his friends, now hits him with the crushing weight of an anvil. Despite the grief he feels, he steels his voice.

The Commander feels the weight of his station compress him into his dock. He sighs in disbelief. Every fiber of his being yearns for him to curl into the fetal position, but he blocks it out. His thoughts revert to his training. *You can't deal with this now; you've got a job to do. We act now and mourn later...* He finally musters a defeated response. "Just get back to the station for a full debrief. Glad to hear you made it out of there, Lex."

"Copy. I was able to tractor in a few pieces of debris from the pirate ship for analysis. Maybe someone can make heads or tails of it."

Braxton looks to his crew, who seem to mirror his sentiments. At the far end of the room, one of the crew members begins to weep. The gravity of loss has crept over the command deck like a dark, looming cloud. As the Commander, it is Braxton's job to address this and rally his crew.

"This is a dark day for Doral Station... I know. But do not forget that this is the reality of our line of work. Those who we've lost...they cannot be replaced. I want each and every one of you here to know that there will be a time to mourn your losses...but right now, I need you all to come together for what comes next. General Dorok Benson will be here shortly, so we have other matters to attend to. I want a status report from every station on this deck within the hour. We need to know what the hell happened out there!"

"I hope by *what the hell happened out there* you mean that you've exceeded your vitalerium quota." The menacing voice comes unexpectedly through the intercom as the viewing wall switches to a video feed. A behemoth of a man donning black and blue armor now glares at Gamma Squadron. His bald head shines in the soft glow of his own ship's deck.

"General Benson!" exclaims Braxton, blindsided by Dorok's comm. He shoots the comms squad member a subtle glare. However, the man only returns a shrug, similarly confused by how Dorok now connects to their feed. Braxton straightens up and responds, "General, I'll be happy to provide you with a full report upon your arrival."

"I look forward to the good news, Commander Hughes. My ship will arrive on station in thirty minutes," replies Dorok.

Great, the bastard will be here early, thinks Braxton behind a stoic expression. Without showing signs of weakness or hesitation, he responds, "We await your arrival, sir. Safe travels."

"See you soon," replies Dorok. His tone is almost sinister. He then reaches forward and ends the transmission. A collective exhale follows from the members of Gamma Squadron as Dorok's face disappears.

"Everyone, you know what you have to do. Get to it," directs Braxton before exiting the command deck and making his way to the docking bay.

First appearing as a speck in the distance, Doral Station soon becomes visible through the viewing window of Dorok's command deck. The structure of the gigantic extra-orbital space station begins to delineate as his vessel approaches with haste. It is comprised of a collection of tarnished, off-white spheres connected by narrow tubes that form walkways between them. The largest sphere is Dorok's destination: the docking bay.

Upon arriving, the black and blue vessel hovers outside the largest sphere of Doral Station, waiting to dock. The off-white panels of the docking bay retract to reveal the vacuum chamber, and the ship glides smoothly inside. Dorok's pilot lands the vessel expertly amongst the other ships, many of which smoke and smolder from their recent pirate encounter. He exhales with relief as Dorok exits the command deck without commenting. An elevator hisses as it lowers Dorok and five armored CP Guardsmen to the docking bay floor. The General's mech armor clanks against the metal panels as he storms through the bay on a mission.

As he traverses the length of the bay, he is met in the middle by Commander Braxton Hughes. The Commander is accompanied by Lieutenant Micah, prematurely woken from her slumber to help collect statements and report on the recent events.

Commander Hughes is the first to speak when they meet their guests. "General Benson, welcome to Doral Station. We've been anticipating your arrival, sir," he starts respectfully.

"Spare me the pleasantries. You know why I'm here. Report," Dorok responds coldly. He is the only one in the group who does not wear a helmet. The blue glow from his five CP companions' headgear casts a judgmental glare on Braxton's face.

Braxton, a noble man at his core, takes a deep breath in preparation for the delivery of bad news. He reports succinctly and without reservation. "Sir, we've had another run-in with vitalerium pirates. We had one of the biggest expulsions in months, but due to unforeseen circumstances, we remain twelve tons short of our goal."

Dorok's snarl is enough to convey his disappointment. He glances back at the Guardsmen behind him, then returns his burning gaze to Braxton. Lieutenant Micah shifts from discomfort at the General's response, but Braxton remains stiff as a statue. His lack of reaction triggers Dorok, who responds disdainfully, "You don't seem to be bothered by your situation, Commander. Tell me, why is it that you find confidence in failure?"

"General, I speak honestly because of my level of respect for you and your position. What you perceive as confidence is nothing more than frustration at having my expectations realized. I have made multiple requests to reevaluate our defensive resources...to account for the attacks we've experienced in recent months. Despite the successes of the unknown enemy we face, we find ourselves severely lacking in defensive firepower and reinforcements. We are fighting against bandits who are heavily armed with new-generation tech, sir. We are at odds with..."

"Excuses..." replies Dorok sternly, interrupting his subordinate. "This is the third time you've come up short, and my patience has all but run out. Consider yourself under review. Clear your schedule—I want a full run-through of all operations on Doral Station!"

Braxton, half expecting this sort of response from his overbearing superior, simply blinks through the saliva that flies in his face from Dorok's lips and calmly responds, "As you wish, General Benson." Without hesitation, Braxton turns on his heels and leads the men to the command deck.

As they walk through the space station, Dorok nudges one of the Guardsmen with his elbow, then stealthily hands him a small copper sliver out of the view of his hosts. The Guardsman discreetly peels away from the group as they continue to follow Braxton to their destination. An automatic door slides promptly open to reveal Gamma Squadron, who still work diligently to recap and record the events of the last hour.

"Commander on deck!" cries Sergeant Litt as the group enters. All members of Gamma Squad stand simultaneously and give the customary CP salute as the group enters solemnly. At the sight of General Dorok and his entourage, the chatter amongst the crew is silenced instantly. The General is the first of the group to speak.

"Show me a recap of the recent expulsion. NOW!" shouts Dorok at Braxton's crew. The comms specialist rushes back to her station and begins to tap frantically on her control panel. A few moments later, the view of the Vital Fracture, now cleared of all activity, is replaced with a video replay of the attack. Green, blue, red, and orange flashes of light gleam on the watchful faces in the room. Many of the crew look away as the scene unfolds, unable to watch the battle for a second time. The recorded voices of Braxton, crew members, and pilots play loudly over the room's speakers, making the situation all the more uncomfortable.

"Stop the replay!" barks Dorok. "Go back ten seconds and then start it." The comms specialist obliges, rewinding the video as requested. The video relives the moment when Commander Hughes tells Gamma Squad not to engage the base's stationary cannon systems. His voice echoes clearly and ominously through the command deck. "No! Do not engage weapon systems. Our ships are too close. That would have been an option if we had seen them coming..."

"Play it again!" Dorok's long forehead vein pulses in his face with anger. As it plays again, he glares at Braxton. "Care to tell me why you ordered your crew NOT to fire upon a clear threat to our mining operation?"

"General Benson, I felt that it would have put our own resources and pilots in jeopardy. The ships were flying in too close of a proximity to ensure success. The weapon system's targeting AI is reliable but not perfect, and in situations like these protocol states..."

Dorok interrupts the Commander by thrusting a finger in his face. "In situations like these it requires strong decision-making. A skill that I am beginning to question in you. Tell me, given the events of the recent past, why in the NAME OF THE FOUR PRIMES WOULD YOU FIND IT ACCEPTABLE TO NOT TAKE ACTION AGAINST A CLEAR AND PRESENT THREAT!"

"For the safety of my crew, sir! I take the now-constant threat of piracy deathly seriously, but I put the lives of my crew first!" replies Braxton, trying his best to shelve his aggravation, which is beginning to boil over. Braxton knows in his heart of hearts that he has made the right decision in protecting his pilots. His values run strong, and in his mind the Doral Station crew, above all else, remains his most important resource. The idea of putting them in danger for some chunks of blue rock seems absurd to him.

"Oh really? For which crew's safety do you mean exactly? The crew of Doral Station, or a different crew?"

"Respectfully, *Sir*, but what exactly does that mean!?" asks Commander Hughes, almost shell-shocked by the line of questioning. He stares fire into the eyes of Dorok, who now stands just inches away from his face. Nothing is said for a few seconds, which feels like minutes to the crew under the weight of the circumstances.

As the staring contest ensues, the doors to the command deck slide apart and the fifth Guardsman enters with his TAB device extended. He promptly breaks the tension by addressing Dorok. "General Benson, Sir? You're going to want to see this..."

"Bring it here!" orders Dorok. The Guardsman, a lieutenant donning armor with green accents and lights, marches over to Dorok and extends his wrist, revealing his TAB device. The holograms surrounding his wrist reveal multiple text conversations. Dorok skims the content, then abruptly grunts, "Explain."

"These were conversations pulled directly from Commander Hughes's private quarters dock. They detail an encrypted conversation with an unknown recipient."

Braxton's feelings of frustration with the intrusion of privacy cause him to lose his cool disposition. He angrily asks, "Who gave you permission to access a superior officer's private quarters, Lieutenant!?" The lieutenant ignores him and looks up at Dorok, who continues to read from the man's TAB device.

"I DID!" shouts Dorok. Then, in an instant, his ferocious scowl morphs into a cocky smirk. "Funny you should have a problem with that, because this conversation seems to document your leaking of detailed information on this morning's Vital expulsion to a non-CP recipient! Care to comment on that, Commander!?"

"THAT IS ABSURD! I BLEED BLACK AND BLUE!" shouts the confounded Commander. His head spins from confusion.

"There's more, sir. I found this in a hidden compartment in his quarters..." responds Dorok's Lieutenant before handing over a small wavecast receiving device. "It seems to be jailbroken to receive unsanctioned media..."

The Lieutenant had only been in his room for a few short minutes. How could he have found his device and supposedly broken into his private comms in that short a time? Braxton's critical thinking finally delivers him to a conclusion. The hidden purpose behind the unlikely sequence of events hits him like a wrecking ball, causing the pit in his stomach to return. A visit immediately after a vitalerium pirate encounter, the unwarranted, unannounced search and seizure of his private property, the supposed "irrefutable" evidence produced out of thin air, and Dorok's incendiary demeanor; an accusatory disposition from the very beginning of his arrival... Braxton is being set up. In that moment, Braxton knows he is powerless, and he knows what comes next.

Commander Hughes straightens his posture, then exhales. "I had no communication with outside entities. That much I know, and that response will not change no matter what false evidence is presented."

"Save it, traitor. By the laws designated by the Coalition for Prosperity Party, you are hereby under arrest for treason." Dorok then motions for the other Guardsmen to restrain him. A Guardsman walks behind him and drops a small metal disc on the ground. The second it touches the floor of the command deck, it expands to cover a larger surface area. The men pull Braxton backward until both of his feet stand firmly on the disc, which latches shut, locking his feet in place. The Commander does not resist, only glares into the eyes of the

General with discontent. Another Guardsman then removes a horseshoe-shaped metal device from his utility belt and slides it onto the back of Braxton's neck. It immediately closes like a vise on Hughes's bare skin and begins to emit beads of blue light. Braxton becomes frozen from the neck down, locked in his standing position. The metal disc begins to hover just an inch from the ground, and the Guardsmen push their captive toward the exit. The crew is left speechless as their beloved Commander is carted off. No one can believe what they are seeing.

Braxton's last words are cutting as he is pushed toward Dorok's ship. "You should have picked a dumber fall guy, Dorok."

Dorok laughs before tapping the side of Braxton's horseshoe-shaped collar, which freezes his head in its place. "Save it for the Cube interrogators, traitor."

CHAPTER 24:

Separate Paths

The Leebrus Red-Light District; dirty, dingy, and teeming with life. As the name implies, the entire sector seems to glow a crimson hue. The bright lights of holograms beaming from surrounding buildings both illuminate and mask the neglected filth covering the streets. Droves of customers weave between each other as they seek outlets for their carnal pleasures. Amongst them, thousands of solicitors disperse themselves throughout the crowded streets. Here, there exists an outlet for every pleasure, and pleasure enough for all to indulge. Women, men, hybrid and non, the surgically altered, trans and everything in between. Even technological indulgences in the form of shapely humanoid Maebots are available for purchase; an option for those who are more...mechanically inclined. They garner their nickname from the first model of robotic AI built specifically for human gratification, which was simply named "Mae." These Maebots walk the streets with their human and hybrid solicitor counterparts, all with the same goal in mind: to fill the void with pleasure. Anything and everything for a price, all for that special someone with enough credits for the intended mission. Whatever the vice, there is undoubtedly both a buyer and a seller on call.

A brothel crier declares the quality of her Maebots loudly for all to hear outside of her establishment, named The Pleasure Mech-A. She is a hybrid woman who wears brimming plumage that stems upward circumferentially from her lower quarters, reminiscent of a peacock's feathers. Her voice is loud and piercing as she addresses the masses. "Come one, come all...that you've got inside you!" She winks at a passerby after her pun. "That's right! Make a visit to every Maebot brothel in this sector and I promise you will find *nothing even close* to the selection we've got here! Experience a pleasure that is beyond that which biology alone can provide! Just ask any of our repeat customers...and oh are they plentiful. Nothing! No, nothing can compare to the downright pristine...the sublime...the divine...the *immaculate* pleasures provided here at THE PLEASURE MECH-A! Take a step inside and feel what it's like to see the face of GOD!"

The Maebots behind her pose provocatively to add theater to her sales pitch, twisting and contorting their bodies in ways impossible for most humans. Some are newer models, clad with fake skin and only a few visible tells of robotic signature. Other, older models display their naked mechanical parts with no intent to disguise. Neither seem troubled in finding consistent work. A female model Maebot cartwheels into a perfect handstand and splits its legs in opposing directions until its feet windmill to the ground beside its arms. Just a few feet away, a shockingly endowed male Maebot with glowing green eyes flaunts its impressive gifts wrapped tightly beneath its acrylic pants.

A heavily tattooed man in white, gold, and black clothing walks past this so-called "holy land" arm in arm with a beautiful young hybrid girl. She lets out a high-pitched laugh as she stumbles in tandem with him through the crowds. The man, clearly less intoxicated, supports the lion's share of her weight as they walk toward a residential building...his residence. They ride the elevator to his floor while exchanging flirty banter and taking short breaks to make out and explore each other preemptively. She runs her fingers across his neatly buzzed hair while his hands disappear into her outfit. The elevator doors open and the two practically explode from its confines into the dingy hallway. As he fumbles with his TAB device to open the door to his apartment, the hybrid girl tosses her bubblegum-pink hair backward, shrieking with laughter. The volume of their antics can practically be heard on the adjacent floors.

Finally, his door chimes and the click of a disengaging lock mechanism follows. They both stumble into the unlit apartment with their lips locked. Once the door shuts behind them, the apartment is pitch-black except for a sliver of light that peeks in from the thin window across the room. As they begin to disrobe in the dark, the man says to his guest, "You just hold on, princess. Let me set the vibe…" After first setting her on his bed, he tosses his shirt to the floor. The man walks to the shelf to find his holoscreen, searching blindly in the dark with his hands as his guide.

"Oou, play something sexy! Like, some Mynx Maloran…or some Valeriya…"

He turns to her and smiles, flashing a grin with two platinum teeth. The man winks and points at her with a sort of slimy confidence, saying, "You got it, gorgeous. It's over here somewhere…" He continues to pat his surroundings but cannot seem to find the familiar shape of the item he searches for. Another few seconds of searching produces empty-handed results. He begins to shuffle frantically through the items on his shelves, scouring the area as if he's lost something important.

His guest is getting impatient. "I'm waiting…" she calls. Her tone is playful and provocative.

"Yea, yea, just hold on! Shut up for a second! Shit, where is it…" he yells, becoming agitated when the device does not turn up. His actions become more pressured, and soon he begins knocking things off the shelving units as he searches in the dark.

"What's wrong, Reggie?" she asks, now concerned by his actions.

"Where is it? Where is it...?" he mumbles. "What the actual fuck!?" In a fit of rage, Reggie tosses all of the contents on the shelf to the floor. The plethora of electronics and miscellaneous junk makes a loud clatter as they hit the concrete.

Unexpectedly, a third voice responds to his question. "Yes, Reggie. What the actual fuck..." The unsettlingly deep voice emanates from the pitch-black, far corner of the room untouched by the narrow ray of streetlight. Believing they had been alone, the noise startles both Reggie and his guest half to death. Suddenly, the lights to the apartment flicker on, revealing a broad-shouldered man in a hooded black coat lounging comfortably in Reggie's love seat. His dirty boots are perched on a small coffee table across from him, and the holoscreen controlling Reggie's apartment features sits on the stranger's lap; now under his control. A black hood covers most all of his features save for his mouth, which moves again to speak as he places Reggie's holoscreen on the nightstand. "As in what the actual fuck were you planning to do with this?" He produces a vial of blue liquid encased in a plastic device. At the press of a button on its surface, a retractable hypodermic needle extends from its tip. "I imagine this is what you were looking for. What were you planning to do with this, Reggie?"

Reggie is a deer in the headlights. His female guest, having backed herself against the headboard, cowers in fear from the opposite side of the bed. She says nothing. Still reeling from shock, she is unable to fully process the situation, and the unidentified man's words register as nothing but a jumble of syllables. Reggie, however, listens closely.

"I hear you like your hybrid women, Reggie. Well, more accurately, I've *read* that you like hybrid women." He taps on Reggie's holoscreen, identifying his source of information. "Tell me, do you just have a thing for freckles, or is there something bigger at play?"

"Hey bro, what the fuck are you doing in my pad!? Get the fuck outta here, bro! Do you know who I work for? Think I wear this black and gold for nothing? You ever hear of the Golden Phoenix!?" responds Reggie, who has finally found his words.

The hooded man turns his attention to the pink-haired girl on the bed. Altering his tone to seem less threatening, he addresses her this time. He slowly shifts in her direction to not startle her again. Lifting his head so only she can see his eyes, his low voice projects calmly, and quietly; almost soothing her. "Hey, listen. You have nothing to worry about. Everything is going to be ok here. Do you understand?"

Staring deep into his eyes, she is unresponsive for a moment. After a few seconds pass in silence, his expression and unbreaking eye contact register as sincere, and she responds with a fidgety nod. The scare she received from this surprise guest has sobered her up somewhat, and now she finds herself locked in a staring contest with the hooded stranger.

"Don't you listen to a word he says, bitch! I told you to leave, motherfucker! You have five seconds!" shouts Reggie. The façade of strength he presents is merely a thin veil and does little to cover his frightened state.

The hooded man ignores him. "This..." he twirls the hypodermic injector between his fingers, "...is a very potent sedative. Your friend Reggie here was planning to put you into a little coma with this so he could traffic you. For what purpose... I'm still working that out." The woman's eyes open wide, and her face drops. She turns to Reggie, hoping to get some kind of hint that his statement is false. Unfortunately, Reggie's response only solidifies it, sending her into a state of despair.

"Yo! Don't fucking talk to my bitch, motherfucker!" shouts Reggie, reaching behind his back into the waistband of his white pants. Before he can produce his weapon, however, the barrel of a pistol extends from the darkness of the open bathroom door behind him. Its steel presses firmly into his temple, putting a halt to his aggression. Reggie freezes as a fourth guest enters the conversation. The voice that follows, this time a female one, delivers a stern message.

"Don't even try it, you GP scum," says the woman as she steps out of the bathroom and into the light of the studio apartment. She moves in closer and removes the pistol from his waistband. A bandana covers her facial features, and her red hair shines from the light fixture above. At first Reggie scowls in defeat, then shifts his eyes to the woman. After realizing her beauty, his demeanor changes on a dime to one of aggressive flirtation. He clicks his tongue and winks at her, then blows her a kiss. She rolls her eyes in disgust before pushing him back a step with the barrel of her gun.

"What is your name?" the hooded man asks Reggie's would-be victim.

She now stares at Reggie in pure disgust. Her brow furrows with anger as she begins to see the real man behind the curtain. The Golden Phoenix thug does not return eye contact. Rather, he looks disdainfully up and away as if ignoring her. She continues to stare him down as she replies, "My name is Kendri."

"Kendri, good. Well, Kendri, I think it's time you left. We have some business with your friend, Reginald."

"Is it true?" she asks Reggie to no avail. He continues to stare at the ceiling without acknowledging her. She leans forward on the bed and asks louder, "IS IT TRUE, REGGIE?" Every fiber of her being is begging for him to give even a breath of rebuttal; a sign of humanity. But his response is only a huffing chuckle as he looks from the ceiling to the floor. Grabbing a pillow on the bed, she launches it at his head screaming, "YOU MOTHERFUCKER!" She searches for anything in her vicinity to throw at him and finds a small ashtray. Tossing it at him, she yells, "YOU PIECE OF SHIT!"

The calm voice interrupts her fit of rage from the corner of the room. "Kendri. You have no need to be mad. You dodged a bullet tonight. Do yourself a favor and leave him to us. We'll take it from here. Go home and sleep it off."

She huffs and puffs, exasperated, after tossing half of the objects in the apartment at him. After a few deep breaths of air, she finally recoils, sobbing from emotional exhaustion. Angry, confused, and scared, she finally grabs her purse and runs out of the apartment. As the door closes, the woman restraining Reggie calls after her, "You can do better. Aim higher next time, sweety."

The man stands and finally removes his hood. Grabbing a chair from the dining room set just a few steps away from his position, he walks it over to Reggie and places it down in front of him. "Sit him down here, M," he directs her, tossing her a bundle of zip ties. She obliges, forcing him into a sitting position before Roman, then restraining his arms behind the backrest.

"Hey bro, do I know you or something? You look like someone..." Reggie asks him poignantly as he scans his face. As Roman gets a closer look, the blue hunk of crystal under his eye catches Reggie's attention. "Hey, what the fuck is up with your face, man? What kind of implant is that?" The response to his question is an unfavorable one.

The two front knuckles of Roman's right fist connect with the bridge of Reggie's nose, immediately breaking it and spraying blood down the front of his tattooed chest. He cries out in pain as his head cocks back before whiplashing to its original position. Now that the three of them are alone, Roman begins to take a very different approach to conversation. "You don't need to know who I am, you Golden Phallus fuck! I'm asking the questions, and you better be straight with me or I will take DAYS slowly cutting you into pieces to get what I want." As he interrogates, Monique walks over to the holoscreen on Reggie's nightstand and turns on the surround sound. The music of Mynx Maloran begins to fill the apartment as she cranks the volume up. Once they have sound cover, Monique returns to her position behind Karnock.

Before Reggie can even make a peep, he receives another swift blow to the face from Roman's fist. This time his cry is high-pitched as his broken nose is struck once again. His eyes begin to water, and he tries desperately to escape, but he is secured tightly to his dining room furniture. Monique uses her leverage to press down on his shoulders with her entire weight, keeping him still. Reggie can no longer breathe through his nostrils, and wheezes for air through his mouth between yelps of pain.

Roman taps his TAB device, prompting a hologram of Windi, Valeriya's cousin, to pop up above his wrist. "We know you like your hybrid girls, so here comes question number one. Do you know this girl? Goes by the name Windi?"

After registering her features, Reggie's eyes shoot open with fear, then immediately look away. A dead giveaway. "I-UH NO, MAN! I DON'T KNOW HER MAN! Looks like any old hybrid bitch on the street!" He is not particularly good at lying. This little fib will cost him, and he immediately receives an uppercut to the abdomen from Roman, who makes no attempt to hold back. Reggie's eyes bulge to the point of visible veins in the whites surrounding his irises. He doubles over as his face turns red as a beet, and he wheezes to the point of vomiting on the floor between his feet.

"I hate to tell you this, brother, but you are not good at this. Like, really bad, actually. I thought you GPs were supposed to take crazy beatings to get initiated…apparently they skimp on the interrogation training though. Let's try something different. You got an 'F' in lying, so let's try the truth. Maybe you've got a chance to make the varsity squad for honesty. Now…" Roman grips the back of his neck and squeezes, bringing Reggie's face within inches of his own, "…do you know this girl?"

Reggie wheezes, then chokes as blood begins to drip from his broken nose down the back of his throat. After finally hacking it up, he spits it out on himself. He looks back at Roman with an entirely different expression. His face curls into one of terror and regret...like a child who has just realized he's been caught stealing. He shakes his head, and on the verge of sobs, he begs Roman, "Please! I... I-I can't, man! This is not your average GP operation, man! I can't! You have no idea, man, no idea! It's bigger than me, bro, bigger than all of us! PLEASE!!"

Roman tilts his head and purses his lips in disappointment. "Sorry bud, wrong answer." Reggie's pleading does nothing to stop Roman, who reaches behind the chair, grabs the index and middle finger on his left hand, and sharply twists. A horrid cracking sound can just be heard over the loud music that fills the room. Reggie screams for entire seconds in agony before actively crying from pain. Tears stream down his face as the realization begins to hit him. He is not escaping this situation. Even Monique takes a step back from his chair at this point, somewhat surprised by Roman's actions.

"If you haven't noticed, I'm breaking your fingers two at a time because I DON'T HAVE TIME FOR THIS SHIT, REGGIE!"

"AHHH! OK, MAN, OK, PLEASE STOP, I'll TELL! I'LL TELL! I'LL TELL—AAHAAAAA!" The tears mix with his blood and drip down to his white pants, staining his legs burgundy. The crying ceases, and after gasping for air, he finally responds. "Alright, yes! Yes, I know her! I know Windi, I know Windi, man..."

Roman pats Karnock on the back after telling the truth. "There we go. Now, how do you know Windi?" Roman asks sternly.

"I took her here. I shot her up with Drexen, that blue shit... then I sent her off with the pick-up crew like the others. That's all I do man, I swear! I swear that's all I do. Only thing I do!"

"What do you mean send them off like all the others? What others?" asks Roman, trying to get the full picture of his operation.

"The hybrid girls. I get the hybrid girls. They make some other whore in the Golden Phoenix lure the guys, but I get the girls. All I know is I'm supposed to get them here, dose 'em up, and then they get picked up."

"WHAT THE HELL FOR!?" screams Monique, horrified by the explanation that spews from the parasite Reggie's mouth.

"I don't know! I swear I really don't know. Something about their DNA, that's all I know. All I do is get them here, and then they get picked up. That's all..."

Roman shoots Monique a concerned look. Even the little bit of information they've uncovered so far does not bode well for their mission, or for Windi. Kneeling down next to Reggie, Roman once again shifts his approach. "We need to find this girl, Reggie. You see, bud, this poor girl...do you know who she is? She's Asa-Valeriya's cousin."

Reggie looks sideways at Roman for a second before asking, "Valeriya? Valeriya who...like...no. No way, the singer Valeriya!?" He stares back in disbelief, waiting for Roman to change his tune, but his face remains stoic. Reggie actually begins to laugh through his pain for a few breaths, but the laughter soon transitions into bawling his eyes out. "Reggie you IDIOT! You stupid fucking idiot..." he says to himself as he continues to cry uncontrollably.

"Reggie, come on. Famous singer's cousin or not, you were bound to get caught by someone at some point. But now, you need to focus. I need you to tell me where they take the girls. I need to know where Windi went."

Reggie continues to sob, only harder now. Through his tears, he once again blurts out, "I can't!" Roman furrows his brow, then reaches back and snaps a third finger at its base without giving Reggie a hint of notice. Reggie once again cries out in pain, but this time, he hits a new gear. After just a moment of crying, Reggie fights through the pain to communicate. He thrusts his face into Roman's and screams, "YOU DON'T UNDERSTAND!! I SAW IT AND I WASN'T EVEN

SUPPOSED TO! THIS IS BIGGER THAN YOU, MAN!! YOU DON'T WANT TO GET ROPED INTO THIS SHIT!! IF HE EVEN FOUND OUT I KNEW, HE WOULD GIVE ME THE RED DEATH, MAN! I DON'T WANT IT! I DON'T WANT TO GET BARBED, MAN!!"

The Golden Phoenix are feared for a number of reasons, even amongst the other gangs on Deorum. Roman had heard of this "red death" once before but had written it off as myth. The Golden Phoenix are rumored to have a special torture reserved for high traitors to their organization. The unfortunate souls are tied to a stake and locked in a room where a Crendarian Barb Centipede is released on them. An indescribably horrid way to go.

Humankind's anatomy was never meant to meet this nightmarish creature. To first describe it, the fully grown Crendarian Barb Centipede looks reminiscent to one of Earth's centipedes if it were capable of flight, and nearly twenty-four inches long. Their mandibles are strong enough to bite through wood, and their forty-six legs each end in sharp talons, with the lowermost six legs having stingers up to four inches long. The species' neurotoxin is not only the most painful neurotoxin known to man, but it has actually been studied to chemically induce an exponential amplification of the brain's ability to feel pain, along with the inhibition of endorphin release: a soul-breaking combination. Roman had been stung by a young one when he was twelve and ended up in the hospital for a full week. It was the most painful, arduous event he had ever experienced in his life. Exposure in large quantities can actually cause neuro-chemical and cognitive changes drastic enough to produce clinical insanity in hive-encounter survivors. However, that's not even the worst of it... When left to a new environment without materials to build a hive, the Crendarian Barb Centipede will instead choose a suitable live host to house its offspring. The barb centipede injects its larvae into its prey with its long stinger. The larvae, upon hatching, release heavy amounts of the Crendarian neurotoxin as they consume their host from the inside out. There are rumors of this method taking as long as a week.

Roman notices the tides of Reggie's resistance turning as he is allowed time to contemplate the repercussions of a Golden Phoenix betrayal. He quickly comes to the realization that he has no choice but to become scarier than the red death itself. This will involve not only skillful deception and a methodical approach, but high-level time management. And so, Roman wastes no time.

Grabbing the leg of the chair, Roman flips the entire seat onto its back with Reginald in it. As Reggie lands, the weight of his body on the chair-back crushes his arms beneath the metal furniture. This produces shock and causes Reginald to scream in pain. Roman has regained his attention. Next, Roman presses his knee into Reggie's diaphragm and applies his entire weight just below his sternum. The pressure that he applies makes breathing difficult, if not impossible, for Reggie. In doing so, Roman has created urgency, a useful tactic to produce results. After that, Roman places his thumb and index finger on one of Reginald's eyes and forces the eyelids wide open. It is important that Reginald see Roman's intentions and has a good view of what is about to happen. Finally, Roman produces the silver and black handle of his blade. After skillfully flipping the knife between his fingers, he ejects the blade from its handle and aligns its sharp tip with Reginald's cornea. This is a clear representation of what is at stake for Reginald. Hopefully, he will be motivated to preserve his sensitive organs, resulting in a full confession. Now, Roman must speak to Reggie's logical side.

"I'LL SHOW YOU RED DEATH!" shouts Roman in his gravelly, booming voice. "DO YOU KNOW WHAT HAPPENS WHEN A BARB CENTIPEDE LAYS ITS LARVAE IN YOU!? IT TYPICALLY TARGETS THE SOFTEST TISSUE AVAILABLE! THAT OFTENTIMES, MY FRIEND, IS YOUR EYES! THAT

FOUR-INCH STINGER IS ONLY TWO INCHES SHORTER THAN MY DAGGER. SO, LET ME ASK YOU THIS! WOULD YOU RATHER EXPERIENCE THE RED DEATH LATER, OR WOULD YOU LIKE TO SEE WHAT IT FEELS LIKE RIGHT NOW!?" This statement, although terrifying, is in fact false. The Crendarian Barb Centipede typically injects its larvae into the victim's abdomen. However, a compromised abdomen typically does not carry the same weight of fear as the eye, a good use of deception. Sixteen seconds have passed: phenomenal time management. Roman becomes so worked up that the blue vitalerium crystal in his face begins to glow, filling with faint gray smoke. The glow becomes bright enough to reflect off Reggie's three chrome dental implants, which adds a new unknown fear to Reggie's long list at hand; exactly the "X-factor" Roman needs to produce results.

"THE TUNNELS!" Reggie forces out the response under the weight of Roman's body on his chest. Clearly, Roman's dagger tip closing in on the moist surface of his bare eyeball has helped him to change his mind.

"WHAT TUNNELS!?" Roman screams. At this point, Monique has turned her back on the events that unfold in the room with her. She has seen no shortage of violence in her career with the Wibetani, but now she sees firsthand the intricacies behind why her father commonly refers to Roman as "extremely effective."

"THE-THE JUNCTION TUNNELS! UNDER CIRCUMSTATION EAST! THEY CONNECT LEEBRUS TO DOROK UNDERGROUND. THAT'S WHERE THEY GO!" squeaks Reggie with the last of his breath. His eyes are open wide with fear. It could be true; it could also be a lie. But as Roman inches closer and closer to Reggie's eye with the blade, even beginning to brush his eyelid with its tip, his response is unchanging. Roman analyzes: deciphering his body language, the cadence of his speech, and his eye contact, he decides that Reggie speaks the truth.

Roman exhales, and as the muscles relax in his face, the

blue glow dissipates. He presses the red gem on his knife to retract the blade back into its handle and starts to shift pressure off Reggie's chest. Another successful interrogation, with only minimal to moderate damage applied. Roman finally relaxes for a moment, as a weight is lifted from his shoulders. Interrogations have never been something he enjoyed partaking in, unlike some people he had crossed paths with in his life. The gravity of his actions sits heavily on his mind. To detract from this, he focuses on the prospect of saving Windi, and the fact that Reggie is a scumbag to his core.

"We have to go! We got really loud there..." whispers Monique.

Roman sighs. "You're right, let's go." However, as he allows room for Reggie's lungs to inflate, he can't help but notice that he is still not breathing. He gazes down at Reggie's face to see his eyes wider than when he was forcing them open. His expression is a harrowing sight, even for Roman.

In the seconds that it took Roman to regroup after gaining the answers he sought, Reginald Karnock finally got a good view of the blade handle in Roman's hand. After a long moment of sustained eye contact, Reggie utters a question just loud enough for Roman to pick up: "Roman? Roman Matthews!?"

Roman is stunned where he kneels. He knows for a fact that Monique had not used his name in the exchange. He also knows that Reggie had looked familiar. Reggie had even acknowledged that he recognized Roman earlier in their interaction, but somehow, he had ignored it in pursuit of the goal at hand. *How does Reginald Karnock, a Golden Phoenix, human trafficking midlevel slimeball know me? Who is this person!?* The questions repeat over and over in his head. Finally, Roman gets his answer.

"Rome, it's me... Roland. Roland from Ion Street..."

The revelation is enough to make Roman's head spin as a dizzy spell sets in, and his legs become weak. His jaw quivers as he is overcome with dread to the point of dropping his blade next to his childhood friend and falling to his hands beside him. *How could I not see it?* He gapes at Roland's face as the man breathes in labored fashion through his teeth...his teeth with three chrome implants in the exact spots where Jace, their former bully, had knocked his real teeth out. The sunken temples. The facial structure. How could he not have seen it was his friend beneath his new face tattoos? Roman's head continues to spin as his world crumbles around him at its very foundation. A person...a friend...one that Roman had once protected, now lays quivering beside him by his own hand. Roman, a stoic, seemingly unbreakable figure, suddenly feels as if he could vomit. With an empty stomach, however, it is impossible. As the collision of his values and all that he despises combust into a fiery inferno in his mind, now Roman is the one whose face streams with tears. "Roland!?" he finally whispers.

"It's me, bro, it's me!" replies the broken man on the concrete floor of his apartment. A bloody, hot mess zip-tied to a chair. Suddenly he wasn't just some GP scum to Roman. He was a person. He was a friend on a path that simply diverged from his own. Roman hangs his head in shame. His mind goes completely blank in the midst of true emotional exhaustion. He reaches into his shirt collar and clutches his pendant, the only memento left from his mother. Roman's fingers trace its silver surface, which has become rough with tarnish over the years. His eyes close, and behind them his mind plays memories of his parents, his childhood, and simpler times. There is no strength left for him to look Roland or Monique in the eye.

With his eyes still closed, Roman finally utters to Roland, "I'm... I'm sorry. I don't know how you got here...how we got here. But you need to stop this...this...kidnapping. It ends now."

"I WILL! I will, man, I promise. I'm so sorry, Rome..." whimpers Roland.

"Get off planet. And do not ever come back," whispers

Roman as he finally musters the strength to stand.

"I will!" cries Roland. "I swear I will! I never wanted this shit! They made me, man, they made me..."

Completely removed from the full scope of information, Monique simply looks on in complete bewilderment as Roman wipes the tears from his face, stands Roland's chair back up on its legs, and starts to walk out of the apartment. Roland remains in his seat, still groaning in pain. When Roman arrives at the apartment's threshold, he stands there for a moment staring at the unfinished concrete floor, trying desperately to process the events. "Let's go" are the only monotone words that escape his mouth. Unsure of what to do, she takes one last look at Reggie, who is apparently Roland now, and follows Roman outside.

Upon reaching street level, Monique stops Roman as he attempts to mount his hoverbike. Still in a state of confusion after watching the events upstairs, she finds herself in need of answers. "What the hell was that?" she asks, placing her hand against Roman's chest in a halting motion before he can get situated.

Roman pushes her hand off him and ignores the question. "Let's just go." His blunted response is all he can muster at the moment.

"No! No, I need to know what happened. I have never seen you like this...like *that*. You can trust me," she says lovingly. "Roman, you just broke down in tears with a Golden Phoenix boss who apparently knows you? And how was Reggie...or Roland, or whatever the hell his name is possibly involved with you!?"

Anxiety starts to build into anger again inside Roman, and he starts to respond with pressured speech but stops when he looks into Monique's eyes. They water with moisture, and although she does not cry, he feels for a brief moment that she truly cares for him. He sighs and pulls her in close for an embrace. As he holds onto the one person that he truly cares for in the world, the anger and anxiety he feels begins to slowly dissipate. "He used to be my friend in the orphanage... back on Ion Street. He's one of the reasons I was able to escape with Jerrick. None of us had it easy there..."

Monique puts her hand on his cheek, and the tips of her fingers caress the blue surface of the vitalerium crystal lodged inside him. It feels warm and soothing against his skin, continuing to ease the pain that courses through Roman's mind. "I'm sorry you had to do that. But he's not the teenager he once was, and neither are you. This world changes people, some for the better, or in Reggie's case, for much worse..."

"How are we different? I just tortured a man! We're just thugs under a different colored flag..." Roman looks down, brooding with guilt and shame.

"At least I know that there's good in you. I've seen it. You would never do what he did to those girls. You're not the same as him; you two took very different paths."

Roman looks away, stern-faced. "I know. That's what bothers me..." He places the burden of guilt from his friend's dark path on his shoulders, believing deep down that he could have helped him avoid it. *Why did Roland have to stay? I could have insisted that he come with me and Jerrick, and not stay at Ion Street. He could have had a different path,* he thinks. The thoughts continue to swirl in his head. What of his other friends? What of David and Ryan? He is once again plagued by his thoughts of "what if."

As he situates himself on his vehicle, his arm brushes against the holster where he keeps his knife. He pats around his pants pockets nervously for the blade; the last remaining memento of his father. The wave of anxiety returns as he realizes that he left it in the apartment with Roland. Immediately jumping into action, Roman dismounts his bike without saying anything to Monique and runs down the alley toward the building's ingress.

"What are you doing?" she calls after Roman.

Racing back into the building, he calls, "I'll be right back! Just be ready to go!" before pushing through the side entrance.

Roman skips the elevator and races up the stairs to Roland's floor, finally ending at his door. The door is still cracked open slightly, and he reaches out to push it open. However, he stops when he hears Roland's voice talking to someone. The intensity of his conversation piques his interest. So instead of barging in, he gently presses the door open another inch to peer inside and eavesdrop.

First, Roman sees an empty chair. On the floor beside it lay the zip ties that bound him; cut apart on the floor. Roland now stands, pacing the kitchen portion of his apartment, ranting and raving to someone on a holo. He tries to wipe the blood from his nose as he recounts the endeavor with another man. Finally, Roman spots the silver and black hilt of his blade resting comfortably on the foot of Roland's bed; Roland must have used it to cut himself free.

"Yes, it was definitely him! He was with some Wibetani slag... I think. She definitely had the colors. They just left...that fucking piece of shit! He broke my nose...my fucking fingers!" screams Roland, huffing and puffing in a nasally voice from his broken beak. He holds up his swollen, contorted hand for the other to see. On the counter across from him lies his holoscreen, which projects the image of an older man above it. The man wears a gold and black tuxedo. His long, wispy hair and glowing yellow eyes are distinct.

"Settle down, Reginald. Your fingers are an easy fix, and of no concern to me. How do you know it was him?" replies a raspy, older voice.

"He had a blue crystal in his face... I saw the thing glow as he was fucking torturing me! It was definitely the same motherfucker! This is your guy, I'm telling you."

The man in the hologram squints his eyes in disappointment. "Are you telling me that you not only lost another hybrid prospect, but you had the very man we've been looking for in your apartment and you let him get away?" the old man replies.

They're looking for me? When did the GPs find out about me? How much do they know about my condition...about my abilities... Roman's teeth grind together as he peers around the edge of the door. He has to find out why.

"Don't worry, I'll find another glow worm bitch for transfer. I'll even get you a couple extra to make up for it. These young university girls have rocks for brains. And as far as the man... You're gonna like this. When his slag was tying me up, I tapped a tracking film on her wrist." Roland's face twists into a sinister grin as he lifts his intact hand up for the old man to see, then extends his index finger. As he does, the tip of his finger separates mechanically from the rest of his digit and opens backward like a tiny hatch. It reveals a cybernetic bundle of black spindles that begin to protrude upward from inside. Tiny lights on the end of the spindles glow light green as they move like tentacles outside of their capsule. "This is the nanite film printer that I asked you to invest in for me. It's what I use to track our little glow worms so I can show up at opportune times. That Wibetani girl of his can't even see it, and she can't wash it off. I can send you the tracking that will lead you right to them."

At first, Roman's heart sinks as he hears Roland selling him out. Although the cynical side of him had thought Roland would not possibly leave the Golden Phoenix, somewhere deep down, Roman was hoping his former friend would choose differently. In the depths of his heart, he hoped he could have been the catalyst for Roland's second chance. It destroys him to see the man openly betray him.

However, now Roland implicates Monique in his betrayal. This man he once called brother puts her in direct danger with an organization that has no qualms with trafficking humans... This man, who talks about innocent people as if they are commodities to be traded like livestock—a man who seemingly has no plans to stop—is no friend of Roman's. This man is not the Roland he once knew. He is a thin shell of a human that harbors a monster inside. Roman sneers as he listens to the exchange inside, clenching his fists until his knuckles turn white.

"Hm..." grunts the old man in satisfaction. "Now that is the initiative I like to see, Reginald. Send me the coordinates this instant. Should this result in his capture, I think I see a promotion in the near future."

"HAHA! Fine with me. Just as long as I get to kill that Wibetani bitch in front of him for what he did to my hand. Oh! Uh... Do you think I could get a nickname with the promo? I mean everyone obviously calls you the Amber Ghost...which is awesome! I could be like...the Seeker? Or the Crystal Hunter... you know, because I helped track him down?"

The old man responds sharply to his request, immediately shutting him down. "I think you speak with too much familiarity, Reginald! If you don't check yourself, the Wibetani girl won't be the only one who dies. Besides, nicknames are earned, not self-ascribed, you fool."

"I-I'm sorry, sir. Please forgive my excitement, Father Riku. I'll send the tracking information to you immediately." Roland immediately walks up to his holoscreen and taps it a few times. "You should have them now."

"That's better. Oh, and Reginald? I hope you are being honest with me here. Because while a capture may result in promotion, if you fail me, I'll not only take back that finger I paid for. I'll take your whole arm..." The sinister tone of Riku's words relays that this is not an empty threat.

Roland gulps, then looks down at the floor nervously before responding. "Understood. Thank you, Father Riku."

The holo ends abruptly, and the visage of Riku Yamasaka, leader of the Golden Phoenix, disappears back into the holoscreen on the counter. Roman's face is as red as the blood clotting on Roland's broken nose. Unbridled rage is now the only feeling. It is both the motive and the goal, the end and the beginning. Adrenaline fills his bloodstream until it tingles his brainstem, and the crystal in his face begins to glow against the metal of the door. Roman pushes the door open, so it thuds against the wall as it swings.

Roland swings around, startled, and with his uninjured hand pulls his gun from his waistband and points it at the figure that stands menacingly in the doorway. When he sees Roman's glowing face, he sighs. "How much of it did you hear?" he asks.

Roman does not speak loudly, but the anger is written on his face, and hangs heavily on his words. "Enough to know that only one of us can leave this room."

Roland shakes his head as he waves his gun in Roman's direction. "You know bro, you don't have to do this. I could just let you go. Give ya' a headstart for old times' sake." The surprise of Roman's presence makes it hard for Roland to make his words seem sincere.

Roman is not falling for that one. There is no room for negotiation. He keeps his eyes dead set on the brash thug, watching his every move. "You're not the Roland I knew. You're a coward and a liar. You'd probably shoot me in the back the second I turn around and walk down the hall. Roland is dead. All I see is Reggie Karnock."

Roland retracts the gun and scratches the side of his head with the barrel. "Hehe...yea that is something I would probably do...guess I let you get too close a look." Pointing the gun back at Roman, he continues his diatribe. "Things have changed, Roman. I took an oath! You think I'm gonna back down from this opportunity because we were boys once!? You really think I'm gonna abandon them for you!? I ain't even know you were alive 'til tonight! You mean nothing to me."

"You're right. Things have changed. I couldn't have stopped what you've become. But I can kill you now." Roman removes his jacket and drops it on the table next to him, causing Roland to tighten his grip on his gun nervously. But Roland starts to laugh as he gets a good look at his opponent.

"Ha! You can't do shit! You don't even have a gun on you! I can see your holster is empty!" Roland gets cocky under the circumstances and begins waving the gun around as he laughs. "This is gonna be the easiest promotion I've ever gotten!"

"You never were that smart, *Reginald*. Never asked the right questions. A follower, not a leader. Do you know the reason that your organization wants to find me? Did you ever think to ask why?"

Brimming with arrogance, Roland replies, "Yea, they want that pretty crystal in your face. Bet it'll fetch a real high price. High enough to get me a nice, cushy new position in the Golden Phoenix."

"They didn't tell you what I can do, did they?" As Roman replies, the vitalerium begins to glow again, brighter and brighter. Then, his torso begins to glow through the divides in his terrain armor from the vitalerium lodged in his abdomen. Roland takes a step backward and raises his gun again.

"Whoa... WHOA! WHAT THE FUCK IS THAT?"

Roman looks through his brows and replies, "Let me show you..." then takes the first step forward, aggressively approaching Roland without a weapon.

"You should have ran!" Roland's gun barrel tilts downward slightly as he starts to pull the trigger. Such inexperience...it gives Roman all the notice he needs. Still feeling the ice in his veins, he produces the bright blue vitalerium shield around himself. Roland's weapon fires, and the bullet races for Roman's midsection. Upon reaching the barrier, however, it flattens like a pancake against the blue barrier and falls to the floor. Roman continues to walk toward him, unscathed, grabbing the blade off the bed as he passes.

Roland's eyes bug out of his head, once again finding himself in a state of shock and awe. "WHAT THE FUCK, MAN!?

JUST DIE!" The thug succumbs to his nerves and begins to quickly empty his pistol's magazine at Roman. Nerves do not make for good accuracy, however, and half of the bullets end up lodged in the walls of his apartment. Any that do hit their target are flattened by the glowing barrier surrounding Roman. Roland continues to stumble backward while firing until his back hits the kitchen wall, the end of his apartment. He pulls the trigger again, but this time, only an unnerving "click" sound follows. No bang, no fire, no bullet. He is out of ammunition.

Roman is only a few steps away and closing in quickly. Roland pulls the trigger again out of panic, as if doing the same thing will produce a different result this time. Roman is only a step away now, and Roland's nerves do not allow him to react functionally. He goes to swing the pistol at Roman, but instead Roman grabs his arm out of the air and pins it against the wall. Then, Roland hears a sound that makes his blood curdle, followed by immense pain, and pressure.

Roman stabs his blade upward into Roland's right side beneath his ribs, piercing his liver. The veins pop out of Roland's neck as he struggles to free himself, but escape is no longer on the table. He is snugly pinned to the wall, stunned by the pain of Roman's blade, and the only free hand he could fight with is severely broken. He looks down at Roman's fist, wrapped tightly around the knife piercing his abdomen. Roland watches in terror as his own blood begins to stream down Roman's forearm.

He looks back at Roman, who stares through him. Roland tries to form words, but the pain of moving his diaphragm is too much to speak.

Roman twists the blade so its edges point laterally, causing Roland to yelp in pain and lose control of his legs. He starts to fall but Roman holds him up by his wrist. Staring fire into Roland's eyes, Roman does not mince his words.

"I'm sorry Reggie, but it seems our paths diverge once

more." Roman then leans in and whispers into Roland's ear, "Your mistake was going after the girl." The second he finishes his words, he rips the blade swiftly across the length of Roland's abdomen from left to right, cutting his liver and internal organs nearly in half. Blood pours from Roland's abdomen like a waterfall, spilling onto the ground and splashing Roman's boots. Roman releases his grip and lets his former friend drop to the ground. Reggie collapses to his knees and slumps against the wall and the side of his refrigerator. Within seconds, he has lost so much blood that his eyes roll to the back of his head: dead.

As he stares at Reggie's body, Roman is surprised to find that he does not feel the way he had earlier. After witnessing the true man Roland had become, he actually feels like a cancer has been removed from the world. As the rage within him dies down, the crystals inside him cease to glow. He looks down at the bloody corpse and notices the index finger of his right hand had popped open again, revealing the wiry tendrils of his implanted device. Immediately, he is reminded of the conversation he eavesdropped on. Roman thinks: *The tracker... I have to get it off Monique!* He also remembers what Roland said, that it could not be washed off, and starts to devise a plan. Roman races to the sink, grabs the detergent beneath it, and washes his knife as quickly and as thoroughly as possible. The blade retracts and is placed back in its holster. Time is of the essence now.

He races back down to Monique, who is walking toward the building when he emerges at street level.

"I heard gunshots. What happened? Oh..." She answers her own questions when she sees Roman's clothes covered in blood.

Roman takes a moment to catch his breath when he reaches her. "Come with me. You're not gonna like this next part..." he replies, grabbing her by the arm and leading her back to his hoverbike.

Roman slaps the left shoulder of his terrain armor under his jacket. It engages the helmet, which forms around his head, covering his face entirely. For a moment he sees black as the screen inside his headgear boots up. It then bursts to life, revealing the world around him again. As soon as the AI greets him, Roman issues a directive. "Scan for anything relaying a tracking signal."

"Uh... What are you doing?" Monique asks, confused by Roman's strange behavior yet again. He takes a step back, scanning her from head to toe through his terrain helmet.

"Just stand still. Don't move..." he replies impatiently. "Reggie put a tracking film on you."

"What!? When?" she screams, now searching herself for anything that looks out of the ordinary.

"Scanning... Scanning... Scanning...." The AI buzzes in his ear.

"You can't see it! That's why I need my helmet. Now stand still!" he yells to try and focus Monique. "Come on, where are you..."

"Signature found. Highlighting area of interest." The AI replies, painting color over a small spot above Monique's wrist.

"Gotcha!" yells Roman as he grabs her wrist and pokes at the spot.

"Ok, how do we get it off?" asks Monique, trying to keep up with Roman's pace.

"That's the part you're not going to like..." he replies, removing the knife from his holster once more and ejecting the blade.

"Whoa, Roman, what the hell are you doing!?" she yells, pulling her wrist away from Roman.

"We don't have time. This is a nanite tracking film; you can't just wash it off. The nanites inside it begin to burrow into your skin the second it touches you. We could remove it with an acid or burn it away, which would be just as painful, or we can cut it out. I don't have any acid, and I don't see any torches lying around. But we definitely don't have time to argue. The Golden Phoenix somehow knows who I am and what I can do with this..." says Roman, tapping the crystal in his face, "...and they are tracking your whereabouts through this little spot here..." Roman draws a dime-sized circle with his finger on the back of Monique's forearm. "They could be onto us any minute. This district is infested with GPs. It's now or never."

Monique thinks about it for a second, grimacing at the thought of what's about to come. However, she knows what will happen if the Golden Phoenix catches up with them. Reluctantly, she extends her arm toward Roman, looks away from the impending surgical procedure, and shouts, "Just get it over with!"

With guidance from his helmet's AI, Roman begins to cut slowly into Monique's skin. She bites her lip in pain, at first trying to hold back any reaction. But as Roman continues to cut, she cannot help but cover her mouth to stifle her cries. The blade is sharp, and the nanites have traveled deep into her tissues.

"I'm almost done! You're almost through this," he shouts, trying to complete the job as delicately as possible. As the blood drips down her arm, she places her hand down on Roman's bike seat to gain another point of contact. Roman finally finishes and removes a thin slice of her skin from her wrist.

"GODSDAMNIT, that hurt Rome!"

"Here, I've got Mediseal in my bike..." he says. Roman quickly rifles through one of the hoverbike compartments and produces the last thin, silver canister of green fluid. "Gonna have to re-up after this. Hold still," he commands Monique, who clutches her forearm. Roman pulls the trigger on the device, and the green mist is released from the canister onto Monique's arm. It causes her to recoil from pain as her wound begins to bubble and scar over. Seconds later, the wound is closed. Monique wipes a tear from her eye, and nods to Roman that she is alright.

Roman nods in response, then smiles proudly at her resilience, saying, "You handled that like a real trooper, but we need to get rid of these nanites and get out of here ASAP." Roman holds up the piece of flesh from Monique's wrist, then motions for them to get moving. They hastily mount the hoverbike and take off.

As Roman rounds the corner, he does not drive quickly. He looks for his target amongst the people who walk on the sidewalks. Just ahead, a flamboyantly dressed man carrying a large, open-topped tote bag walks with a group of friends. They walk slowly, laughing and paying little attention to their surroundings. Roman says to Monique, who is pressed tightly against his back, "There, on the left, green top." She taps his arm to confirm she understands the mission. As he speeds up and pulls in close, Monique leans off the left side of the hoverbike, and delicately drops the nanite-laden tissue into the back of the open tote bag.

The man screams at Roman and Monique as they speed by within arm's length of him and his group. "HEY, WATCH IT, MANIAC!" he yells after them, none the wiser of the new contents inhabiting his luggage. As Roman and Monique continue ahead and disappear from the Red-Light District, three thuggish men wearing black and gold emerge from a perpendicular street and descend on the man and his group, who now harbor the tracking nanites. Surprised to see a skinny man and his friends instead of Roman and his Wibetani compatriot, they forcefully search them. To their dismay, they only find the small bit of flesh tucked away discreetly in his bag. They report back the disappointing news to their superiors: the vitalerium man has eluded them yet again.

When they finally reach Wibetani territory and are out of harm's way, Roman pulls off to the side of the road and tells Monique to dismount.

"What's going on? Is everything alright? Don't tell me you have to remove any more nanites, I will kill you!" she says, remembering the pain of moments prior.

"No. No more nanites, you can grab a skycab here. This is where we part. You need to go home. I'm sorry but I promised Modus," replies Roman.

Monique's nose scrunches as she furrows her brow in disappointment. She nods, but it is not a nod of affirmation. "Ok. I see. And what about the promise you made to me? I told you I wanted to be part of this mission and you agreed! You know how much this one means to me!"

Roman looks away from her scathing gaze, finding it hard to accept her resentment. "I know. And that's exactly why I can't let you come. I have no idea what we're going up against in this next part. The transfer tunnels aren't just walkways. They're CP-controlled transits, which means chances are, Valeriya was right, and they're somehow involved. I can't have anyone who is emotionally compromised partnering with me on this mission. For the safety of both of us."

"EMOTIONALLY COMPROMISED!?" she screams. Roman clearly hit a nerve. She stutters from anger as she speaks. "And what the hell do you call that...that *show* you put on in Reginald's...oh I'm sorry, *Roland's* apartment back there!? Wou...would you call that emotionally compromised?"

This time, it is Monique who hits a nerve, prompting a reactionary response from Roman. "THERE IS NO WAY I COULD HAVE SEEN THAT COMING!" he yells back, standing from his bike to make his point. "WHAT DO YOU WANT ME TO SAY!? That I had a hard go of it? That I'm a little fucked in the head!? WELL FINE! YEA, I AM! But I am not bringing you into a potential firestorm so that you can impress your father!"

Monique feigns laughter at his explosive response, then turns away from him toward the empty street. "OH, that's rich! You too now? Throwing around my relationship with

Modus like every other member of the Wibetani? That's lovely to hear...just great, Roman, really appreciate the support."

What Roman really wants to say is, "I care about you! I love you and I don't want you to get hurt!" but instead, what comes out is, "Yea well, maybe if you acted like an actual officer then no one would have anything to say! You're a Runner, and that means you don't go on missions; you *GIVE* the missions! You should be acting like a leader instead of a grunt!" As the words leave his mouth, he immediately knows he has made a mistake.

She turns back to Roman, her face twisted in disgust. "Ugh...you sound just like him..." She stares at him disdainfully for a moment, then delivers a hard shove to Roman's chest that actually knocks him back a step. Fed up with the conversation, and with Roman in general, she storms down the street in the opposite direction. "Go then! Enjoy your mission. Hope you don't get shot, asshole."

As she walks away, Roman looks down in shame. What she said was not wrong, he had allowed his emotions to get the best of him, and he had dwelled on it the entire ride back. What he had said was not wrong either, but it was not communicated in the way he intended, or in the right forum. *Why didn't I just say what I meant? Why is that so fucking hard for me sometimes?* he thinks. As he looks out onto the empty street, Roman mumbles, "I love you, and I don't want you to get hurt." But Monique has already walked out of earshot. It would have to wait until afterward.

Roman hops back on Rooster and watches Monique walk away. Even her gait seems aggravated. As she disappears into the distance of the dimly lit street, Roman engages his helmet and holos Valeriya. She picks up immediately, as if waiting for the call.

The second her face pops up on his screen, she nervously asks, "Do you have any news?"

"Yea. Our boy Rol..." he starts to say "Roland" but stops himself. An image of the five of them together in the courtyard at Ion Street flashes through his mind. He has to shake it out of his head to get back on track. "...Reginald has been kidnapping hybrid people for a while now, it seems. Apparently, his focus was young women, but there's another arm of the operation out there that's involved in taking others."

"Oh Primes..." Valeriya covers her gasp, then presses her fingers firmly into her eyes. She sniffles and wipes her tears, quickly gathering herself. She looks stressed to her limits, and her makeup runs as if she was crying before their conversation. "Why? What are they taking people for!?"

Roman grunts and replies, "Hm... I don't know yet. Still a lot to figure out with this operation they've got running... Silver lining, though, no one is going to have to worry about Reginald again. And I've got a good lead to move forward on."

With her eyes closed as if expecting bad news, she asks, "Were you able to find her? Do you know where she is?"

"I don't know for sure. But I was able to find out where they take them," Roman says as he starts up his bike and begins riding toward the junction tunnels of Leebrus and Dorok. "Apparently, they get transferred through the Circumstation East Junction Tunnels. Gonna be tough navigating them, but I'll manage."

"The interstate Junction Tunnels!? I knew the CP was involved in this... Are you going there now? You're going to need backup. I'll send some of my men and have them meet you below the east junction station."

"No thanks, I work better alone. I'll handle this," responds Roman who, despite his confident composure, is still unsure exactly how he will pull this one off.

"But how do you plan to get in? Do you even have a plan at all!?" Her questions are valid, and Roman, unfortunately, does not have the answers yet. He still needs to case the entrance. Even if he is to get inside, he does not possess a map of the tunnels. He will be going in blind.

"I'll figure that out as I go. I always do," he responds.

"Roman, this is my family on the line. I know you may think you run the show, but I'm the one holding the UCs. I'd feel much more confident knowing that I have some of my own trusted men on the ground, so I am sending help. And I expect you to work with them."

After killing a former friend and then fighting with Monique, Roman does not have the willpower left to rebut. "Ugh... Fine. But don't crowd me, we need to be stealthy. Two, maybe three people maximum, and make sure they understand I'm running point on this mission. The last thing we need is a group of idiots wanting to do their own thing. They are there for *support only*. Now, who are these people you're saddling me with?"

Valeriya looks offscreen at others in the room and dishes out her orders. "Strider, I need you to take Dieter and Nails with you to meet Roman at Circumstation East. He knows where they took Windi..."

At the sound of the name Nails, Roman's emotional energy is immediately renewed. "Um...no. No Nails. Abso-fucking-lutely not. I am not having that psycho come on this mission with me so he can blow the whole thing up. You want to help me, so you send musicians? Do you even want to get your cousin back!?"

Valeriya, however, is not open to bargaining. "Nails is a man of many talents. And as I mentioned before, he grew up in a tunnel system underground. No one knows how to navigate them like he can. I assure you, he will take this mission *very* seriously, won't you, Nails?"

Roman watches as Nails's face appears on screen next to Valeriya's. He still wears the same bright clothes from when he was on stage. His words are not particularly comforting, either. "Oi! That's right bruv, we're gonna 'ave ourselves an adventure! Break into the baddie's castle, rescue the girl! Now 'ats a fuckin' story book ain't it!" One of his nostrils is still visibly caked with orange Kraken dust.

"Nope. Not happening. I can't have a wildcard compromise the mission and my life if I'm being quite honest. You have to understand that, right?" Roman says.

"AW, PFT!" huffs Nails as he looks away from the screen, deeply offended by Roman denying his assistance. His response is almost childlike, crossing his arms and pouting.

"This is not up for discussion, Roman. I trust these men with my life, and for this mission, you will need to trust them with yours. They'll be at the station in thirty minutes, whether you like it or not."

Roman glances at the "Estimated Time of Arrival" on his HUD's GPS, which reads twenty-three minutes. He sighs so heavily that the inside of his helmet fogs up slightly. "Good gods..." he mumbles back. Feeling less and less confident about the upcoming endeavors, he finally responds. "...Can you at least make him change clothes?"

CHAPTER 25:

They Keep to the Tunnels

The familiar jingle of four horns travels across the cityscape of Kairus, signaling another special edition of Jennifer Baine's nightly news segment. Screens in every city-state light up with the image of the blue CP flag. A large holoscreen curving around the rotund edifice of a Leebrus skyscraper depicts the beautiful face of Deorum's number one news anchor. Her red locks of flawless hair cascade perfectly and effortlessly over her shoulder. The gravity of her message weighs heavily on her voice as she delivers her story to the citizens of Kairus.

"Good evening, Deorum. This is Jennifer Baine, and you're watching a special, breaking edition of the CPN Nightly News. On this segment we will cover the controversy stemming from galactic supermodel Terris Mont-Gematria's social media posts, the growing support for Initiative 919 as it comes into effect incrementally, as well as a glimpse into Overseer Aganon's big plans for planetary expansion. More to come on those topics, but first, our breaking news story comes not from the surface of our beautiful planet, but from just outside its orbit. These heartbreaking revelations may shock you, and the consequences of what we have uncovered at CPN News Network should be enough to rock all us patriots to our very cores. Today, an arrest was made on Doral Station, and to our dismay, it was not at all what we expected. Early this morning, the Vital Cascade Mining Operation was ambushed by yet another pirate raid that ended with the death of four loyal CP-IO pilots and crew members. Their terms of service are recognized with gratitude amongst the CP representatives, and their loss is felt by all. None of us will forget their years of loyal service, which ended with them making the ultimate sacrifice for Deorum."

She places her holoscreen on the desk before her and leans forward dramatically to deliver the next portion. "Following the raid on what officials are now calling 'one of the largest vitalerium expulsions in recent orbits,' three of the four pirate vessels were able to escape with the majority of the haul; with the fourth being destroyed along with the perpetrators inside, and any evidence that may have led to the others' capture. However, as I mentioned earlier, one major arrest was made. During a routine operations evaluation onboard Doral Space Station, Commander Braxton Hughes of the CP-IO was found to have been relaying highly confidential details of Vital Fracture expulsion timelines to individuals outside of the CP via encrypted messaging. According to official reports, based on the content of the messages exchanged, it was determined that he has been collaborating with the pirate organization for some time. Also discovered in his possession were highly illegal communications hardware.

"After further evaluation of the unlawful communications, Hughes's messages also allude heavily to the fact that the individuals he was in contact with are affiliated with none other than the Intergalactic Governing Bureau. A discovery that, if determined to be true, would mean a total and complete act of war from the IGB on Deorum as a whole. The disgraced Commander Hughes has been arraigned on charges of high treason and transported to Sanctum Tower for further interrogation. Let us all hope our *loyal* members of the CP can get the answers they need to bring the responsible parties to justice. As for the pirates and their affiliation, if they are in fact aligned with the IGB, Overseer Aganon has promised that he will do his part in making them answer for their war crimes. His words were solemn and direct. The responsible parties *will* be brought to justice, no matter the cost..."

Roman speeds by the large holoscreen on his way to the Interstate Junction Tunnels. The bright lights emanating from the newscast in his periphery are enough to grab his attention. With his helmet engaged, he cannot hear the words spoken by Jennifer Baine. However, he is able to catch a glimpse of the military headshot of a handsome man with neatly trimmed hair and beard above a banner reading "CP-IO Commander Braxton Hughes arrested on charges of High Treason."

"Hm..." Roman grunts, then mumbles to himself, "...and the klangs eat themselves alive..." He actually revels in the news for a moment, allowing him a respite from the memories of his recent fight with Monique and the unfortunate showdown with Reggie Karnock in the Red-Light District. His respite, however, is short-lived. An alert from his helmet display prompts him to veer off the highway to the lower-level streets. A few sharp turns and a short few minutes later, he arrives at the city-state limits. An enormous, gray metal wall at least forty feet high stands before him. All of the city-states have walls like these, separating the untamed expanses of the Grind from the pristine confines of polite society. However, the surroundings in this area do not register as pristine. No holograms dance on the buildings like the rest of the city. No flashy architecture or cultivated greenery line the streets here. This section is dark, dingy, and industrial. Hundreds of wide gauge pipes line the buildings, connecting warehouses to one another and coursing gods know what to who knows where. The street is decorated with trash and excrement. Most of the buildings, if not all, look derelict; long abandoned, and ripe with graffiti.

Roman turns off his hoverbike lights as he approaches an overpass; the last one before the wall. A sign hangs from the rafters, barely legible through the spray-painted accents that cover it. It reads "Circumstation East." The last drop-off point for a failed public transit project that dragged on for many orbits before it was ultimately abandoned. He slows to a creep beneath the bridge and pulls over behind a giant concrete pylon to conceal his vehicle. After carefully dismounting and retrieving his rifle from the bike's weapon compartment, Roman peers around the concrete slab at the entrance to the Interstate Junction tunnel. What he sees baffles him.

Across the gap are five men: two CP Guardsmen and three men donning distinct black and gold garb of the Golden Phoenix. The Guardsmen stand by the tunnel entrance exchanging words with a man wearing a well-tailored black and gold suit.

"More GPs? And what is an underboss doing way the hell out here?" mumbles Roman disconcertedly. He continues casing the entrance to observe the interactions and find potential opportunities for entry. Unfortunately, the only ingress seems to be through the front door: a large arch-shaped entrance to the tunnel by the Guardsmen.

Just a few steps away from the Guardsmen and the underboss, the more casually dressed Golden Phoenix thugs guide a hovercraft toward the mouth of the archway. Upon landing, the hovercraft's hatch opens, revealing more men dressed in black and gold. They unload three massive metal crates and load them onto a hovering dolly. The men push the crates past the tunnel threshold as the underboss shakes the hands of both Guardsmen.

Roman snaps a picture of the scene with his helmet, then immediately sends it to Modus. He follows it up with a text containing the question, "Since when do the GPs have this kind of partnership with the klangs?" He does not have to wait long for a response.

Modus's reply pops up on his TAB: "Since right after you left the Wibetani…" Roman immediately flashes back to the day he left; the same day that he and Modus fought at his Runner promotion ceremony. The reason why he left. Roman collapses his helmet and rubs the crease out of his forehead, stunned that he had not seen the connection earlier in the mission. Perhaps his mind had blocked out the details of that disturbing day, preventing him from connecting the dots. He replies to Modus, "That would have been helpful information for the mission."

Modus responds: "Honestly, thought you would've known… Good luck out there, be careful."

Roman wipes away his TAB display and grunts at the irony. He sneaks another look around the corner to see what has transpired. Having finished their job, the Golden Phoenix gang's muscle board the hovercraft and close the hatch. The large vehicle whirs to life and takes off. As it disappears behind the city skyline, the Golden Phoenix underboss slides into the back of a high-end hovercar, and the two Guardsmen wave him off before heading into the darkness of the tunnel with their cargo. The car creeps forward slowly, and suddenly turns right on the perpendicular street. He heads directly toward Roman's position.

Roman presses himself firmly against the concrete pylon, hiding his face from view as the sleek black metal of the GP hovercar crawls closer and closer. He holds his breath, completely still, feeling the pounding of his heart press repeatedly into the chest plate of his terrain armor. He begins to slide further behind the structure as he hears the humming of the vehicle grow louder. *If they drive under this overpass, they will undoubtedly see me*, he worries. Preparing for the worst, Roman reaches for the rifle slung over his shoulder. Just as his hand grasps the composite ridges of its grip, the approaching vehicle's gravity resonator roars to life and lifts it into the air. A stroke of luck, it flies directly over the bridge concealing

Roman's position. He huffs a sigh of relief as he relaxes his grip on the rifle and slings it back over his shoulder.

As Roman lets his gaze fall to the dusty gravel beneath his feet, he hears the jarring echo of a familiar voice join him unexpectedly. Still full of adrenaline from the close encounter, Roman's heart skips a beat, and his nervous system jumps into action. His instinct is to reach for his pistol cradled in its holster, but he stops himself halfway when his brain registers the guest.

"Seems the prodigal son finally remembers why he left in the first place." Jerrick's morbid form slumps over the handlebars of Roman's hoverbike. His piercing red eyes glow through the shadows of the secluded underpass refuge.

Jerrick's startling apparitions always send a jolt of fear through him—he still doesn't understand them. Although, this time, he recovers quickly and even musters up a collected, logical response. "I have nothing to say to you. You're just in my head."

"Wow... I mean really, wow. You've an amazing acumen for interpreting reality. Truly astonishing. Obviously, I'm just in your head, numb nuts. Or did they invent teleportation since I kicked the bucket?" replies Jerrick with heavy sarcasm sewn into his multiple voices.

Roman grunts in response, pretending he does not see his friend as clear as day treating his bike like a lounge chair. He does his best to ignore Jerrick by taking inventory before breaching the tunnel. He checks all magazines in his waistband to find them sufficiently full, then checks the barrel of his pistol for one in the chamber. He then swings the rifle around his body to fit snugly in his shoulder crease and does the same. Pulling back the heavy charging handle on his gauss rifle, he sees the shiny brass color of a projectile lodged in its chamber. *Just focus on the mission, and he'll go away... Just in your head...* he thinks.

"Come on, nothing? *You've* got nothing in response?"

asks Jerrick after a short silence.

"Ugh..." grunts Roman, realizing this apparition isn't going anywhere. "...even in death you're a fucking ball-buster."

Jerrick raises his hands as if to celebrate, but even happy expressions seem sinister on his charred face because of his glowing eyes. "There he is! But seriously, think about it. You get into a fight with Modus on the day of your Runner promotion of all days...great timing, by the way...all because of a private conversation you overheard him have about getting into the 'skin game.' You tweak mid-ceremony, leave the Wibetani, and in Modus's state of remorse, he decides to turn down the deal that would have delivered all of Leebrus to Wibetani territory."

Roman locks the magazine back into his rifle with a heavy CLICK and looks up at Jerrick angrily. "What the fuck are you getting at? Don't waste my time with your cryptic lancor-shit."

"Hmph. I like how you've taken to our little encounters," replies Jerrick with a smirk. "All I'm saying is it's a little funny, isn't it? I mean, after that, the gap in the human trafficking market gets filled by the Golden Phoenix, who proliferate like a fungus over the next decade or so...expanding to the point of completely overshadowing the Wibetani in both size and influence in Kairus. All because of your little moral quandary with Modus's conversation..." Jerrick dismounts the hoverbike and begins walking in slow, steady circles around Roman, who remains silent as his brow furrows.

"Almost ten orbits you don't take a mission directly from Modus. And the first real one you're handed...and I'm not talking about that artifact retrieval courier lancor-shit...your first *big break*...is to rescue your little friend Windi from the ruthless gang that capitalized on the Wibetani's faltering. I guess you could say that, indirectly...you are the reason that this mission is even a mission. You're the reason Valeriya's little cousin is down that dark, spooky tunnel." Jerrick stops circling and stands rigidly in front of Roman. He gawks at

Roman with a devilish smirk.

"Fuck off..." replies Roman, trying to shrug off the implication. But he feels his temper begin to flare again. *Why is he so good at getting under my skin?*

"You don't find it even a bit coincidental? Do you not feel the weight of the irony? I told you, Rome. Everything is connected. We are all responsible for everything, Roman, and we all have our place in what's to come. Especially you..."

Roman grits his teeth to the point of almost cracking his molars. *Why the hell am I seeing this? And why does he keep bringing up fate and plans? Am I crazy? Sick? What kind of parasite would cause this type of fever dream...these hallucinations...* Roman cannot make heads or tails of it in his mind. He decides to apply his temper to a different approach. "You say you're in my head, yea?" He takes a dramatic step toward Jerrick, landing just inches from his friend. Removing his pistol from its holster and lifting it up to his temple for Jerrick to see, he hisses, "Then what's to stop me from blowing you out of my fucking mind?" To his dismay, Jerrick howls with laughter in response.

"HA-HA!" Jerrick continues to cackle as he walks to the concrete pylon behind Roman and leans against it. "If I'm in your head, then I'm well aware you're not the type. You're more of the suffer in silence, fight through the pain type. Grit those teeth, GRRR!" he growls back. "Don't bore me with the histrionics. Besides, you've got an important task to complete in your role here. Time's a-ticking..."

Roman experiences a break in his temper. *Histrionics?* he thinks. Roman had gone to a good school as a young teenager. He remembers the word from his vocabulary lessons, and although he can't recall the definition verbatim, he understands its meaning. Jerrick, on the other hand, had never had a formal education. Jerrick's early upbringing was a bit rougher than his own, despite their crossing paths under similar circumstances. And although he had a penchant for discussions of fate and the grand order of things, he was no wordsmith.

"If you were really Jerrick, you wouldn't talk like that. Jerrick used to make fun of long-winded bookworms who talked like that. I knew him better than anyone. He was my best friend, but he was also raised on the streets of Kairus. Even if you were a twisted figment of my own mind's making, I wouldn't imagine him talking the way you talk. So, if you're not a daydream of my own conjuring, and you're certainly not some kind of unholy fucking ghost, then who are you and how are you communicating with me?"

Jerrick's cracked lips curl into a smile. "Now those rusty gears are turning."

"ENOUGH GAMES! I SAID WHO ARE YOU!" Roman's jugular veins bulge out of his neck as he shouts.

"Who the bloody fist-fuck are ya' talkin' to, mate?" asks another agonizingly familiar voice.

Roman spins around furiously to see Nails looking at him suspiciously. With him are Dieter Wuntz and Strider, each with similar expressions of uncertainty. Even Dieter, outfitted with his neuromodulator, lifts a skeptical eyebrow. Roman finds himself caught completely off guard by their presence. He looks behind him to the pillar where Jerrick was perched just moments ago, but he is no longer there. Drowning in embarrassment, he moves his long, oily hair out of his face and begins dusting himself off to detract from the position he finds himself stuck in.

"You got an imaginary friend, yeh? Well shite, I wanna meet the fuckar!! Don't be a prude, introduce us, yea!?"

"I was just..." Roman draws a blank trying to come up with a reasonable response. He finds it easier to deflect. "It was nothin'. Just having a moment. Let's run down the plan."

"Didn't look like *nothin'*..." replies Strider, his deep voice filled with concern.

Roman ignores the comment, and glances back to the mouth of the Junction Tunnel. The Guardsmen manning the tunnel entrance will likely return soon, and their window of opportunity grows smaller each second. He examines the team that was forced upon him to see what he has at his disposal. After just a short scan, he already knows this mission is not going to go as planned.

Strider is tactically dressed...but not for the right job. A jet-black mech armor vest covers his chest, but the gold alloy of his mechanocontractible arms shine like Bios at dawn. His cybernetic legs are hidden, but by camouflage cargo pants meant for blending into a jungle setting. Different shades of bright and forest green swirl together, and actually make him stand out more in the city. A large, automatic gauss rifle rests in his hands, connected around his shoulder by a harness. The weapon has a blue chrome finish, which also does nothing to help his case for a stealthy approach.

Nails wears a white cut-off tank top that exposes his sinewy midriff. Yellow suspenders connect to jet-black parachute pants that scuff the ground by his feet and completely cover whatever footwear he might have on. A black, two-strap backpack hangs from his back, and at least a dozen grenades dangle from the straps that loop over his shoulders. He carries a large pistol in each hand with a holster for neither. And, for the cherry on top, strapped to his abdomen is a bright yellow fanny pack with a hand-painted smiley face. It hangs below his waist from the weight of its contents.

Dieter, supposedly the brains of the group, stands weaponless in a three-piece suit; even more dressed up than when Roman had met him.

"So, this is what I have to work with..." mumbles Roman, beginning to lose confidence in their chances of success.

"Hells yea! Let's blast Windi the fuck outa' this klanghole!" replies an enthusiastic Nails, who does not pick up on Roman's disappointment.

"Uh...no. *Hells no*. None of you are prepared for this. You're going to get us killed. You're all staying here."

"What's that supposed to mean?" replies Strider, crossing

his arms and allowing his gun to dangle from its strap.

"It means exactly what I said it means. Look at you! You look like you're geared up to star in an action movie as the comic relief. And you? Nails? What do you think you're going to do with all those grenades? If we come under fire and a vitalerium charge hits one of those, you're going to blow us all to pieces. Come on! I mean, Dieter looks like he's going to a business meeting at his insurance job!" The arriving crew look at each other, and then down at their mission attire, failing to see the problem. Nails even chuckles a bit at Roman's discontent.

"This is supposed to be a stealth mission. Get in, get the girl, get out. Not some guns blazing bank robbery!"

Nails steps forward and slaps his hand onto Roman's shoulder. "I'm feelin' a bit o' lacking in the trust department comin' off ya, mate. And I get it, I do. But what you don't understand is, this ain't our first rodeo."

"Our first what!?" replies Roman in confusion.

This time, Dieter steps in. "It's an Earth term for a popular event where daring humans ride large indigenous animals. It's of no consequence, but to put your mind further at ease, Roman, I will be remaining here to provide logistical assistance from afar. So, my attire should not factor in your concerns. The three of us have worked together many times before and have escaped far more dire circumstances with all our limbs intact. You would be surprised by the type of work that arises when you're following around an intergalactic superstar..."

"What kind of logistical support can you possibly provide us from here?" asks Roman, still skeptical of the arrangement with Valeriya's trio.

Dieter looks down at Roman's TAB, and its screen instantly blazes to life. A small hologram of what looks like blueprints appears above his wrist. Roman lifts his arm in front of him to get a better view of the map that's been provided. The tunnel system looks much more complicated than he expected.

Dieter's calm voice continues to explain, "I will be tracking your TAB device as you progress through the tunnel. If you run into any trouble with access—gates, doors, etcetera—I will provide assistance via your TAB's Fray connection. Depending on your surroundings, I may also be able to provide you with distractions to help you avoid detection."

Roman is at a loss for words. He actually finds himself somewhat impressed by Dieter's contribution, although he is still unsure what to make of the confidence exuded by the other two. "Hm..." Roman grunts. "I still don't like this..."

Strider approaches Roman and adds his hard-nosed two cents. "Yea well I don't like this either, Mr. Straightjacket. Who's running the show? You, or the invisible girlfriend you were arguing with over there? I wonder what Valeriya would have to say about that..." His stare is bitter, and his nostrils flare aggressively.

Normally, Roman would have walked away from a situation like this. He is not confident in his ragtag bunch of soldiers. What wasn't normal, however, was the number of credits at the end of this finish line. Glancing back at the unguarded tunnel entrance, he repeats in his head: One million... *One million UCs...* Finally, Roman responds, "Fine. But you better keep the pins in those fucking grenades."

CHAPTER 26:

Glow Worm Hunting

The three men line up along the wall by the mouth of the tunnel. Roman peers around the corner slowly, trying not to draw attention, but there's no sign of the CP Guard as far as he can see. A light breeze caresses his face, originating from inside the tunnel, likely from the ventilation system. It carries a musty odor, as if the filters have never once been changed. The pathway is dark, lit only by two solid strips of red lighting. One lines the ceiling of the arch-shaped tunnel, and the other lights the path from the center of the floor. Both are visible all the way until the tunnel curves. The shaft ahead is relatively empty, save for a few pallets carrying cargo containers. Hiding places are sparse, but there is no one in sight. After inspecting, Roman turns back to whisper his orders to Nails and Strider.

"Clear path ahead. Keep an eye out for any purple lights. You'll see them coming from down the path. You see klangs, you find hiding immediately. Do not engage unless we have to. On me..."

Nails stops him from moving. "Oy, hold up. I thought their headlights were blue, no?"

Roman sighs. "They are. But the light inside is red, which

means it will look purple from afar. Blue and red make purple. Now let's go..."

"Alright! Wait a sec. Just gotta reload..." With astonishing speed, Nails retrieves and empties a small baggie of orange powder across the barrel of his pistol. Even faster than it appears, it disappears up his right nostril in a single sniff. His eyes bulge to the size of a Lancor's.

"Are you fuckin' serious!?" Roman yells in a whispered voice. "Can we go!?"

Nails turns to Strider and asks, "Did you know blue and red make purple? He's smart ain't he? Good thing you're leader, mate!" Nails, though his words seem sarcastic, is actually quite serious. Having become familiar with his strange brand of positivity, Strider chuckles at his antics.

"Done chatting? Let's move," says Roman furiously.

Strider nods in the affirmative. Nails clacks the barrels of his pistols together and says loudly, "Let's FUCK these turkeys!" Roman will have to take what he can get.

Tightly hugging the hot cement wall, Roman, Nails, and Strider move swiftly down the corridor of the junction tunnel toward the city of Dorok. As they make their way deeper into its depths, the trajectory begins to slope downward as the channel exits the city of Leebrus. They move quickly and quietly. The sounds, of their careful footsteps and the clinking of Nails's grenades are drowned out by the ventilation system that whirs in the background. As the small amount of streetlight entering the tunnel disappears behind them, Roman engages his terrain helmet and activates night vision.

Twenty minutes of walking leads them to a fork in the path. Immediately ahead is a narrow hallway to a dead end where a ladder scales the wall. A sign next to its metal rungs reads "EXIT TO GRIND SECTION 4181." To their right lays the path toward their destination. As they approach the sharp turn in the tunnel, a bright white light can be seen bending around the corner. Roman lifts his fist to stop the group and checks the map on his TAB. "Alright, the entrance to the central chamber system should be around this corner to the right. Weapons at ready," he whispers to Nails and Strider. The ever-serious Strider simply nods.

"This is so exciting!" whispers Nails. Then at Roman's signal, they round the corner...

"Ugh, son of a bitch!" exclaims Roman as he disengages his helmet to take stock of the well-lit area. The path opens up to a wide, barrel-shaped room ending in a bare concrete wall with no doors. He walks around the space looking for something, anything that will lead them forward, but the layout does not match the one on his map. Aside from a few more pallets of various cargo and an old industrial cargo mover, the room is ostensibly empty.

"Well, that was anticlimactic..." jabs Strider, leaning comfortably on a stack of pallets propped against the wall. Nails scuffs his foot against the cement floor, and then jumps on one of the boxes and pouts for a moment. He exhales dramatically, letting his lips flap together noisily as air passes through them. He looks around aimlessly until he remembers the second baggie of Kraken in his fanny pack.

Roman continues to look for some kind of hatch or panel that might lead them elsewhere, but the walls are as bare as the rest of the tunnel. "They had to come through here. The route we took had no other doors, no forks... Did you guys see anything?"

"It was dark, but no. No other ingress or egress. Just flat concrete," responds Strider, knocking twice on the wall next to him with his golden knuckles. "What's next, mission boss?" His sarcasm does nothing to settle Roman, who feels quite literally stonewalled by the surrounding tunnel edifice.

Filled with frustration, he taps his earpiece and contacts their logistical support. "Dieter, how old was that map you gave me? We're at a complete dead end. According to what you sent me, we should be looking at a three-tunnel junction.

This wall we're facing shouldn't be here." He begins scanning the ceiling in a last-ditch effort to see if he's missing anything.

Dieter responds quickly to assist. "Keep your TAB screen engaged and set to open access. I'll use it as a relay for interface discovery. I will tag what I find on your terrain helmet, so keep it engaged. Running scan now."

Out of options for the moment, Roman obliges Dieter's intrusive requests. "Alright then..." he responds reluctantly. Roman engages his helmet, which ejects from the collar of his terrain armor and encases his face in metal. He follows Dieter's instructions and opens the control panel on his TAB and sets its receiver settings to "open." Almost instantly, the screen begins running code from Dieter. The speed with which he works seems incredible to Roman, for just seconds later, he sees a blue square pop up on his helmet's screen. It directs his attention to a point at waist height on the bare concrete wall.

"I see what you tagged, Dieter, but there's nothing..." But before he can finish his sentence, a rectangular crease forms in the wall, and a small section of the concrete rescinds backward. Moments later, a small control panel replaces it and locks into place. "Did you do that?" Roman asks, astounded. Rather than respond to Roman through his earpiece, a picture of a winking smiley face appears on Roman's TAB, a message from Dieter. Strider and Nails both wear the look of "I told you so" on their faces proudly. Roman sighs, but this time it is a sigh of relief instead of the usual exasperation. He walks briskly to the console to examine.

Its display brightens and presents Roman with a crosshatched set of unlabeled white squares separated into five rows and five columns. It is clear to Roman that a sequence is required. "Dieter...you seeing this? Looks like we need a combination or..." Once again, before he can finish, Dieter interjects.

"Decryption, complete. The sequence is on your screen." Dieter's monotone voice sounds almost computer generated coming through the earpiece. A moment later, a video image of the pin pad appears in Roman's HUD, depicting a sequence of ten squares.

"How did you...?" asks Roman, confounded by Dieter's encryption speed.

"Didn't you hear Valeriya? Dieter's a Blackhat. A Godsdamned genius. Best in the seven planets, don't you listen, motherfucker?" responds Strider.

"Bloke could encrypt your arse into a giraffe if he wanted!" adds Nails after yet another line of his orange Kraken powder.

Confused by yet another one of Nails's nonsensical Earth references, Roman replies, "I don't know what you're saying, but both of you on your feet. Gear up, I have no idea what this is going to do..." Roman carefully enters the sequence from Dieter into the pin pad. The moment his finger touches the tenth square, the console abruptly disappears back into the wall and is replaced by concrete, which smooths over without leaving a trace of its existence.

A heavy tremor shakes the room they stand in, then passes. It knocks Strider off balance, sending him stumbling, and causes Nails to spill the baggie of orange dust. A tangerine plume of powder spews outward onto the ground below him. "Aw nut'er fuck!" he shouts, finally jumping down from the crate he's been perched on. Roman catches his balance and looks for any changes in the room, but none are apparent. Another tremor shakes the room and sustains. Suddenly, the hallway from which they came begins to narrow as the entire room starts to spin. Gears whir and pistons hiss as the bare-walled dead end makes a counterclockwise turn. Slowly but surely, the way they came in disappears behind a concrete wall, and another large, dimly lit room comes into view.

As the room continues to turn into place, a metal grate walkway becomes visible, which connects the tiers of a multilevel cargo room. The space harbors everything imaginable: weapons, ammunition, medical supplies, rations, and other cargo. Across the large room, stacks of gigantic tubular vessels filled with bright green fluid line the far wall. But that is not what grabs Roman's attention. What does send a chill down his spine are the five CP Guardsmen who stand facing the opposite direction on the balcony. Countless others are dispersed throughout the space, unloading crates and completing various tasks.

The trio stands frozen as the room continues to spin, and it becomes imminently clear that they are severely outnumbered. With nowhere to hide, stealth is no longer an option. Their only way out is now through. The gears in Roman's head spin furiously to come up with a plan. "Dieter, we need a distraction, right now..." he whispers as the room continues to spin.

"Working..." replies Dieter calmly.

One of the guards removes his hands from the guardrail and turns around to face them. His head tilts in confusion when he notices the three men standing in the receiving room spinning toward him. He taps one of his compatriots on the shoulder and asks, "Are we expecting another consignment delivery?"

"DIETER WE COULD REALLY USE THAT DISTRACTION!" Roman stresses under duress, but it is far too late to rely on Dieter now. All five men begin to turn toward Roman, Nails, and Strider, who stand next to each other completely exposed.

"Hey! Who are you!?" shouts one of the Guardsmen. The others take notice, and the squad of Guardsmen begin to reach for their vitalerium rifles. However, a shrill sound echoes off the walls of the subterranean cargo hold before any of the armored men can react.

"ACTION!" shrieks Nails, who, having pulled the pins out of two grenades with his teeth, hurls them at the Guardsmen with all he can muster. One grenade makes a loud CLINK sound as it connects with one of the guardsmen's helmets. The other bounces off the metal grate of the balcony and drops swiftly to the level below. Two of the Guardsmen jump for cover while Strider and Nails retreat behind the pallet mover. Roman, flabbergasted by the absurdity of their ill-devised strategy, hunkers down where he stands and covers his face. Focusing on the surge of adrenaline that leaves a tingle in his spine and ice in his veins, time seems to slow...

BOOM! The ear-shattering explosion tears through black and blue armor, obliterating three of the five Guardsmen too slow to react. As the inferno spreads into the rotating room, shrapnel pelts the blue barrier surrounding Roman, who strains to keep it intact. The concussive force of the grenade rocks the pallet mover that Strider and Nails find cover behind. The vehicle teeters on two wheels, and soon the heavy machinery begins tipping toward them. Before it can topple and crush them, it stops as it connects with Strider's golden hands. He exerts the immense power of his cybernetic limbs upward and forces the vehicle back onto four wheels; effectively saving them from a crushing death.

As the two surviving Guardsmen lift themselves from the ground and produce their firearms, preparing themselves for a skirmish, Roman remains one step ahead of them. He quickly lifts his gauss rifle to his shoulder and fires two rounds, both connecting with a CP Guardsman who scrambles for his weapon. The projectiles from a gauss rifle are not powerful enough to fully penetrate their military-grade armor, but they do significant damage. Roman's first shot hits center mass, denting the structure inward and sending pieces of metal and inner workings flying. His second shot connects with the Guardsman's helmet, which sends it flying from his head along with pieces of his face. Roman prepares to target the second guard on the balcony, but a dizzy spell sets in from initiating the vitalerium barrier. His shot misses wide to the right as Roman falls to his knees. The barrel of the Guardsman's gun quickly glows incandescent blue as it is primed to fire, and the man aims to kill...

Another **BOOM!** as the second grenade explodes on the lower level, rocking the grate balcony to the point of fracturing one of its support beams. The ground beneath the Guardsman shifts, and the vitalerium charge from his weapon narrowly misses Roman, instead melting the cement floor beside him. Roman must roll quickly onto his back to avoid the heat of the molten ground. Not a moment too soon, multiple shots ring out from Strider's automatic weapon, crushing the Guardsman's armor and sending him careening over the railing to the lower level.

As Roman's dizzy vision adjusts, he sees a hand connected to a spindly forearm extend from above. Nails shouts over the sounds of chaos and gunfire, "C'MON! WE AIN'T HERE TO FUCK SPIDERS! UP WITH YA, MATE!" Roman grabs his hand and pulls himself to his feet. With vitalerium charges flying overhead from the remaining CP Guardsmen now alert to their presence, there is no time for a thank-you. The two men dash toward the tilted metal balcony to find cover. They spot ideal protection behind a massive titanium crate and jump for cover. Strider, having already found cover behind a support beam, provides cover fire from the bridge. He unleashes a barrage of bullets at the Guardsmen, who return fire from the bridge one level above. He must continuously move as vitalerium charges melt through his cover, turning it into Swiss cheese.

Roman peers below at the two Guardsmen who fire upward on their position. He shouts, "Nails! Take the lower level! Stairs left; I'll cover!" When he finds a break in the fire, Roman flips up the electronic sight on his gauss rifle. Aiming carefully upward, he pulls the trigger and feels the recoil punch his shoulder. A well-placed shot connects with the calf of a Guardsman who stands partially behind cover, effectively shattering his leg and sending him howling to the ground, exposed. Another round to the helmet ceases his howls. *That leaves four; two above and two below*, counts Roman in his head.

As Roman continues to handle the guards above, Nails shouts a resounding, "AYE, AYE!" He then pulls the pin from another grenade with his teeth and lobs it over his head to the lower level. The men below immediately cease fire and run for cover before the grenade turns another set of crates into ashen debris with a thundering explosion. Nails races down the tilted metal catwalk and attempts to jump the gap in the bridge created by his own grenade. Unfortunately, a jagged piece of metal catches his long pants, causing him to trip and fall like a sack of potatoes. The drug-addled Nails slides directly through the gap in the walkway and tumbles down to the story below, crashing painfully through a munitions rack. However, in his Kraken-fueled state, it does nothing to deter his actions, or his attitude. He promptly jumps to his feet and releases his war cry. "FOR WINDI!!" he roars as he charges recklessly toward the other Guardsmen, firing his dual pistols akimbo.

After Strider fires another barrage at the Guardsmen maintaining the high ground, he retreats to cover and checks his weapon. "I'M OUT!" he shouts at Roman. Removing one of the two remaining magazines from his belt, Roman tosses the relief ammunition across the gap. Strider adeptly plucks it from the air and thrusts the cartridge upward into his rifle's receiver.

"MAKE 'EM COUNT!" shouts Roman, who ejects the magazine from his own rifle and replaces it with the last of his ammunition. Another vitalerium charge hits the crate concealing Roman's position. It burns through the metal and strikes the wall behind him. Roman looks back to Strider and points up, referencing the second stairwell leading to the upper level. Nodding, Strider emerges from cover and sprays the upper level indiscriminately with an onslaught of fire. Roman sprints for the stairwell. His heavy breath fogs his display screen as sweat pours down his face inside the helmet. He tries to bring up the barrier again as vitalerium charges fly past him, but nothing happens. He finds trouble focusing as he sprints, and his use of the barrier to defend against Nails's grenades had taken too much out of him.

Arriving on the third level, he rejoins the firefight as he feverishly searches for cover. His eyes pan to a pane glass window separating a small office from the scaffolding. He doesn't waste his opportunity. The glass shatters as the weight of Roman's body crashes through it. He rolls over the control panel and falls to his side on the floor. A groan of pain escapes as he pulls a long shard of glass from his thigh. Blood gushes from the small wound it creates, but he does not tend to it. There are more pressing issues at hand. Ignoring the pain, he checks the magazine in his rifle: three rounds left before he must switch to his sidearm. The two Guardsmen he targets still remain, and blue plasma from their rifles continues to sear the back wall of the office as he ducks for cover.

Two levels below, Nails's rampage has proven astoundingly effective somehow. One officer, having balked at the lunatic's audacious approach, lays dead on the floor. The other, noticing the turning tides of the firefight, retreats into a tunnel on the far side of the cargo hold and seals the large titanium door behind him. Nails now fires his pistols upward ineffectively at the Guardsmen two stories above, but all he hits is the metal bridge below their feet. Strider, still on the second level, is running dangerously low on ammunition once again. A vitalerium charge grazes the front of his mech armor as he is retreating back to cover, sending pieces of the armor flying and exposing part of his chest to the searing hot metal. "ARGH!" he screams. "ROMAN! NEED SUPPORT HERE!!"

As Roman prepares to move to a firing position, he hears Dieter's voice through his earpiece over the sound of gunfire outside the office. "I've connected to the security camera system in your current location, and I believe I have found your distraction..." he says calmly.

"THEN LET IT RIP, DIETER! WHAT ARE YOU WAITING

FOR?" shouts Roman as blue plasma explodes through the console just inches from him.

Sirens suddenly blare behind the remaining two Guardsmen, who turn to the large green vats behind them. The fluid in the stacked vats begins to bubble precariously. Lights and alarms on their frameworks resound a warning to all who stand too close. The firing stops, and the guards have no chance to react before dozens of portholes burst open, unleashing thousands of gallons of fluid upon them. Caught in the tsunami of green gelatinous broth that erupts from the vats, both Guardsmen tumble over the third-floor railing and fall to cement below. One falls directly on his head, instantly breaking his neck. Not even his high-tech armor could save him from the fall. The other strikes the ground with immense force in the prone position.

As the final Guardsman struggles to get to his feet, the last thing he hears is the sloshing of Nails's feet through the river of green fluid that coats the floor. At point-blank range, Nails puts him down with the last bullet in each of his pistols. Turning his sights on the upper levels where Roman and Strider are holed up, Nails lets out an enthusiastic and childish "YAY!"

Roman and Strider poke their heads out from cover and gaze upon the mess that they've created. The cargo hold is in shambles. Vitalerium charges have melted holes in the walls, walkways, and nearly half the cargo. The entire first floor is covered shin-deep in green sludge, and the bodies of several Guardsmen lay strewn about. As Roman limps down the stairs to meet the others, Strider grabs a few of the vitalerium rifles from the bodies that lay motionless on the metal scaffolding.

Upon reaching the lower level, the rubber of Roman's boots creates a disgusting squelching noise as he sloshes through the green muck. He tends to his injuries as he walks, using a piece of torn cloth to tie a bandage around his thigh gash. He winces in pain when he finishes a tight knot. As he approaches Nails, Roman is greeted with an enormous grin. Glancing around at the final outcome of their wet work, Roman exclaims, "I cannot believe that fuckin' worked..."

"See!? 'At's the spirit!" Nails exclaims as he grasps Roman's hand from where it hangs and brings him in for a one-armed embrace.

"Uh...alright then," replies Roman awkwardly.

"Hey guys..." shouts Strider from above, his voice filled with concern, "...any chance you took a look at what's still left in these tubes?"

Roman and Nails turn toward the foggy glass of the vats. Dieter's distraction was extremely effective, though it's clear now that it did not leave the tubes entirely empty... Stepping closer to the glass, they can just make out the struggled motion of something inside. They take another step closer, but a loud thud causes the two men to jump back, startled. A distinctly human face presses involuntarily against the transparent tube. Blue, bioluminescent freckles can be seen glowing through the thick, industrial glass. The hybrid man opens his eyes suddenly and begins coughing up green fluid.

"Whoaa... Now that's something you don't see every day!" Nails says with a fascinated look on his face. He moves in for a closer look, his head tilted to the side with captivation as his nose presses into the glass.

Roman quickly walks to the next tube; then the next one. Upon further inspection, each of the vats contains a struggling, semi-conscious hybrid person. Each slowly returns to life, regurgitating green fluid and desperately searching for a way out of their slime-filled prisons. Roman retracts his helmet and gapes at the utter lack of humanity before his eyes. There are five columns of tubes, stacked twelve tubes high, each with a hybrid captive inside; a soul neatly packaged for processing. Disturbing is an understatement. Roman feels sick to his stomach with disgust. With his voice no louder than a whisper, he comms Dieter. "Dieter... I need you to get those vats opened. Do it now..."

"On it..." replies Dieter. Shortly after his response, the glass cases on the first row of tubes peel back and their inhabitants slide out clumsily. They fall immediately to the ground, weak from their induced sleep and slippery with lubricant. The glass tubes seal behind them, followed by a heavy mechanical whir. A long, thin grate opens below the vats, which begins draining the green fluid from the floor. The entire bottom row of tubes submerges below ground and is replaced by the row above it as the entire wall shifts lower.

"I found her! She's one row up from the ground, far left column!" shouts Strider, pointing toward a vat with a frail young girl inside. Another row of hybrid people slides out of their tubes as the glass opens. They cough and cry, tears streaming down their faces from fear and confusion. Another row of tubes descends into the floor and Nails is there to catch Windi as she falls limp from her vessel. Strider sprints down the stairs to greet her with his partner in crime.

"Windi! Windi!" they shout, trying to jolt her back to life in their arms. Due to her condition, she is unresponsive except to clear her airways. Strider fights back his gag reflex as she expels the green mucous-like substance on his mech armor, which still steams from being shot.

Roman gapes at the dozens of weak, famished hybrids sloshing through the green muck. "We need to get the rest of these people out of here. Get them up that ladder to the Grind. They won't have as much heat there; they can blend."

"Roman, I don't know if we have time, man. There's a lot of people here... We have who we came for. We should go," responds Strider, trying to talk sense into Roman.

"THEN WE MAKE TIME!" he barks back, unhinged by the heartbreaking scene. The hybrid people were kept in appalling condition, and now gasp for air like newborns delivered unwittingly into the world.

Suddenly, Dieter's voice enters Roman's ear. "Gentlemen, we have a problem..."

"General Benson! GENERAL BENSON!!" shouts the CP Guardsman over emergency comms.

General Dorok Ferrous Benson's holographic face does not show even the slightest inkling of interest as it hovers over the console. "What is it? And why the hell are you bothering me on the emergency frequency?"

"Intruders sir! Three intruders have broken into the cargo hold in the Leebrus-Dorok Junction Tunnel! Th-they took the entire room! The entire squadron is dead sir!!" cries the Guardsman.

Suddenly, the General is very interested, and very angry. "WHAT!? ARE YOU TELLING ME YOUR DETAIL SUCCUMBED TO THE LIKES OF THREE RANDOM MEN!?"

"I'm s-sorry sir! We fought the best we could, but they came extremely well prepared! I escaped to the maintenance tunnel and sealed them in on the Leebrus side!" whimpers the man in response.

Dorok's face shakes with anger. Every muscle contracts as the blood rushes to his head, turning him beet-red. He breathes heavily three times through his nose before responding. "Good. Remain where you are. You will be questioned following the result of this." With that, he terminates the holo.

Dorok quickly lifts his TAB device to his face and scans his retina. It chimes, confirming his identity. After scrolling through a few tabs, he enters in an order, prompting a window to pop up on its screen. The question reads: "PROTOCOL 13: RELEASE CYB ALPHA BATTALION, ARE YOU SURE?" Dorok taps the "CONFIRM" option, then sits back uncomfortably in the chair in his office. As the discomfort builds, he screams out into his empty office.

Deep in the maintenance tunnels, a large wall segment slides open, revealing six metallic pods. Machinery whirs as they extend into the hallway just thirty meters from the surviving CP Guardsman, who has since removed his helmet and wipes the sweat from his brow. With a plume of steam, the pods open, revealing the silhouettes of six individuals. After a moment, they step out of the pods in unison, each perfectly in sync with the next. Their cybernetic feet clink heavily against the cement floor.

The Guardsman gapes at them nervously, immediately discerning what they are as he inches his way closer to the wall. He had only heard stories of CYB battalions. What little he had heard was unnerving enough, but to actually see them is a different experience entirely. He had no idea that a CYB battalion was harbored here in the tunnels. Their approach sends shivers down his spine.

Their visage alone is unsettling. The only thing remotely human left of a CYB is their brain, and a few select organs; their entire bodies outfitted with the highest military grade cybernetic implants from head to toe. Even the skulls encasing their human brains are fashioned from shiny, black titanium. Mechanocontractible limbs, reinforced alloy torsos, reflex enhancers, combat processors, and weapons built directly into their metallic frames; pure killing machines. All of the CYB's armor is jet-black, except for the leader, whose torso shines a steely blue chrome in the strip lighting of the tunnel.

The leader approaches the Guardsman and turns toward him. The red optic implants spin in their sockets as they focus on the man standing by the emergency console. "Report," responds his soulless, electronic voice. His jaw does not even move to produce the sound.

"Uh..." he responds, quivering in their presence.

The cyborg bends slightly at the waist to lean in closer to the Guardsman. "Report," CYB Alpha leader repeats.

"Uh...three...three men. One had bionic implants, I think.

They attacked us in the cargo hold. I escaped, but everyone else is dead! I sealed the door shut, but they...they were still in there just a minute ago! You can still catch them!"

"Acknowledged," replies CYB Alpha leader, who returns to an upright position upon collecting the nervous man's report. His head cocks to one side, and his eyes stare up at the ceiling as if listening to something only he can hear. After a moment, his electronic voice responds, "Order received."

CYB Alpha leader's arm extends at lightning speed, and the cold steel of his cybernetic hand grasps the skull of the CP Guardsman before him. The man shrieks with pain, but only for a brief moment. The digits of CYB Alpha leader's hand fully contract, crushing the man's head like a grape. His skull turns to mush as brain matter sprays across the emergency relay console behind him, and his body falls limp to the ground. Without so much as a second look, the cyborg turns down the hallway toward Leebrus, and with machine-like speed, the entire battalion sprints toward the cargo hold simultaneously.

"Not right now, Dieter. And keep emptying those tubes, there are people inside!" shouts Roman into his earpiece. The painful groans of dozens of hybrids fill the cargo hold as they come to. Strider still struggles to stifle his gag reflex at the wheezing captives as they spew green fluid from their orifices.

"I'm detecting a number of entities connected to the tunnel's Fabric system. They are closing in on your location very quickly. Connecting to passage camera systems nearby to identify the threat," Dieter responds before connecting to the cameras in the maintenance tunnel hallway.

"Rome! Pack it up! We can't swing it. It's real noble that you want to get these people to safety, but we just knocked off more than a half-dozen Guardsmen, and we need to get the hell out of Dodge!" Strider insists.

Before Roman can respond, Dieter's voice shouts into his earpiece. His usual, inhuman monotone voice is now distressed, and frantic. The tone catches Roman's attention instantly. "ROMAN, GET WINDI AND GET OUT NOW! LEAVE IMMEDIATELY! DO NOT WAIT ANOTHER SECOND! GO!"

Just then, a shocking **BANG** sound emanates from the sealed metal door, sending a shockwave through the room. The three men cease their bickering and fall silent as they stare at the massive steel door. Another, even louder **BANG** shakes the room as the massive door dents outward sharply. Then again, **BANG**, creating a second, deeper dent. Something on the other side is trying to get in, and that moment is not far off.

"Strider, get Windi out of here NOW! Nails, help me get these people up the stairs!" shouts Roman, jumping to action and lifting two of the frail hybrid people from the ground and stumbling toward the stairwell. Strider sprints up the stairs, jumps the bridge gap, and brings Windi into the rotating concrete room. Nails strains to lift one of the hybrid women onto his back and waddles his way toward the stairs. The room echoes as two more large dents are bludgeoned into the hatch. Roman reaches the gap in the walkway. His arms ache from the weight of the people he carries, but he is compelled to help them escape. He musters up everything he has, and shouts with intensity as he runs toward the precipice and jumps across...

His feet land on the other side, but with his boots coated in green fluid, he slips. Thankfully his momentum launches him forward, and he is able to recover, and bring the two hybrid women into the rotating room. He lays them to rest by Strider's feet, where they struggle to regain full control of their limbs. "Try to get them mobile!" he shouts, before running back to the bridge. Nails stands across the small gap, panting and wheezing with the hybrid woman writhing on the metal grates next to him.

"You..." he says between gasps of air, "...you're a godsdamn TITAN! How the fuck do you expect me to do that!?" calls out an exasperated Nails.

"Just pass her to me!" shouts Roman as he edges down the sloped grate toward Nails. The punk rocker does his best to slide the woman toward him. After much straining, Roman grasps her arms and pulls her across, bringing her to safety beside Strider, who is helping the captives to regain their balance. Nails remains on the bridge with his hands on his knees, recuperating from the arduous task. Roman races back toward the stairwell to help more people escape as they tumble from their vessels to the floor below. However, before he can make the leap across the gap in the bridge...

BANG! The massive steel door flies across the room and crushes a bay station. Nails and Roman look down to the threshold in horror as six cyborg soldiers step into view. With their terrifying stature, they must duck under the frame to enter the cargo hold. After taking a moment to survey their surroundings, their mechanical eyes rest menacingly on the two roughnecks one level above.

Roman quickly measures up the competition, knowing instantly this is not a battle they can win. He gazes down at the dozens of people that lay crawling through the river of green fluid below him. The sorrowful realization hits him like a ton of bricks. *I can't save these people...* His conscience burns with guilt.

Nails jumps the gap with newfound vigor and grabs Roman by his shoulder plate. "OY! Let's fuck off, then!"

The CYB Alpha leader extends his arm, which collapses back, revealing a three-pronged claw, and aims it directly at the pair. The claw launches from its arm with a strange noise, speeding toward Roman and Nails like a cannonball. Nails tackles Roman to the ground, and the projectile barely misses his head. It clamps onto the concrete wall, its prongs piercing through the cement like sand. Roman and Nails look up at the claw and watch as a red ring appears on its back side. Though nothing connects it to the CYB soldier below, it breaks off a chuck of the wall and soars back in the opposite direction to reconnect with the soldier's arm. CYB Alpha leader stares viciously at them as it releases the cement block, then aims to fire again.

"DIETER, ACTIVATE THE ROTATING ROOM NOW!!" screams Roman as he and Nails race down the metal bridge toward their exit. The room begins spinning as they sprint for the exit.

Turrets unfold from the shoulders of the CYB battalion soldiers, and fire streams of blue plasma at Roman and Nails as they sprint for safety. Another launch of the battalion commander's claw narrowly misses Nails, landing on the wall just in front of him. Roman sprints like he's never sprinted in his life, and not far behind, Nails runs while lifting his baggy pants from the floor to refrain from tripping again. The rotating room is already halfway closed now.

Outside of the cargo hold, Strider is already guiding the three slime-covered hybrid people down the hallway to the Grind exit. He does his best to foist the three women up the ladder. They struggle up each rung while their muscles continue to awaken. Though their progress is slow, eventually the hatch opens above them, and they finally reach the surface. Strider, with Windi still draped over his shoulder, climbs the ladder behind the last female to assist her out. "You can do it! Pull up!" he shouts encouragingly. The first two captives, already on street level, offer what help they can by reaching down to lift her from the junction tunnel manhole. Strider continues to climb as she finally passes the threshold, but when his hand reaches the final rung of the ladder, a flashing red alarm blares in the tunnel shaft. The mechanical manhole cover shuts abruptly, sealing him in the tunnel with Windi.

"NO!" he shouts, grasping onto the edge of the door with

his cybernetic arm and attempting to force the door back open. Although its gears strain from the stress, it is not enough to reopen his egress. "SHIT!" he yells furiously. Strider releases his grip from the ladder and descends the twenty-foot drop to his feet at tunnel level. His landing creates a loud **THUD**, with his cybernetic legs taking the brunt of the force. With no time to waste, he rushes back toward the barrel-shaped room carrying Windi. The room has almost completely rotated shut, and to his dismay, his partners are still not in it.

Suddenly, a loud THUD! sounds as Roman and Nails dive through the narrow opening that remains between the cargo hold and the rotating room. Roman jumps to his feet and sprints to Strider. Nails pushes himself up and starts to follow, but when he stands, a horrible sound emanates from behind him just before the wall seals shut. The sound is followed by an indescribably immense pain in his midsection, and a sudden lethargic feeling. Nails watches as Strider's eyes bulge out of his head.

"NAILS!!" screams Strider, his face contorted in horror.

The three-pronged claw grasps Nails's abdomen, with one of the prongs protruding directly through his stomach above his navel. Blood pours from the seam between flesh and metal, and Nails drops to his knees. Just as he looks down at the source of his pain, the red ring lights up on the claw's base. Nails's body crashes against the cement wall of the now-sealed rotating room, pulled by the force of the claw. Roman and Strider sprint back to help him, but as they search for a way to release him from the claw's death grip, a harsh reality sets in.

Nails coughs up a mouthful of blood, which dribbles down his chest, staining his white tank top. Still reeling from the massive amount of orange stimulant in his system, he musters the words "OUF... ARGH, FUCK! More than a...b-bandaid to fix 'at, yea?" He forces a smile to Strider, who places a metal fist to his own face to hide his sorrowful expression. Echoes of the CYB battalion banging away at the concrete wall shake the room, sending painful tremors through Nails's body.

Nails coughs up blood again before speaking. "You...you fucks, g-get W-W-Windi out of here, you h-hear?" His legs dangle limp and motionless from his waist. The claw has punctured his spinal column. However, his hands fumble through the yellow, smiley-face fanny pack and produce one final bag of his orange Kraken; a large one.

Strider removes his hand from his face to show his eyes filled with tears. They stream down the dark skin of his cheeks. He places his cybernetic hand gently on Nails's bloodied shoulder. His deep voice cracks in despair. "'Til the bitter end, my brother. We had some good-ass times..." Roman can see in that moment, for the first time, how close they are, and he feels for them. If truly honest with himself, as infuriating as Nails has been, Roman was just starting to like him as well.

Lifting the bag of drugs to his face with a shaking hand, Nails takes a bump of the powder directly out of the bag. With his eyes wide, his body quivers. Looking at his long-time friend Strider, Nails responds, "Oh, get on ya bl-blubbery fuck! Don't make it s-sad. We saved th-the girl, brotha!" forcing a smile. Strider can't help but chuckle through his tears. Nails then reaches down and unzips the big pocket of his fanny pack to reveal a mango-sized improvised device, its frame crafted of metal and glass with faint blue lights glowing at its center.

"Holy shit, is that a fucking vitalerium bomb!?" exclaims Roman, who stares flabbergasted at the devastating device that Nails has apparently been carrying the entire mission.

Even through the immense pain, Nails shows a look of pride in response to Roman's bewilderment. "Fuck yea!" he shouts before coughing up a load of blood. "M-made it me-self! Now... H-how fast can you mates run a q... ARGH... quarter mile?" He smirks at the end of his sentence.

Roman and Strider look at each other with uncertainty, then back at Nails. The banging continues, and louder now as the CYB battalion begins to break through the wall. "Go... I got them..." whispers Nails on his last leg. The two begin slowly backing up. Strider's eyes do not leave his friend's as he backtracks. Nails flails against the wall as the tremors grow stronger. "GO!!!" he shouts, spewing blood and saliva. Roman pulls Strider by the arm and the two begin sprinting down the hallway toward Leebrus.

Nails twists the key on the vitalerium explosive device to initiate its timer just as a cybernetic arm bursts through the concrete wall. The blinking, glowing lights from inside Nails's fanny pack cast an intermittent bluish hue on his chest and face. He glances painfully to his right to see another hole punched through the concrete just a few feet from where he's tacked to the wall. "Yea...c-come on through...ya' chrome-domes! I've got a new track on deck! A noice little diddy for ya'..." Nails pours the entire bag of powder into his palm and lifts it to his nose. The entire fistful of powder disappears up his nose in a few strained snorts. "AARGH!" he cries as his head cocks back, and a drug-addled grin spreads across his bloody, orange-blotted face.

Another fist crashes through the cement wall. This time, the black metal skull of a CYB soldier pokes through and scans the room. Its face turns slowly toward Nails and glares at him with its red ocular implants. "HAHA I'M GONNA MAKE YOU BOX O' BOLTS DANCE WITH THIS ONE! IT'S A HIT FOR SURE!" screams Nails as the drugs enter his system. The blinking of the V-bomb in his fanny pack begins to quicken. A few more blows from their mechanical limbs and the CYBs break clean through the five-foot-thick cement wall, and begin walking toward Nails, whose head is cocked backward with involuntary muscular contraction. He begins to foam from the mouth, overdosing from the astonishing quantity of drugs in his system. CYB Alpha leader approaches, and a small cannon unfolds from his shoulder, priming for use. Just before Nails's eyes roll to the back of his head in bliss, Nails whispers, "Made ya look..."

Roman sprints as fast as he can up the sloped corridor

of the junction tunnel. He can now see streetlight bending around the curve. Up ahead, Strider sprints with Windi over his shoulder, moving as fast as his metal legs will carry him. Suddenly, a tremendous explosion shakes the corridor to the point that it trips Roman, who quickly recovers and continues sprinting. Behind him, a blaze of blue and white hellfire follows the curves of the tunnel. Roman's legs ache something fierce, but he pushes through the pain as a new surge of adrenaline kicks in. Before the heat of the explosion can reach them, the passage behind them begins to fracture and collapse from the sheer force of the shockwave. Blocks of stone, cement, soil, and clay crash to the ground, completely blocking anything from passing. Before long, the quake from the explosion calms. Roman and Strider both look back at the pile of rubble that now fills the entire girth of the Leebrus-Dorok Junction Tunnel. And for the first time in the mission, there is silence.

At the mouth of the tunnel, Dieter waits in Valeriya's hovercraft, with its boarding ramp extended. "Get on!" he calls over the hum of the ship's humongous gravity resonator. "Roman, your bike is already onboard." The two men jump into the ship with Windi and immediately fall to the floor, exhausted. As the boarding ramp closes, the faint sound of CP sirens can be heard in the distance. Dieter helps Windi into a seat and straps her in snugly. Her head bobbles as she fades in and out of consciousness. When she is safe and well secured, Dieter asks, "Where's Nails?"

Strider, having brought himself to a sitting position, only looks at the ground in silence. Roman, feeling the weight of guilt return as the adrenaline wears off, simply looks at Dieter and shakes his head. Dieter nods solemnly, and replies, "I understand. I am sorry for your loss, Strider..." before returning to the navigation console.

As the hovercraft lifts off, Roman remains on the floor, sulking. He feels cemented to the ground, unable to move from his spot next to the closed boarding ramp. Strider approaches and puts his hand on Roman's shoulder. "We did good in there. *You* did good in there. And for what it's worth... I could tell Nails liked you. He, uh...had a surprising knack for identifying good people. And anyone Nails is down with, I'm down with."

Roman sighs, "Yea... I'm sorry we couldn't save him..."

"Me too..." replies Strider, solemnly. "But that...that crazy fucker..." A chuckle escapes his throat, and he actually smiles for a short moment as a tear rolls down his face. "That crazy-ass bastard went out his way. I knew him a long time, and he'd have been proud to die saving his friends. They're all he's ever had..."

"But all those people...they were transporting those people somewhere...like fucking animals! And I couldn't save them..."

"You saved a few. I thought you were crazy for it in the moment, but we got three more people out of that hell hole. We just didn't have the time..."

"THAT'S NOT GOOD ENOUGH!" shouts Roman as he slams his fist against the metal ramp.

Strider shouts back in response, "Hey! HEY! Now you listen to me. I just lost one of my best friends. Pull it together, motherfucker!" Noticing Roman's eyes fill with water, Strider rolls back his aggression and sighs. He knows that what Roman needs now is space, so he leaves him with what little wisdom he can offer. "Look man...you can't kill yourself over the things you can't control. Especially the horrific ones. You did the best you could. Thinking like that...it'll only leave you with a fractured mind. That much, I know..." With that, Strider taps Roman's armor with his metal fist, and walks away.

With the mission over, and Windi safe, Roman will have more than a million universal credits in his dwindling account soon. He can now return to see Monique, who he misses dearly. But with the blue-freckled faces of the hybrid captives stuck in his head, he cannot find peace. He will never forget those faces filled with disoriented dread; each person's image another tattoo on his brain. Roman cannot enjoy the moment.

A deep-seated feeling of discomfort envelops him, and suddenly he cannot be still. He hobbles to his feet and stares out the window at the smoke escaping from what used to be the Junction Tunnel below. Processing the events of the tumultuous evening will be an arduous task, and he'll likely never forget them. Somewhere deep inside, he feels that the mission is not over, and there is more to be done; that it may never be over.

Their hovercraft takes off into the night sky toward the penthouse at the Gaia Hotel. Valeriya awaits...

CHAPTER 27:

Trifecta

The room is eerily dark, with no windows to allow Bios's light to penetrate its confines. Black furnishings are illuminated only by the small flame of a phoenix-shaped pyre, and the yellow panel lighting that lines the steps of an elevated platform. Upon it rests an ornate leather seat: a throne of sorts. Ancient Gleph artifacts crafted from stone adorn the room, adding a ceremonious persuasion to the chamber. The outlines of Riku Yamasaka's black and gold suit press into the soft leather of the throne as he sits with unnaturally perfect posture. His unblinking gaze falls upon the black brick of the far wall.

Across the room, a group of men dressed in black ceremonial garb descend from the level above by a floating platform. Five of them wear black pants, and a strip of rippling black cloth hangs from each shoulder connecting to a black belt. Tattoos cover the entirety of their bodies, and smooth gold masks cover their faces from their chin to the back of their skulls, effectively concealing any facial features. They stand in a circle around a sixth man dressed in white rags. The faint yellow light of the room casts a glare on his shaved head: a prospective officer.

Once the levitating platform touches the ground, the

masked zealots lead the bald man to the foot of Riku's throne in ceremonial fashion. Riku's ghoulish grin cannot be seen by the initiate, for he dares not lift his gaze to Riku before he has completed the Black Ceremony.

Riku truly relishes the Black Ceremony, a tradition of his own making. As he speaks, his mouth moves in an exaggerated manner to commence the trials. "For what reason does the lesser approach the altar?"

"THE LESSER BELIEVES HE IS WORTHY," respond the masked men in unison, as if chanting.

"Ah...so another believes they are destined for the rank of officer...very well. The lesser may make his case..." responds Riku.

The bald man's rags flutter as he steps forward and kneels before the pedestal upon which the Golden Phoenix leader sits. His head hangs low, never rising; even as he finally speaks. "Father Riku, I have proven myself worthy by establishing a profitable trade route with smugglers from Ventura, allowing the Golden Phoenix to benefit from shipments of weapons, and Guarmatadin, which can be cut with multiple substances for substantial street sale profit. We have already netted just over two million universal credits in the past two months. Similarly, you will now have the opportunity to move Lotusfly off-world to Ventura, expanding your reach to new worlds. These treasures, I grant unto the grace of the Golden Phoenix so it may prosper."

"HM..." grunts Riku as he mulls over the proposal. "Now that does sound tempting. It seems you have shown your efforts can bear fruit. Your skills may yet be of use to Golden Phoenix leadership. But usefulness is not sufficient enough to achieve the rank of officer, *lesser*. You must prove now that you are strong enough to proudly wear the black and gold...as a disciple." The baritone rumble of a deep horn fills the room with unsettling vibrations.

"You have earned your first horn, but two more horns

must sound before your final consideration. One for a successful completion of the Letting Recital, proof of your courage and loyalty; that the Golden Phoenix never be forsaken. One for the trial of Crimson Gold, proof of resilience and enduring strength; that the Golden Phoenix may never crumble upon the shoulders of the weak. You may begin your offering," announces Riku.

Another masked disciple walks toward the prospective officer with a ceremonial dagger cradled in a black stand. Its golden blade is split into two razor-sharp halves that connect to a sturdy, black marble handle. The disciple's steps are silent and slow. His cadence could follow perfectly with the ticking of a metronome. He presents the long, ornate dagger to the kneeling man, who takes the knife after some hesitation. Beads of sweat roll down his forehead, and he hesitates for a moment before pressing the knife firmly against the side of his neck. His breathing quickens, and all eyes in the room fall on him as he builds up the courage for the next step. He takes three deep breaths in succession; then in one quick motion, he swipes the knife across his jugular vein.

Red fluids pour from the small laceration, and intermittent spurts of blood from his neck stain his white rags red. He desperately fights back the urge to recoil with panic and pain as a masked disciple places a golden chalice to his neck wound to collect his offering. With his wide eyes fixed on the ground, the man begins frantically reciting the code of the Golden Phoenix.

"I am nothing, merely a vessel for the golden advance. My family is nothing, may their memories burn to ash in your name. My former beliefs are nothing, for they have only led to less. I believe in only one firm, the Golden Phoenix. I believe in the grand purpose, the one answer to a higher state of being. I recognize no authority outside that of the golden ranks. I offer myself to the infinite progression of this firm. May we select the strong to bolster the cause. May we select the intelligent to apply superior strategy. May we select the savvy to effectively apply our mission..."

He begins to sway where he kneels from the loss of blood, and the chalice begins to overflow and pour down his ragged top. His speech slows, but he presses on, "...I devote my vessel to the grand purpose, that I may apply it as the master sees fit. I pledge loyalty to the black and the gold, that I may strive to achieve what they represent: Black for the darkness of the void, that we may do what is necessary by any and all means: I will steal for the firm, I will lie for the firm, I will kill for the firm, I will die for the firm. Gold for the ambition of material gain, that we may acquire the treasures of kings and want for nothing. I acknowledge the one father, Riku Yamasaka, as my north star, my superior, and my mentor. May my skills fuel your success. For all that I need, and all that I want, the GoldenPhoenix shall provide."

The moment he finishes, the chalice is pulled from his neck. A second disciple produces a vial of Mediseal serum and sprays the greenish mist onto the laceration. It bubbles and fizzes as the initiate retracts in pain, but the once-fatal wound quickly closes into a small scar. With his face pale from blood loss and drenched with blood and sweat, he sighs with relief. The masked disciple walks the chalice of blood to the flaming pyre beside Riku and dumps its contents onto the fiery coals. The fluid sizzles as it lands and fills the room with an awful stench.

Riku announces, "Let the flames of the great idol burn away the weakness of your past, along with any memory of it, so that you may be born anew, in the image of the Golden Phoenix. And let the staining of your garb represent the erasing of the light in you, so that the boundaries of futile morality no longer burden you." Another guttural horn vibrates the room, this one deeper than the last. "I must say, that was quite the offering. You have earned your second horn. One horn remains, earned only following the trial of Crimson Gold. Two minutes to survive. Prepare yourself to receive your blessing."

The initiate stands and removes the blood-stained rags from his body. He steps backward, completely naked, and stands in the middle of the room to wait. The disciples once again surround him, this time facing him directly. Each reaches into their sash and produces a thin, golden rod, which they hold before their masked faces; wielded at the ready. The initiate adopts a fighting stance and prepares for the onslaught. He screams at the top of his lungs and slaps himself repeatedly in the face to psych himself up; an attempt to provoke the animal within.

"Let the trial...begin!" shouts Riku enthusiastically.

One by one, the men charge the initiate, who tries desperately to fight back against the barrage of canes. His fists fly through the air wildly at his aggressors, but few blows land. Severely outnumbered, and without a weapon, he is quickly overwhelmed. The man endures a savage beating from the five disciples. With each blow he receives from a disciple's gold-plated weapon, Riku's smile widens. The man cries in pain as the metal pulverizes his flesh from multiple directions. Shortly after the trial starts, he succumbs to his injuries and falls to the ground. This does not stop the disciples from delivering crushing blows to his torso, arms, and legs. The initiate curls into a ball on the cold, hard floor; his only defense. He prays that the carnage will end soon, but a blow to the head knocks the prospect unconscious. He now lies bloodied and motionless on the floor as the disciples continue to beat him.

Suddenly, "That's enough!" calls Riku to his disciples, who quickly back off and return to their positions encircling the initiate, whose bruised, lifeless body lays sprawled across the stone floor. "Now, time to determine the..." Riku is interrupted by the continuous chime of his TAB device. Annoyed at first, he checks to see who would possibly be foolish enough to interrupt a Black Ceremony, but upon seeing the origin of the comm, his expression changes. "Hm...interesting..." he mutters before addressing his loyal followers. "Check him and let me know the conclusion when I finish," he orders them before transferring the comm to his bionic yellow eyes.

"What a delight to hear from you. I wasn't sure you would accept my offer..." As Riku conducts his business, one of the disciples reaches down to check for a pulse on the motionless initiate. After a moment, he returns to his place.

"To what do I owe the pleasure?" Riku asks. He sits silently for a moment, smiling and content from yet another enjoyable officer initiation. But what he hears causes an immediate response. His eyes open wide, and he leans forward on his throne, breaking his regal posture for the first time since the start of the ceremony. "Where will he be? And how is it that you've come to know this?" Riku listens intently while twisting his wispy beard. "And you are absolutely positive it is him?" he asks the unknown messenger. The smile returns to his face, and Riku returns to his unnaturally upright posture. "Very well. Our deal stands. You will be rewarded for your efforts, I assure you." He then abruptly ends the comm.

Standing from his dark throne, he walks up to the group of disciples and asks, "What has the Phoenix concluded?"

"The initiate has expired, Father Riku. The Phoenix has deemed him...unfit."

An insincere sigh escapes Riku as he looks upon the corpse bleeding all over his floor. "Then the Phoenix has spoken. Such a shame, I had high hopes for this one...clean up this situation and cremate the lesser. It would seem I have reason for an impromptu meeting with the public sector. Oh, and establish contact immediately with his smugglers from Ventura. It certainly sounded like a prosperous opportunity."

Riku steps onto the levitating platform and presses the button for his office. While the floors quickly pass on his ascent, he taps his TAB device and places a comm to an old friend. Moments before he reaches the penthouse, he is connected. "Triconius! My favorite public servant and business partner... I've just received some very valuable news of a particularly sensitive nature. I believe it's time I meet him..."

Zerris paces the black marble floors of his Sanctum Tower office with furious stride. His hands remain clasped behind his back as he rubs his scar vigorously. He awaits a response from his small audience, who sit quietly in their chairs exchanging glances of uncertainty. They can practically feel the rage radiating off their Overseer. When their silence persists, Zerris speaks.

"I'm not hearing any ideas from my *supposedly* capable governors..."

Dorok looks down at the floor, then over to Tye Brenzen as if to pass the buck. Tye, the portly and skittish young governor, lifts a finger and starts to speak, but falters in insecurity and stops himself before he can finish a word. Recoiling his arm, he simply shrugs. "We could try another tour?"

"Another tour? Your solution is another tour? You would burden me with another odyssey of parading around with calming words and a smile? GROW UP!" Zerris shouts back.

The sharp rise of Zerris's voice actually causes Tye to jump in his seat, eliciting a snicker from Dorok. When Zerris's angry stare shifts to Dorok, he lifts a hand to cover his gleeful response to Tye's cowardice.

"We've done the tour. It hasn't achieved the results I had hoped for. We need a new strategy..." Zerris trails off in thought.

"But sir, although the sentiments have not been overly positive on social media, the data shows that you are still received well by many citizens when it comes to your statesmanship. I really think it could make the difference this time..." Tye's placating does not get him far, and Zerris interrupts.

"THE POLLING DATA SHOWS THE PUBLIC DISPLAYING MORE RESENTMENT THAN EVER!" barks Zerris venomously. "Thirty-two percent not in favor!? Thirty-two!? That's almost twice what it was last week! At this rate they'll be storming the tower in a month!"

"We've already erased thousands of these traitors' platforms and arrested a number of the individuals stoking the fire in the Fabric. Eventually the dust will settle, and everything will calm down. People will forget this in a few months," replies Dorok, seemingly undaunted by the situation.

Zerris sighs, frustrated by the idiocy of his closest allies. "Erasing platforms does not solve my problem! Every platform we erase is another platform that cannot further influence in our own favor. And every person we toss into the Cube is yet another body not paying their government dues! Get that through your thick skull, Dorok! The protests are rising! Two in Leebrus and the southern quadrant of the Outer Sphere, and now word of another in Luxenia? Speaking of Leebrus, where the hell is Gunderson!?"

Tye responds nervously, "He-he said he would be here shortly; I think he was held up by an important comm..."

Zerris fumes. He speaks through his teeth as he attempts to contain himself. "What could possibly be more important than reining in these self-important dissenters and ensuring the success of the party? Anti-government sentiments are like a disease. If not contained, they will continue to proliferate and spread like a virus until they become completely uncontrollable!" He walks past a large stone statue of a winged warrior of Gleph origin, and sits down on the edge of his floating desk. He must allow time for the blood to drain from his beet-red face. Next to him, a custom-engineered vitalerium container is displayed on the desk's marble surface. It is larger than most containers and allows for more visibility of its contents. Encased within it, a vitalerium crystal the size of his forearm rotates in midair. It has been painstakingly sculpted into a perfect replica of Michaelangelo's "David"; the ideal human form. The beauty of the piece instills a calming effect on the livid Overseer. Zerris takes a deep breath, followed by a long exhale as he returns to baseline.

Typically, Zerris is not one to lose his temper. He actually despises those who seemingly lack control over their baser instincts. But the stress of recent developments has placed the world on his shoulders, and the obstacles ahead would surely exacerbate the state of affairs as his ultimate plan continues to develop. *I must remain above it, better than... I must detach myself; a calm, collected observer operating efficiently through my own eyes.* Finally, he provides them with the answer he originally had tasked them with sourcing. "Distractions. What we need are more distractions. The Vital Cascade Mining fiasco was a start, but we need more. What does the data report after the story initially broke?"

"Uh...just a moment, Overseer..." Tye fumbles with his holoscreen to bring up the results of his search. A graph displays over the device, depicting a steadily rising line with a sharp downward spike, which then rises steadily again. He enlarges it so the others can see. "It seems like that calmed down the chatter about the initiative for at least last night and this morning...but 919 started to spike again in the Fabric shortly after."

"Ok, good. Then it's time to ramp up our efforts there. I want a fresh news story every hour. Interstellar catastrophes, impending natural disasters, celebrity gossip headlines, and, especially, IGB rumors, all of it; anything and everything we can drum up. I want their heads so filled with extraneous headlines and ongoing events that the sheer quantity of information pushes any misguided uncertainty of government-directed property initiatives out of their feeble minds. I want you each to come up with as many concepts as possible and begin feeding them down to the local city-state networks. Then, after a short break, I want every model, actress, singer, anyone who's anybody brought on board to our cause, and disseminating their positive sentiments about 919. All non-believers to be ostracized! And Dorok, move those detained for Fabric crimes into re-education programs immediately. Their reach will not be wasted."

The dutiful Brenzen responds warily, "Understood sir! Although I have to say..."

"Ugh...what is it, Governor Brenzen?" asks Zerris, seemingly exasperated by the young politician.

"It's just... We should be careful with publishing stories in opposition to the IGB. We have to believe that Grand Regent Wyngor has deployed some kind of...monitoring capabilities to keep tabs on what we publish...you know how paranoid he can be. And his AGI undoubtedly has the ability to parse through all of our media with exceeding speed."

Zerris scoffs at Tye's warning. "I've already taken care of that, *Brenzen*. Do you take me for a fool? The Kairus Skyshield is impenetrable; it cannot be scanned through. Not to mention, I have relay stations positioned around the outer walls that beam a starkly different reality of our IGB allegiance to Wyngor's *not-so-secret* spy satellites. Let me worry about things of that nature, while you focus on carrying out your orders as they are given to you."

"Yes, Overseer..." replies the embarrassed governor.

"I'll work on the counter narrative with Trike whenever he decides to show up. You will be given directives for narrative design when it is decided. For now, both of you handle your local networks, and I'll take care of Jennifer Baine..."

"I'd like to *take care of* Jennifer Baine..." mutters Dorok as he types his duties into the calendar on his TAB. He glances over at Tye for affirmation with a smirk. Tye chuckles nervously to placate his much larger colleague, but ceases when he notices that Zerris is unamused. The awkward silence that ensues is broken when the door to the office opens abruptly.

Governor Triconius Gunderson storms into the room with an urgency that is etched into his face. His representative robe is wrinkled, and a number of its clasps remain undone. His disheveled appearance is an eyesore to Overseer Aganon, whose respect for detail is offended by the very sight of Trike.

"By the Primes..." mutters Zerris as he rolls his eyes. "You better have a good excuse..."

"Overseer! Overseer..." Trike stops halfway across the expansive office and places his hands on his knees to catch his breath. He pants as if he had just run to Sanctum Tower all the way from Leebrus.

"Out with it, Trike! What is it?"

Between gasps for air, Trike blurts out, "Overseer...we need to talk in private... It's... It's regarding XSEC Project... Alpha Gen!"

"What's Project Alpha Gen?" asks Governor Brenzen.

Dorok immediately stands from his seat, then proceeds to lift the overly curious Tye Brenzen from his. "Not for your ears, that's what. As a matter of fact, you never even heard those words put together. Now out with you, Brenzen!" replies Dorok as he aggressively ushers the governor toward the door. Once they are rid of Ytonia's Governor, Dorok locks the doors to the office, then guides Trike to a chair and sits him down forcefully.

Zerris furrows his brow. He speaks sternly, with an almost staccato cadence to relay the gravity of his message. "We. Do not speak. The name. Of that Project aloud. To individuals. Who are not involved. You know this rule, Governor Gunderson. As a matter of fact, that operation ceases to exist."

"I know... I'm sorry, Overseer Aganon..." replies Trike, who finally starts to catch his breath. "But there's been an attack on the Junction Tunnels!"

Zerris nearly loses his footing at Trike's words. "What do you mean?" he growls.

"I mean there was an explosion! The tunnel has collapsed on the Leebrus side!" Trike responds nervously.

Zerris's eyes dart to Dorok, who confidently responds, "I

heard about the breach prior to this meeting. I dispatched a CYB battalion to clear out the intruders." He scrolls through his TAB to bring up a control panel for the battalion, but his eyes bulge out of his head when he arrives at the screen. Six pictures of CYB soldiers display on his wrist; all of them with red "X's" over their icons. None of their vital signs read as living.

"Well, don't leave me in suspense, General..." says Zerris.

"The battalion is..." Dorok fights to maintain his composure, and looks away from his device, embarrassed. He doesn't have to finish his sentence. Zerris is able to read his solemn tone.

"You've got to be kidding me..." replies Zerris, exasperated at this point. "You are in charge of protecting an extremely sensitive supply chain, Dorok! Dispatch a high-security clearance team this instant to investigate. So help me Primes, if my cargo is compromised, Dorok...this debacle will fall on your shoulders!"

"Overseer, Sir?" interrupts Trike. "I know this news is tough to swallow, but I do come with some good news that's come from the incident..."

Massaging the bridge of his nose, Zerris growls, "Unless you've got confirmation that my cargo remains intact, or that you've somehow discovered another fifty *research provisions* in the last five minutes, then spare me."

"I don't yet have word on the cargo, Sir, but based on my new discovery, the cargo could be a moot point. I think I've found the key to Project Alpha Gen's effective completion!"

"I'm sorry but, how exactly? Was I not made aware that you recently became a scientist?" Zerris asks sarcastically.

"Er...no. But I have someone you need to meet, Sir. He's found something, er...*someone* who has figured out the key to our goal."

"Speak directly, Gunderson, you twit!" barks Zerris.

Trike begins tapping furiously on his holoscreen as he

tries to connect. "I think he can tell you better himself..." A moment later, a hologram bursts from the screen on his lap and illuminates the air above it with the figure of an elderly man in a black and gold suit, with long wispy hair.

"Good tidings, Overseer Aganon. It is truly with a humble heart, and with the utmost pleasure that I finally get an audience with the esteemed ruler of our great planet." Riku Yamasaka gives a shallow bow before looking around. He scans the grand office up and down. A slimy grin remains plastered on his face. "I must compliment you. You have impeccable taste."

Zerris glares back into Riku's bionic yellow eyes. Without breaking eye contact with the gangster, he replies coldly, "Governor Gunderson, terminate this comm immediately. The purpose of our *arrangement* was to ensure ample distance between the Overseer's office and certain...unbecoming elements of the operation."

"Oh, that's quite understandable, Overseer Aganon... I simply thought an opportunity to study a successful case of human evolution might pique your interest...but I understand. It was a pleasure meeting you."

"Wait..." blurts out Zerris. "What did you just say?" he asks.

"Oh...forgive me. But that is the reason I collect these... patients for you, correct? You're attempting to produce the next phase of human evolution through vitalerium exposure, no? Similar to the references in deciphered Gleph Scrym, perhaps? Governor Triconius provides the payment, I deliver subjects to your tunnels, where they are then processed through Dorok and delivered to your scientists in Sanctum Tower. It's one of the *many* reasons, I imagine, you are stockpiling vitalerium off the books? Away from the watchful eye of the IGB?"

This time, Zerris breaks eye contact to glare at Governor Triconius Gunderson. His fists ball up until his knuckles turn white. He returns to his unwanted guest, saying, "Unfortunately, you are mistaken; not to mention, significantly overstepping your boundaries, old man. I feel I may be forced to confer with my team to explore different procurement options. That will be all..."

"Zerris Aganon, so quick to react. Ah, the curse of youth... You lie so much better when you have CP news cameras focused on you. But unfortunately, there's no one with quite the same understanding or willingness to access this *market*. And the time it would take to ramp up an operation like mine would cause serious delays in your precious research. No, I fear your options in this regard are quite limited. And don't be so hard on my dearest, Triconius. It's not *all* his fault... I have my own innovative ways of gathering information discerning XSEC goals, and goals of your esteemed office. For instance, I know you are planning to make a power play against the IGB."

At the mention of this, Zerris freezes. *How could he have that kind of foresight? I only just started the campaign!* Zerris's mind races. Even Dorok's brow raises at the mention of this, looking to Zerris wide-eyed for an intelligible deflection, but it never comes. Triconius looks up at Zerris, bewildered by the accusation, only to have his fears confirmed by the Overseer's expression. Zerris declines to respond to Riku, and instead scolds Trike. "This better be worth it. You put us all at risk by bringing this thug into Sanctum Tower..." seethes Zerris through his teeth.

"However..." continues Riku, "...I come to you today, humbly of course, not to gloat, but to offer you a true diamond in the rough. You see, one of your more rugged citizens has actually discovered the key to your experiment. He has evolved, and I come with proof."

The Overseer's ears perk up, and for the first time in the exchange, he pays Riku with something other than disdain. "Well then, let's see this proof you claim."

"Show him the video, darling Triconius," replies Riku, quite tickled by himself.

Trike fiddles with his device to load up the video. After

fumbling for a moment, he finally displays a holographic screen depicting a crowded club and presses play. As Zerris watches intently, his heart skips a beat as the light from the screen flashes blue across his face. Suddenly, he is instilled with confidence in his endless search for answers, and is inspired with hope.

"The Gleph were an interesting race indeed. So much wisdom locked away in their decrepit ruins and old trinkets. I happen to believe this man, who was not particularly hard to find, is the key to their secrets. Now, are you ready to deal?" asks Riku with a smirk.

Zerris straightens his posture into that of a steel beam. He stares stoically into the yellow eyes of Riku, whose holographic image, just moments ago, was an abhorrent sight. Now, however, the same man seems a touch more familiar. To the others in the room, Zerris and Riku are silent for an uncomfortable period of time. Finally, Zerris is the first to speak. With his face entirely devoid of emotion, he replies concisely, "State your terms then, Yamasaka..."

After being delivered to the sliding door of the globe-shaped office, the hovering platform returns to its docking point in the club floor. Roman steps through the first set of doors to the camera-laden waiting room. Before he even has a chance to buzz, the second door opens to Modus's office above Earth Mode's grand space. Idrys sits in the corner with a proud smile stretched across his face. Modus stands at his desk, mechanical arms extended in preparation for an embrace. The ever-insecure Drezz stands next to him. He grimaces and looks away, refusing to acknowledge Roman's success.

"My number one freelancer returns!" Modus shouts over the chatter of red- and black-clad Wibetani Militia convening on the couches nearby. He crosses the loud room and hugs

Roman tightly with his cold cybernetic limbs. Roman reciprocates with a lackluster embrace, partly due to exhaustion, and mostly because his mind is elsewhere. The events of the past twenty-four hours suppress his emotions with the gravitational pull of a small planet. Idrys's smile somehow widens as he stands and begins clapping. The rest of the militiamen follow suit. Enveloped in praise, Roman experiences a lick of warmth for the first time since the mission's start, although he is reluctant to revel in it.

"Hey, HEY! Potential Klippers! Shut up for a minute and maybe you'll learn something." Like an army platoon, the sound of Modus's raised voice prompts the recruits to jump to their feet and stand at the ready. None of them look older than nineteen, perhaps twenty orbits. "This man right here; this is someone who knows how to accomplish a task. More than that, he did so by following orders, using his detective skills, keeping his head on a swivel, and being exceptional at his job. And for that..." with two fingers, he swipes the screen of his TAB toward Roman's. It chimes as the credits transfer, and the holographic numbers "+Ж900,000" hover above Roman's wrist. "...for that he makes cold, hard UCs." The wide-eyed youths drool with ambition over swirling thoughts of money and adventure as they watch the numbers spin on Roman's TAB. The familiar glimmer in their eye is one Roman knows all too well. The flash of pride he feels from Modus's big introduction fades quickly. *These men...boys practically, they know nothing of the world except what's been told to them*, he thinks, returning to his numb baseline.

"But we don't just do it for the UCs, no. We do it for something much greater than ourselves. We do this for each other. We do this for our own vision of the world, one that uplifts our brethren, not some robe-wearing stiffs in Sanctum Tower. One that gives you ownership of a piece of that world. That's right! We don't expect you to become reliant. We expect you to become capable! Ain't no Initiative 919 in the Wibetani,

AM I RIGHT, MEN!?"

"Sir, yes Sir!" shout the men.

"You were all identified as top-notch talent amongst the young Wibetani. But if you wanna be a Klipper, you gotta play your cards smart. As a Klipper, your name is tied directly to the Wibetani in a much larger way. A mistake to your name is a gaping hole ripped into the Wibetani flag," he says, pointing to the red, white, and black flag dangling from the ceiling. "A mistake out there could also mean your life. That's why we don't make mistakes! We operate with excellence and the utmost discretion. We are strong, and unafraid to prove ourselves. And so shall you be, lest you be forgotten."

In unison, the group of men shouts, "Forget not our sword!"

"Runner Idrys has your orders. Dismissed."

"Sir, yes, Sir!" they all respond. After handing off the men, Modus returns to his floating swivel chair behind his desk as the crowd exits. The Runner Left Hand does not leave without laying a firm slap of acknowledgment onto Roman's shoulder.

As the rugged group files out of the office, Drezz's TAB chimes, prompting him to read the message he's received. His eyes widen as they dart back and forth through the text, and he turns away from Modus to read in privacy. Once finished, he immediately deletes it, and hides his wrist behind his back nervously. "I uh...have to check on our new satellite club. Just got word from one of the Klippers that the contractors started building the bar on the wrong side of the fucking room..." His cadence sticks out to Roman, who, even in his state of exhaustion, notices something strange about his demeanor.

Modus squints and rubs the bridge of his nose between his eyes vigorously. "Fucking construction workers...we should be doing our own contracting by now. I want you to make that one of your priorities. We need our *own* teams. Might be a good way to wash creds...should cut costs for future projects too. Get to it then, Runner Right Hand."

"Yes, Sir..." replies Drezz, who then walks briskly past Roman with nothing but a cold glance as he exits Modus's office.

Roman shuffles to the chair in front of Modus's desk and practically falls into its seat. "Beefing up the officer ranks, I see. Still charming young men with the same visions of fortune and fame?"

"Even old men envision fortune and fame, Roman. Might as well invest in the idea in your youth. And we're expanding our base of recruits, so naturally we're going to need more young leaders as the organization grows. You'd know a bit more about that if you stuck around."

"Yea well sometimes it's easier to get the full view of an organization from an outside look in. Free of bias...freer in general, really," replies Roman smugly.

"And freedom without purpose is like hosting an orgy on your farm when you're the last man on Deorum. Sure, you're having an orgy, but I promise you it ain't gonna be that fun... or pretty," retorts Modus coldly.

Roman rolls his eyes and cranes his head to the ceiling of the circular office, adding, "How the clever quips flow from those looking to assert control..."

Modus scoffs loudly and shakes his head. "Look, I ain't tryin' to get into it with you today. I'm in too good a mood. Don't ruin it or I'll put my titanium fist up your ass. Now, you did a damn good job out there. Those UCs are well earned. And..." Modus begins to tap away on his dock. He pushes his chair away from the desk to provide a better view and continues, "I've got a very satisfied client on holo who wants to confirm that claim..." Modus says with a grin before producing a hologram behind him.

The floating image of Valeriya appears. She grins gleefully from her penthouse hotel room. "Roman! So good to see you. I have someone here who wishes to thank you..." A moment later, Windi joins her in the frame. The girl smiles meekly and, having cleaned up since her drop-off, presents a sharp contrast to their last interaction.

Windi chimes in softly and sweetly, "Hi Roman! I uh... guess this is our first time meeting...wasn't exactly all there when we first met."

"Good to meet you, Windi. You look better. Seems like you're recovering quickly."

Windi giggles, responding with a shy, "Thanks, Roman. I... I don't know what they wanted with me. I don't even remember much of it...but you saved my life. I'm grateful, Roman. I just wanted to say thank you myself."

Valeriya interjects with her own words of gratitude. "I don't know how to thank you, Roman, so I'll just say it. From the bottom of our hearts, thank you so much. Because of you, well... I don't even want to think about what would have happened to my Windi if you hadn't found her..." Valeriya caresses the hair of her cousin's head with a loving, almost parental disposition. "I guess what I'm trying to say is, if you ever need anything, we owe you one."

With a slight nod of the head, Roman replies, "Well, the credits are certainly a thank-you enough, but I'll bank the favor either way. Glad you..." The image of dozens of slime-covered hybrid people crawling across the concrete floor flashes through his brain, causing him to momentarily lose his train of thought. "Uh...yea. Glad she's back safe and sound." Suddenly he cannot bear eye contact. He drops his head in shame despite the kudos he receives.

"We're all grieving the loss of Nails. Part of me can hardly believe he's gone...none of us have known life without him for a long time now..." Valeriya wipes tears from her eyes, then wraps her arms around Windi and pulls her in close. "I didn't even get a chance to say goodbye... I think Aramis is taking it the hardest. He hasn't come out of his room since he got back..."

"Is that Roman?" replies a cold, monotone voice from off screen. Dieter steps into frame and places his palm on the shoulder of Valeriya. As he does, Valeriya shifts her cheek to meet the skin of his hand.

Roman, though avoiding eye contact, cocks his head to the side upon noticing this interaction. *Wait, are they together? I thought I picked up on a weird vibe at the meeting,* he thinks.

"Our mission was fraught with unforeseen obstacles. We couldn't have accomplished this without you, Roman. I second Valeriya's statement. Should you need anything, simply comm."

"Uh...yea. Will do. And sorry for your loss. Nails was...he was alright," replies Roman awkwardly. Despite the wording of his compliment, the sentiment is heartfelt.

"Take care of yourself, Roman. And take care of Monique too." The holocomm terminates after Valeriya's farewell.

Modus's chair hovers back behind his desk. "Now there was something I was supposed to tell you... I forget what..." While pondering the message he is supposed to deliver, he finally notices Roman's condition. Across the desk, Roman stares blankly at the floor in his seat. His terrain armor is covered in dust and soot, and splashes of mud fill the scrapes on his face. "You, uh...you alright, freelancer?"

It takes a moment for Roman to snap out of his daze and respond. "Oh, uh...yea. I just need some rest."

"Well, you earned it. OH! I remember now...go see Norvel before you leave. He said he has something for you. I'll tell you what, I've got a mind to hire that science freak full time. I ask it. He builds it. It's incredible! That nerd's gonna launch the Wibetani into a whole new high-tech era!" With that, Modus reclines in his seat and produces a flame with the thumb of his cybernetic hand to light a massive cigar.

"Yea, will do," replies Roman, groaning as he slowly pushes himself from his seat. "See you around, Modus."

Deep in the halls beneath Earth Mode, the clanking of tools and the tones of obscure electronic music echo from a room inhabited by one. With a drill in one hand, and a plasma welding torch in the other, Norvel Mathis bangs his tools on a desk to the beat of the music. He flips the welding torch into the air and attempts to catch it, but misses. The torch crashes to the floor and engages. Flames roar from its nozzle, charring the dirty concrete floor of the basement.

"Ah shit!" he yells, as he scrambles to turn off the device before it starts a fire in his makeshift lab. After finally extinguishing the flame, he chuckles to himself, and continues to dance to the niche music that blares from the speakers provided by Modus. He dances up and down the room, past the wall of outdated tools and improvised equipment made available to him, then back toward his newly finished masterpiece. The small device, consisting of concentric metal rings connected by an apparatus with coils and rods, sits comfortably in its display, on which the final adjustments were recently made. A feeling of pride in accomplishment fills him like a spirit. For a short time, they even shroud the feelings of anxiety and impending doom surrounding his situation; around his love, Mirene's situation. The lab is, and always has been his panacea of respite; a happy place tucked away from the politics and ills of the world. It was a place for science, and science alone. For him, that was enough.

The sound of the lab's heavy door opening interrupts his elated state, causing Norvel to swing his head around. Roman's large frame leans against the doorway with a single brow raised in judgment of Norvel's semi-coordinated gyrations. Norvel stands as still as a statue, pretending like he wasn't just dancing like a fool to strange music.

"Uh, h-hey! Just, uh…" Norvel rushes to the nearby dock to pause the loud music, "…just the guy I was looking for!"

"Oh, I heard…" Roman responds, rolling his eyes. He enters the room and begins scanning the walls and tables. His fingers graze across the equipment strewn about the surfaces as he admires the litany of tools at Norvel's disposal. "Sounds like Modus has big plans for you."

"Yea…your friend Modus is…definitely an interesting one.

Not a particularly *creative* one. I have to say, I was a little worried about this whole arrangement, but...everything he asks me to make is kind of basic. A weapon mod here, an improvised vitalerium rifle there, a lot more surveillance stealth gear... I've actually been kind of bored!" Norvel chuckles.

"Pft...what I wouldn't give to be bored..." mumbles Roman under his breath. He is running on fumes at this point, and suddenly his eyes begin to flutter. It had been days since he had seen a bed. "Hey, listen, I'm not sure where I'm going to stay right now. Not even sure Monique is going to want me around at all after that fight we had... I basically made her walk home."

"Yikes...yea that's...um..." Norvel, being his usual awkward self, is uncertain how to respond. Whether to provide comfort, or to agree with him, to provide advice; he cannot decide. So, he simply trails off. It seems like he's been isolated down here a while.

"You mind if I crash here?" asks Roman, pointing to the two sets of bunk beds pushed against the far side of the room. "I don't want to risk the crossing to the Grind right now...for all I know, my landlord has probably sold all my shit at this point..."

Norvel responds, "Yea s-sure. No problem... Oh, but you have to take the bottom right bunk," he says, pointing to the bunks at the back of the room. "A couple of the recruits are using the other beds. Guess they're in-house recruits?"

Roman chuckles. "The worst possible gig. That was always pure grunt work. They're probably doing stocking for the club. I'm sure their conversation is plenty riveting." Roman throws his utility belt and pistol onto the bed. He removes the chain from his neck and slides it under the pillow with his blade. The red crystal in its handle winks at him as it disappears under the stained pillowcase on his bunk. "Anyway, what'd you want to talk about? I'm fading fast here, so let's make it quick..." replies Roman.

"Uh...right! *So*, while I've been entrenched in boredom, I decided to start tinkering with some prototypes that might help us on future missions... While I was thinking, the recruits brought in a crate of professional-grade Guaniton holo-charges. Kind of a lucky find, I guess. They said it fell off the back of a truck!"

Roman chuckles at Norvel's naivety. "You know that's code for stolen, right?"

"Oh...right. Guess I forget what organization I've gotten myself wrapped up in. Anyway, I was just thinking of different ways to utilize the solid-state hologram technology. The CP uses it for restraints, non-lethal weapons, and a number of other straightforward purposes. But each tool is constrained to a specific use. I wanted to make something for you that was a little more versatile! I was able to extract materio-graphic cores from a number of different types of holo-charges, and created a usable prototype you might find helpful! Especially for our next mission to help Mirene escape." He ignores Roman's eye roll and runs over to the device resting on dual prongs. As he picks it up delicately, its copper-colored metal shines in the fluorescent basement lights. "This!"

"What *is* this? Looks like an arm cannon," replies Roman unenthusiastically.

Noticeably annoyed, Norvel scoffs, "An arm can...ugh. Come on, man, use your imagination! I was just talking about solid-state holographic tech, and you come back with wrist pistol!?" Another eye roll from Roman only motivates Norvel to change gears. He accepts the challenge and continues his pitch. "*This*, is the Materio-graphic Emission Cord. I call it MEC for short. You can load any old holocharges here..." He points to the rear of the device. Norvel then drags his finger across the rods that span the length of the device. "...and it reformats the materio-graphic cores here to take any holographic form you want! You can fire holonets, you can create holoplatforms to bridge gaps... You can even erect a holographic shield with this thing if you need some last-minute cover! If your mind can create it, you can make a hologram of it with this. All you need to do is format your desired configuration on this screen..."

"Norvel," interrupts Roman, to which Norvel's face drops. "I...am tired. I have not had a good day, and I haven't slept in almost two. The room is literally starting to spin. Had I known this was a science project, I would have..." Roman watches as Norvel's face deflates like a balloon. He actually feels bad for stealing the thunder from the excited scientist. "Ugh..." Roman groans. "Look... I appreciate the enthusiasm, buddy. I really do. But I've got a lot on my mind right now. I still haven't seen Monique since we got in a fight, and I'm about ten minutes away from hallucinating. Let me sort out my life, and then I'm all ears for a demonstration tomorrow, cool?"

Reluctantly, Norvel nods in response and places the device back in its display. "Ok, tomorrow then. We can take another look at your...situation tomorrow too," he responds, pointing at the blue crystal in his cheek. "Oh, and Roman? You, uh... I heard about what you saw...you know. Down there in the tunnels...the hybrid people."

Roman shoots Norvel a sharp look, but lacking the energy to discuss the topic, he simply grunts.

"Yea, I was in a meeting with Modus when a guy named Dieter holo'd to fill us in and confirm the job was done. Some real serious tech on that guy... Anyway, I just want you to know I had no part in that. I don't know what the CP is up to, but it sounded...experimental. I mean abducting hybrid citizens? I would never agree to work on anything like that..."

"I know, Norvel. I know you. Besides, if I thought you did have a part in it, I wouldn't have said hello. I would have just shot you," he says bluntly, with a smirk.

Norvel forces a laugh, fiddling nervously with a large wrench. He still has not quite gotten used to how nonchalantly Roman throws around the concept of murder in a humorous light. But at least it's less shocking than it used to be. "Tomorrow, then," replies Norvel.

Roman nods wearily and makes his way out. He uses the doorframe as a crutch to pull himself back into the hallway, but something stops him before he leaves, and his hand remains glued to the wall. He remembers all that he has been through since meeting Norvel: their first meeting, the vitalerium accident, experimenting with his powers in the safe house, and essentially pawning him off on Modus. Despite being in his own predicament, the young scientist has somehow taken everything in stride and continued to aid Roman. As sad as it may seem, aside from Monique, Norvel is probably the closest thing he has to a friend. A familiar feeling hits him, and in that moment, he feels compelled to return the favor for all that Norvel has done. And so, with a heavy sigh, he pokes his head back into the lab.

"Hey..." he calls out. Norvel's head turns around like a top. "I know I promised I'd help you get your girl out. And I need a distraction anyway, so... I guess what I'm saying is I haven't forgotten. We can talk about that tomorrow too."

Norvel lights up like Kairus at night, instantly filled with gratitude. His lips purse into a thin smile. Norvel tries to come up with something to say, but all he can muster is, "Glad you made it back alright, Roman." Roman nods and disappears into the dark hallway.

Each step is more burdensome than the last as Roman makes his way back to the club level. A bed could not come soon enough. *I just hope I can convince Monique to let me back in the apartment*, he thinks. As he climbs, he can hear the prospective Klippers reciting the Wibetani creed in unison. Their voices echo down the stairwell.

> "We commit ourselves to strength, that we may never become reliant on the promises of charlatans. We commit ourselves to excellence, competence, and disavow

mediocrity for the good of all Wibetani. We make a pledge to family, that we uplift the brothers and sisters of the Wibetani to share in its glory. We make a pledge of honor, that our actions reflect the consequence of a free world worth fighting for. We live our lives by the sword, and hone our skills that we may rise up by its edge when the necessity emerges. Never shall rust collect on our blades. We dedicate our sword to the Wibetani, may our independence endure eternally so the brotherhood may flourish."

Emerging from the basement, he sees the same characters from earlier. Idrys barks orders at the group of potential Klippers who stand in formation before him. Not far away, and with a lit cigar in his mouth, Modus oversees the operation from a VIP couch. Only now, another familiar figure joins them.

Her curves are a delight to the eye; they fit snugly into her black and red Wibetani riding suit. Though the Lancor leatherwear looks uncomfortably tight, she wears it with ease. Supple skin emerges from the collar of her clothing to merge with a delicate jaw and features that radiate beauty. Her crimson locks of hair shimmer in the light of the club. The glint of her septum piercing and her subtle tattoo are unmistakable, and her ice blue eyes like stars fit delicately into the statuesque contours of her face. Monique stands next to Idrys with her hands on her hips, and the sight of her alone is enough to reinvigorate Roman. A smile even begins to brim on his callous, dirty face. He does not even care if she is still angry with him. After the ordeal he's been through, seeing her again is more than enough.

Monique wears her heart on her sleeve. I'll know in a single look where we stand... And so Roman approaches to meet her. She notices someone approaching and turns to him. Roman's heart immediately beats faster. Her blank stare meets his, and she...

BOOM! BOOM! Roman falls to the floor, stunned and disoriented. *What the hell was that?* His mind races in all directions with no defined destination. He cranes his neck up painfully to see smoke and daylight billowing into the dark club. A blur of black and blue figures rushes inside, and suddenly the all-too-haunting intonation of vitalerium rifle fire rings out in the dance hall of Earth Mode. Just a dozen feet away from him, the recruits pick themselves up and begin firing back on their assailants. Roman's head spins, and he can hardly distinguish the faces of those around him.

Men donning red and black succumb to the gunfire left and right. Before he can pull himself up, someone crouches next to Roman, just close enough that he can make out her face and helps him up to his feet. "ROME! WE HAVE TO HIDE!" shouts Monique over the barrage of vitalerium charges as they run down the stairs. Modus sprints after them with a number of others, firing as he runs. Idrys and others return fire where they stand, still reeling from the element of surprise parlayed against them. Only a few of their shots land, and most that do simply bounce off the encroaching wave of glimmering black armor.

An army of CP Guardsmen floods into the club, firing upon their Wibetani targets as they position themselves behind the cover of couches and level barriers. One of the Guardsmen, a RoGuard with white and blue armor, rushes forward and takes aim at the dread-locked head of Modus Magni. Within a split second of noticing, Idrys tries to stop him with covering fire, but his weapon only clicks...out of ammunition. With no other recourse and not a second to spare, he jumps toward the General, who sprints by behind him.

The RoGuard's rifle howls as a blue orb of energy screams toward its target. Modus stops dead in his tracks, staring in horror as his Runner Left Hand falls to the ground stiff with half of his face missing. "IDRYS!!" he wails, but before he can run to his loyal underboss, another two fleeing recruits grab him and sweep him down the stairs to follow the others. Modus's eyes are pasted open as he gawks at the smoldering remains of Idrys. He fights the recruits with each step, but his state of shock prevents his limbs from working like they should. As they descend to safety, he calls out to his fallen comrade as he watches Idrys's body disappear above the stairway.

Down the hallway and around the corner, Norvel stands in the doorway of his lab, wearing a giant backpack. He had heard the explosion and preemptively packed his most important possessions. Metal and wire poke out of the overstuffed duffel as he waves down Roman and Monique. "WHAT THE HELL IS HAPPENING!?" he shouts in horrified confusion.

"THE CP JUST RAIDED US! FOLLOW ME, THERE'S A TUNNEL OUT!" returns Monique. Not far behind them, Modus and a handful of recruits sprint after them with the same destination in mind. Norvel jumps into the group of frantic survivors and runs alongside them, his backpack clanging and banging with each step. Monique navigates the group through the basement maze to a small room at a dead end. Except for a folding chair, a card table, and some storage, the room is empty.

"You led us to a dead end!?" Norvel's voice trembles from fear. "I-I-I can't go back there! Zerris will kill me!" The CP Guardsmen continue to close in on their vulnerable position. The noise of heavy metal greaves clanging concurrently against concrete reverberates through the walls of the basement hallway.

"Shut up, Norvel. No one's stealing my new scientist away..." grunts Modus as he enters the room. Having regained his wits, he moves quickly and with focus. Once everyone is inside, he opens a large, dark green storage cabinet and places his cybernetic hand on one of its many shelves. A flash of light emits from the shelf, scanning his hand. Just as the CP Guardsmen round the corner and begin sprinting after the fugitives, a thick steel door drops from the ceiling, encasing them in the room.

A section of the concrete ceiling retracts up and slides away to reveal a hidden passage up to the street. One of the recruits stands on the folding chair available. He reaches into the dark cavern above and pulls a sliding ladder down to the others. "General! You first, Sir!"

"Don't you give me orders, recruit! Monique! Let's go, get up this ladder!" calls Modus. Following his words, rifle charges connect with the outside of the gargantuan door, sending ear-shattering vibrations through the room.

Monique is not focused on her father's words. She looks around the room, frantically scanning faces until she cries, "Where's Idrys!?"

"He's dead! I SAID MOVE!" her father shouts as he starts climbing up the ladder. Norvel does not wait for a second cue. He immediately jumps to the ladder and begins climbing. Others follow as well.

Monique stands in shock at the revelation. Her eyes begin to water instantly at the news. Roman, having finally attuned to the situation despite his exhaustion, grabs Monique by the shoulders and attempts to bring her back to the present. "Hey, HEY!" When her blue eyes meet his, a laconic message follows. "We mourn later. For now, we survive, or we'll never get the chance to."

Monique wipes the tears from her eyes, hardens herself, and nods. Roman leads her to the ladder and begins to assist her up. Her hands grasp the cold metal of the rung as she lifts herself from the floor. She looks down at Roman, who consoles her, saying, "It'll be ok. I'll see you up…"

BOOM! an explosion rocks the room as the steel door splinters inward, sending large pieces of shrapnel through two of the recruits. A chunk of concrete from the doorframe connects with the back of Roman's head, and all goes black…

CHAPTER 28:

A Heart of Cracked Crystal

Roman kicks a rock with his toe lackadaisically. He takes another few steps, and again the spotless, white rubber of his brand-new school shoes sends the rock tumbling a few feet ahead. His clean, pressed uniform feels stiff against his skin. He dislikes the formal clothing and the way it sits uncomfortably on his shoulders. It makes it hard for him to focus. He shuffles along the sidewalk, staring at the cracks in the concrete just a block from his home. Uncertainty fills him as he prepares for his first day of school, though he would never speak a word of it. He is more comfortable in his own head, with his own thoughts.

"What are you starin' at the ground for, kid? You sad or something? Nervous?" asks the bellowing voice of his father, Frank, who walks next to him in the same slow stride that his son affects.

Roman shrugs his shoulders and responds as anyone ten orbits old might. "No..." His voice trails off. Even while his father addresses him, he does not lift his gaze from the sidewalk. He simply scuffs forward with another slow step, then another.

Frank only chuckles in response, placing his hands in his

pockets and looking up at the buildings around him. "Did you know, on my first day of school, I tried to hide from my father when it was time to catch the hovercraft? I guess I just figured that he would eventually forget; that he'd leave fearing he'd be late for work or something... I don't know."

This time, Roman looks up at his father as they continue toward the pick-up zone. "You hid? That's stupid!" laughs Roman.

"That's right, I hid, and I know. I don't know what I was thinking." He laughs back. They walk another few steps before speaking again.

"So...what happened?" asks Roman, whose curiosity begins to overtake his first-day-of-school nerves.

"Obviously my father found me. I had stuffed myself into a small closet in a three-bedroom apartment. There weren't too many places to hide, so it was a pretty short search."

"Then what?" asks Roman.

"Well, my father opened the door to the closet and found me there. Needless to say, he was disappointed. But he never got angry. He simply coaxed me out and walked me to the elevators of the apartment complex, and pressed the button for the roof."

"Did your Education System Craft pick you up on the roof?" asks Roman, excited at the prospect that it might be an option for him as well.

"Hehe, no, buddy. He wanted to teach me a lesson. The roof was on the forty-third floor, so it wasn't nearly the tallest building around. But I remember clearly, I had my head down just like you did, even when we got to the top. But my father looked at me and said: 'Son, never look down at the ground. There's nothing going on down there except mutt shit.' Hearing his father curse elicits a high-pitched belly laugh from Roman. Frank Matthews smirks, then continues his story. "He said: 'Whenever you're feeling low, nervous... down, bad, sad, whatever! Down is the last place you want to look. It'll only take you lower. When you feel that way, don't forget to look up. There's beauty all around you, and a world full of things to be thankful for. Buildings taller than the clouds, and a sky full of stars with endless opportunities. Adventure, success, risks and rewards...and love. You forget about all those things when you stay focused on the ground.' So, uh...just don't forget to look up. It'll make you feel better. That's all."

Roman decides in this moment to look up himself. The light from Bios bends between the tall buildings of Kairus's Outer Sphere and reflects a magnificent orange light on the early morning skyline. Hovercars zip past overhead, weaving between each other. The foliage of green trees peeks out from luxury apartment balconies and catches the beams of orange like a net. They are much nicer than the apartment that Roman lives in, but maybe one day he would have a home like that. With his eyes focused up, he notices a small, glowing sphere move into view near the trees that branch out from the apartment complex. A closer look reveals slight movement, like tentacles extending from its center that wave as it closes in to munch on the building's flora. After squinting through the sun, he recognizes the creature he sees. *A Bulbous Plorion? Those almost never make it into the city,* he thinks, remembering pictures from his father's "Fauna Deorum" encyclopedias.

He does not tell his father what he sees, only watches as the small floating creature disappears into the leaves high above him. Slowly but surely, a smile creeps over his face. His father looks down, and seeing the joyous expression his son affects, he can't help but smile himself.

"So, what happened after that?" asks Roman with newfound excitement.

"Well, I went to school, and found that I definitely had an affinity for the 'adventure' portion of my father's pitch, and I signed up for the Young Spacers program. Ended up leading me to join the Guardsmen down the line..."

"What was that like?"

Frank hesitates as he looks off into the distance. He pats his son on the back, and responds "That, Rome, is a conversation for another day. Just do yourself a favor and avoid the Young Spacers. There are other ways to learn about exploring space." The two continue down the street, weaving through the crowd as they make their way to the pick-up zone for school.

"Don't forget to look up..." A harsh whisper in Roman's ear, and the following clatter of gears wakes Roman from the sweet dreams of a brighter past. His vision is blurry, and his surroundings foreign. At first, he can make out his hand next to his face, which he slowly discerns is pressed against a transparent, red floor, which seems to move beneath him. A sharp pain stings his head and neck as he tries to lift his head. He reaches back and feels for the source on his skull, and finds a large, crusty scab forming beneath his long hair. Returning his hand to the ground to push himself up, he notices his fingers covered in blood. *Great...* is the only thought his tired mind can muster.

As his vision improves, he notices that the walls are the same color as the floor and also seem to be moving. Vertigo hits him, and he begins to feel sick to his stomach. He stifles the reflex to vomit and waits a moment for it to pass before moving. "Ugh, get up, you bitch..." he wheezes as he forces himself up to his knees and attempts to scan his surroundings.

His head spins as he changes position, and the floor still seems to shift beneath him, which does not help. He determines he is in a small, square room about eight feet by eight feet. There is no furniture except for a toilet and a sink with some pipes by the wall. Four recessed lights shine dimly from the corners of the room, the walls of which also seem to be swirling. A closer look brings him to the realization... *The floor isn't moving; the whole room is moving!* All six surfaces that surround him—the walls, the floor, the ceiling—are crafted of some kind of reddish, transparent plexiglass, which glides alongside other cubes just like his. There are dozens...no, hundreds... potentially thousands of them in every direction. Within them, he can see their inhabitants pacing, lying on the floor, or cowering in the corner. He looks up to see his glass case passing by beneath others as well. Directly above him, he sees the two feet of a man who sits on the toilet in his room. His clothes are tattered, and he rocks back and forth violently as he sits with his pants around his ankles. In the next room above his, a man lies dead in a pool of blood that seems to stem from his head.

"Don't forget to look up..." mutters Roman in a raspy voice. It is then he realizes he is thirsty...deathly thirsty. He hobbles to his feet and runs over to the small sink and pulls the lever. The sink sputters and only a momentary flow of murky brown water drips out, and then stops completely. Roman slaps the lever back shut and sighs. "So, this is hell then..." he mutters.

As his room continues to shift, suddenly a brighter light becomes visible. He squints to determine its origin and realizes that his cube is reaching the edge of the others that surround his; neatly stacked on top of each other. When his cell reaches the edge, a platform comes into view in a room that can only be described as gargantuan. Roman looks down as he passes the threshold, and almost has a heart attack as the cube hovers outward over a thin gorge with seemingly no bottom. It descends into pitch-black darkness. A wall of thousands of cubes just like his follow the darkness down to oblivion.

The cube hovers forward out of the larger structure and makes its way to the far left of the room where four men wait. One elderly man in a CP uniform sits at a dock, likely controlling the movement of the cells. The other three are Guardsmen. Two don the usual black and blue armor, but one wears white and blue armor from head to toe: a member of the RoGuard. After a minute or so of floating, Roman's cell lands gently on the platform next to the Guardsmen that await his arrival. He greets them with a less than polite double-handed gesture.

One of the Guardsmen turns to the elderly man and says something Roman cannot decipher. But moments later, the elderly man taps his dock, and a gray smoke begins to fill Roman's cabin. He panics as he looks around for an escape, but none exists. "Son of a…" His field of vision begins to narrow as the fumes fill his lungs. He coughs painfully, then, once again, he succumbs to darkness.

Wake up… whispers a distant voice. Silence.

Waaake UUUuuuup… the voice whispers, somewhat closer this time. Then, silence.

"WAKE UP, ASSHOLE!"

A sharp pain grips Roman as electrical currents course through his body and jolt him back to life. "ARGH!!" he shouts. For good measure, the officer in white armor shocks him again simply for the fun of it. Every muscle in his body tenses and his eyes roll back into his head until the RoGuard turns off the current. "AAHHH!" screams Roman in pain and anger as he regains his bodily functions. "Where the…!" His breathing is rapid and heavy, and his body temperature is high. He would sweat if there were a drop of moisture left in him. Roman stops as he examines his surroundings. He is in a small metal room, rectangular in shape. Nothing but pipes and steel surround him. He tries to move, but the chair he sits in restricts him. He looks down to see metallic clamps around his wrists, arms, and legs. The only clothes he still wears are his tattered pants. His shirt, terrain armor, and boots hang from a pipe near the barricade doors. The shards of smooth, blue crystal in his torso, arms, hand, and face are completely exposed.

"Would you get a load of this freak…" grunts the RoGuard

in a low baritone. The titanium greaves of his white and blue armor bang heavily against the alloy floor as he approaches Roman. There is something strangely familiar about him, but in his chemical daze Roman cannot place him. He is having trouble remembering how he even got into this chair in the first place.

The man wears no helmet, exposing a block-like face riddled with scars. His head is completely shaved save for the back of his skull, where the hair is pulled into a neat, brown top knot. He bends down so his face is only inches away from Roman's. "You fucking disgust me…" he sniffs the air around Roman and says, "…and you smell like shit."

The other two Guardsmen standing by the door chuckle along with him, but the man puts an end to this quickly. "Shut up, you lowlifes! Make yourselves useful and go get the doctor." The men, embarrassed by the scolding they receive, promptly leave to complete their given task. After they exit, the RoGuard removes a canteen from his belt, opens it, and waves it at Roman as if to ask if he wants some.

Roman looks him in the eye, scowling. Despite loathing the man for a litany of reasons, his thirst has become overwhelming. He nods his head slightly, and his captor pours the water into his mouth. Roman drinks ravenously from the stream of water that pours down his chin until the last drop empties from the canteen.

"We can't have you dying of dehydration. Not while the business day is only just beginning…" he says calmly as he screws the cap back on his canteen and retreats back to his dock. "My name…is Colonel Errol Morphet. And I will be your Information Retrieval Specialist for the…well, for as long as it takes, my new friend. Your name…" he taps on his dock to bring up a group of files and begins reading, "…is Roman Matthews, unranked, unaffiliated. You have been detained, *indefinitely*, without bail for a plethora of crimes. Hm…thirty-six to be exact." Errol nods as if impressed. "Among them

I see illegal possession of a controlled element, illegal use and distribution of a controlled element, attempted murder, grand larceny, assaulting an officer of the Coalition for Prosperity Guardsmen, affiliating with a known criminal organization, *and* a number of other fun activities." He presses a command on the dock and begins walking back toward his prisoner. As he does, multiple platforms begin to lower from the ceiling around Roman.

"But let's focus on the ones regarding illicit elements." The Colonel taps on the vitalerium crystal lodged in Roman's face, and grunts. "A thing to marvel at, truly."

Roman does not flinch, but his eyes begin to scan the tables that now hover at chest level. Each is covered with an array of tools: knives, drills, clamps, prods, and strange objects he can't even ascribe a name to. His heart begins to beat out of his chest as he feels his mind retreat to a deep, dark recess. Though he does not know in what form it may come, the solemn truth of the coming events hits him like a hammer to an anvil: suffering. Dreadful, gruesome suffering is around the corner.

"So, let's start from the beginning, shall we? Where did you acquire the unrefined vitalerium to achieve...whatever *this* is, and who aided you in the process?" The Colonel, Errol Morphet, struts from table to table beside Roman, his fingertips gliding along the many tools of terror that rest neatly at his disposal. They shine with a freshly cleaned brilliance on the tables' stainless-steel surfaces.

Roman is very attuned to the moment, and rushes to gather his thoughts. He knows he must remain strong. To outlast his "Information Retrieval Specialist," he must remain focused, and muster every bit of fortitude and discipline he has. He must use every mental trick in the book: deception, deflection, distraction, misleading evidence, the underappreciated red herring. *He must break before I break...* thinks Roman. Sweat drips down his back, making the metal chair he is restrained to slippery. He takes deep, slow breaths in an attempt to calm his heart rate. Roman's eyes scan the man up and down. He does his best to focus on details he can easily pick out. His eyes rest on the man's strange coiffure.

"My main accomplices..." Roman starts, feigning shame as if to come clean right up front. However, his full response is anything but shameful. "...were Zerris Aganon and the rest of your hair." He smiles while he taunts the man. He would have to savor every moment outside of torture to maintain his sanity.

The Colonel snarls in response. "You looked like you might be a challenge. We'll see how you feel in an hour."

This guy is way too serious about his job. I can use that, thinks Roman.

"I had a feeling this was going to be a fun retrieval project." Errol picks up one of the stranger-looking devices from a table, which is connected to the ceiling by a long black cord. The component at the end of the cord looks like a helmet that has been unfolded. It is comprised of small, freely moving metal segments that connect in the shape of an evergreen tree. A red surface coats the bottom of each small steel triangle, and its flexible structure bends and flails as it's lifted from the table and walked over to Roman.

"Let's start off strong, shall we?" Errol says as he slaps the device over Roman's greasy hair, too quickly for Roman to provide resistance. The metal segments conform to the shape of his head, and the pointy tip of its flexible structure rests on the back of his skull. With a twist of the device's handle, it clamps to Roman's head snugly. He struggles in his seat to shirk the headgear, but it does him no good. No matter how hard he shakes, the device remains firmly set. He is barely able to see once its base conforms to his brow, but he can still hear Errol loud and clear.

"This tool is a relatively new one. The Pervasive Nociception Stimulation Appliance, although the clever science fucks that named it call it 'pernoci-stim.' My team, however, we just call it 'Brain-Fire.' It uses nerve induction to hijack your central nervous system to send pain sensations through your body. Supposed to be the most painful thing you've ever felt... Enjoy!"

The chime of Errol's dock precedes a red glow of the underside of the helmet powering up on Roman's head. He barely has time to shut his eyes from the blinding light it produces before...

From the tips of his fingers and toes, to his internal organs, spine, and brain, Roman feels the sensation of blazing fire. His eyes feel as if they will melt from their sockets. Every inch of him wails with the sensation of unending immolation. His jaw locks open, and a scream unlike any noise he has ever produced escapes involuntarily. He cannot think, he cannot move, he cannot even breathe, for his neurons are overloaded with pain in its purest form. For how long, he cannot tell. He has no sense of time, no sense of up or down. Pain is the only feeling. Then, in an instant, it disappears.

Roman vomits what little fluid he retains into his lap. He feels dizzy, nauseated, and cold as sensation returns to baseline from a harrowing hyperbole of noxious stimuli. The light of the room sears his eyes like the morning sun as the device is lifted from his head.

"Some pretty embarrassing squeals you let out. I should have recorded that...oh wait! I did," the Colonel says, pointing to the sheen of a small black lens perched in the top corner of the small room. "You and I are going to record some 'grade-A' content...you terrorist piece of scum."

The door to the room opens with the sound of releasing hydraulics. It swings to reveal the two CP Guardsmen, who reenter followed by a man with a large, oddly shaped bald head. The skin on his face hangs with age, giving him jowls of sorts. He does not wear a CP uniform. Instead, he is draped monochromatically in gray. He removes his gray lab coat and lets it hang on the wall. The man does not speak a word.

"Make it quick, Dr. Leubock. I am in the middle of conducting my interrogation here."

"I will take as long as I please, *Errol*!" he replies spitefully. "In case you've forgotten, he is a subject of interest for scientific purposes first and foremost, a direct order from the Overseer's office. Any and all informational resources to be acquired from him are mere auxiliary gains. Supplementary. *Peripheral*. Do you comprehend? Has your role been clarified sufficiently?"

The Colonel glares into the slits where Dr. Leubock's beady eyes rest. His hatred is palpable, and it looks as if it takes everything in him not to punch the old man in the face. But rather than step into a sparring match with a man who clearly has seniority, he simply looks away. After delivering a verbose, yet swift belittlement, Dr. Leubock diverts his attention to his recovering prisoner.

Roman is still in shock from the "Brain-Fire" device. He simply observes the situation unfold while hunched over in the seated position. Drool and vomit drip from his open mouth as he pants. He scans the weathered face of his prison attending physician. Dr. Leubock's complexion is that of a sun-bleached prune, and crow's feet meet paper-thin eyelids, behind which gleam dark, almost black eyes. His stare is empty, unfeeling; disturbing on a level that Roman cannot quantify.

After poking and prodding the crystals in Roman's abdomen, Dr. Leubock removes a kit from his waistband and unzips it on one of the nearby tables. He produces a medical syringe, jabs it forcefully into the exposed vein of Roman's restrained arm, and begins to draw blood. After filling a few large vials, he continues his specimen collection, which includes hair samples and a mouth swab. Finally, he presses a cylindrical device into Roman's exposed forearm. It leaves a tiny bleed where a biopsy has been taken from his skin.

With his stamina returning, Roman breaks the silence.

"You want a semen sample too?" He forces a laugh to hide how affected he is by the torturous pernoci-stim device.

Dr. Leubock reacts to Roman's sarcasm with the disdain of a man who's just been bitten by his lab rat. "SHUT UP!" he shrieks as he delivers a loud, hard slap to Roman's face. Even his RoGuard colleague raises an eyebrow at the sharpness of the doctor's response.

Roman stares through his long, disheveled hair at the so-called "doctor" who just struck him. His blood begins to boil. There is something utterly creepy, almost inhuman about the old man that stands before him. Whether it is the unhindered willingness to display his psychopathic lack of humanity in front of others, or his choice of an open-handed slap as his mode of attack, Roman is unsure. Perhaps it is the XSEC logo on the man's lab coat coupled with flashbacks of frail hybrids crawling through green slime that compels him. Whatever the reason, he draws a line in the sand then and there. *If, by some grace of the Primes, I live through this... I will kill this man.*

Dr. Leubock packs up his samples and promptly exits. As he leaves, he makes a final remark to the armored men. "Do not let him expire. I will be back tomorrow for more tests."

As the door slams shut, the Colonel walks back toward Roman and picks up the dreaded, red-coated steel device from the table where it rests. "Back to it then, Mr. Matthews?"

"It must kill you to get pushed around by that guy. A guy who you could probably crush between your fingers." Roman leans back in his seat, grinning, surprisingly. He bellows out another forced laugh and musters a raspy voice to say, "Despite all that brawn, all that heavy white armor and the status it brings, blah, blah...you still have the smaller dick when he's in the room!"

Errol's nostrils flare. With a gauntleted fist, he delivers an uppercut to Roman's gut, which leaves him wheezing. He grabs Roman by his hair and throws him against the back of his seat. "You think it's funny? You were only under for twenty seconds last time! Let's see how you do after five minutes!" He then slaps the device forcefully onto Roman's head and twists its handle.

Roman takes deep breaths in quick succession as he prepares for hell. He is all but blind with the device covering his face, but he knows the sound of pain. The faint chime of three bells from Errol's dock sends Roman back into searing pain once again. His screams of pain change by the octave as the device drives needles into his nervous system. The feeling is indescribable, and before long, Roman passes out.

Music blares, all lights remain off, and Roman is alone. His stomach growls painfully, though it is the least agonizing of his ailments. He fidgets in his chair as the music, if you can call it that, rattles through his ear canals to the point of aching. He has not slept. He does not even know how many days it has been. Time is beginning to blur like the boundaries of his sanity. He bounces back and forth from bouts of heavy exhaustion, deliriousness, and microsleeps to intense and uncontrollable anxiety and illusory visions. Every few minutes, he lets out an involuntary scream as they return.

"I need to get out, I need to get out, I need to get out... I NEED TO GET OUT!" Roman yells into the cacophony of sound that blares through the room's speakers. The veins pop out of his neck and forehead like an addict fiending for a fix. A pair of red eyes open and gleam at him from the top corner of the room. "NO!! NOT AGAIN!" he wails.

"Let your weakness get the best of you, and they'll eat you alive," speaks the many voices of Jerrick's apparition, which somehow come through crystal clear over the deafening music. He sits perched in the corner of the room impossibly, his hands pressed against the ceiling and his feet firmly planted on the wall above the room's exit. "It would seem you have let the tides turn...right on schedule."

"HELP ME! DON'T JUST STAND THERE, HELP ME!!" Roman shouts back. The words that Jerrick speaks to him barely register as his brain functions begin to dwindle. His deliberations are disorganized, almost unintelligible. As if they are leaves that blow erratically on a gust of wind, he is unable to fully grasp any of his thoughts for more than a moment. His eyes dart back and forth as they search for something, anything that can ground him. Roman feels he is steadily losing his mind.

"I can't help you. You can only help yourself. Shouldn't be long now before you really make a mess of things..." replies Jerrick, his teeth just barely visible in the dark from his maniacal smirk. "They'll cut you open...tear out your heart. You will perish."

Roman begins laughing hysterically. "I will make it through this just to tear *YOUR* HEART OUT, JERRICK! YOU TURNCOAT! WHOSE SIDE ARE YOU EVEN ON!?"

The music suddenly switches off, and light fills the room, causing Roman to squint. His hair covers his face from fidgeting in his seat. The torturous Colonel Errol Morphet enters the room with his normal detail of two Guardsmen. Despite the clanking of their greaves against the metal floor, the lack of blaring music causes Roman's eyes to become instantly heavy. For one sweet moment, he drifts off.

"Wakey, wakey, Mr. Matthews...aren't you excited for today's mission?" calls out Errol, distracted by the glowing screen of his dock as he prepares for their session. Roman does not respond, only slumps further into his chair as the sweet embrace of slumber grips him tighter. Disappointed by his lack of attentiveness, Errol lumbers over to the chair Roman is confined to and fetches a long, blood-encrusted knife from the table. He taps it on the vitreous shard of vitalerium in his cheek, and asks once more, "Aren't you going to greet your guests?" Nothing more than a snore escapes Roman's airways.

He sleeps through Errol's inquiries, which sends him into a rage.

"How rude... I SAID WAKE UP!" shouts Errol as he buries the dagger deep into Roman's abdomen.

Roman spits blood out of his mouth as his midsection is pierced. He cries out in pain as the smiling face of his malevolent captor mocks him. He looks down at the blade raping his innards up to the hilt, and his eyes bulge. The blade is removed slowly, which is even more painful than the initial stabbing. Errol's armored hand grips Roman's head and locks it in place, forcing him to watch as six inches of steel emerge from his stomach. It leaves a gaping gash next to a litany of scars in his abdomen just like it. Blood pours from the wound like a sieve, but not for long. A cold feeling washes over his body, and a green glow originating from his person begins to reflect off the spotless white armor of the Colonel.

Errol watches with a sort of twisted pleasure as the vitalerium shards in Roman swirl with gray smoke and emit an emerald brilliance. Roman gasps for air while his wound begins to close on its own. Just a few short seconds later, almost the entire gash has healed into a scar. Only this time, the green light dies out early, leaving part of the wound open and bleeding. "I have to say, that never gets old. It reminds me of the Greek myth of Prometheus...*and* it allows us to do all kinds of fun activities I usually couldn't do. Hm...looks like even you have your limits though..." He wipes a gauntlet-covered finger through the blood stream that continues to pour from Roman's nearly closed wound. "No matter, though. We've got nothing but options, *Romey*!" he says, taking a plasma coil and pressing it firmly against the bleeding wound, which cauterizes it shut.

Though Roman recoils in pain, it is nothing compared to previous tortures endured. His mind has been focused elsewhere in response to the Colonel's comments. No one calls him Romey. No one except, *Monique*... thinks Roman, the first coherent thought he has had in a while. The adrenaline he feels from being stabbed and subsequently cauterized is the only thing that allows it. He grounds himself in the pain and follows the thread. *Did she make it out? Did she meet up with Modus and the others? Is she safe? Did she escape?* After getting knocked out at Earth Mode, waking up delirious in a jail cell, and being transferred directly to a torture chamber, it is the first time he has been able to focus on anything other than pain. He forces himself to focus and runs through the chain of events that led him here.

Roman, still gasping for air, decides to find answers. "Argh... Is she alive?" he gargles through the blood in his throat.

"Shut up. I ask the questions. Now we've got a long day. The doc wants to run one more test, and then—" He is unable to finish his sentence when Roman aggressively interjects.

"Is she alive!? IS SHE ALIVE!? TELL ME! TELL ME! IS SHE ALIIIIVE, ERROL!?" His voice affects a crazed, almost melodic intonation as he screams his demands at the Colonel.

Before Errol can answer, the sound of a throat clearing emerges from the doorway, where a man stands in a gray lab coat. "Well, I can see this is going swimmingly, *Errol.*" He steps into the room, followed by two other men in anti-V suits. Their transparent garb, fitted with metal rings, makes a strange, crinkling noise as they move. Each of them carries a small metal container with a thin, transparent port on its side. A blue glow emits from within them: raw vitalerium canisters.

"I will run my final tests now. You may clear the room," states Dr. Leubock coldly.

Errol scoffs at his request. "I'll not be run out of my own office, *Nigel.*" He stands to face the doctor, who glares back disdainfully.

"That's Dr. Leubock to you, underling. Show respect where it is due, or I'll have you for a subject. But no matter. If you wish to stay, you may do so. I hope your suit of monkey armor can repel vital-energy signatures..."

"I'll put my helmet on then..." Errol grunts at the top-ranking XSEC physician.

"Good. I'll be directing from the viewing room." He turns on his heels toward the other men, who await his orders. "You two, as planned! Wait for my cues!" His orders are delivered equally callously to the men on his team, inferring a trend in his communication style.

The door to the room closes and the men begin to set up next to Roman. They clear off the surface of one of the tables, delicately place the containers on top, and produce a set of tools that look like heavy-duty forceps. Errol puts on his white RoGuard helmet and locks it into place with a twist.

Roman, feeling his inquiries are being neglected, becomes annoyed. "I asked you a fucking question..." he mutters through his teeth, hunched over in his chair from exhaustion.

"I heard you. No idea who you're talking about. Keep quiet while the professionals work, huh?" replies Errol.

Dr. Leubock's voice echoes through the room over the intercom. "You may proceed with element extraction!" The men take immense precaution as they follow his orders and begin to open the first vitalerium canister. One man takes notes on his holoscreen, while the other uses his large set of forceps to remove the glowing, swirling crystal from its container.

"YOU WERE THERE! I KNOW YOU WERE! AT EARTH MODE! I SAW YOU!" shouts Roman, flashing back to the single moment of lucidity after being struck in the head. He remembers his consciousness coming and going as the guards flooded the safe room of Earth Mode. The distinct white armor of a RoGuard stepping through the bent metal of the blown steel door and removing his helmet; the strange tuft of hair that unfolded from the white and blue headgear. Roman begins to howl like a crazed loon. "OH ERROL! I SAW YOU, MOTHERFUCKER!"

Errol shrugs his shoulders and retorts, "So the fuck what?

Yea, I was there at the club. My team captured you, and now you're here. Nice math, asshole."

Dr. Leubock gives his next cogent directive via the intercom. "You may proceed with direct subject contact." However, due to Roman's ravings, the scientists hesitate.

"MONIQUE! THE WOMAN WITH THE RED HAIR! WHERE IS SHE!?" screams Roman, practically foaming at the mouth.

"Red hair..." mumbles Errol, his voice distorted through his helmet's speech projector, "...she's dead."

Roman's heart stops. His facial musculature droops as if it melts off his bone structure. He tries to find his breath, but it's as if all the air in the room has been vacuumed out. A moment of awkward silence from Errol follows, and a wave of fear radiates from Roman's chest outward until the hairs stand on the back of his neck. "I... I don't believe you!" he shouts. His entire body now quivers as he yells. "YOU'RE LYING!"

Errol tilts his head in response. It takes a moment for the nature of Roman's reaction to register. When it does, the brute cannot help but laugh. "*Oho!* Wait a second, was that your girl? HAHAHA! It was, wasn't it? Then allow me to be the proud bearer of bad news to an enemy of the state. She's dead as the steak I had for breakfast, *Romey*."

"I DON'T BELIEVE YOU!" shouts Roman as tears begin to stream from his eyes.

"You don't, huh?" Errol walks over to his dock and taps a few times on its workings. After swiping through the light of the dock's holographic projection a number of times, he stops on an image that Roman cannot see from his position. Errol redirects the projection to face Roman with the toss of his hand. "That's about as crimson as I've ever seen. We document every raid! You believe me now?"

The tears stream down Roman's cheeks as the image burns into his retinas. Just a few inches from his face and illuminated by holographic light is the once-sleek form of a woman in a black and red Wibetani riding suit. Her body lies sprawled in a pool of blood on the concrete floor of Earth Mode's basement. A number of large pieces of charred steel shrapnel impale her midsection. Her skin has lost its beautiful tan shimmer, and now imparts a ghost-white chroma splashed with blood, only partly visible through her locks of crimson red hair: the very last person in the world that Roman cared for.

Roman no longer sees the image of Monique's body before him. He does not see the cackling Colonel enjoying every moment of his suffering behind his dock, or the XSEC scientists with the blue glow of vitalerium between their forceps. He sees nothing at all. His entire world crumbles around him and then burns to soot and ash. Roman stares into gaping darkness as the void of oblivion unfurls before him. Its swirling black waves of misery flutter menacingly to his heart's metronome as it engulfs him entirely. His very soul is flooded instantly by a loneliness that is nothing short of absolute; a state of solitary seclusion from any and all. And as his last hope for any shred of a normal life fades into the lifeless image of his love, which taunts his very existence, the void does not simply look back into Roman; it reaches its clawed fist into his chest and climbs inside…

The CP scientists press the raw vitalerium shard into the skin of Roman's forearm, and Roman lets out a boundless cry; not one of pain, but one of pure anguish.

"What is happening? Are you documenting this? Someone, say something!" shouts Dr. Leubock over the intercom. But no response is returned.

The scientists look on in horror as the vitalerium shards lodged in Roman's skin begin to vibrate. The dormant gray smoke suddenly swirls angrily within them, and the once-blue shimmer turns to a deep, crimson red glow that gleams brighter with each passing moment. Roman's scream does not cease, only becomes deeper and more forceful. His eyes open to reveal red orbs that glow as brightly as the crystals in his hide. His entire body emits steam. Heavy plumes of vapor rise from his shoulders as the sweat sizzles from his epithelium, and the room temperature rises drastically. Before anyone in the room has a chance to react, the vitalerium shard pressed against Roman's skin vibrates to the point of shattering between the tongs that stabilize it, and Roman's vision surrenders to black.

A devastating red shockwave echoes outward from Roman's body, the concussive force of which immediately vaporizes the scientists beside him into a red mist of vital fluids. It tears through the armor of Colonel Errol Morphet and splatters him within, reducing his body to a mix of human sludge and RoGuard armor gears. What is left of him is launched backward at incredible speed, but it does not stop for some distance as the walls of the room explode outward as if a large bomb had been detonated. Debris from three floors above them crumbles down to the cracked surface of the ground where Roman's body lays. The components of the chair that once restrained him have been reduced to liquid metal, which begins to burn through the floor around him as he lies there unconscious.

CHAPTER 29:

Friends in Low Places

In the wake of the chaos birthed of Roman's torment, his eyes begin to flutter open to the sound of a blaring alarm. Slowly, his cognizance returns. His joints ache as he rises to his feet. *What the...* Without any recollection of the last ten seconds, he is left in utter bewilderment of the demolished environment that was once his torture chamber. His eyes scan the unrecognizable, ignited wreckage around him and, for a brief moment, he truly believes he is in hell. It is not until he looks to his right that he recognizes his location. The wall is gone entirely, and the red-tinted siding of the dreaded cube sits directly in his view. The transparent walls of its confinement cells lumber over him, and a cleared path becomes visible to the platform his cell was once lowered to. He looks down at his body, which remains somehow unscathed. He watches as the fragments' red glow begins to dwindle, and eventually dissipates to their normal blue hue; an unobserved phenomenon until this moment. Once the color is gone, he is hit with a debilitating dizzy spell that nearly causes him to faint again.

Holy hell...what just happened? thinks Roman as he tries to collect himself. Days of malnutrition and intense physical abuse have left him in a severely weakened state. His thoughts are still scattered from his lack of sleep, but he finds one word to latch onto that moves his feet forward: *Survive.* He has no idea how, and a large part of him even questions why, but he repeats it to himself over and over as he makes his way through the rubble and across the expansive platform toward the elevator. He steps over the body of the old man who controlled the cube dock, knocked unconscious by flying debris from the walls scattered inexplicably across the enormous room. As he shuffles ahead, Roman hears a faint voice call out to him. It echoes off the walls of the massive room, barely decipherable.

Roman glances around anxiously. *Am I still hallucinating?* he thinks. He scratches and rubs his ears, as if to wipe away the voices in his head. It has no effect on him, and the voice persists.

"Hey you! YEA, YOU! OVER HERE!" echoes the voice again.

"JERRICK, I DON'T HAVE TIME FOR THIS!" he shouts, spinning around to the voice's origin. But it is not Jerrick that he sees. What catches his eye is a cell in the lower corner of the cube's great structure. Its transparent edifice shows a giant crack that leads up to a shattered corner where a slab of concrete has lodged itself inside, creating a gaping hole in the cell. A man with short brown hair and a beard has pulled himself up to the crater in the corner of his cell, exposing his head to the stale air of the grand penitentiary. He struggles to wave while maintaining his position a few feet from the floor of his cell.

"Uh... I don't know who Jerrick is, but I could really use some help here. Name's Braxton Hughes, and uh...would very much like to get out."

Roman plods over to the edge of the platform, just inches away from the deep gorge between him and the cube. He struggles to focus his vision to examine the man, but immediately notices his attire. He wears a tight jumpsuit bearing the CP colors. It looks like something he would see a spacefarer wearing, or a pilot. There is something vaguely familiar about this one as well, but again Roman's rambling brain cannot place him. It almost hurts to think at this point. Roman merely stares at the man, snarling from his throbbing headache.

"Yea...nice to meet you too. So, listen, I don't know how the hell you did..." he glances over at the smoldering remains of the torture wing, then back at Roman, "...whatever the hell it is you did, but can you call my cell down? This place really isn't my kind of party."

Between heavy breaths, Roman replies, "Why would I let some CP klang down? As far as I'm concerned, you all can rot in here." Roman turns slowly to limp away.

"WAIT!" yells Braxton frantically at his last chance for a clean escape. "I WAS FRAMED! I'm just as angry with the CP as you are!" but his response receives no answer. The mysterious prisoner who just took down a squadron of men and half a prison wing continues to slog away from him. He must shift gears if he is to ever get out.

"HOW THE HELL DO YOU PLAN TO ESCAPE!?" he shouts back in a last-ditch effort. To his delight, the mysterious, barely clothed man stops in his tracks. Braxton continues to shout, "You can't just walk out the front door like that. You won't even get out of this room without the right codes or clearance. Even if you do, do you even know where you are?"

Roman sighs, then trudges back to the edge of the gorge. "And I'm supposed to believe you can help?"

"I know this facility! I know it well enough to at least give us a shot! And even then, I'm not sure. But I know you DEFINITELY won't make it out on your own! You hear that alarm blaring? It's been going off for about thirty, maybe forty seconds now. In a matter of four or so minutes from now, that elevator door is going to open and unleash an army of Guardsmen into this room. So there is little time for fuckery right now!"

It's not so much the man that Roman does not trust, but the colors that he wears. *He's CP...he could be planted there in case someone escapes? How can I trust some klang? How did I get here? What even happened in that torture room? The torture room...oh gods, Monique... Monique is dead... I'll never see her again...* "ARGHH!" he yells out, gripping his head from a mixture of rapid-fire thoughts, a throbbing headache, and his dilemma.

"Look...you've been in there for days. I saw you get called down, I saw that salty double finger salute you threw the RoGuard, and then I saw you get taken back *there*. I can only imagine what you went through in there, but I can promise you that no matter *how* tough you are, which, *obviously* you are...you're not at the top of your game. On your own, best-case scenario is you get shot and die quickly on your way out. Worst case, they put you back in holding until they can rebuild that torture chamber and then punish you for the extra work you gave them." Braxton readjusts himself on the ledge of the hole in his cell and continues. "Let me down so I can join you, and the best-case scenario is we both get out of here alive! Worst case, we go down shooting."

Even in Roman's delirious state, he cannot argue that logic. Perhaps it is good he cannot think things through normally, for his hatred for the CP would likely have caused him to disregard any suggestion from the klang at all. With the clock ticking, and the alarm ringing in his ears, he finally replies, "Ugh... Fine... What do I do?"

"My man!" yells out Braxton enthusiastically "Ok! Go to that dock right behind you and look for any command key that says, like, 'Extract,' or 'Port,' or 'Return' or something..."

Roman searches the screen for anything similar. His eyes gloss over as he tries to read the words in front of him, but their letters jumble into nonsense in his mind. His eyes finally come to rest on a large yellow icon. It takes him a moment to focus, but the letters finally rest together in his sight to read "Call." He presses it with his knuckle, prompting a hologram to pop up requesting a cell key number.

"It's askin' fer a number!" shouts Roman. His words begin to blend together from exhaustion, and he knows he does not have much time left on his feet.

Braxton pulls himself further up on the ledge that he grips and actually hangs out the side of the cell to get a look at the holographic number displayed on the upper perimeter of his own personal cube. "Ok, you ready?" he shouts. When he sees Roman circle his wrist, gesturing for Braxton to hurry up, he begins reciting the number. "Seven! Seven! One! Two! Seven! One! Six! Nine!"

The sound of shifting gears prompts his cell to jolt slightly and nearly dislodges Braxton from where he is precariously perched. His heart skips a beat as he feels himself slip. The gorge directly below him is so deep he cannot see the bottom. Desperately, he grabs for the ledge or anything that he can latch onto. Braxton's hand grips a piece of the torture chamber wall still lodged in his cell and finally stabilizes himself. He takes a deep breath, then watches as a dusting of concrete and rubble tumbles downward into darkness. "Thank the fuckin' Primes for whatever bomb this psycho smuggled in up his ass..." he mumbles as he pulls himself back into the transparent red walls of his cell, which glides gently toward the receiving bay.

Hundreds of captives watch the events unfold through their cell walls. Some bang furiously on their chambers, begging to also be released, though their screams go unanswered, rendered inaudible by the walls that bind them. Most simply look on with blank stares, having given up on any chance of escape long ago. A few moments later, Braxton's cube hovers to the platform and settles with a loud THUD. Roman presses another button, and the doors to Braxton's cell creak open as the large piece of concrete falls to the floor. Braxton steps out and walks briskly toward Roman. With a smile on his face, and his hand extended confidently, he proclaims "Braxton

Hughes, of the...well, formerly Commander of the CP-IO. You can call me Brax. Whoa...nice implants."

The news story Roman saw on his hoverbike flashes through his mind. He remembers the news banner reading "CP-IO Commander arrested for High Treason," and ponders to himself: *Never thought I'd be in this position...* He scoffs at the extended hand, responding, "Roman. And I'm not shaking that klang paw until we're out of here. What's your plan?"

"Uh...ok. Follow me and be quick about it! We've wasted enough time." Rather than run toward the elevator, Braxton races back down the smoldering corridor of the torture wing of the Cube.

Roman hesitates before following him as unrequested memories of the past few days flood his mind like a raging deluge. The agony of his torture, the sorrow of his loss...the only person left in this world that he loved, perished...they torment him to no end. The blaring alarm in the background, however, acts as the ever-constant reminder that time is of the essence. And so, he forces his thoughts down and repeats to himself the same line he's echoed many times before: *Mourn later, survive now...* and painstakingly runs into the smoke after his unlikely accomplice.

Just a few short minutes later, the elevator doors open on level S100 to the massive platform of the Cube, and a dozen CP Guardsmen file out with ample urgency. The lieutenant with green accents in his armor stops the men in their tracks when he sees the smoldering remains of the wing to his right.

"Halt!" he shouts. "Holy sh... Sergeant! Take four men and sweep the platform! The rest of you, with me!" He leads the group into the smoking ruins of the hallway. They search up and down, both bewildered by the wreckage that extends up multiple floors and disgusted by the gory remains of their fallen comrades. It is enough for one man to remove his helmet and vomit. Their attention is redirected when they hear a voice echo from down the hall.

"OVER HERE! HELP! WE NEED HELP!" shouts the distorted voice of a CP helmet.

The men rush to the rear and enter a room that was once a lavatory. Behind a charred structural beam are two Guardsmen. One lies on the ground, clutching his midsection where his armor is severely compromised, and the other crouches beside him, providing aid. The lieutenant steps forward and aggressively demands, "Identify yourself, Guardsman!"

The crouched man is the first to respond. "Private GR712X, sir!" he stands promptly and brandishes a hasty, off-balance CP salute. He wavers and places his hand on his dented helmet. "I'm...sorry, Sir, I think I may have a concussion..." he responds.

"At ease! What in the hell happened here, private!?" shouts the lieutenant. The men behind him lower their weapons and continue their sweep.

"I... I honestly have no clue, sir...it's all fuzzy. I was here..." he trails off and looks down at the Guardsman on the floor, "...we were in the latrine. It just went off, sir! The blast knocked us on our asses!" He returns to a crouched position by his brother-in-arms. His fallen comrade's hand clutches his flank where the armor has been burned clean through to skin. He moves his comrade's hand slightly, revealing heavy bleeding from an explosive impact. "Sir... Mack, he-he needs help, Sir!"

The lieutenant pauses for a moment, then asks, "Has anyone escaped?"

The indisposed man cries out in pain, and the Guardsman tries desperately to keep him calm. "I... I don't know, sir. I haven't left this room!"

"Get yourselves to the med bay this instant! I will meet you there once we find out what the hell is going on here, and I want a full report, Guardsman!"

"Sir, yes Sir!" shouts the private before lifting the other man to his feet and throwing his arm over his shoulder. He struggles under the weight of his fellow Guardsman, but is somehow able to find his balance. The two stumble down the smoky hallway toward the elevator. After checking in with the sergeant who leads his team of four in a sweep of the platform, the two board the elevator, and the doors close.

"See? I told you you'd have a better chance with me on the team," says Braxton through his dented CP helmet.

"Yea, you're a regular escape artist..." grunts Roman, removing his arm from Braxton's shoulders and standing upright. He lifts his hand from the hole in his armor where his side is exposed and wipes away the blood of some other less fortunate Guardsman to reveal healthy skin beneath. Roman smears the blood from his gauntlet onto the wall of the elevator.

Braxton leans forward and swipes a design into a blue hologram that appears by the doors, which jolts the elevator into motion. Braxton removes the vitalerium rifle from its holster on the back of his armored suit. "Alright, now grab your rifle and hold it at your side to try and hide as much of that hole as you can. And dust yourself off. We need to look normal when we walk through the lobby."

"The lobby? That's your plan? To just walk out the front fucking door!?" asks Roman, baffled by both the stupidity and simplicity of the plan.

Braxton hesitates for a moment, then shrugs his shoulders, replying, "Good as any."

At least two dozen floors whiz by before Roman can comment on the absurd strategy or Braxton's lighthearted energy. When he does, all he can muster up is, "I hate you."

Back on sub-basement level one hundred, the Lieutenant approaches the gorge of the Cube. He looks curiously at the compromised cell that remains open on the platform, then quickly runs to the control dock. He taps furiously on its screen to look up information on the prisoner in cell 77127169. It does not take him long to populate a picture of a man with short brown hair and a neatly trimmed beard. The photo is not a mugshot, but a professional CP headshot. The realization hits him: "That son of a bitch... He knew CP protocol because he IS CP!"

He spins around like a top and screams to his company, "THAT WAS THEM! THE TWO INJURED GUARDSMEN! THEY ARE THE FUGITIVES! AFTER THEM! NOW!"

When the elevator doors open, Brax and Roman slink out of the lift and walk down a winding hallway that leads to a set of fortified metal doors. Braxton scans the ident-patch on his armor, and the doors open up to a bustling lobby floor. They hesitate at the threshold for a moment before pressing onward, attempting to fit as neatly as possible into their environment, where battalions of CP Guardsmen and heaps of government workers flood the lobby of Sanctum Tower. Roman focuses as hard as he can just to walk without limping. Their dusty suits of armor are a sharp contrast to the shining, spotless suits worn by the surrounding Guardsmen, but, somehow, the massive crowds on their way to work pay them no mind. Each concerned with their own personal affairs, not a one gives them a second glance.

"This is insanity," whispers Roman.

"Shut up, it's working!" whispers Braxton in response.

"Where the hell are we right now?" Roman asks.

"Sanctum Tower. Now. Shut. Up!"

Roman's heart beats as quickly as the wings of a hummingbird. He knows that if he does not get rest or food soon, he will likely collapse. *Almost there... Look normal... Keep pushing... Survive...* he tells himself as he walks in tandem with the treasonous Braxton Hughes. After what seems like the longest walk of his life, Roman and Braxton finally find themselves across the impossibly long lobby, staring at the glass front doors—and without receiving so much as a question from prying eyes. The sensors just above the large glass doors sense their ident-patches, and open so the world may receive them.

Bios gleams down on them as they descend the massive set of steps to street level; a light that Roman thought he would never see again. He can feel its heat warm the outside of his CP armor. Despite being entirely surrounded by rows of skyscrapers and covered by the Apex above, a series of gigantic mirrors fitted to the sides of their structures reflects the light of day into the lower levels of Sanctum Core. He is surrounded by megalithic structures, holograms the size of buildings, beautifully crafted fountains, and people...thousands of well-dressed people completely unaware of what has just transpired beneath the soil they tread. Roman has never been inside the Inner Sphere before, never mind Sanctum Core, which only extends a few streets beyond their current position. He looks up and, even in his state, cannot help but marvel at the architecture. The buildings connect to each other through a series of metal walkways and marbled terraces, all of them filled with life. Even through his pain and sleep exhaustion, and despite the torment he has experienced, his father's words echo through his mind: *Don't forget to look up...*

The two men reach the bottom of the grand steps where dozens of hovercars land to be parked. Braxton swats at Roman's elbow to get his attention. "Here's the plan. We go to the valet, and we request to search someone's hovercar. We take it, and we get the f—"

"FREEZE! BOTH OF YOU! YOU'RE UNDER ARREST!" shouts a voice behind them.

Roman and Braxton turn around to see the Lieutenant and his battalion gathered at the main lobby entrance atop the stairs. All of them draw their weapons and aim at the pair. Braxton whispers to Roman, "Just remain calm..." as he tries desperately to think his way through this predicament.

However, to Braxton's chagrin, Roman responds in his own way. "Fuck this..." he replies as he wields his rifle and opens fire. The scream of his vitalerium rifle launches a blue charge through the paned glass of the building directly above the men. Enormous shards of sharp glass rain down upon the Guardsmen's position, along with the gigantic "O" and "W" letters of the famous "Sanctum Tower" sign above them. The dozen or so Guardsmen are forced to dive to safety as the debris crashes to the ground. Chaos strikes the crowds around them, people dashing to safety in any direction they deem fit in their moment of uncertain fear. Roman and Braxton take advantage of the chaos and race toward the hovercars that are now left unattended.

The Guardsmen quickly rise to their feet and descend the steps, searching for the fugitives. When their targets are located, they unleash a barrage of charges indiscriminately upon the sidewalk. The hulls of hovercars melt around them as Braxton and Roman dash between transports, looking for an intact escape vehicle.

"There!" shouts Braxton, pointing to a Cryoxa Scythe. It's fluorescent red paint fades to a reflective black as it sprawls over the vehicle's sleek hull design. An extremely rare, and extremely fast model, the Cryoxa Scythe is a clear leader in high-end performance, luxury hovercars. More importantly, for their purposes, the doors are left wide open, and the red signal lights glow brightly, meaning the vehicle was left started: an easy steal. Roman and Braxton bound over two rows of hovercars and through the onslaught of CP fire to reach the Scythe.

Roman dives in first and closes the passenger door. Not a moment later, Braxton falls clumsily into the driver's seat and groans in agony. Roman looks down at his getaway driver, whose armor steams on his charred left flank. Despite the obvious wound, Braxton bites his tongue, initiates the gravity resonator, and takes off like lightning into the sky, running on pure adrenaline. The men follow the vehicle with their rifle fire, but the hovercraft is too fast. In a matter of seconds, it bends around the nearest skyscraper and is gone.

"ARGH...shit! They knicked Ol' Smoke Drive..." he wails, struggling to maintain control of the vehicle.

"Shit, shit, are you alright!?" yells Roman.

"AAHII'VE NEVER BEEN SHOT BEFORE!!" groans Braxton

as he recoils in pain in his seat while swerving through air traffic.

"Keep it together, Brax! We have to lose them!" Roman reaches over to the console, and pries a panel away from its interior to expose the mechanics and wiring inside. He reaches in and begins to fiddle vigorously with the hovercar's inner workings.

"The FUCK are you doing!?" shouts Braxton.

After a few seconds of twisting wires and removing parts, the holographic dashboard suddenly changes and the "SPEEDING" warning that once flashed incessantly disappears. "Disabled the zone inhibitor so we can fly through red zones and prohibited air space. No more speed governor either."

"ERRGH... NICE," gurgles Braxton.

Behind them, blue lights swirl as the CP response units tack onto their vehicle's location. The two look behind them to see four CP hovercars and a CP hovertank barreling toward their position. They weave between the traffic hundreds of feet above the ground just as Braxton does, but the CP vehicles in pursuit continue to gain ground. The government models are fast, and traffic clears for them due to their flashing lights. Roman and Braxton know instantly that they are in trouble.

Braxton knows they cannot simply fly out of the Spheres. The Skyshield would prevent it upon sensing their approach. He fights through the pain as he tries to come up with a solution. Losing the CP hovercars is proving to be nearly impossible. However, as their newly liberated Cryoxa Scythe approaches the wall to the Outer Sphere at blinding speed, something catches Braxton's eye.

"ARGH OK... I know what to do," says Braxton as he takes the hovercar on a sharp downward descent.

"Whoa, what are you doing!?" Roman quickly remembers why he does not enjoy being in the passenger seat of any vehicle, especially not one being driven by some klang stranger.

A brief pause before Braxton's answer is just about all the

response Roman needs to be afraid. As they barrel toward street level, Braxton finally responds, "You're not gonna like it…"

"BRAXTON. WHAT THE SHIT ARE YOU DOING!?" Roman shouts this time.

"Ok well…whoa…" The hovercar nearly swerves into another one as a dizzy spell hits Braxton. If not for Roman grabbing the yoke and pulling them to the right, they likely would have been reduced to smoldering embers.

"COME ON, MAN, KEEP IT TOGETHER!" shouts Roman, his eyes bulging out of his head in fear.

Braxton grips his side in pain. "UGH…sorry… I'm not doing so hot… So, you see that garbage hauler way up at the wall?"

Roman squints to see what he references, and when his eyes fall upon that massive, multi-trailer hovertanker filled to the brim with rubbish, he immediately catches on to Braxton's bright idea.

"No. NOPE! ABSOLUTELY NOT."

"Oh, it's gonna happen. Because otherwise, they're going to either blow us out of the sky or hit us with a hacking patch to take control of the car… ARGH, and obtain us that way. Also, because…" Braxton is hit with a wheezing cough that launches sputum onto the dashboard of their getaway ride, "… Argh… the seat ejection controls are on my side." He looks at Roman and flashes a childish grin, showing a row of teeth covered in blood.

Roman, with nothing else to do, simply straps his seatbelt on and braces himself, finally replying, "I really fucking hate you. *Hate*."

The CP hovercars follow in hot pursuit. They dive after the Scythe, and one CP hovercar collides with an incoming vehicle from a different lane of altitude traffic. The collision turns the two vehicles into a fireball that showers the streets below with debris. Despite this, the remaining vehicles slowly but surely continue gaining on them. Braxton pulls up sharply on the yoke just shy of the ground beneath them, giving Roman the closest thing to a heart attack since his torture affair.

They hurtle down the road, flying just above the ground traffic, headed straight for the wall. Just ahead, and about to pass through the gate to the Outer Sphere with a full haul of trash for the landfill outside the city, is the massive Waste Management Hauler. Braxton's window will be tight, but they have to make it. With every second that passes, the great steel wall that separates the Inner Sphere from the Outer Sphere gets closer, and Roman clenches his fists tighter. The CP Guardsmen who patrol the wall wave wildly at the approaching Cryoxa Scythe to change course but settle on running for cover when it shows no signs of slowing. Just moments away from colliding steel with steel, and with the CP still a good distance behind them, Braxton says to Roman, "Hold on to your tits! Let's hope they're far enough away to miss *this*..."

Braxton drastically drops their speed and rolls the hovercar one hundred and eighty degrees to the left so the canopy of their cab is facing the hovercars below. At just the right moment, he presses the yolk forward to angle the nose toward the sky, and pulls the ejection lever...

The Cryoxa Scythe, now pilotless, continues on its trajectory until it swoops upward and collides directly with the wall. The front end crunches like a tin can as the gravity resonator flies through the passenger cabin and explodes into a massive blue and orange fireball. The flaming wreckage falls to the ground, sending debris and embers in all directions...just behind the Waste Management Hauler that rolls peacefully beyond the boundaries of the great wall into the Outer Sphere.

The CP response unit arrives at the scene of the crash and immediately lands. The Guardsmen race in to secure the wreckage and block off traffic to the Outer Sphere. The gigantic steel gates of the great wall slam shut. A hovertank positions itself on the bridge that crosses the walls, ensuring everyone inside is totally ground-locked. Above the walls, the Kairus Skyshield becomes visible as it engages a bright orange color. It stems from the top of Sanctum Tower and travels down to the boundaries of the Inner Sphere just past the walls, creating a giant, impenetrable dome over the most valued areas of Kairus. The Guardsmen call in backup, take statements from those nearby, and begin to inspect the flaming wreckage of the getaway hovercar.

Hours pass before the dwindling air in his pod chokes him awake. He had desperately needed the sleep. Roman fumbles around the dark interior for a release latch but fails to find one. Driven by the burning in his lungs as oxygen becomes scarce, his fingers settle on a smooth lever. The steel container of the crash barrier, which protected him in his hovercar seat, pries open. Immediately, he is hit with a foul stench that makes him choke and gag. Fighting through the pungent odor, he climbs his way through the trash of thousands of Kairus inhabitants: old food containers with rotten scraps, plastic bags and rusty shards of metal, broken furniture and animal waste... Finally, Roman reaches the top of the trash mound and gasps for air. When he catches his breath, he takes stock of his surroundings to see if it is safe.

Evening has fallen, and a gloomy, dark layer of clouds covers the night sky, preventing the light of the moons from gracing the street. The concentration of buildings in this part of the city is less dense, and the structures do not extend nearly as high as they do toward Kairus's center. It allows Roman to see a good distance, and about a mile up ahead, a large, expansive structure comes into view. *The wall to the Grind.* A few key landmarks help Roman recognize the street he travels on. As a boy, he had grown up not far from where he is now, though the current state of affairs has drastically changed since those days. This area was never well-to-do, but it now looks vastly worse: homeless men and women shuffle along the sidewalks, and though most of the same buildings remain, many are abandoned. The decay is hard to look at.

Roman pulls the rest of himself up from the trash and calls out for his accomplice, careful not to be loud enough to alert the driver. "Braxton! Brax..." He stops when he sees Braxton's body near the front of the hauler. His legs are still submerged in garbage, and what can be seen of him is slumped over the grime-stained remnants of a flattened cardboard box. He lays eerily still, jostling only with the movement of the garbage hauler, which rolls steadily down the dark backstreets of the Outer Sphere. Roman wades through the garbage to get to him.

"Braxton! Come on, wake up!" but the former CP Commander remains unconscious. Roman quickly removes his helmet and checks for a pulse: *Incredibly weak, but it's there... I could leave him but...* The thought enters Roman's head and nestles for a moment. In the past, it might have been his move: utilitarian, decisive, safe. But something new, an essence of recent origins, ignites that thought into ash, and he springs to action.

Roman tears off the remaining CP Guardsman armor from his own body while crouched behind the edge of the enormous bin he reluctantly sloshes around. Once his armor is removed, he works on Braxton's. After much work to maneuver him out of his escape costume, he takes stock of the wound Braxton sustained to his flank during their getaway. The area around the black char of his impact site is now red and swollen. Launching themselves into a city trash heap certainly did not help his case. Braxton does not have much time—however, given their location, Roman knows he can be saved. Although, he is not particularly excited about where he must go to do so. *It's been more than a few orbits... I hope it's still there...* he thinks.

Roman lifts Braxton's body over his shoulders and peeks over the edge of the hauler's trailer. They are not far from the wall to the Grind, and thus the area around them is relatively desolate. The hauler, which transfers rubbish from the Inner Sphere to the landfill outside the walls, drives straight past mountains of trash that spill into the street. The area looks long neglected by this public service, which actually works in Roman's favor. As they putter along, a pile of trash bags and cardboard boxes stacked particularly high on the upcoming corner catches his eye.

Roman counts down to the second, musters up his strength, and tosses Braxton's body off the side of the hauler. His limp frame lands with a muffled CRASH into the garbage, which dampens his fall. When the truck does not falter on its route, Roman throws himself over the side next. He lands in a pile of cardboard that collapses under his weight, and tips over onto the sidewalk, spilling Roman and other contents onto the concrete. He immediately collects his accomplice and begins walking.

As streets become side streets, which then become alleys, Roman navigates the maze of the Outer Sphere's edge like the back of his hand, although what he sees deflates him. In regard to the buildings and streets, almost nothing has changed since he was a boy, only aged like milk. It looks like a ghost town, as if the dilapidation was allowed because everyone that once lived here just up and left... He used to know people here. But that time seems like an entirely different life than the one he lives now, and though he remembers the way through the backstreets and alleyways, the once-familiar routes seem all but familiar.

Roman stops in his tracks, having finally reached his destination. His labored breathing is matched only by the burning sensation in his arms, and legs. Braxton's body slides off his shoulders onto the pavement next to him, and Roman does what he can to ease him down slowly. The building looming over them is a strange, triangular shape, and its massive front door is situated at one of the rounded corners just before the street. Two blue stained-glass windows hover above the doorway, the light from which casts a blue aura upon the poorly lit street. The distinct sigil of a pendulum is carved into the doors of the concrete temple. Though only two stories tall, the building spans a large area, and remains one of the few intact structures in sight. The majority of the surrounding buildings are either withered to the bare bones of their structural beams, or completely reduced to rubble. Even a tumbleweed would long for company in these parts of the Outer Sphere's edge.

With his head down, he climbs the three steps up to the heavy concrete doors and slams the ornate steel knocker down three times. As he awaits response, he stumbles down the steps and collapses to a kneeling position, facing his unlikely, unconscious companion, whose chest barely rises and falls. It is there, on his knees before a House of the Sacred Order of Equilibrium, a realization hits Roman: *I made it... I survived...and this is what I'm left with...* All of the mourning and emotion that he has pushed aside for the better part of a month suddenly catches up with him all at once.

An evening chill befalls the Outer Sphere. The pitter-patter of droplets cast down from dark clouds overhead pelt softly against the bare skin of Roman's shoulders. Having cast away his CP armor, his one remaining possession is the pair of hole-ridden cargo pants that hug his legs. He has nothing. All his money, belongings, and possessions are gone; stolen by the CP or abandoned in an attempt to avoid capture. He has no one. Monique is gone, and Modus and Norvel likely with her... *Monique...* The gaping hole she leaves in his existence blackens even the whites in his eyes. It brings each step Roman takes into question: *Why? Why even move forward...what is the fucking point?*

The ghosts of Roman's past settle around him like funereal sod, and their memories, like death's grip, pull him deep into the cracks of the streets and squeeze him uncomfortably into his own little hell. One of his own making, and one he believes he deserves. Roman falls to his hands and knees and weeps. The ever-present memories of his loved ones shame him endlessly, yet he's never felt so far from them. His weeping turns to wailing, and he cries out to an empty street. On his last thread of sanity, and just before collapsing to the sidewalk in utter despair, the light from the doorway behind him illuminates the dark sidewalk, and a voice calls out in question:

"Roman? Is that you?"

CHAPTER 30:

Philosophizing and Hard Truths

Roman's eyes flutter through dim blue light. As his vision adjusts, he sees the source of blue ambiance peeking through the open stairwell from stained-glass windows on the first floor. A familiar smell instantly brings back old memories. It would be nearly impossible to forget the musty smell of the church's basement. Roman once had that same odor stuck in his nose for nearly a month...he never got used to it. It has been just over ten orbits since he was last in this building, yet the memory is as sharp as the day he left.

The damp dwelling is not the only thing Roman smells. Something else fills his nostrils, something...savory. He rolls to a sitting position on his uncomfortable cot, inadvertently tossing a pile of robes used as blankets to the cold stone floor. Next to his bed, on the dusty surface of an old storage barrel, is a bowl of steaming soup and a heaping plate of rice, steamed bog ferns, and Lancor meat. He can hardly believe his eyes as he stares down at the food. Practically starving, he lurches for sustenance like a wild animal, blatantly ignoring the utensils placed delicately next to the plate. Before he can get the edge of the soup bowl to his lips, a voice with a distinctly familiar accent interrupts him.

"You had better eat that slowly. You look frail. I don't know when was the last time you ate, but if you're truly starving, you could send yourself into shock..." the deep voice warns him.

Roman turns on his cot to see the tall form of a Sacred Order Seer working diligently over a body laid on a well-lit medical table. The dark black skin of his bald head is a stark contrast to his white and blue robe. With his gloved hands preoccupied by a curette and sterile basin, he uses his shoulder to scratch the graying goatee on his chin. A sight like this, a holy man performing surgery, would likely surprise most, yet Roman remains impassive. He turns back to his dinner and replies, "I'll take my chances..." before feasting ravenously upon the food provided. For a while, no words are spoken while Roman and the Seer occupy the same room with their backs turned to one another. The space remains silent except for the slurping of soup at one end, and the light clinking of medical tools at the other.

Finally, between chomps of his overcooked meat, Roman turns his head to the side and asks, "He gonna make it?" Roman scratches the thick scar on his right shoulder with dirt-covered nails.

The Seer seems in no rush to respond as he tends to the task at hand. "Yes. Didn't think so at first. A piece of armor actually melted into his abdomen. Once I got the metal removed and the artery clamped, he stabilized. Looked like a piece of CP armor. This guy CP?"

Roman gulps down another mouthful of food before tilting his head and responding, "Kinda-sorta..."

"Wow. Roman Matthews saving the life of a CP Guardsman. If I didn't know any better, I'd say you have turned a corner, perhaps matured some," responds the Seer, without looking away from his patient.

"Yea, I've really grown as a person..." responds Roman sarcastically as he picks the last few grains of rice off the plate and eats them. He refrains from any deep conversation, trying to avoid the inevitable. Despite this, he knows at any moment now, a philosophy-laden lecture is headed his way.

The Seer places his incision tools at the end of the table and grabs another tool to seal the fascia in Braxton's side. "Like I said, I might believe it *if* I didn't know any better. Unfortunately, when it comes to you, I *do* know better. All the talent in the world and no discipline…"

"And here we go…" mumbles Roman under his breath.

"Don't *here we go* me. I don't see you for how many orbits? Nine? Ten? You show up on my doorstep! I give you food! I fix your friend! And you give me *here we go*… Grow up…" He inflects a high-pitched whine to mimic Roman's response. It's enough to make Roman chuckle a bit. Once the fascia is sealed, the man picks up a device resembling a gun and stamps its nozzle on Braxton's arm, leaving a small bloody square from the harvest site. He flips a switch, and the device whirs to life, generating a pink serum in its central capsule of Braxton's harvested tissue. Aiming at the wound on Braxton's side, the device sprays a thick, pink film over the gaping hole that rapidly grows into brand-new dermis and epidermis. In seconds, a new sheath of skin has formed over Braxton's injury. The newly generated tissue looks swollen and raised, not unlike Roman's scar.

"Hm… Not pretty, but it will hold," states the Seer as he removes his gloves and turns to face the ruder of his two guests.

"Yea, mine's not pretty either…" replies Roman, pointing to the thick scar on his shoulder.

"Perhaps, though his will look better in time. I only had Mediseal for primary closure back then. The important part is he will live, just like you did after I found you in the Korr Mountains and cleaned you up. And I bet he complains less than you do when he wakes. Maybe if you practiced gratitude, you would lead a happier life," replies the Seer with an almost parental tone.

Roman's gaze falls into his lap, and his head drops solemnly. "Pft... Gratitude...man, do I have a lot to catch you up on..."

"Then catch me up," replies the Seer. His Sacred Order of Equilibrium robe, usually a pristine white cloth with delicate blue lines, is now splattered with bloodstains from his impromptu operation. He sits at the foot of the staircase, facing Roman, and looks at him with an expression Roman knows all too well: flinty, with a hint of disappointment, and perhaps a touch of concern. "So? Let's hear it. Catch up your old friend, Emmanuel, whom you never visit. You can start with what the hell you did to yourself with those...body modifications. What girl did you do this for?"

Roman hesitates for a moment as "the girl" comes to mind. He looks away from Seer Emmanuel, and stares into space as if lost. "Body modifications... Tell me, how does a Sacred Order Seer get into the business of mob-style, backroom surgeries anyhow?" asks Roman, ignoring the question.

"Wow, you ask me questions about me...things for you must be very bad," replies Emmanuel with a smirk. But the look in Roman's eyes tells a different story than usual. This is not the run-of-the-mill sarcastic, religiously skeptical Roman that sits before him. Something different sits behind these eyes, and Emmanuel realizes it is no time for jokes. He simply sighs and decides to take a different approach with the young man.

"Well...eh... Do you know why the pendulum is the sigil for the Sacred Order of Equilibrium?" asks Seer Emmanuel, pointing to the four-pointed blue crystal on his collar that sits just below his throat. It is slightly different from those worn by other Seers of the order. The shape is the same but, rather than a translucent diamond fitted at its center, a red cross is delicately positioned in his holy pendant.

"I'm not in the mood for a diatribe, Emmanuel..." scoffs Roman.

"This is not a diatribe; this is a conversation. Come now, it seems you are at a crossroads. Humor me..."

Roman's gaze drops to his lap. He takes a deep breath followed by a heavy exhale, as if each word burdens him. "Doesn't each point stand for a Prime, or a god or something? Consciousness, Balance, then Interconnectivity...Confidence or whatever?"

Emmanuel smiles. "You are not wrong, my friend. Each point represents one of four Primes; individually, gods in their own right. Together, they form the all-powerful God... the force of Equilibrium. But that is not why the pendulum was chosen. The pendulum was chosen because Equilibrium, like the path of the swinging pendulum, is not a constant. It swings from one extreme to the next, only to correct itself and move back toward the center once it has reached its pinnacle. And then the process begins again. An ever-shifting, balancing act of the universe with biological life as its focus. No matter how extreme things get, no matter how far in one direction the pendulum swings, the universe always finds a way to correct itself, even if that correction may not seem instantly evident. A star explodes, wiping out a dozen planets, only for the universe to breathe life into a million new species on a chunk of rock across the cosmos."

Roman had dismissed the babblings of Seer Emmanuel Ehizome in the past, but for some reason his thick Earth accent lands softer on his ears this time. Perhaps he is just tired enough to listen to Emmanuel's ramblings, or perhaps he needs a reason to take his mind off the cloud of death that clings to him relentlessly; mordantly following wherever he wanders. Whatever the reason, he listens more than usual. "I don't see how that relates to your side gig..." replies Roman.

"Hehe...it relates to everything in existence! Although, I just told you that part because I felt you needed to hear it. It's always a good preface to us dealing with hard times. As far as my practice of medicine..." Emmanuel glances over at Braxton, who remains asleep on the table with multiple lines connected to him. "I started medical school on Earth, then finished my first residency on Ventura after tumultuous times hit Nigeria. Pediatric surgery was my focus. But then, one day, a man comes to me. He says I have been chosen for a unique opportunity...that it was the chance of a lifetime to be on the cutting edge of science and new technology. 'The types of things you could only dream about,' he told me. I was one of three students in the galaxy selected to take part in an exclusive new residency on an IGB star cruiser. That, eh...eventually landed me here." Emmanuel seems somewhat melancholy as he recounts his impressive résumé.

"So then, why aren't you some rich surgeon in the Inner Sphere at Kairus State Hospital? Or in one of the wealthy city-states?" asks Roman, genuinely intrigued. He begins to wonder why he has never asked these questions of Emmanuel before. The Seer has only done right by him in the past, yet for as well as Roman felt he knew the man, it becomes evident now that there is much to understand.

Emmanuel waves off the question, then responds, "Bah... It was never about the money for me. It was a true calling to help those who needed it, because to do so presented a challenge I knew I could rise to! I truly enjoyed it..."

Roman looks confused, sure that the Seer is dodging his question. "But that doesn't explain why you're a Seer. Why not just be a surgeon then?"

"The nature of my second calling...that is a long story. In short, perhaps it was salvation... One day I will tell you, but I do not wish to revisit my dark times today..." Whatever tough times had befallen the man of the cloth, they seem to weigh heavily on him even now. He shifts the focus back to Roman. "In current times, I find my place is providing solace to those who require it most."

Roman scoffs, trying to hide that he fights back tears. "There is no solace for me, Emmanuel. No *salvation*, as you put it. I have nothing left in this world..."

Matching his solemn state, Emmanuel attempts to comfort Roman. "Even in the hardest of times, the darkest times in our lives, it is important we remember that the lifeforce of the universe still breathes in us. And though it may not seem like you have been dealt a hand worthy of your life's actions, the future just might. In the Sacred Order of Equilibrium, we believe that every person has their place in balancing the great scale. Whether you balance that scale toward the element of chaos, or you balance the scale with a more positive force... you are part of a greater picture that we cannot possibly see from our singular perspective."

"So where do you fall on that scale? Sewing up rifle wounds in the thugs and dregs of society in this shit part of town?"

"Hmph...where do *I* fall, yes. Perhaps it is the reason I am assigned to this *shit* part of town as you put it. You see, as a Seer of the Order, we take an oath to be part of the force for good; to only apply positive force to the scale. There is plenty of chaos in the universe, and plenty of those who contribute to it. Our oath is a promise of positivity; an attempt to maintain balance in a world that seems to skew more toward chaos by the day. Unfortunately...others do not agree with my vision for what a positive finger on the scale equates to... I treat anyone who would cross my path: a thief, a charlatan, even a murderer. It is not my position to judge. The actions I put into the world are the same regardless. Some of the more... morally flexible of our ranks...they don't see this as enough. They like to choose sides, and align themselves with the powers that be...those they believe will have a greater impact on Equilibrium. And me? I am forced to work in the shadows. But it is the challenge I accept based on my oath. Politics is not my game."

"Seems like you're the only one living up to your code. Why don't they like what you do?" It bothers Roman to see such a good man eschewed by his own church. Perhaps somewhere in his subconscious, he connects with Emmanuel's story.

"It's not that they don't like me, it's more complicated...

The more I gracefully slip into old age, the more I realize that morality becomes skewed on either end of the flawed binary system of order and chaos. Both extremes are just that: extremes. More like each other than they are willing to admit at times; just opposite ends of the pendulum's apex that would touch each other if they inched just a bit further. Those who brave to walk the line of morality between the extremes are the true change makers in this world; with one foot on the side of order and one on the side of chaos. Perhaps this is what the order strives for now, though their methods concern me..." Emmanuel trails off as he realizes the path of his conversation is a precarious one. He seems almost afraid to finish his sentence. The Seer affects a very serious tone, as if what he says disturbs him. "That is not my calling. I am not suited for it. I simply heal, and tend to my flock..."

As Roman looks Emmanuel in the eye, something inside him that he doesn't understand rebels against the religion-based philosophies touted by the Seer. "Just another reason why religion is lancor-shit."

"Lancor-shit? Why do you say this, lancor-shit?" Emmanuel shrugs, confused by Roman's sudden shift in attitude.

"You just said it yourself. Humans can be full of shit no matter what oath they take. No matter where they fall on the Order's moral spectrum or *your* moral spectrum, they fuck it up. Eventually those in power start acting like they believe they *are* the gods. But they're just people like you, and like me!" Roman jumps to Emmanuel's defense.

Thinking that Roman's diatribe is in reference to him, the Seer jumps to respond. "You are quick to place blame, my friend. I have already told you that I accept my position. I have come to understand my role in the world, and though I may have my philosophical quandaries, I am at peace!" replies Emmanuel, trying to calm Roman down.

"Sometimes people *are* deserving of blame! They stick you out here...practically in the Grind...and you're the only one who lives up to the oath you take! I don't buy it. They're just as corruptible as the CP. Belief is the problem. Belief is what makes people sheep. It's what the wolves use to manipulate others into bending to their will so they can warp the world into whatever hell their twisted minds desire! The vehicle that it comes in has no bearing on the outcome!"

"But that is the beauty of Equilibrium, Roman! It always corrects itself. It is based on the idea that every person is exactly who they must be in their time; that we are literally part of the greatest story ever told: the story of all that is, was, and ever will be. It is the story of the universe! We are crafted by the universe from the very elements that comprise it so the universe may experience a conscious depiction of itself through our eyes! We are but mirrors for the God of Equilibrium, Roman!" Emmanuel's eyes gleam as he pontificates, hoping to impart his cheery cosmic outlook onto Roman. But Roman's response is less than inspiring.

"And as cool of a story as that is, Emmanuel, what good does it do us? What purpose does it actually serve, huh? What does that story do other than provide an outlet for the promise of benevolence, or *so-called* salvation to be preyed upon? Or to coax people into mindless complacency as the world speeds by them? Or for old, bored men to do mental gymnastics? As ironic as it is that you, a seer, saved me and that klang behind us, the concept of religion doesn't save you from the barrel of a rifle. What proof do you have that the Order provides anything other than a quieting hand to the mouths of people caught in the CP's whirlwind of death and destruction!?" asks Roman, becoming more aggressive with each moment that passes.

"Proof?" exclaims the Seer. Emmanuel is actually surprised both by Roman's reaction and his words. He has never seen this type of response from him before; just the normal sarcastic deflections. "Roman, I will not lie to you. You bring up a good point...humanity is a species that, whether through physical construct or through actual spiritual need, has the inclination...the ability to worship. If we do not worship a higher power than ourselves, one that is perhaps beyond the bounds of our reach, we would never strive to be better than we are. We would only put those more powerful than us on the pedestal and worship them."

An internal switch flips, and Roman screams at the top of his lungs, "BUT THAT'S ALREADY HAPPENED, YOU FOOL! AND THEY'VE TAKEN EVERYTHING FROM ME! *HE'S* TAKEN EVERYTHING FROM ME! EVERYTHING!!" Roman as he stands with clenched fists and white knuckles. Veins bulge out of his neck and arms, and the vitalerium crystals in his skin give off a soft blue glow for a moment.

At first, the sudden glow of Roman's skin shocks Seer Emmanuel to the point of covering his face. He can barely believe his eyes as he recognizes the swirling smoke in the crystals just before it dies down. After having time to register what he sees, Emmanuel is drawn to it, and cannot help but stand up and approach Roman to inspect. "What...in the name of the four Primes did you do to yourself, Roman?" He pokes the vitreous shards of crystal that blend with Roman's skin. "These are no body modifications, are they?"

"No. They are not," Roman snarls. "And it's about time I did something useful with them."

"What do you mean?" asks Emmanuel, horrified not by the crystals but by Roman's bombastic demeanor.

"I've sat back my entire life as the CP...as ZERRIS has destroyed my entire world! And I am not the only one; I can't be! How many thousands has he locked up for government dissent? How many who've resisted has he simply killed because it's easier than holding himself accountable? That fucking monster will never stop. Not unless someone stops him..."

"But Roman, you don't seriously mean to..."

"I DO! I mean to kill the man who has taken everything! My parents! My best friend! The love of my life! My fucking

SOUL! And I don't care if it costs me my life. I don't give a fuck where this falls on your morality spectrum. You can count on the fact that I've already stepped over the line into chaos."

"But Roman! You..." Emmanuel tries, but he is unable to get a word in.

"BUT NOTHING!" shouts Roman. But when Emmanuel's face drops in response to his tirade, he realizes he takes his rage out on the wrong person. Roman stops for a moment to take a deep breath. "Ugh... You said it yourself. The universe corrects itself when the pendulum has swung too far. Well, what the hell do you call this?" Roman lifts his hand, displaying the crystal that pokes through the skin of its dorsum. He points to the blue substance lodged in his face and abdomen. "I'd say that's the universe weighing in. A gift to the trampled so he can finally kick back...and I won't waste it!"

Emmanuel watches Roman display an intensity that he has come to expect from the young freelancer. But there is something else in his voice that reads differently than anything he has ever heard from him; something behind his hazel eyes. It is a concern of sorts that seems to carry on his voice and tattoos itself behind his expressions.

"I sincerely hoped this was hyperbole...but it seems this is not the case. Why take the risk to do this? Why now? What has changed in you?"

Roman actually thinks for a moment before responding this time. His anger has subsided some following his fit of shouting. It allows him breath to contemplate. "Because it's the only thing left for me to do...because my life is the only thing I have left. Because what if you're wrong? What if the pendulum gets stuck and never swings back?"

"The pendulum has and always will continue to swing, Roman, until the very end of entropy itself. And I'd say we've got quite a lot of time to deal with that particular problem," responds Emmanuel, having trouble finding the words to talk Roman out of his madness.

"You are, without a doubt, an incredibly intelligent man, Emmanuel. You could argue the stars into submission, and you've always done right by me despite my profession and the characters I've associated with. I respect and I appreciate you for that. But this time might be different. You don't know what Zerris has planned...what he's building... It's either me or him. I've made up my mind. *I'm swinging the pendulum.*"

Emmanuel stares blankly at Roman, trying desperately to come up with convincing reasons to argue. *Has the universe truly chosen this man to do its bidding?* the Seer ponders as he stares at the vitalerium crystals lodged in Roman's body. After a few moments pass, Emmanuel finally concedes. "Then I cannot change your mind. No matter how stupid I think it may be—and I assure you, it is stupid—I will not try to sway you. However, I cannot help you."

"Open your eyes, Seer. You already have," Roman says, pointing over to Braxton, who now coughs weakly as the anesthesia begins to wear off.

"The Guardsman?" asks the Seer, confounded by the allegation.

"Yea well, remember when I said he's 'kinda-sorta' CP? That's because he's not a Guardsman. He was CP-IO...a prestigious Commander, at that. Until they locked him up for treason, that is."

"CP-IO? But...is that..." He looks over at the table where the man lies unconscious. His look of confusion morphs into one of shock as the light bulb in his mind illuminates. The realization actually forces him to his feet. "That's the Commander from the Vital Fracture? The one arrested for high treason!?"

"So, you don't live under a rock...and yes, that's him. He helped me escape from the Cube," replies Roman. He wields blunt honesty like a weapon, for there is more he plans to ask of the Seer.

"The CUBE!? Oh, good Prime of Consciousness, Roman! What have you gotten yourself into this time? What have you brought upon my doorstep!?" Emmanuel begins to sweat and hyperventilate as he contemplates the magnitude of potential consequences; not just for himself for partaking in the harboring of fugitives, but for Roman. "Roman, I don't know how you managed to get yourself in, and I certainly don't want to know what it took to get yourself out. But *no one* escapes the Cube...no one ever has! They will come for you. You must understand, this looks bad for the CP to have anyone escape! It sets a precedent, and they will mean to make an example of you! You need to run; you cannot be here!" He stands up and walks around aimlessly as he imagines their fate.

Roman walks over to the man who has done more for him than he can repay. Perhaps it is part of the reason he was initially reluctant to come here. Roman dislikes debts and is usually unwilling to accept favors because of it; there's a good chance this sentiment even stems from Emmanuel saving his life all those orbits ago. It hurts him to put Emmanuel, a good man, in this position. Roman places his hands on the man's shoulders and guides him to a seated position on the cot nearby. He does his best to calm the old man who clearly cares for him.

In a placid tone, Roman says, "Emmanuel, what's done is done. It's not me you have to worry about. My mind is clear, and I know what I have to do. Unfortunately, this road I walk now is the only one available to me. But this isn't your fight. They will try to get to me through you. So, it's also you who has to run."

Emmanuel glares at Roman. "Run? I do not run! I am a man of the cloth, Roman. It is I who must face what the universe has offered me. My role in balancing the cosmic scale will be what it is. I will not run from the trials that I am to face." The stubborn old Seer takes Roman's words with great offense.

"The universe doesn't tell you that you have to be a martyr! Now who's being stupid, Seer?"

Now, it is Emmanuel who becomes angry with Roman. "You are right! I am a Seer! And this is my home! MY PLACE IS HERE! Do not pretend to speak with wisdom where it is clearly lacking, young one. You run a fool's errand, making an enemy of the Coalition! I thought I taught you better than this..."

"You did...but I also remember what you told me right after I woke up from that very same table," replies Roman, pointing behind them to the blood-splattered metal surface. "Do you?"

Emmanuel hesitates a moment, then sighs with defeat. "Of course I do..." He shifts away from Roman and crosses his arms before reciting a line of Sacred Order scripture. "'And just as the four Primes commune into the one true God of Equilibrium, so do we commune with the universe that begot our very existence. Each soul to traverse their path to the tune of the cosmos' grand vision for itself. And though the path a soul chooses is chosen, the chosen path also guides itself to the soul's choice. No matter the path, whether well-beaten or uncharted; whether ripe with fruit or utterly barren; fair in passage, or exceedingly treacherous; we shall each brave our path and answer the call of the eternal architect as the universe calls through us...'" Emmanuel cannot help but smirk, beginning to realize that he wages a futile fight against circumstance. After a long pause of contemplation, Emmanuel finally finishes with, "I'm glad you listened, at least..."

"Yea well, once in a while I got bored and listened... Once or twice," responds Roman, shooting Emmanuel a look that makes them both chuckle. "Even though I didn't memorize it like you did, the message stuck. My path... it's been pretty much shit from the start, talking about treacherous...and I'm no fan of religion, you know that. But I can at least recognize a calling when I see one. You taught me that. And while mine may not be suturing up gangsters and traitors in the basement of a church or putting a whole heap of good into the world in general...for the first time in my life, I know what I *have* to do."

"Hm..." grunts Emmanuel. "Maybe there's potentially a half speck of wisdom up there somewhere," he says, tapping Roman on the side of the head.

"I've been trying to tell you that since I was a teenager," chuckles Roman.

"Hey, hey, I said *maybe* wisdom. Don't get cocky, now... You still have much to learn. I just pray you live to receive the lessons..."

Roman smiles briefly, but it fades quickly into a stolid stare. "I will do what I set out to do, Emmanuel. Mark my word."

Emmanuel rests his hand adoringly on Roman's shoulder and replies, "And I know that Equilibrium will guide you, my friend. I pray for the universe's current to flow with your path, though I also pray that your path evolves into one of peace. I am no fan of the Aganons...the Order has not been the same since they took charge of Deorum. But committing vile deeds for the sake of good is a slippery slope. You must be wary not to become that which you oppose..."

Roman takes a moment to sit with Seer Emmanuel's words. After a thoughtful bout of silence, he looks back at the man and finally nods, replying, "Thank you, Emmanuel. There is one more thing I need your help with..."

A cough rises from behind them. "Oof, fuckin...ow..." Braxton spews saliva out the side of his mouth as he begins to regain consciousness slowly but surely. Roman and Seer Emmanuel both glance over to check on the Commander as he begins to awkwardly move his limbs. When they can see he is fine, they return to their conversation.

"I will do what my own path allows, Roman," says Emmanuel.

"Well, seeing as there are folks out to kill me, it would be very *orderly* of you to help me get in touch with the only allies I have left," replies Roman with a smirk.

"Hm...well, since you put it like that, I guess it would be my best option to tip the scale for good." Emmanuel smiles. It is the first meaningful conversation he has had with Roman in more than ten orbits, and if honest with himself, it warms his heart to hear him speak in terms of the Order.

"Good. Because I need you to send a message out to Modus Magni. I need to find out if he's alive and where he and the rest of the Wibetani are," responds Roman, well aware of what will come next.

"Good Prime of Consciousness, Roman! I thought you were done with that wretched man! That man does not tip the scale toward order," retorts Emmanuel spitefully. The Seer had met Roman when he was still a member of the Wibetani Militia. Even then, he was no fan of the organization, despite providing medical resources to a number of Gulcher gangs, including the Wibetani.

Roman tries to convince him by explaining his situation. "I'm not a kid anymore, Emmanuel. And Modus, like it or not, is my only shot at getting out of the city. I need him for what's to come. Now, will you help me or not?"

Emmanuel scoffs at the request and returns to his standing position, pacing the floor with his arms crossed.

Another cough sounds. "OoOW! I feel shot... Am I shot? UGH..." spouts Braxton, still in a chemical daze. Drool oozes from his mouth onto the side of the metal surgical table as he tosses and turns.

In a state of desperation, Roman resorts to begging. "Emmanuel, please. I'm begging you. They took everything from me. I have no access to the Fray, or any kind of communications. Please..."

Emmanuel gazes at Roman with disdain for the request. Up until today, he has only seen Roman as a lost soul, a boy without direction who had fallen upon hard times; a product of poor circumstances. However, the man who looks back at him now is nearly unrecognizable. The piercing eyes that look back at him do not relay the sense of aimlessness. There is an invisible aura of undeniable purpose. It is infectious, and somewhat startling for the holy man to witness firsthand Roman Matthews's evolution; to see the fruits of his intervention. In that moment, Emmanuel reconnects with his own purpose.

With a grimacing face and a solemn disposition, Emmanuel walks silently up the stairs to his empty church. Roman does not follow or try to stop him. He lowers his face into the heel of his hand and contemplates what is to become of him. He will have to figure his own way out of the city... Modus was the shot in the dark he was banking on, but without communication, he would be searching blindly. *He may not even be alive...* Roman's thoughts once again begin to spiral into despair. *I will have to find a way past the wall. Maybe a subterranean route? Will I even be safe in the Grind? I may have to get outside those walls as well. Even if I did, I have nothing in the way of survival gear...*

"Ugh, oh...it's healed. Whoa...that's a siiiick scar..." Braxton breaks the vacuum of silence in the room with his post-surgery babbling. He grunts as he pushes himself up to a sitting position on the table and swings his legs to dangle off the side. "Hey, you... Rogan. Wasn't sure we made it out... Hey, you see my badass scar?" he asks, smiling and displaying his bare side.

Attempting to find some kind of distraction from his despair in humor, Roman points to his own shoulder and nods. "Yea. Looks like mine."

"Hehe... Nice, um...where are we?" asks Braxton, looking around the room for a familiar landmark. He flicks the bag of saline that hangs from a metal pole next to him and follows the line that connects to the vein in his arm. "Wha' kinda lancor-shit hospital is this?" he asks as his head sways from one side to the other.

"Middle of nowhere at the rim of the Outer Sphere. And likely stuck..." replies Roman, discouraged by his circumstances once again. He cannot help but hang his head in shame. "Wish I had better news..."

"I'm fuggin' alive! That's good news 'nough for me. We'll, ugh...cross that bridge when we...bridge that gap, or...yea." Braxton blinks his eyes open and closed in succession, struggling to communicate coherently through the pain medication that courses through his veins. "I need more of what*ever* is in this bag!" he exclaims with a smile.

Roman shakes his head in response, mumbling, "We are so fucked..." Embroiled in his own perceived failure, he does not notice the footsteps that descend from the church upstairs.

A commscreen lands heavily in Roman's lap, along with a pile of new clothes and two coats. "I figure a godless man like yourself would scoff at the idea of wearing robes out of this church. Not that you would deserve to wear them. Oh, and your *friend*...he responds quite fast. Must have been hoping to hear from you..." says Emmanuel. "Looks like you are not so fucked, as you put it."

Roman looks up at Emmanuel, who stands over him, refusing to return eye contact; his robed arms still crossed in discontent. Roman rifles through the clothing to retrieve the commscreen, which displays a text thread reading:

Emmanuel: Where to meet RM

Unknown: Where you cut your teeth. Get here ASAP.

Emmanuel: How

Unknown: 533rd & Rim

Unknown: If it's really you, glad you're breathing

Roman, finally presented with a straw he can grasp, cannot hide the elation that he feels. He gazes back at Emmanuel with a gratitude he cannot put into words. "Emmanuel, this is... Thank you. I can't thank you enough."

"You know what it means?" asks the Seer.

"I think so... It's a little unclear, but I..." His elation is cut short when he glances back at the device and opens up the settings. "Emmanuel, please tell me this device is hooked into the Fray and not just the normal Fabric..."

"I am a man of the Sacred Order, not some hacker. Now go. Take your friend and get to safety," responds the old Seer reluctantly.

"Emmanuel...they'll be able to track this. Maybe not Modus...but your communications for sure. What the hell were you thinking!?"

"I SAID GO! For once in your life, listen to my words and obey, you foolhardy boy."

Roman stands from his cot and embraces Emmanuel as tightly as he can, knowing it may very well be his last chance. Emmanuel fights back tears as he hugs back. Roman quickly changes into the clothing provided by the Seer, then helps the unbalanced Braxton out of his tattered garments and into his set of clothes. He moves quickly, knowing he has little time to waste.

Roman guides Braxton to the stairs in their fresh clothing and puts the hood of his cloak over his head. Emmanuel remains by his medical station and watches them leave. When Roman reaches the first step, he turns back to Emmanuel and implores of him, "Please. You have to leave this place. Leave the city. Ditch that commscreen, and get out while you still can."

"Just as you have made up your mind, so have I. I choose my own path, and I am needed here," responds the Seer sternly. Emmanuel gives Roman a slow nod, as if to affirm his decisions. "Go now, Roman."

"Fucking Primes, Emmanuel, you stubborn old fool! Whatever you think you are staying here for, it's not worth your life! You can put your skills to use elsewhere!"

Emmanuel does not raise his voice this time. "And do what? Abandon my flock? Abandon those who need me here?

I may be many things, but I am true to my path. I have undertaken the responsibility of this place of worship. Dereliction of my oath and my duties is not an option, Roman. As a man who so fervently follows his, I expect you to understand that..." Emmanuel begins cleaning up Roman's mess with his back turned. "And don't you take the Primes' names in vain in my church. Blatant disrespect does not suit you. You are better than that..."

Roman stands on that first basement step for what seems like an eternity as Braxton wobbles his way up the stairs. His eyes do not leave the back of Emmanuel's head. He wants so badly to force Emmanuel to leave with them; to drag him out of the church by his robe. However, his respect for the man is too strong. He knows that it is not an option. "Just don't rule it out. Think it over, please," says Roman before he makes his way up the stairs, and lets the heavy doors of the church thud behind him as he and Braxton reach the street.

As the doors slam shut, echoing through the church and into the basement, Emmanuel stops what he is doing and stares pensively up the stairs. In the silence of the old concrete building, Emmanuel mumbles, "Good luck, my old friend. May the great pendulum swing in your favor..."

CHAPTER 31:

An Heir of Consequence

Roman and Braxton keep to the shadows of the abandoned buildings, trekking through back alleys and husks of old structures for as much of the journey as they can. They must travel discreetly, for every so often, the searchlights of hovertanks overhead gleam dangerously close to their location. The full force of the CP Guardsmen diligently hunts for the fugitives who so brazenly escaped their warped sense of justice. After nearly two hours of covert travel, Roman and Braxton stare at the gap between them and the wall to the Grind through an abandoned warehouse window.

"Are you sure this is the right spot? This doesn't exactly look like a viable option..." comments Braxton, whose anesthesia has finally worn off. "I mean, what are we supposed to do? Climb up the side of a forty-foot wall and jump?"

"This is definitely it. This is the warehouse on 533rd Street. And the rim...well, I'm sure you can figure that one out. You were a Commander; you're supposed to be smart," replies Roman coldly.

"I am smart. That's why I know this is a bad fucking idea!" snips Braxton.

"This has to be it. The message from Modus said, 'Where

you cut your teeth,' which is the old Wibetani barracks in the Grind. Shouldn't be far from this point on the other side of the wall."

"Once again, *the wall* is the problem," mumbles Braxton.

Roman searches the expanse of the wall for some kind of sign. *Modus has to have a plan; it can't have been for nothing that the General sent those messages,* he thinks. He scours the edifice of the wall from their position of aerial cover, but it is difficult to see in the dark of night. This decrepit part of town is not well-lit by streetlights. *I just wish I could see it...*

The whirring of another CP hovertank passes overhead, and its multiple spotlights illuminate the streets and buildings around them as it scans the ground below. Braxton jumps for cover, shielding himself from view, and Roman hides behind the cracked concrete wall by the window. Once the beam of light passes over their position, Roman peeks his head around the corner to take advantage of the light provided.

"What are you doing!? Get away from the window!" whispers Braxton, worried that he might give away their location.

Roman does not listen. He focuses on the wall, scanning it up and down for some kind of sign. Some kind of...

"Look!" whispers Roman as he points to a dark segment of the wall.

Braxton waits for the hovertank to pass, then crawls over to the window and lifts his head just enough to see over its ledge. Just along the bottom of the wall, peeking out of a steel panel and barely visible in the dark, is an edge of red cloth. Only a few inches of it stick out of the crack, and the fabric waves in the wind created by the passing hovertank's wake.

"What? That piece of scrap?" asks Braxton, perplexed.

"That piece of scrap is a flag. Come on, this is our chance. We go now!"

The two men stealthily exit the building and check to see if the coast is clear. When the whirring of hovertanks has all but subsided, Roman makes a run for it. Braxton reluctantly follows, clutching his side, and sure that this is the part where they get caught. The two men race through the dark across the dusty road and press themselves against the shadow of the giant steel wall. Roman inches over to the bit of fabric that barely peeks out of the bent edge of the steel panel. He grabs its frayed material and tugs.

It takes all his might, but after straining for a few seconds, the rest of the fabric becomes visible as he pulls a small Wibetani Militia flag from the wall. He tucks it under his arm and begins searching, running his hands over every inch of the panel that hid the flag. Braxton joins him, but all they feel are the solid steel junctures of the barrier. After a few moments of probing, they turn up nothing. Roman leans his forehead against the panel in frustration, creating a loud banging noise that echoes through the wall. Both Roman and Braxton look at each other in disbelief.

"Is that hollow?" whispers Braxton. But Roman does not have time to answer.

The large panel that Roman just banged against is lifted and moved to the side, revealing two Wibetani Militia recruits. They stand inside a hole in the wall at chest height and usher the two men in quietly. Roman and Braxton climb inside, and the panel is replaced just as the next hovertank makes its rounds along the rim of the wall.

The wall of the Outer Sphere was made more cheaply than the Inner Sphere's wall. Rather than forged of solid steel, this wall was made of concrete and then simply covered with steel panels. Roman and Braxton follow the recruits through an astonishing tunnel that has somehow been drilled through the ten-foot-thick wall, creating a narrow passage. The recruits repeat their process, remove a panel on the other side of the wall, and motion for them to climb through.

"Modus is waiting. You know where," are the only words spoken by one of the recruits as they help Roman and Braxton through the hole to the Grind. As they fall to the dirt below their point of entry, the panel is replaced, leaving no trace of the tunnel. The Grind bustles around them, and though no one witnesses their illicit entrance, there are plenty of people nearby for the two to blend in with.

"Your world is just...insane..." mumbles Braxton as they traverse the gap toward the nearest building and replace the hoods over their heads.

Just a few blocks from the passage is a small metal building crafted from the spare components of a repurposed spacefaring vessel. The structure is not much to look at; it is relatively square, only a few stories tall, and decaying in rust. Its windows are covered with heavy metal grates that barely allow light in. Though aesthetically unimpressive, it brings a flood of memories back to Roman as he stands before its brown doors, looking up. Though it looks long abandoned, the front door is left slightly ajar. Roman pushes it open and walks through with Braxton at his heels.

The first floor is dark, and aside from a few tables and old bunk beds pushed against the walls, the space remains empty. Only a sliver of street light shines into the space from the stairwell on the far side of the room. A thick layer of sand and dust coats every surface inside. Braxton paces back and forth with his hands on his head as Roman scans the area.

"I hope you have another secret tunnel I don't know about..." he says to Roman, who walks the length of the room by the wall.

"Shut up, Brax," replies Roman as he lifts one of the many dusty rugs from the floor and then jumps on the space where it once rested. It makes a loud clatter, which catches the former commander's attention. Roman shoots him a smug look before stepping off of the floorspace. Moments later, rustling can be heard beneath their feet. Roman steps to the side, and a metal hatch swings open, releasing a small group of red- and black-clad men wielding large rifles. Roman raises his arms and removes his hood, which prompts them to lower their weapons and retreat down the stairwell that reveals itself.

"Unbelievable...you're like mole people," chuckles Braxton in utter disbelief at the Wibetani's knack for hiding their whereabouts. "Where's the trust?"

As Roman walks down the steps, his voice echoes back up to Braxton. "A little bit of trust'll kill ya' if you let it, Brax."

They follow the recruits down a long flight of steps that opens into a large room filled end to end with Wibetani recruits; dozens of them. They chat quietly to themselves, organize resources, and clean their rifles. Norvel sits in the far corner cradling the MEC device he had crafted for his compatriot. While polishing its frame, he lifts his head from his work and is the first to notice the new arrivals. He stands and gapes in utter disbelief. When Roman and Braxton finally touch down to the dirt-covered basement floor, the entire room becomes as silent as a graveyard. All eyes fall on the two men in brown, hooded cloaks. The crystal shard in Roman's face gleams inexplicably in the warm glow of the hideout's old lighting.

The recruits clear a path for them to the other side of the large space, where a dread-locked head becomes visible. Modus sits alone in a swivel chair that faces the wall. Although he notices their presence, he does not acknowledge them. He simply lifts the open bottle of rum from its perch on his thigh and takes a long swig.

Roman leaves Braxton where he stands and walks slowly across the room to the General's side. Despite standing over him, Roman is unable to see his face. He remains silent for a moment, building up the courage to say anything at all, but the words do not come to him. Fortunately, he does not have to. Modus speaks first.

"You came..." Modus says unenthusiastically, his voice devoid of any emotion. Before continuing, he lifts the bottle to his lips and takes multiple gulps. "Although I have no idea how you made it out of there alive."

"Yea...been surprising myself a lot lately. And of course I came, didn't see any other choice in the matter. We're in the same boat now. We have to work together," responds Roman, somewhat shocked by the way Modus speaks. He is clearly drunk, and though Roman has seen Modus in many states, inebriated had never been one of them.

"And what a shitty fuckin' boat at that..." he responds in the same dead tone. "Take a look around, Rome. Feast your eyes upon the majesty of the Wibetani...in all its fuckin' glory. This is what's left. Both clubs raided, the new barracks set to flames, and so many lights extinguished...rats, forced back into the wall..." He trails off before taking another long sip of rum.

Roman grabs the bottle of rum out of his hand and launches it against the wall that Modus stares blankly at. It shatters into a million pieces and leaves a brown liquor stain that streams down to the dusty floor. Modus barely reacts to the aggression, so Roman grabs him by the shoulder and spins him around in his chair so they are face to face. What Roman sees astonishes him.

Tears stream down the black skin of Modus's cheeks. He stares up at Roman, eyes filled with water, and shrugs with his arms out to his sides. "And here he is. The daughterless leader of the Wibetani Militia... BROKEN! IT'S ALL BROKEN!" he shouts belligerently at Roman.

Roman cringes at the sight of Modus, a man he thought until this point was made of pure stone. Seeing him in shambles sends a humanizing chill down Roman's spine. It is almost too hard to watch, and he's forced to look away as his own eyes begin to water. Without making eye contact, Roman tries to respond. "Monique..."

Leaning forward in his seat, Modus screams, "THAT'S IT! SAY HER NAME! MONIQUE! MY DAUGHTER, ROMAN! They took my fucking daughter from me..." His mood swings wildly between unbridled rage and a zombie-like state. His head bobs from side to side as he retreats back into the cushions of his seat. "I saw her...from the top of the ladder... I went up first...I don't even know why I did... IT SHOULD HAVE BEEN ME!"

"I SAW HER TOO!" shouts Roman in return. "I saw her as I was getting tortured in the Cube!" Roman paces back and forth as he tries to contemplate a meaningful response, but his only reply is, "I loved her, Modus."

"You loved her? *YOU* LOVED HER!? I WAS HER FATHER! YOU MAY HAVE LOVED HER, BUT I WAS RESPONSIBLE FOR HER! I SHOULD HAVE GOTTEN HER OUT OF THERE!"

"Oh yea? So, what are you gonna do about it? Drink yourself to death? Cry yourself to sleep!? SIT HERE AND WALLOW WHEN YOU KNOW WHO IS RESPONSIBLE!?" Roman lifts Modus up from his chair by his red vest and manhandles him vigorously, attempting to shake some sense into the grieving man. He presses Modus's back into the wall and stares daggers into his eyes. "You have no idea what I've been through to get to this point! I've passed through hell a dozen times at the hands of the black and blue! Nearly lost my life and my mind in the process just to survive long enough for this chance! So don't you dare sit there and cry at a time like this. Now is not the time to run or lie down and die. Now is the time to fight, Modus. Zerris needs to die for what he did. And for that to happen, I need all hands on deck. I *need* your help."

Modus begins to cry as he looks back at Roman. "I got no fight left in me, Roman... My fight died with my daughter..." He pushes Roman's hands away, breaking free of his grip, and walks to the corner of the room, head in hand.

Roman cannot tolerate the man that stands before him. This man is not Modus. He lacks bloodlust; an utterly unacceptable coward. Roman needs his general back. And so, he walks over to the man he once called Modus, spins him around, and delivers a punch to his face that sends him to the ground.

"Where's the fearless General Modus Magni? Because

YOU are not him! Are you just gonna let that power-hungry, spoiled little shit get away with killing your daughter!? You're gonna let him get away with taking away the thing you cared about most in the world!? THAT'S NOT THE MODUS I KNOW!" shouts Roman at the man who sits on the ground staring blankly up at him. "You're just a small, scared little man, crying about a problem he's too weak to solve. The way you're acting now, you don't even deserve to call yourself a father!"

Modus's nostrils begin to flare. "You shut up about shit you don't understand..." he sneers.

"WHY SHOULD I? IT'S NOT LIKE YOU'LL FIGHT BACK! It's like you just said, *you've got no fight left in you!* If Monique saw you right now, she would be ashamed to see what her father has turned into! She wouldn't dare call this weak, pitiful, *sniveling* coward her fath—"

"I SAID SHUT UP!" shouts Modus, springing from the floor and tackling Roman to the ground. The two men roll across the floor, punching and grappling each other as the other members of the militia jump out of the way. Modus delivers a punch to Roman's jaw that nearly breaks it, but Roman rolls backward and tosses Modus onto his head. The two men stand and face each other with rage in their eyes. Modus, in an attempt to shut Roman up for good, races toward him and cocks his metal fist back to deliver a knockout blow. But before he can land his punch, the crystal in Roman's face begins to glow.

The bright blue dome comes crashing down to the floor around Roman as he produces the vitalerium barrier. Modus's fist bangs heavily off the barrier that absorbs his blow. He punches the blue shield repeatedly as Roman struggles to maintain it. Again and again he tries to force his titanium knuckles through, until finally, he drops to his knees from utter exhaustion. When he does, the barrier flickers and eventually dissipates, causing Roman to fall to the floor from his own fatigue.

The two men pant just a few feet from each other, gasping for air as they try to recover from the bout. Roman's head spins from producing the barrier for such a long period, and he must stabilize himself with his hands on the floor until his vertigo passes. When it finally does, he speaks:

"You know what we have to do... *I know* what we have to do. Otherwise, more daughters will die. And sons. Mothers... Brothers... we have endured this despotic Overseer far too long. YOU KNOW WHAT WE MUST DO!" Roman stops to take a deep breath and refocus. "Now get off your ass and help me do it."

Modus wheezes for air as he looks at the ground. Besides his heavy breathing, he remains silent for a moment. He looks at the group of men who stand agog to the scene they just witnessed. Finally, his eyes meet Roman's, and having punched out all of his opposition, he simply nods and replies, "Alright then, boss. Make the call."

"What do you mean?" asks Roman, still short of breath and confused by the request.

Modus crawls over to Roman and crouches beside him. After catching his breath, he slaps a cybernetic hand onto Roman's shoulder, and replies, "Look around you, Roman. The Wibetani died in Earth Mode that day. And I... I brought it as far as I could. But I didn't have the strength to build it up to its own creed. 'That our actions may reflect the consequences of a free world worth fighting for'? Just look around, I..." He pauses as he searches for the words but resorts to tapping on the vitalerium shard in Roman's cheek. "I am not you. This thing you've got, this gift...it means something. Something I can't measure up to, and something I can't even pretend to understand... I'm a broken man, Roman. As of today, whatever is left of the Wibetani, any and all my resources are now yours. My sword...is yours. And you better use it to cut that motherfucker Zerris's head off." Modus stands up and extends a hand to Roman.

Roman looks in disbelief at the cybernetic hand offered to him. The simultaneous shuffling of dozens around him attracts his attention to the rest of the room, which stuns him further. Every militia member in the basement now kneels where they once stood. Each holds the barrel of his rifle with its stock planted firmly into the ground. All eyes are on Roman. After seeing the other men move to a kneeling position, Norvel follows suit and takes a knee. Even Braxton, who has been through a short hell and back with Roman, follows the others and kneels. His mouth is agape, and his eyes still bulge from witnessing Roman produce the vitalerium barrier.

"Come on, Roman. Make the call," insists Modus, who extends his hand even closer and nods.

Of all the hypothetical scenarios Roman had played out for this meeting, he had never imagined it would end like this. He imagined that Modus would already have a plan; that he would arrive to orders and an organized militia. He struggles with the gravity of the outcome, and stares blankly as he hesitates to submit any kind of response. *I have no idea how to lead*, he thinks. For as long as he can remember, he has led the life of a complete loner. A million thoughts and questions race through his mind. *Should it really be me? What if I let them down? What if I get men killed? Can I even do this? Am I worthy of this? Do I even want this?* Unprompted, Norvel approaches from Roman's left and crouches beside him, holding something in his hands.

"I, uh... I saved these for you...from the club. Just thought you might want them back..." Norvel says as he holds out his hand. Dangling from Norvel's fingers is Roman's silver chain with its small shield pendant. Resting in his palm is the black and chrome metal of Roman's dagger. The red crystal shaped like planet Deorum twinkles in Roman's eyes from the large knife's handle.

The incessant questions in Roman's mind are instantly replaced by flashes of his time at the Ion Street Orphanage when he proudly stood up to Jace with Jerrick and his other friends; his time at the Wibetani when he received his Klipper promotion; him leading drills with his group of young Wibetani recruits... He remembers his mother, his father, his best friend Jerrick, and Monique...and clarity allows his mind to quiet. *It doesn't matter what I want. I know what I must do...*

He looks at Norvel with gratitude and nods before placing the knife in his pocket and the chain over his head. Norvel walks back to his corner and kneels with the rest of the militia.

Roman's hand connects firmly with Modus's palm, and he pulls himself upright before his new army. They look back with dutiful anticipation as they await orders from their new charge.

"What's the call, Roman?" bellows Modus.

Roman lifts his head slowly, and finally responds: "We move. Tonight."

EPILOGUE:

The Sentinels

A blinding light fills her eyes as they shoot open. She gasps for air as she awakens, coughing as if it's been years since she's taken a breath. Dozens of fluid-filled tubes that connect to portholes in her skin detach one by one, flailing and spraying grayish-blue liquids as they separate from her body. She struggles; panics as she tries desperately to identify her surroundings and ground herself. The stress, fear, and confusion she feels wreak havoc on her overstimulated cortex, preventing her from comprehending any of what she sees. Hard as she tries, she cannot seem to acclimate to the environment that she finds herself in. Unable to discern reality, she screams out in terror.

"REACCLIMATION PROTOCOL, INITIATE," repeats a recorded voice over and over that seems to permeate the great room from an undetermined location.

The mechanical arm behind her, which jacks into her spinal port and suspends her above the lights and panels below, jerks to life and begins to lower her toward the floor. She writhes in its grip, twisting and contorting in her state of anxiety. The lights and sounds of the Dimensional Sight Lab are too much for her to bear in this state, and only add to the traumatic experience.

Finally, the mechanical arm releases her onto the floor of the lab, and though she sloshes around in the grayish fluid expelled from the tubes, she begins to find comfort in the cold metal her body compresses against. The sensation of something tangible after her long sight-dive helps to calm her. An array of pipes positioned around her unleashes a warm mist on her corporeal form. The cloud of murky precipitation fills her orifices with an invigorating sting.

"What did you see this time? What is the status of the Human Species' alternative champion?" The voice does not echo through the lab but rather transfers itself directly to the auditory cortexes of the beings that occupy it.

She is still unable to speak, though she continues to cough. Flexing her vocal cords helps realign her nervous system to her own body. She continues to wriggle on the ground until her ocular HUD becomes visible in her periphery. It reads her vital signs and inscribes messages comprised of complex characters in vertical syntax. In her distracted state, it takes her a moment to recognize what she reads. To feel again...it is an unimaginably satisfying feeling. Sight-diving alters the subject's perception of time. Though her dive was not particularly long in relative terms, to her it seems eons have passed since she last "felt" anything.

"Ubuntis, what is the status of our Deorum-based alternative, Zerris Aganon?" The voice enters her head, more pressured this time.

She does not respond. The artificial light becomes less harsh as her eyes adjust, and finally the room becomes visible to her. Her eyes trace the walls up to the incredibly high ceilings of the lab, presenting an indescribably beautiful view of the stars through the porthole above. The cacophony of sounds begins to delineate in Ubuntis's external auditory structures to their individual sources, and becomes the separate whirs of machinery, vibrating hums of quantum entanglement engines, the steps of her colleagues rushing to her aid on the lab floor, and the inexplicable voice calling out to her...

"Ubuntis! What is the status of Zerris Aganon? We await your report!" the voice says aloud this time.

Ubuntis lifts her head from the floor and then slowly lifts herself to her wobbly knees beside her colleagues. She wipes the grayish sludge from her body and looks up with elation at the beautiful celestial view through the lab's aperture. Her chest wall expands as the thin flaps of tissue on her chest, neck, and shoulders filter the lab's air through her respiratory system. Ubuntis cannot help but display elation in the form of a lateral curving of her posterior extrascapular appendages as she feels herself return to her own body; and with good news, no less. With the empyreal twinkle of the stars reflecting off her glossy eyes, she replies softly to the inquiring voice:

"There is a third option..." she mumbles in their shared language: Scrym, as it is called by humans.

Those that surround Ubuntis look upon her in confusion, unsure as to whether or not she has completely recovered from her sight-dive. They exchange glances and comments without speaking, wondering if what she reports is truth or utter nonsense prattled in the haze of her re-acclimation. The voice calls out to her once more.

"Explain yourself, Ubuntis. What do you mean by a third option? Humanity's points of contact have already been established. The champions have been determined definitively by the Barundglaric."

"There is a third..." she repeats. Their skepticisms are requited when Ubuntis finishes, "...one that has established Serraxis-qui."

Her colleagues, who stand around her in their white, monochromatic lab outfits, are left stunned by the revelation. The statement is in complete opposition to the species' initial biological analysis and forecasted rate of failure, which was calculated to be extremely high. The idea that they would show any additional signs of potential, never mind the establishment of Serraxis-qui by an individual, is unfathomable. It unleashes a wave of chatter in the lab.

"Ubuntis, are you certain? This scenario is highly unlikely. Please confirm your findings. The Barundglaric must be informed of this development at once!" responds the voice in her head.

"I am certain. The Humans may be a better investment than originally calculated." Ubuntis beams as she continues to stare longingly through the aperture above. However, the appendages on her back slowly return to their original position as reality sets in. She looks down at the ports in her skin where the tubes were latched, then at the floor where grayish-blue fluid glides over her feet and down the drains around her. Her eyes rest on the three evenly spaced blue circles embedded in the skin on her stomach. Their flat, vitreous surfaces shine in the light of the lab, serving as a reminder of what is at stake. Accessing her HUD neurologically, Ubuntis disengages her "cerebral communication transmissions." Yellow scripts of Scrym commands flash before her eyes as fast as her neurons can conduct them. She can now contemplate in peace. *Hope is a dangerous emotion to confide in, given our dire circumstances and given the obstacles this species faces. If we are to adopt the Humans as an ally, there is significant work to be done...*

Without looking up, she solemnly speaks aloud for all to hear: "Put me back in... Guidance will be integral."

Humanity... Humanity never changes, and yet, how hard they try. How fervently they pretend to be what they are not; masking their flaws with a façade of perfection as if to present themselves as gods. How dismally short they fall in their quest for a society free of pain and suffering. How brazen to believe that they, alone, sit at the pinnacle of creation. With fatal flaws that run as deep as theirs, our expectations for their species' unification toward the common goal of biological life remain low, and their future is likely a dark one.

And yet...a dull glimmer of potential begins to illuminate in the abyss of their anticipated failure. A species considered to be too young and far too immature to provide any measurable benefit to the greater cause produces a tiny inkling of hope; a sliver of light that shines dimly through the muck of their low expectations and marred reputation. Perhaps they are the vitalerium crystal in the rough, so raw and unrefined that they were initially overlooked and underestimated. Maybe there is, in fact, more to them than meets the eye, doubtful as it may seem. Perhaps they can be of use after all...for we are not without our own challenges. If a united biological front of sufficient magnitude is not established with haste, all species may face the darkest of times; the grimmest of futures.

The coming trials will not be easy, and the hardships ahead will likely bend humanity until they break at the seams. Let us see if they heal at the fractures to grow stronger or perish under the weight of responsibility. As the evaluation stands, humanity will likely never change, at least not in time. However, we will be watching, and we will see how they fare...

ACKNOWLEDGMENTS

<u>A Special Thanks to:</u>

My brother, Matt, for your guidance, and for always being my advocate.

My family, for all your love and support.

My editor, Jon Smith, and everyone at Atmosphere Press.

Phil & Lex, for braving this writing journey with me.

Bianca, for without you, this novel would be in a drawer somewhere.

All my friends, who provided the inspiration to breathe life into this novel.

ABOUT ATMOSPHERE PRESS

Founded in 2015, Atmosphere Press was built on the principles of Honesty, Transparency, Professionalism, Kindness, and Making Your Book Awesome. As an ethical and author-friendly hybrid press, we stay true to that founding mission today.

If you're a reader, enter our giveaway for a free book here:

SCAN TO ENTER
BOOK GIVEAWAY

If you're a writer, submit your manuscript for consideration here:

SCAN TO SUBMIT
MANUSCRIPT

And always feel free to visit Atmosphere Press and our authors online at atmospherepress.com. See you there soon!

For more of the **Vitalerium** series, visit:

https://vitaleriumseries.com/

https://flow.page/vitaleriumseries

ABOUT THE AUTHOR

NICHOLAS KEATING CASBARRO was born in Providence, Rhode Island, in 1990. He attended Northeastern University's Doctor of Physical Therapy Program in Boston, class of 2013. Though he never practiced, he maintained his curiosity and love for the sciences. After college, he worked in the medical device field with a specialty in wound-healing and burn treatment.

In 2021, he joined a regenerative medicine company where he would spend five days a week on a plane, traveling the country to work with burn surgeons and victims. While flying, he experienced a spark of inspiration, and decided to follow the thread. Since childhood, he had a deep love for science fiction, growing to appreciate the greats in sci-fi like Aldous Huxley, George Orwell, Frank Herbert, Isaac Asimov, and many others. Nicholas used his time on countless flights to create the *Vitalerium Series* and its universe. The majority of the first *Vitalerium* novel was written at 36,000 feet. He has six books planned in the *Vitalerium Series* and continues to craft the narrative of Roman Matthews.

Milton Keynes UK
Ingram Content Group UK Ltd.
UKHW030747071024
449371UK00006B/476